J.V. Jones was born in Liverpool in 1963. When she was twenty, she began working for a record label and was part of the Liverpool music scene of the early eighties. She later moved to San Diego, California, where she ran an export business for several years and was the marketing director for an interactive software company.

Find out more about J.V. Jones and other Orbit authors by registering for the free monthly newsletter at www.orbitbooks.co.uk

Praise for
THE BOOK OF WORDS TRILOGY

'J.V. Jones is quite a find . . . a deliciously intricate tale'
Katherine Kurtz

'We have a major new writer here. Bravo! An intriguing tale well told'
Dennis L. McKiernan

'Jones stamps it all with a distinctive touch'
Locus

'J.V. Jones is about to become one of the great fantasy success stories of the 90s'
Mysterious Galaxy Books

By J.V. Jones

The Book of Words Trilogy
THE BAKER'S BOY
A MAN BETRAYED
MASTER AND FOOL

THE BARBED COIL

Sword of Shadows
A CAVERN OF BLACK ICE
A FORTRESS OF GREY ICE

MASTER

✦ AND ✦

FOOL

THE BOOK OF WORDS ~ III

J. V. JONES

www.orbitbooks.co.uk

An *Orbit* Book

First published in Great Britain by Orbit 1997
This edition published by Orbit 1997
Reprinted 1998, 1999, 2000, 2001 (twice)

A CIP catalogue record for this book
is available from the British Library.

ISBN 1 85723 471 5

Typeset in Imprint by M Rules
Printed and bound in Great Britain by
Clays Ltd, St Ives plc

Orbit
A Division of
Little, Brown and Company (UK)
Brettenham House
Lancaster Place
London WC2E 7EN

For Richard

Acknowledgments

I have been helped greatly in writing this trilogy by the work of many scholars. In particular, I am indebted to works by Philip Warner, Frances and Joseph Gies, Elizabeth David, and Reay Tannahill.

I would like to thank Betsy Mitchell for first taking a chance on an unpublished writer, and thereafter guiding my manuscripts with insight and good humor. On plot and character, I am grateful for the advice of Mark Arnold, who challenged me to tie up the storyline as closely as I could, and following his advice, the very character he suggested should be in the final scene is there, center stage (though I'm sorry to say I couldn't manage the marauding pigs!). I am further indebted to Wayne D. Change for a long list of things including moral support, medieval bread, and game tips. I also owe a debt of gratitude to Nancy C. Hanger, Mari Okuda, and all the staff at Warner Books for helping make this trilogy the best it could be. Further thanks are due to Darrell K. Sweet for providing such beautiful and evocative cover art for each volume.

Last of all I would like to thank my brother Paul for Web site services above and beyond the call of brotherly duty, and Richard for, amongst many things, suggesting I change the name Bogger to Bodger.

When men of honor lose sight of their cause
When three bloods are savored in one day
Two houses will meet in wedlock and wealth
And what forms at the join is decay
A man will come with neither father nor mother
But sister as lover
And stay the hand of the plague

The stones will be sundered, the temple will fall
The dark empire's expansion will end at his call
And only the fool know the truth

—Marod's *Book of Words*

Prologue

Drip. Drip. Drip. The waterclock turned another degree, sending a cup full of water trickling to the bowl. One more round and the hour would strike. The same hour on the same day that a month ago had marked her marriage to the duke.

Melli settled herself in the most comfortable chair in the most comfortable room in the house. Even as she drew her feet from the floor, her thumb found its way to her mouth. With her other hand she cradled her belly and then began to rock back and forth. She was a widow with no black to wear, no body to wrap, no wedding night to remember through the mourning. Not a widow at all by Bren's reckoning.

Oh, but they were wrong. All of them: from Lord Baralis to her father, from Traff to Tawl, from the Duchess Catherine to the lowliest stableboy. Each and every one of them as wrong as they could be.

Back and forth Melli rocked. Back and forth, back and forth, back, back, back.

Back to the wedding day. Back to the chapel. Back to the one single hour she and the duke spent as man and wife.

The smell of incense and flowers accompanied them as they turned from the altar and walked down the aisle. The duke's hand was cool, his grip firm. The chapel doors were drawn back and somewhere bells began to ring. One hundred pairs of eyes were focused upon them, yet Melli saw no one but Tawl. In a church full of people feigning joy, the knight's face seemed too honest by far. He bowed as they passed, and as his face fell into shadow, he gave everything away. Regret, raw and unmistakable, was marked in each feature that he bent toward the floor.

Quickly, Melli glanced at the duke. He had seen nothing; his eyes looked only ahead.

Through the palace they walked; guards in blue to either side, Tawl's footfalls sounding from behind. Melli felt as if she were dreaming, everything had happened so fast: the courtship, the proposal, the marriage. Too fast. She felt drunk with the sheer speed of events, dizzy with the importance of it all. This was more than a marriage— this was a strategy for peace. The duke loved her, she did not doubt that, but it was a love prompted by expediency: he needed an heir and a wife to provide him with one. The marriage was as good as a treaty. And the wedding night would be ink for the signing.

Melli knew all this, but as she walked toward the duke's chamber it began to matter less and less. Her heavy satin gown rubbed against her breasts. She could feel the effects of the ceremonial wine on her cheeks, on the furrow of her tongue and belly deep within. Such strong fare for a fastening, the priests must have distilled it themselves. Melli shifted her fingers within the duke's grasp, and he turned to look at her.

"Not long now, my love," he whispered.

The richness of his voice made up for the thinness of his lips. His hand now felt a little damp, whether from her sweat or his own no longer mattered. Yes, this was part marriage of convenience, but love and passion were equal partners at the join. Indeed, tonight they would reign supreme.

They arrived at their destination within a matter of minutes. The last quarter league had been almost a race, with the duke speeding along the corridors just short of a sprint. Tawl had matched him step for step. Eight men waited at the entrance to the duke's chambers, spears crossed in honor, chivalrous in their averted glances. The double doors were opened and the duke bore Melli forward. As he guided her toward the doorway, Melli looked back. Tawl was gone. Her heart fluttered a tiny warning, but the duke's presence—so solid and reassuring—canceled out her feelings of unease. By the time the door closed behind them, Melli couldn't even remember what she was worried about. Nothing mattered anymore.

They were in a small vestibule with a short flight of stairs leading up to the chambers. A matching pair of double doors marked the top. As her foot found the first step, Melli felt the duke's hand on her waist. With a firm grip he guided her round.

"I would kiss my wife on the threshold," he said. His voice was unfamiliar to her: a stranger's voice. Low and guttural, it was thick with something that Melli had no name for. His lips were on hers, pressing so hard she could feel the teeth beneath. His tongue followed after. Thin and dry and tough as old leather, it bore the vestiges of his last meal on its length. Melli's foot hovered above the step a moment longer, and then she brought it to rest against the duke's leg.

Up came her tongue from the bottom of her mouth, back arching inward, arms rising upward, lips pressing forward jaw to jaw. Half-mad with newly discovered need, Melli leant against the duke for support.

He pulled away. "Come, my love, I will take you to our marriage bed."

Before the words were out of his mouth, she was pushing them back down with her tongue. The thing inside of her was too strong to be delayed. To be deprived of the duke's body even for an instant was too long. He fought her at first, arms pushing her forward, hand in the small of her back, but she fought back in her newfound way, biting his ears and breathing moist hot breaths on his neck.

"Damn you, Melliandra," he murmured as he drew her close. "You're enough to drive a man insane."

The words excited Melli more than any kiss. Throwing back her head, she offered him her breasts. A sharp intake of breath, and then she found herself lying back against the stairs. One solitary lantern lit the duke from behind. At first she was surprised by his knowledge of her clothing: it didn't seem right that a man should deal so deftly with petticoats and underdrawers. An instant later she was glad of it. Better a man who knew what he was doing than the fumbling youths at court. The duke didn't bother to unlace her bodice or unfasten the hooks on her skirt; he raised the fabric up around her waist and went to work on the linen below.

The stone steps bit into Melli's back. Consecrated wine ran heavy in her blood, carrying fragments of memory along for the ride: kisses and caresses and touches from the past. Jack, Edrad—Melli stiffened for an instant—and Baralis. A long, crooked finger drawn down a back raised with welts. Despite herself, Melli's spine arched more.

Pain splintered her thoughts. Her legs had long parted of their own accord, and she felt a tearing between. She wanted to scream, but the duke's tongue was whip-sharp in her mouth and Baralis' image was blade-keen in her mind. The pain seemed to fold in on itself, creating a vacuum that demanded to be filled. Melli's fingers no longer formed fists, they became claws. The corner of the step was a hand upon her spine. The man above no more than a silhouette against the light. Need was the only thing that counted, and everything—wine, pain, and memories—served to heighten the need.

Too soon it came. Too quickly it was over. Too little to justify the means. Melli's breaths were ragged, irregular. She wanted more.

Something warm and mercury-heavy trickled down the length of her thigh. Her gaze alighted on the ceiling: stone capped with brass. The duke, for he was now himself once more, stood over her and tore off the fabric at his tunic's cuff.

"Here," he said, handing her the length of heavily embroidered linen. "Clean yourself up. There is a lot of blood." His tone was cold, almost disapproving.

Melli turned away from him and did what she was told. She was ashamed, confused, brought down to earth with an unsettling jolt. Had she done something to displease him?

The blood was not easy to wipe clean. It was dark and fast to dry. Melli had to spit on the cloth to bring it off. As she rubbed away the last of it, the duke spoke up from behind.

"Would that we had waited for the marriage bed. This is not the place to show you love's pleasures."

Melli stood up. Her legs were weak, her senses slow to rally. A dull pain sounded in her side. "You did not enjoy it?" she asked.

The duke came forward and smoothed down her dress. He did not look at her as he said, "It would have been better for you if you were comfortable."

Sensing something close to embarrassment in the duke's voice, Melli stretched out her arm. "Come then, let us try again."

The duke smiled, his first since the wedding. "You bewitch me," he said.

Melli began to ascend the stairs. "I've never been called a witch before, though I was once called a thief."

"You steal men's hearts?"

"No. Their fates." As Melli spoke, a shudder went down her spine. The words were not her own, they belonged to another woman. A woman from the Far South who was an assistant to a flesh-trader. *"Where I come from, we call people like her thieves. Their fates are so strong they bend others into their service. And what they can't bend they steal."*

Melli's hand was on the door. The duke was just behind her. She pushed against the brass plate and entered the chambers first. They were in the duke's study. Melli remembered it well. Two desks were laid out with food. Cold roast beef, ham and venison, sweetmeats, wafers, and pies. The crest of Bren was sculpted in spun sugar.

The duke made his way over to the nearest table and poured them each a cup of wine. For the first time Melli noticed his sword about his waist. Had he worn it through the lovemaking? Surely not.

He held out the cup of wine for her to take. "Let us eat a little to regain our strength," he said, smiling gently.

Melli was by his side in an instant. She took the cup and set it down. With hands shaking, she felt for the hilt of his sword. The duke's eyes flashed a warning. She ignored it and pulled the sword from its loop. It was heavy, solid, good in the hand. "You won't be needing this," she said, laying it flat upon the desk.

"Melli—"

She cut off his protest with a kiss. "Let us eat later. The food is cold, a little longer will do it no harm." What was started on the stairs needed to be finished— for her at least. It seemed the duke had already taken his pleasure. She clasped at his fingers. "Take me to the bedchamber."

The duke's eyes were a match for his blade. He took hold of her arm, not gently. "Very well," he said. "It seems I cannot keep my lady waiting." Twisting her arm behind her back, he walked Melli to the bedchamber.

She saw the assassin first. He was at the side of the door, knife up close to his chest. Melli screamed. The duke pushed her forward with one hand and reached for his sword with the other. It wasn't there. He hesitated for only a half-second, but it was more than enough. The assassin was at his throat. His blade was long, his hand was quick. It was over in less than an instant.

Melli screamed and screamed and no one came. Blood soaked the duke's tunic even before his body fell to the floor. The assassin's name came to her: Traff, Baralis' mercenary. After that one last feat of coherence, her mind seemed to give in. She could remember nothing that followed. Except Tawl. The knight came and although nothing was, or ever would be, all right again, at least he made sure she was safe. Tawl would take care of her always—she didn't need her mind to tell her that. Her heart already knew.

Back and forward Melli rocked. Forward, forward, forward.

The waterclock turned another degree. One month to the minute now. One month a widow, one month in hiding, one month with no blood to show.

There had been more than a wedding that day, there was a union as well. The marriage *had* been consummated, and she was the only person in the Known Lands who knew it. Not for long, though. Melli's hand cradled her belly. The last time blood had flowed between her legs had been on the stairs leading to the duke's chamber. Breaching blood, not menses. There had been nothing since.

A child was growing inside: the duke's child, and if it was a boy, his heir. Melli spread her fingers full-out upon her belly. How would the city of Bren take the news? The answer was quick to come. They would try and discredit her, claim the duke was not the father, or that the child was begotten out of wedlock. Lies and slander would be thrown her way—indeed, by many she was already counted an accomplice to murder. None of it mattered anymore. The only thing that counted was keeping the new life safe.

In eight months time a baby would be born, and everything—her life, her strength, her very soul—would be directed toward its protection. She had taken the duke's sword and stolen his fate, and this was either penalty or payment.

Melli stood up and put a hand to the waterclock, tipping the liquid from the cone. Prematurely it struck the next hour: Melli wished that all hours would pass so fast. She was impatient for the child to be born.

If it were a girl, then she would take her share of Catherine's wealth. If it were a boy, he would have it all.

One

I'm sick of walking the streets day after day looking for work, Grift. My bunions are giving me hell."

"Exactly how many bunions have you got, Bodger?"

"Four at last count, Grift."

"You'll be needing to walk some more then. It's *five* bunions that are lucky, not four."

"What's so lucky about five bunions, Grift?"

"A man with five bunions will never be impotent, Bodger."

"Impotent!"

"Aye, Bodger. Impotence. The curse of men who only take short walks."

"But the chaplain said the only way to cure impotence was a night spent in holy vigil."

"No, Bodger, the chaplain never said that a night spent in holy vigil was a cure for impotence. What he actually said was a night spent with a *horny virgin*. Makes quite a difference, you know." Grift nodded sagely and Bodger nodded back.

The two guards were walking along a street in the south side of Bren. It was midmorning and a light drizzle had just started.

"I suppose we were lucky, Grift. Being thrown out of the guard is a lot better than being flogged and imprisoned."

"Aye, Bodger. The charge of being drunk on duty is a serious one. We got off lightly." Grift stopped for a moment to scrape the horse dung from his shoe. "Of course, it would have helped if they'd given us a month's wages before chucking us out on the streets. As it is now, we can barely afford to buy our next meal, let alone two horses to get us back to the kingdoms."

"You spent all the money we did have on ale, though, Grift."

"Ah well, Bodger. Ale is a basic necessity of life. Without ale a man might as well curl up and die." Grift smiled winningly. "You'll thank me for it in the end, Bodger. Besides, there's still a chance we might find work. The wedding of Catherine and Kylock is due to take place in two weeks, and there's bound to be opportunities for skilled men such as ourselves."

"No one is going to give us work, Grift. Lord Baralis is all but running the city now, and if he learned that anyone was helping us, he'd have their hides whipped." Bodger pulled his cloak close. He hated the rain—it made his hair stand up. "We should do what I said: leave the city, cross the mountains, and go join the Highwall army. Ever since Kylock murdered the Halcus king, the Wall have been taking all comers. Anyone who wants to fight for them gets five coppers a week, a newly cast breastplate, and all the goat's meat they can eat."

"If we joined with Highwall, Bodger, we'd be on the losing side." Grift spat with confidence. "The northern cities might be as mad as a peacock in a pie, but Bren and the kingdoms have never looked stronger. Why, in the last three weeks Kylock has captured most of eastern Halcus. The whole country is virtually his. There's no telling where he'll stop."

"I heard that he wanted to present Catherine with Halcus as a wedding gift, Grift."

"Well, after what happened to King Hirayus, he's all but done it."

Bodger shook his head slowly. "Terrible thing that, Grift. The peace tent is supposed to be sacred ground."

"Nothing's sacred to Kylock, Bodger."

As Bodger lifted his head to nod in agreement, he spotted a familiar figure in the crowd ahead. "Hey, Grift, isn't that young Nabber over there?" Bodger didn't wait for Grift's reply. He dashed straight ahead, shouting loudly, "Nabber! Nabber! Over here!"

Nabber looked around. He was on an important mission and was under direct orders not to loiter, but loitering was in his soul and the sound of his own voice was music to his ears. At once he recognized the distinctly mismatched forms of Bodger and Grift. They looked wet, miserable, down on their luck and, most alarmingly to Nabber, sober as a pair of bailiffs. What was the world coming to?

Bodger ran toward him, a huge grin spreading across his face. "How are you, my friend? It's good to see you. Me and Grift were worried sick about you after the night—"

"The night we parted ways," interrupted Grift, flashing Bodger a cautionary glance.

Nabber gently disengaged himself from Bodger's spiderlike grip. He brushed down his tunic and smoothed back his hair. "Always a pleasure, gentlemen," he said with a small bow.

"Are you still coping with your loss?" asked Bodger in a peculiar meaningful whisper.

"Loss? What loss was that?"

"Your dearly departed mother, of course. You used to spend all your time in the chapel praying for her soul."

Nabber's whole demeanor changed: his shoulders dropped, his back arched, his lips extended to a pout. "It still grieves me every day, Bodger," he murmured tragically. The sight of Bodger and Grift's sympathetic nodding made Nabber feel bad. Swift would not have approved of him taking his mother's name in vain.

Pockets were notoriously sentimental when it came to their mothers. Why, Swift himself had loved his own mother so much that he had named one of his most famous moves after her: the Diddley Delve. A thoroughly sneaky and ingenious move that could deprive any man of valuables he'd concealed about his vitals. Apparently nothing had been safe from Ma Diddley. Nabber hadn't yet aspired to the dizzy heights of the Diddley Delve, and in fact wasn't quite sure he ever wanted to.

Feeling a little guilty about stringing the two guards along, and feeling a *lot* guilty about them being out on the streets with no prospects—after all, he was partly responsible for it—prompted Nabber to make them an offer. "If you are looking for shelter, some hot food, and a chance to protect a certain high-born lady, then I know just the place you can go." As he spoke, Nabber shook his head slowly. No doubt about it, there'd be trouble with Tawl for this. Guilt would be the death of him.

"What place?" asked Grift, suddenly interested. It was telling that he never asked what lady.

Nabber crooked his finger and drew both guards close. In his lowest and most furtive whisper, Nabber gave out the address of the hideaway. "Knock three times on the door, and when someone comes tell them you're there to deliver the snails. Say Nabber sent you." There, it was done now. Tawl would have to take the two guards in— either that, or murder them. Moving quickly along from that particular unsettling thought, Nabber said, "Anyway, I must be going. I have a message to deliver to the palace."

He was just about to step away when Grift caught at his arm. "You're a fool if you go to the palace, Nabber," he said. "If you're caught by Baralis, Borc alone can save you."

Nabber freed himself from the guard's grip, smoothed down the fabric of his sleeve, and tipped a bow. "Thanks for the advice, Grift. I'll bear it in mind. See you later."

With that he was off, losing himself in the crowd as only a pocket could.

He didn't look back. It was getting late and Maybor would be anxiously awaiting his return. Nabber shrugged to himself. He could put it down to the rain: a street full of watery sewage on the move could slow a man down quite considerably.

It really was quite a pity he was on a mission, as by far the best time for pocketing was during rain showers. People jostling into each other, cloaks held above their heads, eyes down—it was perfect. A man could round up a lot of coinage in the rain. Maybe he could put in a little pocketin' later, after the note was delivered. It would certainly be a good idea to keep out of Tawl's way. The knight would be mad as hell about Bodger and Grift turning up on the doorstep, and even madder about the note.

Nabber felt in his tunic: still there. Dry as an archbishop in a desert, and yet another thing to feel guilty about. The problem was that Tawl didn't know about the plan. He and Maybor had concocted this between themselves, and Nabber was quite sure that the knight would not like it one little bit. It was a gamble, there were risks—which in fact was why Nabber had agreed to it in the first place: he could never resist a risk—and, at the end of the day, nothing to gain from the whole thing, only a little personal satisfaction on Maybor's part. Still, Nabber understood the need for personal satisfaction—Swift himself had lived for it. Besides, he liked to be out and about. Being cooped up in the hideaway all day with Tawl, Melli, and Maybor was not his idea of fun. Deals needed to be struck, pockets needed to be lightened, cash needed to circulate, and *he* was the man to do it.

Before he knew it, Nabber found himself by the storm conduit. Bren had no sewer systems to speak of, but it did have a system of drains and tunnels that prevented the city from becoming waterlogged during the countless

storms and rain showers that came down all year round
from the mountains. The problem was, as Nabber saw it,
that the city lay between the mountains and the lake. Any
water that ran off the mountains wanted naturally, as all
water did, to join with its larger watery friends, and Bren
was stuck right in the middle of the course of least resis-
tance. Hence the network of storm channels and drains
that were built to divert the water both around and *under*
the city.

The duke's palace—or was it the *duchess'* palace
now?—being situated right on the shore of the Great
Lake, was naturally well-supplied with such tunnels. And
it was to one of these that Nabber had made his way. Of
course he hadn't counted on the rain. He was going to get
very wet, might even catch his death. There was *one* consolation, though: all the spiders would have drowned.
Nabber hated spiders.

A quick look left, a quick look right, no one around for
the moment, so off with the grille. With speed and agility
that would have brought a tear to Swift's eye, Nabber
swung himself down into the drain channel. His feet
landed, *splash*, in a stream of cold, smelly, and fast-rising
water. He quickly shunted up the wall, dragged the grille
back in place, and then jumped down into the water.
Knee-deep now. He had to get a move on; he didn't want
it reaching his neck. No, sir. No dead spiders down *his*
tunic.

The smell was appalling. The rain brought out the
worst in a city, churning up long-dried horse dung and
slops, carrying blood from the knacker's yard, grease from
the tallow drums, and bearing a circus full of carcasses
along in the swell. By the looks of things, everything had
ended up here, down under the palace. Nabber took a last
longing look around—there were lots of interesting-looking
floaters that were crying out to be investigated—and then
entered the full darkness of the tunnels.

This was familiar territory. No one loved the dark as

much as pockets. Nabber's feet found their way with little
prompting whilst his eyes searched out lightness in the
shade. Up and up he went. Stone staircases wet with
slime welcomed him, barrel-ceilings lined with moss
echoed his every move, water rushed ahead of him on its
way to the lake, and shadows and dead spiders trailed
behind.

At last he came to the entrance he needed: the one in
the nobles' quarters. Putting his eye to the breach in the
stone, Nabber looked out onto a broad quiet corridor that
was lined with old suits of armor. He knew it well. Busy
with servants on their way to light fires and warm baths
in early morning, it was as still as a chapel by midday.
Guards only patrolled here once an hour, and most
noblemen were well away by now. Nabber took a deep
breath, briefly asked for Swift's own luck, set in motion
the opening mechanism, and then stepped onto the hallowed ground of the palace.

Feeling a peculiar mixture of excitement and fear, the
young pocket made his way to Baralis' quarters. He had a
letter to deliver, an answer to be waited upon, and his
own skin to be saved at all costs.

"Concentrate, Jack. *Concentrate!*"

Stillfox's voice was tiny, immeasurably distant.
Outside of time. Still, such was the power of the human
voice that Jack found himself obeying it anyway. He had
to concentrate. His consciousness plunged to his belly
whilst his thoughts focused on the glass.

"Warm it, Jack. Don't smash it."

Every muscle tensing, every hair on end, both eyeballs
drying for want of a blink, Jack tried to do what Stillfox
asked. He sent *himself*—there was no other word for it, he
sent that which made him who he was, what rested in his
mind and bounded his thoughts—outside of his body
toward the glass. It was terrifying. The terrible vulnerability of forsaking one's body, combined with the

bittersweet lightness of the soul. How could men do this? he wondered. How could Baralis and Stillfox and Borc knows who else ever get used to the shock?

"Careful, Jack. You're wavering."

Part of him wanted to shout out, "Let me waver, then." Better half in his body than not at all. Instead, Jack concentrated harder. Through the thin, busy particles of air he traveled, to the hard slick surface of the glass. Only when he got there it wasn't hard. It was slick, but strangely soft: malleable as lead, running like slow honey or a fine summer cheese. He felt the downward push of the glass and began to understand how false and artificial its current state was. It had been shaped unnaturally by man and was quietly fighting its constraints. It would take centuries, perhaps eons, before it reverted back, but it would eventually succeed. Nothing had a memory as long as glass.

Jack knew all this without as much as a single coherent thought. He just knew it, that was all. He also knew, in something more akin to instinct than intellect, that the glass would *welcome* the warming. It would not fight him. The warming would bring it that much closer to its goal.

Strangely, it was this knowledge that empowered Jack. No longer a man with a whip, he became a man with a key. Gently, so gently, tiptoeing with his mind, he melded with the elements of the glass. Fear skirted periphery-close, but he paid it no heed; nothing mattered—only the join. If Stillfox spoke now, Jack didn't hear him.

He became aware of the vibration of the glass: strong, unwavering, almost hypnotic. Jack felt himself falling in time with it. How right it felt, how very *right*.

"Jack! Be careful! You're losing yourself." Stillfox's words carried more weight than speech alone; they were heavy with sorcery. Jack felt the other man's power. It was repugnant to him. The glass was his, and he would brook no interference. Then suddenly, something was forcing its way between him and the glass, a sliver of thought turned to light. It acted like a wrench, cleaving apart the join. Jack fought it aggressively. He had been rocked into quiescence by the vibration of the glass, and now he was a giant awakened. No longer warm, the glass grew hot. An orange line began to glow around the rim.

"Jack, I command you *be gone!*"

Jack felt a powerful shearing, saw a bright flash of light, and then he was torn away from the glass. As he sped back to his body, the glass exploded outward, sending chunks of molten glass flying through the air. Even as he settled himself within flesh and blood, the fragments hit him. Scorching, sizzling, cracking like whips, they landed on his chest and on his arms. Jack, dizzy with the shock of returning, shot up from the chair. His tunic was smoldering, the skin burning beneath. Too new in his body to feel pain, Jack could only feel horror. He had to get away from the glass. Pulling at his tunic, he tore it from his shoulders. Gobs of hardening glass tinkled onto the floor.

The moment the pain started, Jack was hit from behind by a wave of coldness. Reflex-quick, he spun round. Stillfox was standing close by; a large empty bucket rested, dripping, in his hand. Water. The herbalist had poured water on him. He took a step forward. "Jack—"

"Leave me alone, Stillfox," cried Jack, raising his arm in warning. Tired and disorientated, he was shaking from head to foot. "You shouldn't have interfered. I had it. I was in control."

Stillfox's voice rose to a matching anger. "You fool. You were in control of nothing. The glass was controlling *you*. You nearly lost yourself to it."

Searing pinpoints of pain goaded Jack into a rage. "I tell you the glass was mine!" He beat his fist against his side.

The herbalist shook his head slowly. He let the bucket

drop to the floor. When he spoke, he pronounced his words very carefully. "Make an error in judgment like that again, Jack, and I swear it will be your last. I will not step in and save you a second time. I am nobody's nursemaid."

Abruptly, he turned and made his way toward the door. Without looking round he said, "There is ointment in the rag-stoppered jar above the fireplace. See to your burns." The door banged shut behind him.

Jack immediately slumped into the chair. The anger, which had fired his blood only moments earlier, left his body with his very next breath. He felt hollow without it . . . and ashamed. Bringing his head down toward his knees, Jack rubbed both hands against his face. How could he have been so stupid? Stillfox was right; he *had* lost control, losing himself to the vibration of the glass. It had been so hard to resist, though: a siren's song. Jack searched his mind and came up with a few choice baking curses, which he hissed with venom. How was he ever going to learn to master the power inside?

Ten weeks now he'd been with Stillfox. Ten weeks since the aging herbalist had found him hiding in the bushes on Annis' west road and taken him in. Ten weeks of instruction and straining and failure. Every attempt to draw power seemed to end in disaster. Stillfox had been patient at first, slowing his pace, whispering words of encouragement and advice, but by now even Stillfox was losing his patience.

Jack rubbed his temples. He was making so little progress. Sometimes it seemed as if he could only draw power when there were *real* dangers: real-life situations that stirred the rage within. Here in Stillfox's quiet cottage, nestled in a sleepy village ten leagues short of Annis and a mountain's girth west of Bren, all the dangers seemed like insignificant ones. There was no one threatening his safety; he wasn't being hunted, threatened, or conned. The few people he cared about were in no danger, and judging from what Stillfox had told him about the war, it appeared that things were calming down in the north. With nothing and no one to fight for, it was hard for Jack to summon rage and direct it toward a glass, or whatever else the herbalist set before him. These things weren't important to him—skill alone wasn't worth fighting for. There had to be some emotional attachment: someone or something to get angry about. For the first month he had been unable to draw forth anything unless he focused his mind on Tarissa.

Tarissa. The pain in Jack's arms and chest flared to a blaze as her name skimmed across his thoughts. He stood up, kicking the chair behind him. He would not think of her. She was in the past, long gone, as good as dead. He refused to keep her alive in his thoughts. She had lied and betrayed him, and no amount of tears or pleading would ever make it right. Magra, Rovas, Tarissa—those three deserved each other. And he had been so stupid and gullible that he as good as deserved them, too.

Jack walked over to the fireplace and picked up the rag-stoppered jar from the mantel. Over the past few months Jack had learned that he needed to be harsh on both Tarissa *and* himself, it was the only way to put a stop to the pangs of regret. He was a fool and she was a villain, and that was all there was to it. Nothing more.

Taking the rag from the jar, Jack sniffed at the contents. Whatever it was, it smelled bad. Gingerly he dipped a finger downward. The liquid was cold, greasy, and the color of dried blood. Borc only knew what it was! Whenever Stillfox was preparing to use the contents of one of his jars, he would first dab a droplet on his tongue to test that it was still potent. Jack had no intention of tasting this, though. Let it kill him slowly by invading his wounds rather than poison him swiftly on the spot.

Jack began to dab the ointment on his burns, first his arms and then his chest. The process took a lot longer than he'd thought; not only were his hands shaking wildly, making it difficult to target the areas in question, but a natural squeamishness on Jack's part didn't help, either. Yes, it was only stinging, he told himself—and since leaving Castle Harvell he'd endured much worse than a handful of glass burns—but it was the idea of causing *himself* pain that he wasn't happy with. The burns were throbbing away quite bearably until he put the ointment on them, then the real torment began. The ointment stung like lye in an open wound. It seemed to get under his skin with a thousand tiny barbs, then claw its way back to the surface. Was this Stillfox's revenge?

"Jack. Don't use—" The herbalist burst into the cottage. Seeing Jack with the jar in his hand, he stopped himself in midsentence. He shrugged his shoulders rather sheepishly. "Never mind, it won't kill you."

"What will it do, then?"

"It was meant to teach you a lesson." The herbalist's voice dropped to something close to a mutter. "Only I think it taught *me* one, instead: there's little satisfaction to be gained from acting out of spite." He looked up from the floor. "Never mind. The ointment may pain you for a few days, but it should do you no harm in the long term."

Jack was too surprised to speak. He threw an accusatory glance at Stillfox, but really, in the bottom of his heart, he knew he'd deserved it. He had endangered both himself and Stillfox, and when the herbalist had tried to help him, he had fought him off. Jack threw the jar onto the fire. "Let's call it quits," he said.

Stillfox smiled, the lines around his eyes and on his cheeks instantly multiplying. Jack noticed for the first time how very old and tired he looked. "Here," Jack said, pulling the chair near the fire. "Come and sit down, I'll warm you some holk."

The herbalist waved his arm dismissively. "If I had needed someone to look after me in my dotage, Jack, I would have picked someone a lot comelier than you."

Jack nodded in acknowledgment of the reprimand. "I'm sorry, Stillfox. I don't know what's got into me. I'm just so tired of failing all the time."

Stillfox pulled a second chair close to the fire, bidding Jack to sit. He brought a blanket and laid it over Jack's bare shoulders. Finally, when he had settled himself in his seat, he spoke. "I won't lie to you, Jack. Things have not been going well with your training. I think part of the problem is that you're just plain too old. You should have been taught earlier, when your mind was still open and your thought process not so . . . " the herbalist searched for the right word " . . . rigid."

"But I only felt the power for the first time a year ago." A year ago, it hardly seemed possible. His life had been so chaotic for so long now that it was hard to believe there had ever been a time when things had been normal. He didn't even know what normal meant anymore.

"You might have only been aware of this power during the last year, but it has been with you all your life." Stillfox leant forward. "Sorcery doesn't come to anyone in a burst of blinding light. It's real, visceral, as ingrained as instinct and as compelling as a beating heart. You were born with it, Jack, and someone should have taken pains to discover it sooner. If they had, you wouldn't be here today: a fugitive hiding in a foreign land, leaving nothing but destruction in your wake."

Harsh words, but true enough. "Is it too late, then? Is there nothing I can do?"

Stillfox sighed heavily. "You must keep trying, you have no choice. Power will keep building up inside you, and unless you learn to either focus or curb it, it will ultimately destroy you."

"But there are risks even in learning. The glass—"

"Everything is a risk, Jack. Everything." The herbalist's voice had lost all of its country accent. "Walk to market and there's a risk you will be robbed, run over, or stabbed. Marry a girl and there's a risk she'll die in childbirth.

Believe in a god and there's a risk you'll find nothing but darkness on the other side."

"Trust someone and there's a risk they might betray you," said Jack softly, almost to himself.

"Jack, your power is very great. So great it frightens me. The few times when you have managed to focus successfully left me speechless. You have been given a gift, and it would be a terrible tragedy if you never learned to master it."

Jack eased his chair back from the fire. The heat was burning his already tender arms. "Perhaps if I move on to live creatures, not inanimate objects, I—"

"There is even worse danger there," interrupted Stillfox. "Animals can and will fight back. Speed is of the essence in such drawings. You must master the technique of *entering* before we go any further." The herbalist gave Jack a searching look and then stood up. "Now, I think it's time you had some rest. You've had quite a shock and those burns do not look good. A little lacus will help."

Jack was glad of the change of subject. He'd had enough of sorcery for one day. Possibly enough to last a lifetime. He didn't bother to wish he was normal: wishing was something he'd given up long ago.

Baralis rubbed idly at his fingers. It was summer now, but still they pained him. It was the all-pervasive dampness that did it. Tomorrow he would see Catherine about changing his quarters; he was tired of living like a mosquito suspended above the lake.

On his desk lay the various maps and charts. Once the duke's, they were now his. Maps and so many other things: a whole library of ancient books, rooms filled with antiquities and arcane devices, cellars full of secrets, and strong rooms full of gold. The duke's palace was a huge unopened treasure chest, and the duke's death had given him the key.

Oh, but he had so little time, though. Hardly a moment to himself since the funeral. There was so much to do, and so much *to be* done. Just managing Catherine alone took a quarter of his day. She was child—demanding, prone to temper tantrums, constantly craving attention—and he was part father, part nursemaid, part suitor. She would summon him to her chambers at all hours of the day, and he never knew what he would find once he got there: tears, anger, or joy. When there wasn't a problem she would invent one, and she was never satisfied until she had exerted her will over him in some small way. It was all a game to Catherine, and it suited Baralis to let her think that he was just another piece on the board.

Baralis stood up and walked over to the fire. *He* was master of the game, his will was the power behind all of Catherine's moves. The new duchess was just a beginner when it came to the art of manipulation. She might learn fast, though. After all, she was being taught by an expert.

Just how great an expert he was could be judged by the events of the past five weeks. First, he had shifted the blame of the duke's death onto Tawl, Melli's protector; second, he had persuaded Catherine to go ahead with the marriage to Kylock; and last, despite Kylock's heinous act of regicide in Halcus, he had persuaded both the court and the common people of Bren to support the marriage.

Well, more accurately, Catherine had persuaded them. Three days after the news of King Hirayus' death had reached the city, Catherine had, on his instructions, gathered her court around her. In no uncertain terms she told them that she fully intended to marry King Kylock, and anyone who objected to the match should come forward now and let their misgivings be heard. One man made the mistake of coming forward: Lord Carhill, one-time advisor to the duke and a man whose only daughter was married to a well-to-do lord in Highwall. The minute he stepped from the ranks, he was seized by the ducal guard.

He was executed, then and there, before the court. That night his sons were hunted down and beheaded, and the following day his land was seized in the name of the duchess.

The sting was taken from the whole affair by one single calculated act of compassion. Catherine had taken Lord Carhill's wife into the palace, publicly proclaiming that the poor widow would never want for food nor shelter. This little performance was for the benefit of the people, not the court. *Catherine might be firm*, they said, *but at least she is not without charity*. Baralis pursed his lips in distaste. The common folk were easily swayed by such showy acts of mercy.

In fact, public opinion was the least of his problems. Catherine was seen to be a tragic figure: her father murdered, a heavy responsibility newly fallen upon her shoulders, alone in a world drawing perilously close to war. Of course, it helped that she was young and beautiful. Beauty was yet another thing that swayed the common folk.

Baralis shook his head slowly. No, his problems were not with Catherine and the people of Bren. His problem was with Kylock. What would the new king do next? Maybor's eldest brat, Kedrac, was finishing off Halcus for him, yet would he stop there? Was Annis next in line? And if it was, when did he plan to take it? Baralis only hoped he left it till after the wedding. Bren might support the marriage at the moment, but it was an uneasy, suspicious support, easily shaken by unfavorable news. And never would there be news so unfavorable as Kylock's overwhelming greed.

There was such a delicate balance to be maintained: Annis and Highwall were now certain to move against Bren. The question was would they leave it until after the wedding, or would they move before? Baralis received daily reports from the two mountain cities, and there was no mistaking their intent: mercenaries, armaments, siege engines, and chemicals were flooding into both cities. Tavalisk was underwriter to them all. The chubby, interfering archbishop was seeing to it that Annis and Highwall had unlimited funds with which to purchase the necessities of war. It seemed the south was willing to pay a high price to keep trouble away from its prosperous shores.

Baralis sighed, not deeply. All would have to be dealt with as it came.

Then there was his second problem: Maybor and his wayward daughter. Where were they? What did they know or guess about the assassination? And what did they plan on doing next? Would they quietly leave the city, content that they were at least alive? Or would they try and make some claim upon Catherine's inheritance? Knowing Maybor, it would most likely be the latter of the two; the lord of the Eastlands had never styled himself a shrinking violet.

Just then, Baralis was distracted from his thoughts by the sound of a commotion at his door. A few minutes earlier he had been aware of a knock, but had paid it no heed—Crope was ordered to send everyone away except Catherine. A shrill scream pierced the rain-clear air, and Baralis rushed across to the reception room.

Crope was in the doorway. Huge arms stretched out in front of him; he had a boy dangling by the scruff of his neck. The boy was squirming and kicking with venomous gusto, but Crope had him firmly in hand.

"You kicked Big Tom," accused the hulking servant.

"Leave it out, Crope. It's only a rat!" cried the boy. "You should count yourself lucky old Thornypurse hasn't set eyes upon it. She would have had it squeezed and bottled by now."

"No one's gonna bottle Big Tom," said Crope, lifting the boy higher into the air.

"If you don't put me down this instant, Crope, I'll personally see to it that old Thornypurse is rubbing Big

Tom's oily remains into her wrinkles before the day is through."

"Put him down, Crope," ordered Baralis.

"But master—"

"*Down, Crope.*" The tone of Baralis' voice killed all protest instantly and Crope lowered the boy to the ground. "Leave us now," said Baralis.

Crope flashed Nabber an evil look, muttered something comforting to the large and rat-shaped bulge in his tunic, and then backed away.

Baralis turned to the boy. "So, Nabber, what brings you here? Come to turn your friend the knight in?" He stretched a smile designed only to show the sharpness of tooth. "He's wanted for murder, you know."

The boy looked a lot more scared now than he did when he was in Crope's clutches. He was trying to cover it, though, smoothing down his collar with a nonchalant air, and then raising his fingernails to the light to check for dirt.

Baralis was extremely pleased by this surprise visit. If one waited in one's web long enough, the prey would always come. "You've been wading, I take it?" Baralis indicated the boy's britches, which were soaked to the knee. "I must say, it's just the day for it."

The boy looked most indignant. "What about you, Baralis? Attracted any new crawling insects lately?"

"Come inside," hissed Baralis, annoyed at himself for stooping to trade insults with a mere boy.

Nabber looked quickly to his left and right. "I'm not sure that I want to."

"Aah," Baralis said slowly, in the manner of one about to draw a logical conclusion. "Then you're afraid."

"I am not! Let me past." The boy stomped into the room.

Baralis smiled behind his back.

The boy made a quick survey of the room. Once satisfied that they were alone, he pulled a sheet of sealed and folded paper from his tunic. Before he handed it to Baralis, he said, "I'll be wanting an answer straightaway."

Baralis snatched it from him. The bloodred seal was Maybor's: the swan and the double-edged sword. Like the man himself, it took quite a breaking. Quickly, Baralis read the spidery, uncultivated script. Once finished he turned to the boy. "Why does he want to meet me?"

Nabber shrugged. "Don't ask me. I'm just the messenger."

Baralis took a thinking breath. The boy was a liar—and not a bad one at that. "Am I to understand that I am to come with you now?"

"Yes. Here and now. No henchmen, no weapons, no chance to warn the guard."

"How do I know this is not a trap?"

Nabber smiled sweetly. "Who's afraid now, Baralis?"

Baralis curbed his desire to strike the boy. "And what if I refuse and send for the guard anyway? I could have your secrets out of you on your very first scream." As he spoke, Baralis noticed that Nabber was edging, none too discreetly, toward the door.

"Ah well, my friend," said Nabber, hand upon the latch, "you'd have to catch me first."

The boy was young and therefore could be excused his stupidity. "Do you really think I would let you out the door?"

The latch was up, but Baralis' hand was faster. "Nay, boy. Leave it be! I will agree to come with you." Baralis found himself breathless. There had been a brief instant when he had considered drawing power against the boy, but curiosity overcame caution. He *wanted* to see Maybor. He wanted to hear what the great lord had to say. Maybor had taken quite a risk sending a boy who could disclose his own whereabouts, and presumably his daughter's, straight into the heart of the palace. There must be a good reason behind it. Oh, Baralis knew he could seize the boy and scrape the truth right off his plump, youthful tongue, but his love of intrigue had been sparked. There was a game to be played here, and after all, what good was power without the thrill of power games?

"Take me to him," he said.

Maybor ordered a second mug of ale, then settled back in his chair. He was not exactly drunk, but he was definitely pleasantly potted. It was good to be out. A fine tavern, a blazing fire, and a buxom serving girl to flirt with; why, he hadn't enjoyed himself so much in a long time. For the past nine weeks he'd been holed up like a squirrel in a jar, and now, having managed to escape for a short while, he was determined to enjoy himself.

Still, enjoyment took many forms and the best was yet to come.

The ale arrived, its fine head frothing over the brim. The girl who brought it took great pains to place it carefully on the table. Her bodice was cut modestly enough, but additional cleavage was revealed during the process of the slow bend. Maybor liked women who played coy.

"So, my beauty," he said to the girl. "Does the tavern-keeper here have strong-arms in the crowd?" He had intended to ask this question of the tavern-keeper himself, but he rather liked appearing mysterious to the young and comely girl.

The girl giggled foolishly. "Oh aye, he does that, sir. You can never be too careful when it comes to the riffraff."

Maybor ran his fingers down the plump arm of the girl. When he reached her hand, he pressed a single gold coin into the waiting palm. "A man in black will soon be coming here to visit me. Ask the tavern-keeper to set a watch on the door, and if he is escorted by anyone other than a young boy, I would appreciate it if they were held there, until I make my escape." Maybor allowed his leather pouch to gape open. It was loaded to the drawstring with the duke's own gold. "I trust this place has another way out?"

Greed improved the girl's looks, brightening her eyes and bringing a flush to her cheeks. "Oh yes, sir. There's more than one way to leave the Brimming Bucket."

Well pleased, Maybor nodded. "I trust I can count on you to let my wishes be known?"

The girl hesitated a moment. "Well, sir, naturally I'd be glad to help such a fine gentleman as yourself, but—"

"You'll need some extra coinage to ensure the word is well spread."

"Well, I hate to ask, sir, but you know what men are like. They hate to do anything on just the *promise* of gold."

Maybor handed her a fistful of coinage. He knew exactly what men were like. "And when you've done that," he said, "bring me a footstool for my feet. The floor is running with ale, and I want to give my shoes chance to dry."

As the girl cut across the tavern to its keeper, Maybor's eyes flicked toward the candle on the sill. Down a notch since he'd last looked. Damn! Where was the boy? What was keeping him? Had Baralis decided to hold him in the palace and torture the truth out of him? Maybor brought the second mug of ale to his lips. Somehow he doubted that. He knew his enemy well, and Baralis would come, not just because he was curious, but also because he was compelled to do so.

Maybor downed a throatful of the golden brew. He wasn't a superstitious man, indeed, hated any mention of mystics and magic, but he and Baralis were connected in some way: their fates were intertwined. They fed off each other. And it had been a long time for both of them since their last meal.

Nabber wasn't at all sure that he liked being Baralis' escort. The man's presence had a distinct effect on those around him: people scattered like rats in torchlight whenever he walked by. Nabber shook his head grimly—the man would never make a pocket. He had the *feet* for it, though. He and Baralis had been walking for quarter of an hour now, and not once had Nabber heard a single footfall from his black-robed companion. Swift would die for feet like that.

The rain had stopped the moment Baralis passed under the palace gate. The streets were damp, steaming, fragrant with a variety of rainy smells. As they walked south the district changed: fine stone buildings gave way to precarious wooden structures that leant against each other for support. The fare offered by the street hawkers changed accordingly. Near the palace they had sold fresh lampreys, artichokes, and saffron. Here they sold meat pies, pease pudding, and bread.

As they turned onto the street that boasted the Brimming Bucket, Nabber risked a quick glance sideways. Baralis did not look happy. In fact, he looked rather venomous, his features no more than a pale insignificance when compared to the darkness of his eyes. Nabber sniffed solemnly. He hoped Maybor knew what he was doing.

The Brimming Bucket was lit up in anticipation of the night. Smoke and candlelight escaped from the shutters and the boldly painted sign creaked brightly in the wind. Nabber noticed a man standing by the door; his right hand was resting inside his tunic and, after one quick scope of the two of them, he directed his gaze toward the floor. A lookout, no doubt set to watch by Maybor. Well, he certainly could have been more discreet about it. Nabber doubted very much that the man's purpose had gone unnoticed by Baralis.

"Here we are," said Nabber, hoping to distract Baralis' thoughts away from the lookout. "Maybor is waiting for you inside."

Baralis nodded once. "I know."

*

Inside he went. Poorly rendered tallow gave off smoke that stung his eyes. He was all senses, a being purely of perception: if there was danger he would search it out. Even before his eyes grew accustomed to the smoke he had eliminated sorcery as a threat. *He* was the only one in the room with power beyond flesh. The knowledge brought confidence in its wake. No matter what happened now, he would be able to deal with it.

Baralis looked around the room. Thirty pairs of eyes were gazing upon him. The floor was awash with slowly souring ale: the tavern reeked of it. Maybor was sitting at a lower level in front of the fire, and Baralis didn't spot him at first. Silhouetted against the light, Maybor stood up and beckoned him forth. Baralis crossed the room and stepped down into the enclosed space of the fire-well. Two other men sat there: old men who drew in their chairs when Baralis entered their domain. Unlike the rest of the tavern floor, which was raised off the ground and paved, the floor in the fire-well consisted purely of packed-down earth. It was even wetter than above, and the old men sat cross-legged, one foot apiece resting in the pool of ale.

"Aah, Baralis," said Maybor, with an expansive sweep of his arm. "I'm so pleased you could come."

"Cut to the meat, Maybor," hissed Baralis.

"As charming as ever, I see." Maybor sat down. When Baralis made no motion to sit, he said, "Stay where you are and you give me no choice but to shout my news all over the tavern."

"News!" Baralis' voice was scathing. "The petty intelligences of a fugitive on the run do not count as news to me."

Maybor was not in the least affected by this tirade. Calmly he drummed his fingertips against the wood. "If you didn't come here to listen to what I have to say, then I am forced to conclude that you came to see my handsome face, instead."

"As ugly as your face is, Maybor, it still might be the greatest of your charms."

Maybor beamed. "I'm glad you think so, as I'm hoping to pass my features down in the blood."

Baralis felt the skin on his cheeks flush. He had a sudden, overpowering sensation of foreboding. As his stomach constricted, the world shifted and refocused. The Brimming Bucket turned from tavern to snake pit. Maybor changed from drunken fool to fiend. "What do you mean?"

"I mean, my dear Baralis, that in less than seven months time I shall be a grandfather. Melliandra is with child and—"

"*No!*"

"Oh, yes. The child is the duke's. The marriage *was* consummated."

"You are lying."

"Why, Baralis, you're trembling. I thought you would be pleased."

Baralis, annoyed at showing weakness, drew breath before moving close to Maybor. "Your daughter is a whore who has rutted with every man who crossed her path. Don't expect either me or the good people of Bren to believe a single word of what you say."

Maybor reached out and grabbed Baralis' robe close to the throat. "My daughter was a virgin when she married the duke."

Baralis was aware that the noise in the tavern had died down. He was also aware that two well-built men had moved from their position at the bar to the top stair leading down to the fire-well. The only movement was from a sick-looking cat padding through the ale toward the fire.

"I wouldn't be so sure that Melliandra was a virgin if I were you, Maybor," Baralis said slowly. "She certainly showed me a few new tricks when I had her."

Baralis saw the knife flash. By the time it raked against

his cheek, a drawing was on his lips. He let it build on his tongue while he pulled away from the table. The two men behind had moved to the second stair. Maybor remained seated; he seemed content to have drawn blood.

"Your lies will not win in the end, Baralis," he said. "Melliandra's son will have Bren to himself."

Baralis didn't even acknowledge the words. He stepped upon the first stair of the fire-well, and then let the sorcery out. Beneath his palms the air shimmered. It crackled with a blue light: a charged streak of lightning aimed straight at the beer-covered floor. With his back to the room only Maybor, the two old men, and the cat saw it flash. Baralis spun round as the ale began to sizzle.

One of the old men screamed first. Then everyone began to scream—one voice indistinguishable from another. The smell of hops was carried on the warm ripple of air that hit Baralis' back. The two men who had moved from the bar made no attempt to stop him. Baralis felt the familiar wave of weakness. People rushed past him toward the fire-well, shock on their faces, eyes cast downward to avoid his gaze. He had to get away from here, to get back to the palace. There was one thing he must do, however. Weary though he was, he formed a second drawing as he walked across the room.

A compulsion weaved its way through the air, fine as sea spray yet wide enough to cover thirty people. It settled like dust and was drawn into the lungs like a fragrance. The very air itself became a message, and it was quickly translated by the blood. After Baralis left, no one would remember his passing. He would be a mysterious man in black, nothing more. Every person in the tavern would give a different description of him and no two tellings would be the same. He could not risk his identity becoming known.

By the time he reached the door, he could barely walk. Outside he stumbled, legs buckling under him, heart racing ahead. A man with a mule loaded with cabbages stood in the street watching him.

"Take me to the palace," he murmured. "And I will make you a rich man." Even then, when nothing seemed left, he squeezed forth enough to put a compulsion behind the words. It nearly killed him.

The last thing Baralis saw before he fell into darkness were two baskets full of cabbages being thrown onto the road.

Maybor wasn't entirely sure what had just happened. In the small area of the fire-well all hell had been let loose, yet he had remained untouched by it. The two old men lay slumped against their table, hair on end, feet and ankles blackened as if burned. The cat lay dead on the ale-washed floor. Its paws were still smoking. All around him people were fussing and panicking and muttering about a man in black. It was time to get out of here. Swinging his feet from the footstool to the floor, Maybor stood up and pushed his way toward the door.

Two

$\mathcal{J}$ack was beginning to hate herbs—particularly the smelly ones.

He was waiting in the darkened storeroom, barely moving, barely breathing, while Stillfox dealt with his unexpected visitor on the other side of the door. Bunches of mint and rosemary hung above Jack's head, tangling in his hair and tempting him to sneeze. He'd been here for quite a while now, and his left leg was beginning to cramp. He couldn't risk stretching it out, though, so with teeth firmly gritted, his mind searched out diversions.

Frallit used to say that the best way to stop cramp was to strike the offending limb with a good-sized plank of wood. Jack had once been the unlucky recipient of this "cure" and had quickly learned never to claim cramp in Frallit's hearing again. Jack smiled at the memory. They were good days.

Or were they? The smile left his face: could he honestly say he'd been happy at Castle Harvell? He had a bed to sleep in every night, food to eat, and a measure of security about his future, but was he *happy*? People whispered behind his back, naming him a bastard and his mother a whore. As a mere apprentice he was treated badly by everyone around him, and Frallit was not the kindly father-figure that his memory seemed intent on creating. He was nothing more than a sadistic vengeful bully. And Jack bore the scars to prove it.

No, Castle Harvell wasn't some wonderful peaceful haven where worries and heartache simply didn't exist. It was filled with people who allowed him no freedom, who beat the will from his mind and drained the strength from his body. And he should never have allowed himself to look back at it through a romantic haze of longing. The past was all it was good for.

Jack was strangely exhilarated by these thoughts; there was power in them. Why hadn't he seen all this before?

Then, from the kitchen, he heard a word that stopped all thoughts dead:

"Melliandra."

Jack was sure the name was hers—he heard it often enough in his dreams. Without moving as much as a finger's breadth, Jack trained every sense and focused every cell upon the wood-paneled door separating him from Stillfox and his uninvited guest.

Stillfox was speaking: "Who can say what Catherine will do to—" The scrape of iron poker against grate cut off the end of the sentence.

Jack cursed all things metal.

"Well, I wouldn't like to be in her shoes," said the stranger.

Did he mean Catherine or Melli?

"Ah, well," Stillfox said, "we have our own troubles to worry about. I hear our generals travel to the Wall today . . . "

Jack got the feeling that Stillfox was deliberately changing the subject.

A week after he'd first come to stay with the herbalist, Jack had told him a shortened version of his life since leaving Castle Harvell. He had been very selective with the details—no one would ever know about Tarissa's betrayal—but he had confided to Stillfox about Melli.

He had told him who she was, how they had met, and how they had come to be separated in Helch.

Even before the story was free from his lips, Stillfox had told him the news. "Maybor's daughter is to marry the duke of Bren."

On hearing those words, Jack felt a confusion of emotions: relief that she was safe, wonder at how she had come to end up with the duke and, if he were honest, disappointment that she had finally succumbed to convention and married a man with position and wealth. He was jealous, too. Melli had been his to protect, his dream had been to save her. All gone now. A duchess in a fine palace needed saving from nothing except false flattery.

There had been no word of her since.

Until now. Stillfox's uninvited guest had brought news of Melli's marriage and, judging from the few snatches of conversation that Jack had managed to hear, things did not sound good.

Jack *willed* the stranger to leave. He needed to talk to Stillfox, to find out if Melli was all right. The ointment on his glass burns itched with gleeful intent. The storeroom began to seem impossibly small and confining. Herb dust choked in his throat, and the darkness fueled his fears. The idea that Melli could be in danger worked upon his brain like a poison. The longer he waited, the wilder his thoughts became. Had the duke decided to rid himself of his new bride? Had Baralis somehow discredited Melli? Or had Kylock abducted her in a fit of jealous rage?

At last the kitchen door banged shut. Jack was in the kitchen before the shutters stopped rattling. The light stung his eyes. Stillfox was leaning against the fireplace. He looked a little stiff, as if his position were posed.

"Sorry to keep you in the storeroom for so long, Jack. There's no getting rid of Garfus."

"What did he say about Melli?" Jack hardly recognized his own voice. It was cold, commanding.

"Why, Jack, give me a minute to get settled and I'll tell you all he said."

"Tell me now."

Stillfox made time for himself by raking through the ashes then pulling up a chair. Finally he spoke. "Nine of Annis' best generals are heading to Highwall to assist in coordinating the invasion."

Despite his determination to learn about Melli, Jack couldn't help but ask, "Invasion of what?"

The herbalist shrugged. "Bren, of course."

"Why 'of course'? Why not invade the kingdoms, or try and rout Kylock's forces on the Halcus field?"

"Because Bren will soon belong to Kylock."

Jack felt a single tremor pass down his spine. "I thought the duke's marriage had put an end to that."

Stillfox tried to backtrack. "Ah well, when he marries Catherine it's as good as his. And Highwall isn't the sort of city to split hairs in matters of war."

He was lying. Self-righteous anger—so briefly tasted earlier while he thought of Castle Harvell—began to build within Jack. Stillfox was keeping something from him. He was playing him for a fool. "What happened between Melli and the duke?"

Stillfox looked nervous. "Jack, I have my reasons for keeping things from you—"

"*Reasons!* I don't want to hear your reasons. I want to hear the truth."

"You're not ready to run away to Bren yet. Your training has barely started." Stillfox took a step forward.

Jack stepped toward the door. "You are not my keeper, Stillfox. My life is my own responsibility, and I'll have no one deciding what is and isn't right for me to hear." Jack was trembling. Anger was flowing through him and he made no effort to control it. "Now either tell me what happened to Melli, or as Borc is my witness I will walk out this door and find out for myself."

Stillfox raised his arm. "Jack, you don't understand—"

Jack's hand was on the latch. "No. You're the one who doesn't understand, Stillfox. I've had a bellyful of lies, they've destroyed everything I ever had—I'm sick to the death of them. And today I've finally heard one too many." As Jack spoke he thought of Tarissa, Rovas, and Magra: they were all liars. Even his mother had practiced deceit. Who was worse, he wondered: people who lied outright like Rovas and Tarissa, or people who kept the truth to themselves like his mother and Stillfox?

Jack brought down the latch with his fist. He couldn't really see the difference.

"Jack! Don't go," cried the herbalist, rushing forward. "I'll tell you everything."

Opening the door, Jack said, "Too late now, Stillfox. I doubt if I'd believe you anyway." Stepping out into the warm summer rain, he slammed the door behind him. He set a course to meet with the high road. If he was lucky, he'd reach Annis by dusk.

Tavalisk had just come from his counting house where he'd been counting out his money. Such a trip always served to reassure him. Gold was the ultimate feather pillow—whenever one had to fall back on it, one could be sure of a cushioned blow. The archbishop's stockpile of gold was the nearest thing he had to a family; it was always there to comfort him, it asked no questions and told no lies, and it would never ever die and leave him helpless.

Tavalisk did not remember his real family fondly. His mother might have indeed brought him into the world, but she chose both the place and the circumstance badly.

Born in a beggar's hospice in Silbur, his earliest memory was watching his mother's pig die of swine fever. It just lay in the rushes amidst its own filth and willed itself to death. Tavalisk remembered scraping around in the dirt to bring it acorns, but the creature refused to eat them. It simply stayed in its corner and never made a sound. Tavalisk had loved that pig, but when it *let* itself die, making no effort to save itself, he turned against it. He beat the last breath out of it with a warming brick he'd snatched from the hearth. Even at such a tender age, when he was still breaking his milk teeth, Tavalisk knew that self-preservation and self-promotion were the only things that counted. And the pig, like his mother, had been sorely lacking in both.

Once the pig died, they had no choice but to eat the tainted flesh. He and his mother were the lowest amongst the low, the poorest amongst the poor. The only things they owned were the clothes on their backs, a sackful of turnips, and two tin spoons. They had no knife, so his mother was forced to drag the pig's carcass to the meat market to be butchered. The butcher had taken everything but the head in payment. Tavalisk could still remember the butcher now, rubbing pig blood into his mustache to make it stiffen whilst offering to take less pork if his mother agreed to bed him. Tavalisk would never forgive her for turning the man down: it would have meant cutlets, not tongue.

Such self-indulgent sacrifice had haunted his early childhood. His mother had taken a position as a church cleaner for no other reason than she didn't like to live off charity. Tavalisk quickly learned that priests were more miserly than moneylenders. Generous gifts of food were kept under lock and key, the level of blessed wine was marked against the bottle each night, and every holy sweetmeat was counted after mass.

Oh, but the ceremony was breathtaking, though. Priests were part magician, part actor, part king. They performed miracles, granted forgiveness, and held congregations of thousands in their thrall. They wielded power in this world and the next. Tavalisk watched them from his hideout behind the choir stall. He saw the glamour of it all: the gold and crimson tapestries, the snowy-white wax candles, the jewel-encrusted reliquaries, and the silver-robed choirboys who sang with angels' voices. It was a world of gaudy enchantments, and Tavalisk vowed he would be part of it.

One year later his mother died and he was thrown out on the street, penniless. His love for the Church, quite understandably, diminished, and it was many years and half a continent later before he felt its lure again. When the call finally came, however, it didn't take Tavalisk long to realize that in the politically sensitive hierarchy of the Church, there was more than one way to reach the top.

Smiling gently, the archbishop moved across his study to his desk, where a splendid meal awaited him. His remembrances had acted like a fine white wine, honing an edge to his appetite, wetting his tongue for more. But, as with wine, Tavalisk was careful never to overindulge his memories—he wasn't about to end up a quivering, sentimental fool.

He brought the duck thigh to his lips, and all thoughts of the past vanished as the oil-rich flesh met his tongue. By the time he'd swallowed the meat his mind was firmly in the present.

Gamil chose this moment to knock upon the door.

"Enter, Gamil. Enter," called Tavalisk, rather pleased that his aide had arrived. There were matters he needed to discuss.

"How is Your Eminence this day?" asked Gamil entering the room.

"Never better, Gamil. The duck is crispy, the wine is tart, and war draws nearer by the hour."

"It is the war that brings me here, Your Eminence."

"Aah, a meeting of the minds." Tavalisk was genial. "How very fortuitous. Tell me your news." He grabbed another thigh from the platter, dipped it into the pepper dish, and set about tearing flesh from the bone.

"Well, Your Eminence, nine Annis generals are set to meet with their Highwall equivalents in three days time."

"And like a romantic couple they hope to set a date, eh, Gamil?"

"Yes, Your Eminence. They mean to discuss invasion plans."

"Hmm . . . " Tavalisk toyed with the remains of the duck. "When do you think they'll head for Bren?"

"It's hard to say, Your Eminence. I think it's wise to assume they won't do anything until the wedding has taken place. After all, their grievances are with Kylock, not Bren."

"That will take us into high summer, then. If they have any sense they will make their move while the wedding bed is still warm."

"They may move into position before then, Your Eminence. It could take the Wall nearly two weeks to bring its foot soldiers and siege engines through the passes. If they were to wait until the wedding, the delay might prove crucial."

Tavalisk dislodged the wishbone on the duck. He always liked to pull both ends himself—that way he was sure to receive all the luck. Oddly enough, this one snapped right down the middle. "Can't be done, Gamil. You must send a fast messenger out to represent the southern cities in the talks."

"But, Your Eminence, Annis and Highwall won't listen to us."

"Of course they will, Gamil. Who do you think is financing the damn war for them in the first place? The northern cities might be strong and well-peopled, but they are woefully short on cash. Why, Annis couldn't even finance a pleasant mountain hike, let alone a full-blown siege." Tavalisk threw the offending pieces of wishbone on the fire: something about their matching length and symmetry sent shivers down his spine. "At the end of the day, Gamil, they will listen to us because they have no choice."

"What message would Your Eminence have me convey?"

"In no shape or form should Annis or Highwall make a move against Bren—and that includes taking up positions—until the marriage has been legally consummated."

"May I be permitted to know Your Eminence's reasons for this?"

"Gamil, if I were to throw you into a pond you would surely sink straight to the bottom."

"Why, Your Eminence?"

"Because you're about as dense as a piece of lead!" Tavalisk snorted with good humor. He always enjoyed pointing out how much cleverer he was than anyone else. "Really, Gamil. Don't you see? If Annis and Highwall make any move before the wedding is legally fixed, then there's a chance the whole thing might fall through. Do you really think the good people of Bren are going to cheer their favorite daughter down the aisle when an army, the size of which has not been seen in over a century, is poised in the passes ready to invade?" The archbishop finished his speech with a chorus of disappointed tut-tutting.

"But surely if an army were in place, and the wedding was canceled, then all our problems would be solved?"

"The only time our problems will be solved, Gamil, is when Tyren and the knighthood have been sent crying back to Valdis, and when that demon Baralis lies cold in his grave. Neither of which is likely to happen, I hasten to add, unless the whole northern crisis comes firmly to a head."

"But—"

"Say that word once more, Gamil, and I swear I will have you excommunicated on the spot!" The archbishop brandished the bare drumstick like a weapon. "Think, man. *Think*. Just suppose the wedding didn't go ahead, where would that leave us?" Tavalisk didn't wait for an answer. "It would leave us with Kylock still ruling a third of the north, and very liable, with the knights' help, to conquer more. Baralis would still be behind it all, scheming and maneuvering, and Tyren—Borc rot his greasy little soul—would eventually be set to gain control of the Church in the north. The only thing the wedding changes is the time scale. The marriage of Catherine and Kylock will only serve to accelerate events that have already been set in motion."

Gamil looked suitably contrite. "I see Your Eminence's point."

"There was never any question that you wouldn't," said the archbishop, flashing his aide a distinctly cool glance. "Now. What I need you to do, Gamil, is scribe a persuasive letter to the duke of Highwall. Tell him that the south still stands beside him, and more money is on the way, and so forth. Then inform him, in no uncertain terms, that we will completely withdraw our resources if he moves so much as a single soldier eastward before the marriage is in place."

"Very well, Your Eminence. Is there anything more?"

"Just one more thing, Gamil. Would you mind going down to the market district and buying me a fish?"

"What sort of fish, Your Eminence?"

"One in a bowl, Gamil. Ever since my cat had that unfortunate accident with the tapestry, I've been missing having a friendly creature around. I fancy a fish this time."

"As you wish." Gamil bowed and made his way toward the door. Just as he stepped from the room, the archbishop called out:

"Oh, and Gamil, I'm sure you will want to pay for it yourself. The Feast of Borc's First Miracle is coming up, and I feel a fish would be an appropriate gift, don't you?" Tavalisk smiled sweetly. "No cheap one, mind."

Tawl sat in the sun-drenched windowseat and whittled at a piece of wood. The cushion, which had rested invitingly atop the stone, lay discarded on the floor. Comfort was something that he just couldn't get used to.

Every so often, when a splinter of wood fell to the floor or his knife sliced into a knot, Tawl would look up through the open window and search for any sign of Nabber in the street below. The boy had been gone four days now and Tawl was worried sick about him. Oh, he knew *why* the boy had gone missing—he was keeping a low profile after what had happened at the Brimming Bucket the other afternoon—but bad deeds done with dubious intentions were Nabber's trademark, and Tawl could neither curse him nor condemn him. He'd done much worse himself.

Maybor had returned to the hideout in early evening the day before last. The man was a little shaken and confused and had finally admitted that he had a meeting with Baralis, and that Nabber had acted as go-between. Maybor was unrepentant. He railed on most indignantly about his right, as an expectant grandfather, to inform anyone he wished of Melli's delicate condition. When Tawl questioned him about the details of the meeting, Maybor was unusually reticent; a blank look came over his face, and he mumbled something to the effect that he wasn't about to be questioned like a prisoner in the stocks. Tawl suspected the great lord simply *couldn't* remember. Which could only mean one thing: sorcery.

Tawl shook his head, quickly glanced down to the street, and resumed his whittling. Maybor had no idea how lucky he was. He had been a fly who thought that just because the spider was out of its web, somehow it was rendered less deadly.

Two days back Tawl had gone down to the Brimming Bucket to find out for himself what had gone down. The patrons, besides being blind-drunk to the last man, were united in their confusion about the events of the day before. A mysterious black-robed figure had shot lightning onto the floor, said one man. Another disagreed with him entirely, stating that the very ale on the floorboards had begun to sizzle of its own accord. One thing they all seemed to know, however, was the fact that Melliandra claimed to be with child by the duke.

The word was out now. All the city knew that Melli was pregnant. Just this morning, Cravin had visited the townhouse, bearing tales of people's reactions. "Most say Melliandra is a brazen liar and a whore," he had said. "But given time I should be able to whip up some support."

Tawl felt like murdering Maybor. With one single act of bravado, the man had endangered not only his own life, but his daughter's, too. Now that her pregnancy was common knowledge, Melli was more vulnerable than ever. At this very minute Baralis would be having the city searched door to door. Posters offering rewards for details about Melli's whereabouts could be found on every street corner. The net was closing fast, and Maybor's little rendezvous had ensured that Baralis would pull it in all the way.

"I've got the pies, Tawl," came a voice from the bottom of the stairs. "Should I take one to the lady?"

"Make sure she gets the finest, Bodger," Tawl replied. "And test the milk before she drinks any—it must be fresh and cool."

"Grift's already done that, Tawl. Ain't nobody like him for telling when the milk has turned. He has the nose of a dairyman and the hands of a milkmaid."

Groaning, Tawl said, "Just take it to her, Bodger."

"It's as good as done, Tawl. Grift always says that . . . " The words padded into the distance along with the footsteps.

The two chapel guards had turned up on the doorstep the other day, looking decidedly sheepish and reeling off Nabber's secret entry phrase. Tawl had no choice—as Nabber was well aware—but to take them in. They were a risk; they knew the address of the hideout. The only other alternative would have been to kill them—and he hadn't felt like murder that day. Despite everything Tawl couldn't help but smile. Those two guards were quite a pair.

And Melli owed them her life.

He only wished the duke had a similar debt.

Tawl stabbed at the windowframe with his knife. Why was he destined always to fail? Why did he fail those he was sworn to protect? Again and again the knife came down. Why, whenever he felt as if he was getting ahead, did something always happen to pull him back? The knife hovered in the air an instant, then Tawl let it fall to his lap. Now was not the time for self-reproach. Melli was here, and keeping her safe was what counted. His oath as the duke's champion was to protect the duke *and* his heirs. The duke might be dead, but his widow and his unborn child were still served by that oath and Tawl was bound to guard them with his life. The whole of Bren had heard him swear it.

A quick look out the window—still no sign of Nabber. They needed to leave the city. Baralis was tracking them, and Nabber and Maybor with their secret meetings and nighttime forays were practically asking to be caught. Of course, they both thought they were as clever as could be. But Baralis was cleverer by far. It would only be a matter of time before they were caught. Unless they got clean away.

Sighing heavily, Tawl took up his piece of wood and began to whittle once more. His hands seemed intent on making something, but they hadn't yet informed his brain what it was.

There were two problems with leaving the city. First, every gate, every road, every dip in the wall was being watched by enough guards to take a fort. Baralis knew they would try to leave at some point, and he was taking no chances. The passes were being monitored, the walls were patrolled by archers, even the lake boasted a ring of troops around its shore. There was going to be no easy way out. Secondly, even if there were an easy way out, Melli might be too sick to take it.

The pregnancy was not going well. Melli was losing

weight. She was now so thin that it tore at Tawl's heart to look at her. For two weeks after the duke's death, she had simply refused to eat. She was in shock, unable to eat, talk, or even cry. Then slowly she began to come round, taking bread with her milk, washing her face and hair, and even smiling at Nabber's antics. Thinking back on it now, Tawl guessed that Melli began to look after herself about the same time she began to suspect she was pregnant. Still, even now, when her appetite had all but returned, she could barely keep her food down. No sooner had she eaten something than it could be seen, as Nabber put it, "returning like an ugly sister."

Everyone spoiled her. Nothing was too good, or too much trouble. Pies were baked fresh each day, Maybor had purchased a hen so she would have newly laid eggs, and Nabber brought her flowers and fruit. Despite all this attention, however, Melli's health was not improving.

Tawl had lost loved ones. He knew what it was to grieve. Daily he wrestled with the soul-destroying *what ifs*. Melli had watched an assassin cut her husband's throat, and she would have to deal with her own set of regrets. What if she had entered the bedchamber first? What if she had only screamed louder? What if she had never married the duke at all?

No, Tawl shook his head softly, it was hardly strange that Melli was not well. That she got through each day was miracle enough.

Tawl checked the street as a matter of course. No Nabber, no strangers, no guards.

What was he going to do about Melli? Should he place her unborn child at risk by taking her from the city? Or should he place the child's health first and stay put? If they left the city, there would be many days of hard traveling, mountains to cross, soldiers to evade; they would have to live rough and be light on their feet in case they were chased. If they stayed in Bren they risked capture, but at least Melli's pregnancy would run smoothly.

Tawl looked down at his hands, and saw for the first time what he was sculpting: it was a child's doll.

Was his first loyalty to Melli or the baby?

Jack's feet felt as if they had been run over by a loaded cart. The rest of his body wasn't doing too well, either—particularly the glass burns. Stillfox certainly knew how to turn an ointment into a weapon. For two days now his arms and chest had been throbbing, but over the past four hours his feet had stolen the show.

He had finally made it to Annis. The city lay ahead of him, its gray walls gleaming in the moonlight. The road to either side was lined with houses and taverns, their shutters and lintels painted many shades of blue. People were everywhere, driving cattle home from pasture, bringing unsold goods from market, walking slowly to evening mass, or briskly to well-lit taverns. The wind was cool and smelled of wood smoke. Stars glinted high above the mountains, and somewhere water skipped noisily over a quarry's worth of rocks.

The road consisted of crushed stones that crunched with every step. Jack could feel their sharp edges cutting through his shoes. He was nervous. Surely people were staring at him. Yet he looked no different from anyone else. His clothes, which had been provided by Stillfox, were much the same as any man's. True, his hair was long, but it was tied at the back of his neck with a length of Wadwell rope. Jack's hand stole up to check it—a gesture he caught himself doing more and more these days—and he found the rope was still in place. Nothing made by the Wadwells was likely to wear out, drop off, or break. In fact, Jack was pretty certain that the rope would have to be buried with him.

Smiling, Jack looked up. A young girl was staring straight at him. As soon as their glances met she looked away. Jack moved on. He made a point of walking where the light from the houses couldn't catch him.

It had been ten weeks since he first met Stillfox and over three months since the garrison burned. Could the Halcus still be looking for him? With the war all but lost and an invasion of Bren planned, did they really have time or resources to search out one man?

All thoughts vanished from Jack's head as he reached the outer wall of Annis. The gate was being drawn closed for the night. The portcullis was being lowered, the overhead timbers creaking with the strain. Jack ran toward it.

"Watch out, boy!" came a gruff warning. "Or the spikes will have your shoulders for mincemeat."

Jack took a step back. "I must enter the city tonight." As he spoke, Jack attempted to mimic Stillfox's way of speaking—his kingdoms accent would give him away.

A second man, situated high atop the wall, shouted down. "Slip us a few golds and I'll hold the gate while you pass."

"I don't have any gold."

"Then I don't have the strength to hold the gate." The portcullis plunged toward the ground. Jack contemplated making a run for it, decided it wasn't a good idea, so hissed a few choice curses instead. The spikes fell straight into the waiting pits and the city was closed off for the night.

"Try us in the morning, boy," said the gatekeeper pleasantly. "My strength might have returned by then."

Jack smiled up at the man, while calling him a smug devil under his breath. How was he going to get into the city now?

With nothing else to do and nowhere to go, Jack began to walk around the walls. Made of light gray granite, they had been finely polished and then chiseled with a diamond's edge. Demons and angels had been carved side by side, the sun shared the sky with the stars, and Borc and the devil walked hand in hand.

"Annis is a city of intellectuals," Grift had once said. "They're not happy unless they're confusing, confounding, and acting as devil's advocate." Jack remembered that Grift's first wife had come from Annis, so that probably explained a lot.

The temperature was dropping sharply and the wind from the mountains was picking up speed. Jack knew the wise thing to do would be to turn around and head back to Stillfox's cottage. Wearing only a light wool tunic and britches, he was not dressed for the night. His limbs were aching and his feet were sore and chafed. The herbalist would take him in, feed him, give him medicine and brandy, and now, after their argument this morning, very probably tell all he wanted to know about Melli.

Yes, Jack thought, the *wise* thing would definitely be to go back. Only pride wouldn't let him. He had left swearing to Stillfox that he would find out the truth on his own, and so by Borc he would! Even if it killed him.

Annis was turning out to be quite large. The walls towered so high above him and stretched out so far ahead that they disappeared into their own dark shadows, merging into the night. Jack had to constantly watch his step; water pipes, sewer ducts, and rain channels all led away from the wall. Once out of the city, these carefully constructed conduits simply ended in pools of stinking slop. Jack grimaced as he was forced to jump over one. It seemed even intellectuals were capable of embracing the idea of out of sight out of mind.

An owl called shrill and close. Jack was so startled, he stepped right back into the puddle he'd just safely jumped. *"Borc's blood,"* he hissed, scraping the soles of his shoes against a rock. Owls weren't supposed to live by mountains!

Just then he heard a soft whisper carried on the wind. Jack froze in mid-scrape. A second whisper chased after the first: a man's voice beckoning. Looking ahead, Jack tried to make out the details in the shadow. A row of high bushes cut straight across his line of view. Strange, the bushes led directly to the wall. A man's head appeared above the leaf tops, then another, and another. Where were they coming from? As far as Jack could make out, the bushes sloped away from the city and then curved into darkness down the hillside.

Very slowly Jack placed his foot on the ground. There were no twigs or dry leaves to give him away. He began to creep toward the bushes. More heads bobbed over the top, all heading for the wall. As he drew near, Jack could feel his heart banging against his chest. Saliva had all but abandoned his mouth, leaving it as rough as a dog's snout.

Suddenly a hand slapped over Jack's mouth. Pudgy, moist, and broad, it cut off the air to his lungs. Jack whipped around, elbow out like a club. The man the hand belonged to was massive; rolls of fat quivered in the moonlight. Just before Jack slammed his elbow into him, he let out a mighty roar:

"Miller!"

The word was a battle cry, and even as its caller went down, a score of men rallied to the cause. The bushes opened up and an army of fat men dressed in baker's white came out brandishing sticks and knives. Jack knew when he was outnumbered. He raised his hands in submission.

The man on the ground made a quick recovery, flesh trembling as he pulled himself up. His army drew close, no longer running but with weapons still held before them. Jack felt the return of the pudgy hand.

The white-aproned men formed a half circle around him. "He looks like no miller I know," said one of their number.

"Aye, Barmer, but you know millers—sneaky through and through." This comment, made by the fattest of the group, elicited several grunts of approval.

The pudgy-handed one spoke up from behind. "Do we give him a chance to speak, or club him where he stands?"

"Club him!" cried the fattest.

"Search him first for gold," cried Barmer.

The hand that was pressed against Jack's mouth smelled strongly of yeast. "Well," said its owner, "I think we should question him anyway. Suspend his vitals over a hot griddle and we'll soon learn what the millers are up to." The word *millers* was spoken with an enemy's contempt.

Jack was beginning to realize what he had chanced upon. Snapping back his jaw, he jerked it quickly forward and bit the pudgy-handed man squarely on the thumb. Free from the man's grip for an instant, Jack cried, "I'm not a miller! I'm one of you. I'm a baker."

Three

*I*t seemed a lot darker in Bren tonight than any other night Nabber could remember. Not that he was scared of the dark, of course. It was just a little worrying, that was all. Swift had once said, *"Some nights just aren't right for pocketing,"* and this was most definitely one of those.

Nabber was weaving his way through the south side of the city, about a league east of Cravin's townhouse. He'd been skirting around the hideout all day, hoping to muster enough courage to face Tawl. He knew the knight would give him a lashing, the worst kind, too—a verbal one. After all he deserved it, sending Bodger and Grift round with the password, getting Lord Maybor nearly killed. Why, all he needed to do to top it all off would be to bring the duke's blackhelms to the door!

Nabber spat in self-disgust. Swift would have revoked his pocketing privileges and cast him out on the street for less.

Oh, he knew he had to go back—and in fact had pocketed more than enough gold to ensure a welcome return—but the thought of seeing disapproval or, even worse, disappointment, on Tawl's noble face kept his feet from making their move. He still kept an eye on the hideout, though. Just to make sure that everyone was safe and no guards had turned up to take Tawl and Melli away. He wouldn't be able to live with himself if that had happened in his absence. Scratching his chin to aid reflection, Nabber carefully considered such an occurrence. Well, he might be able to live with himself after all—but he'd be sorely ashamed.

Slap! Thump! Tap!

For the first time Nabber's brain registered what his ears already knew: someone had stepped from the alleyway and was following him. Someone with a bad leg and a stick. To test the man out, Nabber made a point of crossing the cobbled road.

Slap! Thump! Tap!

The man followed suit. Now, looking like a penniless, scrawny low-life as he did, Nabber didn't think old Bad Leg's intention was to rob him. Which left only two other possibilities: Bad Leg was either a tunic-lifter, or one of Baralis' spies. Either way, Nabber knew it was time to move on.

Remaining as calm as Swift had taught him, he began to walk a little faster. Bad Leg matched him step for mismatched step. He walked real fast for a man with a stick. Nabber's eyes searched out likely doors and alleyways. He was beginning to feel a little afraid.

Slap! Thump! Tap!

Bad Leg was gaining on him. The sound of his lurching footsteps sent a shiver down Nabber's spine. There was no one on the streets to watch them pass. Straight ahead lay a series of archways where the poultry sellers sold their birds by day. Nabber knew this area well: swan and peacock sellers were famous for their loose coinage. To the right was Duck's End, a short alleyway that most people believed finished in a dead end. Nabber knew differently. A small drainage tunnel led under the wall. If he hadn't grown too much in the past three weeks, he should be able to squeeze through it. Old Bad Leg wouldn't stand a chance.

Nabber feinted to the left, then waited until the last possible moment before cutting a sharp right.

Slap! Thump! Tap!

There was no fooling Bad Leg.

Duck's End was a dark spot in an already dark night. A trickle of sweat slid along Nabber's temple and then down his cheek. *It's just getting a little hot around here,* he told himself, wiping his face with his sleeve. Bad Leg was only a shadow behind him now. Nabber picked up his pace. The ground was always wet in alleyways regardless of the rain, and Nabber's shoes squelched with every step. The dead end loomed close. The drainage tunnel was a black puddle at the bottom corner of the wall. Nabber began to gravitate toward it.

Slap! Thump! Tap!

So did Bad Leg.

Sweat was now running unchecked down Nabber's cheek. The sound of the man's footsteps had his nerves on edge. Feet away from the tunnel now, Nabber gave up all semblance of dignity and made a run for it. Water splashed round his ankles, air raced past his face. The violent thumping of his heart drowned out all other noise. A whiff of air rose up from the tunnel: the foul stench meant freedom.

Feet first? Head first? Nabber had only a split second to decide. Taking a deep breath, he dived for the tunnel.

The entrance engulfed him, dark and inviting. He slid down into its moist and furtive depths. Hands, head, shoulders, body, legs . . . Feet! Nabber felt something clawing at his feet. Close to panicking, he kicked out wildly. His hands searched the curved wall of the tunnel for something to grip on to. His kick had no effect: Bad Leg's fingers still grasped at his feet. They felt like talons.

Then a hand moved up to his ankle. Nabber tried to crawl forward, but Bad Leg pulled him back. The sheer strength of the pull took him by surprise. For some reason Nabber had thought the man would be weak. Scrambling for a handhold, Nabber was dragged from the tunnel. His belly scraped through the mud. His heart was beating so fast it was surely going to burst. The hands moved up to his knees and one sharp tug brought him out into the night.

Nabber twisted around and came face to face with Bad Leg.

Dark though it was, he recognized the man's features. Or at least the look of them.

Gripping his wrist, the man smiled. "Nabber, isn't it?" he said. His voice was as thin as wire. He was not out of breath, not even breathing fast. "You might already know me. I'm Skaythe, Blayze's brother." He smiled again, twisting Nabber's wrist behind his back. This time when he spoke, his breath caught the side of Nabber's face. "We met the night of the fight. I was Blayze's second."

Nabber tried not to breathe in the man's breath—it smelled like sweet things turned bad. Skaythe was a shorter, wiry, and less handsome version of his brother. His teeth were like Blayze's only slightly crooked, his eyes were a little narrower, and his lips, unlike his brother's full and sculpted ones, were nothing more than a jagged line. He didn't have Blayze's flair for fashion, either—his clothes were plain and boasted no frills. He was strong, though. Nabber couldn't remember ever having felt a grip so powerful.

"What d'you want with me, then?" said Nabber, trying very hard to inject a measure of defiance into his voice.

Another twist of his wrist was all it got him. "You know what I want, boy," hissed Skaythe. "I want Tawl."

Nabber tried to pull free, but the grip just got tighter.

"And you're going to take me to him."

Something glinted, catching Nabber's eye. It was the tip of Skaythe's stick; molded onto the end of the wood was a spike of darkened steel. Nabber's heart stopped at the sight of it. The spike came toward his face.

"Where is he?"

Nabber wasn't at all sure if he was pleased when his

heart started again, as it seemed to have moved up toward his throat. "I don't know where Tawl is. I ain't seen him since the night of the murder."

Skaythe drew the spike under Nabber's chin. Its progress was so smooth that only the warm trickle following it told of its slicing action. Nabber froze.

"Tell me where Tawl is, or I'll cut more than just skin next time."

Nabber didn't doubt he was a man of his word. "Tawl's in the north of the city—hiding out in Old Knackers Lane."

The spike came close once more. "Why are you in the south, then, boy?"

Unable to move forward, Nabber slumped back against the man's side. The action forced Skaythe to readjust his grip on the stick. Nabber used this diversion to raise his right knee and then slam his heel into Skaythe's bad leg.

Skaythe stumbled back. Nabber kicked his stick near the base, stopping him from gaining his balance. He didn't wait around to see if it worked. Gathering all his strength, Nabber sprang for the tunnel. Skaythe sprang after him. Nabber knew what to do this time. Sprinting forward, he brought up his legs and leapt into the tunnel feet first. The cool filth enveloped him. Skaythe grabbed at his hair. Much though Nabber was attached to it, he snapped his head forward and let the locks go.

Sidling down the tunnel he made his escape. He was missing a fistful of hair, a cupful of blood, and about ten years from the lifespan of his heart. It was time he went home to Tawl.

Jack had, by means most extraordinary, gained entry into the city of Annis. He was sitting around a large, well-lit, well-burdened banquet table enjoying the somewhat skeptical company of the Baking Master's Guild.

"How would you slow down a dough that rises too

fast?" asked Barmer, a baker with a huge, bristling mustache and a face as red as the wine he was drinking.

"You put it in a tub full of water and wait until it rises to the top." Jack's answer met with grudging nods of approval. He was getting quite used to the interrogation. For the past hour and a half—ever since he was caught outside the wall and dragged through a cleverly concealed gate into the east side of the city—the members of the baking guild had been throwing him questions to test his claim. It wasn't enough to *say* he was a baker, he had to prove it as well.

"Any miller could know that," said the only slim baker in the room, a hollow-cheeked man named Nivlet.

"Let the lad off the hook," said Eckles, the baker who had first slapped his pudgy hand on Jack outside the city. "It's obvious he's one of us."

"No, Eckles," countered Scuppit, a short baker with forearms as broad as hams. "Nivlet's got a point. That *is* the sort of thing that a miller might know. Best to ask the lad one more question, just to be safe."

"Aye," mumbled the rest of the bakers in disunion. They were about twenty in number, and were all currently stuffing themselves with a banquet's worth of food. For the first hour, Jack had looked on as the Baking Master's Guild discussed guild business such as the rising cost of bread tax, the weight of a penny loaf, and this year's candidates for apprenticeship.

Millers were the enemy. The main aim of the Baking Master's Guild was to outlaw, outwit, and outdo the Milling Master's Guild. Millers mixed cheap grains in with good, milled flour either too coarsely or too finely, and had an unbreakable monopoly on the price of meal. If you told a baker that a miller had murdered his family and ate them for supper, the baker would nod and say: "Aye, and I bet he saved their bones for his mill." Millers were notorious for grinding anything that could be ground, and then passing it off as flour.

Jack had stumbled upon the Baking Master's Guild's monthly spying expedition. Eckles, who in addition to being one of the guild chiefs was the only person who believed Jack to be a baker from the start, had told him that once a month, when the Miller's Guild were busy with their monthly meeting, the Baking Master's Guild sent spies out to all the mills within a league of the city to check the miller's stores. The number of grain bags at each mill was carefully counted and recorded, and then, as the month progressed, the bakers would keep an eye to the amount of flour produced from each individual mill, ensuring that any excess was duly noted. Too much flour meant that foreign substances had been mixed in with the grain.

Each baking master was assigned a specific mill, and when the counting was done they met in the bushes south of the city and smuggled themselves through the wall via the hidden gate. Spying on fellow guilds was considered a thoroughly dishonorable crime punishable by lifetime expulsion from the professional classes. The Baking Master's Guild were taking quite a risk.

Jack rather admired their nerve.

"All right," said Barmer, swallowing a mouthful of food. "Let's ask him a tough one." The baker slipped a sweet roll between his lips to aid the thinking process. "Nice texture, Scuppit," he remarked to the baker by his side.

Scuppit bowed his head graciously. "I added a half-measure of clotted cream to the dough."

Barmer let the bread roll on his tongue. "Never tasted better, my friend." He swallowed and then turned his attention back to Jack. "Very well, lad, what sort of buttermilk is best for unfermented bread? Fresh or sour?"

Jack was beginning to enjoy himself. He liked the bakers; they were a good-humored group who loved their creature comforts and were passionate about their trade. "Sour," said Jack. "The soda in sour buttermilk will help a flat bread rise."

Eckles looked up from his food. "The boy knows his stuff, Barmer."

"That he does," agreed Scuppit.

"I still don't trust him," said Nivlet.

Barmer waggled a bread roll at Jack. "All right. One last question, lad. If you add more yeast to make the dough rise faster, will you need to add more salt, as well?"

"No. Too much salt slows down the yeast." Jack smiled at the company of bakers. "And makes the crust too firm."

Barmer stood up, walked over to Jack, and clapped him hard on the back. "Welcome to the guild," he said. Food permitting, other bakers followed his lead, and Jack was slapped, patted, nudged, and even kissed in congratulation. All came forward except Nivlet, who sat back in his chair, eyeing Jack with open suspicion. After watching the back-slapping for some time, Nivlet left the room.

"Eat, boy, eat," said Eckles. "The Baking Master's Guild never lets a guest go hungry."

Jack didn't need much encouragement. He hadn't eaten since breakfast—which seemed at least two days back now—and the food in front of him looked a lot more appetizing than anything Stillfox had ever cooked. Glistening baked hams rested beside pies as large as butter churns, cheeses were split open and stuffed with fruit, and fat strings of crisp-skinned sausages shared bowls with roasted onions. Everywhere there was bread: barmcakes, soda rolls, sweet breads, bloomers, griddlecakes, and loaves. Jack had never seen such a variety. They were glorious to behold; some with hearty crusts, others softly glazed or sprinkled with seeds, many had been slashed before baking to give interest to the tooth, and a few had been formed into shapes as elaborate as could be. All of them were fresh, fragrant, and cooked to perfection.

As Jack ate, he began to feel guilty about his treatment of Stillfox. The herbalist had been kind to him—teaching, feeding, healing, asking no awkward questions—and he had repaid it all by storming out in a fit of indignant anger. Jack shook his head slowly. Tomorrow he would go back to the cottage; he wouldn't apologize for his words—for he said only what he truly felt—but he would apologize for his anger and the way in which he left. He owed Stillfox that much.

With that decision made, Jack poured himself a cup of ale. For ten weeks the herbalist had treated him well, and it didn't seem right to let one bad incident come between them. Jack downed the thick country beer, relishing its bitter taste. Hadn't Falk told him all those months ago to accept people for what they are, with all their faults and frailties? Stillfox had accepted *him*, not blinking an eye about him being a wanted war criminal and a dangerously unstable sorcery user. So, thought Jack, if *he* had faults, surely he should make allowances for them in others? Yes, Stillfox had kept something from him, but perhaps his motives had been nothing but good.

Jack's eyes focused on a far distant point. He no longer saw the baker's lodge; he saw Rovas' cottage and Tarissa by the fire. A world of good motives couldn't justify what she had done to him. And then there was his mother with her half-truths and her desire for death. And back a decade more was his father: a man who had left him before he was born. Both his parents had deserted him, and no amount of excuses could talk their deeds away.

Here, in the bakers' lodge, with a score of noisy bakers busily eating themselves sick, Jack began to wonder if there was purpose behind the pain. Did his mother's death, his father's abandonment, and Tarissa's betrayal mean something?

Jack's cup was filled by an attentive pudgy hand. "Deep in thought, eh?" said Eckles.

Jack was annoyed at the distraction. There had been an instant where he felt the answer was within reach. Eckles' words had chased it away.

"You best come with me now, lad. Bring your cup and

as much food as you can hold." Eckles began to walk toward a side door and Jack followed him bringing only his cup. His appetite had left him. The huge, round-faced baker led him to a small sitting room where a fire burned brightly in the hearth. "Sit. Sit," he said, motioning to a bench that was pulled up to the grate.

Jack did as he was told. "Are you going back to the meeting?" he asked. Obviously the Baking Master's Guild had secret matters to discuss.

"Me? No." Eckles shook his head firmly. "I've heard it all before, and I already know the outcome." He didn't as much sit as *land* on the bench next to Jack. "They're deciding whether to make their ancient prophecy be known."

Jack felt his face grow hot. "What prophecy?"

Eckles looked at him carefully. "Well, lad, you're a baker, that's for sure, and as you've already stumbled across our best-kept secret, I can't see that telling you another will make any difference either way." He had brought in a skin of ale from the banquet hall and filled Jack's cup for a second time. Jack was hardly aware that he'd drunk the first cup. "The Baking Master's Guild has been meeting in Annis since before it was even a city. When it was just a scholars' retreat we were kneading dough for the philosophers, putting bread to rise for the wise men." Eckles leant forward. "Contrary to popular belief, Annis was built on bread, not brainpower."

Jack managed a smile: bakers were nothing if not proud.

"Anyway," continued Eckles, "one day, over a century ago now, a baker baked a loaf for a man who called himself a prophet. Only when the loaf was delivered did the baker find out that the man had no money to pay for it. The prophet was close to starvation and begged the baker to give him the loaf. Now, the baker was a good man and took pity on the prophet. Of course he didn't give him the freshly baked loaf—after all, he was a tradesman, not a fool—but he did give the man the left-over loaves from the day before. The man thanked him for his trouble, and from that day on the baker always sent his stale bread to the prophet.

"The following winter the prophet caught the tubes—thinkers just don't have the constitution of us bakers—and on his deathbed he called the baker to him. The baker was master of the guild by now, but he came to the man's summons as if he were just an apprentice. The prophet took the baker's hand and said, 'I have asked you here to repay my debt. As you know, I have no money, but what I do have is insight, and so that is how I will pay you.' Well, the prophet then told the baker his prophecy, and it has been a guild secret ever since. Passed from generation to generation, from father to son." Eckles finished his tale with a dramatic flourish worthy of an actor.

Whilst the story was being told, Jack felt the palms of his hands growing damp with sweat. He felt guilty, but wasn't sure why. "And what does this prophecy concern?" he asked.

"A baker, of course."

Jack nodded. He wasn't surprised. "Which baker is this?"

"One who will come from the west and bring an end to the war."

"What war?"

Eckles looked him straight in the eye. "The one that's building between the north and the south. *This one*." He rubbed his hand over his mouth. "I can't tell you the whole verse, lad, not until the guild gives the nod, but the last two lines are:

> *If time turns twice, the truth will bring*
> *Peace into the hands of a baker, not a king.*"

Jack looked away. Time turning. The memory of eight score of loaves flashed quickly through his brain. Aware that Eckles was still looking at him, Jack worked hard to compose his features: he didn't want to give anything away.

Abruptly he stood up. Prophecies, lies, secrets: he'd had enough for one day. The subject needed changing— it was time to talk of truths, not shadowy foretellings. "Tell me what's happening in Bren," he said. "How is the duke and his new wife?"

A curious expression came over Eckles' face. "Boy, where have you been these past nine weeks?"

Jack was immediately on his guard. "I live in a cabin in the mountains. My master and I are cut off from the world. He only sends me into the city when we need some supplies. The last time I came was two months back." Jack turned his face to the fire. All the time he'd spent despising deception and here he was, turning out to be quite a liar himself.

"Then you won't know the duke is dead." There was a slight edge to Eckles' voice. "And his new wife has gone into hiding to escape Catherine's wrath."

"What would Melliandra have to fear from Catherine?" Jack no longer cared what Eckles thought: all that mattered was learning the truth.

"Half the city says she let the duke's murderer into the bedchamber. Catherine wants her executed."

"Is she still in Bren?"

"Most people believe so. If she left the city, Lord Baralis would know it."

Baralis? Jack could hear the blood pumping through his veins. "Why would Baralis know it?"

"*Lord* Baralis is all but running the city now." The emphasis Eckles placed on the word *lord* was a question in itself. "Just today I heard a rumor that the Lady Melliandra is with child—apparently her father is stirring up trouble in the city, swearing that the unborn babe is the duke's issue. Whether it's true or not, I can't tell you, but you can be sure that Lord Baralis won't like it one little bit."

Jack's throat tightened. Melli was in danger. "Is she alone?"

"Her father and the duke's champion are said to be with her. There are those who say the champion is her lover." Eckles shrugged. "None of it will matter before long."

"Why?"

"Because within a matter of weeks Bren will be razed to the ground."

The room seemed to have shrunk as they spoke. Jack paced its length. He had to go to Melli—*now*. He had to go to Bren.

Eckles took a swig from his ale skin. "You seem mighty agitated, lad, for someone who lives quietly in the mountains." He gave Jack a shrewd look.

Jack forced himself to take a deep breath. His throat fought him all the way, but he swallowed hard and willed his muscles to relax. He couldn't afford to give Eckles reason to be suspicious. The last thing he felt like was a drink, but he took one all the same, purposely taking a long, slow draught to give himself time to think.

Going to Bren tonight just wasn't practical; it was too late, too dark and his shoes and clothes were too flimsy for the mountains. Besides, he needed to see Stillfox. Jack could guess why the herbalist had withheld this information, but he wanted to hear it from the man's mouth. They had things to talk about, and another lie wrapped in good intent was just the first of them.

"Look," he said to Eckles, "I need somewhere to stay tonight. I'll be gone before sunup."

"Sunup comes late to Annis," the baker said. It was his way of saying that Jack could stay. "You can sleep here by the fire. We'll not trouble the others with the details; they'll all be going home soon anyway. Just be gone before the maid comes to spread fresh rushes in the morning."

*

Nabber decided to take the long way back to Cravin's townhouse. After his encounter with Skaythe, he didn't trust anyone or anything. If a drunk as much as stumbled in his direction, a prostitute gave him an earful, or an alley cat gave him the eye, then he'd backtrack, sidestep, or change his path. Sometimes he did all three. A man couldn't be too careful when returning to his lair. Once, in the space of a single night, Swift had circled Rorn three times, rowed from the north harbor to the south harbor in a crab boat, changed horses and traveling companions twice, and donned no less than four separate disguises just to throw his pursuers off the scent. Nabber sighed wistfully. Such extraordinary evasive maneuvers were the stuff of legends in the pocketing world.

Inspired by the thought of Swift braving salt water, strange streets, and a dress—the third of Swift's four disguises had apparently been as an old milkmaid, complete with wooden buckets, shoulder yoke, and a limp— Nabber decided to make one final detour before heading back toward the townhouse.

Spying a street lined with taverns, brothels, and pie shops, Nabber set his sights in that direction. The fact that plenty of candlelight spilled from the doorways and shutters of various establishments only put him more at ease. He'd lost his appetite for the dark.

As he walked along, Nabber spit in his palm and smoothed down his hair. He wanted to look presentable when he finally saw Tawl. After a few moments of smoothing, probing, and measuring, he was quite sure he'd located a bald spot the size of a five-copper bit just above his left ear. Alarmed, for Swift always said that once a man lost his hair it never grew back, Nabber paused in midstep to search through his sack. After a little discreet fumbling, accompanied by much under-his-breath cursing of Skaythe, his fingers finally closed around the wooden handle of his preening mirror.

Having assured himself that no one was looking,

Nabber sidled up to the nearest building, and standing on tiptoe to catch the light escaping through the open shutter, he brought the mirror up to his face. After much twisting and rotating, he eventually managed to find a position where the light fell directly onto the offending bald spot.

Strange, it didn't look nearly as big and bald as it felt. In fact, it looked rather pathetic.

Disappointed as much as he was relieved, Nabber went to move away from the shutter. Just as he settled back onto the heels of his feet, something bright flashed in the mirror. For a quarter of a second the interior of the building was fully visible in the reflection.

Nabber caught his breath.

A figure sat in the room with his back to the window. Dark haired and robed in black, the oyster pale flesh of his neck was all that was visible of the man. Yet Nabber recognized him all the same. Four days ago he had followed that neck across half a city: it was Baralis.

Nabber's first instinct was to run. His second instinct was to creep ever so quietly away—he'd had quite enough excitement for one night, what with Skaythe and his metal-spiked stick and everything. His third instinct, however, was to stay put and see if he could discover just what old Insect Features was up to, conducting a meeting in an unmarked building bordered by a pastry shop and a vintner's, in the south side of the city after dark. Nabber seriously doubted that the man had developed a late-night fancy for a glass of wine and a pork pie.

Nabber wavered between his second and third instincts. He really did want to go home; right now there was nothing in the world he fancied more than a hot toddy, a spot of supper, and a freshly stuffed pallet for the night. Yet what if Baralis was up to something devious in there, something that Tawl and the Lady Melliandra needed to know about? Perhaps if he discovered something useful, Tawl might be so pleased with him that he'd totally forget about the fiasco at the Brimming Bucket. Nabber smiled, mind made up. He might even get a warm welcome to go with the hot toddy.

Crouching down to hide himself from view of the window, Nabber slipped his preening mirror back in his sack, his thoughts racing ahead of his hands. This was obviously a secret meeting of some sort: why else would Baralis choose to meet someone away from the safety of the palace? Which meant that Baralis had probably either come here on his own, or brought only his rat-loving servant along for protection. Nabber slipped into the shadows. There would be no armed guards to give him chase.

As the building was in the middle of a row of six, there was no alleyway running down the side, so Nabber had to walk to the end of the row before he could find a way to approach the rear. A narrow, walled walkway provided access for deliveries, and Nabber had to keep count of the number of gateways he passed to ensure he picked the right building. They all looked the same from the back.

The vintner was obviously having some sort of late-night party, as the sounds of laughing, coughing, and singing escaped from between the partially closed shutters. Nabber was glad of the noise when he entered the middle building's yard, as piles of scrap metal and rotting wood made it difficult for him to move quietly.

A sudden noise caused Nabber to freeze in midstep. A dark form close to the building's rear wall moved. Nabber's heart turned to a dead weight in his chest. He didn't dare move, didn't dare breathe. The sound came again, this time followed by a second noise. A low, nickering animal noise. It was a *horse*! Annoyed at himself for being scared of an old nag, Nabber risked moving in closer. Tethered to a holding timber jutting from the rear wall, the horse was on a very short lead. Looking at it, Nabber was forced to admit that it was an extraordinary animal: tall, with a finely muscled flank and neck, and a slim but gleaming belly. Not an old nag by anyone's counting, but rather a Far South purebred.

Nabber could see now why it was on such a short lead: its owner wouldn't want to risk the animal injuring itself on a chunk of scrap metal, or a nail-encrusted plank. The horse whinnied in Nabber's direction. Nabber shook his head softly. There was no way he was going to go near it. All horses were dangerous as far as he was concerned—especially purebreds.

The horse whinnied again, louder this time.

"Ssh," hissed Nabber under his breath.

The horse wasn't about to be quieted. It stamped its forehooves on the ground and pulled against its reins. Panicking, Nabber darted forward and grabbed the horse's bridle. Unsure of what to say to calm a horse, he threatened it with all manner of dire punishments in his softest, most encouraging voice. It seemed to work. The horse settled down, moving closer to the wall and letting the reins fall slack.

Nabber heaved a sigh of relief. As he took his hands from the horse's noseband, he noticed something black on his palm. Bringing his hand closer to his face, Nabber inspected the mark, first rubbing, then smelling it. It was soot.

A small thrill passed down Nabber's spine. Quickly, he glanced over at the horse's noseband. Even in the dull light spilling from the shutters, he could clearly see a stripe of yellow on the leather. Two minutes earlier it had been entirely black. Someone had gone to great trouble to conceal the true colors of the bridle. Nabber leant forward and ran his hands over the leather. A second yellow stripe emerged from beneath the soot.

Yellow and black.

The colors of Valdis.

Suddenly the back door of the building opened, and the backyard was flooded with light. Nabber dived for the shadows behind the horse. Something sharp caught at his left shin, and he had to clench his teeth together to stop himself from crying out.

A figure moved into the doorway, blocking out part of the light. Nabber used the cover of increased shadow to move into the corner where the building and the wall met. The jutting timber the horse was tethered to provided further cover.

Not daring to rub his throbbing shin, Nabber brought his hand to his throat. The cut that Skaythe had opened earlier was encrusted with dried blood. It stung when he touched it. Nabber gulped. He should have followed his first instinct and run straight home to Tawl.

The figure moved from the doorway into the yard, and then a second, taller man followed.

"The guards at the west gate will turn a blind eye as you pass," said the second man to the first.

Nabber rubbed at the dried blood on his throat. That voice belonged to Baralis.

"Like a gaggle of maidservants on a wedding night, you think of everything, Baralis."

The dark figure that Nabber now knew to be Baralis bowed toward the stranger. "I do my best."

Both men took a few steps in Nabber's direction. Nabber could now smell the scent of the stranger: exotic, foreign fragrances and horse sweat. His dark hair was slick with oil and his teeth flashed white as he spoke.

"You do know Kylock is camped outside the south gate?" he said, bringing a finger up to his temple to smooth a misplaced hair. Although he was wearing a leather tunic, he made no sound as he moved.

"There's no need to bother the king with the details of our little meeting," said Baralis smoothly.

"My thoughts exactly," replied the stranger after a carefully lazy pause. Just how careful the pause was could be judged from watching the man's left hand. As Nabber looked on, the stranger balled his hand into a fist and relaxed it five times before speaking.

Judging from the colors of his horse's bridle, the stranger had something to do with Valdis. And although Nabber didn't know much about these things, he had a feeling the man was more than just a knight.

The stranger moved toward his horse. Nabber pressed his body flat against the wall. The horse nickered softly. The stranger's hand automatically came up to calm the animal, but Baralis chose that moment to speak, so his attention was diverted away.

"In fact," said Baralis, moving toward the horse, "the less the king knows about our . . . how should I put it? . . . our *understanding*, the better. After all, he will soon have a new marriage, a new bride, and a new dukedom to contend with. I see no need to bother him with the petty details of power."

Nabber shivered. There was something about Baralis' voice that chilled him through and through.

"Yes," agreed the stranger. "Whatever religious activities transpire in Helch and any other occupied territories should be of little interest to the king." The stranger's voice wasn't as cold and deadly as Baralis'; it was smoother and more detached. In fact, everything about the stranger was smooth: his leather tunic, his oiled hair, his movements.

"Know this, my friend," Baralis said. "The king's feelings in this matter are exactly the same as my own. As long as the knights join us on the field, and order is maintained in the occupied territories, we care little about your intent."

The stranger smiled. His teeth were small and perfectly even. Once again, he paused before speaking. Three fists this time. "I'm glad to hear the king has the same feelings about religion as we do." The faint hint of mockery in his voice trailed away as he spoke the next sentence. "The north has been too long under the spiritual guidance of Silbur and Marls and Rorn. We shouldn't be beholden to the whims of a southern Church."

The stranger took a breath, preparing to speak again, but Baralis cut him short:

"Do whatever you have to do, Tyren. Just keep Helch on its knees until Highwall is broken, and no questions will be asked about your motives."

Tyren. A hard lump rose in Nabber's throat. He tried to breathe and found he couldn't. Tyren was the leader of the knights. He was Tawl's idol, his savior, his mentor. And here he was making secret deals with Baralis that involved performing Borc-only-knew what atrocities on the unsuspecting people of Helch. Nabber wasn't fooled by the words "religious activities." He'd lived with smooth-talkers for too long not to see the truth behind a well-chosen phrase. Tyren wanted to convert the people of Helch to his own religious doctrines, and judging from what had been said tonight in this yard, neither he nor Baralis were fussy about the means.

Listening to the two men plotting, Nabber vehemently wished that he had never stumbled upon the meeting. This wasn't the sort of information Tawl would thank him for coming back with. In fact, Nabber was beginning to wonder if he should keep the details to himself. It would crush Tawl to find out the truth about Tyren. The leader of the knighthood was the one person left in whom Tawl had any faith.

Nabber felt a sharp pain in his neck. Without realizing it, he had pulled the scab off his throat. Skaythe's spike wound reopened and a trickle of blood slid down Nabber's tunic. He forced himself to breathe, taking fast, feather-light breaths. *Stay calm,* he told himself. *Stay calm.*

Baralis and Tyren had been speaking all the while, and as Nabber concentrated upon what they were saying once more, Tyren reached over to untie the reins of his horse.

Baralis spoke. "I don't want to hear any rumors of torture or worse coming out of Helch. Whatever you choose to do, it must be done quietly. It's too early in the game to risk the south getting wind of our plans."

"Don't worry, Baralis," Tyren said, long, gold-ringed fingers tugging gently on the reins to loosen the knot. "I'll make sure that nothing leaks out. There are countless different methods for discrediting a tattletale, and more than half a dozen ways to kill one."

As Tyren was speaking his eyes flicked from the wooden beam to the horse. For the briefest instant, he looked straight into the dark corner where the wall and building met. Less than six paces away from where he stood, separated only by the horse and its shadow and the wooden holding beam, Nabber tensed.

Tyren hesitated for a second. His hand moved from the reins to his face. He peered into the darkness.

The lump returned to Nabber's throat. It was as heavy as lead this time. Sweat trickled down his nose.

Suddenly the horse pulled on its reins, stepping away from the wall. Tyren was forced to move along with it in order to keep hold of the reins.

"Well, Tyren," said Baralis, nodding at the horse. "It looks as if your gelding is eager to be on his way. I think our business for this night is complete. We both see eye to eye on the religious future of the north."

Tyren checked the position of the saddle and the buckles on the stirrups and then mounted the horse. "And when the king decides to expand his empire outwards?" he said, settling himself down in the saddle. "I trust Valdis will be allowed to address the religious practices of the south, as well?"

Baralis smiled slowly. "Oh, most especially the south."

Hearing Baralis' words, Nabber's stomach collapsed inwards, leaving an aching hollow in his chest. He felt as if he might be sick.

Tyren nodded, satisfied. Baralis looked on as he guided his horse toward the gate. Neither man bid the other farewell.

Baralis stood in the center of the fan of light escaping from the doorway and watched as Tyren rode away. When the sound of the horses' hooves could no longer be heard, Baralis took a thin breath and then smiled.

"Tavalisk," he said softly, speaking into the darkness, "it may have taken me nearly twenty years, but I *will* have my revenge."

Baralis waited a moment longer and then turned and walked back to the building.

As soon as the door closed behind him, Nabber took a long, deep breath. He thanked Borc and the spirit of Swift's dead mother for keeping him safe and sound—he even thanked the horse. Sending his right hand down to explore his throbbing shin, he discovered a large, bloody lump that was unbelievably tender to the touch. The spike wound on his throat was still bleeding, and his tunic was soaked in sweat. Although there was nothing in the world he wanted to do more than to run as fast as he could from the yard, Nabber forced himself to stay put until the lights went out. Even then he didn't dare move until a fair length of time had passed. He was taking no more chances tonight. Chased, accosted, threatened, trapped, and very nearly caught: he'd had quite enough excitement to last him all his life. Well, certainly a good part of it.

Stiff from standing still for so long, cold, tired, and shivering, Nabber made his way out of the yard. He couldn't muster any enthusiasm for throwing potential pursuers off his track and took the shortest, quickest route back to Tawl.

It had been a long time since Kylock last measured the powder as Baralis had taught him. No longer did he bother to spread only enough grain to cover the dip in his palm. Now he took his drug by the fistful. Into his glass he sprinkled it, the powder flashing as quick and bright as an arrowhead shot to a mark. A cup of red wine wetted it for the taking. Only when the powder had been washed down his throat could Kylock breathe easy again.

The terrible flashes when his skull crushed his mind, and when his thoughts turned inside out revealing the raw meat of brain beneath, would ease for a while now. The drug did that at least.

As he drew the glass to his lips a second time, two guards carried the girl's body away from the tent. It had been an especially unpleasant attack. Passion brought out more than the beast in him.

"Get her hand off the floor," he commanded to the men. The fools were carrying her too low and her hand was trailing the length of his carpet. It was tainted now, along with the pillows and the sheets. The whole place reeked of her. Everything would have to be destroyed. Kylock pushed past the men to the tent flap and made his way into the night.

The sky was always dark when he was under it. And Kylock was not displeased to note that Bren's purple-and-black expanse acted no differently from the rest.

They were camping just south of the city—so close they could see the walls, taste the wood smoke, and hear the wagons creaking through the streets. Kylock cast his gaze upon the high battlements of Bren. Yes. This city was for him. Not an overbloated town like Harvell, not an ancient shabby hovel like Helch, but a glorious youthful city, growing, burgeoning: a terrible child. Bren didn't sit in its own squalor like other cities: the mountain air carried off the stench each night and the rain washed the dirt to the lake.

The lake, the mountains, the walls: Bren's defenses were unmatched in the Known Lands. It was made to be the center of an empire. The long line of its dukes had prepared the city for him, constructing strong walls, impregnable gatehouses, and ringing the city with a network of portcullises. Now that they had done their job, it was fitting they were gone. Bren had seen the last of its dukes.

Kylock drank the last sip from his glass. The drug was a sweetener for the wine. The smell of roasting flesh met his nostrils and he guessed the guards had thrown the girl on the fire. Burning was the best way to render a corpse unrecognizable. No one but he and the guards would know who the girl was or what had become of her. Her chest cavity would be split by the actions of the flame, and her two broken wrists would be reduced to so many charred and disjointed bones. Kylock shrugged. It might even burn the expression of terror right off her pretty face. She would just be another disease-racked whore who was torched for the good of the camp.

He was feeling a lot better now. The drug was working its commission: the world was heavier, darker, and infinitely more solid under its thrall. It calmed the rage inside. Something alarming was happening to him. More and more he lost control of himself: violent schisms ripped through his body and his thoughts. Always there was the taste of metal in his mouth. Just earlier, when he was abed with the girl—when he had tied her wrists to the post and her neck to the board, and when the wax was hot enough to blister—his body had been racked by a violent contraction. It was as if a hand had squeezed his gut, sending bile flooding to his mouth. His brain grew large, or his skull shrunk small, and suddenly his thoughts were too many to be contained. A shocking pressure built up within and the only way to release it was to tear at the girl beneath.

He fell on her like an animal. Teeth became fangs and fingers became talons. Blackness came to overwhelm him, and by fighting the girl he fought the monster off. If she screamed, he never heard it; if she struggled, he never noticed. All he felt was the cooling spray of her blood on his cheek and the feeble push of her second to last breath. By the time she took her last, he had clawed his way back to the light. Gut rested against liver once more and the pressure had lifted from his head. A trickle of his own blood had run down from his nose, and he spat in a cloth to remove the aftertaste from his mouth.

"A missive has arrived from Halcus, sire."

Kylock spun around. He had not heard the guard approach. As the man handed him the sealed parchment, he noticed the guard's eyes fall to his tunic. The girl's blood formed a dark patch upon the gold. Kylock spoke very softly. "Blood spilled in secret is a bond between men. Go now, my friend, and tell no one of what you saw."

The man fell to the floor. "Sire, I would spill an army's worth of blood on your saying."

Kylock nodded softly and gestured for the man to rise. "Your loyalty will not be forgotten."

The man bowed and walked away.

Kylock smiled. Every day he discovered new powers that were made for kings alone. The ability to inspire unquestioning loyalty was a gift straight from the gods. What men would not do for money, they would do in an instant if it was a matter of belief. His men had faith in him: he won wars, took risks, and was hated by his enemies. He promised his men spoils and made sure that they got them: women or children, whatever their tastes. Gold, grain, appointments . . . destruction if they fancied. A town set alight in a frenzy of blood-lust was often the best reward after a day on the field. Nothing inspired greater contempt for the enemy than watching them burn.

Kylock broke the wax seal. Yes, he had the loyalty of his men, and the contents of this letter proved it.

Tonight, just before dawn, his mother would meet her death. Her castle in the Northlands would be raided by a rogue Halcus war party. None would survive to tell the tale. Kedrac, Maybor's eldest, had planned every detail, right down to the rape and desecration of the dowager queen. The truly inspirational part had been his own, though. The queen's body, when it was done with, was to be laid out on an Annis banner. The implication would be that Halcus was working in conjunction with the mountain city. The kingdoms would be outraged when the news came to light, and support for his next move—which just happened to be the invasion of Annis—would be all but guaranteed. What country would let the rape and murder of its beloved, and so recently bereaved, queen go unavenged?

Of course the invasion of Annis would be merely a feint. His army would be needed elsewhere, but it suited him to let his enemies believe that they were too entrenched in a siege of honor to be moved. Kylock's eyes searched out the dark lines of the battlements of Bren. It would be quite a surprise to all when his plans took their final turn. Of course Annis would be his eventually anyway—a few months here or there would make no difference in the end.

Kylock read on. Kedrac was clever enough to write in code. Not only had he arranged the queen's demise, he'd also timed the conquering of the last Halcus towns to perfection. Kylock was well pleased with Kedrac's work. It meant that the day he married Catherine, he could present her with Halcus as her own. A magnificent gesture, but an unworthy gift: nothing was too precious for Catherine.

He couldn't wait to meet her. He would come to Catherine as a free man. With his mother gone he would be bound to no one. He would give himself wholly to his new bride, and when he came and knelt at her feet, she would cleanse him forever of the taint of the womb.

Kylock turned back toward the camp. His manservant knew him well enough to have heated some water in his absence. He was dirty and needed to be clean. His hands and clothes stank, and it wasn't fitting to even *think* of Catherine whilst he smelled of the whore he'd just killed.

Four

$\mathcal{J}$ack was dreaming about Tarissa again. His thoughts, which so carefully avoided her during the daytime, seemed to gang up on him at night. She was always there; one moment laughing, tempting, merry as a dairymaid, the next she would be crying, pleading, falling on her knees and begging him to take her with him.

Always, even in his dreams, he walked away.

Only tonight he heard her footsteps following him.

Jack's heart raced to hear them. He turned to face Tarissa, but she wasn't there. Still the footsteps came, nearer than ever now. Jack spun around. Where was she? The footsteps were so close the ground vibrated with their resonance.

"He's in here," came a voice.

Not Tarissa's voice. Not a familiar voice. Not even a dream. Jack jumped up. His senses came after him. He was in the baker's lodge and the light peeking in from the shutters told of a new dawn.

The door burst open. Four men fully armed barged into the room. Nivlet, the one thin baker in the Baking Master's Guild, stood behind them.

"That's him!" he cried. "He's the one the Halcus are looking for."

Two of the men came forward. Jack's hand was already on his knife. His mouth was dry and his thoughts were still reeling with sleep. As he moved to meet the guards, he cast his gaze from side to side, taking in the details of the room. Searching for distractions. The wood shuttle lay to his left, well-stacked with logs. Jack made a jump for it, kicking it toward the guards. The logs went careening forward, forcing the two guards to step back. Jack sprang with them. His knife was ahead of him, drawing ever decreasing circles in the air. The blade caught one of the guard's arms. Jack put his weight behind it and sliced through muscle as well as skin.

Something nicked him from behind. Spinning around he came face-to-face with the third guard. He had red hair, a large red mustache, and the longest knife Jack had ever seen.

"Come and get some, boy," he encouraged. His sideways glance gave him away. He was hoping to distract Jack long enough to enable the second guard to slice him from behind.

His eyes never leaving Red Hair for a moment, Jack took a guess at where the second man stood. He pivoted his weight to his left leg and then kicked back with his right heel like a horse. He caught the man's knee dead-center. Groaning, he fell forward. Jack made straight for Red Hair's blade. At the very last instant, he pulled sharply to the side. Red Hair was already in motion, and his momentum carried him forward. He went smashing into the second guard, who was rocking over his knee.

Jack had no time to watch the outcome. The air burned in his throat and his lungs seemed ready to burst. He turned his attention back to the first guard with the wounded arm. The fourth was still in the doorway, biding his time. Wounded-arm had gotten a spear from somewhere. He teased Jack with it, stabbing wildly at his chest and thighs. Jack grew angry at the man's cowardice. Keeping a safe distance between himself and the spear tip, he raised his knife to his face. Wounded-arm's blood was still drying on the blade.

"Hmm," said Jack, hoping to get the man to look down at his wound. "I'd see a physician if I were you. Your blood looks a strange color to me."

The man smiled. "I'm not so easily fooled, boy." He jabbed his spear forward.

Jack was forced to step back. He realized he couldn't go any farther, as he was now backed up against the wall. Something had to be done. He returned the guard's smile. "I still think you may have to see a physician after all, my friend. About that terrible slash near your eye."

Just as the man's face registered confusion, Jack tensed his knife arm like a spring and then shot his wrist forward. He released his grip on the haft and the blade went shooting straight for the man's eye. Once again, Jack didn't wait for the show. Now unarmed, he sprang away from the wall. Red Hair had recovered, but the second guard was on the floor. There was blood on Red Hair's blade. The fourth guard had moved to his side, and both of them now blocked Jack's path to the door.

Two men, armed and ready, faced him. Jack knew it was time for sorcery. He concentrated on the metal in the blades. He felt it dense, rigid, resisting with all its might. Doing exactly what he had been taught, he entered the cool-metal hardness. This wasn't one of Stillfox's training sessions where the dangers were mostly imagined and the outcome carefully monitored like an experiment under glass. This was real.

Split seconds were all he had. There was no time for straining or finesse, no time to be entrapped by the substance he entered. Jack fed off the urgency and the danger. His mind conjured up an image of Tarissa. She was there in a blink of an eye, Rovas in front of her, and gently she raised her hand to feel the heat from his forehead. Jack felt sorcery build. Shame was underneath, but he had no time to deal with that now. He let the power flood up from his belly whilst his thoughts swept down from his mind. The two met in his mouth and the metal bite of sorcery slithered down along his tongue.

Straight to the blades it went. Jack's mind formed the intent as it raced through the air. He molded the sorcery like a sculptor, and once it hit it was fully formed. It passed with his thoughts into the substance of the knife, and just as it did what it was made for, he pulled himself back from the blades. The knives became red-hot pokers. Both men screamed, opening their fists and dropping the blades to the floor.

Jack felt a wave of weakness sweep over him. Fighting it off, he pushed past both men toward the door. Neither Red Hair nor his friend had any desire to stop him. They were both holding up red, raw palms and looking wildly around for some way to cool them.

Jack stepped over the threshold and walked straight into Nivlet. Frallit had once said: *"Never trust a skinny baker,"* and it seemed that he was right. Jack punched Nivlet squarely in the face. Nivlet fell to the floor and Jack stepped over his body. "See to it those guards get some water for their burns." He didn't wait to hear the man's reply; he turned his back and walked away.

Feeling strangely elated, Jack made his way from the lodge. *He had done it!* He had made sorcery do his bidding! It was exhilarating. He felt powerful, confident, ready to take on all comers. As he walked through the banquet hall, Jack swept all the remains of last night's food from the table. Loaves, chickens, and fruit went flying into the air. He threw his head back and laughed out loud. Finally he had done something right.

Footsteps again, either Nivlet or one of the injured guards. Time to move on. Jack's smile fell from his face. It looked like he wouldn't be seeing much of Annis after all, as he'd be going out the same way he came in: by the back door. Jack picked a particularly nasty-looking carving knife from the rushes, filled his tunic with bread and cheese and, as an afterthought, downed a cupful of ale in a toast to himself. Grimacing—sitting around all night had done little for the ale—Jack turned on his heel and slipped out into the dawn.

"Your Grace, may I present His Royal Highness King Kylock, Sovereign of the Four Kingdoms." Baralis stepped back and let Kylock come forward to meet Catherine.

Kylock looked magnificent. Dressed in black silk and sable with spun gold at cuffs and collar he looked more than the king he was. Tall and fine-limbed he carried himself with casual pride. His features were harder to judge; strangely shadowed despite the sunshine beaming down from the windows, they eluded both words and light.

He stretched out an elegant hand and Catherine raised her own to meet it. He brought her pale fingers to his lips. His breath was cool, cooler even than his lips. A tiny thrill passed through Catherine. She hadn't intended to curtsy when she met him—the mistress of Bren bowed to no man—yet she knew how very becoming she looked from above: how enticingly the cleft of her bosom deepened, how full her bottom lip became when gilded with light.

"It is an honor to welcome you to our fine city, Your Majesty."

"The honor," said Kylock, "is mine."

They stood in the great hall surrounded by courtiers. Garlands of summer roses decked the walls. The windows were glazed with stained glass and the sun's rays shining upon them were converted to the colors of state. Royal blue, midnight blue, purple, and scarlet: colors her father had chosen. The colors of the cloth they had wound around his corpse. Catherine shivered despite the warmth of the sun.

Kylock still had hold of her hand. "Say the word if you are cold, my lady," he said softly. "And I will burn a city to warm you."

Catherine's sharp intake of breath was not the only one. The courtiers who heard Kylock speak shifted uneasily in their places.

Baralis stepped in to fill the awkward silence. "Your Majesty must be tired after your long journey. If you will permit me, I will show you to your chambers."

Kylock did not look at him. He did not take his eyes from Catherine. Still he had hold of her hand. His fingers pressed against her bone, stopping the blood from flowing to the tips. "You are right, my chancellor, I must rest. Today I have seen my future wife, and the sight has all but stolen my breath." Abruptly he let her hand drop.

Catherine had willed him to let it go, but now that he had she felt lost. There was such power to him, and while he held her hand it was as if she was party to it. She spoke to hold him an instant longer. "My lord, I trust you will find your chambers to your liking. I saw to the furnishings myself."

He moved swiftly forward. Catherine panicked for a moment and took a step back—for some reason she had thought he meant to strike her. He bowed instead, dipping his head low and exposing the white flesh on the back of his neck. His nostrils quivered as if he were taking in her scent. "My lady's thoughtfulness is matched only by her purity."

Catherine dug her fingernails into her palms to stop herself from blushing. *Purity?* Such an odd word to use. She began to feel uncomfortable. Bowing her head, she murmured, "I trust I will not disappoint you."

Kylock's eyes met hers. Dark, they were, but the color escaped her. He smiled, showing even white teeth with a slight inward slant. "My lady will not disappoint me." He moved away from her so quickly that she was unable to focus on his form until he was still once more.

Turning to Baralis, he said, "Chancellor, lead me to my chambers." Baralis came to the king's side and began to guide him from the hall.

Catherine watched the pair go. There was something strange about the two of them . . . they were matched in height and coloring. Even their very movements seemed the same. No footfalls sounded as they walked. Catherine shook her head slowly, unwilling to carry her thoughts further. Kylock and Baralis were from the same country, the same court; it was hardly unusual that they bore the same façade.

Overcome with a sudden desire to rest, Catherine dismissed her court with a wave of her hand. She was tired, drained, sharply aware of her vulnerability. Kylock was so much *more* than she had expected, and his presence had unnerved her. In eight days she would be his wife. Turning, she made her way to her chambers. Never in her life had she felt more *alive* than when King Kylock held her hand.

"The trout is coming along nicely, Grift. A few more minutes and it will be as fine as fish can be."

"I've never cared for fish myself, Bodger. But it *is* good for a man's plums."

"His plums, Grift?"

"Aye, Bodger, his plums. A man will never have a problem with his hernies as long as he eats lots of fish."

"Why's that, Grift?"

"Fish increases a man's power of suspension, if you get my drift, Bodger. Two trout a day and your plums will be so supple they'll be bouncing off the floor."

Bodger looked doubtful. "I'm not so sure that sounds like a benefit, Grift."

"It's not for me to decide what's best, Bodger. I'm merely here to give you all the facts." Grift nodded wisely and Bodger nodded back.

"Here, d'you think I should take a trout to Tawl, Grift?"

"No, Bodger. Best stay clear of him today, it being the Feast of Borc's First Miracle and all. It's the most holy of days for knights, and bringing Tawl a fish will only serve to salten the wound."

"Aye, Grift. I think you're right. I saw him earlier and he looked right through me. Lady Melliandra tried to comfort him, but he just sent her away."

"You can hardly blame the man, Bodger. Every knight who was ever knighted lets his blood for Borc today. Tawl will be feeling the loss of his circles keenly."

"How does the story go again, Grift?"

"Well, Borc, as you know, was a shepherd in the foothills of the Great Divide. One day he's protecting his flock and along comes a pack of hunger-crazed wolves. They chase Borc and his flock right up to the Faldara Falls. Well, Borc has nowhere to go and so he pleads to God for guidance, and before the words have left his mouth the falls turn to ice. Every spit of water, every fish on the fin: all frozen in an instant. So Borc and his sheep cross the falls, and as soon as the wolves step onto the ice, everything melts and the predators go plunging to their death."

Bodger sighed impatiently. "Everyone knows that story, Bodger. It's how Valdis fits in that I'm not clear on."

"Right. Why didn't you say so in the first place, then?" Grift downed a mouthful of ale and settled himself back on his chair. "Well, as you know Valdis was the first man to become a disciple of Borc's. And when Borc traveled to the Far South in search of truth, Valdis stayed in the north to spread the word. Anyway, ten years to the day after the miracle at Faldara Falls, Valdis is preaching along its bank to an angry and disbelieving mob. They begin to shout at him, saying there was no miracle and that anyone who tried to cross the falls would surely die.

"Well, being flesh and blood like he was, Valdis knows there's no way he can perform a miracle, so he does something else instead: the First Act of Faith. He jumps into the river and lets the current take him over the falls.

"Naturally everyone thinks he's a goner, he'd likely be crushed by the rocks the minute he hits the falls. So the mob walks home to their wives and children and promptly forget all about him. But somehow Valdis survived—how, no one knows for sure, though most say it was God's reward for his faith—and he makes his way back to the village. The villagers are so overcome by the sight of him that they fall to their knees and pledge themselves to Borc. Valdis kisses each and every one of them on the forehead, and then leaves, telling them it is their duty to go forth and spread the word." Grift drained his cup, indicating the end of the story.

"Valdis was a very brave man, Grift," said Bodger softly.

"Aye, Bodger, and the knighthood he started was supposed to carry on his ideals."

"Poor Tawl. It must distress him to see the way the knighthood has fallen."

"If you ask me, Bodger, he's lucky to be out of it."

"If you could have seen his face this morning, Grift, you'd know that's the last of his thoughts. He just sat in his windowseat and looked out toward the south."

"The city of Valdis lies to the south, Bodger."

"Aye. And Tawl's heart lies with it this day."

Baralis closed the door behind himself. He thought for a moment and then drew the bolt. Kylock was in the palace now, and somehow his presence changed everything.

The boy had grown in many ways since Baralis had last seen him. Indeed, he was no longer a boy at all. A man. A king. A ruler of men. Oh, how his presence dominated the great hall! How everyone strained to hear his every word, and how they all breathed a sigh of relief as he left. There was no doubt about it: Kylock was born to be an emperor. He was *begot* for it. But he was so young, so inexperienced, so bright with all the ruthlessness of youth. He had to be molded, his decisions gently guided, his policies shaped to curves of greater subtlety.

Seeing Kylock this morning had been like seeing a different person. He would be no willingly manipulated half-man. He was whole, vibrant, and ready to take control. Baralis permitted himself the smallest of smiles. Well, not quite whole. The sparkling drug named *ivysh* had already seen to that. *Ivysh* stopped sorcery from flowing through the body, and while Kylock continued to be addicted to it he would be unable to draw upon the source. The fact that the new king was still taking it was no longer in doubt. He reeked of it: his hair, his clothes, his breath. The side effects he covered up well, though.

Ivysh promoted madness in some, paranoia in others, and destructive delusions in all. Men in Hanatta took it to bring themselves closer to God. Women in Hanatta took it to forget about the cruelty of their men, and children in Hanatta were given *ivysh*-coated rags to suck on when they cried too much. Baralis had tasted it only once, in the mouth of his teacher's young niece. He never tried it again: self-control was not something he relinquished lightly.

The fact that Kylock managed to take the drug and still retain the semblance of sanity was nothing short of remarkable. Five years he had taken it. Baralis could not begin to guess at the long-term effects of its use. Yet despite everything Kylock appeared to be faring well. A remarkable young man, indeed.

Baralis felt a trace of paternal pride. He worked quickly to suppress it: now was not the time for self-congratulation. There were things he must do, tasks he had been putting off for several days now, while he gave his body a chance to recover from the incident with Maybor at the tavern.

Baralis sat by his fire and Crope came to pour him some holk. "Ready my potions, Crope. I have a long journey to make." The drawings he had performed at the

Brimming Bucket had left him badly weakened, and only now did he have the strength to forsake himself. Baralis drank his holk slowly, putting off the final moment for as long as possible. He hated leaving his body. When mind was separated from flesh, when the soul pulled away from the body that fed it, and when the heart pumped blood around an empty shell, time was of the essence—and dangers as terrible as insentience and madness lurked in dark spaces waiting to strike.

Taking a deep breath, Baralis began his preparations: the powder, the leaf, the blood. He inhaled the mixture deeply and then fell back into the waiting arms of Crope.

The terrible lightness never failed to shock. Baralis kept his thoughts weighty, lest his mind rise high above the firmament never to return. His body screamed in protest, but already he was too far away to acknowledge the loss. Up and up he went, through layers of clouds and thinning bands of air pressure, the rotation of the world bending his ascent. Strange how he felt the cold. Heat, wind, and water left him unaffected, but the cold had a power all its own.

Before he knew it he was there. The temple at Larn lay below him: a stone rectangle on an island that was shaped like a pear. Down through slate and rock and wood he traveled, into the chamber they had prepared for his mooring. Four men, a table, four candles, and a bowl.

"Welcome, Baralis," said the first of the four.

Baralis took a moment to still himself. If he'd had breath he would be breathless. This time he did not make the mistake of shaping himself a form—he would not waste his energy on a trifle to please the priests. "I have come in search of answers."

"You have come to the right place, but what will you give us in return?"

"Not my soul, if that is what you think."

"You have no soul, Baralis. You survive on ambition alone."

Baralis flexed his will and all four candles went out. "I will listen to no condemnation from Larn."

The eldest of the four spoke quickly. "Say what you want, Baralis."

They already knew why he'd come, he was sure of it. They just liked to play their games. "The duke's newly bereaved wife is with child. I need to know if it is a boy or a girl."

The four were silent for a moment, exchanging whatever secret messages they needed to exchange. After a moment the youngest priest spoke up. "Ill tidings for you, I'd say, Baralis."

"A boy, then." It was as direct an answer as he was ever likely to get from Larn. He moved quickly along: it was never wise to give the priests too long to think. "When will Annis and Highwall move against Bren?"

The youngest tut-tutted. "Now, now, Baralis. A favor for a favor first."

Baralis was prepared for this. If there was one thing Larn was famous for, it was always extracting its price. He spoke slowly, relishing every word. "I know the identity of the one whom you fear."

No one breathed for the longest moment. Then the eldest whispered, "Go on."

"A baker's boy from Castle Harvell is the one who can destroy you. Jack is his name, and he used to be my scribe."

"Where is he now?" hissed the youngest.

Baralis was beginning to enjoy himself. He wished he had shoulders to shrug. "Somewhere west of Bren— Helch, Annis, who knows?"

"What makes you so sure of what you say?"

"Aah, my friend, do I ask you how the seers spin their tales?" Baralis wasn't about to tell them of Marod's prophecy—let them figure that one out on their own. Marod spoke of many things that were no concern of Larn's.

"And what of the knight who seeks the boy called Jack?"

"I believe he is still in Bren. 'Twould be near impossible for him to smuggle a pregnant woman and her aging father out of the city." Baralis couldn't resist a jibe. "But surely you know that already?"

"We cannot force our seers to see."

"You would if you could." Baralis changed the timbre of his thoughts. He was tired of trading jibes, and time was running out. "Tell me what you know of Highwall's plans."

"Their plans are no longer their own. Their troops will not leave their city until the marriage has taken place."

"Why will they wait until then?"

"Because the one who pays the piper picks the tune."

Tavalisk. Rorn's scheming archbishop was financing the buildup to war. Yet what benefit would he gain by waiting? Baralis felt himself wavering. The blood-pull of his body called him back.

"Going so soon, Baralis?" taunted the youngest.

"A proposition before you do," said the eldest. "Track down and destroy the knight and the boy, and we will direct your hand in the war."

The words *I agree* sounded over half a continent as Baralis succumbed to the cravings of his flesh.

Jack felt the hairs on the back of his neck bristle like a dog's. It was damp and cool with a light breeze blowing, but nothing could explain the sensation he'd just felt. It was as if a dark shadow had passed over him.

Jack pulled his new cloak close. The sky was growing dimmer by the minute. It was dusk, and from where he stood, at the side of the road leading up to the mountains, Jack could see all of Annis below him. He had decided not to return to Stillfox. There was too much risk: the city would be crawling with people looking for

him. The road leading to the herbalist's village was too
busy—a hundred people might recognize him. In fact,
walking to the city in the first place had been nothing
short of foolish. According to Stillfox, his likeness was
posted all over Annis.

No. It was for the best that he didn't go back. He
would only be placing Stillfox in danger. And even
though the man may have hidden the truth about Melli
from him, he hardly deserved to be branded a traitor.
Jack didn't know what the penalty for harboring a notorious war criminal would be, but he could guess it would
involve torture, then death.

Jack began to walk up the narrow mountain path. Even
though he knew he was doing the right thing by not
returning to say farewell to Stillfox, he couldn't help but
feel bad. The herbalist would assume that he had taken
off in a fit of anger vowing never to return. Well, that was
what life was all about, wasn't it? A series of misunder-
standings, half-truths, and regrets?

Jack drew his lips into a thin line that might have
passed for a smile in candlelight. Sometimes, just sometimes, one was given the chance to silence the softly
scathing voices of regret.

For months before he had found out the truth about
Melli, he had tortured himself with thoughts of what had
happened to her in the chicken coop. If only he hadn't left
her. If only he had fought harder to get away from Rovas.
If only it had been *he* the Halcus caught instead of her.
Now he had been given a second chance. Melli was in
danger and this time he would be there when she needed
him.

Stillfox had kept the information about Melli's plight
from him, knowing full well he would want to go to her.
Perhaps the herbalist would guess his reasons for not
returning after all. He was not a stupid man.

The moon appeared from behind the clouds and the
last of the daylight faded away. An old woman he'd

spoken to this morning said there were two roads to Bren. The Duke's Highway was wide and cut into the rock where it could, only narrowing to accommodate the pass. Soldiers and messengers and merchants walked its mighty length, so the old woman said. But if he was looking for a quieter way to Bren—a way that could only be traveled in summer and early autumn, a way that was narrow and winding and might add ten extra leagues to his journey—then the Old Goat Trail would do. Only spies and goatherders walked the trail, she said. Jack had given her a wedge of cheese for her trouble, and with lips as dry as paper she had kissed him on his cheek.

He had seen only one goatherder all day. The man had given him a suspicious look and Jack guessed that he thought he was a spy. Feeling a little mischievous, Jack had openly taken a head count of the herder's goats as seriously as if they were enemy soldiers. Rather sheepishly for a man who spent his time herding goats, the herder had approached him.

"Are you counting numbers for Annis or Bren?" he asked.

"Neither," replied Jack, quickly realizing that there was a chance for gain here. "I count only for the Wall."

The goatherder acted as if this information merely confirmed a prior suspicion. He nodded knowingly and sucked in his cheeks. "Highwall," he said. "Aye." He looked at his goats, looked at Jack, looked at a distant point on the horizon, took a deep breath, and then spoke. "What will it take to cut those numbers by half?"

Jack was ready with his request. He motioned toward the herder's coarse wool cloak. "Do you keep a second cloak for feastday best?"

The herder, who smelled of goat dung, goat cheese, and goats, brought his hand up to his face and scratched his chin. "So you'd settle for my best cloak?" he said, his voice a peculiar mixture of surprise and relief.

"No. I want the one you're wearing now."

"This old thing's stiff with goat dung," said the herder.

Jack clamped his teeth together to stop himself from laughing outright. After a moment he said, "It will do." Anything was better than freezing to death on the dark side of a mountain. Summer it might well be, but once night came seasons would have little meaning. Dressed as he was at the moment, in a light tunic and undershirt, he wouldn't stand a chance. Jack was tempted to have the man's boots as well, and would have taken them if it wasn't for the fact that the herder's feet were most definitely not a match for his own.

The herder handed over his coat. "How many goats do I have now?" he asked.

Jack had counted two scores. "Owning only a handful like you do, you're hardly worth a mention in my report." He took the cloak from the man. It didn't smell as bad as he thought.

The man nodded his approval. "My wife will thank you for taking that thing off my hands. She's been trying to make me get rid of it for years now."

"Tell her she has the Wall to thank, not me." Jack bowed to the herder and took his leave, purloined cloak firmly in hand.

Borc! but he was glad of it now, though. With the appearance of the moon, summer seemed to have given up completely. The very same breeze that had been blowing against him all day had decided to turn nasty and was worrying away at his bones. Jack began to slow his pace, pausing every few steps to check to either side of the path. It was about time to find somewhere to sleep for the night.

He had, thanks to the Baking Master's Guild, enough food to last him for a few days, and if he ran out, well, he could always con another unsuspecting goatherder out of his cheese. Jack smiled at the thought of the herder going home, cloakless, to his wife. He'd obviously learnt more from Rovas than just how to defend himself. Some of Rovas' cunning must have rubbed off along the way.

A cluster of rocks caught Jack's eye: it was about as good as he was going to get tonight. He left the path and headed toward them. The wind whipped down from the mountain and this time it brought rain for the ride. A few specks splashed against Jack's face, then a few more, and before he knew it he was in the middle of a squall. He raced for the rocks, cloak pulled tight about his chest.

The rocks formed a rim around a dip. It promised great protection from the wind, but in the rain was little but a bowl waiting to be filled. Jack looked up at the sky. The moon was still visible behind shifting banks of clouds, which meant the rain would probably be light. He decided to risk the rocky dip. A few young saplings were growing to the left of the rocks, and Jack took his knife to them. He hacked an armful of branches and laid them in the space between the rocks. Now he wouldn't have to lie on the wet ground. He collected a few more branches for good measure, and then settled into his den, spreading the extra branches out on top of him. Not bad really, he thought as he snuggled down amidst the fragrant summer leaves.

Jack immediately began to feel sleepy: it had been a long two days. The old woman had said it would take over a week to get to Bren by the Old Goat Trail. Well, it might take a while, and his feet might never forgive him, but one way or another he would make it to Melli's side. With that comforting thought on his mind, Jack fell into a dreamless sleep. Raindrops pattered softly for a while and then gradually faded away.

Five

Melli counted the weeks backward to her wedding day. Eleven. Could it really be that many? That made her nearly three months pregnant. Her hands stole to her belly as she tested for any sign of swelling. Nothing. Well, perhaps a slight thickening around her waist.

Just this morning Nabber had returned from a foray bearing several new dresses for her to wear. Melli was rather alarmed at the size of them: they were as large and billowing as priest's cassocks. Not to mention the fact that they were all various shades of red. Following her beating in Duvitt, Melli had developed a strong dislike for the color. Now, having been married in red, she despised it even more. Nabber, however, loved red, and everything he brought her—purses, flowers, ribbons— was either scarlet, ruby, or crimson. She didn't have the heart to tell him that she would have preferred blue instead.

Everyone was always so kind to her. Bodger and Grift would force fancies and sweetmeats on her like a pair of maiden aunts, Nabber brought her gifts like an over- ardent suitor, and Maybor checked in on her by the hour like a nursemaid. Tawl was different, though. He alone allowed her breathing space. Oh, he was always there, on the other side of the door sitting in his windowseat, but he never intruded upon her thoughts or her time.

Every so often she would hear his footsteps just outside the door, and she knew he was listening for her. There was no right word to describe the way those footsteps made her feel: secure, certainly, but something more as well. Something much more. Tawl would lay down his life for her, Melli knew as surely as she knew her own name. Yet that was only part of it. Tawl spent his days on guard outside her door and his nights sleeping propped up against it. Loyalty kept him there, but it was *love* that made him tiptoe up to the wood and listen for the sound of her tears.

And it was this unassuming unspoken love that kept her going from day to day.

Once, almost two weeks back now, Tawl had left the hideout without telling her. Melli had come out of her room to ask him something, and when she found he wasn't there, her heart started to pound. Tawl was *always* there. He had sworn never to leave her side, and for one terrible moment, she thought he had abandoned his oath. No one knew where he'd gone. Nabber wasn't around, either. Melli started to panic: without Tawl she was vulnerable, alone in a world that wanted her dead. Then he had come back. The front door opened and in he came, and instantly he saw all on her face.

Always chivalrous, the only thing he said was, "I will not leave you again."

Even as he spoke, a shiver passed down Melli's spine, and she knew in her heart that he would.

Strangely, her premonition had made her stronger. It had focused her thoughts on herself. She had always been strong, yet since the duke's murder she had somehow stopped relying on herself. Tawl took care of her completely, and she had willingly relinquished control. Ever since the day of Tawl's absence, she had slowly been claiming it back. Her premonition had told her he would go, and she wanted to be prepared when he did. She had to be strong for her baby.

Tawl loved her, she had realized that the day she married the duke, and in a way she had used that love. It had given her comfort in a time of chaos. For weeks after the wedding her life had been a bleak and distant dream, and it had been Tawl's quiet strength that had helped pull her through. His footsteps outside her door, his gentle considerations, and most of all the knowledge that he was in control, had given her peace of mind through the long hours of her grief.

A gentle tapping came upon the door. "Melli, are you awake?" It was Tawl.

"Come in. I'm awake, I'm alert, and I'm as sick as a dog."

Tawl entered smiling. "Do you need the bowl?"

The bowl was the bane of Melli's existence. It followed her around the house, waiting to serve. "No. I don't feel like I'm going to be sick just yet."

Coming to stand beside her, Tawl reached out and took her hand in his. "You know the wedding of Catherine and Kylock is today."

Melli nodded. "I know." She didn't want to think about it. The marriage was nothing to her.

"There is a good side to it," said Tawl softly. "Baralis has been so busy pulling everything together these past ten days that he's had little time to search for us. The streets have been quiet."

"Too quiet for a city whose favorite daughter is married today."

Tawl took a quick breath. "You know, we should leave. Just last night Nabber found a sluice gate that leads under the wall. He says there are only two guards within striking distance on the other side. I could easily take them out."

"No. I'm not ready to leave. We're safe for the moment—you said so yourself." Melli turned her back on him. "I don't know if I could manage it if we were chased by the guards. I can't run. I can barely stand up without being sick. The baby's health is too important to risk. Grift says that once the first three months are up it will be safer to move me."

"What about the risks here?" Tawl said, grabbing hold of her shoulders and spinning her round. "They would give up searching for us if they thought we were out of the city—"

"Would they?" Melli cut in harshly. "Now that my father has blurted out to a tavern full of drunkards that I'm with child, how long do you think it would be before Baralis came after us?"

"Baralis has no power in Annis or Highwall. We could go there. Leave it too late and the whole of the north will be one huge battlefield."

"You go, then," said Melli, suddenly angry. "Right now they are looking for you, not me. Half the city still believes it was you who murdered the duke." As soon as the words were out of her mouth, she regretted them. She bowed her head. "I'm sorry, Tawl. I don't know what I'm saying. Pregnancy seems to rob me of my wits." She wanted to say more, to tell him that the feeling that he would leave her was never far from her thoughts, and that it had pushed the harsh words right out of her mouth.

Tawl slid his forefinger under her chin and tilted her face up to meet his. "Melli," he said, his blue eyes looking straight into hers, "I would do anything to keep you safe, and if I thought for a moment that my presence endangered you, then I'd be gone before you took your next breath."

His voice was heavy with emotion. Something dark and hurting lay just beneath the surface. Melli realized how little she knew of him. He never spoke about himself or his past. He had left the knighthood, that much she knew, and just last week, on the Feast of Borc's First Miracle, she had seen how much pain that had caused him. He was a man who'd lost his soul that day. But everything else he kept to himself: his family, his origins, his dreams for the future. Day and night he kept watch outside her door, yet if he ever crossed the threshold it was never to speak of himself.

Melli took a step forward and up came Tawl's arms, guiding her toward his chest. She rested herself against him, feeling the mighty beat of his heart. She wanted to beg him never to leave regardless of what was best for her and the baby, but something, perhaps pride, perhaps instinct, stopped the thoughts from forming words in her mouth.

Jack entered the city of Bren late in the afternoon. The Old Goat Trail had taken ten days of solid walking to bring him here. He had been lucky with the weather; a little rain, a pesky wind, and temperature that dropped sharply at night were the worst things he'd had to contend with. Of course, the walking was another matter: his feet now boasted more blisters than an army full of flat-footed soldiers on the move. Or at least they felt like they did.

His food had given out three days earlier and right about now he was ready for a meal. In fact, even as he walked through Bren's southwestern gate, Jack was planning exactly how he'd get his hands on some food. No unsuspecting goatherders here, that's for sure. He would have to rob someone, and after three days of not eating, he wasn't particularly fussy about who—the first man he saw with a hot pie, most likely.

The scale of the city took his breath away. There were buildings of stone and brick and timber, two, sometimes three stories high. The streets were wide, and most were either paved or cobbled. Shops and taverns and warehouses crowded side by side, leaning against each other for support, all jostling for recognition with brightly painted signs and carvings above their doors. Above it all towered the wall. It dominated the city, rising high above the buildings and casting its long shadow to the east. Jack had never seen anything like it in his life. Annis' wall seemed like so many naked stones compared to this.

Stillfox had said that Annis and Highwall would lay siege to Bren. Jack cast a last admiring glance at the battlements: he would like to see the army that would try to breach these walls.

Jack began to walk the city in search of food. The place was a lot quieter than he'd imagined. Yes, it was late in the day, so stallholders were upping stakes and shopkeepers were closing shutters, but those people who were on the streets seemed strangely subdued. There were no riotous drunks, no children chasing pigs, no old women gossiping in groups. Even the beggars were quiet.

Jack approached an aging stallholder who was busy loading his mule with unsold goods. His baskets were filled with apples, not pies, but Jack decided to try him anyway. He had a kind-looking face. "Can I help you with those baskets, sir?" he asked.

The stallholder looked him up and down. "You're welcome to, young man, but only expect the sour ones for your trouble." He indicated the baskets to be lifted. "From your accent I suppose you're here for the war. People from all over have been flooding into the city hoping to have a go at Highwall's army."

Jack shook his head. "No. I'm not here for the war." He began loading the baskets on the mule. They were heavier than he thought, and he wondered how the old man had managed to do the job every night.

The stallholder seemed to read his thoughts, for he said, "Any other night, young man, and I wouldn't have needed your help. Business has been terrible slow today. I've got so many apples left they just might break my poor mule's back."

Jack was thinking just the same thing. The old man must have someone else deliver the apples in the morning, as the mule did not look up to it. "So you normally sell them all?"

"Aye, that I do. But not today." The stallholder spat reflectively. "Never seen a day like it in all my life. It's like the whole city's in mourning."

Jack felt his stomach twist into a knot. "Why? What's happened?"

The stallholder looked at him as if he were mad. "Where've you been these past months, boy? Living under a rock? Today is the day that Catherine marries King Kylock." He looked up into the deep blue sky. "And if I'm not mistaken, the ceremony will be over and done with right about now."

Right on cue, a distant bell began to ring. It tolled three solemn notes. Jack's blood quickened to the sound: it was almost as if the notes were for him alone. He stood, apple basket in hand, unable to move a muscle or take a breath, and listened to the sound of Kylock's fate. It tolled strong and clear, setting the whole city vibrating in time. The very walls rang with it. Jack felt it in his soul like a message, like a warning, like a blade. Ever since the first morning he'd woken in Stillfox's cottage and seen a vision of the war, Jack knew Kylock and he were destined to oppose each other. And the ringing of the bell marked the beginning of the match.

Jack lost his hold on the basket and the apples went careening to the ground. He'd come to the right place at exactly the right time. Bren had called him for so long, and now that he'd finally arrived it was no coincidence that Kylock, Baralis, and Melli were here, too.

As if the very city itself were confirming Jack's thoughts, a hundred separate bells began to chime. Chapels throughout the city were marking the wedding, each one bent on out-pealing the last. High and low they rang out their notes, no two of them ringing in time.

The wedding feast had been torture to Kylock. Hundreds upon hundreds of people had touched him, holding out hands to be clasped and cheeks to be kissed and cups to be shared in toast. His whole body was tainted with their saliva and their sweat. Minuscule fragments of their skin clung to his sleeves, and his lungs were filled with their breath. He would have liked to burn them all for his suffering.

But he wouldn't. Oh no, he played the game, instead. The game of courtly manners, smiling and bowing and gracious to a fault. Promising positions and pensions and elevation to those who counted, whilst barely deigning to acknowledge those who did not.

Through it all one thought had kept him going: tonight Catherine would be his. Just to look at her calmed him. Her face so pale and serene, her eyes so blue and pure: she was an angel, created for him alone. The only part of his body that was clean were his fingertips, for she had kissed them before they left the hall.

Up to their chamber they walked, the lamp-holders stepping before them, the court watching quietly from below. Baralis waited at the top of the stairs, his eyes flashing a caution as he bowed his head toward the floor. Kylock paid him no heed. He stretched out his arm and his new wife rested her hand upon it.

"My lord chancellor," he said, "you have done your duty well. Your presence is no longer called for this night." Beside him he felt Catherine shudder, her breast pushing gently against his arm.

"As you wish, sire," murmured Baralis as they passed.

The double doors to the chamber were flung back as they reached the nobles' quarters, and the heady scent of roses crept forth to meet them. Kylock turned to one of the servants who was holding back the door.

"Get those flowers out of here. *Now!*"

The servant darted forward to do his bidding. Kylock stepped into the room with Catherine. His eyes took in all the details of the chamber. Good. A tub full of scalding water steamed away in the corner. "Draw a screen around the bath," he commanded to the servant whose arms were now full of roses. The man off-loaded his burden to another and began to pull the screen out from the wall.

When the screen was in place, Kylock ordered the servants to leave. He and Catherine stood side by side until the double doors closed behind them. Kylock then turned to face his new wife. Catherine was radiant in the firelight: more than an angel now, she was a goddess. Her golden hair glowed like a halo and her skin was as smooth as a statue. She was a holy icon, and it was only fitting that he kneel at her feet.

Catherine shifted nervously as Kylock stepped forward. Her hand fluttered up to her chest. Looking down at him, she saw to her amazement that he was lifting the hem of her dress. She couldn't stop herself from shuddering. He was so solemn, so intent—like a man possessed. His neck arched further and he kissed the fabric of her satin bridal shoes. Even through the fabric she could feel the cool touch of his lips.

Part of her was thrilled by the gesture—here was a king supplicating himself before her—yet part of her knew it was wrong. She felt out of her depth. Kylock was a stranger, an unknown entity who seemed intent on worshiping her. Uneasy, she took a step back.

Her withdrawal seemed to break the spell. Up came Kylock's head. His eyes took a moment to focus. There was a trace of spittle on his lips. "My love," he said, so softly she had to strain to hear him. "I can hardly believe that soon you will be mine."

"Why soon?" Catherine said. "Why not take me now?" Reaching back, she pulled at the lacings of her dress. She wanted to be naked before him. She didn't want to be worshiped, she wanted to be desired.

Kylock raised up his hand. "Not now, my love. Not like this." His voice had an edge to it, and Catherine let the laces fall. Satisfied, Kylock continued, "I must ready myself first." He motioned toward the screen.

Catherine hid her disappointment. She had hoped Kylock would be like Blayze: unable to resist her. Shrugging her shoulders, she said, "Very well, my lord. As you make ready, so will I." She turned her back on him and walked over to the dressing table. By the time she had poured herself a cup of wine, he had disappeared behind the screen. Catherine breathed a sigh of relief and downed her drink in one.

Well, it was obvious she was going to have to work a little harder to gain Kylock's interest. He was no Blayze, that was for sure.

Catherine cast her gaze upon the mirror. Her own beauty never failed to please her. Slowly, she took the pins from her hair, relishing the fall of every golden lock. Next she turned to her beauty box, dipping two fingers in to scoop up the rouge. She had deliberately not worn any cosmetics in Kylock's presence, thinking that he would prefer his women unadorned. Now it seemed she would need all the help she could get. She would not have Kylock regarding her as a holy relic to be worshiped. She was a woman with a woman's needs, and when he emerged from his bath he would see her for what she was.

During the banquet she had been unable to drink or eat. Her excitement over her wedding night had drawn her stomach to a close. It had been many months since she had been with a man, and she missed the rough-soft excitement of passion. Kylock was darkly handsome with a mouth that was marked by a cruel downward twist and eyes that were deeply set and thickly lidded. Catherine had felt sure he would be aggressive, even rough, in his lovemaking. Now, when they were finally alone, the first thing he wanted to do was take a bath!

Catherine smiled and poured herself another cup of wine. She would make sure that her feet were the last thing he'd want to kiss when he emerged from behind the screen. She rubbed the rouge into her cheeks and then her lips, turning them from pale pink to bloodred. Once finished she took up her cup. The wine was unwatered and went quickly to her head, making her feel wicked and lustful. For centuries people had said that the women of Bren were like cats in heat, so there was little point in denying it now.

Rather merrily, Catherine tugged at the strings of her bodice. As the fabric cleaved apart, she turned to the mirror and paused to admire the high curves of her breasts. A flash of inspiration came to her, and she rubbed a spot of rouge into each nipple. *Oh, yes*, she thought, arching forward to admire her handiwork, *Blayze would have loved this!*

What next? Catherine picked up a jar of scented oil and began dabbing behind her ears, at the base of her neck, and anywhere else that she fancied. As she finished her toilette, she listened for telltale signs of readiness from behind the screen. She could hear nothing at first, then her ears picked up the sound of water splashing . . . and something else. She couldn't tell what. Slipping out of her underskirt and stockings, she walked over to the screen. Without her maiden's belt she felt strangely light, not herself at all. Early this morning Bailor had passed her the key, and she had now been without the belt all day. Catherine almost missed it: the pressure and the chafing had delivered a subtle pleasure all their own.

Coming to stand beside the screen, Catherine started to brush a stray hair from her face when she noticed there were still spots of rouge on her fingertips. Naked now, she went to wipe her hands upon a nearby tapestry. At the last moment she stopped herself, a chuckle of delight sounding deep within her throat. Instead of wiping the rouge on the tapestry, she rubbed it into her pubic hair instead. The blond down became a blushing pink. Catherine bit her lip; she wanted to laugh out loud at the sight of it.

The faint rubbing sound that was coming from behind

the screen put a stop to all her delight. There was something unnerving about it: here was a man on his wedding night, with his new bride waiting for him, yet he chose to spend their first hour alone together scrubbing himself in a tub. Catherine felt a cold chill skim down her spine: this wasn't right, it wasn't normal.

She crept along the length of the screen until she came to the end. Then slowly she peeked her head around the corner of the screen.

Steam rose up from water hot enough to scald most people. Kylock sat in the tub with his back toward Catherine. A series of red scratch marks ran from his flank to his waist; some still had flakes of dried blood attached to them. He was bent forward, intent on something set before him—Catherine couldn't see what. She swung out a little farther. Now she saw what he was doing. He was scrubbing his hands with a small wooden brush. Back and forth the brush went, so quickly it was only a blur.

Catherine watched for a moment thinking, *Surely he will stop before he rubs all the skin from his bone.* But he didn't. He continued scrubbing with a terrible blind purpose. It was as if nothing else mattered.

Looking up from his hands to the slant of his cheek, Catherine realized that his jaw was moving. She could neither see his lips nor hear the words, but the muscles in his cheek kept working and his jaw jerked up and down.

Catherine withdrew back behind the screen. She had seen enough. The sight of Kylock muttering to himself while he rubbed his hands raw had changed her mood entirely. There was something very wrong with her new husband: it almost seemed as if he wasn't quite sane. Catherine shook her head. No. She wouldn't think such thoughts. After all, only two days back, Kylock had learned of his mother's death. All of Bren was talking about it.

By all accounts she had died horribly, at the hand of a

Halcus raiding party, raped and dismembered, her body wrapped in an Annis banner. No wonder Kylock was acting strangely: the news must have upset him deeply. In less than a year he had lost both his parents, and Catherine knew just how difficult a loss that was to bear. No. Her new husband wasn't crazed or demented, he was simply a man who didn't know how to deal with his grief.

Having come to this conclusion, Catherine felt a lot better. It was her duty, as a wife, to help her husband through this difficult time. She knew from experience that whenever Blayze was worried about an upcoming fight, or angry with his brother, that nothing took his mind off his troubles more than a night of fiery passion.

Whilst she was thinking, Catherine had poured herself a third cup of wine. She took a hearty gulp and then called out, "Kylock, my husband, your wife grows weary with the wait." She listened for a moment, and then heard the sound of water splashing from behind the screen. Her cry had obviously broken his trance.

Her smile was smug as she glanced one last time toward the mirror: tonight was going to be glorious. In her mind, she was already creating a fantasy where Kylock, weak from many hours of glorious lovemaking, broke down and wept in her arms.

Passion first, though, grief later. Crossing over to the bed, she blew out the surrounding candles one by one until she was happy with the light. In one hand she held her wine cup, in the other the jar of scented oil. Giggling, she began to sprinkle the oil upon the bed. When that was done to her satisfaction, she finished the last of her wine and slipped gaily between the sheets.

Encouraging sounds came from behind the screen: sounds of footsteps and drying and dressing.

Catherine began propping pillows up to support her neck and back. She tried several poses, thrusting out her chest, squaring her shoulders, spreading her hair out like a fan on the pillows. Nothing seemed quite right. She wanted to delight *and* surprise Kylock when he emerged from his bath. Judging from the increased activity behind the screen, she didn't have much longer to decide. If only her head was a little clearer; she had drunk too much wine by far, much more than was proper for a lady on her wedding night. Still, it made her feel so delightfully uninhibited.

Sucking on her thumb, Catherine came up with a plan: she would pose for him *under* the covers. Above he would simply see her face looking maidenly and modest, whilst below, she would be spread-eagled and waiting. It was perfect!

Smiling, Catherine adjusted the covers and then waited, a little impatiently, for Kylock to appear.

Kylock was not as clean as he would have liked to be for Catherine. Even now, with his mother new in the grave, he still couldn't rid himself of the stench of her. She clung to him from whatever hell she had been damned to: the smell, the taint, the sin. Queen Arinalda was a whore who had died a whore's death, and he would not allow himself to be dragged down with her. Tonight he would finally be rid of her—death alone was not nearly enough. He needed to be embraced by Catherine's purity to banish the last traces of his mother's lust.

He was a bastard, and that could never be changed, but his union with Catherine would give him his own private legitimacy. He would be born anew in the sanctity of her womb.

Eager now, Kylock ran the cloth over his hair, rubbing out the last of the wetness. On his instructions, a clean robe had been laid out in the corner over a chair. He ran the fabric between his scalded fingers. Good, it was silk.

In less than a minute he was ready to face his new wife. He was anxious, excited, his breath coming light and fast. Stepping out from behind the screen, he looked around the room. Everything had changed: the light was dimmer, more intimate, the cloying smell of perfume filled the air, and Catherine was no longer standing. She was already in bed, waiting for him.

She smiled as he approached. "Today you laid Halcus at my feet, my lord, and I haven't yet repaid you."

Kylock started to return the smile, then he noticed that Catherine herself had changed: her lips and cheeks were painted red. Whore's red. He felt a tiny muscle beginning to pump at his temple's edge. In all his dreams of rebirth Catherine had never looked like this. He took a step closer. The smell of perfume grew stronger, and underneath it was another smell: the smell of wine. The place stank like a brothel. Slowly, Kylock began to shake his head. This was not right.

Catherine smiled up at him, as brazen as a tavern wench. "Come now, husband," she said. "Your wife is waiting to pleasure you."

The candles cast their light on Kylock's back, sending his shadow out before him. Catherine fell under it as he walked toward the bed.

Throwing the covers from her body, she whispered, "I am ready, my lord. Take me now."

Kylock looked down upon his bride. She lay open-legged upon the bed, her back arching upwards, her hips thrust toward him.

The world began to dim for Kylock. The pressure point on his temple stretched across his forehead, becoming a tight band of pain. His vision blurred. His breathing stopped. His body became as rigid as a board. Terrible pressure built within his skull: something was pressing against his brain.

Catherine paled. She said, "My lord, what is wrong?"

Kylock's stomach churned bile into his throat. He gazed upon Catherine's naked body. The nipples were grotesquely bright, redder even than her lips.

He took a deep breath. "No," he murmured. "No."

And then he saw her sex. It was smeared with the same

foul redness. She had prepared herself like a trollop. She was no blushing, inexperienced maiden. She was a craven, licentious whore.

Just like his mother.

Kylock snapped. His tenuous link with sanity was severed in an instant. Catherine screamed. He punched her in the mouth to quiet her. Her head went reeling back into the pillows. Kylock sprang onto the bed. Everything smelled of her: the awful cloying stench of decay. He had to be rid of it. Catherine reached up with her hand, raking her nails across his cheek. Dark, terrible anger rose within Kylock, and he took Catherine's neck in his hand. Blood ran from her nose. It was the same color as her lips, her nipples, *her sex*.

He slammed her neck back against the headboard. Something cracked. Catherine's body stiffened for an instant and then slumped back against the sheets. Kylock dropped his hold and her head fell against the pillow at an unnatural angle. There was blood on the headboard, and blood seeping on either side of the pillow.

The pressure in Kylock's head was too much for him to bear. He felt a sickening contraction in his stomach. His bride lay still beneath him. *"No!"* he screamed. And as the word left his lips something real and metal to the taste came with it.

Baralis was in his chambers when he felt it. He was massaging oil into his hands when he felt a wave of warm air that stopped him dead. *Sorcery!* Here, within the palace. He shot from his chair. Every hair on his body prickled a warning, all his senses were intent upon perceiving the source. The salty glaze upon his eyes evaporated in an instant, causing him to blink repeatedly to water them once more. His tongue rested in the base of his mouth, and as he inhaled he drew in the aftertaste of the force. It was known and yet unknown to him. Familiar to a point and then entirely alien.

It was something new. Something dangerous. And it made Baralis afraid.

"Crope," he called. "Crope!"

As he waited for his servant to appear, Baralis paced around the room, a hound on the scent. The waves were coming from the east of him—that meant the nobles' quarters . . . "Borc, no," he whispered under his breath. It meant Catherine's chamber, as well.

Crope entered the room. "Come with me," Baralis ordered, making his way to the door. A cold feeling of dread settled within his stomach. There was no time to lose; he had to know what had happened. Down corridors he sped, robe flapping behind him, Crope padding at his heels. The waves of the drawing grew stronger with every step. They led him straight to Catherine's door. The two guards who watched the hallway crossed their spears as Baralis approached.

Baralis had no time to deal with them. He shaped a compulsion, part soporific, part delusion. A deep instinct within warned him not to use too much of himself. Borc only knew what he might find behind the door. The faces of both guards slackened, muscles falling limp. Crope came forward, grabbed both guards, and guided them toward the floor. Baralis nodded to him. "Good." The huge servant came and stood by his side, and together they stepped toward the doorway.

Never in his life had Baralis been so afraid; every fiber of his soul screamed out that something was terribly wrong. He took a deep breath and opened the door.

The aftermath from the drawing lapped over his body in waves. The light was dim, very dim. The room reeked of exotic fragrances. Dampness filled the air. The only movement came from the base of the bed. Kylock was kneeling on the floor, his hands resting on the bed. He appeared to be stroking something. Baralis didn't want to step forward, didn't want to see, didn't want to know what had happened, but he knew he must. Above all he was a shaper of destinies and his work was as much about dealing with catastrophe as it was about creation.

One step was enough to reveal the naked body of Catherine. She was lying on a heap of sheets and pillows. Her head was bent impossibly far back from her body, and there was blood on the pillows to either side of her face. Kylock knelt over her, muttering words to himself whilst gently stroking her feet.

The headboard had been completely destroyed. Not burnt, but rather blasted away. All the glass and the metal in the room was hot to the touch, some of it glowing. A mist of water vapor hung in the air like a pall.

Baralis recognized the signs of an unfocused drawing: hot metal, evaporated water, mild unspecific destruction. Despite the formidable suppressing powers of *ivysh,* Kylock had drawn power from within. Crude, yes. Unfocused, certainly—but the sorcery was there all the same. Baralis shuddered. What sort of man could draw so strongly that he broke through *ivysh*'s restraint? It should not have been possible. Still, violent emotion could work strange effects upon a man's body and mind.

Baralis shook his head, purposely dispelling all possible implications from his thoughts. He could not afford to dwell on them now. He had more immediate problems to deal with. He gestured to Crope to close the door and walked toward the bed.

Kylock did not acknowledge Baralis' presence; he simply continued stroking his dead wife's feet.

Reaching up, Baralis touched Catherine's neck with his fingertips. She was already growing cold. There was no pulse. He slid his hand behind her neck; her spinal cord had been broken. Lifting his hand up, he cupped the back of her head; her skull had been cracked near the base. Nodding softly, Baralis withdrew, pausing to wipe the blood on his robe.

He stood there, looking down upon the newly deceased duchess of Bren, and began to formulate a plan.

Catherine's body took on the look of a corpse as he thought. A minute, perhaps two at the most, passed; then turning to Crope, Baralis gave his instructions.

An hour later he was ready. Crope had brought him potions, drugs, herbs, and props. A subtle compulsion had ensured that no one would mark the huge servant's passing. Crope was now busy replacing the destroyed headboard with a similar one from Baralis' own chamber.

Kylock had to be dealt with first. Baralis knelt beside him at the foot of the bed and very gently guided his hands away from Catherine's feet. "Ssh," he murmured as he brought the cup to Kylock's lips. "Drink this, my lord. Drink it now." Like an obedient child, Kylock drank his medicine. It was a special strain of sleeping draft used by warriors from beyond the Northern Ranges to dispel battle-terror and weariness on the field. In less than an hour Kylock would wake refreshed, strengthened, clear of mind and sound of body. At least that was what Baralis hoped—the alternative didn't bear thinking about.

"Crope," he called. "Take Kylock and lay him to rest behind the screen." The drug worked quickly, and by the time Crope moved from the head of the bed, Kylock's eyes were already closed.

Baralis turned his attention to the room. The shutters had been pulled back to enable the water vapor from the bath to escape. Crope had brought fresh linens for the bed and a bowl of warm water to wash the blood from Kylock's hands and Catherine's hair. Moving around the room, Baralis checked all glass and metal items. The candlesticks surrounding the bed were the only things that needed discarding: the metal had grown so hot that it had melted, running thickly to the base. Candle wax formed grotesque shapes over the metal. Crope would have to bring new holders and candles.

At the time of the drawing the wine jar had been stoppered, so there were still a few drops remaining in the bottom. Baralis took his flask and filled Catherine's jar one cup short of the brim. Next he turned to her cup. It was a thing of unusual beauty: smoothly carved silkwood with parchment-thin sides and a goodly weight at the base. It was perfect in every way.

"Crope," said Baralis, "when you've finished with the headboard, I want you to take your sharpest knife and carve two circles in the base of this cup. One inside the other."

Crope was excited. "Like the knight's circles, master?"

Baralis smiled, his first of the evening. "Yes, exactly like the knight's circles." He thought for a moment, then added, "Oh, and be sure to carve a line that cuts through the circles dead center." Exactly like one particular knight, who would find himself wanted for murder come the morning. Baralis turned his attention back to Crope. "Once that's done, go to my chambers and fetch me some candles and holders."

Crope nodded enthusiastically. He liked nothing better than being useful to his master.

Now it was time to see to himself. Baralis took a small vial from the dresser and emptied its contents upon his tongue. The viscous liquid stung going down. It would not strengthen him exactly, rather prolong what strength he already had. He would now be able to function after the drawing to come. Of course, there would be a price: at some point tomorrow he would simply collapse and it might be as long as a week before he recovered his senses. That wasn't important, though. What counted tonight was eliminating every little thing that could tell of what had happened between Kylock and Catherine. One wrong move, one item overlooked, and *everything* would fall apart. His plans had stretched over three decades and nothing, absolutely nothing, would stand in the way of his mastery of the north.

Baralis took a deep breath and came to stand beside Catherine. Her body was now blue and stiff. "Turn her

for me, Crope," he murmured, "and fetch me a chair so
that I might sit." Crope did his bidding, and a minute
later Baralis was sitting by the side of the bed, looking
down at the broken bones in Catherine's spine. The crack
in the skull was nothing: more blood than bone, a simple
knitting would suffice. But the spine—Baralis shook his
head—the spine would require a surgeon's skill.

A jagged bone pressed against the skin at the base of
Catherine's neck. Baralis placed his palm over it. During
his time on the plains he had seen many broken bones.
The herdsmen had a way with them, knitting together the
white and porous husks with a combination of potions,
sorcery, and sacrifice. Never had he seen them repair a
broken spine. It was too delicate an operation, too much
could go wrong: nerves could be trapped, blood vessels
could be destroyed, and the bone might fix improperly,
causing lameness or worse. Baralis bit down on his
tongue, preparing for the trance. None of that mattered to
Catherine: a corpse's spine required no such consideration. As long as it looked all right, that was enough.

Crope handed him leaf and bowl, and the fat beads of
Baralis' blood dripped readily down from his tongue.
There would be no sacrifice to help the process—he
would rely upon his own strength alone.

Down he sent his consciousness, down into the corpse.
He had worked on freshly killed animals many times, but
no amount of training could prepare one for the appalling
shock of the dead. Cold, corrupt, actively decaying: a
corpse was no place for a sorcerer to linger.

Baralis' fingers went to work, warming, shaping, shifting. His hand pressed the bone backward, while his mind
prepared the rest. Once the fragment was in place, he
began the knitting, stirring tissue to join with bone. He
had no time for finesse, no time for a surgeon's subtlety,
and he concentrated purely upon the join. When he had
finished, Catherine's neck was rigid. The top four verte-
brae were now more firmly linked in death than they had

ever been in life. Baralis transferred his consciousness to Catherine's skull. The stiffness would be put down to the poison.

Compared to the spine, the skull was an easy task, a mere knitting of bone to bone. Baralis wasted little effort with show as any bruising would be covered by Catherine's thick, golden hair. As long as her head felt smooth when the physician ran his hands over it, that would be more than enough.

Baralis worked quickly, conscious of the nearness of Catherine's brain and unnerved by the last futile firings of her nerve cells. By the time the task was complete, he was weak beyond telling. Withdrawing from the corpse, he was dazzled by the light, warmth, and freshness of life. For Baralis it merely confirmed that survival at any cost was the most important thing of all. There was little glory to be had in death.

He slumped back in his chair and regarded his patient. Her neck was as smooth as a swan's, and once the blood was washed from her hair, her skull would pass for normal. Glancing over at the candles on the wall, he saw that two notches had burned whilst he worked. Crope had left and returned, and was quietly replacing the mis-shapen candlesticks with new ones. When he noticed his master was conscious, he came over with a glass of mulled holk. Baralis took it from him. "Turn the duchess onto her back and then wake Kylock for me," he said.

"Should I change the sheets first, master?"

"No. That will be done last. I haven't finished here yet." Baralis watched as Crope disappeared behind the screen. He was so tired, all he wanted to do was rest. Bringing his hands together, he massaged his aching fingers. Behind the screen came the sound of Crope imploring Kylock to wake. Baralis braced himself and stood up. His legs ached from sitting too long, but he forced himself to walk to the dresser. Resting on top was Catherine's wooden cup, which now boasted two circles in the base. Baralis poured a splash of poisoned wine into it. Bringing it over to the bed, he sprinkled a few drops upon Catherine's perfect lips, prying apart her teeth to make sure the liquid went down, and then set the cup on the nearest chest.

Kylock appeared from behind the screen. "What have you done?" he demanded.

Baralis permitted himself a tiny sigh of relief: the king was lucid. "I have made it look as if your wife died from poison. Everything is as it was before——" Baralis caught himself. "Everything looks normal. Your story is that when you went to sleep Catherine looked well, and when you woke she was dead. She offered you a drink from her cup, and although you declined at first, you took a tiny sip to please her. In the morning, just before you raise the alarm, you will take this." Baralis indicated a vial on the dresser. "It will mimic a case of poisoning, but will not harm you greatly. Valdis' circles are carved on the base of Catherine's cup, but you will not discover them—let someone else do that. Your part is to act shocked, outraged, and tear the city apart looking for the man who did this."

Kylock nodded once. "Who?"

"Tawl, duke's champion. As soon as the cup is discovered, all the servants will be questioned. When I leave you now, I will *convince* one of the poor wretches that he was bribed into delivering the wine and cup by a certain golden-haired knight." Baralis was curt. "Have you got everything?"

"Yes."

"Good. Now Crope will stay with you to change the sheets and help with positioning Catherine's body. The blood must be cleaned from her hair and the rouge wiped from her body. When you have finished with her, she must be dressed in her nightgown——"

Kylock interrupted him. "What do you mean, finished with her?"

"I take it the marriage has not been consummated?"

"No."

"Then legally it is no marriage at all. For you to retain rights in Bren there must be no question that a joining took place."

Kylock shook his head. "No. No. *No!*"

"*Yes!*" insisted Baralis. "I have not gone to all this trouble to see everything wasted. The first thing the physician will do is examine her for seed. They will be looking for any possible way to wriggle out of the marriage." Baralis raised his voice. "I don't care how you manage it, but it must be done." He moved over to the door and turned the handle. "*Now do it!*" he hissed as he walked across the threshold.

Six

*T*avalisk loved his new fish. It had tiny little fish-teeth, and it tore at anything that was dangled into its bowl. Currently Fang, as the archbishop had named him, was intent on savaging a rather inert, but not entirely defenseless, sausage. Size alone ensured it a measure of protection, for Fang in addition to being deadly was also rather small. The sausage was twice the size of him. Tavalisk only wished that the glass bowl was more transparent, for the thick green swirls prevented him from seeing all the action.

Just as Fang got a decent grip on the sausage, in came Gamil. No knock, no ceremony, waving a small gray piece of paper. "Your Eminence. Such news!" Gamil proceeded to fan himself with the paper. He was out of breath, red of face, and his hair had want of a brush.

Like a priest among lepers, Tavalisk chose to keep his distance. Holding out a restraining palm, he said, "Gamil, much though I appreciate your speedy delivery of important messages, I simply cannot tolerate seeing a man such as yourself sweat. Who knows what vile substances are secreted with the salt." Tavalisk sent a pointed glance to his aide, who looked ready to burst if he wasn't allowed to speak. "Very well. Step no closer and I will permit you to tell your news."

"Your Eminence, Catherine of Bren is dead. Poison, they say."

"When did this happen?"

"Four, perhaps five days back. I just received tidings by bird."

Tavalisk, forgetting his previous warning, came up to his aide and snatched the paper from his hand. If Gamil's sweat was upon it, he didn't give it a second thought. "Is this all?" he said, once he'd read the note.

"Yes, Your Eminence. We'll know more in a few weeks when the swift messengers arrive."

Tavalisk crushed the paper in his fist. "Poison, eh?" Baralis had a hand in this. Why, he, himself, had provided the know-how. Tavalisk's libraries had been five years in Baralis' keep. There were dozens of books on poisons in his collection, and doubtless the lovely Catherine had fallen victim to one of them.

Now, if Baralis *had* poisoned Catherine, then that meant the blame would fall elsewhere. Baralis was no fool; he could shift blame as easily as other men changed their clothes. So, who would Baralis choose to implicate? Anyone from Highwall or Annis would help his cause, inciting passions in Bren against its two northern rivals. Tavalisk nodded slowly. Or he could try and eliminate a more immediate threat: the claim that Maybor's daughter was carrying the duke's child. By all accounts Lord Maybor was seeding the city with rumors that his daughter's unborn child was most definitely the heir to Bren. Implicate Melliandra or one of her supporters in Catherine's murder and her claim would be instantly discredited. That was it, Tavalisk was sure of it. At this point in time Baralis had more to fear from Melliandra and her unborn child than the armies of Annis and Highwall combined.

Kylock would doubtless claim Bren for his own, yet if there was a possibility that a rightful heir existed, then the good people of the city would send him running back to the kingdoms with his tail between his legs.

Tavalisk smiled his special secret smile. Baralis was

vulnerable, and it was high time that *he*, the chosen one, played upon that vulnerability like a bell-ringer at the rope. "Gamil," he said, crossing over to the fishbowl, "what do we know about the movement of Highwall troops?"

"Well, Your Eminence, we know they received your message to wait until after the wedding day before making their move, but we can only guess how the news of Catherine's death might affect their plans."

Dropping the crumpled sheet of paper in the bowl, Tavalisk said, "*Guess*, Gamil! I am not in the business of guessing policy. I am in the business of shaping it." Fang approached the paper with all the intent of a shark after prey. The sausage was now so much flotsam and jetsam floating murkily on the surface. "Indeed, Gamil, I think it's high time I became a champion."

"A champion, Your Eminence?"

Fang's little fish-teeth tore at the paper, shredding it into a hundred tiny pieces. Tavalisk watched the process with great satisfaction. Perhaps he should place all his sensitive documents into the bowl. "Yes, Gamil, a champion, or more precisely, Melliandra's champion. In fact I think that all of us—the four southern cities, Highwall, Annis and what is left of poor defeated Halcus—should take up the good lady's claim. Don't you see? It's perfect. No longer will we be fighting out of fear, we will be fighting for a *cause*! We will be fighting to place the rightful heir to Bren on the ducal throne."

Tavalisk, in his excitement, had inadvertently rested his fingers on the side of the bowl. Fang, being a fish with no powers of discrimination, promptly leapt from the water and bit the archbishop's thumb. "Aah!" cried Tavalisk, pulling back his hand. Blood oozed from a small but perfectly serrated wound. The archbishop sucked the wound closed: he liked the taste of his own blood.

Flashing a hateful look at Fang, he continued, "Today, Gamil, I need you to send messages to those parties concerned. From now on our allies must officially support Melliandra's claim." Tavalisk smiled, regaining a little of his good humor. "I can imagine nothing that would annoy Baralis more! This will cause a lot of trouble for him in Bren. Might even divide the city if he's not careful. Disputes over ascendancy are notorious for starting civil wars."

"So is religion, Your Eminence."

"I neither want nor require any words of wisdom from you at this juncture, Gamil. When I am in the middle of formulating policy, a simple, 'Yes, Your Eminence,' will suffice. Is that clear?"

"Yes, Your Eminence," said Gamil sourly.

"Good. Now in addition to sending messages to Annis and Highwall—whose armies are probably on the way to Bren as we speak—I need you to track down Maybor and his daughter. I'm sure they are still somewhere in Bren: ask the local priests and clergy to keep an eye out for them. The girl must be found and removed to a place of safety." Tavalisk paused for a minute, contemplating his plan. "Of course, the strange thing in all of this is why Baralis moved against Catherine so swiftly. I simply can't understand it. He has just destabilized his position." The archbishop shrugged. "Still, everyone makes mistakes, and all a clever man like myself has to do is simply wait around for an opportunity to exploit them."

"Yes, Your Eminence."

Tavalisk shot a suspicious glance at his aide; he did not like the tone of Gamil's voice. "You may go now. Make sure the messages are sent promptly." The archbishop waited until Gamil was at the door before he added, "Ah, about the fish . . . "

"Would you like me to take it away, Your Eminence?"

"No, Gamil. I've taken quite a liking to the feisty little creature, but its water *is* rather dirty, and I'd be grateful if you'd clean it."

*

"You must leave Bren today," said Maybor, trying but not quite succeeding to keep his voice low. "Every minute you stay is another minute that Melliandra is in danger."

"Melliandra's reputation is of the utmost importance, Tawl," Cravin said, his tone smoother and more calculating than Maybor's. "She now carries Bren's only living heir, and for her to be associated with a suspected murderer is nothing short of disastrous. There are many lords in the city who would help us back her claim, yet none will come forward if you are by her side. All of Bren thinks you murdered Catherine, and whilst that may be untrue, I'm sure you'll agree that the evidence certainly *looks* damning." Cravin took a step closer to Tawl, putting his elegantly manicured hand on his arm. "Stay and you bring Melliandra down with you."

Tawl pulled away. Cravin had a reptile's touch. He turned his back on both men and walked toward the fire.

They were downstairs in the hideout, Cravin's townhouse, and for the first time since they had been staying here, the owner had decided to pay them a visit. Lord Cravin had arrived an hour earlier and had spent most of that time in private conference with Maybor. About fifteen minutes ago they had called him down.

Even before the call came, Tawl knew what they would say. Catherine had been dead for five days now, and on the dawn of the second day, he had been proclaimed her murderer. A cup with his mark carved upon it had been found at her bedside. There was poison in it, the same poison that was found on Catherine's lips. There was also a servant who, when tortured, had confessed to taking gold from a man who looked like the duke's champion in return for placing the cup and the poisoned wine in Catherine's chamber. Fifty pieces of gold had even been found in the servant's room.

Tawl balled his hands into fists. Cravin was right—it *did* look damning.

Someone had done a very good job of making it seem as if he'd murdered Catherine. It was different than the duke's murder, where no one really knew what had happened. Yes, accusations had been thrown at him, but despite all of Baralis' efforts, no one could say with conviction that he had done it. There was only suspicion, nothing more. But this . . . Tawl shook his head. Baralis had outdone himself this time.

"Tawl, today Kylock's forces are sweeping southeast of the city. Tomorrow, they will be here." Maybor was trying to speak quietly, so there would be no chance of Melli overhearing the conversation. "There's little chance they'll miss us this time."

"Yes," agreed Cravin. "The search is door to door, room to room. By midday tomorrow they will have reached this street." He lowered his voice to the level of a threat. "We cannot risk Melliandra being caught."

Not in a house owned by you, thought Tawl. He didn't say it, though. Instead he said, "Even if I were to leave, the search would still continue."

Cravin was ready for him. "You are right. It is not enough for you to leave, you must also be *seen* to leave. Only then will Kylock call off the search."

Tawl suddenly felt very tired. He leaned forward, supporting his weight on the mantel. The heat from the fire had lost its power to warm him. He was cold, colder than he could ever remember being before. The thought of leaving Melli chilled his very soul. She was all there was in the world for him. Even if he had never taken an oath, he would still be here at her side. He lived to keep her safe, yet now it looked as if the very protection he gave her was just one more danger.

Maybor came and stood beside him. Out of the corner of his eye, Tawl saw him exchange a glance with Cravin. "Look, Tawl," he said. "I know you've done a lot for all of us, and we all thank you for it, but now it's time for you to go. Unless you leave tonight, Melliandra will fall into

Baralis' hands." Maybor shook his head slowly. "And no oath in the world will be able to save her then."

"You must not forget your oath, Tawl," said Cravin from behind him. "An oath to protect the duke's wife, but more importantly, his heirs." Tawl could feel the man's breath on the back of his neck. "The unborn child must be protected at all cost."

"We could all leave tonight," said Tawl, whipping around to face Cravin. "I could take Melliandra from the city after dark."

Once again Cravin was ready. "No. She cannot be moved. She is not well, the risk to the baby is too great."

Maybor waved an arm, stopping Cravin from speaking further. "Just go away for a little while, Tawl," he said gently. "Just until the uproar over Catherine's death dies down. Come back later—in a month, say."

"In less than ten days time the armies of Highwall and Annis will be setting camp outside the city." Tawl was losing his temper. "War is coming, and Bren will be the battlefield. It's madness to keep Melli here."

"No, Tawl," said Cravin. "What's madness is you staying here knowing full well that your presence endangers Melliandra. Now, I know you're no longer a knight, but I thought at least I could rely on your sense of honor."

"*Honor!* You know nothing of honor." Tawl swept all the candles from the mantel. "All you care about are politics and your own precious neck." Trembling from head to foot, Tawl wanted nothing more than to beat the life from Cravin. "You should be thankful of Valdis' codes of honor at this moment, Cravin," he murmured. "For if I hadn't learnt them well, you'd be a dead man now."

The two men stared at each other for a minute, then Tawl had the satisfaction of seeing Cravin back away.

Maybor stepped in to fill the gap. His tone was conciliatory. "Tawl, I know you are honorable, and I am relying on you to do what is right. Forget about Lord

Cravin and the baby, just think about Melliandra. We can't allow her to fall into Baralis' hands."

Tawl sighed heavily, his anger toward Cravin leaving him as quickly as it came. What Maybor said was right: Baralis must never be allowed to capture Melli. Kylock's forces would be here tomorrow. Only this morning Nabber had come back from the market with horrible tales of the searches—houses were being burned, people tortured, anything that might lead to Tawl's capture. The whole city was looking for him.

And then there was Blayze's brother, Skaythe. The man had accosted Nabber not far from the hideout, and it wouldn't be long before he tracked them down. From Nabber's account of the incident, Skaythe sounded like a man bent on revenge. Tawl knew Blayze's brother wanted to see him dead, so by leaving the city he would eliminate yet another threat. Skaythe would either give up his search altogether, or leave the city in pursuit of him.

"If I were to leave, how would you protect Melliandra in my absence?"

"I will set my own men to watch the district. At the first sign of any danger, I will see to it that she is moved to another place." Cravin gave Tawl a hostile look. "Once *you* go, the danger will be greatly reduced. The search parties will be called off and the city will get back to normal. Keeping Melliandra safe shouldn't be too difficult, then. After all, she's been here three months without being discovered."

Much though he hated to admit it, Cravin had a point. Melli *was* safe here, or she would be as long as tomorrow's search didn't go ahead. It was just so hard to think of Melli being here without him. Tawl found himself wishing he'd never taken the duke's oath. He felt as if he was trapped by it. Melli and the baby would be safer in his absence, and so he was oath-bound to leave them. He knew it was the rational thing to do, but his heart and his soul cried out to stay.

Nine years ago he had left the little cottage by the marsh to go to Valdis, only to return three years later and find his sisters long dead. It was the defining failure of his life; it guided all his actions and made him who he was. Every day he was forced to struggle with the memory, and every day he realized anew that he could never make it right. It haunted his dreams, his days, his mornings, and his nights. And Tawl knew he wouldn't be able to live with himself if the same thing happened to Melli. There was only so much guilt a man could bear.

Yet tomorrow Melli might be captured or killed, and it would be his presence that brought Kylock's minions to the door. The search could not be allowed to continue. If guards broke into the house, Tawl knew he would defend Melli with his life: but that was it, he only had one life, and once that was gone, Melli was on her own.

"I will go now," said Tawl. He had to—for Melli, for the baby, for the oath he'd sworn to the duke. Loyalty took many forms, and the hardest part of all was knowing when to walk away.

Maybor patted him on the back. "It's for the best, Tawl. Lord Cravin and I will look after Melli."

"And Nabber," added Tawl. He put more store in Nabber's ability to look after Melli than either of the self-serving lords before him.

Maybor nodded. "It will be so."

Crossing the room, Tawl paused by the door and turned to look at Cravin. "If one hair on Melli's head is harmed, I swear by Borc I will see you dead for it."

Closing the door behind him, he raced up the stairs, taking them three at a time. Nabber was waiting for him at the top. Tawl ignored him at first and began stuffing his belongings into a sack. His sword and his knives took up most of the space.

"How did it go with old Cravin and Maybor?" asked Nabber, growing impatient with being overlooked.

Tawl swung around. "Nabber, I am going away for a

while—don't worry, I won't be far away. Look after Melli for me while I'm gone."

"But, Tawl—"

"No questions. Just do as I say." Tawl clasped Nabber's hand. "I promise I will be back."

Nabber nodded rather solemnly. "I understand, Tawl."

He probably did, as well. Taking up his sack, Tawl slung it over his shoulder. "Take care, Nabber. Tell Melli my thoughts will always be with her."

"Aren't you gonna say good-bye?" Nabber indicated Melli's door.

Tawl shook his head. She would only beg him to stay. And once he heard her voice, nothing on earth could make him leave. No, he wouldn't say good-bye: her safety mattered more than his own personal fears. Melli was different than his sisters—older, wiser, stronger—she would be safe without him. She had to be.

Just before he made his way down the stairs, Tawl crept up to her door. Not a sound came from the other side. Turning away, he raised a hand in parting to Nabber and quietly left the house.

Jack was in the south of the city. Of all the districts that he had walked around, he felt drawn to the south side the most. In the deep purple shadows of twilight, it was a maze of narrow streets and darkened alleys. Taverns, brothels, and bakeshops crowded around tiny squares. The smell of the abattoir and the tanners combined with the smoke from the charcoal burners and the fumes from the dyemakers to create an especially challenging test for the lungs.

Foul air aside, Jack was actually enjoying being in the city. He didn't have to hide his face here—no one cared about a Halcus war criminal in Bren—and for the first time in his life he felt free to do as he pleased. No Frallit, no Rovas, no Stillfox: he was his own man, and as he walked the streets of Bren, he was beginning to appreciate the joy of it.

It was a good feeling to walk down a darkened alleyway and know that if he was jumped by a robber, a cutthroat, or a pimp he would be able to deal with them. Thanks to Rovas he could handle himself well now. The thought of a surprise attack held no fear for him. As long as he had a blade and a little room to work in, he could deal with most challengers.

He only wished he had a similar confidence in his sorcery. After the incident in the bakers' lodge in Annis, he knew he could draw sorcery at will, but there was still a part of Jack that was frightened of using it. Even now, he was afraid of doing the wrong thing, of mistiming the drawing, of becoming too involved with whatever he was trying to change, or, worst of all, of drawing too much. He knew he was powerful—what had happened at the garrison had proven that beyond question—but he had little faith in his ability to control that power. Like a giant picking daisies, he felt too blundering and big-handed to do the job with the delicacy it required.

There was nothing tangible to hold and see: no blade to dodge, no handle to grasp, no blood to judge the blow. It was all in the mind; the attack had to be planned and shaped in the thoughts, and by the time you could taste the metal on your tongue it was all over and done with.

The dangers were as real as with swordplay, yet because there were no thrusting blades and no opponent's skill to gauge, it didn't seem as threatening. When a man has his knife to your throat, instinct warns you to proceed carefully. With sorcery it was different. The dangers were to the mind as much as the body, and sometimes it was difficult to judge the line between safety and self-destruction. More than once Jack had nearly lost himself to the lure of inanimate objects. It was so easy to fall in time with them, to be influenced by them, and then to forget to pull away. Pulling away was hard. It was like coming to sit by a warm and cozy fire and then forcing yourself outside into the cold.

A thin gust of wind razored down the alleyway and Jack pulled his goatherding cloak close. Coming to a crossroad, he took a turn to the left.

Hard though pulling away was, it wasn't the hardest part of the drawing. Not for him, anyway. The hardest part was generating the *spark*: the thing that gave the sorcery its life. Always, right down to the last time he'd drawn sorcery in the bakers' lodge, he used the image of Tarissa to conjure up the power. It seemed violent emotion was the only way he could make it happen, and perhaps that was the reason why he had never gotten very far with Stillfox's teaching. It wasn't easy for him to conjure up false emotion.

Stillfox had tried to show him other ways, telling him over and over again to *"focus your thoughts on forming the intent,"* but Jack had focused until he was owl-eyed and head-sore and nothing had come. In fact, up until the morning in the bakers' lodge, he wasn't even sure if he knew what *focus* meant.

Reaching the end of the street, Jack chose a second turn at random. Picking a path down the center of the road, he steered well clear of the filth-strewn gutters.

Jack sighed to himself and the newly arrived night. His learning was far from done. In his heart he knew it wasn't right to use his anger toward Tarissa as a spark. He should have paid more attention to Stillfox, should have tried harder, should have practiced more. One day, thought Jack, he would return and finish what he had started. He owed it to Stillfox *and* himself.

For the time being, though, that was in the distant future. Finding Melli was what he had to do now.

Five days he'd been in the city, and he was still no closer to discovering where she was. Strangely, Jack wasn't too worried. He felt sure that something would turn up.

In the meantime all he had to do was find food each day and a doorway to sleep in each night, neither of which was turning out to be difficult. Somewhere along the way he'd even picked up a new pair of shoes—he had an unsuspecting cobbler to thank for those. Not once had he gone hungry, but there'd been more than a few times when he'd been tempted to mug the first man he'd seen with a full skin of ale: so far his skills hadn't extended as far as acquiring a decent drink. All things considered, though, he wasn't doing too badly, and he was actually enjoying having to rely on his own resources for a change.

As for tonight, well, it was about time to find a place free from the wind. Jack looked around. Without realizing it, he had made his way to Bren's southern wall. It loomed high above the rooftops, less than a meadow's length away. Cutting a path toward it, Jack quickened his pace. It seemed as good a place as any to find shelter for the night.

Just as he altered his course, Jack heard the sound of footsteps behind him. He looked back and saw a man running up the street. Close on his heels were a group of armed men. The man ran faster than anyone Jack had ever seen. His golden hair streamed behind him, and his chest rose and fell like a waterpump. As he came closer, Jack could see his face; his eyes were bright with fierce intensity, and his mouth was a sculptor's tale. In his hand he held a beautifully polished sword.

The man passed Jack in an instant, not even seeing him, his sights set firmly ahead. Jack followed his gaze: he was making for the wall.

There was something about the sight of the man, something about his hard and beautiful face and his terrible focused intensity, that affected Jack deeply. His golden hair provoked memories of dreams long past.

Hardly aware of what he was doing, Jack sprang toward the pursuers. He wanted to give the man time to escape: he didn't know why, perhaps it was the brightness of his blade or the sheer desperation of his plight, but Jack felt in his soul that the man needed his help.

He made a blundering leap into the snarl of armed men. Surprise was the only thing he had on his side. Then men were forced to stop in midstep to deal with this new development. Jack fell facedown on the ground like a drunkard. He did not draw his knife. He felt a blade trained upon his spine and another at the back of his neck. Two of the men carried on running after the golden-haired one.

That meant four had stopped for him. Jack hiccuped loudly. He could deal with four alone if it came to it.

"You stupid, drunken fool!" said one of the men, pushing his spear into Jack's thigh. "What d'you think you're doing stopping Kylock's guard in full chase?"

"Sorry, mate," mumbled Jack, "I thought you were a press gang, what with the war and all." He didn't bother disguising his accent. The city was crawling with troops from the kingdoms making ready for the war.

The two men who had dashed ahead came running back. They were both out of breath. "He got away, Captain," said one of them. "One of the sluice gates was open and he jumped right into it."

"Why didn't you follow him?" barked the captain.

"Once he was in, he fixed the gate so that me and Harold couldn't open it. If you'd been there with your spear, we could have pried it open."

The captain stabbed at Jack's thigh with the spear. "This drunken bastard kept me from him." He hissed a mouthful of foul curses, kicking Jack in the abdomen with each one.

Jack tasted blood in his mouth: he must have bitten his tongue when he landed. He endured the kicks passively, groaning a little for effect. Now that the golden-haired man had escaped, he had his own neck to save.

"Kylock and Baralis ain't gonna be pleased about this," said another man. "We had Catherine's murderer right in our grasp . . ." He shook his head.

"Now listen, you lot," said the captain, "ain't no one here gonna mention that we got stopped by an ale-crazy fool, d'you hear? I'm not having anyone thinking we're a gang of bungling amateurs. If anyone asks, tell 'em the champion had accomplices on the wall who shot at us." The captain surveyed each of his men in turn. "Is that clear?"

"Aye," said the rest of the men in unison.

"What do we do about this one here, then, Captain?" said the one who had his blade to Jack's spine.

"Let him go, Civral. He won't be telling any tales." He kicked Jack one more time. "Will you?"

Jack twisted his neck around and said, "No, sir. No tales from me." He smiled, adding, "Got any beer on you?" Bracing himself for another kick, Jack was surprised when the captain began to move away.

"Come on, lads," he said. "We gotta get back to the palace and tell 'em to call off the search." He turned to the man named Civral. "You go to the gate and tell old Greengill to search the area just south of the wall."

Realizing that he was being let off, Jack rolled around in the dirt for good measure. The captain watched him with distaste. "Dirty beggar," he said as he walked away.

Jack waited until the men had rounded the corner before picking himself off the ground. He was filthy: horse dung, slops, and mud clung to his cloak and britches. His thigh was bleeding, but nothing that a few minutes worth of pressure wouldn't stop. Brushing himself down, he decided to head toward the wall. For some reason he wanted to see the place where the man had escaped. He found the sluice gate straightaway. It had been jammed up against the stone and was impossible to move. Jack ran his fingers over the metal grille. He knew it had been madness to help the golden-haired stranger, but somehow it just felt *right*.

After a few minutes he settled down against the grille, making a bed of it for the night. Sleep came quickly and his dreams, when they came, were all of the man he had helped escape.

Seven

Melli knew it would be better just to lie in bed a little longer and wait for the nausea to pass. She knew that was the right thing to do, but she didn't do it anyway. Instead she swung her feet onto the floor and sat herself up. The all too familiar churning in her stomach sent her fumbling wildly for her bowl. As always she found it just in time— even when there was no Tawl to find it for her.

Melli's whole body heaved and she vomited into the bowl.

"You all right in there, miss?" It was Nabber, shouting through the door. The boy had ears like a bat.

Melli spat to clean her mouth: for some time now she had given up trying to be ladylike about the whole affair. All sorts of unpleasant things were happening to her body, and surrounded by a household full of men, there was no one who could tell her how to deal with them or what to expect next. So she had come to treat her pregnancy with a sort of suspicious stoicism: she was constantly on the lookout for new symptoms, and when she found them, no matter how distressing they were, she would grit her teeth and deal with them like a man. She absolutely refused to have a fainting fit over a rash on her neck or a bout of constipation. Maybor's daughter was made of hardier stuff.

"Should I call for Grift?" came Nabber again.

Grift was as near to an old wife as a man was likely to get. He had a remedy for everything from toothache to lost limbs. Melli adamantly refused to take his advice about morning sickness. There was no way she was going to eat three unripe apricots every night. "No, Nabber," Melli said, walking to the door. "Don't call Grift." She opened the door. "I want to talk to you, instead."

Nabber spit on his palm and slicked back his hair. "Me, miss?"

"Yes. Come inside." Melli returned to the bed, pausing to kick the bowl under the frame.

Nabber followed her in. He made a great show of brushing himself down and pulling his britches up. "It's an honor to be invited in, miss," he said. He looked around speculatively, and Melli guessed he was appraising the worth of the waterclock and the various other contents of the room. "Right nice set-up you have here, miss."

Melli smiled. "Thank you, but none of it's mine. It's all Lord Cravin's."

"Aye, he's just the sort for secret stashing."

"It's just as well for me that he is, or I would have nowhere to hide."

"I'd find a place for us, miss. You just say the word." Nabber looked at her with all the confidence of youth.

"I believe you would, Nabber." She indicated a chair and bade him sit. "I want you to call me Melli from now on."

"Say no more, Melli," he replied, regarding the chair warily. "Though I'd prefer to stand if you don't mind. Good friend of mine, name o' Swift, always maintained that a man heard nothing good sitting down."

Melli was surprised to hear herself laugh. After yesterday, when she had learnt that Tawl had left her, she thought that everything was coming to an end. But there were no ends, just heavily veiled beginnings. The duke's death had been a beginning, and so was Tawl's departure.

Life always continued, and laughter was never far behind.

Leaning forward, she said, "Nabber, I want you to tell me all you know about Tawl. Who his family were, why he left the knighthood, what he was doing when you met him. I need to know."

"He will come back, you know, Melli. He promised me he would." Nabber's face was a picture of conviction. He believed very deeply in his friend.

Melli felt a sudden pressure in her throat. Ever since the pregnancy she had known such terrible mood swings: one minute laughing, then crying like a baby the next. Now she wanted to cry; the boy's faith in Tawl made her sad. "Just tell me what you know."

Nabber pulled a handkerchief from his ever-present sack and handed it to Melli. "Right. Where d'you want me to start?"

Melli was surprised and then touched by Nabber's attention. She thought she had concealed her sadness well. "Tell me about when you met him."

Nabber took an actor's breath. "Well, that was in Rorn. Beautiful day it was, a good many months back now. Tawl had just returned from the cursed isle of Larn, and he was looking to deliver some letters. I volunteered to help him find the addresses. Even then it was obvious he needed me, and we've been together ever since."

"What was in the letters?"

"Nabber shrugged. "I can't say. What I can tell you is that he went to Larn to talk with the seers about a boy. He was on a quest, you see, to find this boy, and he'd come up blank. Well, Larn put him straight, and me and him were traveling to find this boy, when—" Nabber's narrative came to a dead halt.

"When what?"

Nabber was silent for a minute, thinking. "When the man who sent Tawl on his quest got killed."

Melli detected something strained about the boy's voice. "Killed?"

Nabber dashed ahead. "Aye. It sort of set Tawl going, you know. If he did find the boy now, he'd have no one to take him to, so he just lost all his will to carry on. And then we ended up here, in Bren—him fighting in the pits, me making sure he didn't get beaten. Teamwork, you know."

Melli nodded slowly. "Was giving up the quest hard for Tawl?"

"Harder than I can say. He lived for finding the boy. Sworn to it, he was. For a man of honor like him to give it all up . . . " Nabber shook his head. "It's a tragedy."

"Is there any way we could persuade him to continue his quest?"

The effect this simple question had on Nabber was nothing short of amazing. He began to pace up and down the room, shaking his head and muttering. Once or twice, Melli heard the word "Swift" muttered under his breath. After half a minute, Nabber turned to face her. From his sack, he pulled out a sealed letter. It looked old and pocket-weary, stained yellow with time and sweat.

"This," he said, holding the letter up, but not out toward her, "could have changed everything."

"What is it?"

"Letter from a dead man."

A breath of cold air passed over Melli's body. She pulled the bedclothes about her. "The man who sent Tawl to look for the boy?"

"That's the one. Bevlin he was called. Nice man, couldn't cook, though. He sent this letter to the Old Man in Rorn, with instructions that he give it to Tawl if he died."

"And why haven't you given it to him, then?"

"Someone tried to, but Tawl wouldn't take it. He just left it on the street for anyone to pick up. Me, I just came along and pocketed it. Holding it, I am, for Tawl."

Melli knew that Tawl had left her because he wanted to make sure she was safe. She also knew exactly how hard that must have been for him. He did not take his oath lightly, but it was more than just an oath to him: he loved her. And Melli had known Tawl long enough to realize that he was not a man to give his love lightly. Indeed, Melli couldn't imagine Tawl taking anything lightly. He was not that sort of man.

Melli never knew who looked up first: herself or Nabber. But somehow their eyes met, and Nabber's dark and twinkling brown eyes held the exact same thought as her own.

"Without you, miss, Tawl has nothing to live for." Nabber's voice was soft. He dropped her name out of respect.

Melli stood up and crossed over to him. A ripple of nausea threatened, but she fought it with fists clenched. When it passed, she laid her hand on Nabber's shoulder. She could feel his bones through the fabric of his tunic: he was very small and very young. It was easy to forget just how young he was. "You know Tawl very well, don't you?"

"Yes."

"And this letter," she said, brushing her fingertips against the parchment. "This letter only arrived after he'd sworn his oath to the duke." It wasn't really a question, for Melli knew the answer already. Once Nabber nodded, she continued. "And his oath to the duke prevented him from opening it?"

"I think that's about the long and short of it, miss."

Without realizing it, Melli had gradually shifted her weight so that she was leaning against Nabber for support. She pulled away, drawing herself up to her full height. "Nabber," she said, her voice ringing clear and strong, "you must take it to him now. Find him wherever he is, and tell him—" Melli thought for a moment. "And tell him that I command him to read it."

"But—"

"No, Nabber. I will hear nothing more. I know he

asked you to look after me, but right now the one thing you can do to give me peace of mind is find Tawl and deliver the letter. It has been unopened too long."

Nabber's face was a study of barely concealed joy. Oh, he protested and objected, and tried very hard to make a case for staying, but at the end of the day all he wanted to do was go to Tawl. His heart was already there.

After a few minutes he allowed himself to be talked into it—Melli didn't begrudge him the show. "Well, seeing as you're insisting, miss," he said. "I best be on my way."

Melli smiled as he bowed and then dashed out of the room. As soon as the door closed behind him, she fell back on the bed. Tears welled fast and heavy, but she wiped them away, telling herself it was just another symptom of an overactive womb.

Jack couldn't get the golden-haired stranger out of his mind. His dreams had been filled with him. Just before dawn, he'd dreamt that instead of helping the man escape, he had actually followed him under the wall and out of the city. When he woke, Jack found himself strangely disappointed. He was still in Bren, and the golden-haired stranger was long gone with the night.

It was midmorning now; a day in high summer, warm and breezy, with thin streaks of clouds whisking across the sky.

The city was full of soldiers. Ever since he'd arrived six days back, Jack had noticed that more and more troops were flooding into Bren. The taverns and the brothels were crawling with them: mercenaries, the duke's guard, blackhelms recalled from the field, and even some of Kylock's troops, wearing the blue and the gold of the Royal Guard. Jack made a point of keeping his distance from all of them. Soldiers waiting for action would pick a fight just for the sake of it.

Still, he didn't want to stray too far from them—they,

like him, had gravitated to the south of the city, and Jack most definitely wanted to stay where he was. Melli was somewhere on the south side: last night having proven what he'd already guessed.

The guards had referred to the golden-haired stranger as the duke's murderer. Jack had heard the rumors about the man; he was said to have been the duke's champion, a failed knight, Melli's protector, and ultimately Melli's lover. Which meant that last night he had abandoned her: the man had left the city alone. Jack couldn't begin to guess what was truth and what was fiction, but he had seen the man's face for himself, and although it was very easy to believe that the golden-haired stranger could take someone's life, it was hard to believe he would do it without just cause. Jack had looked into his bright blue eyes and seen the nature of the man.

No. Even if the duke's champion *had* run from Melli, Jack still didn't regret helping him. Sometimes things went deeper than right or wrong; sometimes they were just meant to be.

Jack picked a busy street and headed for the largest density of people. There was a market up ahead, and it was as good a place as any to find food to eat and people to watch.

Walking through the crowds, Jack searched the faces of everyone who crossed his path. He didn't really know what he was looking for. Some sort of clue, certainly, perhaps someone who was acting suspiciously, or someone he recognized. The golden-haired stranger had run down a street less than a quarter of a league away from here, and Jack had the distinct feeling that Melli would not be far away.

Jack spent the last of the morning milling around the market, helping a butcher with his carcasses in return for a roasted chicken, gossiping with two old women about the duke's murder—he now knew the golden-haired stranger's name: Tawl—and finding out about the area from a man who sat on the road carving toy boats from chunks of firewood.

Apparently, even though the area was notorious for crime and prostitution, only two streets down from the market was a small square where some high and mighty lords at court had discreet townhouses. "For keeping their easy wenches," said the wood-carver with a wink.

With nothing better to do, Jack decided he would take a walk over to the square. The roast chicken lay heavy in his stomach and the scope of his search lay heavy on his mind. His steps dragged; he wasn't expecting anything to come of the walk, it was merely something to pass the time.

When he finally arrived at the square, he was disappointed to find that it looked like countless other squares he'd seen: dirty, strewn with filth, the buildings unremarkable and badly in need of repair. There was even the usual fountain gurgling unpleasantly in the middle, surrounded by several old flower-sellers who were busy watering their stock.

Jack was about to turn from the square when he decided that since he was here, he might as well take a drink of water. The chicken was a heavy load that needed lightening.

As he approached the fountain the flower-sellers scuttled away like beetles. Jack couldn't help but smile— women being afraid of him was something he hadn't quite gotten used to. He had always been tall, but only after his training with Rovas had the rest of his body begun to match his height. He was broad now, with muscles that tested the stitching on his tunic, and with arms and legs that gave him the look of a professional fighter. Even his hair, which fell in a chestnut ponytail down his back, must make him seem like a wild man. Jack quite liked the way he looked and, until last night when he saw the stranger running down the street, he fancied himself as looking quite tough. Compared to the golden-haired man, though, he was nothing more than a spring sapling.

Jack smiled and bent forward to take a drink from the fountain. The water was cool and tasted of lead. He edged a little nearer and thrust his whole face under the stream, enjoying the wetness on his face.

Just as he was going to pull away, he noticed a man leaving the house in the far corner of the square. Even through the filter of running water, there seemed something familiar about him. The man turned to the side and Jack got a glimpse of his profile: huge nose, large pot belly. Stepping back from the fountain, Jack rubbed the water from his eyes. The man was turning down the far street. Not pausing to think, Jack ran after him.

He knew this man. He had listened to his bad but kindly offered advice, watched in amazement as he downed cup after cup of ale, and been ordered around the palace by him as a boy. It was Grift. Castle guard and expert extraordinaire. Jack raced toward him, calling out his name.

The man turned around. He looked at Jack, and then began to run away.

Jack called out, "Grift! It's me, Jack. From Castle Harvell!"

Grift slowed his pace. After a moment he spun round. He watched as Jack drew level with him, his eyes squinting with strain. A minute of silent scrutiny followed, and then he said, "By Borc's own balls! It is indeed you." He moved forward and caught Jack up in a huge bear hug. He smelled wonderful—just like a brewery. An instant later he pulled away. "No offense, lad," he said. "Doesn't look good, us men hugging too much in public. It's bad for a man's reputation."

Jack's heart was filled with joy. "Count yourself lucky I didn't kiss you, Grift. You're the best sight I've seen in months."

"Aye, lad. Less of that." Grift beamed back at him. "Why, if you hadn't said who you were I would never have recognized you. You've got as big as a barn and as mean-looking as Widow Harpit on the rampage."

Jack laughed. Some things never changed. "You look about the same as ever, Grift. Your beer belly is still one of the nine wonders of the world."

Grift patted his belly smugly. "Aye, lad. Ain't nothing catches a wench's eye better than a gut the size of a battleship."

Before the laughter had died down, Grift pulled him into the shadows. He looked both ways to check that no one was watching and then whispered, "You here for the war, lad?"

"No, Grift. I'm here to find Melliandra. I've got to make sure she's safe."

Grift looked him straight in the eye. "Why would you care about her? It's Kylock who everyone from the kingdoms is backing."

"I don't care a damn about Kylock. It's Melli I've come here for."

Grift nodded slowly, as if he'd received the answer he needed. "You look like you can handle yourself now, lad." He motioned toward the knife in Jack's belt. "Know how to use that, do you?"

Jack shrugged. "You could say that."

"All right, lad. You wanna find the Lady Melliandra. Well, it so happens that she's a lot closer than you think."

"She's in the house you just came from?" Jack could barely contain his excitement.

"Aye. Come on, lad. Let's get back there so you can meet her. She's been right down since last night, and perhaps the sight of you might cheer her up a bit." As he spoke, Grift started retracing his steps toward the house.

Jack had to physically stop himself from dashing ahead. At last he'd found what he had come here for. The walk seemed over before it started. The door was knocked upon, greetings were exchanged, and bolts were drawn back from their casings. And then Bodger appeared on the other side, speaking words of welcome that Jack could barely hear.

Without being told, Jack made for the stairs. He felt hands upon his back, patting or restraining, he didn't know which. Grift spoke a caution. Jack had no mind to acknowledge it. He passed a window with a windowseat and then came upon a closed door.

Less than a heartbeat later it opened. Melli stood upon the threshold. Her lips moved, yet she made no sound. Her arms opened, and before he knew it, he was there, close against her chest, kissing the sweet flesh of her neck, and thanking Borc with every breath for showing him the way.

"The combined armies of Annis and Highwall will reach the city sometime in the next four days." Baralis was standing, but he would have preferred to sit. He was still weak from the drawing to correct Catherine's spine, but he didn't like showing that weakness to Kylock. So he stood in the king's presence and leant against the mantel when he needed to.

"You merely confirm my own reconnaissance," Kylock said with detachment. "By tomorrow I will know their numbers."

"I think we can safely say that their numbers will be more than enough to mount a full-scale siege." Baralis was annoyed at Kylock's aloofness. Less than a week ago he had come close to ruining everything; now he stood calmly pretending that there was nothing to worry about.

Although they were in Baralis' chamber, Kylock was treating it as his own. He lounged indolently upon a cushioned bench and had already poured himself a glass of Baralis' wine. "I have my plan in place," he said.

Baralis' thoughts had already moved on. "I have recalled all of Bren's forces from the field, but the ones in the east will take several weeks to return. If I were you, I'd talk to Lord Gresif—he knows Bren's defenses like the back of his hand. Get him on our side. Promise him whatever it takes."

Surprisingly, Kylock nodded. "You are right. I'm sick of the sight of charts. I need someone to talk me through them. Send him to me tonight."

"Very well." Baralis ill-liked being ordered around. But for now, with Bren under the immediate danger of a siege, he judged it best to hold his tongue. "And the gates—all but one should be closed tonight. No foreigners must be allowed to enter the city from now on. In two days time the final gate should be barred. Notices must be posted to that effect today." Baralis thought for a few seconds. "As far as supplies go, we should be all right: the last of the grain and cattle arrived this morning. If we need any more, we'll have to bring them in on the lake."

"What about the grain in the field?"

"Harvest is a few weeks off yet."

"Anything that cannot be harvested within the next three days must be burnt."

Baralis took a deep breath. "Do that and you'll have a riot on your hands."

Kylock took a single sip of wine. "Then we'll have to burn the rioters, as well." He shifted his position on the bench, swinging his feet down to the floor and sitting upright. "You know we cannot afford to have crops in the field when the Highwall army arrives. We'd be as good as feeding them if we did. I will not tolerate the Wall stripping our fields and using our grain as their own." By the end of the sentence, Kylock's voice was metal-cold.

Baralis looked at him a moment. What he said made sense, but the way he spoke caused Baralis to feel wary. What toll had the wedding night taken upon him? To look at him, one would never guess the horror of the deed he had done. He was dressed beautifully and with care, his dark hair newly trimmed, his chin shaved smooth, his clothes all the subtle shades of black. Confident to the point of nonchalance, there was no sign of any strain or inner torment.

Yet if one watched closely, which Baralis did, one glimpsed strange little habits from time to time: the way Kylock drank from his glass, always pausing to clean the rim; his peculiar distaste for touching anything that a servant had handled first; and then there were his fingertips—always red and marked with sores. Yes, thought Baralis, Kylock might look normal on the surface, but he was a locked chest of secrets beneath. Doubtless *ivysh* was the key to them all. Madness, paranoia, delusions: they could all be traced back to the sparkling white drug.

Baralis couldn't guess what had caused Kylock to break Catherine's neck, but he had a strong feeling that Kylock's rage had been *ivysh* induced. The drug had summoned his demons, and the king had been brought down by their weight on his back.

Why Kylock murdered Catherine wasn't important— the deed was done and then suitably disguised—but what was important was the fact that Kylock had somehow managed to draw sorcery. With huge amounts of *ivysh* running in his blood, coating the very vessels that it flowed through, Kylock had successfully performed a drawing. It shouldn't be possible. Nothing was stronger than *ivysh*. Yet Kylock had done it anyway, overriding the drug's considerable powers of suppression, blasting through its bone-white restraints.

Still, it could have been one of those freak happenings, brought on by strong emotion, the likes of which are seldom felt. Perhaps, because it was his wedding night, Kylock had decided to take less of the drug— even Baralis did not know what effects *ivysh* had on sexual prowess.

Anyway, whatever the cause, it couldn't be allowed to happen again: Kylock's doses must be increased. Already Baralis had seen to it that everything Kylock ate was salted with the drug. After a couple of weeks of this, when the "salt" was withdrawn, Kylock would find himself with a greater need and be forced take more accordingly.

"Today I will send a contingent of the Royal Guard out into the city," said Kylock, interrupting his thoughts. "I need them to put the fear of the devil into anyone who dares speak Melliandra's name. I will not tolerate anyone supporting her or her child." He curled his gloved hand into a fist. "Examples must be made of those who would oppose me."

Kylock's eyes grew blank as he spoke. Seeing his gaze shift inwards, Baralis shivered. The new king had a taste for sharp blades, burning flesh, and spilt blood. Baralis found himself pitying the poor wretches who dared to stand against him.

After a moment, Kylock's gaze refocused. Uncurling his fist, he said, "While the Royal Guard are out they can deal with the blacksmiths, too. There are still some who are flouting my orders and forging candlesticks and belt buckles when I need arrowheads and spears."

"Send the duke's own, instead," said Baralis. "The blacksmiths will be less hostile if they're confronted by their own countrymen rather than foreigners."

Kylock scowled. "Always the diplomat, Baralis."

"Someone has to be," snapped Baralis.

The two men looked at each other a moment, the air between them bristling with quick tension. Baralis knew it would be up to him to break the silence.

"Besides," he said, "I want the Royal Guard to resume their search of the city. The area to the south was untouched." This statement dissipated the tension immediately, just as Baralis knew it would.

Kylock stood up. "But the duke's champion has left the city. Six guards chased him and then watched him skulk under the wall like a rat."

"Not quite like a rat, Kylock," Baralis said softly. "More like a red herring."

"You think he's back in the city?"

"No. I think he left because he knew we were getting close." Baralis moved nearer to Kylock. "Think, sire. Why would he escape in such a public way? He had already loosened the sluice gate beforehand, so why didn't he leave then?" Baralis' smile was as succinct as he could make it. "I believe he wanted to ensure that you and I knew he'd left the city."

"So we would call the search off?"

"Exactly. And by doing so we have played right into his hands. I say tomorrow we search the area we missed. We probably won't find a murderer, but we may find a certain lady, instead."

Kylock nodded. "So be it. The search will begin before dawn."

Eight

*O*ccasionally there are nights that one never wants to end. For Jack, this was such a night.

Already it was close to dawn. He and Melli had watched candle upon candle burn down, pool in their own wax, and burn out.

They had talked, laughed, shared wine and bread and silences, held hands, touched shoulders, and swapped tales. It was a night of surprises and gentle understanding. Melli was beautiful, more radiant than Jack ever remembered her, but tougher, too. There was a streak of steel running down her spine, and sometimes when she joked an edge of bitterness was revealed. Yet, if she was more bitter, she was also more vulnerable. He'd seen tears in her eyes twice so far this night. Once when she talked of her reunion with Maybor in the banquet hall of the palace, and the second time when she talked of the man named Tawl. No tears had been shed for the duke.

From the way she spoke, Jack could tell that Melli was in love with Tawl. Strangely, she had denied the charge, stating that it was Tawl who was in love with her. Jack wasn't fooled. When a woman talks of a man the way that Melli talked of Tawl there is only one conclusion to draw. Melli just didn't know it yet.

When Jack told her that he had seen Tawl escape from the city, she had gripped his hand so tightly that her knuckles turned white with the strain. "How did he look?" she asked.

He told her that Tawl had looked glorious as he ran, and it was nothing but the truth.

Lord Maybor had entered the room after that, and all talk of Tawl ended. Jack sensed a little tension between father and daughter and guessed Tawl's departure was the cause.

Lord Maybor had been grudgingly cordial to Jack, his manner only warming somewhat when he learned that Jack was good with a blade. He'd left after a few minutes, muttering words to the effect that it was a sad time indeed when lords were forced to rely on kitchen help for security. Melli began to apologize for her father, but Jack halted her. "I stopped being kitchen help a long time ago," he said, "but I'll not take offense when my past is spoken of. I'm not ashamed of what I once was."

After that their mood had lightened. Bodger and Grift had tapped discreetly on the door, and when they walked into the room they brought a full-blown banquet with them. There was wine and ale and cheese and ham. Grift advised eggs for the digestion and eels for the soul, cold mutton for the travel weary and unripe apricots for the sick. They had eaten till their stomachs strained, and drank till the room spun out of focus. By turn they were joyous, silly, melancholy, then maudlin—Grift always first to lead the way.

Later, after Bodger passed out and Grift was forced to carry him from the room, things had mellowed to a slow, sleepy hush. He and Melli sat close, dropping in and out of sleep, exchanging secrets one moment, softly snoring the next. He had told her about Tarissa, then: only part of it, only the good part. And as he spoke of Tarissa to Melli, his perceptions began to change. For so long he had thought only of what was bad, and now to say out loud what was *good* had a profound effect upon him. As Jack told Melli of Tarissa's spirit, of her skills at fighting, and of her sparkling hazel eyes, he relived them as he spoke. Pain softened to hurt, and even hurt became tempered with understanding. Tarissa had done what she had to. She had lied about Melli's death so she wouldn't have to kill Vanly herself.

Melli had been nothing but kind through the telling, though she had dogged him about Tarissa's appearance until he was forced to admit that Tarissa wasn't so perfect after all and that her nose had been a little crooked. "Just like yours," Melli had replied, her vanity now gratified— *her* nose was perfect.

They had joked and teased each other for a while after that; once Melli kicked him in the shin, then pinched the muscle on his forearm. He, in turn, pulled her ear and squeezed the tip of her nose. The blows were swung with neither force nor rancor—mostly it was just an excuse to touch each other.

Now they sat quietly, waiting for the dawn, neither one of them wanting to be the first to take their leave.

Jack was just drifting off into the hazy state that led to sleep when he heard a loud banging noise. *Ignore it, it's a dream,* his mind told him. The banging came again, louder, more insistent. Jack opened his eyes. Melli's were already open. The whole room reverberated with the sound of the banging.

Melli looked at him. "They've come for me," she said.

Jack sprang up. "Stay here." He checked his blade and raced from the room. The stairs were nothing but a blur as he took them. At the bottom he found Bodger and Grift. Bodger had dark circles round his eyes and dry skin flaking from his lips. The two guards were carrying a large wooden plank between them, and they were attempting to bar the door.

The banging began once more. *"Open up! Open up!"* came a voice from the other side. *"King's business."*

Jack took Bodger's end of the bar. "Go and find Maybor," he said to the guard. "Wake him and tell him to get to Melli's side. Then make sure Melli is dressed in a warm cloak."

Bodger hesitated for an instant.

"Go!" cried Jack. Bodger moved away, and Jack then turned to Grift. "Right, let's get this bar in place."

"If you don't open up on the count of ten," shouted the voice through the wood, *"we're breaking down the door."*

"What's your guess of their number?" asked Jack, as he and Grift swung one end of the bar toward the door.

"Ten!"

Grift spoke over the counting. "If they're the same search party as Nabber saw last week, then they're six in number. They'll have blades, halberds, and torches, and they won't blink an eye at burning the place to the ground."

"Six!"

With the first end in place, Jack struggled to wedge the second end into the space between two timbers. Behind him, he heard footsteps racing up the stairs. The count was drawing to an end.

"Three!"

Sweat was pouring off Jack's brow onto the wood. Every muscle was straining. The plank was a fraction too large.

"Two!"

But, by Borc, it was going in. Jack shifted his hold a fraction. He shoved the first end hard against the door. With all his might, Grift pushed on the first holding timber, forcing it back just a fraction.

"One!"

Jack rammed the end of the plank into place, missing Grift's fingers by less than a hairsbreadth. Jack thrust so hard that the surface of the holding timber was razed to splinters.

"Right! We're coming in!"

Jack was breathing fast and heavy. His tunic was soaked with sweat. Grift looked at him and smiled. "You did well, lad."

There was silence from the other side of the door for a few seconds and then a terrible, house-shaking boom as the door was beaten with a battering ram.

The bar held firm.

At the top of the stairs Melli, Maybor, and Bodger appeared. Jack spoke to Maybor. "Is there a back way out of here?"

Bodger answered for him. "There's a door in the kitchen—it leads off to a back street."

Crack! Another blow against the door. This time the sound of splintering wood accompanied the jolt.

"Right," Jack said. "You're going to have to risk that. Have you all got blades?" Everyone including Melli nodded. "Right, all out. I'll stay here and make sure they don't come after you."

"But Jack—"

"No, Melli," interrupted Maybor. "The boy's right. We don't stand a chance with the guards after us."

Crack! More splintering.

"Have you got somewhere to go?" asked Jack.

Maybor nodded. "Lord Cravin keeps a storage cellar not far from here—under a butcher's shop I think." He told Jack the address. "We'll meet you there."

Crack! The whole door jerked forward. The hinges were beginning to give.

"Go!" cried Jack, nerves frayed by the constant battering. "I'll catch up with you in a few minutes."

Grift laid a hand on his shoulder. "Don't do anything foolish, lad."

Melli, Maybor, and Bodger raced down the stairs and to the kitchens, Melli pausing once to mouth the words, *Take care*.

Jack was relieved when Melli was gone. At least she stood a chance of escaping now.

Jack's relief was short-lived, as another jolting blow came against the door. The first of the hinges gave way. The timbers began to crack and separate. Then, straightaway, another blow followed. The second hinge caved. The whole door fell back, the plank giving way ahead of it.

Jack glanced toward the kitchen—the others had been gone less than a minute. He had to give them time.

The door collapsed backward in a cloud of dust and splinters. Jack drew his blade and stepped forward. Two men with halberds came to meet him, stepping over the remains of the door. They wore the colors of the Royal Guard. There were more men behind; Jack couldn't tell how many. He had to make sure they all came after him: Melli needed time to escape.

Halberds jabbed at his gut. Jack could not stop the two men from moving forward. A knife was no match for a halberd in length, and he was forced to back away from them. Jack's thoughts were with Melli. He wanted to go after her, make sure there were no guards round the back. She wouldn't be able to defend herself. She was pregnant!

The guards coming through the door angered him: they were preventing him from going to Melli's side. As he dodged their thrusts, stepping ever backward, a familiar tension began to build within Jack. It was fueled by the thought of Melli being captured, hurt, abused. Tight bands of pressure clasped against skull, his stomach began to contract. He didn't fight it. Instead he let it build, encouraging, shaping, working on the very air itself.

The entry hall was full of guards now. Jack took one final step back, and found himself against a wall.

One blade against seven men with halberds—he wouldn't stand a chance.

Jack deliberately pushed his thoughts on to Melli, *her* plight, *her* safety: anger rose more easily that way. And anger was what he wanted: it was the only thing that would provide a spark.

The guards moved forward warily. Even with his

thoughts in another place, Jack still took defensive actions with his blade, aiming deep, circular thrusts at the men.

Jack's mind was on the air immediately in front of him. He perceived its loose-knitted nature; he felt it dance.

Someone swung a halberd at his face. Jack dodged—with the wall behind him there was nothing else he could do. Split seconds were all that he had.

He concentrated on the air, gathering it close, thickening. It fought, then beguiled him. Jack ignored both. He felt a spike jab into his arm, then the axlike blade of a halberd ran across his shoulder. Wildly, he swung his knife. Desperate, scared, back against the wall, Jack *willed* the air into a ball. At that instant his stomach contracted sharply. He tasted metal on his tongue. The pressure in his head was unbearable. In his mind Melli ran through the streets chased by guards.

The air became heavy like oil. It roiled in upon itself as it contracted. The guards began to back away. It was impossible to breathe. Jack felt the sorcery on his tongue. He held it in till he could take no more, and then *pushed* it toward the thickening air.

The air blasted forward, hitting the guards full on. Three men slammed into the front wall. Another hit the doorframe, and another shot through the doorway. Jack was pinned against the wall by the sheer force of the backlash. The noise was deafening, painful. Jack's ears ached. He still couldn't breathe. The sickening crack of breaking bones tore through the air. If anyone had breath to scream, Jack didn't hear them.

Then, just as quickly as it started, the chaos ended. The air shimmered, then stilled. Scraps of fabric, hair, dust, and skin came floating to the floor. Jack took a deep, gulping breath. His body, released from the push of the backlash, slumped forward, and he had to grab onto the nearest timber to stop himself from falling to his knees.

He was weak, dazed. His body seemed heavier than he remembered it.

Before him lay the results of his drawing. The hallway looked as if it had been hit by a tornado. Chunks of wood and carpet lay scattered about the doorframe. The door itself had been ripped apart. Some of the men were groaning, rubbing blood from their faces, or testing their broken limbs by attempting to stand. Some made no noise; the effort of moving their heads from the floor, or their arms from beneath their bodies, consumed what little strength they had left. Some didn't move at all.

Jack turned away. He had seen enough. Looking down at his hand, he saw that through all of it he had still kept his grip on his blade. Rovas would have been proud. Jack managed a grim smile. It was time to catch up with Melli.

If he was away from a city for too long, Nabber began to suffer withdrawal pains. City life was in his blood. He fed off the excitement on the streets: the tension of choosing a mark, the thrill of the lift, and the pleasure of a move well taken. There was nothing else like it. The city was full of wonders: fragrant rubbish piles that needed investigating, wads of coinage crying out to be circulated, and dodgy-looking characters spoiling for a fight. Everywhere people were cutting deals, exchanging goods, and selling services. Business was being done.

Being a man of business himself, it was the commerce that Nabber missed the most. Why, out here in the fields, the only deals to be struck were with field mice and farmers! A man might as well curl up in the wheat and sleep until harvest.

Not that curling up in these fields would be a good idea. Not unless you fancied being baked to a crisp along with the kernels. Nabber shook his head slowly as he focused his gaze toward the stream of black smoke gathering on the horizon. Kylock was burning the fields.

All morning Nabber had passed company upon company of soldiers, all carrying torches and wooden casks. Nabber didn't know about such things, but he was sure the casks were filled with just the sort of thing to make the fields burn faster. Probably kerosene, he concluded—either that or rat oil.

Whatever it was, it was doing a fine job. The smell of burning dominated the early afternoon air, flakes of burnt matter sailed with the breeze, and the column of thick smoke drew nearer by the minute. All the crops that weren't ready for harvest were being burned.

Now, normally Nabber would have liked to stay around and see the burning for himself firsthand, but he found himself uncharacteristically sobered by the torching. Somehow it made the war seem real and inevitable. Yes, there had been talk of it for weeks—even months—but it hadn't appeared real to Nabber until now. The burning fields represented the *reality* of war: the heedless destruction, the wasted resources, and the sheer madness of it all.

The soldiers with the torches were happy, festive, glad to be doing something rather than passively waiting for the enemy. The farmers and village folk were in a frenzy, some attacking the soldiers with their pitchforks and clubs, others busy harvesting what they could, whilst a few sat by the roadside and wept.

For the most part, Nabber tried to steer well clear of it all. He picked quiet lanes lined with summer crops that had already been harvested and sleepy little hamlets that dealt in livestock not grain. Still, nothing could stop his gaze from wandering to the black smoke on the horizon and his small shoulders shuddering when he thought of what was to come.

Everyone was on the move. The main roads were packed with people heading into Bren. They were seeking protection from Highwall's army behind the city walls. Whole families with laden mules and livestock walked beside monks from monasteries with carts full of wine and millers with sacks full of grain, rolling their millstones before them. Soldiers, knights, and mercenaries barged through the crowds, spurs drawing blood, their warhorses baring yellowing teeth. Young women, livestock, produce, and horses were regularly snatched from the throng. Anything the troops fancied they took. Old women screamed as their spring lambs were loaded onto wagons and their household belongings trampled to kindling in the fray. Chickens' necks snapped as soldiers twisted them, and children wailed as their mothers were dragged away.

Nabber didn't like any of it. He'd never experienced war before and was quite certain he would rather do without it now.

Yet, he thought, stretching the word as long as the treacherous notion that sparked it, *there was money to be made during war*. Bags full of it. There was black-marketing, hoarding, confiscations, extortion, and profiteering to name but a few. Which, at the end of the day, was why he *really* needed to be in the city: opportunity beckoned him from Bren's fair streets, and here he was, stuck in the country, unable to heed its call.

In fact, if he hadn't been on a mission from a beautiful high-born lady, he would never have left in the first place. Well, perhaps that wasn't entirely true—in his heart he did want to find Tawl—but why was it that good deeds always conflicted with commerce? Why couldn't he do something good *and* earn money from it?

Nabber spat, smoothed back his hair, hitched up his britches, and turned away from the smoke and burning crops. He couldn't afford to waste any more time dawdling around, wishing he was back in the city one moment, feeling guilty the next. It just wasn't productive. His mission was to find Tawl and give him Bevlin's letter, and that was what he had to concentrate on. It was about time he used his head.

Since he left Bren yesterday, he had spent his time visiting all the nearby towns and villagers, looking for any sign that the knight had passed through. Not surprisingly, there were no signs. Tawl would be keeping a low profile wherever he was; he wouldn't want to risk being picked up by the authorities. Tawl would be somewhere near—he wouldn't want to be too far away from Lady Melliandra—but he would be somewhere discreet. Might be a barn, or a tumbled-down cottage, or even a chicken coop. With everyone leaving their homes for the city there were a thousand places to hide.

Thinking about Tawl out in the country on his own, Nabber couldn't help but be glad that he hadn't yet told the knight about the meeting between Baralis and Tyren. Things were difficult enough for Tawl at the moment without adding to his problems. Oh, he had *meant* to tell Tawl about the meeting, but the night he returned to the townhouse he had been too tired, and then the day after that it was the Feast of Borc's First Miracle, and there was no way he could tell the knight about Tyren's treachery on that most sacred of days. Tawl had spent most of the day at the window, staring south in the direction of Valdis.

Nabber sighed. He knew he would have to tell Tawl the truth at some point, but the longer it went on the more difficult it became.

Well, one thing was sure, he wasn't going to mention the meeting to Tawl when he found him. Delivering Bevlin's letter was the thing that counted now, giving Tawl reason to return to his quest.

That settled, Nabber felt a lot better. Now all he had to do was figure out where Tawl could possibly be. Putting his hand on his chin, Nabber concentrated as hard as he could. Swift, who was always tracking down someone for the purpose of revenge, retribution, or murder, had once said, *"A rat might leave a sinking ship, but it will always make its home amongst the wreckage. Men are no different—given a choice, they'll always pick the familiar over the unknown."* So, supposing what Swift said was true—and up till this point Nabber had absolutely no reason to doubt the man's wisdom—then that meant Tawl would go somewhere he'd already been. Somewhere not far away.

Nabber was now gripping his chin so tightly, the blood had stopped flowing to his lips. This thinking lark was a lot harder than it looked.

Then, suddenly, like a gift from the gods, the answer came to him. The duke's hunting lodge! Of course, why hadn't it occurred to him sooner? Tawl would go there: he knew the place, he'd first met Melli there, it wasn't far from the city, and now with the duke's death and the war and everything, it would probably be deserted.

Nabber was so excited with his brainwave that he actually jumped in the air and clicked his heels. A second later he had composed himself again: excitement was one thing that it didn't do to overindulge in.

Having assumed his former nonchalance, Nabber began to walk northward. He knew the lodge was somewhere northwest of the city, about six hours ride by horseback, but that was all. The rest he would have to find out as he went along. Nabber shrugged to himself. That sort of thing was never a problem for him. And who knew? If he was lucky, he just might hitch a ride along the way.

The day was drawing to a close. Clouds with their backs to the sun were black in the darkening sky. Already a breeze worthy of the night was blowing down from the mountains. It was cold at the base of the mighty peaks, cold enough for a fire and a winter cloak. Cold enough to chill Tawl to the bone.

He sat on grass that had not been clipped for at least a month and gained shelter from the wind behind a wall belonging to a building that had been unoccupied for just as long. He was outside the duke's hunting lodge, biding his time in the foothills of the Great Divide.

This morning Tawl had discovered that if he climbed

up to the roof of the lodge and turned his gaze southeast, he could see the city of Bren. It really wasn't far away at all. All day he'd spent on the roof, trying to make out details of streets and landmarks in the sunshine, and then when the light faded, looking at the dark form of the city and imagining where Melli lay within it. Eventually the wind and cold had brought him down. His hands were riddled with splinters from the roof beams and all his limbs were stiff. Still, looking up at the roof now, Tawl knew that at first light tomorrow he'd be up there once more.

Melli was in his thoughts constantly. Every idea, every image, every movement he made led in some way back to her. Even now, in the fire, he could see her face amidst the flickers of the flame.

Should he have left her the way he did? With no explanations or farewells? Tawl ran his fingers through his golden hair. Should he have left her at all?

Tawl turned the rabbit on the spit. One benefit of being on the roof was that down below all manner of creatures gathered unawares. It was easy to throw a stone and bag a meal for the night. The meat smelled delicious, fragrant, and smoky. The fire sizzled with every drip of its fat. There would have been enough for Melli if she were here.

Standing up, Tawl moved away from the fire. The smell was suddenly abhorrent to him. Why hadn't he just picked her up and carried her—kicking and screaming—from the city? Why had he listened to Maybor and that slick, maneuvering Lord Cravin? Why? Why? *Why?*

Tawl slammed his fist against the wooden wall of the hunting lodge. The pain gave him the answer. Because Melli was safer without him. And that was everything: keeping Melli safe.

With the quest and the knighthood lost to him, Melli was the one precious thing he had left, and now that she no longer needed him it was hard for him to let her go.

Yet in his heart he knew he must. He only wished it didn't hurt so much to leave.

He had to let go of his old fears. Just because his sisters had come to harm while he was away didn't mean that Melli would. It was nearly ten years later, the situation was different, Melli wasn't a child who couldn't fend for herself.

It was so hard to put his fears behind him, though. So very, very hard.

Without realizing it, Tawl had stepped back to the fire. He picked up his knife, turning the blade in his hand. Sometimes he'd rather be dead than live with the memory of his failures. Anna, Sara, the baby, Bevlin, his quest, and the knighthood: he'd failed them all. And right now, looking into the bleak face of the Great Divide, it didn't seem as if he'd ever be given the chance to make up for all his mistakes.

Just then Tawl heard a rustling sound. He whipped around. The noise was coming from the bushes. He shifted the grip on his blade, making ready for an attack. The rustling came again. Tawl stepped back into the deep shadows of the lodge. A figure emerged from the bush. A small figure with sloping shoulders.

"Nabber?" called Tawl softly.

"Aye, Tawl. It's me!" Nabber came forward, stepping into the place where moon and firelight met. "I've come to deliver something to you." He began rooting around in his sack.

Tawl slipped his knife into his belt. "Is Melli safe? Was the search halted?"

Nabber continued to root. "Melli's fine. They halted the search the morning after you left."

"I told you to stay by her side."

"Aye. And she told me to come"—Nabber pulled something flat and cream-colored out from his pack—"and give you this." He held it out for Tawl.

Tawl didn't move. Nabber held a sealed letter. The

parchment shone in the moonlight, flapping gently with
the breeze. He knew what it was. He had been offered the
letter before. He knew the seal, the folds, the paper. And
when he'd last seen it, it was lying in the dirt on a dark
and narrow street.

Tawl's throat was dry. His heartbeat slowed. "Where
did you get this?" he said.

"The same place where you left it: little street right by
the abattoir." Nabber thrust the letter toward him. "Take
it. Melli wants you to open it."

Tawl looked at the letter. Bevlin's letter. He had
thought he would never see it again. Hadn't wanted to see
it again. But here it was, being offered to him by a boy
who was his only friend. "Nabber," he said softly, "if I
open this it will change everything."

"I know. Melli knows, too. I told her about the quest,
and Bevlin——"

"Bevlin?"

"Don't worry, Tawl. I told her only what she needed
to know."

Tawl looked in Nabber's eyes. He was a truly remarkable boy—and not just an only friend, a best one, as well.

The wind calmed. The letter was still. Tawl and
Nabber stood facing each other, the letter in between.

"Take it, Tawl," said Nabber, his voice gentle. "Never
in my whole life did anything feel as right as this."

Tawl's vision blurred. He felt something wet streak
down his cheek. "To open this letter will be to open the
past."

Nabber's eyes were bright with tears of his own.
Slowly he shook his head. "Tawl, your past has never
been closed. You live with it every day."

How did one so young become so wise? Tawl wiped
the tears from his cheeks. "You've held that for many
months now," he said, reaching out his hand toward the
letter. "It's time I took the burden from you."

The parchment was smooth in his hand and warm

from Nabber's touch. Tawl looked up. Nabber was gone.

Tawl sat beside the fire. The moon was full, brilliant, just like an oil lamp. He bowed his head and spoke a simple prayer, and then broke the seal on the letter.

Dear Tawl,

If you are reading this, then I am dead. For some time I have known that my life is due for the taking, and that is the reason that I write you this letter. There are things I must tell you, things to be explained, and I am now no longer sure that I will be allowed the chance to say them to you. So I write where I would rather speak, and hope the written word carries all the affection of speech.

First, Tawl, I must tell you that my heart is ever with you. My burden will always be that I set you a near impossible task, and by doing so robbed you of a life of your own. I ask forgiveness, here and now, for I am an old man and do not wish to rest in my grave with such a weight to bear me down. You are a good man, I feel sure you will give it gladly.

Now we must talk of your quest. When I first sent you on your way, with Marod's prophecy ringing in your ear and your eyes bright with purpose, there was much that I still didn't understand. I didn't know the true meaning of the prophecy, or the role of the boy whom you seek. The only thing I knew for certain was that war would play a part.

Over the years I have discovered more. I now believe that Bren and the kingdoms are the two houses who will meet in wedlock and wealth. And war will come from that union. All the portents tell that it will be a war the likes of which we haven't seen in a thousand years. Unless it is halted in its infancy it will rip the continent asunder.

I fear that Bren will have unnatural advantages at its side. Larn, the island of the seers, will feed its armies with information. The two places are connected, by what or whom, I do not know. The temple must be destroyed; it will ally itself with Bren and lend the city the power of its seers. Larn must be broken if Bren is ever to know peace.

Larn. The place haunts my dreams. I fear it will dog me to the grave. Tawl, find the boy. He alone can destroy that cursed place.

And now, before I go, there is one last thing that I want to lay to parchment. Larn is not the only thing that haunts my dreams: I also see a man with a blade standing above me. Every night I see this and every night I wake before the blade falls upon my heart. One night I fear I will awake and find it real. In my dreams, the one who holds the blade is moved by strings, like a puppet. His actions are not his own.

Tawl, whoever kills me is not responsible for my death. Send them my forgiveness and tell them not to blame themselves. An old man like me is never far from the shadow of his grave.

Farewell, my good friend. May Borc speed your journey. I forever remain in your debt,

Bevlin.

Tawl brought the letter to rest against his lap. He looked upward to the night sky. It was full of stars. Strange how he had never noticed how peaceful it was here before now. How beautiful the mountains were, how very fresh the air.

The rabbit on the spit had some time ago passed the well-done stage and was now black and charred. Tawl took it from the spit and set it to cool. He had a feeling it would taste good despite the burn. Without letting go of the letter, Tawl stretched over and took the smaller of the two flasks from his sack. He removed the stopper and took a deep draught of Maybor's best brandy. Just one. The golden liquid warmed him to his belly. He stood up and walked a few steps until he was clear of the side of the lodge. Bevlin's letter was still in his hand.

Before him lay a huge, moonlit valley. Trees were dark against the grass, and in the distance water flowed like a thin thread of purest silver. It was perfect: silent and lofty as a cathedral. A place of rest, a place of reverence, and most of all a place of forgiveness. Gentle were the breezes, softly shone the stars, the vast darkness of the sky was a salve upon his soul, and the earth beneath his feet held him firm.

Tawl stood, he would never know for how long, and let nature and Bevlin's forgiveness take their course. When he finally turned back to the fire the rabbit was cold, but it still tasted better than any meal he could remember. In the warm halo from the fire, he curled up for the night, and with Bevlin's letter pressed fast against his heart sleep came quick and deep.

Nine

No, Bodger. Clean the wound first with a little wine, *then* apply the ointment." Grift lay on a wooden pallet surrounded by fragrant grasses and proceeded to physician himself. "Circular movements, Bodger. Dab rather than wipe." Then, after a few seconds, "Watch out for my appendix, Bodger. Damage that and I'll never rollick again. Key to a man's sexual appetites is his 'pendix. Why, without it a man might as well shave his legs and call himself a woman."

"I've heard that there's men that do that, Grift." Bodger tried valiantly to dab, even though it felt a lot better to wipe. Grift was still losing blood. Not as much as yesterday, but still a fair amount. Every time Bodger dabbed, the cloth came up red.

"Aye, Bodger, some men do dress as women. Men from Marls generally. Apparently the women there are so ugly that the men— *Aagh!*" Grift screamed as Bodger dabbed directly on the wound. Grift had been sliced low in the abdomen by a kingdoms halberd during the escape from the townhouse the day before. Bodger was very worried about him. The wound needed to be seen to by someone who knew about these things. Someone like Tawl.

"Do you think there's any chance that Tawl might come back, Grift?" Bodger said, trying his best to sound nonchalant.

Grift's face was covered in sweat, his brow creased into many folds. Even so, the pain lifted instantly the moment the question was asked—Grift *lived* to give his opinions. "Can't say as he will, Bodger, but even if he did return he'd have no way of finding us now. Stuck in a wine cellar below a butcher's yard, with no one knowing that we're here. . . . " Grift shook his head. "Why, he could walk right past and not even spot us."

Bodger nodded his head slowly, his gaze dropping down to Grift's wound. He hoped very much that this was one of those rare instances when his dear old friend was wrong.

"Jack, if you don't stand still while I clean out this cut, I swear I will hit you with that bowl over there." Melli stamped her foot to underline her statement. Why were men always such pig-headed fools?

Jack glanced toward the bowl. "Not full, is it?"

Melli managed to turn a smile into an indignant snort. She dashed across the room, picked up the bowl, and threw it toward him, crying, "See for yourself!"

Her aim was true, but Jack was fast, and he dodged the bowl by executing a magnificent sideways leap. He didn't land too well, though, crashing into a row of wine barrels, sending them careening across the cobbled floor.

Melli rushed over. "Are you all right?" She looked down at Jack, who lay spread out on the damp floor.

He rubbed his head. "It was empty, then?"

Melli made no effort to hide her smile this time. She was feeling a little guilty; she just wasn't cut out to be a nursemaid. "I've had no need for the bowl for the past couple of days," she said, offering Jack a hand. "My first three months are behind me now." She hauled him up. "I haven't been sick since . . . " *Since the day after Tawl left.* The words wouldn't come out. Quickly, she turned from Jack. There was a hard lump in her throat and try as she might, she couldn't swallow it.

Where was Tawl? Had Nabber found him yet? And, if Nabber had found him, would she ever see him again? If the letter was as important as Nabber said, Tawl might leave the north never to return.

Melli gulped hard, determined not to feel sorry for herself. Tawl wouldn't leave without coming to see her. He was a man of honor, and such men always said good-bye.

"Melli, what's the matter?" Jack's hand came to rest on her shoulder.

"Nothing." Melli turned to face him. The tenderness in his voice brought the lump right back to her throat. Jack had aged so much the past year. His brow was lined, his eyes more knowing; he was no longer the same boy who had come to her aid by the roadside all those months ago. He was a man now. Suddenly she didn't feel the need to hide everything behind a show of strength. Taking a quick breath, she said, "Jack, I'm just . . . "

Before she'd finished her sentence, Jack caught her up in his arms and guided her toward his chest. Melli rested her head on his shoulder, nuzzling her cheek against the soft fabric of his tunic. The past few days had been madness: Tawl leaving without saying good-bye, Jack turning up out of nowhere, the escape from the townhouse, and the scuffle with the guards. Her nerves were worn thin and her emotions worn out. Everything was happening too fast, the dangers were too real, and the outcome was too far in the distance to see.

Since yesterday morning she'd hardly had a chance to catch her breath. When the armed men had come banging on the door, she and Maybor had left by the back way. Two guards were waiting for them. Melli had watched as Maybor and Bodger and Grift fought with the two men. Grift was badly wounded. There was a lot of blood. He could barely walk. Bodger had half-dragged, half-carried him to the butcher's yard. Just as they arrived, Jack caught up with them. He was bleeding, too, but his wounds did not appear serious. He didn't want to talk about what had happened back at the house.

Donning Maybor's cloak to hide the blood, he'd had a few quiet words with the butcher. A measure of Maybor's gold changed hands, and the butcher led him to a wooden trapdoor in his courtyard, below which lay Cravin's wine cellar. The butcher never saw the rest of their party—Jack made sure of that.

The wine cellar stank of sour wine and damp. The ceilings were low, the walls were wet and dripping, and springy mosses grew like a carpet on the floor. There were four chambers in all, linked together by a series of passageways. The largest chamber, which they were in now, was located directly below the trapdoor. It was by far the dampest of the four: the door let in water and slops from the courtyard, but little light. Grift had been placed in the smallest, driest chamber, and Bodger was tending him there now. Melli had spent the night sleeping on a wooden pallet in another chamber, and Jack and Maybor had shared the fourth.

All night they had been without light, rushes, food, or medicine. Early in the morning Bodger had volunteered to go out for some supplies, and they now had lanterns, a brace of roasted pheasants, three bundles of fragrant summer grasses, and some strange-looking grease in a bowl. "Medicine," volunteered Bodger, before being asked.

Whilst Maybor busied himself with trying the various vintages—most were, he pronounced, "ruined by the damp"—Bodger tended Grift in the small chamber, and Melli saw to Jack, here, in the main cellar.

Right now, though, it felt as if Jack were looking after *her*. Melli withdrew from his embrace. Here she was perfectly well, feeling sorry for herself over nothing at all, damp-eyed and helpless like a princess in a tower.

"Come on," she said briskly. "Roll up your britches so I can put some of this medicine on your leg."

"Later," said Jack, walking away. "I want to make sure this trapdoor is secure first, and then I'm going to see how Grift is getting on. My injuries can wait. They're flesh wounds, nothing more."

Melli didn't protest. She hadn't really known what she was doing anyway. For all she knew the medicine was supposed to be swallowed, not applied. She sat on an upturned wine barrel and watched Jack prop a bar against the door.

"Tomorrow I'll get a hammer and some nails," he said, "and fix a bar in place. It'll make it more secure." That finished, he jumped down from the crates and asked, "When you looked around earlier, did you come across another way out?"

Melli shook her head. "No. That," she motioned upward to the trapdoor, "is the only entrance."

"I'll have to make my bed here from now on, then." Jack began to push the piles of crates away from their position under the trapdoor. "If anyone breaks in, we'll need all the warning we can get."

It was on the tip of Melli's tongue to say that they didn't have any warning yesterday, but she stopped herself. She knew Jack wouldn't like to be reminded about what had happened. So she nodded instead, and offered him her hand, and together they went and saw Grift.

Tawl woke late. The sun was high in the sky. It was midday. Despite the lateness of the hour, the fire was still alight. In fact, not only was it alight, it was boasting freshly cut logs and a pot full of something hot. Looking into the murky depths of the pot, Tawl discovered a concoction of dried apples, sweet rolls, honey cakes, cider, and cheese. Nabber. Only a boy of twelve could come up with such a dish. Grinning, Tawl stood up and shouted out the boy's name.

Nabber duly appeared from behind a leafy bush. "'Bout time, too," he said, walking over to greet him. "I thought you'd never wake up. Five minutes longer and I would have eaten the stew."

"Stew?" Tawl's grin widened. He felt as happy as a child. "So that's what you call it?"

"Well, I must say, this will be the last time I cook for you. Never seen such a show of ungratefulness." Nabber sat down beside the fire and began tending his stew. "No one's gonna force you to eat, you know."

Tawl sat down beside him. "No. I want some. Dish it out. Plenty of the soggy sweet rolls for me."

Tawl watched as the boy dished out two large portions. As he handed him one of the bowls, Tawl realized that Bevlin's letter was still crumpled up in his fist. He'd hardly realized it was there. He slipped it in his tunic and took the bowl.

"Nabber, we're heading back to the city today."

Nabber now had a mouthful of food. "I thought we might be."

"I've got to see Melli one last time before I go away." Tawl thought about the contents of Bevlin's letter—he would never have to read it again, he knew it by heart. Everything was now clear to him: he knew what he must do and why he must do it. Last night he had been given a rare and wondrous gift. No, not one gift—two gifts.

The first was Bevlin's forgiveness.

The second was that he now had a chance to fulfill his oath to the duke *and* his promise to Bevlin. He was sworn to protect Melli and her child. When he spoke the oath in front of the duke and the people of Bren, he thought that there was no going back. Valdis, Bevlin, and the quest were doors that were firmly closed. But last night as he read the letter, he realized that although they might have been closed for many months, the locks had never been turned.

Indeed, by swearing the oath, he had only bound himself more surely to the quest.

Melli's child was the rightful ruler in Bren. He was

bound to protect the interests of the duke's heir. Only by finding the boy named in Marod's prophecy would Melli's unborn child ever be able to take its place as leader. Larn had to be destroyed, the war had to be halted, and Kylock and Baralis had to be eliminated before his job was done. Then, and only then, would his oath be fulfilled. Melli and her child would never be safe until Bren was at peace and her baby was formally recognized as the duke's sole heir.

It was the baby's birthright to rule Bren, and the one who could make this come to pass was the one whom Bevlin had searched for.

Tawl took a deep breath of mountain air. Everything had been connected all along, and it had taken Bevlin's letter for him to see it. As Catherine's murderer, Melli could no longer afford to be associated with him, yet this way he could still work for her even though he wouldn't be at her side. He would be working for her long-term protection. And with an oath that bound her to him for a lifetime, the future was something he had to consider.

Up until now he had been thinking in terms of weeks and months, never planning too far ahead. Now he had to think in years, perhaps even decades. If Baralis and Kylock won the coming war, Melli and her child would be forced to live in hiding all their lives. They would be hounded like criminals, always on the move, unable to trust anyone, living with fear day to day.

He could not and *would not* allow that to happen.

"Eat up, Tawl. The stew's going cold."

Tawl blinked, emerging bleary-eyed as if from sleep. "I'm sorry, Nabber. My thoughts were"—he shook his head—"a long way away."

"One taste of my stew will bring you down to earth again, Tawl. It's the special combination of melted cheese and cider that does it."

Reaching forward, Tawl patted Nabber's shoulder. "You're a rare friend, Nabber."

"I'm only doing for you what Swift would've done for me." Nabber refused to meet his eyes, suddenly developing an intense interest in scraping all the ash into a pile.

Tawl smiled. He knew·it was best to change the subject. "Right then, let's finish our meal and then make our way back to the city. If we hurry, we can get there by dark."

They walked all day, stopping only once to rest by the roadside. The weather was warm, but the sun did not shine quite as brightly as it could, for the sky was filled with smoke. Most of Bren's harvest was being systematically destroyed. The two companions passed field upon field of charred wheat, rye, and oats.

Villages were all but deserted now. Everyone had gone to the city, taking with them whatever livestock and possessions they had concealed from the mercenaries. Already looters were moving in, ransacking deserted homes and terrorizing those who were either too old, too stubborn, or too infirm to leave with the rest.

Once, during the day, Tawl caught sight of Valdis' banner in the distance. The yellow-and-black flag was at the head of a large company of knights. Tawl couldn't make out too much detail, but he caught the flash of their steel armor and watched the dust rise as they passed.

The knights were not the only fighting men on the move. As they drew nearer to the city, the roads became blocked with troops wearing the blackened helms of Bren, soldiers dressed in the blue and the gold of the kingdoms, mercenaries with no colors to boast of, and peasants brandishing pitchforks and scythes.

As the day wore on and the hard facts of war pushed close in all directions, Tawl knew in his heart that he had made the right decision. His duty was to put an end to this. Oh, right now everyone was happy and festive, confident, excited, ready to do battle. But all that would change over the next few weeks. The scream of the siege engines and the blast of artillery would haunt every waking moment. Many would see their loved ones die, their sons maimed, their fathers bleeding to death for want of a surgeon, and their brothers scarred for life. Eventually people would begin to feel trapped inside the city as the streets and the lake began to stink of the dead. And if the siege went on long enough, starvation and disease would take more lives than a whole year's worth of fighting.

And this one great city was just the start.

Baralis and Kylock would not stop at Bren. If they foiled the siege and routed the Highwall army, they would send their troops out and chase them back across the mountains. They would take Highwall, take Annis, and then they would turn their gaze to the south.

They had to be stopped. Larn had to be destroyed. The boy must be found.

Approaching the city walls, Tawl and Nabber bypassed a near-riot at the gate, as it had just been closed for the night and the gatekeepers could offer no guarantee that it would open again in the morning. Tawl looked at the hundreds, perhaps thousands, of people waiting for entry: two-thirds of them were men wanting a fight. Baralis would let them in.

He and Nabber skirted the angry mob and made their way down into the drain channels. A few stragglers and beggars had made the drains their home, sleeping on their bundles, blankets pulled close, eyes carefully down as the two strangers passed. Tawl let Nabber lead the way. The boy waded down tunnels knee-deep in water, shuffled along ledges meant only for rats, and crawled into openings that were too dark to see. Tawl found it hard to keep up with him. Eventually, a glimmer of pale moonlight came into view ahead. It was the sluice gate.

Someone had gone to great trouble to fit it firmly in place. Tawl and Nabber went to work to loosen it. Half an hour later, they had worn away enough stone to free the metal grid from its hold.

Wet and exhausted, Tawl pulled himself out from the ditch. Spinning around, he offered a hand to Nabber. The boy grinned as he was hauled up. "We made it again, Tawl."

"No one knows the back ways like you do, Nabber." Tawl looked around. The street was a quiet one: no shops, taverns, or brothels to attract people into walking its length. "Come on," he said. "Let's get back to Melli."

Tawl's heart soared as he made his way to the town-house. He had so much he wanted to say to Melli, so much to share and explain. Yet more than anything else he wanted to take her in his arms and tell her that he loved her. She was everything to him, and before he left the city to renew his quest, he would make sure the words were said.

As soon as they turned toward the square, Tawl knew there was something wrong. The house was dark. He raced across the square. The door had been kicked in. The hallway was destroyed. Tawl took the stairs four at a time. Melli's clothes were gone. The room had been turned upside down. Frantic, Tawl searched amongst the wreckage. Where was she? What had happened to her? Why in Borc's name had he left her alone?

"Tawl." It was Nabber, standing in the doorway. "I think they got away."

"Why?" Tawl was a madman desperate for meaning. He had to stop himself from shaking the answers out of Nabber. "What makes you say that?"

"There's blood in the hallway, but there's also blood outside the kitchen door. It looks like someone escaped."

Tawl tried to calm himself. He grasped onto the possibility that Melli might be safe—it was the only way to keep his sanity. Taking a deep breath, he forced his mind to focus on what he could do to find her. "Where would they go?"

"I think Cravin's got other places in the city."

"Do you know where they are?"

Nabber began to shuffle his feet.

Tawl knew the pocket didn't like being caught short of answers, so he spoke quickly to cover the silence. "Well, in that case we have to find Cravin himself."

"He'll most probably be at court at the moment," said Nabber, visibly relieved at being able to contribute something useful, "what with the war and everything. That Lord Cravin strikes me as the sort who doesn't like to be left out of the reckoning."

Tawl nodded; Nabber was right. "You know a way into the palace. Go and find him, and demand to know what's happened." Tawl's thoughts raced ahead. Cravin would be in a delicate position right now: Baralis may have discovered who owned the townhouse. "If he doesn't appear talkative, threaten to tell the whole city that we used his house with his permission." The way things were in the city at the moment it would mean a hanging, at least. "Have you got that?"

Nabber was all business. He nodded. "Anything else?"

"Find out the names and addresses of every building he owns in the city. And then meet me back here. I'll be waiting for you."

"It could take me a good many hours, Tawl. It's quite tricky traveling around the palace when you don't know where you're going."

Tawl didn't hesitate. "I'll come with you."

"No: You'd only slow me down." Nabber's voice was surprisingly firm. "Besides, walking through the streets with the most wanted man in Bren on my arm is not my idea of keeping a low profile. No offense, mind."

"None taken," murmured Tawl. He stretched out his arm and touched Nabber on the cheek. He didn't want to let the boy go, but it seemed he had no choice. Quickly he tried to find words that spoke of caution and love. When nothing seemed right, he said, "Whatever you do, Nabber, keep yourself safe."

Nabber snorted. "That's like telling a bear to eat

honey. Don't worry about me, Tawl, I'll be back before you know it." With that he was gone, running down the stairs and into the night.

A distant bell tolled out two hours past midnight. Two long sleepless hours for Jack. He couldn't stop worrying—about Grift, about Melli, about the safeness of the wine cellar. A slim wooden bar, held most precariously in place, was all that stopped those outside from coming in. First thing tomorrow he would make it more secure. Second thing was to find a physician for Grift. Jack couldn't stand by and watch the man slowly ebb away. He needed attention, and although getting help was a risk, both he and Melli agreed it was one they had to take.

Jack shifted his position on the pallet. With only a blanket between him and the wood, it was highly unlikely that he would get a good night's rest. Not to mention the rats. Jack hated rats. Ever since Master Frallit had insisted on sending him to the granary the first day he came to work as an apprentice, he had disliked the fat, yet skinny-limbed, rodents. Even now, eight years on, Jack lay on his wooden pallet, intent on keeping his fingers and toes from hanging over the sides, in case the rats decided to chew on them.

The night was filled with noises. The rats scraped and scurried, the timbers creaked as they cooled, and thunder rolled in the distance, gathering momentum for a late summer storm.

Then came another noise. It sounded overhead. Footsteps. Jack felt the hair on his arms prickle a warning. He jumped up from the pallet, fumbling around for his knife. Silence. He moved toward the trapdoor. It was so dark he could barely make out the square outline above him. Footsteps again, this time directly over the door. Jack was scared. His heart pumped wildly as he drew his knife to his chest.

Suddenly there was a loud cracking noise. Wood splintered. The holding beam loosened. The trapdoor caved in, and a man jumped down into the cellar. He called something out, but the noise of the beam crashing to the floor drowned out the meaning of his words.

Jack sprang forward. The man was nothing but a dark silhouette. Jack felt his knife slice into the soft flesh of the man's outer arm. Then a fist smashed into his stomach. He went reeling backward, falling against the crates he'd moved earlier. Even before he caught his breath, his attacker was on him again. Jack saw the glint of his teeth. The man's free arm caught his wrist. His grip was like steel, and his fingers pushed for the bone.

Jack couldn't take the pain any longer. At the same time he dropped his knife, he brought up his knees and smashed them into the man's chest. His attacker wavered backward, but did not fall. Jack inhaled sharply. Any other man would have gone down.

With knife gone, Jack tried to back away to give himself time and space. He sprung to the side, arms ahead of him searching for something, *anything*, to put between him and the dark shadow that was his attacker. Jack's palm brushed against a wine barrel—only half full, thanks to Maybor—and hauling it up, he flung it in the man's direction. He heard it crash against the cobbles, but it was too dark to see where it landed.

Just as he put his arm out to feel for a second barrel, something sharp jabbed against his forehead. He lost his footing and fell against the wall. Warm blood trickled down his cheek. Then a blade pressed against his throat.

"Stop!"

Light filled the room. Melli came rushing forward.

Jack looked into the face of his attacker. Blue eyes, golden hair: it was the man he'd helped escape. Before either of them could take a breath, a drop of Jack's blood dripped from his chin onto the man's bare arm. It landed directly on the gash that Jack had opened only seconds before.

The two bloods met. There was a perceptible hiss, like a candle snuffed out by hand.

Both men were locked together. Neither moved. Neither breathed. Their bodies were as stiff as statues.

Lightning flashed, forking straight down the space where the trapdoor had been. Thunder rolled after it and the whole building shook, and by the time the cellar was still once more, the whole nature of the night had changed.

Still Jack stared into the blue eyes of the stranger. He knew this man. He had seen him in his dreams.

The man's eyes were all the colors that blue could ever be. Deep with unreadable emotions, light with unquestionable faith. In a movement so fast that Jack could not follow it, the man withdrew his blade from Jack's throat. Bringing up his bloody arm, he pressed it against the gash on Jack's forehead.

Jack felt his whole body respond. His own blood seemed to pull upward toward the stranger's. He felt a rushing sound in his ears. A film of clouded matter seemed to fall from his eyes and his memories, leaving sharpness and clarity behind. Every dream, every thought, every hope he'd ever had crystallized in an instant, and something new was born.

His heart beat in time with the stranger's. They fell into a world where only they existed: the wine cellar, the trapdoor, Melli and her lantern were so many shadows cast upon them. The space between them was charged with energy, it crackled with every intake of breath.

Still the stranger looked at him. His gaze did not waver.

Jack felt his body being renewed. Skin, membranes, senses were changing, reshaping, making themselves anew. Hours passed in the space of seconds. A lifetime of memories were relived in one blink of the stranger's eye.

Jack remembered his mother as she had been before her illness: beautiful, clever, fingernails caked with soot. He remembered Baralis probing his mind, searching for answers that he'd very nearly found. He saw Kylock as a young boy, slamming a sack containing two kittens against the study wall. He traveled back to the hunting lodge and spied the old crusty book lying at the bottom of a chest, and when he took it in his hands, the letter from the king fluttered to the floor once more. He recalled Falk's words, *"Don't be bitter, Jack,"* and he heard Tarissa say, *"I love you."*

Just as quickly, everything passed, and he and the golden-haired stranger were alone in the present.

"You are the one I've searched for," Tawl said.

"Yes," replied Jack. "I know."

And as he spoke, the glass cocoon surrounding them shattered, sending out sharp-edged splinters to puncture the night.

Baralis awoke with a start. His heart had missed two beats. The darkness disorientated him and his dreams lingered on past his waking. For the first time in years he knew what it was to be completely afraid. Something was out there. Something that could destroy him.

His hands shook as he felt for flint and tallow. The spark was slow in coming, and the flame it produced was strangely subdued. The air it burnt in had changed imperceptibly. It was thinner, it tasted bitter, and something akin to sorcery, but not *quite* sorcery, hung upon it like smoke.

Perhaps, if he hadn't felt something very similar only the day before, he might not have recognized it. But he had, and he did, so he well knew who was responsible for the change in the very fabric of the night. It was Jack, the baker's boy.

Yesterday morning at dawn, a drawing had taken place at a house in the south of the city. Baralis knew of it before the reports came in, and at once he recognized the aftermath. His former scribe had helped Melliandra escape from his clutches. The drawing was almost an exact copy of one that had happened nearly a year earlier now, just outside a disused hunting lodge in the heart of Harvell forest. Almost, but not quite. The result was the same—a blast of thickened air—but the technique was subtly different. It was more sophisticated, more controlled, designed from start to finish. The first drawing had been the work of a dangerous amateur. The second was the work of someone who had been taught how to wield power properly. Still a little unsure of himself, still lacking in timing and subtlety, but a definite improvement nonetheless.

And now, a day later, this had happened.

Baralis reached for a package of his pain-killing drug. He emptied the powder on his tongue, swallowing it dry.

Truth be known, he didn't really know *what* had happened. It wasn't sorcery, it wasn't foretelling; it was something minutely different from both, but infinitely more dangerous than either.

Baralis stretched his mind to encompass all possibilities. What did he know about Jack? Larn had told him the knight was searching for a boy. *He* knew in his soul that the boy was none other than Jack, apprentice baker and blind scribe. Yesterday had proven that Jack had somehow caught up with Melliandra. . . . Baralis curled his hands into fists—that was it! Melliandra was the link. First protected by the knight, now protected by Jack.

What if the knight had stolen back into the city? What if the two had met, here, tonight?

Baralis' thoughts raced on unchecked. And if they had met, then Marod's prophecy was one step closer to coming to pass. The northern empire, *his* empire—first dreamt of, then forged by him alone—was in danger. Indeed, the very fact that both Jack and the knight had aligned themselves with Melliandra and, presumably, the

claim of her unborn child, showed beyond a shadow of a
doubt that the two men were meant to oppose him.

And Larn. They were also meant to oppose Larn. The
powers that be on the island already knew it. The seers
were probably babbling on about it even now.

Leaning back amongst his pillows, Baralis relaxed, letting the pain-killer run its course. He noticed the candle
began to burn more brightly.

Larn would help him track and kill the two—they had
as much interest in destroying Jack and the knight as he.
Yet destroying only two of them was not enough:
Melliandra had to be killed, as well. Only then would the
future empire be safe.

Feeling calmer, Baralis began to drift off into a light
sleep. Tomorrow he would journey to Larn.

Tawl stepped forward and clasped the hand of the boy
he'd been searching for. No, no longer a boy. A man.
Tall, well-built, with sensitive hazel eyes and chestnut
hair that fell in a mane down his back.

His grip was as firm as his gaze.

Tawl felt as if the earth had changed beneath his feet
and the air that he breathed was somehow thicker and
sweeter. Emotions crowded upon him, then dispersed
leaving nothing at all. By turns he was elated, confused,
frightened, content, then drained.

He and the boy had been transformed. They both felt
it. Their bloods had met and mingled, and the bond that
was forged had changed everything. Six years ago, Bevlin
said, "You will know him when you find him." The wiseman had been right. When the boy's blood dripped into
his, it had been like a message from God. Something
holy, a communion, passed between them and now they
were forever linked in purpose.

And to think, seconds earlier, he had nearly killed him.

Just over an hour ago, Nabber had returned from the
palace. He had talked with Cravin, been forced to resort

to threats, and had eventually gotten the man to confirm that Melli and her party had managed to escape the search party. Cravin went on to admit that he had two more places in the city, which he had mentioned to Maybor last time they met. The first was a disused stables situated close to the east wall, and the second was a wine cellar that lay underneath a butcher's courtyard. Tawl had sent Nabber to check out the stables, while he saw to the wine cellar himself.

Finding the trapdoor barred, he had simply smashed it in, using a nearby butcher's block to break it. When he jumped down into the cellar and found himself in the pitch-black, being jumped by a stranger, he'd had no choice but to defend himself. He had been surprised by the strength and quickness of his opponent, but Tawl had yet to meet the man who could beat him one-on-one.

Then, when his blade was ready to slit the boy's throat, Melli had screamed and lit a lamp.

The scream and the light were two things he would be forever grateful for. Not only had Melli sent Nabber to deliver Bevlin's letter, but she had also prevented the greatest tragedy of all. Yes, he and this boy before him were linked together, but Melli was also part of the join.

Letting go of the boy's arm, he turned toward Melli. Her face was pale. The lantern trembled in her hand. "I knew you would return," she said.

The clear certainty in her voice was the most beautiful thing Tawl had ever heard. This brave and magnificent woman had faith in him. Suddenly nothing mattered except feeling the warmth of her body next to his. Tawl dashed forward, scooping Melli up in his arms. Everything had been made anew; the world was now fresh with joy and light and hope, and the only thing that mattered was the truth. "I love you, " he murmured into Melli's dark hair. "That's what I came back to say."

When she replied, "I love you, too," it was more than his heart could bear. First Bevlin's forgiveness, then the man he'd searched years for turned up at the end of his blade, and now this. Tawl hugged Melli tightly, his fingers spreading wide to touch all he possibly could. She was real, beautiful, tough as could be, and he couldn't believe she was his.

Finally Melli pulled away. "What happened here just now?"

He suspected she already knew. "I've found the one I've been searching for." Tawl glanced at Jack. He was looking toward them, his face unreadable.

Melli nodded. "Yes. Jack," she said softly. "Yesterday, he saved my life. Months ago he rescued me from Baralis' dungeon, and months before that he scared away a robber who was attacking me by the road." As she spoke, Melli held out her hand and Jack came forward and took it.

He raised it to his lips. "And you," he said, looking into the deep blue of her eyes, "dragged me halfway across the forest when you could have left me for dead."

Tawl looked from Jack to Melli. His hand followed his eyes, moving gently from shoulder to shoulder. He was glad they knew one another—it seemed right, fitting. It connected everything into a perfect self-contained circle. Tawl did not begrudge their friendship for an instant. Jack looking after Melli, saving her life before Tawl ever knew her, was an unexpected blessing. Jack cared for Melli, and that meant he had a greater ally than he could ever have hoped for. Together they would work for Melli and her child.

"Tawl," called Melli softly, "Grift is badly wounded." Of the three of them she was the least surprised by what had happened. Already, she had moved on to practical matters.

Tawl pulled a crate forward, stepped onto it, and then swung up through the space where the trapdoor had been. Grabbing his sack, he jumped down and said, "Take me to him."

Then, for many hours, Tawl tended Grift. He cleaned

his wound with witch hazel, cauterized the broken blood vessels, stitched up the skin, and administered willow-bark tea for fever and inflammation. Later he massaged Grift's muscles with a fistful of lanolin and gave him a measure of brandy to help him fall asleep.

By the time he had finished, dawn had broken. Jack and Melli had stayed awake with him, heating the iron, brewing the tea, listening all the while to Grift's advice. At some point during the night, Nabber had found his way to the cellar. Like Melli, he was strangely unsur-prised that the boy in the prophecy had turned up right under their noses. He had nodded wisely and said, "Swift says the only thing worth betting on is the unexpected."

He was asleep now, curled up on a pallet in the corner of the large cellar, snoring with all the boundless gusto of youth.

Bodger had fallen asleep by Grift's side, and Maybor, far away in a separate chamber all his own, had slept through the entire night. Jack and Melli were still awake, though. Tawl looked at both of them. Melli was exhausted; there were dark circles under her eyes, and her hands were shaking as she folded the last of the blan-kets. Jack looked tired, too; he sat quietly on a wine barrel, head down, waiting.

"Let's get some sleep," said Tawl, laying his hand on Jack's shoulder. "It's too late to talk now. Tomorrow I will tell you everything."

Jack looked up. He managed half a smile. "I feel like I've been to heaven and hell and all the places in between tonight."

Tawl matched his smile. "You're not the only one," he said softly.

Ten

*T*avalisk was eating fish. Not just any old fish, mind, it was the very creature that Gamil had bought him as a pet. The archbishop's chef had prepared the small fish whole: guts, head, fins, and all. Tavalisk now had the once-aggressive little fish by its tail and was sucking it into his mouth, scraping the scales off with his teeth as he went.

Once that was done, he swallowed it intact and spat out the scales into a cloth. There! That would certainly teach the little devil not to bite the hand that fed him.

Footsteps pitter-pattered behind. They were followed by an apologetic cough.

"Come in, Gamil," said the archbishop, sighing. "As you see, the door is open." Every door in the palace was open today. Every door, every window, every coy virgin's blouse. It was high summer in Rorn and the heat was unrelenting. The city was festering, and even in the hallowed ground of the palace, the smell of fertile, abundant decay was unmistakable.

As a rule, Tavalisk did not fare well in the heat. His many rolls of flesh became a breeding ground for odors, and the fine silk beneath his armpits grew uncomfortably wet with sweat. At times like this, when even the *thought* of moving his considerable bulk off the chair was enough to cause discomfort, the archbishop liked to remember back to his far distant past.

He had not always been a chubby man. In youth he had been beautiful—too beautiful, some had said, with his sensuous lips and smooth skin that never wanted a razor's edge. When his mother died and he was thrown out on the streets, he was but seven years old. He soon came to learn all the ways that a pretty child could earn money in a city full of priests. He would wait outside the great libraries of Silbur, sitting on the steps close to the important meeting houses where men of influence and men of God met. Here, his strikingly feminine looks would catch the eye of scholars, clerics, and noblemen.

First three coppers, then two silvers, then one gold to take him home.

Most young boys hung around the old fish market, the more traditional place for such delicate assignations. But not he. No. Tavalisk knew he was special. Different. He wanted no dealings with the tawdry merchant classes, with shopkeepers who stank of their wares and farmers in town to buy feed. No, he solicited only from the top ranks of Silbur's society. They smelled better, they washed regularly, they were superior in every way.

Except for the sex, of course: that was always the same.

Tavalisk had learnt the value of appearances during his time on the streets. To attract the eyes of the men he most admired, he styled himself anew. He dressed like a nobleman's son who had fallen upon hard times. He changed his voice, his manners, and his bearing. Affectation came naturally to him, and he soon sloughed off the dirt and manners of the street.

He would sit outside the library, perhaps with a sketch-book and a length of charcoal, and pretend to be engrossed in high thoughts of art and beauty. Men always approached him. A conversation would take place, followed by a little casual touching—the man always touching *him*, never the other way around—and then an offer would be made: supper, the man's apartments. Supper would be a heady affair. The man—drunk on wine, lust, and Tavalisk's own beauty—would become pathetic; begging for favors, kneeling at his feet. Either that, or he would blow out the candles and show him the whip.

As the years passed, Tavalisk learned to refuse the whip, learned to tease, to toy with the men, to create obsessions in them. And then to blackmail them.

Even then he was a hoarder. He saved nearly all of what he earned. Fine clothes were his only expense. Everything else was paid for by his friends. By the time he was nineteen, his savings had grown to substantial proportions. Money allowed him time to think, and he began to realize two things: one, that his beauty was slowly fading with his youth; and two, that if he was ever to make anything of himself, he would have to shape himself anew. In his current incarnation as a male prostitute he was known to too many people in Silbur.

As providence would have it, at the exact time that Tavalisk was coming to these conclusions, he met a man who provided him with the perfect solution. He was an aging and infirm priest called Venesay. This man, besides having conveniently poor eyesight, was revered as a great scholar, a man of letters, and a renowned traveler. Tavalisk quickly ingratiated himself with him and soon found that Venesay was interested in a disciple more than a bedmate. Of course, the fact that Tavalisk could warm his bony body at night was an added bonus, but really Venesay yearned for a son.

Always a chameleon, Tavalisk took on his second persona: surrogate son, pupil, clerical assistant to Venesay.

Together they traveled the Known Lands. Venesay taught him how to read and write, about philosophy, history, and the Church. It was a comfortable time for Tavalisk, for Venesay was very rich. Fine dining in fine cities fattened him, and servants ever-ready with plump cushions and silken wraps spoiled him. At the same time he developed a taste for luxury, he also renewed his interest in religion.

Venesay was a high-ranking priest, well thought of
wherever he went. He enjoyed the veneration of his infe-
riors and the respect of his peers. Tavalisk began to crave
such adulation for himself.

One day Venesay announced they were going to travel
north, over the ranges and into barbarian territory.
People tried to dissuade him, Tavalisk included, but he
refused to be put off. There was a great scholar who lived
there, a mystic, whom he was anxious to visit.

The journey took six weeks. The cold was unbearable:
it chilled day and night, and the wind was at their heels all
the way. Venesay was now too old to sit a horse and was
carried through the mountains in a covered cart. By the
time they arrived in the northern territories, Tavalisk's
nerves were as bruised as Venesay's bones.

The man who Venesay came to see was part priest, part
monk, part sorcerer. Rapascus, as he was called, was
famed throughout the Known Lands for his learning.
Once a priest destined for the episcopate, he had been
thrown out of the Church because of his interest in the
occult. Exiled from his former land, he settled at the foot
of the great Northern Ranges. He lived like a hermit,
seeing no one and working himself to death: reading,
translating, and reinterpreting holy texts, writing religious
poems and commentaries, experimenting with magic and
the occult. His keen mind never stopped probing, and his
fierce desire for answers allowed him no peace.

Venesay had long conversations with Rapascus about
God. Tavalisk had longer conversations with him about
sorcery. It was a time of great awakening for Tavalisk. He
discovered that there were more layers to the world than
could be seen by the eye, and many more roads to power
than achievement alone. When the time came for Venesay
to leave, Tavalisk decided not to accompany him. He
wanted to stay and learn.

With the old priest gone, Rapascus became more specific about magic. Instead of the history and morals

surrounding sorcery, they spoke of its use and purpose. After Rapascus discovered Tavalisk had a little inborn ability, he taught him a few simple drawings. Months passed, and Tavalisk craved to know more. Rapascus shook his head and said that if greatness was what he craved, then he would have to take another route rather than sorcery's dark path—he didn't have the talent for it.

Tavalisk grew bitter. He knew from reading the great man's correspondence that there was one to whom he was teaching all his wisdom. One named Baralis. Every week Rapascus would dispatch notebook upon notebook to the young scholar living in Silbur. Whenever a party of merchant traders passed Rapascus' house, they would bring letters bearing Baralis' name. Tavalisk would wait until Rapascus slept, then he would read them all.

One night he read that Baralis intended to visit Rapascus in order to complete his training and learn from the great man firsthand. Tavalisk was instantly jealous: he saw Baralis as a rival, a threat, and a favorite. Why should this person, this young upstart whom Rapascus had never even met, be party to all the wiseman's teachings? Tavalisk scrambled around on the desktop, searching for Rapascus' reply. He found a letter addressed to Baralis. It was finished, but unsigned. In it, Rapascus stated that Baralis was welcome to come and see him. He went on to say that he had many books and gifts he would give him, and that he was looking forward to the visit. Then, on the final line he wrote, "By the time you come, I will be alone once more. I have taught my current pupil as much as he is able to know."

Tavalisk put down the letter, careful to place it exactly where it had been left. Sitting back in Rapascus' comfortable chair, he wondered what his next move should be. He wasn't ready to be ousted just yet. As he thought, Tavalisk absently ran his fingers over a collection of books that were strewn across the desk. His eyes were drawn to a slim leather-bound volume. Gold lettering rubbed onto the spine proclaimed: *Poisons, Their Making and Their Uses*.

That night Tavalisk sloughed off his third incarnation as pupil to a wiseman and took on his fourth: poisoner and shaper of his own fate.

It took Rapascus five weeks to die. Tavalisk, being a novice, was inclined toward caution. Rather a slow, debilitating sickness followed by an almost inevitable death than a quick and suspicious demise. Rapascus hadn't known a thing—so much for his knowledge of foretelling. In fact, near the end, the wiseman had become rather touching, begging Tavalisk to see to it that his books, his writings, and his possessions were sent to the great library at Silbur. It was his way of reaching out to the Church that had excommunicated him.

He was also anxious to ensure that certain books and scrolls were sent to the young scholar Baralis. "He is a man of rare genius," said Rapascus in one of his last lucid moments. "Yet his conscience needs to be shaped. He must learn the value of goodness and mercy. And I hope, with these books I send, to be able to teach him both."

Rapascus died the next day.

The books were never sent. None of them.

That night Tavalisk rode as fast as a fat man on a horse could ride. He headed to the nearest village, eager to find out if any parties were due to cross the ranges. He was lucky, a caravan of traveling performers was due to leave the following day. With Rapascus' gold, Tavalisk bribed them to return to the wiseman's house with him and begin their journey a day later.

Early the next morning, Tavalisk began to sort through all of Rapascus' belongings. Space was limited in the caravan, and he could only afford to take the best of Rapascus' collection. He loaded chests with rare books and scrolls, hating every decision that involved leaving something behind. He would have had it all if he could. Finally, he came to Rapascus' religious works: his poems, his commentaries, his reinterpretation of the ancient texts. They were a heavy lot, and Tavalisk was just about to leave them when an idea occurred to him. Hastily, he flicked through some of the papers, eyes scanning the works for rare jewels. He found brilliance, insight, faith; great leaps of intellect lay only paragraphs apart from humble affirmations of belief. The man had indeed been a genius.

Tavalisk promptly repacked the trunk, throwing out many books to make way for Rapascus' theological works. The books that the wiseman had specifically asked to be sent to Baralis were not discarded, however. Tavalisk would keep them with him to the grave.

Finally, he was ready to leave. The wagons were loaded up, and the performers were anxious to be on their way. Tavalisk looked around Rapascus' house one last time. There was an oil lamp still burning on the desk. As he walked toward the door, he picked up the lamp and dropped it on the pile of abandoned manuscripts. They crackled into flame the moment he closed the door.

By the time they'd ridden to the foothills, the house was burnt to the ground.

Gamil coughed, bringing the archbishop back to the present. "Your Eminence seems a little distracted," he said. "Should I bring you a little something to awaken you?"

Tavalisk's hand shot out, catching his aide by the arm. "I am not an invalid to be nursed, Gamil," he said, releasing his grip. "Now tell me your news and be off."

"Highwall's army is due to arrive in Bren today, Your Eminence."

Tavalisk immediately put all thought of the past behind him. The present was what counted. "And Annis? Is that intellectual little city represented in the numbers?"

"Yes, Your Eminence. Two battalions. Most Annis troops have stayed behind, though. Ever since Queen Arinalda was found lying dead atop an Annis banner, the city has lived in fear of invasion by Kylock's troops. In fact, just this morning I heard news that the largest part of Kylock's army was last spotted heading toward Annis, not Bren."

Tavalisk made a smacking sound with his lips. "Kylock avenging the death of his dearly beloved mother. How touching." He poured himself a glass of cool, white wine. "Of course, with Kylock's troops tied up in Annis, Bren will have a greater fight on its hands. The armies of Highwall are not to be sniffed at."

"Certainly not now that Your Eminence has donated so much money to the cause."

"*Donated!*" said Tavalisk, bringing pudgy hand to chest. "No, not donated, Gamil. *Loaned.* War is just another commodity like grain and rare spices, and it is up to me to invest our money wisely. A war loan to Highwall is just such an investment."

Lesson given, the archbishop turned his thoughts to other matters. "If Kylock's forces are on the move to Annis, then how is he managing to keep Halcus in line?"

"He's left a full quarter of his troops in Halcus, Your Eminence. And there are the knights, too. Currently Valdis is as good as running the city of Helch. Tyren has ordered the execution of all the lords and noblemen who insist on attending rites given by the old priests and bishops. He's keeping the whole thing quiet, but our spies have discovered that he ordered his knights to confiscate the worshipers' houses, their assets, and their women. We've even heard rumors of torture and worse."

"Tyren's after gold as well as converts, Gamil."

"That may be true, Your Eminence. But Tyren has to make out he's only after converts, or the knighthood wouldn't stand behind him. The knights can't kill men for personal gain, it's against their deepest beliefs."

"Beliefs take second place to loyalty in the knighthood," snapped Tavalisk. "Absolute obedience to one's leader is the founding tenet of Valdis. The knights will do anything

Tyren wants—including murder or torture—they have to. They have sworn an oath of loyalty. Oh, some knights may be stupid, and others may be rogues, but for the most part it's blind, unquestioning faith that enables Tyren to get his way. Tyren knows this, of course, and uses it to his advantage at every turn." The archbishop eyed Gamil sharply. "Tyren is one man who can count on the dedication and discretion of his underlings."

Gamil coughed nervously.

Normally Tavalisk would feel pleased at delivering such a thinly veiled insult, but he was too worried to enjoy the embarrassed flush that rose up Gamil's neck. Baralis' decision to let Tyren have free reign over Helch troubled the archbishop. He could see why the man had done it: he had more pressing trouble in Annis and Bren, and he lacked the manpower to deal with all three cities, so he left the one he'd successfully conquered in the hands of someone who could manage it for him. Obviously Baralis wasn't fussy about who his bedfellows were.

Or did he have a choice? "Gamil, have you any reports about knights heading north toward Bren?"

"Yes, Your Eminence. There are reports of knights leaving Valdis every week now. All fully-armed and heading for Bren."

Then Baralis had given Tyren Helch in return for the knights' support in the siege. Having discovered the truth behind the strange relationship, Tavalisk began to feel a lot better: he hated things he couldn't understand. But the concept of tit for tat was one he was very familiar with.

Now he only had one thing to worry about: why was the main part of Kylock's army heading for Annis, when it was so obviously needed in Bren?

"So the wiseman Bevlin is dead now?"

Tawl bowed his head. "Yes." He intended to say no

more, but Bevlin's letter had changed things. Freed him—not from guilt, but from *blame*. "He died by my own hand. I held the blade, Larn directed my actions."

Behind him, Tawl heard Melli take a quick breath. There was silence for a minute, perhaps longer.

Jack looked at him during the silence, his gaze never faltering. Finally he said, "So now we are on our own."

Once again Tawl was surprised by Jack. All morning he and Jack had talked, yet still he couldn't take the boy's measure. One minute he would be mature, grave, even, like now. The next he would be full of wonder, excited, and sometimes naïve. But then he was just a boy, after all—nineteen, no more—so what did Tawl expect?

Slowly, through tales told and experiences exchanged, they were coming to know each other. Tawl had just finished his story. He told Jack about how, nearly six years ago now, Bevlin had sent him to look for a boy out of a prophecy. He went on to tell him the prophecy, and Bevlin's interpretation of it. He told him about Larn, and why the island had to be destroyed.

Jack surprised him for the first time by telling Tawl that he had heard of Larn. He recounted a story of his own, one told by a man named Stillfox, which involved a girl born on the isle. Tawl was pleased that the boy had knowledge of Larn: just like the fact that they both knew Melli independently of each other, it drew the circle closer.

The most difficult part for Jack was revealing his own story. There was no mistaking his reluctance when he finally admitted he could use sorcery. He told how he was forced to leave Castle Harvell, how he met up with Melli and they were both captured by Baralis. How they escaped, and how, during the cold Halcus winter, they had been separated. He skipped over the following months, murmuring that he was taken in by a Halcus family. From the look on the boy's face when he spoke, Tawl guessed there was more to the tale. He didn't press

Jack for details, though, remembering Bevlin's words: *"There is much in all of us that bears no questioning."*

The wiseman had been wise in so many different ways.

Jack went on to tell how he was taken in by a sorcerer in Annis and was learning how to curb his powers, when he heard that Melli was in danger in Bren.

Lastly, in a voice barely above a whisper, he spoke about his feelings toward Kylock. "I feel we are connected in some way," he said. "Whenever I hear his name, something pulls against my blood. All along I felt as if I had to head to Bren, yet it seems only right that I didn't arrive until Kylock was here, too."

Tawl had nodded. The picture grew clearer with every word Jack said. Their lives were laced with connections: Melli, Baralis, Larn, Bren, and Kylock. Even Bodger and Grift. Hundreds of leagues apart they had been, yet they drew closer with every breath.

All through the telling, Melli had sat quietly on a pallet. Sometimes Nabber was there, sometimes not. Bodger was in the small cellar watching over Grift, who was still sleeping, and Maybor, despite everyone's protests, had gone out.

Now there were only three of them: it was time to talk of tomorrow. Tawl felt a light pressure on his shoulder. Melli's hand brushed against his cheek.

"You two must leave," she said softly, relieving Tawl of the burden of saying it himself. "Highwall's armies are due here any day now, and once they arrive it will be difficult to escape from the city." She tried, unsuccessfully, to keep the strain from her voice. "Besides, with a full-blown siege to attend to, Baralis' attentions will be diverted elsewhere. He won't have time to search for me."

Tawl almost believed her. But he knew Baralis: give him a thousand diversions and he would still track Melli down. "We will leave tomorrow." As he spoke, he raised his hand and linked fingers with Melli. He never missed an opportunity to touch her. "Time is running out.

Already it might be too late. Kylock is getting more powerful by the day; he has the Four Kingdoms, Bren, and Halcus in his pocket. Annis may be next." Tawl shook his head. "If you and your baby are ever to be safe, Kylock and Baralis must be stopped."

"I know," said Melli. "I want you to go." She withdrew her hand, bringing it to rest on her belly. "I am carrying the only living heir to Bren. And it is your duty, Tawl, to see that the baby takes its rightful place." Her words were formal, prepared. While he and Jack had been talking, she had obviously been planning this. Tawl was touched by her bravery. Even now, when she had the most to lose, she was making it easy for him to go.

"How far is Larn?" asked Jack.

"A few weeks away." It was much more than that, but Tawl wished so hard it was less that it didn't feel like a lie.

"We'll need supplies and horses."

"We'll get them once we're clear of the city." Tawl looked quickly to Melli, unsure of how she would take such talk. He should not have doubted her strength, for straightaway she said:

"Nabber should have enough cash on him to purchase a battleship."

"Nabber will stay with you," Tawl replied.

Melli shook her head. "No. The boy is lost without you, Tawl. He'll just moon around until you get back. Let him go with you." There was fierce determination in her deep blue eyes.

And no end of steel in her soul. "Very well," he said. "Nabber will come with us. Now, you must promise me something." He didn't wait for her assent. "Bodger knows the secret way out of the city. When the Highwall army has settled in, I want you to send Bodger with a message, telling them who you are, whose baby you are carrying, and requesting safe haven. If they agree, I want you to leave the city straightaway and make for the Highwall camp." Tawl looked Melli directly in the eyes. "Unless you promise me this, I will not leave your side."

Melli nodded once. "Better the enemy than Baralis," she said, echoing Tawl's thoughts exactly.

"Highwall isn't the enemy," said Jack. Tawl and Melli both looked at him. "They don't want Bren for themselves, they just want to send Kylock cowering back to the kingdoms. If Melli comes to them carrying Bren's heir, then they'll welcome her with open arms. Even if they conquer the city, they know they can never rule it. They'll just be creating another empire. Putting Melli's child in its rightful place will be the only way to stabilize the north once Kylock has been beaten. Bren must have a strong, unchallenged leadership if the north is ever to know peace."

Tawl and Melli exchanged glances. What Jack said was absolutely true: the northern allies *did* need Melli. Tawl began to feel more hopeful. Melli could easily slip under the wall and into the enemy camp. "I didn't realize you were a politician, Jack," he said.

"Neither did I."

All three of them laughed—their first that day.

Three sharp raps sounded on the trapdoor. "Let me in," came Maybor's voice. "It's as wet as a middens after a banquet out here."

Jack scooted up and drew back the door brace. Maybor made a dignified entrance into the cellar, lowering himself like an avenging angel into hell.

"Highwall's army has just been spotted on the rise," he said. "The war begins today."

The rain stopped only when the night came. It had poured heavily all day, cleaning the slate before the start of war.

Baralis stood in a protected alcove high atop the duke's palace and looked south toward the rapidly growing encampment of the enemy. A thousand campfires flickered in the darkness, each one marking a small part of the whole.

Tents and siege engines were being erected in the lee of the hill. Now, since the rain had stopped, Baralis could hear the sound of timber being sawn and bolts being hammered. The rise served to conceal their activities well, but Baralis could guess what constructions they were preparing: battering rams with roofs of hardened leather to protect troops from hot oil and fire; assault towers borne on rollers, built to match the exact height of Bren's own walls; timber galleries with iron roofs, beneath which teams of miners would begin digging tunnels under the wall. Other items such as trebuchets, catapults, and scaling ladders would be already built, brought whole and in working order across the mountains.

Baralis knew all this, but he was not afraid. The duke of Bren had spent a lifetime fortifying the city and the palace in countless minute and unassuming ways. The crenelations were shuttered with iron, not wood. The curtain wall was now the thickest in the north, two horses in width and splayed at the base to send dropped missiles ricocheting into the enemy. Even the gatetowers had been built anew, accommodating all the latest designs in portcullises, together with much-needed additional height. A heavy stone dropped from Bren's gatehouse would hit the ground with enough force to smash a battering ram.

The newly deceased duke had made so many modifications that Baralis had lost count of them.

At the very worst, if Highwall did succeed in breaching both the curtain wall and the inner wall, the palace would be secure. For, despite its dainty name, the duke's palace was the best protected fortress in the Known Lands. None could match its rounded towers, or its intricate network of portcullises, traps, and murder holes. Even its position, perched high above the Great Lake, was second to none. The only viable approach was to the south.

Yes, thought Baralis, bringing a crooked finger to rest against the stone, even if the city of Bren did fall, it would take an act of God to break the palace.

Food would be the biggest problem of the siege. This past week people had been flooding into the city. Farmers and freeholders brought their own grain and livestock with them, but mercenaries and opportunists traveled light. At the moment the city was well stocked with provisions; however after weeks, perhaps months, of being held captive things would begin to look very different. With no way to get supplies into the city, the bloated populace would start eating whatever they could lay their hands on: dogs, horses, rats.

Baralis shrugged. Even then, starvation wasn't really a worry. Hunger made men desperate, and desperate men won wars.

Withdrawing from the battlements, Baralis didn't pause to look back. Highwall's campsites didn't frighten him, but a certain baker's boy from Castle Harvell did. It was time to journey to Larn. Today an army had arrived. Last night an adversary had been born.

Swiftly, he traveled downward. He could always find his way in the dark. Shadowed walkways were his mistresses and unlit stairwells were his friends. Dusky corridors, galleries, and hallways ushered him through the night, and before he knew it the very palace itself had seduced him back to his chambers.

Crope was waiting, crucible in hand, fire stoked up to a blaze. He drew chair to hearth and brought silk slippers to replace leather long gone damp. Master and servant had known each other for over twenty-five years, and at times such as this there was little need of words.

Baralis slumped in his chair. He made the exact same incision, on the exact same spot, that he had done so many times before. The skin was thickened by constant scarring, but blood came quickly to the surface nonetheless.

The potion's vapors propelled him upward and his willpower pushed him ahead.

Tonight the journey was not an easy one. The over-world was troubled by unfamiliar currents. Distortions pulled at what little there was of him, spiraling him upward to meet the cold glitter of the stars. He had to fight it all the way. By the time he arrived at Larn he was weary to the very bones he'd left behind.

The four waited. They always did.

Baralis had neither time nor energy to mince words with Larn tonight. "I believe the knight has found the one he seeks. A boy named Jack—my former scribe. He has great powers at his disposal, and if Marod's prophecy is to be believed, he will soon come here to destroy you." Despite his fatigue, Baralis found much to relish in this statement. It was pleasing to see the four visibly distressed.

A discreet inner dialogue passed between them. Finally the youngest shaped his thoughts to words. "Are you sure?"

Baralis snapped back, "I am not a servant to be questioned."

"What do you want of us?" It was the eldest now, speaking to calm.

In no mood to be calmed, Baralis carried on. "I want your help in tracking the boy down." He thought a moment, then added, "And I want you to fulfill your promise about the war. You said you would help Bren's cause. What aid can you give?"

"We will set our seers to work on the boy," said the eldest, his voice edged with reprimand. "And as for the war, Baralis, your memory is woefully short. Last time we met, did we not tell you that Highwall wouldn't attack until after the wedding?"

"One prophecy does not a transaction make."

"We give you information as we receive it ourselves. For now I can tell you that Annis will not fall under Kylock's first siege, and that Highwall's army is planning to dig a mine beneath the northeast wall directly towards the palace. They will break ground tomorrow."

At last something specific he could use! Nothing was as dangerous in a siege as a well-constructed mine. Once dug, then set alight, it could collapse entire buildings. Baralis was well pleased. No one could have guessed that Highwall would try and mine straight for the palace. "Anything else?"

The eldest spoke in thoughts, not words, but even so he managed a fair copy of an indignant snort. "You would have the blood of our seers if you could. There is no more. Be content with what you have." The eldest was about to speak further when he was distracted by another of the four. They exchanged their secrets, and then the eldest continued. "Today one of our seers spoke of the girl, Melliandra. Soon she will be yours." The elder lowered his tone. "Is that enough for you, Baralis?"

"Plenty."

"Then leave us. I will contact you when we know more about the boy named Jack."

Baralis didn't care to be dismissed like a disobedient squire, but he let the matter drop. He'd just heard that the one thing he wanted most would soon be his. Speeding back to his body, leaving no farewells in his wake, Baralis risked a glance toward the heavens: the broad arc of the firmament had never seemed more like a crown.

Eleven

No, Nabber. Keep some for the journey." Melli pushed Nabber's sack back toward him. "I can't take it all." She turned away quickly, glad of the darkness of the cellar. No one would see her eyes heavy with tears.

Everyone was being so kind, so thoughtful. Jack and Tawl were speaking in hushed voices, pausing every now and then to squeeze her hand and ask if she would be all right. She felt like she was at a funeral. And it seemed suspiciously like her own.

It was early morning. As yet there was no light coming in from the cracks around the trapdoor, but there were plenty of unsettling sounds. Sounds of battle. The first missiles were being flung against the south wall. The blasts were jarring, fierce; from time to time the entire cellar rattled and creaked. Melli's nerves were on edge. She wanted Jack and Tawl to go, to leave right now, so that she could compose herself and find some peace. The noise of battle she could bear, but the terrible guilt-laden atmosphere created by the three who were leaving was more than she could stand.

In the shadows, she wiped her eyes. Turning around, she said to Tawl, "Look, you really should go now. You've already left it far too late as it is. First light is less than an hour away. Come, get your things together." She knew she sounded angry, but the anger in her voice was the only thing that stopped it from breaking.

Tawl looked at her gently.

Melli couldn't bear it. "Tawl, I am neither an invalid nor a holy relic. Please ease my mind by leaving now." Tears welled bright despite herself. Once again she turned to the shadows.

Tawl was one step behind her. This time he didn't take her hand. This time he kissed her lips, instead. It was no holy kiss, no invalid's kiss. It was a kiss between lovers—their very first—and it was passion, not concern, that parted lips. Tawl's arms came up around her shoulders and he held her very tight. Too soon he pulled away. Cradling her chin in his large and capable hands, he said, "Swear to me that you will be here when I return."

She looked into his eyes and said nothing.

"Swear it."

Never had she seen him like this. His whole body was shaking. His grip bit into her chin. The look on his face was almost frightening. Melli realized he *needed* her to say the words.

"I swear it," she said. And as she spoke, Melli knew she meant it—she would keep herself safe until he returned, no matter what it took.

Hearing her words, Tawl visibly relaxed. He let her go.

"Tawl, are you ready?" It was Nabber, coming up from behind. "Dawn's just around the corner, and we have to slip out of the city before it gets light."

Tawl gave Melli one final, searching look and then turned away. Grabbing hold of his pack, he said, "I'm ready, Nabber. What about you, Jack?"

Jack hadn't said much since they'd been woken two hours earlier by Highwall's predawn attack. In fact, he hadn't said much yesterday, either, and last night, when everyone else tapped into a barrel and turned the eve of their parting into a festive affair, Jack had drunk the least and was the first to go to his bed.

Melli came over and stood beside him. He must be in turmoil, she thought. Yesterday he learnt that he alone could put an end to the empire that Kylock and Baralis were creating. Melli couldn't begin to imagine what such a responsibility would feel like. She chided herself for indulging in self-pity when others, most particularly the man before her, had much more to bear than she. All she had to do was keep herself safe and give birth to a healthy baby. Jack had to end a war.

"It hardly seems like we've only been together three days," she said, smiling gently.

He nodded. "Better three than none." He caught and held her gaze, and they both knew there was nothing more to say.

Nabber coughed tactfully. "Here you go, Melli," he said, offering her his newly lightened sack. "Kept a little back, just like you said."

Melli smiled. By the time she looked up, Jack and Tawl had moved beneath the trapdoor. They were loaded down with supplies, bedrolls slung over their shoulders, packs around their waists. And weapons, so many weapons: knives slipped beneath tunics and swords hung over belts. Tawl even had a shortbow at his back.

Jack went up first, then Nabber, and last of all went Tawl. Bodger lifted the remaining supplies up to them. Grift was sitting on a pallet against the wall. He was still weak, but he was getting better. Tawl had spent much precious time this morning demonstrating to Melli how to care for his wound.

Maybor was not in the least bit sorry to see them go. He had no faith in anything they were doing, but he wasn't above encouraging them to leave anyway. Melli looked for a moment at her father. She loved him, but he was wrong about this.

Grift shouted out some last-minute advice for the journey, then everyone said good-bye. Hearing Tawl say farewell, Melli suddenly lost her composure. She scrambled over the crates, up toward the trapdoor. "Tawl," she cried, hating herself for her weakness. "Tawl!"

Tawl crouched down by the opening. He reached out for her and lifted her up with one mighty pull. "Swear you will come back," she said.

"I swear that as long as there is breath in my body and blood in my veins I will make it back to your side." It was an oath and was spoken as one.

They looked at each other for only a moment, then Tawl laid a single kiss on her forehead. Nothing else was said. Gently he lowered her into the waiting arms of Maybor. The last thing Melli saw of him was the glint of his sword as he walked across the courtyard.

"Master, there be someone here to see you."

"Tell whoever it is to go away, you dithering fool. I am far too weary to see anyone this day."

"But he's a cripple, master. He's got a stick to help him walk."

Baralis was well aware of Crope's weakness for cripples: the huge servant carried a three-legged rat on his person at all times. "Very well," he relented. "At least tell me who it is."

"He says his name is Skaythe, master. Says he's Blayze's brother."

Baralis sipped his holk. He was sitting in a comfortable, high-backed chair close to the fire. He was dressed, for no matter how weak he was, he always took care to present an appearance of strength. His journey to Larn had left him drained of all physical energy, but his mind was as active as ever. So Blayze's brother wanted to see him. Baralis motioned to Crope to bring him forth. His curiosity had been aroused.

In walked a man who was a long way from being a cripple. He had a stick, yes, and his left leg was stiff about the knee, but Blayze's brother moved like no doddering invalid. He was confident, stood well, and had an arrogant manner about himself. He strode up to Baralis and offered his arm to be clasped.

Baralis shook him away. He had no desire to show his hands to a stranger. Skaythe sat without being invited, resting his stick against the desk. It was long and straight, with a swelling about a hand's length below the top. The swelling was ribbed, obviously for gripping, but above the knot of wood jutted a spike of polished steel. The walking stick was a barely disguised lance.

Baralis regarded the man to whom the stick belonged. He was like Blayze, yet older, smaller, harder. "Speak your business swiftly, then leave."

"My business is your business, Lord Baralis." Skaythe smiled, showing sharp, uneven teeth. He waited a moment before he explained himself, making a show of settling down in his chair. "The man who murdered Catherine also murdered my brother. You want him found. I want him found. I say we work together to achieve what neither of us can do alone."

Baralis ill-liked anyone pointing out his failings, but he bit the retort right off his tongue and swilled it down with a little sour wine. He could use this man. "What do you want from me?" he asked.

"Money, information"—Skaythe shrugged—"access to your special skills."

Baralis leant forward imperceptibly. He breathed in deeply and let the air tarry in his lungs. Things were growing more interesting by the moment. Skaythe was a user of sorcery. That could prove very useful, indeed. Skirting around the subject, Baralis said, "So you want to track the knight down?"

"No one knows the city of Bren like I do. Next time you get a *tip*," Skaythe emphasized the word to illustrate that he knew very well how such a tip might be procured, "you might come to me first. I won't blunder in and let everyone get away like the Royal Guard did."

Baralis arched an eyebrow. Skaythe obviously thought a lot of himself. "What if I were to tell you that the knight plans on leaving Bren and heading south?"

"Then I will head south, too." Skaythe was unruffled. Idly his hands toyed around the knot of his stick. "I know the south well enough. I ride faster than any man you care to pit me against. No one in Bren can match me with a knife, and I've yet to miss a target I set my sights upon."

This was turning into a most fortunate meeting. Skaythe was just the sort of man he needed: driven, skilled, deadly, and, most of all, expendable. Baralis decided to test the man a little. "What would you say if I told you there was another man I wanted killed? One who will be traveling with the knight."

"I would say it will cost you more than my expenses."

Baralis smiled, showing teeth more deadly than Skaythe's would ever be. "Then you have a deal, my friend."

Skaythe's face betrayed no emotion. "If I am to leave the city, I will require two hundred golds minimum. I may need to change horse, give bribes, pay for intelligence, not to mention the usual traveling expenses."

"Not to mention them," agreed Baralis, nodding faintly.

"I will, of course, require more the farther south you send me."

Baralis continued nodding. "Of course."

Judging from the sun, which was straining for attention behind a bank of high clouds, it was close to midday. All morning they had crawled through mud on their elbows and bellies, now they were crawling through burnt chaff. Jack smiled grimly. The mud had been a lot smoother.

They had left the city just as dawn was breaking. The Highwall army was attacking the southwestern wall, and they left to the southeast. Already the bodies had begun to pile up. The gates had obviously been closed last night, and people waiting until morning to gain entrance to Bren had been slaughtered where they stood.

Tawl insisted they hit the soft and bloody ground straightaway, else risk being picked out by a keen-eyed marksman. Nabber had taken to the mud like a leech, slithering along chin down, nose up, bedroll trailing behind him like a disobedient child. Tawl's movements were silent, efficient—he had obviously done this sort of thing before. His face was dark and easy to read; it said: *Do not talk to me, do not bother me, I have my own problems to deal with.*

Seeing him with Melli earlier, Jack could guess what those problems were. Tawl had to physically wrench himself away from Melli this morning. The parting had been more than difficult; it had been devastating. And the haunted look in the knight's normally light blue eyes told that although his body was here, on the burnt grainfields of rural Bren, his soul was in the city with the woman he loved.

Jack did not trouble him. So in silence the three crept through the smoking fields. Ash and burnt chaff stole into their lungs with the air, and dry and blackened stalks scraped against cheek and shin. Everything was dead: grass scorched to the pith, field mice charred to the bone, and thousands upon thousands of insects reduced to tiny filigrees—like snowdrops, only black.

Occasionally they would come across roads. There were still some people wandering their lengths, poor dazed souls who had nowhere to go now that the city had shut down for the siege.

Sometimes they caught sight of Highwall soldiers; they carried torches and were busily burning what little of the countryside was left: barns, villages, farms. It seemed to Jack that there was little difference between Kylock burning the fields and Highwall burning the buildings. Ashes from one looked pretty much like the other.

The sun managed to push past a cloud for an instant,

flooding the fields with light. Jack swung round for a moment and looked back at the city. Its walls shone like hammered silver. Highwall would not find it easy to break Bren.

Jack was surprised by how near they still were. They'd been on the move for six hours now, yet they were still close to the city. Or was it that the walls were so tall and substantial that it just seemed that way?

Shrugging, Jack moved on. After a while, Tawl raised his hand. It was a sign for them to stop. More Highwall soldiers? wondered Jack. Tawl beckoned them forward, and Jack and Nabber came level with him. All three of them lay belly-flat on the ground.

"This is the last of the grain fields," hissed Tawl. "Up ahead is open country. Nothing but grazing land. It's going to be harder to keep ourselves hidden. If we spot anyone now, the chances are that they'll be mercenaries or stragglers hoping to reach Bren. If anyone asks, we're traders from Lanholt, leaving the city, yet afraid to travel west because of Highwall. I'll do the talking. Right?"

"What if we see any soldiers from the Wall?" asked Nabber.

"Up to three and we kill them. More than that and we run." Tawl looked at Jack, and Jack nodded. "Now, there's a small thicket of bushes directly ahead. I say we make it as far as there, then take a break for a while. I for one intend to pick all this cursed dry grass from my tunic and have myself a decent drink. Are you with me?"

Ten minutes later, they were sitting around a small puddle that might once have been a pond, eating honey-cakes and sipping on Cravin's best brandy. Yesterday Tawl had put Nabber in charge of provisions, and the boy obviously had no liking for traditional traveling fare, for there was no drybread or drymeat on the menu, just items that were well-honeyed or sugared or both. And cheese.

Everyone ate in silence. Nabber had produced a pair of

tweezers from his pack and was pulling burnt stalks from
his britches with all the finesse of a court dandy. Tawl
simply took off his tunic and beat it against the nearest
tree trunk. Jack hadn't begun his extraction yet. He was
still trying to keep up with everything. In fact, that was
what he had been doing for the past three days: just trying
his best to keep up.

Even now he couldn't take it all in. According to Tawl,
he was the one named in an ancient prophecy, the one
who was supposed to bring an end to the war and the
suffering at Larn. Three weeks earlier in Annis, he had
learned of another prophecy that he guessed he was part
of. He had deliberately not thought about the baking
master's verse since then, but now, having met up with
Tawl, everything was becoming harder to ignore or deny.
Jack felt as if ancient forces were ganging up on him,
shaping his fate, controlling his movements, forcing him
to see himself in a new and terrifying light.

For the past two days he had been in a sort of dazed
shock. It was as if some invisible force had punched him
in the gut and was now dragging him south for the kill.
His whole body was still reeling from the blow. He
couldn't even think straight. He tried to remember the
exact wording of Tawl's prophecy, but the details eluded
him. Something about two houses and a fool knowing
the truth. Jack would have liked to ask Tawl to tell it to
him one more time, but he didn't want to admit that he'd
forgotten something so important.

Everything had happened so fast. There was too much
to take in. Jack glanced quickly at Tawl. The knight was
now leaning against a tree, restringing his bow to suit the
weather. Jack found it hard to believe that the man standing opposite had spent five years of his life searching for
him. It was the sort of thing that legends were made of.
He didn't feel worthy of such a search. He was just a
baker's boy from Castle Harvell, not a savior of the world,
not a skilled and fearless hero.

Larn must be destroyed, said Tawl. Kylock must be displaced.

How in Borc's name was he supposed to do such things? Why should the responsibility have fallen to him? Surely there must be others better equipped than he? Highwall had an army. The knights had their brethren. Kylock had Baralis, and Larn had its seers. He had no one.

Well, that wasn't entirely true. He had Tawl and Nabber, but he didn't want the responsibility anyway. Give him a battalion of troops and an armory of blades and he still wouldn't want to be the one.

Tawl and Melli had treated him exactly the same: they just assumed he'd be willing to do what they said. No one had asked if he wanted to go to Larn, it was just taken for granted he would. But why should he? Oh, he'd heard all about the seers, and he had to admit that being bound to a rock for life didn't sound too appealing, but the practice had been going on for hundreds of years now, so why should everyone suddenly decide that he was the one to stop it? He had no connection with the island. The seers of Larn weren't his responsibility. Surely the obligation of destroying the place should fall upon someone who had once been involved with the island, or had a grudge to bear. Like Tawl.

Jack brushed his hair from his face. He felt tired and confused. It was all so overwhelming. There was so much to consider and so much that was unexplained.

What was he supposed to do once they reached their destination? How could he possibly destroy Larn? Yes, he could manage a few tricks with air and metal, but he couldn't bring about an earthquake or a tidal wave, or anything else that was liable to make an entire island disappear.

And what if he didn't succeed? What would become of Melli back in Bren? Jack didn't know anything about prophecies, but Tawl seemed quite adamant about the need for Larn to be destroyed before Melli's child could take its rightful place. Jack suddenly felt like running all the way back home to Castle Harvell. There was too much responsibility for him to bear. Too much at stake, too little information to go on. The truth was, he was just plain scared. Tawl and Melli had put their faith in him, and he wasn't at all sure if he was worthy of it.

But for all his doubts, Jack never once questioned that he was the one in the prophecy. In a way he had known it long before he met Tawl. Not about the prophecy, of course, but about his connection with Kylock and Baralis and the war. For months now he'd felt as if he had some part to play in everything, and all along he'd been traveling toward Bren. It was no coincidence that Tawl had found him when he got there. No coincidence at all.

Jack became aware that Tawl was no longer leaning against the tree; the knight was standing behind him. Reaching forward, he rested a hand on Jack's shoulder.

"You're not alone," he said.

Jack spun round to meet his gaze. He had a bitter reply ready, but when he saw Tawl's face, the words died on his lips. He wasn't the only person to be given no choice—the man before him had no choice, either. Not in a million years would Tawl *choose* to leave Melli. He did so because he had to.

Suddenly the knight's words meant more than one thing: they meant many things, and all of them bound him and Tawl closer together. He *wasn't* alone, and it just might prove to be more than a comfort: it might be his only advantage.

"Come on, Jack," said Tawl, offering Jack a hand up. "Let's get a good start on the rest of the day. He was glad to see that the boy returned his smile. He had been watching Jack for some time now, and it wasn't hard to guess what he was thinking about. That was why he came over: to give him what reassurance he could. Fancy words failed him, of course; they always did. So he offered his hand instead, and said the only thing that really meant anything: *"You're not alone."*

Tawl had lived long enough to know the value of those words. Many years before, Tyren had changed his life by saying the very same thing to him.

Time has little meaning to the imprisoned, the tormented, and the grieving. Days and nights are just shadows in the greater darkness of existence.

To this day, Tawl still didn't know how much time passed between the moment he learnt of his sisters' deaths and the night he ended up in Valdis. Weeks and months take on all the power of a lifetime when a man has lost his soul. For that was what Tawl lost that day in the marshes: the center of his being—his heart, his family, his soul. His sisters were dead, and while he had been busy claiming glory at Valdis, they had grown cold in their graves.

He couldn't blame his father. The man was a drunken, worthless fool, and Tawl had known that for as long as he could remember. He should never have left his sisters with him. He should have known better than to be fooled by a few fine words and a pocketful of gold. His father might have won at the carding table, but *he* should have known that winning never changed a gambler, merely vindicated him, instead.

Tawl cursed himself. He simply didn't think. He just took off for the Bulrush at Greyving the moment his father stole his place.

Looking back on it now, Tawl could still relive the anger he felt at his father's return. He remembered the quick flare of jealousy when he saw how much his sisters loved their papa, and recalled the slow-brewing rage that carried him out of the house before dawn. Funny, but at the time he told himself he was finally free, yet freedom began with a bitter taste even then, and it was many months before his mouth was free of the tang.

Three years later, he paid the price for his rashness and

his rage. The day he returned to the marshes was the day his life came to an end. Hope died that morning, and everything was tainted by the loss. Valdis, his newly branded second circle, his dreams of greatness, and his hopes for the future all became things with no meaning. His own pride had brought him to this.

Tawl had cut through his circles and cast away his sword and rode as hard and fast as he could. He had no destination, just the burning need to be as far away from the marshes as possible. It was the worst time in his life. The only way to stop himself thinking was to ride like the devil and never once look back. His horse finally collapsed beneath him. Tawl picked himself off the ground and cursed the exhausted beast. He stormed away from the horse, leaving it to a slow but sure death. He felt ashamed of that now, especially when he considered where the horse had brought him.

When dawn came the next day, Tawl found himself in familiar territory. He was in the valley just south of Valdis. For so long he had ridden with no thought to time or place that he was genuinely surprised at where he was. Dimly he wondered if he had been heading here all along. Looking down at his circles—clotted with blood, swollen with infection—Tawl decided he would go to Tyren and tell him that he could no longer be a knight. He owed the man that much.

Tyren was now head of the order, yet despite his high position, he came down to see Tawl as soon as he knew of his presence. He had a letter in his hand, which he tucked beneath his tunic as he drew Tawl forward into a warm embrace.

Tawl stiffened and pushed the man away.

"What is the matter, my son?" said Tyren. His eyes flicked toward Tawl's arm. "What has happened?"

Tawl finally broke down. He fell to his knees and sobbed like a baby. "They're dead," he kept saying. "They're dead."

Tyren put his arms around him. From somewhere warm blankets and two flasks of fine brandy appeared. "Your family are gone?" he asked gently, offering one of the flasks.

Tawl nodded. He tried to speak, but the words wouldn't come. There *were* no words to tell of what had become of his family. Instead, he said, "I can no longer be a knight."

Tyren's fingers rose to his tunic. The imprint of the letter could be clearly seen beneath. "My son," he said with great gravity, "the knighthood needs you. I need you. I will not let you go."

Tawl shook his head savagely. "How can a man with no soul be a knight?"

Then Tyren said the one thing that made a difference. "You're not alone," he said. "All of us have to live with despair. Gaining the third circle is nothing unless it is paid for with blood and sacrifice. You must know pain and suffering before you can know greatness. You are not the first knight to lose his family. Everyone who comes to Valdis forsakes all that has gone before.

"What you must do now is give your sisters' deaths meaning—that is the only way to regain your soul. Leave here now, and I guarantee you will regret it for the rest of your life. You will live and die in shame, unfulfilled and tormented till the end of your days. Stay, and do what I ask of you, and I swear you will be redeemed."

Tyren looked like a god as he spoke. His brown eyes were fierce with divine light. Tawl *believed* in him.

He bowed his head low in deference to the greatness of the man before him, and said, "What would you have me do, my lord?"

Tyren pulled the letter from his tunic. He waved it toward Tawl, but never unfolded it. "Today I received this from a wiseman named Bevlin. He asks me to send him a knight. He needs to find a boy who has the power to stop a world war before it starts . . ."

Twelve

"No, Bodger, you take it from me, the worst thing a soldier's got to worry about isn't Isro fire."

"But Isro fire burns everything it touches, Grift: stone, iron, hardened leather. It even burns on water."

"Aye, but it's nothing a good friend couldn't put out by pissing on you, Bodger. Nothing's faster than urine for extinguishing the Isro flame." Grift shook his head wisely. "No, Bodger, the worst thing a soldier can have thrown at him is a dead rabbit."

"A dead rabbit!"

"Aye, Bodger. It's common knowledge that there's nothing in the universe that smells worse than a dead rabbit. Horrible for a man's constitution, it is. Makes me sick just to think of it."

"But why rabbits, Grift? Why not skunks?"

"I thought I'd already told you about the strange mating practices of rabbits, Bodger."

"That you did, Grift."

"Then I think it's about time you took a great leap forward and finally put two and two together, Bodger."

Bodger drew his eyebrows together, looked puzzled for a moment, took a draught of wine, and then smiled triumphantly. "Aah. Say no more, Grift."

Grift beamed like a proud teacher. Settling himself more comfortably on his pallet, he said, "Eh, it was a bit of luck Kylock finding that Highwall tunnel and all."

"Aye. Who would have guessed that Highwall would have tried to mine toward the palace?"

"Not everything's going Kylock's way, though. After the wall was breached yesterday, about five hundred blackhelms died trying to cordon it off. By all accounts it was a right bloodbath."

"The wall's still not secure even now, Grift. Saw it with my own eyes, I did. They timbered it up and dug a trench around it, but my guess is that one decent attack could reopen it."

Grift nodded his head. "Won't be our problem this time tomorrow, Bodger. Have you got the letter on you?"

"Aye, but it's sealed. The Lady Melliandra gave it to me about an hour ago. Says I'm to take it to the enemy before first light tomorrow."

"You're not worried, are you, Bodger?"

"Well, I was wondering if I should carry a white flag or anything. Just to let them know not to shoot at me."

Grift thought for a moment. "I think you should, Bodger. Just to be safe. 'Course, once they realize who the letter's from, they'll welcome you with open arms. Lord Maybor said he spotted the duke's colors flying above Highwall's siege tower. So they're already claiming to be fighting for the duke's rightful heir."

"Lord Baralis ordered the colors to be shot down as soon as he saw them, Grift."

"Aye. That's the last place he'd want to see 'em, Bodger."

Bodger drained his glass of wine. After looking around the cellar to make sure they were alone, he said in a low voice, "Highwall aren't the only ones taking up the Lady Melliandra's cause. There's people in the city who'd rather back her claim than Kylock's. Just today, I saw the duke's guard leading two men away from Old Taverner's Square. The men had drawn quite a crowd, claiming they'd rather have the duke's bastard son as their leader than a bloodthirsty foreign king."

Grift shook his head slowly. "Kylock won't tolerate talk like that, Bodger. He'll cut out the tongue of any man who dares to challenge his rule."

The two guards suddenly grew silent as Lord Maybor walked through the main cellar, toward the trapdoor.

"Keep an eye to Melliandra while I'm gone," said Maybor to Bodger. The lord pulled his cloak close and climbed up the newly installed ladder and out into the night.

"That was strange," said Grift, nudging Bodger with his empty glass.

Bodger promptly refilled the glass with wine from the nearest of the three barrels that were surrounding them. Gradually the guards were working their way through every barrel in the cellar. They'd found quite a few sour brews so far, but none that couldn't be drunk.

"What's strange, Grift?"

"Old Maybor wearing a heavy cloak like that on a night like this."

"You've got a point there, Grift. It's got to be the warmest night of the year."

As soon as Maybor let the trapdoor fall behind him he took off his cloak and stuffed it in a darkened corner of the butcher's yard. The place reeked of blood, but Maybor wasn't overly concerned where he put the gray, flea-ridden thing. He'd been sleeping on it for months now and it had long lost what little style its tailor had first intended.

Although it was growing dark, Maybor still found enough light to admire the deep crimson color of his tunic. A color that was certain to impress the wenches. Maybor smiled, well pleased with what shadowy grandeur the twilight revealed, and made his way across the courtyard and onto the city streets.

As he walked, the Highwall bombardment shook buildings and lit up the southwestern sky. Having grown bored with attacking the wall all day, the northern allies had decided to set their catapults higher and were now sending missiles *over* the wall and into the city. The noise was the worst thing. The terrible stomach-churning rumble of the siege engines, the hammering of stone blasting against stone, the soft whip of the longbow, and the high, haunting screams of the wounded.

Listening to the sounds of war as he traveled eastward through the city, Maybor could hardly wait until tomorrow. Tomorrow Melli's letter would be read by Lord Besik, the leader of the Highwall army. Only today the man had ordered the flying of the duke's colors to signify that he was behind Melliandra and her child—Maybor could guess whose jeweled and pudgy hand was behind that one—and he and Melli were now assured of a warm welcome into the enemy camp. Then at last he would be able to take an active part in the war instead of hiding in a wine cellar like a coward.

Maybor had spent many of the last few days quietly surveying the city and had come up with a few ideas on how best to defeat it. The wall was its strength, and although the allies had managed to break through a small outer section, it had taken them nearly a week to do so. The lake, however, was its weakness. The lake was the lifeblood of Bren; every well in the city drew upon its cold and glassy water. Thousands of people depended upon it for survival. Poison it and those very same people would be on their knees within a week.

Highwall should be sending out divers into the lake. Nabber had told him that there were gateways beneath the surface that led straight to the heart of the palace. If there was already a network of tunnels beneath the palace, then a mine should be built under the lake to join up with it. The whole thing should be filled with hay and timber, then set alight. The foundations would crumble in no time.

And as for the late duke's colors, well, he'd have them flying on every tent, every scaling ladder, every crossbow in the field. There were many in Bren who would prefer to back Melli's claim rather than Kylock's—they just needed a little encouragement, that was all. Cravin was currently working to whip up support for Melliandra. It was, Maybor grudgingly admitted, a decidedly risky endeavor. So far the handful of noblemen who had expressed tentative support for Melliandra had all wound up dead. Of course, the official word was they were missing, but Maybor was far too old and wily to believe official word.

Maybor was distracted from his thoughts by two young ladies who were standing in a doorway and calling out to him:

"Hey there, handsome! Fancy a little brawl between the sheets?"

"You can lay siege to my door anytime, matey."

Maybor, having quickly appraised their charms, or rather lack of them, bowed politely to the two women in passing. "Not this evening, ladies. Another time, perhaps."

The girls giggled in appreciation of his courtesy, then promised him special rates if he passed their way again later.

Maybor made a mental note of the street. If he didn't find the place he was looking for soon, he just might take the ladies up on their offer. After all, the plain ones were usually the most inventive in bed. One thing was certain, though, tonight he *would* have a woman.

He had been without one for so long, he'd almost forgotten what to do with one. Such severe abstinence could kill a man! After tomorrow, when he joined the Highwall camp, he probably wouldn't be able to enjoy a woman until after the siege ended, so that was why he'd taken to the streets tonight: it was his last chance to bed one.

Now, as fortune would have, while he was out earlier, he dropped by a tavern and was given the address of the most profitable brothel in the city. One which boasted a girl of such extraordinary beauty that men came from far and wide to bed her. Hearing of the girl's charms, Maybor became determined that she would be the one he would spend his last night in Bren with. His long days of self-restraint would be made up for in one glorious—and very probably expensive—coupling.

Eventually, after many turnoffs and a little backtracking, Maybor found the place he was looking for. The red shutters were flung open to the night, and smoke, noise, and fragrances leaked out to lure customers in. Maybor checked the name scribed in the alcove, put his hand on his purse for good measure, and rapped loudly on the door.

A woman answered. She looked him up and down, patted her heavily powdered hair, and said, "Why, welcome, fine sir. Come in and brush the siege dust from your shoes." She grabbed on to his arm with a pincerlike grip and dragged him across the threshold.

Maybor's natural reaction was to back away. The woman was neither young nor pretty, and she smelled like dead rodents. Just as he was about to make his exit, the woman called out:

"Moxie! Franny! Come and see to this gentleman." Two young girls came rushing forward and the woman relinquished her grip. The two girls arranged themselves, one on either side of him, and the woman thrust a jug of ale into his hand. "Special brew," she said.

Considering there weren't many candles lit, there was an awful lot of smoke. The light was dim, the fumes were heavy, and the place was crowded to the rafters. Maybor took a sip of his ale. Strangely familiar, it tasted like the stuff they brewed in the kingdoms.

"Never had so much business since the war started," said the woman. "Nothing like manning the battlements all day for making a man randy at night." She smiled coquettishly, adjusting her curls to frame her face.

Maybor was feeling a little bemused. The smoke and the strong ale were working their effects, relaxing his mind and his senses. The rodent woman still looked ugly, though.

"Tell me," he said, "where is your beauty?"

The two girls to either side of him moved closer.

The rodent woman's smile widened. "Aah. Well, handsome sir, Cherry is busy at the moment. She'll be free a little later, but in the meantime why don't you enjoy Franny and Moxie, instead?"

Franny and Moxie blew kisses at opposite sides of his neck. Both girls looked pleasant enough, but he had a feeling they'd look a lot worse in daylight. "I'll sup with them for a while," said Maybor. "But send Cherry to me as soon as she is free."

The woman hesitated. "Very well, sir. But it'll cost you double for all three."

Maybor let himself be led to a bench at the side of the room. Moxie and Franny began kissing and petting him. "Don't worry about the cost, woman," he shouted above the din of drink and chatter. "Just send me the best you have."

Mistress Greal's bat ears could pick up talk of money a league away. She had just heard her two favorite sentences in all the world: *"Don't worry about the cost,"* and *"Send me the best you have."* Her small heart thrilled to their musical sound. There was obviously someone here tonight who could afford the very best.

Not that she needed the money, of course. Ever since she'd purchased her great beauty, business had never been better. Men came from all over the city to see Cherry's formidable charms. Pale blond hair, skin like silk, eyes as green as emeralds. Not to mention a bottom the size of a beer barrel! The girl was quickly becoming a phenomenon; songs were sung about her in taverns, her likeness had been painted on several missiles destined for the enemy, and just last night King Kylock himself had sent for her.

"Dearest sister," came Madame Thornypurse's high and nasal voice from behind. "I think we have a slight problem."

"What now, sister dear? Someone else griping about the smoke?" Mistress Greal was scathing. No one could fuss up a storm over a trivial complaint like her sister. Last night it had been beetles in the special brew!

"Well, dearest sister," said Madame Thornypurse, dropping her voice to a whisper. "A right fine gentleman has come in asking to see Cherry. From the way he's dressed he can afford to pay her double."

Mistress Greal saw the problem. "Have you given him Franny, instead?" After Cherry, Franny was the second best girl in the establishment. If it wasn't for her long nose and buck teeth she would have been a true beauty.

"Yes, dearest sister, but he's still asking after Cherry."

"Well, he can't see her," snapped Mistress Greal. "No one can until she's better."

Only this morning Cherry had returned from the duke's palace. As well as a broken arm, she had three small burn marks on her right shoulder. The girl swore she fell down the stairs and went crashing into a table bearing lit candles. Mistress Greal thought otherwise. She knew from experience that some men had a liking for inflicting pain upon women, and she had a feeling that King Kylock was just such a man.

Normally Mistress Greal would turn a blind eye to such practices, particularly for someone who paid as well as the king did, but her greatest business asset was now out of commission for at least a week. Cherry could work with a broken arm—might even add to her mystique— but the bruises and burns would have to be healed before she could appear in public once more. It really was most inconvenient. Especially when there was a rich man willing to pay double for her favors.

"Point the fine gentleman out to me, sister dear."

Up came Madame Thornypurse's finger like a divining rod pointing for gold. "He's over there," she said. "The one in the scarlet with his back to us."

Mistress Greal's eyes had already outpaced her sister's finger. She had seen the scarlet, recognized it as the finest silk, and was about to step toward the man when he turned his head to the light.

Mistress Greal stopped dead in her tracks. The air turned to dust in her lungs. All the smoke in the world was not enough to conceal the identity of the man in scarlet. She saw his face every night in her dreams. Mistress Greal brought her thumb up to her lips and pressed gently against the yielding softness. Softness where once there had been teeth.

"What's the matter, dearest sister? You look like you've seen a ghost."

With great effort Mistress Greal took control of herself. She smiled her own peculiar smile, pressing her lips together and forcing them into a thin line. "No, sister dear," she said. "I've just seen something much more profitable than a ghost."

Madame Thornypurse trembled like a blushing maiden. "What, dearest sister? What?"

"The second most wanted man in all of Bren," whispered Mistress Greal, more to herself than her sister. Who would have guessed that Lord Maybor would end up here of all places? Her smile widened. There was vengeance *and* profit to be extracted here: the two most satisfying things in the Greal universe.

It would be a good way to ingratiate herself with Lord Baralis, too. Oh, she knew she had something on the great lord—she alone in all of Bren knew he had conspired to assassinate the duke—but the truth was she was a little afraid to use her knowledge. People who messed with Lord Baralis had a nasty habit of ending up dead. If he could murder a duke, and very possibly a duchess as well, then he certainly wouldn't think twice about murdering someone who was trying to blackmail him. It was far better to get to know Lord Baralis first and see just how generous he could be. Blackmail could come later. In her experience secrets like the one she held always grew more potent over time. With the money she was going to make by turning Maybor and his tart of a daughter in, she could well afford to wait.

"You," she said to her sister, "must keep that man occupied until I return."

"But—"

Mistress Greal's hand was already up. "I don't care what you do. Have the girls dance naked, for all I care. Just make sure that old bastard doesn't leave."

Madame Thornypurse looked shocked. The habit of obeying her elder sister's every word was so well entrenched by now, however, that she duly nodded her head. "You won't be too long, dearest sister?"

Mistress Greal had already pulled on her cloak. "No, sister dear. I'll be back before you know it."

Baralis had just finished his first sending to Skaythe. The man had left the city five days back and was currently heading south, hoping at some point to run into Tawl. Although Baralis had suspected for some time that the knight was no longer in the area, up until this morning he hadn't known for sure. Now, thanks to those busy little seers at Larn, he not only knew *where* Tawl was heading, but he also knew the route he would take. Down along the peninsula past Ness, Toolay, and Rorn.

The powers that be at Larn had contacted Baralis in his sleep. It was telling that they waited until early morning to contact him—they had hoped to glean his secrets from his dreams. Baralis smiled to himself. It would take more than the seers of Larn to fathom the dark maze of his unconscious mind.

They were obviously becoming very worried on their

faraway isle. They tried to be their usual aloof selves, but there was an undertone of urgency in their desire to tell all they knew. Larn wanted the knight and the boy killed, and they would go to great lengths to help him do so. Besides telling him what route the two fugitives would be taking, they also bribed him with more intelligence about the war. Apparently Highwall was waiting on the arrival of two thousand mercenaries. The men were fully equipped and paid for, courtesy of the venerable archbishop of Rorn.

Baralis had wasted no time passing the information along to Kylock. After all, war was the king's specialty.

Politics and loose ends were *his*.

Smiling, Baralis poured himself a glass of red wine. Skaythe was turning out to be a useful find. He could have hired any number of men to do the tracking, but Skaythe, with his amateur knowledge of sorcery, could be contacted en route. To send a message was difficult, but to *receive* one was easy. All Skaythe had to do was concentrate and listen without using his ears. Any fool could do that.

Skaythe had received the sending and was now adjusting his route accordingly. Baralis had great faith in the man. He might not be as skilled as Blayze in armed combat, but he was infinitely more cunning.

A sharp rap on the door broke Baralis' line of thought. Crope was usually away at this time of night, tending to the animals. Baralis stood up. Before he'd crossed the room, the rap came again. Whoever was on the other side was most impatient.

He flung the door open. "Who dares disturb me at this hour?"

A woman stood in the corridor. Her expression was severe and her body had all the charm of a knotted rope. "Someone who can lead you to the biggest whore in all of Bren."

"And who might that be?" Baralis glanced along the corridor. Who had let this madwoman in the palace?

"Why, Maybor's daughter, of course."

"You know where Melliandra is?" Perhaps she wasn't so mad after all. She had the narrow-eyed look of the greedy, not the insane. "Step inside a moment." Baralis waved her into his chambers. "Would you care for a glass of wine?"

"Just a little drop to wet my throat." The woman patted the dry bit.

Baralis poured her a brimming glass. "And who might I have the pleasure of speaking to?"

"Mistress G." The woman spoke with a minimum of lip movement.

"Well then, *Mistress G*, perhaps you'd like to tell me where the young murderess is." Baralis turned his voice into a honeyed trap to catch his fly. "And once you've done that we can talk of rewards."

"I'd rather speak of rewards first, if you don't mind. In my line of business you soon learn that it's best to take your payment up front."

"Go on."

"Well." The woman looked around the chamber for inspiration. "There's cash, of course."

Baralis nodded. "Of course."

"Say five hundred golds."

"And?"

The woman smiled with all the satisfaction of a hangman measuring the drop. "Well, we both know how important finding the Lady Melliandra is. If she makes it to the enemy, then it could lead to civil war." Mistress G shook her head sadly. "There's more than a few in Bren who would rather see her child in the palace than Kylock—though the way the king's cracking down on her supporters, no one dare come out and say it."

"Speak what you would have."

The change in Baralis' voice did not go unnoticed by the woman. She betrayed her first sign of nervousness by taking a deep draught of her wine. For the first time,

Baralis noticed that her two front teeth were missing.

Having gained a little courage from the drink, the woman looked him straight in the eye. "I would have a position here in the palace. Housekeeper, recordkeeper, cellarer . . ." As Mistress G waved her arms in illustration, a look of unmistakable malice sharpened her tight, little face. "I could even look after the whore herself."

Try as he might, Baralis could not keep the smile from pushing against his lips. The woman would make a formidable jailer. "You may have whatever position you wish," he said. "Now tell me—"

"I must ask for the gold and your word before we go any further," interrupted Mistress G.

Baralis crossed over to his desk. He quickly drew up a promissory note, signed it, then stamped it with his seal. He handed it to the woman.

She read it slowly. "I'll still need a deposit."

"If you don't tell me where Maybor and his daughter are this instant, you will not leave this palace alive." Baralis drew very close to the woman. "Now accept what you have, or lose everything."

With a shaking hand, Mistress G slid the note into her bodice. "Very well, then. Lord Maybor is currently being entertained in my sister's establishment. Send some men over to follow him home. He'll lead you straight to Melliandra."

Baralis' hand was on the bell rope. "What establishment is this?"

"A little place in the south of the city. I'll travel back with the men to make sure they find it all right."

"Very well," said Baralis. He had already lost interest in the woman—she could lead the chase for all he cared. The seers at Larn were never wrong. Melliandra would soon be his.

Maybor had long since given up trying to remember all the girls' names. Moxie and Franny came first, but after that the rest of them were just pleasant, scantily clad bodies.

Smoke that would choke a charcoal burner, combined with special brew so strong it could kill one, had left Maybor in a sort of dazed semiconscious state. The only thing he knew for sure was that it was time to be going home, and the woman who smelled of dead rats wouldn't let him. Every time he walked to the door, she would block his path and push another naked girl his way.

The place was virtually empty now. A few drunken no-hopes lay snoring on the floor, one man was quietly weeping into his ale, and another was singing about his wife. Even the smoke was starting to clear.

Maybor pushed the girls away from him and stood up. The room took a moment to settle beneath his feet. The rat woman loomed into his field of vision.

"Oh sir, don't go just yet," she said, gripping his arm. "You haven't seen Esmi dance."

Maybor slapped at her fingers. "As Borc is my witness, woman, I am leaving now! And you are not going to stop me." He lurched toward the door. It opened before he got to it. A woman poked her head round. Or at least he thought she did, for when he focused his gaze, she was gone.

The rat woman, who had been one step behind him, suddenly turned to her girls. "Say goodnight to the fine gentleman," she prompted.

"Goodnight, handsome," echoed the girls.

Maybor instinctively knew that now wasn't a good time to risk a bow, so he waved an arm in acknowledgment, instead. The rat woman let him walk out of the door unchallenged.

Maybor took a deep breath of night air and tried hard to remember the way home. With eyes focused firmly on his feet, he walked to the end of the road. Everything seemed familiar enough and he turned to the left, then made his way across the market square. It was quiet now.

The Highwall army had given up their bombardment for the night, and the only sound was the trickle of the water in the fountains and the rustle of his satin tunic as he walked.

All in all it had been an unusual night. He'd learnt a rather disappointing lesson from it: even naked women could get boring after a while. Still, a man needs to get thoroughly, disgustingly drunk once in a while just to stop himself from going to seed. Judging from the quick pitter-patter of his heart, seed would be the last place he'd go tonight.

As he walked through the city, Maybor began to sober up a little. A light breeze blew the smoke from his lungs, and the foul air from the open sewers had a greater reviving action than the finest smelling salts.

With increased lucidity came a certain wariness. His heart wasn't the only thing that was pitter-pattering. Maybor stopped in midstep and, sure enough, the footfalls stopped, too. Someone was following him. Probably a pickpocket, or a cutthroat attracted by his fine clothes and his drunken stupor. Maybor hurried on. He wasn't far from the cellar now.

A few more turns, a quick check to the left and right, and Maybor entered the butcher's courtyard.

Borc! but it was dark. Maybor stumbled into the center, his eyes searching the ground for the flat square that marked the trapdoor. Once he found it, he banged his foot against the wood and hissed, "It's Maybor! Let me in." Hearing some movement from below, Maybor grunted with satisfaction. Those lazy beggars were still awake. Just as the trapdoor opened up, Maybor realized he'd left his cloak in the corner of the courtyard. "I'll be back in just a minute," he murmured to Bodger down below.

Maybor wasn't exactly sure which corner of the courtyard he'd left his cloak in. They all looked the same in the dark. As he veered off toward the farthest point in the courtyard, a harsh cry broke the silence of the night:

"Get 'em!"

Swords slithered from sheaths and suddenly the court-yard was full of shadowy forms heading for the trapdoor.

Maybor saw two men coming straight for him. He drew his knife and backed into the deeper shadows of the wall. His hip smashed against something. It was the butcher's table. Cursing, he made his way around it.

Looking up, he saw a group of armed guards jumping into the cellar. Someone screamed.

The two men were only paces away now, and Maybor slashed out with his knife. One of the two backed away. Grabbing hold of the butcher's table, Maybor pushed with all his might. It went crashing forward into the second man. Maybor dropped onto the ground. He scrambled around in the dirt until his hand brushed against the softness of his cloak.

The second man was pinned under the butcher's table. He called to his companion to help him lift it off.

Several men emerged from the trapdoor. One of them was carrying someone. Someone who neither screamed nor struggled. It was so dark Maybor could make out no details, but he guessed it was his daughter. Melliandra would meet the guards with dignity. Maybor's heart leaped when he saw the figure move. The starlight caught the flare of a skirt. It was Melli, and she was alive and well. Two guards stood on either side of her.

"Trevis! Brunner! Have you got the old goat yet?"

"We've got him cornered, cap'n." A loud crash followed as the first man levered the butcher's table off the second man's foot.

Maybor knew he had only split seconds to decide what to do. Melli was caught, and he doubted if he could save her. There were too many men to fight single-handedly. He had to pull his wits about him. For Melli's sake.

The two guards came closer. They made wary, sweeping actions with their blades. Maybor was deep in the shadows, and he guessed that neither man could see him.

He knew the best thing he could do would be to escape. He'd be no good to Melli caught or dead. If he remembered rightly, there was a service gate halfway between him and the butcher's kitchen. Maybor grabbed hold of his cloak. He cast it like a net, letting it flare out and catch the air. It glided away into the center of the courtyard. In the quarter-light it looked like a man.

"There he is, Trevis!" cried the first man. "He's making a run for it." Both men shot off toward the cloak.

"Father! *No!*" screamed Melli.

Maybor's stomach churned when he heard her—she must have recognized his cloak. He hesitated for an instant, then scrambled in the opposite direction from all the commotion, along the wall, toward the gate, making accomplices out of the shadows as he went. The air was burning in his lungs and he wheezed with every breath. He didn't need to look back to know that his feint had been discovered. A crossfire of footfalls and calls sounded behind him.

Maybor reached the gate. His hand was shaking so much, he couldn't draw the bolt.

"He's there against the wall!" cried someone.

Maybor gripped the bolt with both hands and drew it back. The gate opened outward. He risked one look back.

Melli was causing a minor riot. She was kicking and screaming and trying her damnedest to distract the guards from running after him. Maybor felt his heart would break. She was the bravest daughter a father ever had.

Footsteps charged up behind him and he knew it was time to go. He would not let Melli's efforts go to waste. He slipped through the gate, slamming it closed as soon as he was through. There was a little more light in the alleyway, and Maybor immediately saw that the entire left wall was stacked with apple crates. Dashing forward, he shouldered his whole body into the end stack of crates. They came tumbling down behind him. Splinters cracked, boxes smashed, and apples went careening to the floor. The gate was opened and two guards came through just in time to be bombarded.

Maybor didn't have the energy to relish the sight. He turned quickly and ran down the alleyway. Every step was torture. There was a tight band of pain around his chest. His fine tunic was soaked with sweat. Gradually, as he became lost in the great maze of the city, his run slowed to a walk.

Fully sober now, Maybor felt no joy in his escape. His mind kept replaying his last sight of Melli, and the image haunted him until dawn.

Thirteen

We have to assume we're being followed," said Tawl. "At all times."

"You never said a truer word, my friend," chipped in Nabber. "Swift himself swore he'd been trailed so many times that one day someone would follow him straight into the grave."

Tawl smiled. He looked quickly at Jack. He wasn't sure how Jack would take this last statement. There was so much he didn't know about him.

Jack continued building the fire. "I've assumed we've been followed for the past week now."

"Is it something you've sensed?"

"Not sorcery, if that's what you mean, Tawl." Jack placed a pointed emphasis on the word *sorcery*.

Tawl accepted the reprimand. He deserved it for not speaking plainly. "Why, then?"

"Because Baralis has ways of knowing what people are up to. He can follow their trails if they use sorcery." Jack threw the last of the logs on the fire. "And because he's tracked me down more than once before."

A cool wind blew through the flames. The sun slid behind the hills to the west and the last of the day went with it. The horses nickered softly, then turned their attention back to the grass. Tawl had an uneasy feeling, and he suspected that Jack shared it.

They had been gone from the city for nine days now. Nine days of late nights and early mornings, of hard travel, long hours, aching limbs, and little rest. A week ago they purchased two horses from a farmer who was so scared of being robbed or beaten that he'd practically given them away. The horses were a little long in the tooth, but sturdy and well used to hard work. Tawl had let Jack have the bay, which was the smaller of the two, and kept the dun for himself. Under protest, Nabber rode at his back.

Up until now, the horses had actually slowed them down. Nabber hated horses and Jack had never learnt to ride. Tawl kept forgetting that Jack had been a baker's apprentice. He didn't look like one, didn't act like one, and he held his blade like a killer, not a kitchen boy. But he *was* young, and there were many things he didn't know. Simple things like how to ride, how to pack his belongings to keep them dry, how to follow the stars at night, and how to dampen the fire in the morning.

Slowly Tawl was teaching him all he knew. Jack learned fast. Already he was a better horseman than Nabber. Tomorrow, Tawl expected they'd actually make good time. Within a couple of days they should be in Ness. Once there they could exchange their horses for faster ones and ride to Rorn within two weeks.

Tawl smiled. He knew he was being overly optimistic—it might take twice as long as that—but he just couldn't help himself. Melli was in Bren, and all he could think about was getting to Larn as fast as possible and then speeding back to her side. He dreamt of it every night.

"Tawl, we're not going to do any more traveling tonight, are we? I'm as bowlegged as a wishbone." Nabber made a sweeping gesture with his arm. "Besides, this is a real nice spot to kip down. Right secluded, it is."

Tawl looked at the fire. It was burning brightly now. Ever since Jack had mastered the art of building a quick fire, he used every opportunity to demonstrate it. Nabber was right. They shouldn't go any farther tonight. They had a pleasant fire, a good place to sleep, and with only half a moon on show, there wasn't much light to travel by anyway. Tawl had planned on riding for a few more hours, but he knew Nabber was tired. "Very well," he said. "We'll go no farther tonight."

Nabber stood up. "I'm off to fill the flasks. There's a stream beyond those trees."

"Watch out for wolves," said Tawl, smiling. Nabber wasn't as interested in collecting water as he was in the possibility of pestering newts and frogs. Tawl watched the boy until he was out of sight, making a mental note of the exact direction he was headed.

"Still feeling uneasy?" asked Jack.

Tawl hid his surprise. "I never take anyone's safety for granted."

Jack was quiet for a while after that. There was a pot on the fire, and he was stirring lentils and dried meat into it.

They were in a gently sloping glade in a sparsely planted wood. The trees that surrounded them clustered in loose groups like old women. There were oaks, beech trees, and hawthorn bushes. Everything looked like it had been here a long time. Even the grass had the jaundiced look of the elderly.

Tawl made himself comfortable. He leant back against the trunk of a gnarled old oak and watched as Jack tended the stew. After a while, he said, "So Baralis has tracked you down before?"

Jack nodded. "And Melli, as well. We ran away from Castle Harvell together. He found us twice."

"Why did Melli run away?"

"Her father was forcing her to marry Kylock."

"So she just took off and ran away?"

"Yes. She left the castle in the middle of the night."

Tawl suddenly felt very happy. He could picture Melli

working herself up into an indignant rage, then deciding to do something reckless. He'd never met a woman with more spirit. "What was she like when you met her?"

"Uppity." Jack took the pot from the middle of the fire and set it amongst the ashes to the side. He picked up his pack and came and sat close to Tawl. "Her hand was bleeding and she'd just been robbed, but she still refused my help. It took her over an hour just to tell me her name." Jack smiled, remembering. "She was beautiful, though."

Tawl smiled with him. "Yes, she *is* beautiful."

"And strong. To this day I still don't know how she managed to drag me across the forest to Harvell's eastern road. She even persuaded a pig farmer to take care of me. Told her I was injured in a hunting accident."

"And the pig farmer believed her?"

"Melli has a way of saying things that makes it difficult for people to contradict her."

"You mean she bullied the pig farmer?"

"What do *you* think?"

Both men laughed. Tawl's heart filled with joy. He liked sitting here, in the glade under the pale moon, and talking of Melli. It was the next best thing to being with her.

"You care about her very much, don't you?" he said when the laughter died down.

Jack looked up. "Yes, I do."

Tawl sensed some reluctance in his voice. By not speaking he encouraged Jack to say more.

"But I'm not in love with her, though. Not like you are."

In his own way, Jack was telling him he had no rival. Tawl lifted his hand and brought it to rest on Jack's shoulder. The world seemed like a good place. There was honor and friendship and love. "And what of you, Jack?" he said softly. "Who do you dream of at night?"

Tawl smiled. He knew he'd caught the boy off guard.

Jack moved toward the fire. His back was to Tawl, and when he spoke his voice sounded far away. "There's a girl in Halcus. Her family took me in. She was beautiful, not perfect like Melli, but . . . " Jack shrugged. "But beautiful all the same."

Sensing Jack's mood matched his own, Tawl settled himself back against his tree. He shot a quick glance in Nabber's direction—all seemed quiet—and then said, "So, tell me her name."

"Tarissa."

Tawl could tell a lot by the way Jack said her name. There was longing in his voice, and something else. A certain hardness. Not used to such conversations himself, Tawl's instinct was to tread lightly. "What did she look like?" He thought he'd asked the wrong question, for several minutes passed with no reply.

The wind died down and the moon lost itself behind a bank of clouds. The fire crackled and popped, spitting flecks of green summer wood up with the smoke. Finally Jack spoke: "Her eyes are brown and sparkling. Her hair is chestnut and gold. There's a tiny bump in the middle of her nose and her dimples deepen when she smiles."

As Jack spoke, Tawl looked at Jack. His hair was the exact same color as the woman he'd just described.

A soft whirring sound whipped through the dark.

Tawl felt a cool wisp of air brush against his face.

Crack!

"Get down!" he shouted. Directly above him, an arrow jutted from the trunk of the tree. Its shaft was still vibrating.

Jack dropped to the ground.

"Kick the fire out."

Tawl followed the direction of the arrow's flight. The archer was to the north of them. Behind him, Jack threw soil on the fire. It banked, then died. "Crawl over and untether the horses." Tawl spoke to Jack, but his mind was on Nabber. "Bring them to meet me by the stream.

Hold their reins to the side and put their bodies between you and the archer." Tawl was going to ask him to draw his knife, but a single gleam of steel caught his eye. Jack was already ahead of him.

Tawl scrambled over to the campfire. The pot of stew was overturned. No supper tonight. Grabbing hold of the packs and bedrolls, he made a run for the stream.

It would be impossible for the archer to get a good shot now. His targets were on the move and there was no firelight to set his sights by. The trees would make it difficult for him to get a clean line, as well. Strange, but Tawl never doubted for an instant that it *was* a lone archer. If there'd been more than one he and Jack would be dead by now.

No. This was one man working alone. And Tawl had the distinct feeling they'd just been sent a greeting. The arrow was too well placed to be a mark gone awry. A handspan above his forehead, centered between his eyes—it was a classic warning shot. Someone not only wanted them to know he was out there, but also that he was in no hurry to kill them just yet. He wanted to scare them first.

Looking ahead, Tawl spotted the bright glimmer of the stream. There were shadows moving in front of it. The horses. He sprinted toward them. As soon as he spotted Jack, he shouted, "Is Nabber with you?"

Jack didn't get a chance to reply.

Nabber piped up: "Hey, Tawl, what's been going on? A boy can't take forty winks round here without finding himself in the middle of an uproar." He walked forward into the moonlight. His tunic sported several wriggling bulges.

"Leave the toads here, Nabber," said Tawl, resisting the urge to hug the boy. "We're going to be on the move tonight, after all. We've got to put some distance between ourselves and the man who fired that arrow."

*

Skaythe rarely smiled. At times such as this, when he had reason to be pleased, he permitted himself a satisfied tightening of his lips. Nothing more.

From his position on the top of the rise, he could just make out the slow-moving forms of the two horses. He couldn't see if they were being ridden or led. It didn't matter. He had accomplished exactly what he set out to do tonight: he'd thrown down the red marker.

Too bad Tawl hadn't spared a glance for the arrow, or he just might have guessed the game.

There is something sacred about an arrow. It speeds through the air carrying a message of death, propelled only by muscle and tensile force. Every part of the arrow could tell you something about the archer's intent. Messages within the message, like a secret code within a letter.

Skaythe was a little disappointed that Tawl had not taken the time to read the arrow on the tree. After all, he had once been a knight, and knights knew all about the secret language of archery.

If Tawl had but looked he would have seen a small arrowhead, finely shaped for accuracy. Not a hunting arrowhead, a sporting one, designed to hit a target, not a beast. It had never been aimed for a kill, rather a well-placed threat, instead. As for the shaft, it was shaped from finest cedar. Not something a casual archer could easily come by, but something a *serious* archer would make it his business to acquire. The shaft was a thing of beauty: smooth enough to rub across a lady's cheek, straight enough to set your sights by. It was a shaft that told of the archer himself. It told of his skill, his perfectionism, and his knowledge of his trade. Only professionals used cedarwood.

Then there were the fletchings, the most specific feature of the arrow. The archer's chance to show off his true colors. They were the arrow's banner, its flag waving in the breeze for all to see once it had hit its target. The fletchings of Skaythe's arrow were unique.

Red silk and human hair.

Red silk for the marker that was thrown into the pit the night that Blayze was murdered. Human hair shaved from Blayze's corpse the day before they laid him in his grave.

The arrow was a tribute to his brother's memory and a sworn oath of vengeance.

Skaythe had been with Blayze when he died. He had watched the fight in the pit, watched the knight beat Blayze's skull against the ground until his brain splattered the dirt walls, watched his body being carried to the palace, and watched him die without once gaining consciousness.

Tawl hadn't fought a man that night, he had *murdered* one. He could have stopped sooner; Blayze was out as soon as his skull smashed against the stone for the first time. The knight could have stopped then and there and claimed victory. But no, he continued on and on, only stopping when his second pulled him off. Blayze could have walked away from that fight with his life, able to fight another day, to regain his lost dignity, and to settle old scores that hadn't yet been settled. But the knight had put an end to all of that.

Skaythe fastened his quiver to his back and mounted his horse. He urged the gelding forward toward the glade.

Now he would never have the chance to beat Blayze one on one.

They had been rivals first, brothers second. They were born exactly nine months apart. Skaythe was the eldest. People said that Blayze had the charm and good looks, while Skaythe had the skill and the brains. They were fighting before they could walk. By the time Skaythe reached his sixteenth year there seemed no limit to what he could achieve. He fought like a demon. No one could beat him, though his brother always came close.

They were good days, then. Their rivalry spurred them both on; they lived for it, and it shaped them into the fighters they became. As soon as Skaythe mastered a

new move he would use it against Blayze, then teach him
it after he'd won. Sometimes, but not often, Blayze would
learn a new technique first. Oh, the fight would be glorious then. Skaythe was never happier than when he was
faced with new challenges. There was joy in every thrust
and parry, meaning in every blow.

People watched them and shook their heads. Never
were there two such brothers, they said.

Then, when Blayze turned sixteen they had their last
fight. It was dark, and they had both been drinking.
Skaythe had downed one skin; Blayze, always lacking in
moderation, had two. The fight was sloppy, undisci-
plined. It took place in the courtyard at the back of their
father's shop. One oil lamp and two candles were the only
light they had.

Ale not only made them slow, it made them bitter.
Before long the fight became nasty: long-held resent-
ments surfaced in the fray. Blayze was always the favorite,
beloved of both their parents, his handsome face a guarantee of success. Skaythe was the arrogant one, a
bad-tempered bully, unable to control his moods. Insults
came faster than blows.

Skaythe was the most clear-headed of the two, and he
took the advantage when it came, raking his knife along
his brother's arm and then pressing it into his chest.
Normally in a friendly bout, as soon as blood was drawn
from the torso the fight was won. Skaythe turned his back
on his brother and began to walk away. He felt a sharp
blow to his head. Stumbling forward, he fell to the
ground. He spun around in time to see Blayze standing
over him with a rock in his hand. The rock blasted into
his leg. His knee exploded in pain. The night became
light as he screamed, then darkened as the agony of splintered bones pushing against muscle became too much for
him to bear.

Skaythe's face was grim as he remembered. His knuckles were white as he held the reins.

After that day he never fought again. The knee healed in time, but the limp remained. Neither Skaythe nor Blayze mentioned the fight again. Skaythe put all his efforts into helping Blayze become a champion. Blayze's victories were his victories, and his failures were too few to count. While his brother fought his way through every pit in Bren, Skaythe quietly kept up his skills, practicing archery instead of the longsword, and the lance instead of the flail. He had a local blacksmith forge a spike for his stick and turned a weakness into a weapon. He could walk without his stick now, but it suited him too well to give it up.

Ten years had passed since the incident with the rock. Blayze eventually became duke's champion, and Skaythe was at his side all the way. Right until the final fight.

Even now, Skaythe found it hard to believe that Blayze was gone. Every day of those ten long years he had imagined that a time would come when he and his brother would fight again. And he would beat him one last time.

Only now there would never be a fight. And all the victories left were hollow ones.

Skaythe dismounted his horse. He stepped into the glade and moved toward the tree where the arrow was lodged. Taking the shaft in his fist, he pulled it from the trunk. The wood split in his hand.

The knight had a lot to answer for.

All the apples and crates were gone. Someone had cleared them away.

Maybor stood in the same shadows that had helped him escape four nights earlier. He was in the alleyway and had just opened the gate into the courtyard. It was dark and quiet. There was no sign of movement, and not a single sliver of light shone up from the cellar's depths.

For three hours he'd been here. Watching. Waiting. Making sure that no one was watching and waiting for him. The butcher's lights had gone out two hours back.

Then the butcher himself had come out and relieved himself against the wall. Nothing else had happened since.
No footfalls, no muffled coughs, no calls. The courtyard
was empty, and it looked like the cellar was, too.

Maybor only knew one prayer. It was self-centered
and immodest and used the word *me* a lot, and he chose to
speak it now as he crept toward the door.

The wooden panel had been moved back into place.
Maybor nudged it with his foot. It was loose. Bending
down, he scooped his fingers under the corner and pulled
the trapdoor up. It had not been fastened on the inside.
There was no bar to prevent it from being kicked in.
Maybor peered downward. It was very dark. It stank of
sour wine. The guards must have split a good few barrels
open.

Without pausing to look around, Maybor lowered
himself into the cellar. He landed with a jolt. The crates
that were usually underneath were gone. Rats scattered.
His shoes quickly soaked with wine.

"Anyone there?" he called softly.

Nothing.

Maybor fumbled in the dark until he found a candle.
The wick was wet and wouldn't take a spark from the
flint. "Damn," he hissed.

Just then he heard an unratlike noise: scraping.
Something was being scraped across the floor in the cellar
to the right. "Who's there?" demanded Maybor. His
voice did not reveal his fear.

More scraping. Followed by a barely audible whisper:
"Lord Maybor, is that you?"

Maybor hurried in the direction of the voice, cutting
across the large cellar, through to the smaller one and
then under a low arch to the storeroom. Grift was lying
on the floor. There was a single candle by his side. Blood
was soaking through the bandage round his stomach. His
lips were pale and cracked.

The first thing he said was, "Is Bodger with you?"

Maybor shook his head. "He was taken with Melliandra."

Grift began coughing. Softly at first, then hacking uncontrollably, his whole body shaking.

Maybor fished in his tunic and pulled out his flask. There were only a few drops of brandy left. He knelt down and supported Grift's back while he drank it. The man was in bad need of medical attention. Food and water probably wouldn't go amiss, either. Maybor wondered how he had managed to go unnoticed by the guards.

"Have you got a spare candle?" he asked, when Grift had calmed down. Grift indicated a supply on a high shelf. Maybor took one and lit it. "I'll be back in a moment," he said.

He made his way to his own little room. The place had been ransacked; his clothes were gone, the bedding had been torn, and several barrels were split at the seams. Everything was soaked in wine. Maybor bent down and lifted the soaking rushes from his pallet. The box wasn't there. Scrambling, Maybor turned the pallet on its side. His gold was gone! He couldn't believe it. Falling to his hands and knees, he searched every corner of the room. By the time he had finished his clothes were soaked right through.

The guards had taken his gold. All two hundred pieces of it. He had nothing left. Sitting back in the pool of sour wine, Maybor made a decision.

He took the candle and went back to Grift. The guard was lying exactly where he left him. "Can you walk?" he asked.

Grift's response was to struggle to his feet. He got halfway up, then his legs began to buckle. Maybor came forward to steady him.

"Do you know the way out of the city?"

"Aye, but it's quite a way. I don't think I'll be able to make it."

"You'll make it all right. Even if I have to carry you."
Maybor hauled Grift up all the way. "Come on, lean on
me now."

Grift took a lurching step forward. "But we could get
caught or shot at."

"I don't care if we get bombarded with headless
corpses," said Maybor. "We're leaving this city tonight."

Nabber's thighs were sore, his back was aching, and his
feet had gone numb. Everyone was tense. The slightest
sound stopped them in their tracks, and every quickly
shifting shadow drew knives. Tawl walked with his shortbow in his hand, his knuckles white and strained against
the wood. Jack rode six paces behind him, eyes darting
from side to side, fingers resting on the hilt of his sword.

It was impossible to tell how many hours had passed
since the shooting. Lots of them, was Nabber's best
guess. Yet it was still very dark, and whenever he spied
the stars between shifting banks of clouds their positions
hadn't changed. Time passed slowly for the guilty.

Nabber glanced over at Tawl. The knight was staring
straight ahead, intent on keeping to the trail. He hadn't
spoken since they'd upped camp, just silently led the way.
Taken by a sudden impulse, Nabber coughed loudly, pretending to clear his throat. Tawl's head whipped round in
his direction. "Nabber, what's the matter?" he whispered.
"Are you all right?"

Feeling even more guilty than ever, Nabber nodded.
He had just wanted to look at Tawl's face, that was all. He
knew by coughing he would attract Tawl's attention, but
he hadn't counted on his concern. He thought Tawl
would tell him off for making a noise when he should be
quiet. Nabber slumped down in his saddle. That was the
knight's problem: he was just too trusting.

"Tawl, let's swap over," said Jack. "I'll lead the horses
now. You need a break."

Tawl had been leading the horses on foot since they

left the camp. There was no moonlight to light their way and the horses were skittish, so the knight had walked while Jack and Nabber rode.

"I think we'll stop for a while," Tawl said. "We haven't eaten anything all night, and Nabber sounds as if he needs a drink."

Nabber was surprised at Tawl's decision—he hadn't thought they would be getting any rest tonight, not after the shooting—but he wasn't about to argue. He was beginning to feel a desperate need to exchange a few words with the knight.

They pulled off the trail into the cover of some tall pines. Glistening spiderwebs trailed like nets from the slender trees. An owl cried out in the distance and moths fluttered from branch to branch before settling flat against the bark. The minute Nabber clambered down from his horse, he took his waterskin from his pack, and having checked that no one was looking, he emptied the contents into the grass.

"Tawl," he hissed, a moment later, "the skin must have sprung a leak. There's no water left."

Tawl had clambered up a rock and was looking back in the direction they had just come from. "Jack, have you got any water on you?"

"Only a few drops. We'll need to get some more."

"I heard a stream about five minutes ago. It was to the east of the trail, I think." Nabber tried his best to sound nonchalant.

"You two wait here," Tawl said, jumping down from the rock. "I'll be back as soon—"

"No," said Nabber quickly. "Don't go. I wanted you to look at my throat. It feels sore."

Tawl glanced quickly at Nabber.

"I'll go, then," Jack said, looking from Nabber to Tawl. He dismounted his horse and started back up the trail. "Be sure to save some of the cheese and drybread for me."

Tawl waited until Jack was out of sight and then came and stood next to Nabber. "Now that we're alone, what's really the matter?" he said. "I heard you draining the water from your skin."

Even in the dark, the knight's eyes looked very blue. He didn't look angry or amused like other men might in similar situations. He simply looked concerned. Suddenly Nabber wasn't sure he had done the right thing. It was the guilt, of course. It always made him do things that were . . . well . . . just plain *strange*.

"Nabber," said Tawl, speaking softly, "you can tell me anything. Anything at all."

The gentleness in Tawl's voice made everything worse as far as Nabber was concerned. How was he supposed to tell such a trusting and caring man that the one person he revered above all others was rotten to the core?

Nabber sighed. He was going to have to do it all the same. The shooting had changed things, made it harder for him to keep the truth to himself. The instant Jack came rushing through the trees, shouting out that Tawl had been shot at, Nabber knew he'd been wrong to conceal the truth. What if the arrow hadn't missed? What if Tawl had died here, far away from home and the woman he loved, without ever learning the truth? Nabber didn't like to think of things like that. Didn't like to think of Tawl dying—ever. Tawl was his friend, his traveling companion, his *partner*. He trusted Tawl, and Tawl trusted him.

Only ever since the night when he'd stumbled upon Baralis and Tyren meeting in the south side of Bren, he had kept something from him. Something Nabber was certain that Tawl would want to know.

For weeks now, Nabber had kept the truth in, saying to himself that he just had to find the right time and the right place. Tonight had shown him how tenuous life was. Wait too long and the chance might never come again. Nabber looked up at Tawl. He took a quick breath and said, "You know the night when I nearly got caught by Skaythe?" Tawl nodded and he continued. "Well, I didn't run straight back to the townhouse like I said. I hung around the south side of the city making sure I wasn't being followed. That's when I sort of ran into Baralis again."

Tawl was immediately tense. "Did he harm you?"

Nabber shook his head. Somehow nothing he said turned out the way he meant it. "No, he didn't see me. You see, I was in this yard, and there was a horse whose bridle was black. Only it wasn't black, not all the way. Someone had rubbed soot on it to hide the yellow stripes."

"Yellow stripes?" Tawl's voice sounded strained.

"Yes, yellow and black." Nabber knew he had to continue fast and get the whole story over with before Tawl had a chance to say another word. He dashed ahead. "It was Tyren's horse, Tawl. He and Baralis came out into the yard. They'd been having a meeting in the building, and they came out so Tyren could collect his horse. They were talking about Helch, about converting its people, and keeping them on their knees until Kylock had dealt with Highwall." Nabber couldn't look Tawl in the eye. He stared at the knight's boots. "Tyren's a bad man, Tawl. He's gonna kill anyone who spreads rumors against him—I heard him say it. He wants to get his hands on any other territories Kylock conquers, including the south. He's after breaking up the Church."

Nabber wanted to continue talking, but he couldn't think of anything else to say. He risked glancing up at the knight's face. Tawl's gaze was focused on a distant point. A muscle pumped in his cheek.

Without looking at Nabber he said, "It's no secret that Tyren wants to change the face of the Church. Everyone in the knighthood has known that for years. Tyren has always believed that Silbur has had too much influence on the north, and that its priests were becoming soft, forgetting the true word of God."

Nabber didn't like the look on Tawl's face one little bit. He looked dazed, like a sleepwalker or a drunk. "Tawl, I was there. I heard Tyren talking. He didn't sound like a man concerned with the well-being of Helch's people. He sounded . . . " Nabber struggled for the right word ". . . *greedy*."

Tawl's expression hardened. He looked Nabber straight in the eye. "Tyren wouldn't make an agreement with Baralis without good reason. We don't know his true motives. He could be luring Baralis into a trap, fooling him into giving Helch over to the knighthood, trying to catch him out. *Anything*. He could have said all the things he did because he knew they were exactly the sort of things that Baralis wanted to hear."

"But, Tawl—"

"No, Nabber. You're wrong." Tawl went to touch Nabber's arm, but Nabber pulled away. "I know Tyren. He helped me during a very bad time; saved my soul and my life. He isn't the sort of man to become involved in . . . in such an agreement without due cause."

Nabber opened his mouth to say something scathing, but Tawl's eyes were shining and his brow was creased into many lines. He looked worried and upset. Someone had tried to shoot him earlier and would probably try again. Nabber suddenly felt very tired and about as old as he'd ever felt in his life. Tawl was everything to him, *everything*, yet here he was upsetting him, telling him that the one man he respected above all others was a rogue. It wasn't the night for it. He'd been wrong to bring it up now, whilst Tawl was still shaken from the shooting, hurting from parting with Melli, and nervous about the journey ahead. He had enough on his mind without having to deal with the problem of an old friend turning bad.

Tawl looked at Nabber, waiting for a response. Slowly Nabber nodded his head. "Come to think of it, Tawl," he said. "You're right. Tyren could have been up to anything in that yard. It was a dark night, I could hardly see a thing, both men were whispering, and I only caught the final minutes of the meeting. Who knows what went on before?"

Tawl looked at Nabber closely while he was speaking. After a moment he reached out his hand again. Nabber didn't pull away this time, instead letting the knight draw him close to his chest. The knight smelled of good honest things, like sweat, bay leaves, and horses. Unlike Tyren, there was no scented hair oil or slick foreign fragrances to conceal the true smell of the man. Nabber hugged Tawl hard. Although he would never, ever say it, he loved his friend very much.

A minute passed, and then Tawl gently pulled away. "Come on," he said. "Let's go and meet up with Jack. I'm not happy about him being on the path by himself."

Sad, tired, but not in the least bit doubtful that he'd done the right thing, Nabber followed Tawl down the trail.

High atop the palace, high above the lake, a woman stands alone in a room that has no angles, only curves: a tower room with a door that is locked and bolted from the outside.

There is no window, but there is an arrow loop that is shaped like a cross. If she stands upon her toes and presses her body to the stone, she can snatch a view of the stars from the night. The stone is cold against her belly, though—cold and hard and damp. And her legs and feet ache if she stands too long.

She doesn't spend much time looking out.

They do not give her candles at night, so she feels her way to the bench in the dark. Strange, but she has never noticed before just how warm wood can be. Compared to stone it is a living, breathing thing. The wood of the bench is her only comfort, and she wraps her arms around it as if it were a friend.

There are no blankets, so she curls herself up into a ball. The wood can only warm where it touches, so much of her body is chilled. She closes her eyes to shut out *their* dark and to replace it with some dark of her own. Now she only wishes that she could stop her body from shaking with fear and make it shake with cold, instead.

Even though she knows tomorrow will be just the same, she tries very hard to go to sleep. Her dreams scare her more than her surroundings, and she awakens in the middle of the night. Sitting up, she draws her knees under her chin and pushes her lips together very tightly. She will not cry. She is approaching her fourth month of pregnancy, and she doesn't want the sound of her crying to be the first thing her baby ever hears.

Fourteen

Jack urged Barley up to the top of the rise. It was a severe slope and the horse took its time, choosing its steps carefully, like a young boy at his first dance.

The air changed on the way up. It became cooler, faster, fresher, and it began to taste of salt. Barley took the last stretch with growing confidence and Jack eased up on the reins. He even sat back a little on the saddle.

Nothing prepared him for what he saw at the top. Barley scrambled onto the flat ground and Jack looked out at something he'd never seen before in his life: the ocean.

Dark and sparkling, impossibly wide, it stretched out into the territory where the earth met the sky. Above Jack's head seagulls turned and circled, calling and diving, white specks amidst the blue. The air smelled of so many things that were new and unfamiliar. So salty he could taste it, so complex he could never hope to name the parts. Jack's breath was literally taken away and replaced with tidings from the ocean. Caught up in a tangle of emotions and sensations, Jack felt like he'd come home.

They had been traveling for several weeks now. Southeast at first and later just south. They'd skirted around the shores of Lake Herry and crossed the northeastern plains. Meeting up with the mountains in the east, they had followed them down as far as Ness. Two days they spent in the busy farming city. Nabber had enough money in his pack to exchange their horses for better ones, and Tawl had gone missing for the day. Later, when he joined up with them he had a beautifully crafted longbow strapped to his back and a red-haired girl waving him good-bye from the crowd.

Tawl refused to speak about his absence, but later Nabber told Jack that the girl in the crowd had once tried to seduce Tawl, and that Tawl had felt bad about it since. Tawl's mood certainly seemed better after that day, and Nabber wisely concluded that Tawl must have stopped by to apologize. Either that, or *he* had seduced *her* this time.

They spent the next weeks following the mountains farther south, and just today they crossed over to the coast. Tawl said they would be in Toolay by this time tomorrow.

The weather had been with them all the way. Late summer curved into autumn and trees changed their wares from green to gold. The rain, when it fell, was light and warm, and the wind only blew after dark. They made good time up until Nabber was shot in the arm.

It was a shock to all of them. In a way they had grown used to the shadowy presence who was constantly at their backs. Over the past three weeks other arrows had been shot. Expertly aimed, they skimmed breath-close but never hit. Jack had gradually begun to relax—even Tawl had let down his guard. And then five days back an arrow was aimed straight at Nabber's chest. No one had got much sleep since then. Nabber's bone had been chipped and his arm was now resting in a sling. The boy didn't seem too upset by the incident, saying that at least it wasn't his pocketing arm.

Even though things had been quiet since the shooting, Jack suspected they wouldn't remain so for long. Someone was playing a game with them, and if Nabber hadn't suddenly swiveled around to catch an escaping frog, it would have been a deadly one. The arrow had been meant to kill him. It hit the exact spot where, less than a tenth of a second earlier, Nabber's heart had been beating.

Tawl was on his guard day and night. They all were. The problem was that the archer never showed himself. He had a longbow and could fire from the sort of distances that were impossible to spot him over. And he had a definite preference for waiting till dark. Ever since Nabber was wounded, they hadn't had a fire. They couldn't risk one. The flames glowed through the night like a target.

Sometimes they would catch a glimpse of him. When they crossed the plains they had spotted him twice. He was on horseback, that much was clear, but further details were hard to make out. At the time, Tawl had only a shortbow, and the shots he had taken were hardly worth the nocking. Not now, though; he had a beautiful yew-wood longbow. Curving more wickedly than a tavern-maid's hips, it promised that the next time the archer was spotted would be his last.

"Hey! Jack! What you doing mooning over the ocean? Come over here and have some blackberries."

Jack spun around. Tawl and Nabber had reached the top of the bluff ahead of him and were already off their horses and settling down to eat. Jack felt a little disorientated. He wasn't sure how much time had elapsed between him cresting the rise and Nabber calling out. Just how long had he been sitting here, staring at the sea?

Tawl stood up and came over to him. He patted Barley's neck and offered Jack a hand down. "Are you all right?" he said quietly.

"I'm fine. The ocean just"—Jack jumped from his horse—"caught me off guard. I wasn't expecting it."

Tawl took Barley's reins and began leading the horse

toward the makeshift camp. "You've never seen the ocean before, have you?"

"No. Harvell is a long, long way from the sea."

"You know that Larn lies out there in that ocean?"

Jack drew in a quick breath. "Whereabouts?"

Tawl's face looked grim. He turned to the south and then a fraction to the east. "It's a couple of hundred leagues over there."

Jack followed his pointing finger. The horizon was darkening and the sea turned from blue to black. It was about four hours past midday, but the mountains to the west were already taking in the sun for the night. Jack suddenly felt cold. His gaze rested far on the horizon, and it took Tawl's words to pull him back to shore:

"Jack, come on. You need to rest."

Jack turned to face him. The knight's eyes were clear and blue. "Do you feel it, too?" he said.

Tawl looked down. "There's not been a day since I went there that I haven't felt its presence."

The two men stood side by side and watched the ocean glisten like a jewel. The seagulls were quiet now.

Barley broke the spell by pulling against his reins as he sniffed out an especially fragrant clump of grass.

Tawl surprised Jack by calling out to Nabber: "Go and collect all the wood you can find. This looks like a good night for a fire."

Nabber scurried off. Jack waited for Tawl's explanation. The knight refused to meet his eyes, and Jack guessed that he was not the only one who felt chilled to the bone.

An hour later the fire was crackling and bright. Smoked sausages wrapped in dock leaves were warming in the embers, and a jug full of holk sat in the flames. In addition to Tawl's longbow, Ness had provided them with an abundant variety of food. True, all the meat was lamb's meat and the cheese was made from ewe's milk, but up until they reached the city they had been surviving on Nabber's highly subjective ideas of traveling fare, and anything that wasn't sticky with honey or snow-drifted in cinnamon was more than a welcome change.

"Blackberries, anyone?" Nabber held out a handful of berries. When no one came forward to take them, he rubbed his injured arm. "Last time I go collecting fresh fruit for you lot. Risked my neck, I did. And what do I get for it?" Nabber answered his own question. "I'll tell you what I get. Two men looking at me as if I'm offering them poison."

Jack smiled. Nabber was very astute when it came to sensing mood changes. He saw that he and Tawl were quiet, counted this as unacceptable behavior, and decided to lighten the atmosphere with a spirited burst of self-pity.

"Here. Give me the berries," Jack said. "I'll eat them."

"What, all of them?"

"Yes. Even the ones with the slug trails on them."

"Slug trails! There's no slugs been on these beauties. Why, slugs couldn't even fit on 'em."

The look of wild indignation on Nabber's face made Jack laugh. After a moment Tawl joined in. It was easy to feel protective toward Nabber. Even with his brusque, I-can-look-after-myself manner, the boy could not conceal his vulnerability or his youth. The night he was shot he hadn't cried once. And although he *had* fainted, he held that it wasn't a girlish sick sort of faint, but rather a manly, pain-blocking, strength-saving sort of faint.

There had been a lot of blood. The arrowhead was wide and soft. Nabber's bone bent the metal as it broke. As always the fletchings were crafted from red silk and human hair. Jack didn't know what it meant, but he suspected that both Tawl and Nabber did.

Jack glanced quickly at Tawl. The knight was measuring the length of his arrows against his chest. More than a thumb-length past his fingers, and he cut the arrow short.

"Why the fire, Tawl?"

Tawl dropped the arrow he was shortening, then brushed his hair from his face. "Look around, Jack. Why do you think I brought us here?"

Jack did as he was asked. They had camped upon a small rocky cliffside. Directly ahead of them lay the ocean, below them lay more rocks, and behind them lay the hills that they had spent the best part of the day crossing. In all directions the view was unhindered. The world was laid out below them, and the full moon illuminated every bush and strand of grass.

"You're laying a trap."

"You could say that. If our mysterious friend tries anything tonight, I'm counting on spotting him first."

"He's not so mysterious, though, is he?"

Tawl sucked in his breath. "I think I know who he is."

"Who?"

"A man whose brother I killed."

"You didn't kill him, Tawl. You beat him fair and square." It was Nabber, stepping forward to defend his friend. "That Skaythe's just a mad devil. That's all."

"How do you know it's him?" Jack felt annoyed for some reason.

"The red silk on the arrows," said Nabber. "Same color as they use in the pits."

"And the hair?"

"Well, I couldn't testify to it myself, but it looks about the same color as Blayze's. Doesn't it, Tawl?"

"Why only tell me this now?" Jack was looking at Tawl and his voice held an accusation.

"Because he's not interested in you, Jack. He wants me."

"Didn't stop him from shooting Nabber, though, did it?"

Tawl whipped around. "What is your point?"

"My point is that you should have told me. The danger here concerns all of us, and at the very least you owe me the truth. I will not be treated like a child who needs protecting. If there's trouble coming, I want to know exactly what to expect." By the time Jack had finished speaking he was shaking.

A minute passed. The wind picked up a little, blowing sparks from the fire toward the sea.

Tawl took a deep breath and then spoke. "You're right, Jack. I'm sorry, I should have told you everything the minute I guessed what was happening." He looked Jack straight in the eye. He didn't lessen his apology by making excuses. After a few seconds, he said, "So, how are you with a bow?"

Jack smiled, recognizing Tawl's attempt to include him in his plan. "Not good," he said.

Tawl had moved over to the horses. He untied the shortbow from the back of the gelding and handed it to Jack. "How about me giving you a few lessons while we wait?"

"Do you think we'll have to wait long?"

"As long as it takes." Tawl looked over at the hills. Nothing moved that the wind wasn't blowing. "All night, perhaps."

Jack tested the string on the bow. "Then you just might have time to teach me a thing or two."

Tavalisk was in his chamber enjoying a fine meal of slow-roasted dove, whilst he and his aide discussed various details concerning the siege at Bren. There was nothing like eating a bird of peace when one's tongue was busy wagging about the war. The birds themselves were a little scrawny, of course. But the archbishop found that nothing savored a dish better than a healthy sprinkling of whimsy. Besides, the doves were only the start. The fatted calf was next.

"Gamil, you slice it from shoulder to flank. Not the other way round." Tavalisk was having his aide do the duties of his cook. "Not so thin, either, Gamil. I want to be able to chew on the slices, not wear them as an under-garment."

"Yes, Your Eminence."

"Now then, have we discovered how Kylock learnt about the two thousand mercenaries yet?" Tavalisk took a dove and broke its spine. The meat slipped off more easily that way.

"No, Your Eminence. But someone obviously informed him, for he not only knew their numbers, but he also knew the exact route they would be taking to get to Bren."

"That was certainly some ambush. Fifteen hundred men killed! Their horses slaughtered and their equipment flung into the lake. It was an outright disaster!" Tavalisk was so upset that he let the dovemeat slide to the floor. He had lost his taste for fowl. "Kylock is always one step ahead of us. If we mine a tunnel, he knows it. If we send supplies, he steals them. If we change our strategies, then he changes his before we've even made a move. Someone is feeding him information, and I want to know who it is."

"I will look into it, Your Eminence," said Gamil, placing slices of calf on a platter.

The sight of red meat heartened the archbishop. "Have we any news about Annis?"

"Nothing's changed, Your Eminence. It's a very strange situation. The backbone of the Four Kingdoms' army is still camped outside the city. They're engaging in a sort of half-hearted siege: keeping a round-the-clock watch on the walls, whilst never getting close enough to incur any damage."

"It's not strange at all, Gamil. It's brilliant. By laying siege to Annis, Kylock is not only wearing the good people of the city down, but he's also preventing their army from fighting at Bren. No man is going to leave his home to fight someone else's battle when his own country is in danger." Tavalisk took the platter from Gamil.

"Kylock is effectively keeping Annis under lock and key. And it's costing him nothing to do so."

Tavalisk speared a chunk of meat with his little silver skewer. "What worries me is that at any point Kylock could give the order for his troops to up stakes and cross the mountains. Now, if that happens, the Highwall army is in serious danger of being outflanked."

Gamil nodded slowly. "Yes, Your Eminence does have a point."

Tavalisk certainly did have a point, and he used it now to spear Gamil's arm. "If I wanted condescension, Gamil, I would go to God. Not you." Removing the silver skewer from his aide's flesh, Tavalisk said, "Slip of the wrist, Gamil, I had intended to spear the calf."

Gamil did not look pleased.

"Come on now, Gamil. Stop sulking. It was only an accident." Feeling a tiny bit contrite, the archbishop offered his napkin to wipe away the blood, then quickly changed the subject. "So, is Maybor's daughter still under lock and key?"

Gamil got what revenge he could by bleeding profusely onto the silk napkin. "No one has heard anything about her since Lord Maybor left the city, Your Eminence. Baralis and Kylock are both denying knowing anything about the abduction. They're claiming that Maybor is a madman."

"But they do have her, though?"

"Either that or they've already killed her."

"It makes no difference to us if she's alive or dead, Gamil. As long as no one can be sure what has become of her, we can still go on fighting in her name." Tavalisk ran a chubby finger along the rim of the platter. "Has she any support within the city?"

Gamil shook his head. "Anyone who openly supports the Lady Melliandra is seized by Kylock's forces and hanged by the neck. The executions are carried out in public for all the city to see."

"Hmm. And what of those who support the good lady in secret?"

"A fair number of noblemen have gone missing in the past months, Your Eminence. They disappear from their quarters in the middle of the night, leaving friends and family frantic."

"Missing, eh?" Tavalisk's smile was almost wistful.

Gamil cleared his throat. "I did take the liberty of having our spies look into the matter, Your Eminence. I've learned that Kylock has secret intelligence sources placed throughout the city. Any lord who as much as breathes Melliandra's name over the dinner table is likely to disappear."

Tavalisk sighed. "Too bad. If Kylock wasn't cracking down so hard, I'm sure the city would be liable to turn tail."

"Lord Maybor is causing quite a fuss in the Highwall camp, though, Your Eminence. He's got all sorts of plans to infiltrate the city and bring the siege to an early end."

Tavalisk waved an *I told you so*. "I always knew the time would come when he would need my help, Gamil. See to it that he gets whatever manpower and resources he requires. Might as well let him have a go. The Highwall generals have been sadly lacking in brilliance so far. A few wall breaches are nothing to get excited about."

"Very well, Your Eminence. If there is nothing further, may I take my leave?"

"By all means." Tavalisk smiled like a concerned passerby. "I'd pay a visit to the surgeon on the way out, if I were you, Gamil. That cut looks like it might need a stitching."

Melli forced herself to eat the last of the bread. She had no water left, so she swallowed it dry. Next, she turned her attention to the pork joint. It was mostly skin and fat, but she tore away at it as if it were the finest meat. She didn't want to, but she *had* to. And she would eat a lot worse if it came to it.

The light was beginning to fail. A thin streak of gold caught the edge of the arrow loop, and Melli knew from experience that it would soon fade away. The *anticipation* of darkness was the worst thing of all—much worse than the darkness itself. At this time Melli always felt tense. She would look around the small curved room, memorizing. Then she would make last-minute adjustments, moving her bowl, shifting the straw, chasing the beetles from the bench. Last of all, just as the daylight skimmed softly out of sight, she would glance down at her belly and whisper words of comfort to her child.

True darkness is hard to come by. Melli had spent every night of her life in the dark, but the darkness of a comfortable chamber—with candlelight creeping under the door and embers glowing softly in the hearth—was a world apart from the darkness she knew now. Some nights it was like being in a grave. If you can't see your hand in front of your face, it's easy to believe you don't exist. That was how Melli felt when there was no moon— as if somehow the world had passed her by.

So the words of comfort were really for herself, but it suited her to pretend they were for the child.

Melli now kept track of the moon. Tonight she was expecting a full one. Whether or not she would see it depended on the clouds. The great lake often allowed sunlight in the day, only to send the clouds in overnight. Melli hadn't yet come up with a way of predicting the cloud cover, but she always knew when it would rain.

Being pregnant had done it. When her ankles began to ache with a needling fussy pain and her legs swelled slowly like rising dough, then it was a sure sign that the skies were going to open, and icy little droplets would soon come spitting through the loop.

Facing the lake as it did, the arrow loop was an open invitation to the wind and the rain. For the first week or so it was warm. Flies would buzz up from the water and the sun would warm the back of the stone. Now, a month later, the weather was changeable. Suffering from the growing pains of winter, it couldn't really decide what it wanted to do: one minute it would rain and howl, the next the sun would come out and cast a remorseful rainbow across the lake. Yesterday there had even been hailstones.

The nights were always cold. Bren was at the mercy of the mountains after dark. The temperature dropped sharply and the wind stopped blowing and started cutting, instead.

Once, Melli had attempted to block the arrow loop off with her shawl. It hadn't worked. The wind just blew it back against the wall.

Melli tried to keep track of the days as best she could. At first she had made marks against the stone: one line for every day. But after two weeks the lines began to mount up, and what had started out as a record began to take on the look of a last will and testament. She imagined people finding her body and shaking their heads sadly as they counted all the lines.

For the most part, Melli tried to keep macabre thoughts at the back of her mind. She told herself that if they were going to kill her, they would surely have done it by now.

She was brought food and water once a day. Two guards came. One unlocked the door, let his friend with the tray pass, and then held a halberd in her face until yesterday's tray and chamberpot had been retrieved. Melli had tried asking them for warm clothes, candles, and some wood to block the loop, but they didn't acknowledge her voice. Wouldn't even look her in the eyes. Obviously they were under strict orders from someone. Someone they were so scared of that they hardly dared to breathe in her presence, lest they risk provoking the man's displeasure.

Baralis. It was no other. There was no one to match him when it came to breeding fear. He was certainly doing a good job on her. If he had come to visit her just once—if only to refuse her requests, or gloat over her ever-worsening state—then she would have feared him less. She could hold her own with any man. She knew that if she saw Baralis in person, the myth she had created in his absence would be dispelled.

But he didn't come. And so her mind created a monster and his motives, and she had a nagging little feeling that that had been his intention all along. He wanted her to be afraid. It pleased him: fear was at the heart of his power.

He didn't get it all his own way, though. No, not at all. She was strong. It would take more than solitude and walls of rounded stone to break her back. They fed her slops; she ate them. They refused to bring her blankets; she did without them. They took away the light, and like a fungus she flourished in the dark. She would not give in to Baralis and his henchmen. She and her baby were not merely surviving, they were growing tougher and more vital by the day.

Melli heard a distant banging. She paid it no attention—with the siege going on the night was full of noises. The banging came again, nearer this time. Melli stood very still. This was no Highwall siege engine. Light as thin as smoke crept under the door. Someone was coming.

All her earlier bravado drained away faster than water down a grate. No one ever came at night. No one.

The banging turned into distinct footsteps. The light was now a band around the door. Melli steadied herself against the stone wall. She was shaking. There was something hard blocking her throat. She drew her hand down to her belly and lifted her head high as the key turned in the lock.

The door swung open. Melli was dazzled by the light. A figure stood in the doorway. From his shape, she knew it was Baralis. Slowly, he drew the lantern up to his face.

Fifteen

So, what did you really feel when you saw the ocean?"
Tawl sat hunched close to the fire. The longbow was to
his left and the arrows were to his right. He tended the
fire, but his eyes looked to the hills.

Nabber was sleeping. He'd grown quickly bored of the
archery. Wrapping himself up in all the good blankets, he
had extracted solemn promises from both Tawl and Jack to
wake him up if anything happened, and then promptly fell
asleep. That was about an hour ago now, and Nabber's
vibrant snoring could currently be heard above the breeze.

It was very bright on the bluff. The full moon shone
on the chalky cliffs and the ash-colored rocks and then
bounced the light created down to the hills below. There
weren't many nights like this in the year. Nights when
there was enough light to teach a man archery by.

Jack was on the opposite side of the fire. He lay on his
blanket and looked up at the stars. He didn't answer
Tawl's question.

Perhaps he hadn't heard. It was late, he was tired, the
wind might have blown the question out to sea. Tawl
didn't repeat it. They had both had a long day.

Searching in his pack, Tawl pulled out a small jar of
beeswax. He scooped some into a cloth and began to work
it into the bow. The best way to stay awake all night was
never to let your hands or mind be idle.

"It was like recognizing a long lost friend."

At first Tawl didn't realize what Jack was talking about. The question had drifted from his thoughts.

Jack continued speaking. "I knew it. The smells, the sound, the colors—they were all familiar, and yet"—with his hand, he made a small helpless gesture—"strange. Foreign. Like something I'd dreamt about long ago."

Jack's voice sounded small and lost. Tawl had to remind himself that he was little more than a boy. Not through his twentieth year yet. He'd been given no choice, no guidance. Nothing to prepare him for what was to come. Yet he was here anyway, trying very hard to appear calm on the outside, while he quietly worked through the chaos underneath.

Tawl wiped the wax from his fingers. It was different for *him*—he'd had years to prepare for this. Bevlin had given him plenty of warning. And at the end of the day, it was always his choice to be a knight, to search for truth and honor, to take risks and *"find merit in the eyes of God."* Jack had no creed to follow.

He was on his own.

"Tawl, tell me the prophecy again."

The request took Tawl by surprise. It was the last thing he expected. Glancing quickly over at Jack, he saw that the boy was still looking at the stars.

Tawl began to say the prophecy:

"When men of honor lose sight of their cause . . ."

As he spoke the first line, Tawl heard his voice faltering. The words might have been written for him alone: *he* was the one who had lost sight of his allegiances and his oaths. He was the one who had brought the knighthood into disrepute. Not Tyren, as Nabber had tried to tell him, but *he* himself.

Tawl swallowed hard. The pain was always there inside him—it never got any smaller, or hurt any less, just shifted gradually into discernible layers: each one a band of steel around his heart. Dropping his gaze to the ground, Tawl took two deep breaths to calm himself before continuing. No matter how hard things got, he had no choice but to carry on.

> *"When three bloods are savored in one day*
> *Two houses will meet in wedlock and wealth*
> *And what forms at the join is decay*
> *A man will come with neither father nor mother"*

As Tawl paused to take a speaking breath, Jack shifted his position on his blanket, moving closer toward the fire. The light from the flames fell upon his hair, brightening it with colors that the moonlight had all but robbed. Colors of chestnut and gold. Tawl's mind skimmed over the next line of verse.

> *But sister as lover*

In that instant, a small warning sounded in his head. He didn't give it any thought, didn't question it in any way, but when he spoke, he found he'd skipped the line entirely:

> *"And stay the hand of the plague*
>
> *The stones will be sundered, the temple will fall*
> *The dark empire's expansion will end at his call*
> *And only the fool knows the truth."*

Everything was quiet after he finished. Jack didn't move, the wind didn't blow, even the ocean stopped sending waves to the shore.

Tawl knew he had to break the silence. More for his own good than for Jack's. There was nothing to do in the silence but think. And Tawl did not want to spend a minute speculating about what he'd just done and why.

"Does any of it mean anything to you?" he asked.

Jack's reply was slow in coming. "Yes and no," he said at last. "My mother is dead, and I never had a father. And I suppose the two houses that meet are Bren and the kingdoms."

Tawl nodded. He was glad of the opportunity to shift his thoughts onto less treacherous ground. "And the men who have lost their honor are the knights. The temple is Larn and the dark empire is being forged as we speak."

"Kylock."

There was something akin to longing in Jack's voice as he spoke, and Tawl turned his head to look at him. No longer staring at the stars, he was enthralled by the flames.

"You knew him, didn't you?"

Jack nodded. His gaze didn't leave the fire. "I think I'm meant to destroy him."

Tawl felt his spine prickle as surely as if someone had poured ice down his back. Out of the corner of his eye he spotted a thin line of light. It moved upward as he watched. Already unnerved from what Jack had just said, Tawl was immediately on his guard. Keeping his gaze even, he whispered, "Lie down slowly, Jack. Pretend you're bedding down for the night."

Jack faked a yawn, smoothed out his blanket, and lay down. His face was turned to the hills. His hand was on the shortbow. "Where is he?" he hissed.

"On the hill to the left, a third of the way down. Just above the tree line." Tawl barely moved as he spoke. He kept staring straight ahead. It was the archer. No doubt about it. He was on foot, and as he walked his bow caught the light of the moon. Tawl couldn't see the man's horse, but he guessed it was hidden back in the trees.

Slowly Tawl reached for an arrow. As his hand closed around the shaft, he spoke to Jack: "On my word throw the blanket on the fire."

The shadowy figure in the distance stopped moving. The light slanted upward as he raised his bow.

They would only have a split second once the archer saw the light go out. The opportunity was too good to miss, though. Skaythe was now a standing target.

Tawl snatched his own bow from the ground. He nocked the arrow and drew back the string.

"Now, Jack. *Now!*"

Tawl aimed his arrow.

The light went out.

The bend of Skaythe's elbow told of a bow drawn and ready. Tawl kissed the string and then relaxed his hold. The arrow exploded from the plate and shot toward its target.

The instant his fingers were free of the string, Tawl dove toward the fire. He heard the whir of an arrow, felt the head graze past his face. A hot searing pain followed, then the fletchings brushed against his cheek.

He slammed onto the blanket. It was hot and smoking. His momentum sent his body careening into Jack.

Jack had the shortbow up and nocked. Tawl grabbed his ankle and brought him down.

"Did I hit him?" Tawl could barely breathe. His right eye was full of blood. He twisted Jack's ankle, preventing him from standing.

"I don't know. He went down maybe a second after you." Jack kicked against the grip. "If you hadn't pulled me down, I would have got a shot at him. I had him in my sights even after he'd hit the ground."

Behind them, Nabber shifted in his blankets. "What's going on?"

"*Stay down.*" Tawl wiped his eye. The cut was on his right cheekbone and the blood was flowing into the socket. "Where is he now?" he asked Jack. He still couldn't see properly.

"He's gone. In between you pulling me down and me looking up again, he got away."

Tawl hissed a curse. Skaythe would have made it below the tree line by now. If he had been hit, it obviously hadn't been fatal. The fact that he fell to the ground meant nothing. They both knew what game they were playing: two archers, two arrows, two shots. It was a duel. Skaythe would have had the same instinct *he* had—release the string, then get the hell away.

Tawl almost admired the man. He had loosed a fine arrow.

"Come on," he said, standing up. "It's about time we upped camp."

"I ain't getting up. No, sir," said Nabber from the ground. "No one's gonna take a free shot at me."

Tawl tore a strip from his linen undershirt and pressed it against the cut on his cheek. "He won't bother us again tonight."

"Why? Did you get him?"

"Perhaps. I don't know."

"If you can't be sure," said Jack, "what makes you think he won't fire again?"

"Because it's not what he wants."

"So what *does* he want, then?"

Tawl looked into the distance, searching for the spot where he'd last seen Skaythe. "He wants a contest, Jack. He wants to beat me one on one. That's what he got tonight: me against him, even odds, my skills pitted against his."

"Why?"

"Revenge for his brother. A chance to prove he can beat the man who beat Blayze." Tawl shrugged. "I don't know his motives." He began to move around the camp, putting pots and flasks in his sack.

"So what do you think he's doing now?" Jack's voice was hard. He hadn't liked being kept in the dark about the mysterious archer.

"If he's injured, then he'll lie low until tomorrow when we're well out of the way. If not, then he'll probably follow us south. Either way he'll be planning his next attack."

"But what if you got a real good hit, Tawl?" said Nabber, finally plucking up the courage to rise from his blanket.

"Then I've slowed him down by a few days. Perhaps even weeks. I just don't know." Tawl crossed over to the horses and threw the saddle on the back of the gelding.

Jack was one step behind him. "This man might want some sort of duel with you, but he's not above killing Nabber and me in cold blood. Is he?"

Tawl looked quickly to Nabber. The boy was busy rolling up his blanket. "Look," he said quietly, intending his words for Jack alone, "I think you're right. I think he's out to kill all of us. Now I've got to stop him, but he's good, and he's tracking us as if we were game. The only time he'll come out in the open is to take a shot at me. You and Nabber he'll shoot from the shade. That's why I've got to make myself a target—like tonight. Our only chance of killing him is when he's intent on killing *me*." Tawl fastened the girth around the gelding's belly. "So that leaves us with no choice: we've got to force him to come out and fight."

"Why didn't you let me take a shot at him?"

"You have a shortbow. He has a longbow. You were making yourself vulnerable for no reason."

"It wasn't because you wanted to play his game, too? Beat him man to man?"

Tawl shook his head. "No. A man who'll shoot a defenseless boy in the dark deserves no such honor. You spot him, Jack, you kill him. That's fine with me. I'll pull you down every time, though, if I think you haven't got a chance in hell of hitting him."

Jack smiled. "I see your point." He began strapping the saddlebags in place. "So, I suppose we'll be purchasing our second longbow in Toolay?"

Tawl felt tired but pleased. In his own way, Jack was telling him that he wouldn't be left out of this. It was a good feeling to know that someone else was willing to share the danger.

"You'll need to practice," he said. "If there's an archer in you, I haven't seen him yet."

They both laughed. Tawl reached out and clasped Jack's arm.

Jack returned the grip. "I appreciate you being honest with me."

"And I appreciate all the help I can get."

The two men stood for a moment, both looking at each other, revising their opinions. For the first time in many weeks, Tawl felt that everything might just turn out all right.

Up came the lamp. Melli's eyes strained to find detail in the brightness. Instinctively she took a step back. Her ankle struck stone. There was nowhere for her to go.

On its way up, the light cast long shadows over the man's face, turning it into a savage mask. He took a step forward.

"It's been such a long time, Melliandra."

Melli took a sharp breath. It wasn't Baralis, it was Kylock. They were perfectly matched in figure and height. Even their coloring was the same. Melli felt a growing sense of dread. At least with Baralis she knew what to expect; he was calculating, cunning, a man of method. But Kylock was a different creature altogether. A dangerously unstable one.

Determined not to show fear, Melli tilted her chin upward and said, "So, have you come to set me free?"

Ignoring her, he looked around the room. His dark hair shone sleekly in the lamplight. Dressed in a black kidskin tunic and black silk undershirt, he looked as if he had just come from an official dinner. After a few seconds he nodded softly. "Not doing too well now, are we, Melliandra?"

"I'd be doing a lot worse if I'd married you. Your wife was cold before the wedding night was over."

Melli felt something hard slam against her face. She

went toppling backward, banging her head against the wall.

Kylock stood over her, wiping his fist on his tunic. "I'd be careful what you say if I were you, Melliandra. Your tongue's too glib by far."

Melli rubbed her aching jaw. She moved to stand up, but Kylock pushed her down.

"I think I'll have you stay where you are for the moment." He spoke like a painter posing a model. Stretching forward, he brushed a lock of hair from her face. "Yes, just there."

Melli tasted blood in her mouth. She didn't dare move. Kylock's eyes were blank and unfocused. He looked like he'd been drinking.

In a movement so swift, Melli thought he was going to strike her, he came and knelt at her side. He saw her flinch and smiled. "Not so sure of yourself now, eh?"

His breath held no trace of alcohol, but there was an unnatural sweetness to it. There were a few specks of white powder on the corner of his lip.

"You know what I think?" he said.

"No. Why don't you tell me?" Without realizing, Melli had slid both her arms around her stomach. She wanted desperately to lash out at Kylock, both physically and verbally, but she stopped herself. She had her baby to think of now.

"I think you deserve better than this." His hand came up, but this time he stroked her cheek.

Melli preferred the slapping. "Is that why you came here?" she said, slowly edging her cheek away from his touch.

Kylock was very close now. The skin on his face was very pale. There were dark circles under his eyes. "I came to see how they were treating you."

"Well, as you can see, *they* are treating me badly." Melli wasn't really sure who he was referring to: Baralis, the guards, perhaps both.

"Hmm." Kylock's hand moved down from her cheek to her throat. His fingertips were as soft as a baby's.

Melli wrapped her arms more tightly across her stomach, and then asked the only question worth asking: "Why come here now? I've been here weeks, you could have seen me at any point."

Kylock smiled softly, curving his beautifully sculpted lips upward. "Baralis wants you executed tomorrow."

Very still. She kept herself very still. Not a single muscle on her face betrayed her. She didn't blink, didn't tremble, didn't form any expression at all. She still breathed, though. Long, deep breaths.

"Yes, they're going to come for you in the morning. The water they give you will be drugged to make you . . . " Kylock took pleasure choosing the right phrase, "more compliant. Then they will put a blade through your heart. You'll never have to leave this room, it will all happen here." He smiled as if doing her a great courtesy.

"When the two guards have finished, they will lock the door and descend the stairs, only to be slaughtered before they reach the last step. After that's done, the lady who supervises your comforts will also meet an unfortunate end. And that will leave no one to tell of what happened."

All the time he was speaking, Kylock's hand was on her throat. Now that he had finished, he moved it lower. Down to her breast and then along to her belly. "That's the plan, anyway."

Melli made no attempt to move away from him. She let his hand rest where it was. Her mind had seized on the tone of Kylock's voice as he spoke his last sentence. Was it reluctance she detected? Inching her little finger forward to touch his, she tested him. "*Is* the plan, or *was* the plan?"

He pulled back from her. With his other hand he raised the lantern, bringing it close to her face. "No rouge on *your* lips, I see."

Melli's heart was beating fast. The lantern was so close she could feel it hot against her cheek. Despite all her efforts, she felt the beginnings of panic. She didn't know what Kylock wanted from her. Couldn't understand the shift in conversation. "No," she said, feeling as if she were stumbling in the dark. "Not on mine."

Kylock brought the lantern closer. The flame was now less than an eyelash length from her face. "You've never painted yourself like a whore, have you?"

Melli felt her skin burn. She could take it no longer. She raised up her fist and sent it smashing into Kylock's arm.

Kylock lost his grip on the lantern. It flew into the air. Melli heard it clatter against the stone. The light wavered. Kylock's fist punched into her jaw. All the bones in her neck cracked at once. Kylock fell on top of her, tearing at her clothes.

She screamed.

He placed his hand right under her jaw and slammed her head into the back of the wall.

Pain burst into her skull. The world shot out of focus. Still she screamed.

She felt Kylock's fingers probing under her bodice. She fought him, but her hands weren't responding the way they should. She felt like she was drunk. He got a grip of the fabric and ripped the bodice from her.

Through eyes that saw everything as blurred, Melli became aware of a bright glow behind Kylock's shoulder. The rushes on the floor had caught on fire.

Either sensing the heat or smoke, Kylock pulled away from her. Standing up, he kicked the thin layer of rushes with his boot, sending them to the far side of the room. The wooden bench was near Melli's foot and so was removed from the danger. Everything else was stone. Kylock stamped at the rushes around the edge of the blaze. The flames licked at his shins. Spinning around for something to dampen them with, he stopped in his tracks.

Melli hadn't moved. Her breasts and torso were bare. The curve of her belly was highlighted by the flames.

Kylock stared at her. He stared at her swollen stomach.

As Melli watched, she saw his expression change. The blind look of rage crystallized into madness. In that instant she felt fear so concentrated that it pushed the air from her lungs. She felt it rush through her lips like her last chance of hope.

Kylock's gaze rose to her eyes. Behind him the fire began to dim, muffled by the stone and frustrated by the lack of fuel. The room became thick with smoke. The vacuum in Melli's lungs was like a hunger. She needed to breathe, but was afraid of drawing in a substance more deadly than smoke. The back of her skull was bleeding. She felt the blood trickle down her neck. Her eyes were watering.

The smoke was black and speckled with soft burnt flakes. Kylock raised his hands and took a step toward her. Melli opened her lips and took in the smoke. For a second her body resisted her and she started to choke, but she fought it, breathing in more and more. The smoke was bitter at first. Hot and acrid, it burnt her lungs. But then Kylock's hands were upon her, and what had been her poison became her savior.

The world fell away and left Melli in the dark.

By the time Skaythe dragged himself into the trees, his tunic was soaked in blood. He had taken the arrow high on his left shoulder blade, and the tip had pierced his bone. He had crawled to safety on his stomach, using his right arm to pull himself forward.

His horse was tethered to a slender ash tree and she whinnied softly as she caught his scent. "Ssh, Kali," he murmured.

The trees still carried most of their foliage and the leaves cut out much of the moonlight. Skaythe preferred it that way. He always worked better in the dark.

Grasping hold of a nearby tree trunk, he hauled himself off the ground. Pain coursed down his side. He felt physically sick and had to stop himself from vomiting by holding back his head and gulping hard. His left hand made a fist just as his right did. Good. That meant the muscles in his arm would be all right.

After a moment the nausea passed, leaving nothing but a sharp taste in his mouth. He stood up all the way and then rested against the trunk for support. Making a soft clicking noise with his tongue, he urged his horse forward. The filly came as near as her reins permitted, and Skaythe was able to take the saddlebag from her back.

More pain and nausea followed as his shoulders bore the weight of the bag. He found what he needed: ointment, sharp knife, linen bandages, and a small flask of hard liquor. He took the liquor first, drinking all but a mouthful in one go. It burned a path down his throat and then glowed like an ember in his belly. He had to work quickly now: liquor like this didn't leave much time between dulling your senses and robbing you of your wits. The last of the liquor he poured onto half the bandage and then cleaned the area around the wound, the bottom portion of the arrow shaft, the blade of his knife, and his fingers.

He had already broken the shaft halfway down, and about a hand's length of wood now projected from his shoulder blade. Taking the knife, he cut into the wound, opening the flesh to either side of the arrowhead. The knight had used a standard V-shaped blade. Just the sort of head you'd expect a man of honor to use. Not barbed, not razored, not beveled. Skaythe shrugged. He had pointed a barbed, serrated head the knight's way.

Once he'd freed the flesh on each side of the V, Skaythe took the remaining shaft in his hand, willed his body to stay relaxed, and pulled the arrowhead free.

The pain was hot, white, and clawing. It shot down his arm and across to his heart. Urine splashed down his leg.

Even though he had made space for the V, the edges still gouged flesh as they went. He didn't scream. He never screamed—even as a child.

Once the head was out, Skaythe slumped back against the tree. Taking the other half of the bandage, he pressed it hard against the wound. His blood was black in the moonlight. He was weakening fast. The liquor was reaching the point where it robbed him of his wits.

As he held the cloth to his shoulder blade he cursed Tawl with all the hate of a man defeated. The knight had taken a chance—he had deliberately aimed his arrow to the left. Tawl had bet that he would jump, and then taken a further bet on which way he was likely to go. Skaythe had thought he was leaping to safety, but he had been leaping straight into the arrow's path. If the knight had aimed his arrow straight at the heart, then he would have emerged without a scratch. But no, he had pointed his sights at thin air, and by doing so drawn blood instead.

Skaythe shook his head grimly. The blood was slow to stop.

There was one consolation to be drawn from tonight's match, however. Tawl had been lucky, that was all. Skaythe knew all about luck, and he knew that, without exception, it always ran out in the end. A man who was lucky one day would likely be cursed the next. So when he met Tawl again, the odds would be in his favor.

And he would meet Tawl again.

Tomorrow he would find someone to stitch up the wound. After that he'd probably need to rest for a few days, to give the skin time to heal. In the short term he might lose track of the knight, but ultimately he knew where Tawl was heading, knew where he would return to, and with just one sending from Baralis, Skaythe could find him in the dark.

Sixteen

*T*he wind was lively and smelled of fish. The morning came early and bright. The white buildings of Toolay trailed golden shadows in the sunrise, and the sea played songs for the cliffs.

They had traveled all night and were weary, but somehow the sight of the little city perched high above the ocean acted like breakfast and tonic in one. Jack knew he wasn't the only one to feel it; Nabber's face lit up and he muttered a long and happy sentence in which the words *prospecting* and *at last* were repeated several times. Even Tawl seemed pleased. He couldn't smile much, though. The cut on his cheek might be stretched open by a smile.

"Goat's milk and ale," he said, urging his horse forward.

"Goat's milk and ale?" Jack kicked his heels into his gelding's flank. He wasn't about to let Tawl get to the city first.

Tawl's eyes twinkled brighter than the sea. "That's what they serve a man for breakfast here."

There was a little furtive rivalry in the air. Jack could clearly see Tawl building up for a gallop. "What do they serve the women, then?"

"I've seen the women here, Jack," said Nabber. "And by the looks of them, they get just the ale."

With that, Tawl's horse sped ahead, leaving Nabber's muffled cries of complaint in its wake. Jack chased after them. It felt good to be here, right now, with the sun warming his face and the wind salting his lips, riding through dust left by friends.

Friends they might be, but he was still going to beat them. Jack dug his heels deeper and gave Barley his reins. Tawl's horse was more powerful, but it had to carry two. Barley found reserves of strength and was soon on their tail. Nabber kept his head low, whilst his voice bellowed like a foghorn:

"This is the last time I'll ever get on a horse with you, Tawl!"

Jack smiled as Barley passed them. "I don't blame you, Nabber," he yelled. "It's only worth riding with the best." He didn't risk turning to look at them. First, because he didn't want Tawl to see him smile, and second, he was terrified. He'd never ridden this fast before. Beneath him, Barley had turned from a sweet and gentle creature to a warhorse on the charge. All Jack could do was hang on and hope for leniency.

On his way to victory, Barley demonstrated latent talents for jumping over ditches, picking paths through rocks, and delaying his swerves around trees until the last possible moment.

Finally, horse and rider made it onto the high road. Seeing carts, people, and other horses had a profound effect on Barley and, like a naughty child in front of visitors, he became a model of good behavior. He slowed his pace to a trot and even stepped to the side to let people in a hurry pass. Jack was so grateful that he'd stopped galloping that he didn't have the heart to chide him. He merely whispered in his ear, "If you've any more tricks up your sleeve, save them for your next master."

"Hey! Jack!" Tawl and Nabber drew level with him. Tawl reached over and patted Barley's flank. "If I'd known he was that good, I would have picked him for myself."

Jack had the distinct feeling that if it wasn't for the

newly scabbed cut on his face, Tawl would be laughing out loud by now. "Come on, then," he said, urging Barley forward. "We can't keep the goats waiting."

The city of Toolay was bustling. Merchants, farmers, barrow-boys, and fishermen crowded the narrow, winding streets. People were shouting their wares, calling greetings to acquaintances, haggling, harping, and gossiping. Jack liked the place immediately, his only reservation being that there were a lot of geese roaming the streets. Having been chased by a pack of the vicious, honking birds last spring, the only acceptable goose to him was now a roast one.

Suddenly feeling hungry, Jack was glad when Tawl picked a nearby tavern to stop at. The Lobster's Legs was small and cozy. The tavern-keeper, a hearty red-jowled man named Blaxer, greeted them warmly, sending out a boy to look after their horses and personally warming the goat's milk himself. His exceedingly handsome son brought them a breakfast of hot oatmeal and cold lobster, and then offered to prepare them a room.

Jack hoped Tawl would agree. They hadn't slept at all last night, and the idea of sleeping in a comfortable, safe bed rather than on hard ground out in the open was pleasing to say the least. Tawl looked quickly at Nabber. The boy stifled a theatrical yawn.

"Very well. We'll stay the night here and leave for Rorn in the morning."

The tavern-keeper's son nodded politely, poured ale into their goat's milk, and then took his leave. His father watched all this from the corner of the room, his face bright with paternal pride.

They ate their breakfast in silence, all of them too tired, or hungry, or caught up in their own thoughts to talk. After they had finished, Tawl stood up. "You two go and get some rest. I'll be back in a couple of hours."

Jack shook his head. "No. I think I'll come with you, instead."

Tawl gave him a hard look. "I'm just going to find someone to put a couple of stitches in my cheek."

"That's fine with me. After that we can see about getting an extra longbow." Jack wasn't going to be put off.

Tawl began walking across the room. "Come on, then," he said as he reached the door.

Feeling like he'd just won a small victory, Jack followed him outside. The sunlight made him squint. The streets were still busy, but a little more ordered now that every market-trader's stall was in place and everyone else had settled down to the serious business of buying. Tawl accosted the first person who walked past, asking her the name of a decent surgeon.

"Sir," said the old lady, "for an injury such as the one on your cheek, any barber on Letting Street will suffice." She smiled pleasantly, bid them good morning, and was off, large empty basket held out in front of her like a shield.

Jack and Tawl exchanged a smile. The people of Toolay were certainly unique.

By the time they found Letting Street it was close to midday. All together there were about half a dozen barbers vying for business along the way. Their shop fronts were open, showing displays of sharp knives, hacked-off topnotches, and gallstones in jars. "This one will do," said Tawl, indicating one enterprising barber who had hung a carving of a huge wooden leech above his door.

"Aah, sirs! I see two men in need of a haircut." The barber came rushing over to them as soon as they stepped through the door. He was a thin man with a red leather belt around his waist and a razor-sharp knife in his hand. He caught sight of Tawl's cheek. "Why, sir, sit down. Sit down. That's a four-stitcher if ever I saw one."

Tawl sat in the proffered chair. Jack stayed where he was. He had grown accustomed to his hair the length it was, and he had no intention of letting the barber near him.

The barber had turned tutting into an art form, and as he examined Tawl's cheek, he made several highly telling tuts in a row. "Oh, sir," he exclaimed shaking his head. "Such a tragedy. A fine face such as yours and now . . . " several fast tuts followed, "*disaster!* Do you already have a wife, sir?"

Tawl shook his head. He winced as the barber began to clean out the wound with clear alcohol.

"Then this calls for my finest work." The barber began to unravel a large bundle of black thread. "By the time I'm finished with you, your own mother won't be able to tell the difference. You will be able to pay the extra, won't you, sir? Fine little stitches, eight instead of four."

"I'll take four," said Tawl.

"No," said Jack. "Give him the full eight."

Tawl turned a frown Jack's way. "We've got to purchase a longbow."

Jack shook his head. "I'll make do with what I've got." Then to the barber, "Give him whatever it takes." Tawl might not be interested in his appearance, but Jack wasn't doing it for him. He was doing it for Melli.

The barber nodded judiciously. "A man of reason, I see." He looked Jack up and down, and then tutted. "But also, if I may be so bold, one who's badly in need of a little grooming."

Jack edged nearer the door. "Stitch him first, then we'll see if we've any money left over for grooming."

The barber executed his most expressive tut so far. With one click of the tongue, he said, *Borc save me from these barbarians! They have no sense of refinement whatsoever.* He did his duty, though, picking out his finest needle and changing the thread to match. "Brandy, sir?" he asked just before he put point to flesh.

"Will it cost me extra?"

"Two silvers."

"I'll do without."

The barber conveyed his surprise by simply not tutting at all. "Very well. Brace yourself."

Jack looked away.

The barber spoke as he stitched. "So, have you men come from the north?"

"No," said Jack.

"Pity. I was hoping you'd have some news."

"About the siege?"

"Hmm." The barber was silent a moment. Jack didn't want to know what he was doing. "And about the Lady Melliandra."

Jack spun around. "What about her?"

"Well, she's the one who married the duke, you know. Quite a beauty by all accounts."

Tawl's arm shot out and he grabbed the barber's arm. "Get to the point."

The barber tutted, pried his arm free, and continued his stitching. "Well, her father escaped and went over to the enemy and is telling everyone that Kylock has captured her. Of course, it's all just a rumor at the moment."

Tawl made as if to stand, but the barber pushed him down. "Just another minute, sir."

"How long ago did this happen?" asked Jack.

The barber shrugged. "I don't know. News takes a while to reach us here." With that he finished his job, tied a knot, cut the thread, cleaned the new blood from Tawl's face, and splashed the skin with a little ointment. "Seven days and then they come out."

Tawl stood up. "How much?"

The barber seemed disappointed that his work hadn't been appreciated. "Two golds."

Jack handed him the money. "Nicely done," he said.

The barber bowed and started to say something, but Jack didn't catch what it was, for he and Tawl were already heading out the door.

"We travel today. Right now," said Tawl as the door closed behind him. "We get Nabber, change the horses, and leave within the hour."

"Leave for where?" Jack wasn't sure if Tawl meant to continue on to Rorn or head back to Bren.

Tawl's normally light blue eyes were as dark as the sky at midnight. "We go to Larn as planned."

"What in Borc's name do you think you're doing? The girl has to be killed."

Melli had been hearing words for some time now, but these were the first ones that her brain could be bothered to understand. She was emerging from a smoky haze. Her first instinct was to cough—to hack and spit and splutter. Her second instinct was to keep both her eyes and her mouth firmly shut. She took a deep breath and used it to calm her lungs.

"No, Baralis. The girl doesn't have to be killed. The child does."

"They are one and the same right now."

Melli shuddered. She couldn't help herself. She recognized both speakers—Kylock and Baralis—and the sound of their voices chilled her to the bone.

When Baralis spoke again his tone was lower. "Look, as long as the girl is alive, she is a blade in our side. Maybor is running around telling everyone we've got her, half the people in Bren would rather see her son in the palace than you, and Highwall is actually claiming to be fighting on her behalf. The girl must die."

The last words were taut with controlled fury. Not even a second passed before Kylock replied, "No. She won't die. I won't let her."

"If you want her, take her now and be done with it. Just don't lose sight of what she is."

"And what is she, Baralis?"

"She is your only rival."

Melli became aware of a splitting pain in her head.

The urge to cough grew stronger, but she fought it.

"No, Baralis," said Kylock softly. "She isn't my rival, her child is."

The tension in the room was unmistakable. The air grew close and heavy, like before a storm. Melli smelled something metal like sword steel. Her skin prickled as a wave of warm air passed over her.

There was silence for a moment, then Baralis said, "Very well, if you insist."

"I do insist, Baralis." Kylock moved near to the bed. Melli sensed his gaze upon her. "Oh, and she will stay here for the time being. The tower is no place for her to sleep."

With light steps Baralis walked across the room. "She will need to be watched closely at all times."

"The woman will do it."

"As you wish." Baralis' voice was hard. "I will send her here to make arrangements." With that Baralis left the room, closing the door behind him.

Melli didn't know whether to be relieved or frightened. She knew Kylock was close to her, watching her. She felt something touch her cheek. Opening her eyes, she found herself looking straight into his.

A black band ringed his irises. "Aah, the mother-to-be awakens." He was wearing gloves. His finger trailed from her cheek down beneath the sheets. Slowly it moved across her breast and down to her belly. He paused a moment and then poked her stomach as if testing a fruit for ripeness. Melli's hand shot up to stop him. Kylock grabbed her wrist. He slammed it against the bed. "No. No, my love, this is not the way to repay a debt."

Melli wanted desperately to cough. Her lungs felt full of dust. Kylock twisted her wrist so she couldn't move her arm. "What do you want from me?" she cried.

Kylock shook his head slowly. "I don't think it's your place to ask questions," he said. A tiny drop of spittle appeared at the corner of his lip. He dug his gloved fingers into the bones of her wrist.

A knock came upon the door.

"Who is it?" snapped Kylock.

"It's Mistress Greal, sire. Lord Baralis bid me come."

Mistress Greal. Melli started choking. Her head came off the pillow and she coughed and spluttered, unable to stop herself.

"Come."

The door opened and a woman walked in. Melli's eyes were full of tears. The woman looked different: smaller, and the lower part of her face was oddly misshapen. Then she spoke. There was no mistaking her thin, clawing voice. "I see the little bitch is pretending to be ill." She stepped toward the bed. Kylock moved away. Grabbing a handful of hair, she yanked Melli upright and then thumped her hard in the back. "There. That should do it."

Melli stopped coughing.

Kylock regarded Mistress Greal with distaste. He crossed the room toward the door. "See to it that she gets a bath," he said.

"But—"

"Do it."

Melli had the fleeting pleasure of seeing Mistress Greal flinch. The door slammed shut. Mistress Greal turned to face her. "So, landed on your feet again, have you?"

"What are you doing here?"

Mistress Greal snorted. "I ain't answering to no slut." She looked around the room with a proprietorial air. "They should have kept you in the tower. This place is too good for you. Fancy bed, carpets . . . you'd think you were a princess, not the biggest whore in Bren."

Melli was trying hard to keep her sanity. It felt as if she'd woken up in the middle of a bad dream. Baralis, Kylock, and now Mistress Greal. Who next, she wondered, Fiscel and Captain Vanly?

She forced her mind to stay focused. "What do you know about the tower?"

"I picked it for you, that's what. Nice and bare. No frills. No blankets, no candles—I made sure of that." Mistress Greal smiled. She looked hideous; two of her front teeth were missing.

Realizing that Mistress Greal didn't mind answering questions when they gave her a chance to show off her authority, Melli continued. "So Baralis left you in charge of my welfare?"

Mistress Greal almost simpered. "Yes, he did. Told me anything I saw fit to do, just go ahead and do it. He didn't want nothing to do with you. Can't say as I blame him, either."

Melli sat back against the headboard. The picture was becoming clearer now: Mistress Greal had been the one supervising her imprisonment, not Baralis. He had washed his hands of her. Melli felt a tiny spark of disappointment, then told herself she hadn't. Quickly, she moved on. "Baralis must trust you a lot."

Mistress Greal was helping herself to a glass of wine. The bones around her wrist jutted out at odd angles. "He owes me, does Lord Baralis."

"Owes you for what?"

Mistress Greal whipped around. "Getting a little nosy, ain't you?"

Melli tried a different approach. "You must have done him a great service to be given such responsibility."

"D'you think me a fool, missy? I've been managing young girls since before you were born. I know every trick a slut like you can pull, and flattery is just the first of them."

As she spoke, Mistress Greal's grip slipped on her wine cup, and wine went spilling down the front of her dress. She shot Melli a venomous look. Coming toward the bed, she held out the cup in front of her. The damage to her wrist was plain to see. "So you want to know what

I did to get here, do you?" She leant over the bed and thrust her wrist under Melli's nose. "Well, take a good look at that, missy. That should tell you all you need to know."

Melli refused to be frightened by her. She pushed the wrist away. "An unhappy client, perhaps?"

Mistress Greal slapped Melli with her good hand. Melli's head snapped back. Her skull hit the headboard. The impact wasn't great, but the pain it produced was dizzying. Slowly, she brought up her hand to feel the back of her head. She winced as her fingers touched the sore spot. Her hair was stiff with blood.

"Your father did this to me." Mistress Greal thrust the wrist back into Melli's face. "And my teeth. Robbed me of my good hand and my looks he did, and that's something I'm never going to forget."

Melli hid her surprise. Her father must have found out what went on in Duvitt! She felt a moment of pure, spiteful pleasure. He must have given the old witch quite a blow to take out her teeth.

"So you've been extracting what petty vengeance you can through me?" she said.

Mistress Greal waggled a bony finger. "I wouldn't say finding the most wanted woman in Bren is such a petty thing. Would you?"

"You found us?"

"Your father was wenching in my sister's establishment. Can't take his ale, you know."

"He got away, didn't he?" said Melli casually, trying not to betray the importance of the question.

"That old bastard's got the luck of the devil."

Melli's whole body relaxed. Up until now she hadn't realized just how tense she had been. All her muscles ached, her head was pounding, and her heart was beating wildly against her ribs. Somehow none of it mattered anymore. She was all right, her baby was still alive, and Maybor had managed to get away.

"A scalding bath will soon knock that smile from your face, missy," said Mistress Greal on her way to the door.

"Bring out your hottest tub, woman," said Melli. "It'll take more than boiling water to kill Maybor's daughter."

"Tawl, go back to Bren," said Jack. "I'll go to Larn on my own."

They were in the stables. The new horses were saddled and ready. Nabber was wiping the sleep from his eyes. The tavern-keeper's handsome son had just returned with the supplies Tawl had asked for, and now, just when they were ready to leave, Jack came out with this.

Every day Tawl learned more about Jack, and every day he realized he'd underestimated him once more.

Tawl shook his head. He didn't trust himself to speak just yet. He knew a genuine offer when he heard one, and he also knew the sound of fear well hidden. Jack couldn't be aware of what he was volunteering to do. Or could he? Tawl didn't want to underestimate him again.

Catching hold of Jack's arm, Tawl guided him into the dark area beneath the hayloft. "Jack, I can't let you go to Larn on your own."

"Do you know what I'm supposed to do when I get there?"

"No."

"Then you can't help me." Jack spoke calmly. "So you might as well return to Bren and try to rescue Melli."

His words sounded rational, but Tawl doubted if Jack actually believed them. *He* didn't. "It's not as simple as that. Larn is no place for a man to go on his own."

"You went on your own."

"Yes. And look what it did to me. I murdered the one man who could have helped us." Tawl's voice hardened as he spoke. "I can't let you go there alone, Jack. I'm coming with you."

A cow lowed gently from behind a wooden stall. Tawl looked at Jack. He was already working on his response.

Tawl knew what it would be, but didn't give him a chance to say it. "Jack, you know what one of the last things Bevlin said to me was?"

Jack shook his head.

"He spoke of you and me. He said, 'There is a link between you, and it is your destiny to help him fulfill his.'" Tawl felt his emotions respond to the words. He could clearly remember Bevlin saying them; his eyes sparkling, his voice strained, his chest rising up and down with the sheer force of the prophecy. For that was what it was: a prophecy, every bit as compelling as Marod's verse. Jack was not the only one forced to live by the words of a dead man.

"But what about Melli, Tawl?" said Jack. "What will become of her?"

He had said the one thing that Tawl hoped he wouldn't. It was so much easier to suppress his fears when he kept them all to himself. Now Jack had spoken them out loud, and like a floodgate opened, it let in the swell.

Tawl kicked the stall door. "I don't know what will become of Melli!" he cried. "*I don't know*. If I go back to Bren now, she might be dead by the time I get there. If I come with you, the risk is even greater. Don't think for one second that I'm not considering Melli. She's why I'm here today. She's why I wake up every morning and breathe. She's the only thing that matters, and right now I'd give anything to be by her side. But I can't. I've got to go to Larn and follow the whole damn thing through to the end. Then, and only then, will Melli be truly safe." Tawl was shaking by the time he'd finished. His skin was slick with sweat.

Jack couldn't look at him. He stared at the floor instead. "I'm sorry, Tawl. I know how you feel about Melli."

"Then why are we standing around wasting time? Let's get on the horses and go." Tawl knew he sounded harsh, but he had to leave. The stables were beginning to feel like a prison. "Come on, Nabber," he called, walking over to his latest mount. "Let's get you up here."

Half an hour later they were out of the city. The sun was still up and shining, but to Tawl it made little difference what hour of the day it was. Melli was to the north and he was heading to the south. Everything else paled in comparison to that one irrefutable fact. He had to believe she would be all right until he returned, that somehow time itself would wait for him. It was the only way to keep his sanity and force his horse forward instead of back.

Kylock listened to what Lord Guthry said. The man was concerned about Highwall's lakeborne advances. The siege army had built a huge raft for their largest trebuchet and had spent most of the day launching missiles at the north wall and the palace itself. The two north towers had been damaged and the domed ceiling, which was the palace's greatest weakness, had taken several well-aimed hits.

At times like this Kylock never thought, he simply reacted. "Right, I want the carpenters up on the roof tonight. I want a wooden scaffold built over the dome. I want it strengthened with metal sheets, and I want ten score of archers up there while they work.

"As for the raft—"

"A storm's predicted tomorrow, sire. The lake will be too rough for Highwall to man it."

Kylock regarded Lord Guthry coolly. "Never, ever interrupt me," he said. Lord Guthry began to speak, but Kylock waved a silencing arm. Apologies held no interest for him. "Now, I want the raft destroyed tonight. As I understand it, the problem is the raft is beyond our firing range—their trebuchet can fire twice the distance of ours. So, as soon as it goes dark, I want you to send out two divers under the lake. They will carry skins of lamp oil

with them and they'll set the raft alight. Is that understood?" Kylock knew it would be certain suicide for their
divers. With his gaze he challenged Lord Guthry to crit-
icize him.

The man didn't have the guts for it. He walked over to
the desk and poured himself a cup of wine. Kylock made
a mental note of the cup he used and other surfaces he
touched.

"Is there anything else, sire?" Guthry asked after
draining his cup dry.

"Yes, I heard a report today that thousands of dead
fish were floating on the surface of the lake."

Lord Guthry nodded. He was a large man with a red
face and graying hair. He had been the late duke's closest
military advisor. "Aye. I saw that with my own eyes this
morning. Mighty strange it is."

"I don't think there's anything strange about it at all,"
said Kylock softly. "I think Highwall's poisoning the
lake."

"You could be right, sire." Lord Guthry was a man
who tended toward caution. "The best thing we can do is
warn everyone not to draw from the wells for a few days,
just in case. It will give the poison chance to dissipate.
There's no possible way that Highwall could have poisoned the entire lake. If they've done anything at all, it's
to the water around the shore."

"Yes, you're quite right," Kylock said. He thought for
a moment, then added: "I only want the warning passed
on to the military. There's no need to panic everyone in
the city."

"But the women. The children—"

Kylock's hand was on the desk. With one quick movement he overturned it. The wine jug and cups went
crashing to the floor. Papers floated slowly down.

Lord Guthry took a step back. The color drained from
his face.

Kylock took a quick breath. His gaze flicked over the

cups on the floor. No longer could he tell which one belonged to his guest. All of them would have to go. When he spoke, his voice was calm. "Just do as I say. Women and children never won a war."

Oh, how Lord Guthry wanted to speak; the words practically pushed against his lips. But he didn't say anything. He simply bowed and took his leave.

Only when the door shut behind him did Kylock see fit to remove his gloves. With the desk overturned the chamber was in disorder. It disturbed him, and he had to turn his back on the chaos of cups and papers to think clearly. More and more these days, everything had to be perfect for him to concentrate; one fleck of ash on the grate, one curtain fold amiss, and his mind would go no further than the fault.

People disturbed him more than ever, too. All of them were dirty, disgusting. Fingers that picked noses, raised glasses; hands that held sexual organs to piss with, minutes later were cupping the salt. The smell of sex, sweat, and urine could be detected on every palm.

His chambers reeked of Guthry's breath. Of his last meal and his last drink and the slow decay of his teeth. Kylock could hardly bear it. Never again would he let that man enter his private domain.

Catherine was to have stopped all this. Beautiful, innocent Catherine. Only she wasn't innocent. She was a whore, just like every other woman. And she had died a whore's death, and with her went his last hope of salvation.

Or so he had thought until last night.

He had visited Melliandra out of curiosity. She was due to die the next day, and he thought it would be interesting to see fear in her eyes. And indeed it had been. She was more beautiful than he remembered, her eyes large with terror, her bottom lip trembling while she pretended to be brave. But then he had ripped the clothes from her back and everything changed.

The fire glowed on her skin, accentuating her belly's curve. Like a holy statue she was surrounded by light. Her breasts heavy with pregnancy, her stomach swelling with the new life beneath—she was a symbol of the only thing that was good in women: their ability to renew life.

As long as Melliandra was with child, she was beyond all womanly vices. Pure like an angel, she had been cleansed by a force of nature. When she gave birth to her baby, she would give birth to him, as well. Once her womb had been purified by the passage of new life, he would take her and be made anew. Melliandra had been sent to him as his savior, and he would use her to wash the sins of his mother away.

Catherine had failed him. His mother's death had left him strangely unmoved. Now more than ever he needed someone to sacrifice herself for him. Life was crowding too close; it teemed, it reeked, it drove him forward into oblivion. He had to start again. His very being must be freshly shaped.

Melliandra would be the vessel in which he cleansed his soul. Her child's life would be short—not even a full step in the dance of fate—but it would live long enough to do what it was conceived for: to clear a sacred path for the king.

Seventeen

*I*f there was anything in life worse than traveling, Nabber couldn't think of it. He had a lot of time to try, too. For nearly nine weeks now he'd sat on the back of Tawl's horse, spending his mornings wishing for midday and spending his days wishing for dark. And never had there been a less profitable, less comfortable, and less interesting thing to do.

Tawl set a hard pace—especially after Toolay—and it was up every morning before dawn, riding long hard hours until noon, then half a day more until dusk. It was enough to kill a man.

It wouldn't have been so bad if they were traveling through lands exotic and unfamiliar; there would be scenery to appreciate, strange creatures to pocket, and new food to stuff in his pack. As it was, they were making their way down the barren peninsula north of Rorn, and there was nothing more interesting than ground rats and rocks. It was a sad testament to a man when all he had in his pocket was a large rodent and a chunk of limestone.

It was high time they reached Rorn. If they didn't get there soon, Nabber was quite sure he'd go under the barrel. Or was it *over* it? Well, one way or other there'd be a barrel in his future and he'd very probably end up dead in it. According to Swift, guilt wasn't the only thing that could be the death of a pocket. Lack of practice was another. *"A pocket who loses his feel might as well hit himself over the head with a mallet,"* Swift would say. *"Either that or wait till the bailiffs do it for him."* Losing your feel was the one thing that kept pockets awake at night. Fear of it sent them out onto the streets in sickness, bad weather, and plague. A pocket simply couldn't function unless he had his feel.

Nabber had intended to get some practice in Toolay—stay a few days, do a little pocketing, add to his dwindling contingency—but Tawl had put a stop to that. One mention of Melli in danger and the knight had turned into a demon. He'd had them out of the city in no time, galloping through the streets without as much as a please or thank-you to anyone. It had been the same ever since. If they came to a river, then they'd cross it then and there, not bothering to trek downstream and look for a bridge. If there was a ditch, they'd jump it; if there was a tavern, they'd ride right past it. When they met other travelers, Tawl would ask them if they had news of the duke's widow, and when they didn't, he just turned his horse and moved on.

He hardly talked at all. Anything that might slow him down was not tolerated. There was no washing, no cooking, no resting. There was riding and sleeping and nothing else.

At least they hadn't heard from Skaythe in the past few weeks. Tawl must have aimed a decent arrow, for there had been no sign of old Bad Leg since the night on the bluff. A fact that pleased Nabber no end: his arm was only now out of the sling and he didn't fancy having to put it back there any time soon. He'd had enough of splints, bandages, and slings to last a lifetime. The only good thing about being injured was the brandy, and they'd run out of that two days past Toolay.

Nabber looked up at the sky. There was no time like midmorning for outstaying its welcome. It had been midmorning for the better part of a day now—Nabber was sure of it.

He let his gaze drop down onto the horizon. He was sick of blue skies and eastern breezes, sick of rocks and hills and dust. Just as he was about to direct his gaze elsewhere, he spotted a speck of white in the distance. A speck of white with the ocean as its backdrop.

"*Rorn!*" he cried. "Tawl, it's Rorn."

Tawl nodded. "We'll be there by tonight."

Nabber could hardly believe it. Over the past few days, they'd traveled through a few villages and seen a good number of people on the road, but nothing prepared him for Rorn's closeness. "None of this seems familiar, Tawl," he said.

"We've traveled close to the coast this time. When we left all those months back, we went straight up the middle. That's where most of the towns and villages are. There's little but hills this way."

"You can say that again." Nabber beamed at the back of Tawl's head. Now that he'd seen the city, he felt like jumping off the horse and running all the way to the sea. Rorn was his home; it was where his business associates lurked, where Swift held court, and where he knew every street, alleyway, and crevice.

"We'll stop here," shouted Tawl to Jack.

Was it midday already? What had happened to mid-morning? Nabber tapped on Tawl's shoulder. "I could manage a bit further before we stopped."

Tawl laughed: his first in a long time. "Either my hearing's going, or someone snatched Nabber away in the night and replaced him with you, instead. Since when did you start volunteering to spend more time in the saddle?" As he spoke, Tawl guided his horse from the track. There was a stretch of grass on the sheltered side of the hill and he headed toward it.

"Ain't no pixies taken me," said Nabber, sliding off the horse. "Just thought I'd do my bit, that's all. It'll be the last time I do a good deed, I can tell you." Nabber sorted through the items in his sack—he was now reduced to a truly pathetic selection—and picked out a stale honey-cake to munch on. "Some people ought to learn to be a bit more grateful."

Jack tied his horse to a rock and came to join him. "Any more of those in your sack?" he said, pointing at the honeycake.

"Seeing as it's you that's asking, Jack, and not a certain thankless knight who's currently unbuckling the saddle from his horse"—Nabber threw a withering look Tawl's way—"then I think I can manage one." He rooted once more and came out with the last edible thing he had on him—not counting the ground rat, of course. "Here you go. Just pick off the hairs and it'll be as right as rain."

Jack brushed the cake against his leg. "So you've never been this way before?"

"No. Me and Tawl went another way last time." Nabber looked into the distance. Rorn had somehow disappeared into thin air.

"Is this way quicker?"

"There's not a lot in it," said Tawl, coming up to join them. He gave Jack a searching look. "As the crow flies, this way is shorter, but you've got the hills to contend with. The other route is longer—"

"But you've got people to contend with," finished Jack.

Tawl didn't bother to contradict him. "Just being cautious, that's all."

"Cautious of what?" asked Nabber. He hated conversations that beat around bushes.

There it was again! That glance swapped between Jack and Tawl. The same one that always appeared when there was talk of danger. Nabber wasn't going to let the matter drop, though. Those two could trade looks until their eyelashes fell out for all he cared. If there were dangers, he needed to know about them. "Who exactly are you trying to avoid, Tawl? Is it Skaythe?"

Tawl shrugged. "Yes."

"But there's more, isn't there?" said Jack. "It's not really about Skaythe. It's about how he found us in the first place. About who told him where to look."

Nabber had the distinct feeling that he might as well be invisible at this point. Somehow he'd been squeezed out of his own conversation. This was between Tawl and Jack now.

Tawl turned to look at the way they'd come. Hills and more hills. "If Skaythe is alive, he'll find us again. If he's dead, they'll send someone else."

"Baralis?"

"And Larn. They're probably working together." Tawl's voice betrayed the strain of the journey. "I've seen those seers. I know what they can do. Their powers are neither superstition nor legend. They're real, and the priests know how to exploit them."

"So they'll be tracking us?"

"You, Jack. They'll be tracking you." Tawl spun around to face him. "They'll know everything by now—Marod's prophecy, what it means, the fact you're on your way. They know you're coming to destroy them, and they're not about to sit back and let that happen."

Jack's face was pale. Nabber couldn't understand why Tawl was being so hard on him.

"I'm not a fool, Tawl," he said. "Don't you think I know the risks? Or did you think I just followed you to go on a grand adventure?"

The two men had been drawing nearer with every word and they were now only a breath apart.

"Why don't you tell me why you came?" said Tawl.

"I came because I have to." A long moment passed. "I was born for it."

Nabber shivered. At that moment the breeze from the ocean was as good as a blade. No one moved. Jack and Tawl stood opposite each other. Nabber began to understand what had passed between the two: it was a test. Tawl had been testing Jack.

Nabber knew all about men's pride and standoffs. He knew that no man wanted to back down to another. Swift himself had said, *"Back down to a man and you'll spend the rest of your days regretting it."* Now Tawl and Jack had reached such an impasse. If someone didn't do something, those two would be standing there until Rorn sank into the sea. And there was no way Nabber was going to let that happen. No, sir. Rorn was no good to him underwater.

Reaching in his sack, he pulled out his darning needle. Lock-breaker, weapon, gold-tester, and insect-impaler: Nabber never went anywhere without it. He cut across to the horses, smiled sweetly at Tawl's gelding, whispered, "this is for all those hours of torture," and thrust the needle into the horse's flank.

The horse reared up and began bucking. It squealed like a pig. Snapping back its head, it pulled its reins free of the rock.

The deadlock was broken. Tawl leapt forward. Jack followed after him. The horse galloped down the hillside.

Nabber shouted, "I'll keep an eye on things here." He patted Jack's horse on the nose and then settled down to wait.

"His Highness has been in to see her just this morning, my lord," said Mistress Greal.

"How long did he spend with her?" asked Baralis.

"Less than an hour."

Baralis didn't like this one little bit. Kylock was visiting Maybor's daughter on an almost daily basis. This meant trouble. He walked across the room, thinking. With the iron shutters drawn over the windows, his chambers were as dark as night. A fistful of candles burned on the desk, but they did little except send shadows into the gloom. "Next time he calls upon the lady, I would appreciate it if you could . . . "

Mistress Greal leapt into the pause. "Keep an ear to things."

"Yes," said Baralis, trying hard not to show his distaste. "I am interested in knowing what passes between
them."

"I can tell you that already, my lord. He goes in there
and beats her up. She's always got either a black eye or
bruises on her arms, or a bloody lip." Mistress Greal
spoke with a certain grudging respect. "You've got to
give him that, my lord. His Highness ain't about to be
fooled by a pretty face."

"And what about you? How do you treat the girl?"

"I treat the girl like the slut she is. She might be in a
fancy chamber, but I see to it she gets only the bare minimum. No fire, no candles. One cold meal a day."

"And how does she look?"

"She's a tough one, that's for sure. She's well into her
fifth month, by the looks of things. Her belly's rounding
out now. I'd say she'll be birthing in midwinter."

"Leave me now," said Baralis. He had no liking for the
woman before him. She was far too familiar with him
and he didn't trust her. By the sounds of things she'd
already been spying on Kylock and Melliandra.

Mistress Greal curtsied in her crablike way, smiled as
if they were co-conspirators, and left the room. As soon as
the door closed, Crope emerged from the bedchamber.
"Is the toothless woman gone now, master?"

Baralis nodded. His servant had no liking for Mistress
Greal. "Yes, you can come out now. Stoke up the fire
and pour me some holk."

Crope had been handling his little wooden box and
promptly stuffed it into his tunic before doing as he was
bidden.

Baralis came and sat by the fire. His thoughts
returned to Kylock once more. The king was becoming
increasingly unstable. He was growing obsessed with
Maybor's daughter. Baralis had challenged him twice
about it: once the day after he took her from the tower,
and again last week. Both times Kylock had come close

to drawing sorcery. The first time Baralis actually had to draw power himself to contain it. Kylock was potent, strong, the sorcery rolled off his tongue into the air, and the only thing that stopped it from causing damage was the quickness of Baralis' reflexes.

It seemed the drug was no longer enough. A lifetime of use was impairing its effectiveness. Either that or Kylock was growing more powerful.

Baralis doubted if Kylock knew what he was doing when he drew sorcery. It was a product of rage, not intent, and that in itself was worrying. Kylock could not afford to make the people of Bren any more wary than they already were.

The city was holding up well under the siege, but over the last six weeks Highwall had been making progress. First they attacked the north wall of the palace, then they poisoned the lake, and just yesterday they set fire to a mine and collapsed a whole section of the curtain wall. Tavalisk was seeing to it that Highwall had all the mercenaries, provisions, and armaments they needed. Larn stopped perhaps three-quarters of the supplies from getting through, but the quarter that was left was enough to ensure that the siege army had no need to return home.

Meanwhile the people of Bren were becoming nervous. The Royal Guard regularly swept the city looking for traitors, and they weren't fussy about matters of evidence or guilt. Food was short, and what little was available was ten times its normal price. Several hundred people had died last month from drinking the poisoned lake water. Lord Guthry had been executed over the scandal that followed. Apparently he had given the order that only men of fighting age were to be warned of the danger. Oh, Baralis knew who was really behind the order, but he made sure that no one else did. Kylock had to be protected from scandal at all cost.

Baralis reached over to his desk and pulled down the letter he had been reading before Mistress Greal's arrival.

It was from Tyren, head of the Knights of Valdis. In it, he expressed his nervousness about the moral tone of Kylock's leadership. Apparently Tyren was having a little difficulty convincing his brethren to follow the cause when it was widely rumored that Kylock had kidnapped the woman who was carrying the legitimate heir to Bren.

People outside of Bren soon forgot that Melliandra's camp was responsible for murdering both the duke and his daughter. Baralis threw the letter onto the fire. Tyren would have to be reminded of the facts one more time.

Not that Tyren was interested in morals. Money and power were the only two things that mattered to him. That was why he had written this letter in the first place: it was purely an opening gambit. He wanted to meet and renegotiate the deal they had struck in Bren three months back. Now that he had exhausted the spoils of Halcus and ripped all the assets from its Church, he wanted more. More gold, more influence, more of anything that would advance his cause.

Helch was now too much of a backwater for the leader of the knights.

Baralis rubbed his aching hands. There was so much for him to do. A second meeting with Tyren would have to be arranged, Kylock needed monitoring, the Highwall army had to be beaten back from the wall, and the people of Bren had to be watched closely for signs of insurgency. So far Kylock had done a good job suppressing Melliandra's supporters—there was nothing like a hanging for sealing would-be traitors' lips—but the fact that he still had to resort to public executions was telling. Kylock was not well loved in Bren.

Baralis sighed, but not heavily. Then there was the other side of events to deal with: the baker's boy had to be found and destroyed. Skaythe was now over a week behind him, and that meant Jack and his little party could be landing a boat on Larn before Skaythe even reached Rorn.

Just last night the priests at Larn had contacted him. They were beginning to panic. They knew Jack was on his way and were desperate for help. They had told him many secrets to secure his cooperation. Baralis now knew the exact date the winter storms would start in the mountains, he knew the fundamental military weakness of the city of Ness, he knew there would be an uprising in Helch during the first winter thaw, and he had learned who was responsible for the recent change in tactics of the siege army: Maybor. In one night Larn had traded more information than in six months of verbal parrying.

Baralis smiled as the vapors of the holk reached his nostrils. He would have to see what he could do in return.

The door opened. Even before he saw who was on the other side, Baralis stood up. Only Kylock dared enter his chambers without knocking.

"Aah, Baralis, you look quite the old man warming yourself by the fire." Kylock strode into the room. He walked around a little and then came to stand by the desk. He rarely sat.

Today he was without his gloves. His leather boots were damp. The soles left dark imprints on the rug, which meant that Kylock had probably just come from the dungeons. Baralis already knew better than to ask what Kylock did there. He neither wanted, nor needed, to know the details. "I believe you saw Melliandra earlier," he said.

"You are not my keeper, Baralis. I see who I want when I want."

There was an edge to Kylock's voice and Baralis decided to let the matter rest for today. After last night's sending from Larn, he felt too weak to cope with Kylock's rage. "Did you get the note I sent you?" he said, changing the subject.

"Yes. That's why I'm here." Kylock poured himself a glass of wine. Baralis knew he wouldn't drink it. "I've been waiting on news of the winter storms."

"Why?"

Kylock's gaze was shrewd and clear. He smiled slightly. "According to our friends at Larn, the first winter storm will hit the mountains in two weeks time. Once that happens the passes will be blocked with snow and ice for many months, and conditions will be so bad it will be virtually impossible for an army to cross the mountains. Today I will send the order for my army at Annis to cross the mountains immediately. They have been on standby for several weeks now and can move on a moment's notice. They will take the pass just ahead of the storm."

The smile came again, and then Kylock continued. "Doubtless the Annis army will try to follow us over the mountains, but they're not expecting our move and it will take them a good week or so to get organized. By the time they're ready the passes will be closed. They will be forced to spend the winter at home.

"Meanwhile, the kingdoms' army will arrive in Bren and proceed to outflank and then destroy Highwall's army."

It was a simple and brilliant plan. Baralis had long wondered why Kylock had positioned his troops outside of Annis. Now he knew why. The king had been waiting for a chance to maroon the Annis army in their own city. Up until now, he couldn't risk moving his troops without fear they would be caught between Annis on one side and Highwall on the next.

Kylock was still smiling. He was well aware of his own brilliance. "On the day the kingdoms' forces are due to come down from the mountains, I want Bren's army to wage their most aggressive attack on Highwall. The siege army will be so busy defending themselves, they won't even see our troops coming. As soon as they're spotted, Bren's army will come over the wall and attack Highwall full on.

"Highwall won't stand a chance. Bren will be in front

of them, the blackhelms to the east, the mountains behind them, and the kingdoms' forces will come from the west. It will be a bloody massacre. No prisoners. No mercy. No chance of retreat."

Kylock put down his cup of wine untouched. He looked directly at Baralis. "So, Chancellor, what do you think?"

"I think the entire north will be ours in less than a year," replied Baralis. He believed it, too. Kylock was many things—unstable, irrational, cruel to a fault—but he was a genius where military strategy was concerned. No one in the Known Lands could match him. Feeling suddenly more confident than he had in months, Baralis said, "I will arrange to have your orders sent today by eagle, sire."

Jack tapped Nabber on the shoulder and said to the tavern-maid, "I'll have what he's having."

"Very wise, Jack. Very wise." Nabber beamed. The tavern-maid beamed. Only Tawl didn't join in the merriment. The knight's attention was elsewhere; out of the corner of his eye he was watching two men who were sitting near the back of the tavern.

"Would you like a crust of pastry or turnips on your pie, sir?"

Jack looked to Nabber, who supplied the answer, "He'll have the pastry, miss. He's hoping to get some sleep tonight."

Jack didn't bother asking Nabber to explain the relationship between turnips and sleeplessness—he was too busy studying the men who had attracted Tawl's attention.

The Rose and Crown was a large and busy tavern. It was dark by the time they arrived, and although Jack hadn't seen the sea, he knew it was close. The Rose and Crown was full of swarthy men whose faces were reddened with salt and wind. Sailors, Jack guessed. The two men Tawl was watching looked different than most of the other clientele. It wasn't just their fair coloring, it was their size and their bearing. Like Tawl, they managed to study everyone in the room without once lifting their gaze from their drinks.

The tavern-maid returned with the beer. The huge pewter jug brimmed with froth, and Nabber set about pouring it into cups with all the skill of an innkeeper's son.

They had been in Rorn for less than an hour. As soon as they passed the city gate Tawl had them steering a course for the harbor. The sun spent little time setting, and most of the journey through the city was done in the dark. Jack had little chance to form an impression of the most famous city in the south, except that it smelled really bad and the buildings were nowhere near as white as they appeared from a distance. There were a lot of dodgy-looking people on the streets, too—and quite a few of them were women.

No women in here, though. None except the tavern-maid.

Jack pushed Tawl's drink his way and said under his breath, "Should I have my knife ready?"

Tawl raised the cup to his lips. "Always have your knife ready, Jack," he said before he drank. He brushed the foam from his lips, then spoke to Nabber. "Go and see the innkeeper about a room for the night and stabling for the horses."

Nabber hesitated.

"Now."

Mouth closed in indignation, Nabber did as he was told.

The fairest of the two men in the back stood up. He was looking straight at Tawl. Under the table, Jack's hand was damp around his knife. The man walked toward them. He was large and well built. His gaze never left Tawl. His hands were empty, but the too-straight line of his tunic told of a weapon barely concealed. He stopped less than a handspan away from the table. Even though Jack was neither touching nor looking at Tawl, he could sense the knight's readiness. He smelled like an animal prepared to fight.

The man checked to left and right, and then hissed, "Have you been sent by Tyren to bring us back?"

Tawl's stance didn't change. "Why? Are you deserting him?"

"Are you?"

Jack didn't understand what was going on. He was beginning to suspect that the fair-haired man and his companion were knights, but that still didn't explain the exchange.

Neither man had relaxed. "What are you doing in a city that executes knights on sight?" said the stranger.

"Same thing you are. Passing through."

"Where are you heading?"

"That's my business." Tawl leaned forward a little. "I don't think there's any need to ask you yours."

The stranger sent a quick look to his companion. A "bide your time" look if Jack ever saw one. "Have you been in Helch over the past five months?" he asked Tawl.

Tawl shook his head.

"Then you only *think* you know my business." The stranger's voice was low and harsh. "I'm not about to be judged by a man who's been playing it safe in the south while the war's been raging in the north." He made a quick movement.

Tawl's hand came out. He grabbed the stranger's arm. His grip shook as the man fought his hold. "Go back to your table, my brother," he said. "You're right, I'm in no position to judge anyone. And I have no wish to fight you tonight."

The man pulled his arm free. "Tyren is murdering the soul of Valdis," he said. "And a body with no soul needs to be buried deep in an unmarked grave." He held Tawl's gaze a moment, then turned and walked away.

His companion stood up and joined him, and together they left the tavern.

Jack was trembling. Strong emotions thickened the air: pride, bitterness, shame. He glanced toward Tawl. The knight was looking down. His golden hair fell over his face, and slowly, very slowly, he shook his head from side to side.

"Has it come to this?" he said, his voice plain and small like a child's. "When knights slip away from Valdis like prisoners from jail?"

Jack knew Tawl wasn't talking to him, but he had to know. He had to understand. "Those two men are knights like you?"

"Not like me. No." Tawl didn't look up. He managed a bitter smile. "Then again, they might be exactly like me. After all, I deserted the knighthood first."

"So they're deserters?"

Tawl nodded. "Yes. They thought I had been sent to bring them back." The bitterness of the smile now extended to a laugh. "Me. The one man in the knighthood who's not fit to stand in Valdis' shadow. A traitor to bring back traitors."

"That knight who just left didn't sound like a traitor to me," said Jack. "He sounded like a man with no hope."

At first Jack didn't think his words had any effect on Tawl, for he made no attempt to reply. A candle burnt low at the center of the table. Liquid wax shot over the wood like a stream of glistening jewels. They both watched in silence as it solidified, becoming milky and dull once more.

Brushing the hair from his face, Tawl looked across the tavern in the direction the two knights had taken. "No hope, you say?"

Jack was nervous, yet didn't know why. It was suddenly very important that he say the right thing. "If you were still in the knighthood, how would you feel about fighting at Kylock's side?"

"I would do whatever Tyren asked of me. Loyalty is the one thread that binds the knighthood together."

The candle began to gutter, then die. There was no more wax left to burn. The flame changed from yellow to orange to red, and then went out, leaving a thin strand of smoke heading up toward the roof.

"I asked how you would feel, not what you would do." Jack desperately wanted a drink. His mouth was as dry as sawdust. He didn't dare take one, though. The slightest movement might ruin what was happening between him and Tawl.

For the first time Tawl looked directly at him. His blue eyes were bright—with tears or dreams, Jack didn't know. "You're right, my friend," he said. "I would feel like a man with no hope."

"But you are different from the two who just left. You can make your own hope." Jack leant closer. "Together, we can stop this. Everything good doesn't have to pass. The knighthood can be glorious once more. Peace can come to the north."

"Jack, you're young. You don't understand."

"Then help me understand. Tell me."

Tawl made a small, helpless gesture with his hand. "The leader of the knighthood, the man who those two are running away from, was like a father to me. Tyren first brought me to Valdis. He made me who I am. When others rejected and ridiculed, he was there backing me all the way. When my life was no longer worth living, he gave me reason to carry on." Tawl's voice was close to breaking. "What sort of man would that make me, if I turned against him now?"

Jack's heart was beating fast. What Tawl said affected him deeply. There were whole worlds in the layers between the words. There was tragedy and truth and lies. More than anyone Jack knew there were always two sides to people. They could do good things, say good things, and behind your back create a landscape of deceit. Tarissa and Rovas, Stillfox, even his mother—they had all smiled at him whilst they lied.

"It would make you human, Tawl," he said. "The knight who came over to speak to you wasn't a liar. He wasn't a traitor. He was disillusioned. There must have been a time when he believed in Tyren as much as you."

"What are you saying, Jack?"

"I'm saying that just because Tyren's been good to you, it doesn't mean he can't be bad."

Tawl smiled, this time without bitterness. "You said that like you know what you're talking about."

Jack shook his head. He didn't want things to become too personal. Not here, not now. "The only thing I know for sure is that you and I are on opposite sides from Tyren. He is fighting against Melli, and that makes him our enemy." Jack's mind caught at something half-forgotten in the intensity of the moment. "As soon as you saw those two knights, you assumed they were sent by Tyren to assassinate us both. That's why you sent Nabber away."

Tawl didn't deny it. He stood up. "This morning you told me why you agreed to come to Larn—you said you were born for it. Well, let me tell you what I was born for: I was born to serve. First my mother, then my sisters, then Tyren. Now Melli. I'm not a fool, Jack; I recognize that Tyren is my enemy. I would even oppose him if it came to it. But know this: until I have seen proof of his wrongdoings myself, I will hear no word against him."

Tawl began to walk away. "You don't serve someone to cast them aside as soon as another obligation comes along."

Jack watched him head out the door. He had probably gone looking for Nabber. Stretching out his arm, Jack grabbed at the jug of ale. He swallowed the remaining brew, then followed Tawl outside. The knight might be wise in many ways, but he still had one hard lesson to learn.

Eighteen

As always, Melli scraped the dripping from the bread. Mistress Greal allowed her no butter, so she had to make do with what she got. Bacon grease today, by the smell of it. Hitching up her dress, she rubbed the grease into her belly. Her stretched and tautened skin drank it up.

As she worked, she spoke to the baby beneath: gentle words of nonsense mixed heavily with love. This was her favorite part of the day; too early by far for a visit from Mistress Greal or Kylock, she could sit in her uncushioned chair with her shawl pulled close around her shoulders and imagine that Tawl would soon be coming to take her far away.

It was strange, really. All her life, she had believed people who daydreamed were weak and mindless fools. Now she knew she was wrong. There was strength to be found in dreams. Lots of it. And when there was nothing else in life—only violence and the fear of it—the strength drawn from make-believe worlds was enough to carry on.

So she sat and rubbed and dreamed. If she was careful enough, and didn't look at her hands or her legs or her arms, she sometimes managed to forget where she was.

It was amazing what the body could bear. Her pregnancy seemed to make her body more resilient. If Kylock bound her wrists, which he did often, the rope burns would take less than two days to heal. The wax burns took longer, but the bruises often went away overnight. At the moment, her right palm had a burn the size of a flame tip upon it, and one of the bones in her right wrist was bent out of shape.

Her face may, or may not, have been bruised—she couldn't tell. There was no mirror or glass in the room. But even if her skin *was* marked, Kylock had not done it. He never beat her on the face. Only Mistress Greal did that.

Neither face nor belly, that was Kylock's way.

The bolt on the door whirred softly. Melli pushed down her dress, wiping the grease on the hem. Her stomach contracted and the baby protested by kicking against her abdomen. No matter how healthy she felt, how strong her daydreams made her, the noise of the bolt being drawn back destroyed all courage in an instant.

Kylock entered the room. Straightaway, Melli knew he was lucid. His eyes focused sharp like a fox. "Good morning, my precious," he said. He moved like no other. Like a dancer with knives: graceful, guarded, deadly.

Melli had come to know him over the past month. She knew what to say and what not to say. She knew his moods and the signs of those moods.

She knew what he wanted.

It was very early, and he was dressed finely, so there would be no blood. He was wearing gloves, silk not leather, so that meant there was a good chance he would touch her. Folding her arms across her belly, she inclined her head in greeting. "I am glad you chose to come today."

The words stung like salt in a wound. They hurt her baby, her pride, and her father's memory, but she spoke them all the same. Yes, she knew what Kylock wanted. She also knew her one chance of survival was to go along with him. She'd be dead within an hour if she didn't.

Kylock was insane, Melli was sure of it. And that insanity led him down paths that were black and twisted.

Somehow that night in the tower, when the lantern fell
and the rushes began to burn, she had become a beacon of
light along the dark road of Kylock's madness. He
thought he needed her. He thought she could save him.
She couldn't yet guess what his ultimate plan for her was,
but she knew that her pregnancy was important to him.
The only time he ever laid a hand upon her belly was to
feel the child beneath.

Kylock was not the only person with a plan. Melli had
one of her own. She was trapped here, that much she
knew. There was no chance of escape: the Highwall army
would not be coming to rescue her, though her father
would surely try; she was guarded day and night; the door
was always firmly locked, and she was never allowed out
of her room. Her only hope was Tawl. When he and Jack
were finished in the south, he would come back and save
her. Castle walls, siege armies, Kylock, and even
Baralis—nothing and no one would stop him.

All she had to do was stay alive until he returned.

And since Kylock was the one person who was stopping Baralis from executing her, she would tolerate,
encourage, and even respect him. Whatever it took, she
would do.

Kylock came and knelt beside her. He took her hand in
his. Flipping it over to look at the burnt palm, he said,
"Has the pain enabled you to see more clearly?"

By now she knew the question was a trap. Answer no,
and he would inflict a separate pain on her, on a different
part of her body. Answer yes, and she would get more of
the same. Melli managed a grim smile. At least he gave
her a choice.

She cursed her hand for shaking and her heart for
beating fast. Taking a calming breath, she stretched her
arm full out before her. There was a long distance
between her belly and her palms. A safe distance. "The
pain clarified my thoughts, sire," she said. "Last night I
saw my sins laid out before me, classified and labeled like

specimens in a jar." It was amazing what nonsense her mind came up with. Quickly, she glanced at Kylock.

He nodded once then stood. Without looking, she knew what he would reach for: the candle by the bedside. Mistress Greal allowed her the candle, but not the means to light it. Kylock never came without a flint.

The flint was struck. Melli closed her eyes. A child's terror came upon her: the fear of burns and pain and monsters. Her stomach squeezed in upon itself. Her entire body shook. Kylock drew near, candle glowing brightly in his hand. His eyes were growing blank. Melli felt a burning sensation in her throat. She swallowed deeply, and as she did so, she distilled all her thoughts into one, concentrating on the only thing that mattered in the tortured madness that had become her life.

Daydreams weren't her only access to power. The baby inside was, too.

It was only a short walk down to the harbor, but somehow they managed to lose Nabber along the way.

As far as mornings went this one was definitely a first, thought Jack. By his reckoning, it was growing close to winter in the north, yet here in Rorn the breezes were barely cool. The sky was blue and full of seagulls and the sun was large and golden. The harbor was bustling. People, pigs, crates, and donkeys jostled for space on the road. The air smelled as if it came straight from the sewers, and the sights to be seen were so numerous that Jack had a hard time choosing where to look.

If there was a choice between a boat and a pretty girl there was never much contest, though.

All three of them left the tavern less than quarter of an hour back, but now, as they approached the wharf, only he and Tawl were casting shadows to the west.

As soon as Tawl realized Nabber had gone, he simply shrugged his shoulders and said, "The next time we see him, he'll need a cart for that sack of his." Jack took this to mean that Nabber was off doing some pocketing, and by the sounds of things that suited Tawl nicely.

The knight was even more withdrawn than normal this morning. His face was tense, his words were sparse, and his movements were pared down to the bone. Judging from the dark circles beneath his eyes, the incident last night in the tavern had robbed him of sleep. Jack would have liked to ask him how he felt, but he knew Tawl wasn't one for talk. Jack couldn't help but admire Tawl's continuing faith in Tyren—even as he knew it was an illusion waiting to be shattered. Believing in something against all odds was the hardest thing of all.

Jack kicked at the wooden boards of the wharf. He hadn't managed such a feat with Tarissa. The first sign of wrongdoing and he had condemned, punished, and abandoned her. He bitterly regretted that now. He had been too harsh, too judgmental, seeing only black and white. Nothing gray.

Tawl tapped Jack on the arm. "This way," he said.

Jack was glad of the distraction; thinking about Tarissa was dangerous. Regrets were dangerous. Everything in the past needed to stay in the past—at least until this journey was over. Too much was at stake in the present.

Tawl led him down a narrow wharf that trailed between two lines of boats. The planks were wet, slippery with salt, barely suspended above the water. On either side sailors were busy unloading their wares. They threw huge crates at each other, catching them deftly, then toting them down the wharf as if it were the firmest, flattest road.

"Well, call me a randy walrus! If that isn't our old friend Tawl, then I'll eat nothing but fish-ends for a week!"

Jack looked up. A large boat was docked at the end of a wharf. Perched on the highest of its two masts was a man with shocking red hair and the grin of the devil himself.

Tawl waved his arm high above his head. "You reek like a randy walrus, Carver. I can smell you from here."

Another red-haired man popped up on deck. "I've heard he rollicks like one, too. Lots of honking and self-applause."

"Fyler!" Tawl dashed ahead. He leapt across the gang-plank and onto the ship. The second red-haired man captured him in a huge bear hug.

The first beamed at him from high atop the mast. "Finally got a hankering to see me after all this time, eh, Tawl?" he shouted.

"Well, it was a close call between your handsome face and Captain Quain's special reserve."

Jack made his way forward. He was amazed at the change in Tawl. It was hard to believe that this roguish, bantering man was the same person he'd walked here with.

Tawl caught sight of him and beckoned him onward. "Come on, Jack. Come and meet the finest sailors ever to raise anchor in Rorn." Tawl was now surrounded by a group of mostly red-haired men. Insults flew faster than the seagulls overhead, but there was no mistaking the warmth of the sailors' welcome.

"*Jack*," cried the man from the mast. "That's a worse name than Tawl. I wouldn't call the ship's cat Jack."

"You would call it dinner, though, Carver," chipped in the one named Fyler. "I saw you eyeing that cat up last week. You were fancying how it would look in a pie."

Carver nodded his head merrily. "It would be a damn sight more useful as a pie than a rat-killer."

"If we let old Tawl here bake the pie, we'd all end up dead—including the rats."

Everyone laughed. There was much muttering about raw turnips and landlubbers not knowing how to light a ship's stove. Out of the corner of his eye, Jack spotted a man emerging from below deck. Sporting red hair like the rest, he was older and more heavily set.

"What's all this hue and cry about?" he shouted.

The sailors all stopped talking at once. They stepped away from Tawl, revealing him to the older man.

"By the tides! If it's not our old shipmate Tawl." The man moved forward, arms stretched out. He clasped Tawl's hands. "My heart grows larger for seeing you again."

Tawl's face was hard to read. His knuckles were white as he clutched the older man's arms. "It's been too long, Captain," he said.

The man shook his head. "Nay, lad. There's no such thing as too long between friends. The timing is always right."

Hearing the genuine affection of the captain's words made Jack feel left out. He had never experienced the welcome of an old friend. He always moved forward, never back. Slowly, he began to ease away from the crowd of sailors. His movement was spotted by Carver up in the mast, who shouted at the top of his voice:

"Eh, Captain. Tawl's brought another green-face along with him. Name 'o Jack, I'm sorry to say."

The captain turned in the direction that Carver indicated. Jack stopped in his tracks. The man's sharp gray eyes focused upon him.

"Captain Quain," said Tawl, "this is my good friend Jack."

Jack watched as the captain, a large man who looked as healthy as a dog, brought his hand to his chest and fell backward onto the deck.

"Don't know what came over me," said Captain Quain, bringing the glass of rum to his lips. He swallowed its contents in one. "Aah. That's better." He slammed the glass down on the banded wooden table. "I've sailed the high seas for close to half a century now, and I've never had such a turn in my life."

Jack noticed the captain's eyes avoided him.

They were belowdecks in a small, brightly lit cabin. Fyler had just left. Even though the captain had insisted on walking down the stairs, "with nothing but my sea legs beneath me," Fyler had stayed by his side until he was safely in his chair.

"So, Captain," said Tawl, "have you just got in from Marls?"

Jack glanced at Tawl. It seemed an abrupt change of subject following so soon after the captain's turn. The knight shot him a quick hard look, and Jack suddenly understood what he was doing. Captain Quain was a proud man, and proud men don't like to show weakness. Tawl, by not dwelling on the incident abovedeck, was helping the captain regain his pride.

"Aye. First light. I've a shipload of Isro silk aboard. Worth a fortune, it is." Quain took the bottle of brandy and refilled all three glasses. As he leant over to fill Jack's glass, his gaze was firmly down.

"Is silk your normal cargo, Captain?" asked Jack, determined to make the man look at him.

The captain downed his second glass before he looked Jack's way. When his eyes finally came up, he actually smiled. "Silk, spices, siege powders—anything I can get my hands on."

There was a discernible expression of relief on the captain's face. It was as if he'd jumped into water he thought would be cold, only to find it warm instead. Still looking at Jack, he continued: "Business is booming at the moment, lad, what with the war and all. Those who *are* fighting need everything they can get their hands on, those who are *considering* fighting are busy stocking up, and everyone else is so damn nervous they're hoarding just for the sake of it."

"So you wouldn't consider taking *The Fishy Few* on a charter?" said Tawl.

Captain Quain stood up. His large presence took up most of the cabin, and his booming voice filled what little was left. "I don't need the cash, lad. I'll be honest with you there. Right now Rorn to Marls and back is about as profitable a run as it's ever going to be. I could sail blindfold and still make a living." The captain turned his back on them, pausing to look at a wide, banded shelf lined with books. After a moment he said, "But there is one small problem, though."

"What's that, Captain?" asked Jack.

Quain turned to face him. "The straits, lad. This time of year the sea between Rorn and Marls is as thick as slow-pouring custard. There's no wind, no waves, no swell—nothing for a man to get his teeth into. Why, *The Fishy Few* practically sails herself." The captain shook his head sadly. "Right disheartening, it is."

Jack didn't need Tawl's pointed look to catch on this time. "How about the sea to the east, Captain?" he said. "What's that like this time of year?"

"I'll not mince words with you, lad. The eastern run's a bitch at the moment."

"How about the run to Larn?" said Tawl.

The captain didn't blink an eye. "I thought that's what we were talking about, Tawl." He smiled. His gray eyes sparkled like the sea itself. "Larn is the charter you're after, isn't it?"

Jack was beginning to like the captain. He liked his loud gruff voice, the coziness of his cabin, and the mischievous glint in his eye. Quain had known what they wanted from the start, probably from the very moment he set eyes on Tawl. Jack drank his second glass of rum. Brandy was lamp fuel compared to this golden brew.

Tawl leant over the table. "We need to get to Larn as soon as possible."

The captain rubbed his jowls. He looked at Jack and then back at Tawl. "A pressing matter, I take it?"

"The future of the north depends on it," said Tawl.

Jack thought for a moment, then added, "And the life of a beautiful woman." Tawl sent him a puzzled look, but Jack knew he was right to say it. Captain Quain didn't seem the sort of man to be swayed by thoughts of saving the north.

"A beautiful woman, eh?"

"The most beautiful," said Jack. "Eyes the color of the midnight sky, skin as soft as silk, and hair . . . " He shook his head. "Hair as dark and fragrant as a tropical wood." As he spoke, Jack looked only at the captain. For some reason he didn't fancy meeting Tawl's gaze.

Quain held the rum bottle up to the light, found its contents wanting, and brought out another from a cabinet. The top was corked and waxed. The captain took one of the candles from the shelf and put the flame to the wax. Catching Jack's puzzled glance, he said, "Aye, lad, I know what you're thinking. If I broke the seal by hand I could get to the rum sooner. But if I did I'd be missing out on the most important pleasure of all."

"Anticipation?"

The captain smiled his way. "I like you, Jack. You're a smart lad." He gave Jack a quick searching look, as if he were trying to put a name to a face. Only he knew the name already. Shaking himself, he brushed the last of the liquid wax from the bottle top. Taking a cork that was barely blackened in his fist, he pulled the bottle open. He made a quick gesture to Jack and Tawl, urging them to drink the last drops in their glasses, and then poured three new measures of rum. In silence they downed the brew.

Finally, when his glass was empty once more and enough time had passed for the rum to mellow on his tongue, the captain spoke. "A woman whose eyes are the color of midnight is a treasure well worth sailing for. *The Fishy Few*'s anchor has been raised for a lot less, I can tell you. Men sail for many reasons: for gold, for adventure, to escape their pasts or to find a new future. I sail for one thing and one thing alone: *for the love of it*."

Quain's eyes were no longer focused on any point in

the room. They were seeing something that was not there. "I sail because the sea changes color from day to day, because the wind whips and chides one minute and caresses like a lover the next. I sail because my body has more salt than blood in it, and my soul never follows me ashore." Slowly, the captain's eyes refocused on the present. He looked directly at Jack. "I'll sail to Larn, my friend. I'll sail for a beautiful woman and for the love of the sea, and because a sailor never knows a place until he's been there thrice."

Jack's heart was pumping. Captain Quain spoke with such emotion, such rhythm in his voice, it was impossible not to be carried away by his words. Jack felt the pull of the sea, the same pull that Quain spoke of, yet up until today he'd never been on a boat in his life. He hastily downed his rum. Nothing made any sense.

"How soon can we sail?" asked Tawl.

"How soon do you need to?"

"Tomorrow. First light."

The captain smiled. "Tide's no good tomorrow morning, lad. It'll have to be tonight or not at all."

Jack and Tawl looked at each other. Neither of them had hoped for this. "Captain, I don't know how to thank you," said Tawl.

"Oh, I've got an idea or two," said Quain, eyes twinkling. "I've got a hold full of silk for one thing. Can't move until it's been off-loaded. And then, I'll need someone to get me supplies for the journey—plenty of rum o' course. And, seeing as there's two of you this time, I'll not need to send the cook ashore, but he'll certainly need some help for the extra hands."

"What about Nabber?" said Jack to Tawl.

"He stays here. Larn is no place for a young boy." Tawl turned to Quain. "We have no money to pay you now, Captain, but our friend may have secured enough once we return. If he hasn't, then I'll give you all we have, both our horses and a promissory note."

"No help from the Old Man this time, eh?"

Tawl shook his head.

"Good. I like it better that way. Not that I've anything against the Old Man, mind. It's just that I feel happier knowing that my hand's on the tiller, and your hand's on the coffers." The captain opened the cabin door. "I'll take whatever you have when we return. You're a man of your word, Tawl. I don't think you'd leave the crew with empty pockets."

"They'd keelhaul me if I did." Tawl stood up and walked through the door. Jack followed him. They took turns grasping the captain's hand and then headed onto the deck. They had a hard day's work ahead of them.

Tavalisk was racing frogs. His cook, Master Bunyon, had turned up with them only a few minutes earlier with the intent of asking the archbishop which one he fancied delimbing first. Tavalisk had immediately thrown the rubbery little amphibians onto the floor and was currently encouraging them to jump by promising to eat the loser in a lemon-garlic sauce.

Neither frog was taking much notice of him—a fact that caused the archbishop so much consternation that he was just about to stamp his foot on the most lethargic of the two when in walked Gamil.

"Know anything about frogs, Gamil?"

"A frog is a tailless amphibian, Your Eminence." Standing where he was—by the door—Gamil had not yet spotted the frogs in question. "Their most distinctive feature is their long hind legs, and they are found most commonly in damp or aquatic habitats."

Splat!

"Hmm," said the archbishop. "They squash well, too." Tavalisk beckoned his aide forth. Together, they studied the remains of the frog. "You're quite right, Gamil. No tail."

The sudden obliteration of its brother-in-arms caused

the second frog to rethink its position on jumping, and it bounded across the floor, managing to successfully evade both Gamil and Master Bunyon by leaping under the archbishop's desk.

"Get up, man!" snapped Tavalisk, as his aide dove under said desk in search of the runaway frog. "Really. I expect a little dignity from those who serve me." Tavalisk knew Gamil had chased the frog to please him, but he liked to keep his aide in a constant state of bafflement: it kept him on his toes.

Tavalisk turned to Master Bunyon. "What are you staring at?" He pointed toward the squashed frog. "Don't just stand there, scrape it up and cook it."

"But the legs, Your Eminence. They're ruined."

"Well, scramble it with some eggs, then. Bake it in a pie. I really don't care what you do with it as long as I'm eating it within the hour. Now go."

Master Bunyon nodded, scraped, and then left.

As soon as the door was closed behind him, Gamil stepped forward. "Your Eminence, we must take action."

Tavalisk groaned. "What now, Gamil? Have the knights taken over Marls? Is Kylock calling himself a god?"

"No, Your Eminence. The knight has returned to Rorn, and by the looks of things he's setting sail for Larn."

Riddit, riddit, went the frog under the desk.

"This is interesting. When did he get in?"

"He was spotted last night in a tavern by the dock. He's still got the pocket in tow, but he's also picked up someone else. A young man, by all accounts. They headed down to the docks together this morning. And as luck would have it *The Fishy Few* had just come in from Marls." Gamil looked a little edgy as he talked. His brow was slick with sweat, and he dabbed at it with the sleeve of his robe. "We've got to stop them from leaving the city, Your Eminence."

"Why on earth should we, Gamil? What's it to us if they go to the godforsaken isle of Larn?"

"But the knight is wanted for the duke of Bren's murder. Catherine's, too. He's a notorious criminal."

"Not by me, though. It's Baralis who wants the knight's head on a stake." Tavalisk took off his left shoe; the sole was slippery with frog scum. "I think we should just watch and wait as usual."

"But it's your duty to act, Your Eminence. You're the chosen one."

What was this? Flattery? Gamil was certainly acting strangely today. "What would *you* have me do, Gamil?"

"Send out a band of armed guards to pick up the knight and his new companion. Bring them in, torture, then kill them."

"That seems a little hasty."

"But, Your Eminence, you've said all along that the knight had a part to play in the coming conflict in the north. What if his part conflicts with your own? He could rob you of your only chance for glory."

"Gamil, a man such as myself has many chances for glory." Tavalisk wriggled his pudgy toes. "Glory is my element. It shines upon me like sunlight. No one person is going to come along and rob me of it—unless of course it's the reaper. Even then I think I'd make a glorious corpse."

"You would indeed, Your Eminence."

Tavalisk looked up sharply. Gamil was looking down. *Riddit, riddit.*

"Where are they staying?" asked the archbishop with a heavy sigh. "It won't do me any harm to bring them in for questioning."

"The Rose and Crown, Your Eminence."

"Very well. I'll send someone round there early tomorrow morning. A predawn raid should catch them nicely unawares."

"Couldn't we act today, Your Eminence?"

Tavalisk was beginning to feel a little suspicious of Gamil's eagerness. "No. I will take no action before tomorrow. If the ship just came in from Marls, then it certainly won't sail before morning." The archbishop handed Gamil his shoe. "Once you've caught that damned frog, Gamil, be so good as to see if you can remove the stain from this." He thought for a moment, then added: "Oh, and I'll need you in the palace for the rest of the day. You can help me with His Holiness' paperwork."

"But, Your Eminence, I have other matters to attend to."

Tavalisk's plump lips turned as tough as a dried fruit. "You will stay here with me, Gamil, and that's the last I want to hear of it."

Tawl watched the last mooring rope being pulled up from the quay. Carver and another crewman were winding out the sails. It was nearly dark. Soon Rorn would be a white city that glowed across the waves. A spot on the horizon, like the early moon. Who could tell what would happen between now and when they saw it next? Perhaps they might never see it again.

Larn was the closest thing to hell on earth, and the devil always protected his own.

Even now Tawl could feel the island. It was out there in the eastern sea, expecting them, waiting. Confident.

Tawl glanced at Jack. He was asking Fyler why Carver had called him a green-face. Seasickness was the answer: first-timers were notorious for suffering from it. Smiling, Tawl looked away. Jack was a green-face in more ways than one. Here he was, heading to Larn, without the faintest idea of what was expected of him once he got there. Tawl knew his part was easy compared to Jack's. All he had to do was provide the opportunity, find a way in there, clear a path, and keep the priests at bay. Jack had to do more. So much more that Tawl couldn't bear to think about it. How could one man raze the temple to the ground? It was the sort of responsibility that could crush a man's spirit and turn a sound mind bad. Yet, Jack was on the deck with Carver, chatting away as if he didn't have a care in the world.

Tawl made his way to the bow of the boat. He would do the worrying for both of them.

Nabber still hadn't shown up. Which was probably a good thing: the boy would only stamp his feet and demand to come along. Tawl would have to ignore his pleas. He would rest easier knowing Nabber was in Rorn. If anything should happen to them on Larn, at least he knew the boy would be safely back in the city he called home.

Larn was not Nabber's affair. It was for him and Jack alone. In a way Tawl wished it was just for him. He had earned the right to bring it down. Larn had destroyed his life, his dreams, and his quest. Its priests had made a murderer out of him, and it was time they paid the price.

The timbers of *The Fishy Few* began to creak and roll, and the sails grew fat with the wind. The ship was on its way.

Tawl moved away from the bow. He was going belowdecks. He didn't fancy testing his sea legs just yet. As he drew back the bolt of the main hatch, Jack looked over at him. Their gazes met, and Tawl suddenly knew he'd been wrong about him. Jack was no carefree adventurer: he was a young man with fear in his eyes.

Nineteen

*I*t was easy to fall into the old habits of Rorn: nodding discreet *hellos* to fellow pockets, keeping a safe distance between you and the pimps, pilfering hot pies from slow barrow-boys, and always keeping an eye out for friends of the Old Man.

It certainly was the life! A boy could get right comfortable here, make a home and a living for himself. Make a boatful of coinage, too. In fact, ever since Jack and Tawl had sailed off into the sunset nearly four days back, there'd been little else to do but acquire loot.

Now, it wasn't that he thought Jack and Tawl were in the wrong about going off without him—a man's life was his own and he could do with it whatever he wanted, no questions asked—but a few words of parting might have been nice. You know, *"Bye Nabber, see you in a few days. In a week. In a month. In the afterlife."* Something had been called for. As it was, he'd had to figure the whole thing out on his own.

And the fact that he was good at figuring out was beside the point. Tawl should have let him know the plan from the start. Right dishonorable it was, them taking off in the middle of the night. Another boy might have considered it a mortal insult. Another boy might just have wiped his hands of the whole affair.

Not him, though. Grievously hurt as he was, he would

do his duty by them. And it was more than either of the thankless traitors deserved.

He knew they'd need loot when they returned. A ship as large and fancy as *The Fishy Few* didn't set sail without the assurance of gold, and as far as Nabber knew, Tawl hadn't got a penny on him, which meant that the knight had promised payment to the good captain when he returned. That was the first thing Nabber had figured out.

The second thing was that Tawl was obviously expecting him to come up with the loot in his absence—like his own personal treasurer. Talk about taking a boy for granted!

Indeed, if it hadn't been for the third thing Nabber had figured out, he might well have chucked the whole thing in and gone back to work for his old friend Swift—if he could ever find him, of course. There was no one like Swift for lying long and low. But no, that was out of the question now. Jack and Tawl were in danger the minute they returned to Rorn. The archbishop's henchmen were after them. A band of armed men had raided the Rose and Crown in the wee hours of the morning looking for them. It was lucky for Jack and Tawl that *The Fishy Few* had sailed some seven hours earlier, else they'd be deep in a dark dungeon by now.

Anyway, the raid was the reason why Nabber had to stick around. Someone had to warn Jack and Tawl about the archbishop's plan before they got off the boat. Nabber shook his head sadly. Those two just weren't as smart as him when it came to dodging men with knives.

Coming to a fork in his path, Nabber chose the way that looked most interesting: the dark alleyway with the foul stench and the greasy-looking cobblestones. He'd been wandering around for some time now. The first pocketing shift of the day—the market hours between sunup and two—had been nicely profitable. And the second shift—the wenching spell between eight and midnight—was still a good few hours ahead. So, he had nothing to do at the moment but kick dirt and revisit his old hunting grounds.

Strange, but nothing seemed quite as good as he remembered. Oh, it was dodgy all right, and rife with as many possibilities as a bishop on the make, but it just wasn't all he'd expected.

Feeling a little disheartened, Nabber decided to head back to the market district. As he spun around, something dark and smelling of figs was thrown over his head. *"Murder!"* he cried at the top of his voice. *"Pimps! Help!"* He was grabbed, lifted from the ground, and the sack-thing was pulled tightly across his face. Screaming, he was carried away.

Baralis was nervous. Tonight he would do something he'd never done before. Something so unpredictable and strength-depleting that it could conceivably harm himself.

He was in his chambers. It was twilight, but Crope had stoked the fire to a furnace and lit so many candles that it now looked like day. The newly born calf was in a copper bath by Baralis' feet. Barely alive, it still managed to whine for its mother. Crope had purchased it fresh in its caul this morning, yet already it was losing the special luster that accompanied a creature from the womb.

There was power in birthing. The herdsmen of the Great Plains knew it, his teacher in Hanatta knew it, and now, as he sat but a hand's length away from a creature who had drawn its first breath only nine hours earlier, Baralis knew it, too.

The womb was not just tissue and muscle and blood. It was a barrier between worlds. On one side was life: fertile, abundant, decaying. On the other was existence and the *beginnings* of existence: vulnerable, pure, benign. When the two sides met—when water broke and young were expelled and muscles contracted like a mighty olive press—power was generated. And that power was granted to the newborn.

Rich with the secrets of the ovaries, heavy with the blood of the placenta, nothing provided as strong a sorcery as a life taken fresh from the womb.

During his time in the Great Plains, Baralis had seen the herdsmen harness the power of a newborn babe to create the lacus. It had taken six of their wisemen to contain it. Even now Baralis could remember the terrible backlash, feel the searing heat on his skin, and smell the burning flesh as the arms of two of the six were charred to the elbow. Baralis shuddered. Afterward the wisemen, drunk on grain alcohol and valerian root, swore the drawing had been a success. Lost limbs were nothing compared to the value of the lacus. Wisemen's arms were expendable—the tribe's hunters had to be healed regardless of the cost. Baralis ran a finger across his lips. He would never dare to take a newborn child himself.

Crope made the arrangements, bringing cup, knife, and powder. Baralis settled down in his high-backed chair and watched his servant prepare the beast.

Debts were dangerous bedfellows—especially if they'd been accrued at Larn's expense. The priests on that windswept isle kept short tally, and they always demanded payment in full.

That was what tonight was: payment in full. They had told him their secrets and now he would act on their behalf. The baker's boy had to be stopped. He was on his way to Larn to destroy the temple, and if he succeeded Baralis knew it wouldn't be long before his former scribe headed back toward Bren. Oh, Larn was a valuable asset in the war; it fed them information direct from the gods themselves. But it wasn't essential. He could dominate the north without the help of its seers. So tonight Baralis wasn't only repaying a debt: he was working on his own behalf.

Jack was the one person who could prove a serious

threat to his plans. Wrapped in an ancient prophecy, he had powers that defied all reason. First he turned back time and then last summer he destroyed an entire garrison, sending shockwaves throughout the Known Lands. He had to be destroyed, Baralis knew that as simply as a child knew the sky was blue.

Only tonight, over a certain section of the sea southwest of Larn, the skies wouldn't be blue at all. They'd be blacker than the deepest pits in hell.

Baralis leant forward and sliced the shaking calf. Blood spattered his face and tunic. The calf screamed like a baby. Crope hovered close with his hearth-warmed bowl. Baralis bit down on his tongue, his teeth piercing deep into the muscle to draw the tissue-rich blood. Baralis braced himself, then railed against the physical world. His body let him go. Reaching out, he caught the essence of the beast. It hit him like a jolt from a lance.

It sent him reeling. The soul of the calf was still its mother's, but the power was all its own. Baralis was borne upward by it. At first he was confused, disorientated, drunk with the sheer potency of the force unleashed by the blade. Then, as always, his will rose up to meet the challenge, compelling, reshaping, claiming the power for its own. Like God, Baralis fashioned the creation in his own image. He made it his alone.

The power was breathtaking: the room could not contain it. Baralis stopped rising upward and expanded *outward*, instead. He stretched across the palace, then Bren, then the north. No longer a loose scattering of particles, he was a deadly force of nature. Southward he sped along the coast, causing the tides to reverse in his wake.

"So, Captain," said Jack, "you said this will be your third trip to Larn?"

Quain looked at him sharply. Four days they had been sailing now, and every time the captain crossed his path,

Jack got the distinct feeling he was being studied like a chart marked with buried treasure.

This was the first time they'd been alone. Tawl was on deck, trading insults with Carver, no doubt. Either that or sharpening his knives. The knight spent a lot of time seeing to his weapons, and over the past two days had taken to rubbing grease into the blades to protect them from the damp, salty air.

A bottle of rum was never far from Quain's hand, and he tilted one now in the direction of two short glasses. Just as the rum level rose to the top of the second glass, the ship suddenly lurched to the side. Amber liquid went spilling across the table, where it pooled against the wooden band.

"Swell's rising, Captain," said Fyler, popping his head around the doorframe.

"Aye, man. Keep an eye to it," said the captain. Fyler nodded then disappeared, and the captain turned his attention back to the rum.

Jack was aware that the sea was growing restless; he could feel the boat rolling and jawing beneath his feet. But he was strangely unaffected by it: no seasickness, no queasiness, no fear. A born sailor, Carver had said. Reaching out to take his glass of rum, Jack prompted the captain again: "So when did you first visit Larn?"

The captain managed a grudging smile. "You're persistent, lad. I'll give you that."

"Let's drink to my persistence, then," said Jack, raising his glass and smiling like a rogue. "And your knowledge of the sea."

The captain's glass came up to meet his. "The sea."

They both downed their drinks in one. Quain slammed his glass down on the table. "Aah. It gets your blood running every time." He leant back in his chair and took a while to savor the rum before he spoke again.

"The first time I sailed close to Larn it nearly cost me my commission. Over thirty years ago it was now. I was on a big merchant ship name o' *The Bountiful Breeze*. Four masts it had, and a crew of close to forty men. It was my first time out as a navigator and I was shaky as a jellyfish. Thinking back now, I'm amazed that anyone would have let me within a galley's length of the wheel. Still, Rorn was booming at the time, and the merchants were willing to take on any man as long as he knew the stern from the prow.

"We were due to sail up the coast to Toolay. Pick up seafood and drop off silk threads for their embroidery. Well, the minute *The Bountiful Breeze* left the harbor, things began to go wrong. The wind was blowing from the northeast—now, that in itself was strange, as it was early winter, and the northeasterlies never hit until spring. But that wasn't the only thing that was odd. The ship's compass started to play up, spinning around like a top one minute, dead as a rusty anchor the next. Then came the storm. . . . "

Captain Quain shook his head. *The Fishy Few* rocked back and forth. Outside, Jack could hear the wind picking up.

"It was a bad one. Came out of nowhere, it did. There were waves crashing into the foredeck, water leaking into the hold. The sails were ripped straight from the masts and we lost three men overboard. It lasted three days. By the time it was over, the ship's cat had about as good an idea of where we lay as I did."

As the captain spoke, Jack was forced to hold onto the table to stop himself from being thrown from his chair. The entire cabin was creaking. With every roll of the ship, glasses, books, and instruments were thrown against the wooden bands on the shelves. There was an oil lamp hanging from the wall, and it swung back and forth like a drunkard at a dance.

Quain was as calm as ever. He continued speaking in his warm, gruff voice, and soon nothing mattered but what he said.

"Well, I gets out my spyglass and takes a quick shifty round. On the horizon is this little rocky isle. So, I consult my charts and find no sign of it, then talk to the captain, who takes a look for himself and pronounces that the isle is Larn. 'Best get a move on out of here, boy,' he says. 'Lest the devil catch us all unawares.' I tell you, I turned that ship round as fast as if it were a rowboat—no one's as superstitious as a sailor lost at sea.

"Anyway, we're just setting back the way we came when I takes another shifty from the glass. That's when I see her."

"See who?"

"The girl from Larn. She was adrift on a skiff with neither sails nor oars to get her moving. Right away I can tell she's in trouble, for she's just lying there, not moving a muscle. So the first thing I do is turn *The Bountiful Breeze* round once more. Up comes the captain cursing and yelling and orders me to turn her about. Well, we have a terrible row. He doesn't want to pick up the girl. He says it's bad luck and we'll all be cursed. I says it was no coincidence that *The Bountiful Breeze* was blown off course, and that we were fated to rescue the girl. Soon the whole crew's involved, and the captain has little choice but to go along. Sailor's superstition works both ways—I managed to convince the crew that it would bring us all bad luck if we left the girl to die."

The storm outside was building. Jack could hear the crew calling to each other, shouting to be heard above the roar of the waves.

"The poor thing was as good as dead when we got to her. There was nothing in the skiff: no food or water, no spare clothes. She was hot with fever. Delirious. She rambled on in her sleep, crying out a boy's name over and over again. Aye, but she was beautiful, though. A slip of a girl with long dark hair. I think everyone on board fell in love with her—including the captain. You just couldn't look at her without wanting to make everything right.

We all chipped in our rations; the cook made her special broth and the captain broke out the special brew. I tended to her day and night.

"Her fever broke the day we docked in Rorn. I asked her what she was doing cast adrift on a skiff off Larn. You know what she said?"

"No."

"She said, 'Please don't force me to lie. What happened at Larn is between God, the priests, and myself.'"

The lantern swung back and forth, sending shadows darting across the captain's face. Everything in the room was moving in time with the storm: the table, the chairs, the rum. Jack's heart raced ahead of them all.

"Why do you think she was cast adrift?" he asked.

"She was running away." Quain met his eye. He searched Jack's features for a moment and then dropped his gaze to his glass. Neither man spoke for a while.

An ear-splitting crash broke the silence. The ship pitched sharply to port. All of the captain's belongings smashed against the bands. A collection of rolled charts went spilling to the floor. The oil lamp slammed against the wall. Lightning flashed.

The captain leapt from his chair. "It's time I was on deck. Dampen the lights, then follow me up."

"Wake up, boy! Wake up! It's disrespectful to sleep in the presence of the Old Man."

Nabber was shaken, prodded, cajoled, and finally freed from his bindings. His first instinct was to smooth back his hair. His second instinct was to feel for his sack. Gone. Bleary-eyed, sore-headed, and indignant, Nabber took in his surroundings. Nice. Very nice. A good fire, gold-embellished furniture, and enough fresh flowers to bury a family of four.

"You should count yourself lucky, young man," came a voice from behind.

Nabber swung around. An old man was sitting in the

corner. He was dressed well but plainly, and had no hair to call his own. Thinking he'd got the gist of the situation, Nabber said, "I tell you now, sir, I've got nothing against you types, but it's just not my meat of choice."

The old man burst out laughing. The man behind joined in.

Unsure what to do next, Nabber finally settled for a long, sweeping glare. As he caught the eye of the one who'd brought him, a tiny little shift took place in his brain: he recognized this man. It was the smaller of the two cronies who had delivered the letter to Tawl in Bren. What was it he said when he woke him up? It's disrespectful to sleep in the presence of *the* Old Man, not *an* old man. Nabber took a gulp big enough to swallow an apple whole. He was in the Old Man's lair. And the person who he'd just insulted was none other than the Old Man himself.

"Moth, would you be so good as to leave us alone?" said the Old Man.

"No problem, Old Man. Me and Clem will be waiting outside." The one named Moth bowed and left.

The Old Man turned his attention back to Nabber. "Sit. Sit," he said, indicating a chair near the fire.

Nabber sat. When in the presence of Rorn's greatest crime lord, it was best to do as you were told. "Nice arrangements," he said, nodding to the various vases filled with flowers. "Must be hard to get your hands on such a variety at this time of year."

The Old Man smiled a dry little smile. "I do my best."

Nabber cursed himself for not knowing more about flowers. He could hardly tell a tulip from a turnip. "Smell real nice, they do. Brighten the room up considerably."

"We all have to have our little indulgences. Mine is fresh flowers; yours, I hear, is a certain wayward knight." Nabber went to speak, but the Old Man didn't give him a chance. "Now, as I said earlier, you are quite lucky, my friend. I could have had Moth and Clem give you a real nasty blow to your skull. Instead they brought you in the nice way, with just a sack over your head."

"That sack nearly killed me!" Nabber wasn't about to have anyone, including the Old Man, tell him he was lucky when he'd nearly died of suffocation. "I passed clean out. Couldn't breathe to save my life."

"Yes, that *was* unfortunate." The Old Man smiled again, this time rather merrily. "I think it's time we got down to business. I believe your friend has left the city—heading to Larn, so I've heard. Now, as far as *he* is concerned I have no choice but to wipe my hands of him. He murdered a dear friend of mine, and I couldn't call myself a man of honor unless I acted honorably, could I?"

Nabber nodded. The Old Man had a point there.

"So that leaves me with a choice. I could either sit back and do nothing—my duty to Bevlin ended the minute the letter was delivered—or I could do what little I could to continue the wiseman's cause."

Nabber was sharp enough to realize that he wouldn't be here if the Old Man had decided on the first option. He remained outwardly nonchalant, though. Let the Old Man say his piece.

"I think I owe Bevlin more than a letter. Many years ago now he saved my daughter's life. Not with sorcery, mind, but with his potions. Daisy was bad with red fever and everyone said it was too late. Bevlin was in Toolay at the time and I sent word to him by pigeon. That man was in Rorn three days later—how he managed it I still don't know—but he made it anyway, and he saved my sweet Daisy's life. And that's why I brought you here today. I still don't think I've done enough to repay that debt."

The Old Man got up, walked toward the fire, and rearranged the flowers on the mantel, throwing all the red ones into the flames. "I can never speak with or see Tawl again, but I'd be fooling myself if I didn't admit that Bevlin would have wanted me to help him. Even after all that has happened." He turned to face Nabber. "So that's why I've brought you here."

"Because you can't talk to Tawl, so you'll talk to me, instead?" Nabber's eyes were on the arrangement above the fire. Without the red ones it looked decidedly odd.

"Yes. So listen hard, for I'll say this only once." The Old Man moved close. His sharp little face was nothing but a backdrop for his eyes. Almost black, they shone with all the cunning of a fox. "First of all, don't expect any help from me in terms of money or favors. Information is one thing, but I'm not about to go out of my way to help the man who murdered my friend. Tawl probably knows this already, but I'm stating it here and now to ensure there's no misunderstanding.

"Second, the archbishop is holding an old acquaintance of Tawl's in the dungeon below the palace. She's a young prostitute called Megan and she's been there for over a year now, so Borc only knows what state she's in." The Old Man paused to take a quick breath. "Last, we come to the venerable archbishop himself, or rather his chief aide, Gamil. The man has been sending and receiving messages from Larn at regular intervals over the past five years. I'm pretty certain the archbishop himself has no knowledge of this correspondence, and I'm also certain he wouldn't be too pleased if he found out." The Old Man gave Nabber a pointed look.

Nabber gave one back.

"You are aware that the archbishop intends to pick up Tawl the moment *The Fishy Few* docks in Rorn?"

"I'm ahead of you there, Old Man."

The Old Man was not displeased. "Well, that's everything I mean to say." He walked toward the door. "Tawl's on his own from here."

Sensing an imminent dismissal, Nabber stood up. "No, sir, Tawl's not on his own."

"You're right. He's got you." Opening the door, the Old Man raised an age-spotted hand to his face. "You know what, Nabber, when all this business is over with, I think you should come back and see me again. You and I would make good business partners."

Try as he might, Nabber couldn't quite stop himself from beaming from ear to ear. "Might take you up on that, Old Man."

"Might be obliged if you did."

Nabber bowed at the compliment. Just as he was out the door, he remembered his sack.

"Moth will see you get it back," said the Old Man. "Oh, and tell him I said to go easy on you on the way back. Perhaps just a fold this time, eh?"

"A fold sounds good to me." Nabber stepped out into a dimly lit chamber. The door closed behind him. Well, well, well, he thought as he was frisked for valuables by Moth, the Old Man had good as given him a plan.

"It came out of nowhere, Captain," shouted Fyler above the roar of crashing waves. "An hour ago and the sky was as clear as a mountain pool."

Tawl never heard the captain's reply, as a mighty wave crashed against the hull of the ship. A mountain of frothing water was driven over the deck and the entire ship pitched starboard. Holding on to the railings with all his might, Tawl brought his head down to his chest to stop the rain lashing at his face.

Lightning struck. It forked blue across the sky, lighting up the night with a single chilling flash. Thunder followed less than two seconds later.

Tawl watched as the captain barked out orders. A team of men were already bringing in the sails. The deck was secure and the last of the hatches was being barred. Fyler was at the wheel, but the smooth oakwood round was spinning out of control beneath his fingers.

There were three lanterns on the deck: one above the anchor mount, another above the wheel, and a third nailed against the mainmast at man height. All three of them were burning, yet their pale, bucket-sized halos of light did nothing but emphasize the dark. The temperature had dropped rapidly in the past hour. The wind had gone from a healthy breeze to a full-blown gale. It cut across the sea, slicing the tops off the swells and driving the rain hard and fast against the boat.

Out of the corner of his eye, Tawl spotted Jack emerging from belowdecks. He watched as Jack struggled to close the hatch against the wind. The ship rolled and lurched, both masts rocking wildly from side to side. The flag above the crow's nest was torn from its rope, a quick flash of yellow consumed by the dark.

Another wave hit. Tawl's left side was blasted by the surge. Water skimmed across the main and foredecks. Having secured the hatch, Jack made his way forward. Tawl was surprised at how well he moved. The deck was running with saltwater and the ship rocked like a pendulum, yet Jack's footing was sure. The rain was coming in heavy white sheets now, and Tawl couldn't make out Jack's expression until they were an arm's-length apart.

Jack gripped the rail. His eyes were dark. A muscle in his neck beat a pulse.

The crew darted about them, fastening lines, sweeping the decks, drawing in the rigging. There were two pairs of hands on the wheel now: Fyler's and the captain's. Tawl didn't know much about sailing, but he had a feeling that the only thing steering the ship was the storm.

More lightning. Thunder right behind it.

Tawl got a clear look at Jack's face. What he saw scared him. The boy's lips were drawn to a thin line. His eyes were blank. He seemed to be looking *through* the storm, not at it.

"Captain, the swell's rising fast. It'll match the hull before we know it." Carver dashed past them to the wheel.

Jack followed him. Tawl was reluctant to leave the railing, but he knew something was wrong with Jack and he had to find out what. His hands were numb with cold.

He pried them free from the railing and followed Jack to the wheel. The deck was as slick as a frozen pond. Tawl skidded with every step. The rain beat him back. Waves hit from all sides. There was a powerful gust of wind and then Tawl heard something crack.

"Whoa! Watch out!"

Instinct more than sense made Tawl leap to the side. He dived for the railings and hit an oncoming wave full-on. Water smashed against him. It was in his eyes, his nose, his throat. He couldn't breathe. A high, creaking sound split through the air. The ship rolled sharply to port. Tawl was forced to hold on to the railings with all his might to stop himself from rolling with it.

Crack!

With sea salt stinging in his eyes, Tawl watched as the aftermast crashed to the deck like a felled tree. It went smashing into the port railings, crushing them like tinder-wood.

"Cut the rigging!" cried the captain.

The cables attached to the aftermast were pulling against the mainmast. The huge central mast was listing to the port. Tawl could hear the beam creaking with strain. Carver dashed forward, knife in hand. Tawl felt for his own knife. He was up before he knew it. As soon as his left foot hit the deck, pain coursed up his ankle. He ignored it. He had no choice. The winds were high and the mainmast was listing, ready to crack. If that fell, the entire ship would go down with it.

Tawl scrambled toward the fallen aftermast. The rigging ropes were wrist-thick. They were so taut they hummed in the wind like the strings of a bow. Carver and two other crewmen were busy hacking. The mainmast towered above them. It was visibly bending. Waves beat against the hull. Surf spewed across the deck. The ship no longer rolled, it *heaved*.

Lightning flashed. Thunder roared. The wind cut the rain into razors.

One by one the rigging ropes were cut. The usually quick-tongued Carver was silent. Tawl worked by his side, sawing the ropes with the edge of his blade. Finally there were only four ropes left: those that secured the top of the aftermast to the top of the mainmast. Tawl's gaze traveled to the end of the aftermast. It was jutting out two horse-lengths across the sea. He stood up.

Carver put a hand on his arm. "No, Tawl. This is my job."

Tawl opened his mouth to protest.

Carver gripped him hard. "No, Tawl. You did me a favor once by insisting you row to Larn on your own. I haven't forgotten that, and I'm not about to let you risk your neck out there when I can do the job faster and better than you."

Tawl brought his hand up and clasped it against Carver's. "You're a brave man."

"No. I'm just a man who loves his ship."

No one on the ship spoke as Carver moved toward the broken railings. The aftermast gleamed with saltwater. Like a sapling in a gale, the mainmast leaned toward it. The last four rigging ropes bound the two masts together as surely as a leash between master and dog. Carver hoisted himself onto the aftermast and began to shunt along the beam. The blade of his knife was between his teeth, as he needed both hands to hold on. Tawl crept alongside the mast, only coming to a halt where the deck came to an end.

Thirteen men watched with baited breath. Carver was now suspended above the open sea. The waves swelled up to meet him. Reaching the end of the mast, he took the knife in his right hand and began to work on the first of the four ropes. Rain drove against his face. His legs were entwined around the beam for support. The first rope snapped back to the mainmast. A massive wave smashed against the port side. Carver was engulfed by white foam For a second no one could tell what had become of him, then the foam fell away and Carver could clearly be seen spitting saltwater from his mouth and holding onto the beam for dear life.

Everyone cheered.

Carver tipped them a nod.

Without realizing it, Tawl had stretched out along the beam, ready to catch Carver's foot or britches if he fell.

The second rope was cut and then the third. Carver hacked away at the last. The mainmast creaked like a rotten staircase, and then, as the final rope was cut, it bounded back toward the starboard side. The aftermast, which had been in part suspended by the rope, shifted downward, crushing more railings and coming to rest at a lower point above the sea.

Tawl didn't wait. He shunted out onto the beam and grabbed Carver's leg. Carver was barely above the swell line. Holding on to the beam was like holding on to a greased pole. Together, Carver and Tawl crawled back to the ship. Jack had grabbed hold of Tawl's legs, and someone else grabbed hold of him. Carver was reeled in like a fish on a line.

As soon as Tawl's feet were on deck, Jack said to him, "We've got to get off this ship now, or everyone will be killed."

Tawl, high on exhilaration and relief, was brought down in an instant. Quickly, he made sure that Carver was all right and then grabbed hold of Jack's arm and dragged him to the side of the bos'n's cabin.

"What d'you mean?"

Jack was soaked to the skin. His long hair was loose and the wind blew it into his face. "I mean this storm isn't natural. It's been created by sorcery. Can't you smell it?"

Tawl could smell salt and the sharp chemical tang of the lightning. "No."

"I don't know how it's been done, but it's been created to kill us. You and me, Tawl, not the crew. And unless we get off this ship right now, it'll take all the sailors along with us."

Tawl had never see Jack so firm. There was no question of arguing with him. "How strong is it?"

"Still strong, but given enough time it will die down. No one can keep this up for hour after hour and not be weakened."

Tawl nodded. He trusted Jack's judgment implicitly. "How far are we from Larn?"

"Captain says that when the storm hit, we were twenty leagues to the south. Borc knows where we are now."

More lightning. Thunder right behind it. Jack was right; this storm wasn't passing over, it was staying right on top of them.

Two waves hit the ship in quick succession. *The Fishy Few* bounced off the first only to plow headlong into the second. A crest of water blasted across the bow and foredeck.

"If we take a boat now, the chances are it'll be ripped apart."

Jack looked Tawl straight in the eyes. "It's either us or the entire crew."

"You think we can draw away the storm?"

"I think we can give it a try."

Tawl nodded. "Let's do it."

The rowboat was winched down to just above water level. Already it was carrying water, courtesy of the waves that kept lapping over the sides.

"I don't like this," said the captain, watching as the little boat swung back and forth on the ropes. "It's suicide to put down in a storm." As he spoke, the wind whipped through the rigging. The fall of the aftermast had left the mainmast vulnerable, and everyone tensed until the gust tapered off.

Jack didn't know what to say to the captain. He didn't want to lie, yet he wasn't sure how the captain would take the truth. He looked around for Tawl, but he was belowdecks, collecting together whatever they needed. Jack took a deep breath. "The storm's not going to pass as long as Tawl and I are here."

The captain nodded. "I'm not a fool, lad. I know." He looked across at the wheel. Fyler was struggling to gain control of the ship. His huge muscles could be seen straining in the lamplight. "A storm like this doesn't come fresh out of the blue sky of its own accord." Quain looked at Jack and smiled. "You don't sail the high seas for forty years without learning a thing or two about life."

"Boat's ready, Captain," shouted one of the crewmen.

Jack was beginning to realize why all sailors had loud voices: they needed them to shout over the roar of the waves. Making a small gesture toward the sky, he said, "I'm sorry, Captain. I would never have come on board if I thought anything like this would happen."

"Nay, lad. Don't be sorry. *The Fishy Few* isn't ready to pay her respects to the seabed just yet."

"A big one's coming in, Captain."

Jack and the captain looked out to sea. Amidst the black and the gray was a gleam of pure silver. It was the top of a swell and it towered high above the deck.

"Brace yourselves, shipmates," cried the captain.

Everyone hunkered down against the deck, grabbing at railings, mooring heads, anything that was at hand. Jack watched the swell roll forward. It was a massive shimmering wall. Sucking in his breath, he held on to the mooring head with all his might. He heard a low rumbling—like thunder, only gentler, more ominous. And then the swell collided with the ship.

The noise was a deafening rush. *The Fishy Few* rocked on its keel. The starboard deck tilted downward, and a solid cliff of water blasted into the ship. Jack's whole body felt the impact; his limbs felt as if they were being torn from their sockets, his face felt as if it had been slammed against a door. Still the water came, churning and bubbling like a mighty river. Wood splintered, lanterns smashed, someone shouted out to Borc to help save them. A high, splitting sound came from the mainmast.

The ship rolled back from the port and the last of the swell caught the hull.

Jack's fingers were frozen against the mooring head. His hair was plastered against his face. All around him, the crew jumped up and began sweeping the water from the deck, checking the lines, and running to brace the mainmast.

Tawl staggered up from belowdecks. He, too, was soaked to the skin. He took in the chaos of the scene, saw the visible crack running down the length of the mainmast, and said, "Captain, we're going now. We'll try and set a course to the north. You head away from us as fast as possible."

The captain nodded. Like everyone, his gaze was fixed on the mainmast. "Go now, then. When the storm clears we'll be back to pick you up."

Jack had difficulty catching his breath. He already knew the captain well enough not to protest. "Thank you," he said.

Captain Quain opened his mouth to say something, hesitated, then said, "Borc be with you, lad."

Before Jack knew it, they were climbing down the rope ladder. Knees, ankles, and chins took a beating against the hull. Jack could see white bands across the ocean where the wind was cutting through the swells. The rain took turns whipping then falling in sheets.

By the time he reached the boat, Jack was sporting two bloody knees, a bloody elbow, and a sprained ankle. Tawl, who was following him down, looked in even worse shape. He caught Jack staring at him and grinned.

"This is either the stupidest thing I've ever done in my life, or the bravest."

Jack grinned back. He was glad to the bone that Tawl was with him.

Working together, they untied the mooring knots and pushed the rowboat away from *The Fishy Few* with their oars. The crew leant against the railings, waving their farewells. It was too dark to make out faces and too windy to hear what was said. It didn't matter. That night Jack learnt that goodwill didn't have to be seen or spoken to be felt.

And then they were off. A wave cleaved them from the ship, bouncing them southward and filling the rowboat with cold, foamy water. Tawl bailed while Jack rowed.

The wind was slower, but colder close to the surface. The swells seemed impossibly large, yet whereas *The Fishy Few* sat high in the water and blocked their path, causing the swells to break, the little rowboat bobbed right over them.

They were fine for a while. *The Fishy Few* faded to a dark silhouette in the distance, and then, a few minutes later when Jack looked back, it had disappeared completely. That was when the storm came in for its last attack. Jack sensed that the storm, or rather the power behind it, had been waiting for a chance to get them alone. He was frightened by the *breadth* of the sorcery behind it. It was powerful, wild, beyond his ken. He wasn't fit to challenge it. He should have stayed longer with Stillfox, should have learnt more, listened better, tried harder.

The sorcery used in the storm's making was not just powerful, it was a sophisticated, many-layered construction with an iron will at its core.

Jack felt it now, coming in for the kill. The metal tang was unmistakable. The very air was charged with it. The swell rose and the wind picked up. The little rowboat was flung from wave to wave like a leaf in a stream. The sea was a rabid dog: angry, frothing, out of control.

Tawl stopped bailing and began tying. At first Jack didn't understand what he was doing. The knight threaded a thick mooring rope beneath the bench Jack was sitting on, then he pulled the rope tight across Jack's lap. Jack felt the beginnings of panic. He was being bound to the boat. Twice more Tawl looped the rope under the bench and over Jack's thighs. Then he sat on the opposite bench and began to bind himself. He never uttered a word.

Jack felt trapped. He couldn't move his legs. The rowboat pitched and spun. The rain drove against them. Water poured in from all sides. Tawl's face was grim. He was holding the second pair of oars. The swells were coming fast—too fast for the boat to right itself after each one.

Shin-deep in saltwater, Jack tried to concentrate on the sorcery behind the storm. Lightning blazed in front of them. Thunder blasted behind. The rain and the wind began to spiral around them. The boat was flung prow-first into the oncoming swell. Jack was thrust forward. The rope burnt against his thighs. Suddenly he was underwater.

He couldn't see. He couldn't breathe.

He was dragged down with the boat. The sea itself seemed to twist in on him, crushing, wrenching. There was a dull cracking noise, and a sharp pain coursed through his head. He thought he heard Tawl call his name. And then everything went black.

Twenty

*W*inters in Rorn were a little cooler than summers, but for some reason the sunshine always seemed brighter. Perhaps the wind thinned the air, or water crystals magnified the sun's rays, or maybe it was just a trick of the light. Gamil didn't know. But, as he walked across the palace courtyard on his way to an early morning meeting, he made a mental note to find out.

Gamil liked to know things. Indeed, he *lived* to know things.

Some men said that knowledge was power—and they were right—but it was also much more than that. Knowledge could bestow many more gifts than power alone. Satisfaction, for one. Who could not help feeling that peculiar mix of smugness and triumph as one dined amongst friends whose most intimate and terrible secrets were known to one? Who could not feel glee at knowing—and meticulously cataloging—all the weaknesses and vices of one's workmates?

Besides satisfaction, knowledge bestowed confidence. It bred upon itself, creating a dynasty of influences gained, favors owed, mutual respect, and fear. A silk merchant with an illegal fondness for young boys would willingly offer up the latest gossip from Isro; shipbuilders who designed holds suitable for carrying slaves would gladly share either profits or information with a silent but knowledgeable friend. Illicit business deals, unlawful sexual practices, shady pasts, false fronts, and well-covered trails: they were the currency Gamil dealt in.

Oh, he could have made a fortune by now—a blackmailer could retire for life on the scandals he knew—but money wasn't what Gamil was after. Knowledge was what counted. Why take a payment in gold when you could take it in information, instead? Gold might be legal tender, but it was as bloodless as a corpse, whereas knowledge was a living, breathing thing.

Gamil was on his way to receive just such a payment this morning. He was due to meet a man in a tavern who could tell him of all the latest developments in the north. Gamil was hoping to discover if the notorious Lady Melliandra was alive or dead. Either way, it would have to be a short meeting. He was expected back in the palace within an hour, doubtless to suffer more indignities at the hands of the fat, lazy windbag who was known as the archbishop of Rorn.

As he passed through the palace gates, Gamil tried not to dwell on Tavalisk's latest penchant for making him scrape dead animals from the floor. Last week it had been snails, the other day it was frogs. What would His Eminence think of next?

"'Scuse me, sir. If I might have a word?"

Gamil jumped back in horror. Some lowly street vagrant had actually touched him. Quickly, he looked around. The palace guards were within calling range. He took a shouting breath.

"I wouldn't do that if I were you, sir. You wouldn't want me to be caught and tortured by the guards." The person who was speaking was a boy of about twelve years old: dark eyed, dark haired, and as thin as a pole. He grinned. "There's no telling what I might say under pressure."

Gamil knew a veiled threat when he heard one—random coercion was one of the few drawbacks of knowledge. He put a hand on the boy's back and bundled him down the road. Only when they were out of sight of the guards did Gamil see fit to stop. "Now, what's all this about?" he said, turning to face the young lowlife.

The boy made a great show of smoothing down his tunic. "I'm surprised you don't know me, my friend."

Gamil ran down a mental list of all the people he was currently dealing with. A twelve-year-old boy rang only one bell. "Are you an associate of the knight named Tawl?"

The boy nodded. "That's me. Nabber's my name. Though I suppose you know that already. After all, that's what you're famous for: knowing other people's business."

While the boy was speaking, Gamil took the opportunity to look around. No one but an old orange-seller was within sight. The district around the palace was thankfully a discreet one. Still, there was a shadier area to the right, and Gamil steered his newfound friend in that direction.

"What do you want from me?" he asked.

"I want you to set up a meeting between me and the archbishop. A discreet one, mind. Just a quick in and out."

Gamil stepped back from the unsavory boy. He was obviously quite mad. A meeting with Tavalisk! Who did he think he was? "That is out of the question. His Eminence never gives audiences to"—Gamil shuddered with distaste—"people off the street."

The boy was unruffled. "He would if you set it up."

"And why would I want to do that?"

"Because you wouldn't want old Tavalisk finding out you're in league with Larn."

Gamil didn't move. He neither blushed nor batted an eye. Having spent years being insulted and harangued by the archbishop, he was a master of giving nothing away. His stomach, however, was a different matter entirely. It felt like someone had given it wings and it had taken to fluttering around his heart. Knowledge bestowed many gifts, but bravery was unfortunately not one of them.

Mentally he pulled himself together. His first job was to find out how much the boy knew. "Boy, you are a liar. And as such can be prosecuted by a judge."

"Why don't you run along and get one, then?" replied the boy. "I've got time enough to wait." With a great show of nonchalance he examined the dirt under his nails. "I know, while you're gone I'll pass the time thinking about all those letters you received from Larn."

Gamil's stomach was no longer fluttering, it was coming in to land. This was his worst fear: the archbishop finding out about his association with Larn. Why, Tavalisk would have him dismissed and banished on the spot! Gamil felt a trickle of sweat slide past his ear. No matter how much he loathed the archbishop, his position as chief aide was everything to him. He tolerated being a lackey in the palace, because in the city he was as good as a king. He had a network of spies and informants under him, men feared and respected him, stallholders offered trade discounts, and prostitutes granted favors for free.

The last thing knowledge conveyed was a sense of entitlement, and that's how Gamil felt about Rorn. It was his city. He knew more about its people, its history, and its politics than any other man alive. By squirreling away every day, collecting information from a hundred different sources, he had *earned* the right to run it. And now this young upstart was threatening to take it all away.

For what? For Larn. It just wasn't worth it. The only reason he'd taken to corresponding with the priests was to gather information from afar. What the seers knew could not be gleaned from gossip in a tavern, or read about in books. The seers knew the future: the most provocative knowledge of all.

In return for that knowledge Gamil had granted Larn a few favors here and there. Nothing much, nothing that would compromise his position. Until a week ago. That was when he received a letter from the high priest himself. The hooded one stated that the knight would soon pass through Rorn. In no uncertain terms, he demanded that Gamil prevent the knight from boarding a boat and sailing to Larn.

Gamil had done his best, but by the time Tavalisk had begrudgingly sent out the troops, the knight had sailed off into the sunset. Which meant that he had aroused His Eminence's suspicion for nothing. Now, Tavalisk was many things—gluttonous, narcissistic, indolent, and sadistic, to name but a few—but above all he was suspicious. Little things lingered long in his mind awaiting connections, affirmations, or denials. Gamil was quite sure that the conversation that they'd had over the knight would be one of those little things. All it would take for Tavalisk's suspicions to be confirmed would be this young ruffian in front of him. True, the boy would never be able to see Tavalisk face-to-face, but he could start rumors, send messages, impute from a distance.

Gamil shuddered at the thought of it. He simply couldn't take the risk. Beckoning the boy closer, he said, "If I did agree to set up an audience with His Eminence, I take it there would be no mention of Larn?"

The boy smiled broadly. "*Larn?* Never heard of the place."

Tarissa was mocking him. Her voice was shrill and her laugh was cruel.

"*Jack!*"

The cold stuff passed over him once more. Cold, salty, and wet, it rushed along his side and into his mouth. It didn't make him choke. Some deep unconscious instinct forced him to swallow, not breathe.

"*Jack!*"

The cold stuff drained away, leaving him heavier, colder, and vaguely aware of his own discomfort. Jack didn't mind: he knew it would be back.

Tarissa was above him. Screeching. He made an effort to turn away from her. Pain sizzled across his thighs. He couldn't move his legs. The cold stuff hit again. This time it came higher, past his mouth to his eyes. Jack knew he had to do something, but he was just so content where he was. Whatever lay beneath him was shaped for him alone. It dipped to accommodate his elbow and rose to support his head. In fact, he was so comfortable that if it hadn't been for Tarissa harping on he would have fallen into a nice dark sleep by now.

"Jack!"

Someone was calling his name. Not Tarissa, though. Too deep for her. Jack kept very still. The pain in his thighs had subsided to a background hum, and that was the way he wanted to keep it.

"Oh, my God, Jack!"

And then someone was shaking him, brushing the hair from his face, slapping his cheeks, turning him on his belly and slamming their fists against his lungs.

"Come on. *Come on!*"

He was turned over once more. His chest was pumped. His mouth was cleared. He was dragged by his arms up a slope.

Tarissa started screaming again at about the same instant the pain hit; Jack didn't know which was worse. Searing, nerve-twisting spasms raced across his thighs while he was laughed at from above by the woman he still loved. It was too much. He opened his eyes.

Seagulls in a blue sky. Their cries were shrill, almost human. Jack felt disappointed: it hadn't been Tarissa after all.

"Jack, are you all right?" It was Tawl. He had a knife and was leaning over him. "I'm just going to cut the ropes."

Jack tilted his head forward. He saw the sea, the seashore, and then the beach. Looking farther down he saw his thighs were bound by rope. Underneath them lay a rectangle of wood: the bench from the rowboat. Tawl was hacking away.

The action of moving triggered something in Jack's stomach, and he turned to the left and vomited. Water, salty and bitter, heaved up from deep within his belly.

"Good," said Tawl, coming forward to support his head. "You'll feel better once you've lost all that salt-water." He smiled. "I think you're going to be all right. Try and move your legs."

Jack threw a resentful look at Tawl. He knew he wasn't going to like this one little bit. Beginning with his toes, he sent a warning message down along the nerves of his legs, braced himself, and then squeezed the muscles in his feet and ankles. Pain in bright, vivid flashes overwhelmed him. It shot up his thighs with vicious abandon, leaving Jack feeling dizzy and sick.

Another turn to the left was in order. More water was thrown from his belly.

Tawl slapped him on the back. "Good. Your toes moved." Grabbing Jack under his armpits, he dragged him up from the sand. "Come on. We're too exposed out here. We've got to find some cover."

Weak from vomiting, pain, and delirium, Jack most definitely did not want to move. "I don't think my legs can take my weight."

Tawl's hands moved down to his waist. "I'll carry you, then."

Jack pushed him away. "No. I'll try and walk." Weak or not, no one was going to carry him like a baby.

He ended up leaning heavily against Tawl. His legs buckled every few steps, he was shaking from head to foot, and he had a problem keeping his body level. Left on his own he would simply keel over in the sand. Together they stumbled up the small beach and then along the cove until they found a place where high rocks cast long shadows to the east.

They sat down in sand that was wet and pitted with

pools. All around were rocks speckled green and brown and white. Water trickled down through cracks in the stone, and mineral deposits glistened beneath the flow. Crabs scuttled away in search of shelter, and strangely formed insects with short legs and flat bodies buried themselves in the sand. The roar of the ocean echoed around the rocks, blocking out the call of the gulls.

Jack's brain was taking longer to come around than his body. He remembered the storm and being cast adrift on the rowboat, but after that there was nothing. "What happened?"

Tawl shrugged. He leant back against a rock. "A couple of big waves hit the rowboat, sent it underwater, and then broke it up. We were carried along with the wreckage."

Jack remembered the rope around his thighs. He shuddered. "Is that why you lashed us to the boat, so we'd be carried along with the wreckage?"

"I knew there was a risk we'd capsize, but you saw the storm, Jack. It wasn't going to stop until the boat was torn apart. I had to do something, so I took a chance that the boat would break up before we capsized."

"And we'd float to the surface with the driftwood?"

Tawl nodded. "I suppose so. I didn't really think." He looked tired. For the first time Jack noticed what bad shape he was in. His face was bruised and swollen. There was a large gash on his forehead and a smaller one above his lip. His britches were torn at the knees and the thighs, and his tunic was in tatters. Bloody flesh showed through all the various tears.

Catching Jack's gaze, Tawl smiled. "You should take a look at yourself."

"I'm not about to do that," said Jack. "Last spring I spent a couple of weeks in a Halcus prison. I'd been chewed up by a pack of dogs and I wasn't a pretty sight. That's when I learnt the art of *not* seeing my body."

Tawl lifted a bloody arm up to the light. "You'll have to show me how to do that sometime."

Both men laughed. The joke wasn't particularly funny, but the laughter was more than just merriment, it was a celebration of their survival.

After a while, the laughter died down. Strangely, Jack felt closer to Tawl now. Throughout the journey, Jack had thought the knight was infallible; there was nothing he didn't know about horses, weapons, traveling, and medicine. He knew so much that at times he seemed almost too perfect. Now, by admitting that he'd bound them to the boat out of pure desperation, rather than calculated knowledge of the sea, he began to appear more human.

"*The Fishy Few* was lucky last night," said Tawl.

"Why?" Jack tried to find a comfortable spot to lie down in amidst the wet sand and pebbles.

"Because we were nearer to Larn than anyone knew. The place is circled by shallows and rocks, and the way that storm was blowing it's a wonder the ship didn't run aground."

"We got off just in time," said Jack absently. His mind had already moved on. So they were here, on Larn. It wasn't a surprise really. Where else could they be? It was just that up until now he hadn't given his surroundings any thought. There was a beach, some rocks, and the sea. That was all that had existed for him so far.

Things suddenly began to seem different. The air was colder, the light harsher, the wet sand beneath his fingers turned to mud. "Do you think they know we're here?"

Tawl gave Jack a sharp look. "Do you?"

"I haven't got a sixth sense, Tawl." For some reason, Jack felt annoyed. "I knew about the sorcery last night because I could smell it, *taste* it, not because I'm a conjurer with a crystal ball."

"I'm sorry, Jack. I just don't know about these things."

"Neither do I." Jack looked at Tawl for a moment. They both needed some rest. "Did you manage to salvage anything from the boat?" he asked, changing the subject.

"No. We lost all our supplies. All we've got is my knife."

"So what do we do?"

Tawl leant forward. "We have to assume that they don't know we're here. If they caused the storm last night, then there's a good chance they think we're dead. Our best option is to lie low until the middle of the night, then take them by surprise. I say we get some sleep for now, and when it's dark we make our way up the cliff-side."

Jack nodded. He was amazed that he was managing to appear calm when inside his stomach lay a solid block of fear. He was just beginning to realize that Larn, the prophecy, and the quest were more than fireside stories. They were real.

Nabber was experiencing a strong sensation of déjà vu as he walked down the palace corridors on his way to his audience with the archbishop. Gamil strode ahead of him, setting a fast pace and acting like a nervous bloodhound. No matter how fast he scurried, though, Nabber still had time to take in his surroundings. And that was why he was beginning to feel distinctly . . . *familiar* with the contents of the palace.

Gold urns, marble statues, paintings, tapestries, jeweled reliquaries—Nabber had the curious feeling he'd seen them all before.

Furtively he reached out to touch a gold urn ensconced in a recess in the wall. It didn't feel quite as warm as gold. Only one thing for it. Reaching into his tunic, he pulled out his darning needle, and then shouted, *"Rats!"* at the top of his voice.

Whilst Gamil was busy hopping and panicking, Nabber scraped the needle along the urn. Just as he thought: base metal beneath.

"There are no rats." Gamil swiped Nabber across the ear. "What are you up to?"

Nabber slipped the needle up his sleeve. "Could have sworn there was, my friend. Great big hairy ones. Two of 'em."

Gamil made an annoyed clicking sound in his throat, grabbed Nabber by the coattail, and hurried him along. "Any nonsense like that with His Eminence, and you'll be leaving the palace minus your tongue."

Nabber tried his best to look contrite. They walked across a lofty gallery, down a short flight of stairs, and into a marble-lined corridor. A set of double doors marked the end. Nabber, who had taken the trouble to change into his best for this occasion, smoothed down his tunic and tried hard to swallow the lump in his throat.

Gamil reached out to knock on the door. Nabber stopped him.

"One question before we go in, my friend," he said.

Old Gamil didn't look at all happy at this. "What?"

"The treasure in the palace. All the urns and statues and things. They are real, aren't they?"

"Of course they are. The tributes have been collected over centuries. They are priceless. The holy treasures of Rorn are second in value only to those of Silbur."

"Hmm. Very interesting. You can knock now."

Gamil sent him a withering look and knocked, very softly, upon the door.

"Enter!" came a muffled cry.

They walked into a glorious, golden chamber. Light poured in from arched stained-glass windows and the rugs on the marble were at least two toes thick.

"Your Eminence, this is the young man I talked to you about. I promised him but three minutes of your time."

Nabber stepped forward. Like everyone else in Rorn, he knew the archbishop by sight—the man could never turn down a parade. He was dressed in exquisite silks of yellow and cream and rustled like a wealthy monarch when he moved.

"Most unusual this, Gamil," he said. "Caught me in the middle of my lemmings."

"I apologize, Your Eminence. If you would prefer I'll—"

The archbishop waved a heavily jeweled hand. "No, no. I'll see the boy now." And then to Nabber: "What's your name, boy? Nobber?"

"Nabber."

"Very nice. You can go now, Gamil."

"But, Your Eminence—"

"Go, Gamil. I'm sure young Nibber here would like to talk to me, man to man." He smiled benignly at Nabber.

Gamil was gripping Nabber's shoulder very hard. Under his breath he whispered, "One word about Larn and out comes your tongue."

"'Nuff said, Gamil," murmured Nabber between gritted teeth.

Gamil gave his shoulder one final skin-piercing squeeze and reluctantly took his leave.

The archbishop waved a beckoning hand. "Come over here, young Nibber. How do you feel about lemmings?"

"Never heard of them. And the name's Nabber."

"Good. Care to try one?" The archbishop brandished something small and squirrel-shaped impaled upon a stick. "I have these brought in from beyond the Northern Ranges, you know."

"I think I'll have to decline. Tempting though they look, Your Eminence."

The archbishop sighed. "All the more for me, then." He took a dainty bite at the squirrel-thing, then said, "Now, while I'm eating perhaps you'd like to tell me how you managed to coerce my aide into setting up this meeting. For this is the first time in my recollection that Gamil has ever brought me a boy off the street." Up came the lemming to his lips. "Are you blackmailing him, by any chance?"

The fat man was not as stupid as he looked. Nabber

revised his opinion of him. To buy himself time to think about his reply, he turned his back on the archbishop and looked around the room. All that glittered was most definitely not gold. Nabber smiled, suddenly more confident. A change of plan was in order. "If I *was* blackmailing Gamil, Your Eminence, I couldn't possibly tell you the reason why."

The archbishop now had a silver goblet in his hand. "Boy, I could have any information I wished out of you in an instant. My torturers are second to none. Now kindly tell me what you know about Gamil."

"Can't do that, Your Eminence. Once I've done a deal, my lips are firmly sealed." Nabber had come to the palace with the idea of bluffing the archbishop into giving him what he wanted. He knew about the archbishop's storehouse full of loot, and he had planned to state that unless His Eminence agreed to lay off the knight, the whole thing would be torched before nightfall. Nabber was even going to invent an accomplice who was poised outside the storehouse, flame in hand, ready to set it alight if he'd heard no news within the hour.

Nabber hadn't been entirely happy with the plan, but it was the only thing he could come up with on short notice. And, as Swift always said, *"when everything else fails, an inspired bluff is your best resort."* Things looked different now, though. There'd be less bluffing—inspired or otherwise—in what he was currently concocting.

"Boy, you do realize that I will have you tortured unless you speak?"

"Do you realize that the one thing you look for in a blackmailer is the ability to keep his mouth shut?" Nabber grinned. He took the liberty of coming forward and running a hand over the treasures on the archbishop's desk: gilded boxes, goblets, jeweled candlesticks, and incense holders. He selected a particularly pretty gold statuette: Borc's sainted mother, if he wasn't mistaken. Holding it up to the light, he said, "It's really not bad for a fake."

Four skewers worth of lemmings clattered to the floor. A soft whisking noise escaped from the archbishop's lips. His fingers strayed to the large ruby ring on his left hand. Nabber knew rubies; this one was a little too bright, a little too brazen to be real.

"I see that's one, too," he said pointing to the ring. "Of course, no one would spot it unless they knew what they were looking for. Take me, I would never have guessed all these things were fake if I hadn't seen the originals for myself."

The archbishop looked a little lost for words, so Nabber decided to carry on. "You and I both know where the holy treasures of Rorn are, and they ain't in this palace, that's for sure. They're in a smart little house just off Mulberry Street. Right nice place, it is. Looted to the rafters." Nabber knew what he was saying was right. Three years ago he'd been in that house, checking out the prospects for Swift. Of course, as soon as they'd learned that the archbishop owned the place, they'd backed away from the job. But the memory formed by the treasure was a lasting one, and the minute Nabber walked into the palace it all came flooding back: the golden angels, the enamel boxes, the jeweled chests, the countless paintings of Borc and his disciples. Old Tavalisk had ripped them all off.

"Boy, you are deranged. I'm going to ring for the guards." The archbishop reached for the bell rope.

"Torture me, kill me, and the word will still get out." Nabber was beginning to feel more confident. He was back on his own territory again: inspired bluffing. "You don't think I'd walk into the lion's den without helpers in the field?"

Down came the hand. "Are there others who know of this foul lie?"

"Just me and a good friend. But you needn't worry about that, Your Eminence. We're the two discreetest people you're ever likely to meet."

"What do you want?"

"First of all, I want you to lay off the knight. When he gets back into Rorn, I want him to get off the boat and leave the city in one piece."

"And?"

"I believe you're holding a friend of the knight's. A lady, name o' Megan. I'd like her released. Today. Right now. She can leave with me." Nabber didn't have the vaguest idea who Megan was, but she was obviously important enough for the Old Man to mention her. Besides, any friend of Tawl's was a friend of his.

During the conversation, the archbishop had been slowly changing color, and now he was rather an alarming shade of puce. He tugged on the bell rope. "Boy, let me make this very clear to you. What you have accused me of is an outright lie. Unfortunately a great man like myself simply cannot allow his reputation to be sullied by such slanderous lies. And that—and only that—is the reason why I'm agreeing to your requests."

Nabber judged a bow was in order. "Of course, Your Eminence."

The archbishop poured himself a cup of wine. "Suffice to say, if I hear as much as a whiff of this ugly rumor, I will not rest until you and the knight are so much rotting flesh. Is that clear?"

Nabber shivered. He couldn't help himself. The archbishop issued the threat in such an off-hand manner, that you just knew he was serious about it. Swift had been right not to mess with him.

A knock came upon the door and in walked Gamil.

"Aah, Gamil. Your young friend here is ready to leave. See to it that the prostitute Megan accompanies him."

"But—"

"Do as I say, Gamil." The archbishop waved an almost fond farewell. "Remember what I said, Nabber. Not one whiff."

Twenty-one

"Come on, Jack," said Tawl. "What are you stopping for?"

A pale ribbon of mist-filtered moonlight slanted across Jack's face. "Tawl, I can feel it. I can feel the rock . . . " He shook his head. "It's throbbing, like a heartbeat."

Tawl could hear fear in Jack's voice. Fear and something else: wonder, perhaps. He reached up and touched Jack lightly on the arm. "Let's go."

They had just found the tunnel that led up through the cliff face. For over two hours they'd circled around the shore looking for a place to climb up to the top. The cliffs were too sheer, though, and slick with condensation from the mist.

Even before it started to go dark, the mist began to roll in from the sea. Having grown up in the marshes, Tawl was used to fog and mist, but he'd never seen anything like this before in his life. There was no gradual buildup, no gentle clouding, no delicate swirling and thickening. It came from the sea in a solid bank, as dense and real as the waves it glided over. The mist came in with intent. It didn't accompany the night, it *made* it.

Now, as they climbed up a tunnel that cut through solid rock, the mist came after them. Tawl wasn't given to idle fancies, but even in the dark he could tell there was no mist ahead of them. It was only behind. He and Jack were leading the mist up the cliff.

It was bitterly cold in the tunnel. The rock underfoot was damp, greasy; rivulets of water trickled down along the depressions, flaring out when the path ran smooth. Every step had to be carefully placed. Overhead the rock coverage varied, one minute dipping low to meet their heads, the next soaring high and shaping echoes, and occasionally pulling back and allowing glimpses of the sky.

The darkness in the tunnel had a quality all its own. At first Tawl couldn't work out what was wrong, what made it different from other darkness, but as they struggled ever upward, he began to see what it was. Most of the rock surfaces were either damp or dripping, but instead of catching the occasional flash of light from the much-absent moon, the water running down the walls, ceiling, and floor of the tunnel *glowed*. There was a faint phosphorescence to it—not nearly enough to banish the darkness, but enough to alter its nature.

Tawl shivered. He needed a drink. He was thirsty, hungry, and his body hurt in a hundred different ways. Glancing back at Jack, Tawl saw a mirror of his own emotions: fear, apprehension, a strong desire that the whole thing be over and done with. One knife they had between them. One single-bladed knife.

They had been walking uphill for some time now and Tawl felt sure the tunnel would end soon. So far things looked good: they hadn't seen anyone, which could mean that the priests didn't know they were here. It could also mean that they were waiting in their temple like spiders in a web. There was just no way of knowing. Thinking back, Tawl tried to remember if any of the hooded men he had seen were armed. There were definitely no guards, that was certain, but were the priests trained to defend the temple? Tawl shrugged. Trained or not, they would defend it with their lives.

Suddenly a cold breeze blasted against his face. The air was fresh, mist free. The path began to lighten ahead. Tawl dropped to the floor. "Get down," he hissed at Jack. The tunnel was about to end, and from here onward they had to take every precaution they could.

On their bellies, they pulled themselves forward, finding handholds in the rock. The mist was no longer behind; it was on top of them, hovering overhead like smoke above a fire. The sensation of wet rock beneath and clammy mist above was so unpleasant that Tawl actually grinned. It reminded him of early mornings at his fishing hole, lying still between the fog and dew while he waited for the fish to bite. Strangely, the memory gave him strength—he'd never come home without a catch.

Abruptly the tunnel ended. Tawl had grown so used to the dark that the moonlit night seemed impossibly bright. It was dazzling. Tawl felt exposed, vulnerable, as if a score of lanterns had been turned on him. The only mist up this high was the white swirls escaping from the tunnel. Swinging to the left, Tawl saw the low oblong form of the temple. His mouth went dry. It was just the same as he remembered it: oppressive, primitive, its very shape telling of power passed down over time. Tawl had seen it in his dreams: it was the place that nearly destroyed him.

Jack moved next to him. "I feel like I've been here before," he whispered. His voice was thin, strained.

Tawl could feel the tension in his body. He wished he knew how to reply. Jack needed some reassurance, but he had none to give. "The place is dark. That's a good sign," was all he could think of to say.

Jack nodded, as if he understood the intention behind the words. "What do we do now?"

The wind whipped low over the ground, buffeting their bodies and sending ripples through the flattened grass. It was warmer here than down below. Tawl looked up at the sky. The moon was hanging to the west. "It's

past midnight now. I say we go in." He had planned on
waiting longer, but ever since he'd learned that Melli had
been caught by Baralis, waiting had become intolerable to
him. Everything had to be done as soon as possible. The
one thing that kept him moving forward was the burning
desire to get back. He had to return to Bren, to Melli, and
an hour longer than necessary was a lifetime too much.

He pulled his knife from his belt and offered it to Jack.
"Here, take this."

Jack shook his head. He patted his tunic, and for the
first time Tawl realized that it was looking decidedly
bulky. "Rocks," he said. "I might be no good with a bow,
but I can throw a rock with the best of 'em."

Tawl smiled. Again he wanted to say something, and
again the words failed him. "Good thinking," he said,
when what he really meant to say was, *If the worst happens
here tonight, I promise you we'll go down fighting, together*.

"Come on, then," said Jack, scrambling on all fours.
"Let's see if we can make it to the temple while the
moon's behind that cloud."

Tawl raced after him.

Breathless, backs aching and shins throbbing, they
arrived at the temple a few minutes later. The cloud had
failed them in the last thirty seconds. The wind, however,
had blown hard and long, muffling the sound of their
footfalls with all the timing of a third accomplice.

Jack had to run with a hand clamped to his waist to
stop the rocks in his tunic from beating against his chest.

They stood to the side of the temple steps and caught
their breaths. There was no one in sight. No light escaped
from inside. All was quiet apart from the wind.

Jack wanted to sit down. The muscles in his thighs
hadn't recovered from being bound and they were
screaming for rest. He ignored them. He didn't want to
appear weak in front of Tawl. Leaning against the rise of
the step for support, Jack noticed the stone wasn't quite

as cold as it should be. Granite should feel cool to the touch, not barely below tepid.

Everything about the island was unnatural: the water, the mist, the rock. Its differences jangled against Jack's nerves like a song played out of tune. Dimly, he was aware that the place was having a physical effect upon him, tightening the muscles around his heart, causing the skin to pull taut across his face and his breath to come quick and ragged. First he tried to excuse these as after-effects of the wreck. Now he just ignored them.

The one thing he couldn't ignore was the *rhythm* of the place. It permeated everything: the waves lapping against the shore, the water dripping from the rocks, the rocks themselves, even the wind. Everything was moving in time. The sensation grew stronger as they made their way through the cliff side, and now, breath-close to the temple, it was so strong it was almost overbearing. At first Jack's heart had actively fought against the lure of the rhythm, now it was trying to fall in time.

Suddenly scared, Jack said, "Let's try and get inside." The sound of his own voice should have been a comfort, but the words carried the cadence of Larn.

The steps were low. Worn to curves by centuries worth of footsteps, they cradled Jack's every step. For a moment it seemed as if the place was almost welcoming him. Jack firmly dispelled the thought, but even as he did, he started to place his feet on the ridges between the curves.

Tawl had drawn his knife. The tip was down, the blade was forward. As he climbed, it flashed in the moonlight.

The door to the temple towered above them. Fashioned out of oak, it was old, dark, and weather-beaten. Seeing it, Jack realized that it must have been shipped here, for there wasn't a single tree on the island. He pressed against it, lightly at first, and then harder when there was no give. "It must be bolted on the inside."

Frustrated, he swung back his arm, ready to beat against the door.

Tawl caught his wrist before it came down. "We'll find another way in."

Heads down, hugging shadows, they made their way around the side of the temple. There was now an unspoken sense of urgency between them, and each step lost a measure of caution to speed. The temple was shaped from massive blocks of granite. Ancient beyond telling, it boasted no adornments, no pillars, nothing to relieve the eye. High above their heads was a series of barred vents. Jack didn't waste a minute thinking about them; the only way they could be reached was from the roof.

The temple flared out toward the back. Granite slabs jutted from the main wall, breaking the line of the building. The stone was cleaner, its angles more defined—obviously a later addition. Just as they reached the end of the annex, Jack caught the smell of woodsmoke in his nostrils. He looked at Tawl, who nodded at him. Woodsmoke meant people.

Drawing level with the end corner of the building, they peered around the back. A collection of sheds and lean-tos clustered close to the temple. Old, rickety huts shaped suspiciously like parts of ships.

"They built these from shipwrecks, by the looks of them," whispered Tawl. "They're probably storage huts or servants' quarters."

"Then there'll be a way in." Jack scanned the buildings. He saw the glow of a fire, and then something moving back and forth right by it. Rocking. Someone was sitting in a rocking chair, rocking to and fro in time to the rhythm of the island. Jack felt a cold chill claw down his spine. It was an old woman.

Her chair faced the temple and she rocked toward it with blind intent. Jack followed the line of her rocking. Straight ahead of her, in the temple's back wall, there was a dark rectangle marking a door.

Jack knew, more surely than he had ever known anything before in his life, that the door would be open. The
old woman was showing them the way.

He tapped Tawl lightly on the shoulder. "We're safe
for now. Let's go." Jack had come to know the knight
well, for he guessed Tawl wouldn't question him—and he
was right. Tawl simply nodded once and then followed
him forward.

If the old woman saw them, she never gave anything
away, just kept on rocking back and forth.

The door swung back the moment Jack touched it.
Cool, stale air brushed against Jack's cheek, and he
stepped into the temple at Larn.

The rhythm was strong, compelling, pulsing like a
heartbeat. Jack felt it all around him, stifling yet strangely
familiar. His own heart was now only split seconds out of
time.

They were in a dim, low-ceilinged room. Bare stone
walls, bare stone floor, and several wooden tables stacked
high with pots. The light was coming from the corridor
opposite the door. Jack made straight toward it. Tawl
put a restraining hand on his arm. "Me first," he said,
dropping his gaze to his knife. Jack pulled two fist-sized
rocks from his tunic and let him past.

The air was so cold their breath whitened before them,
yet once again the stone in his hand didn't quite match
the surrounding temperature: it was a fraction warmer.
They walked down the narrow torch-lit corridor.
Occasionally there were doors leading off to the sides.
Tawl ignored them. He seemed to know where he was
going.

Something creaked behind them. A voice called out:
"Who goes there?"

Jack was pushed out of the way by Tawl. His head hit
the stone wall. A jolt raced through his nerves, setting the
hair on the back of his neck prickling. He looked up in
time to see Tawl knifing a hooded man in the chest. The

knight's large, well-shaped hands were firmly clamped over the man's mouth.

"Help me get him back into his room," hissed Tawl.

Jack was still reeling from hitting the wall. He felt almost light-headed. By the time he reached Tawl, a dark pool of blood had formed around the dead man's feet.

Tawl was shaking. Together they lifted the man and placed him on a stone bench in what looked to be his own personal chamber. They were in the priests' living quarters. Tawl paused to clean his knife against the dead man's habit and then they left.

Footsteps scuttled lightly in the distance.

Jack and Tawl exchanged a glance. There was nothing to do but move forward. Jack's head was throbbing. He couldn't understand why; Tawl hadn't shoved him hard, yet he felt as if he were punch-drunk.

The corridor took a sharp turn to the left. Four hooded men blocked their path. They were armed with curved swords. Jack didn't pause to think. He hurled a rock toward the first man, catching him on the arm. The second rock followed straight after, but it missed its target and went smashing into the stone wall. Tawl sprang toward the man with the injured arm. Jack reached in his tunic for more rocks and threw them at the remaining three, hoping to buy time for Tawl.

The knight made a quick, jerking movement, and the first man fell to the floor. Knife out before him, he spun around to face the other three.

Jack had run out of rocks. He knew Tawl needed help fast. He centered his thoughts upon the hooded men's blades. He felt the cool-metal hardness, the solid form of iron shot with carbon. He formed the intent, forced his stomach to contract, and then *nothing*. No push, no energy, no coppery tang upon his tongue.

Tawl was backed up against the wall; two hooded men held him at sword's point. Desperate, Jack concentrated again. This time he thought of Rovas laying his hands upon Tarissa. The image was bright, biting, more vivid than he had expected. The emotions that came with it were like a slap in the face. His feelings hadn't changed: he still loved her.

Still there was no spark. Jack felt as if the temple, as if the very stone that surrounded him, was stopping the sorcery from coming through.

There was no time to wonder why. Grabbing a torch from the wall, Jack plunged ahead. The third man came forward to meet him, his sword slicing half-circles around his body. Even now, even after everything that had happened, Jack still remembered Rovas' advice: *"Do anything to throw your opponent off guard: dance, laugh, cry. Anything."* Everyone was afraid of fire, thought Jack, and he thrust the burning torch right for his attacker's face. It didn't come even close to burning him, but instinct made the man step back.

It was all Jack needed. His mind was on the space surrounding the first man's body. His eye was on the blade. Switching the torch from right hand to left, Jack thrust forward. Streams of flame and smoke trailed from the torch. Sweeping down, Jack grasped the hilt of the first man's blade. Then he threw the torch at what he hoped was the third man's vitals—it was difficult to tell, as the man was wearing a long unbelted habit.

Whether he reached the target or not, the effect was still the same. The man backed away, screaming. His habit caught fire, and Jack let him burn. He didn't have time for a mercy killing.

Swinging around, he tackled the nearest of Tawl's attackers. The rhythm of Larn was throbbing in his head, and instead of fighting it, Jack made it his own, thrusting and hacking with each beat. The tempo fitted him like a glove. He felt exhilarated, powerful, in control. The hooded man was a bloody corpse within a minute.

Tawl finished the last man off. Jack was shocked to see a gash running down the knight's side.

Shouts and more footsteps came from behind. Bending down to pick up one of the curved blades, Tawl thrust his fist against the wound. "You go ahead. I'll hold them off for a minute to give you time to get to the cavern." As he spoke, blood ran between his fingers and down his thigh.

"No. We'll go together." The cries and footsteps were getting louder. Jack held out his hand. "Come on."

Tawl reached out and grasped it. They stood for a moment, bound together by the knight's blood, and then they pulled apart and ran.

The air above the Great Divide was perfectly still. Diamond-clear and diamond-cold, it cut through a man's bones to the marrow beneath. Ice had formed on the path and the rocks and the broadsides of plants. Wafer-thin, fossil-white, it gained mass beneath the moon.

The moon itself kept its distance. It hung above the mountains with the dispassion of an ancient god.

Kedrac, Maybor's firstborn and heir to the most valuable estate in the kingdoms, stood on a narrow rise and surveyed his troops. Six thousand men stood ready. Six thousand men fully-armed, fighting-fit, and impatient for a kill. It had been a long dreary summer at Annis. Their restlessness affected Kedrac like a drug. Sleep, he had told them five hours earlier. He might as well have told the dead to walk.

No one had slept. They sat in circles unlit by fires, not drinking, not talking, just waiting. Those wearing plate armor were forced to sit ramrod straight, those in mail could have stooped. But they didn't.

The sound of blades being sharpened and buckles being fastened had long since faded away. Now the only noise was the nickering of the horses and the jangling of tack. The men wanted to get started, they'd bided their time long enough. It would take a good four hours to march down from the mountains and onto the southern plain of Bren. Kedrac looked up at the moon. If he gave the order now, they'd be there by dawn.

He raised a gloved fist into the cold, crackling air, held it for six seconds—one for each thousand—and then brought it down to his side.

The mountainside began to move. A swarm of dark forms rose up above the ice; banners were raised, horses were mounted, loose circles of troops became columns. Kedrac chose not to address the men—in their present state words would have no meaning. They knew the plan. They would take no prisoners. They were ready to slaughter the Wall.

Kedrac turned and made his way down from the rise. The storm was behind them, Bren was ahead of them, and if he met his father on the field, then so be it.

They raced down corridors, their swords wet and dripping, the blood slow to dry in the damp air beneath the stone. Jack's lungs were burning, ready to explode. His head felt as if someone was beating it with a hammer.

They were descending quickly now. The corridors sloped downward and began to look like tunnels, the rock only planed smooth where it jutted too far from the wall. The narrowness of the ways worked in their favor—the hooded ones could only tackle them one at a time.

By setting light to a corridor lined with bookshelves, they had managed to slow their pursuers down. In reality, there was more smoke than flames and it had probably given them an extra minute at the most. Even so, they still had priests ahead of them to deal with. Jack glanced around the naked stone. There was nothing to burn here, that was for sure.

Down and down they went. Hacking men out of their way, choosing the darkest paths, never pausing once to catch their breaths. Instead of dropping, the temperature was actually rising. The air was thickening, warming, *pulsing.* Jack felt it brushing against his face in waves. He was too exhausted to be afraid.

Then he heard the sound. High, discordant, it was like the braying of hounds on the scent. Every hair on Jack's body bristled. It wasn't hounds, it was the seers, and they were waiting for him. That was it, he thought, *waiting.* The old woman rocking in her chair had been waiting, the rock he hit his head against had been waiting, the island itself had been waiting. Not the priests, not the hooded ones, but the land, the stone, the soil.

Tawl was by his side, clearing a path. Blood spattered over Jack's cheeks and forehead. He let his sword drop to the ground. He could no longer hold it. Stepping ahead into the crowd of milling, panicking priests, he made no effort to defend himself. That was why the knight was here, so he let him do his job.

The visual world was sloughing away. The seers keened, the rhythm beat, the blood cooled his skin as it dried.

Then he was there, in the cavern, where he was meant to be. A domed ceiling glowed with seams of crystal, below it rows of stones were laid out in neat rows. Bound to each stone was a man. Wailing and shifting gracelessly against their bindings, they had little meaning to Jack. They weren't important. It was the cavern itself that counted.

It was the source, the heart. It throbbed with power, setting everything resonating in time. Jack felt his own heart racing to fall in with the rhythm. The pounding in his head already matched the beat.

Tawl was at his back, at his side, in front of him. The red and silver blur of his sword was as good as a shield. Clashing metal, ragged breaths, and death cries diminished to so much background noise. The pulse was everything. Jack was drawn to the back of the cavern. His eyes no longer saw, but his blood pulled him forward nonetheless.

Reaching the end wall, he stretched out both his arms and laid his flattened palms against the rock. A jolt like the one earlier, only stronger and more compelling, raced down Jack's spine. His muscles tensed and his body jerked. Warm air blasted down his body. Jack felt the cavern's heart, felt its ancient and terrible power.

And then he knew what he must do.

Ignoring all instincts for survival, Jack relaxed, leaving his body open to the pulse. Panic swept over him. He ignored it. His legs shook beneath him. He paid them no heed. His heart had to beat in time with the cavern; only then, only when his blood pumped through his arteries at the same rate as the power pulsed through the seams in the rock, could he do anything. No sorcery could be drawn. No risks could be taken. Nothing could be done without the bond. Fear was a sprung trap within his stomach. He felt its cold metal teeth tearing away at his resolve. He was sick, sweating. The world his senses had shaped for him was lacking markers. Jack felt as if he had been cast adrift upon a sea of blood-warm oil. Unable to get his bearings and unwilling to break his connection with the stone, Jack took his chances in the dark.

The two beats were close to matching. Off-kilter by a tenth of a second, they jarred against each other, the stronger of the two exerting all the pressure of a mountain's worth of rock. Jack felt his heart racing, pumping, aching with the strain. A sharp, needling pain darted up his left arm.

His heart stopped.

His lungs sucked in air, but there were no takers.

There was an instant of pure blackness. Like death. With it came glimpses of secrets, memories left like an aftertaste in his blood. He knew this place. He was familiar with the power. Coming here was like coming home.

And then a strong contraction racked Jack's body and his heart began to beat in time. Close to swooning, Jack slumped against the rock face. It was warm against his chest. An almost sensuous pleasure swept over his body; he felt calmed, soothed, held in a gentle embrace. It seemed natural to draw his power now—it was made of the same substance that surrounded him. Why hadn't he seen it before? Why hadn't he recognized his own?

Slowly the sorcery began to flow. There was no need for nasty scenes, no anger to be used for fuel. It flowed out of him to the rock, to the cavern, and down into the island's core. It was so easy, it just drained away on its own. Jack knew such peace, such a sense of belonging, all he wanted to do was join with the rock.

Niggling little things kept buzzing through his head: sounds, sights, instincts. He went deeper so they wouldn't distract him. The cavern enveloped him like a womb.

Jack! Be careful! You're losing yourself.

What was Stillfox's voice doing down so deep? Jack pushed it aside. It was just another memory amongst many.

You fool. You were in control of nothing. The glass was controlling you. You nearly lost yourself to it.

Oh, but this wasn't glass. And he *was* in control. Deeper and deeper he went, power flowing from him like a river to the sea.

Stillfox's voice seemed to have left open the gate to his senses. Irritating noises barged in on his thoughts. Swords ringing, footfalls sounding, the high shrieking cries of the seers. It was bedlam compared to the tranquillity of the stone.

"Do what you were born for."

It took Jack a moment to realize that the words were separate from his thoughts. He tried to push the voice into the background. Only it wasn't in the background, it came from right beside him.

"Do it now."

There was a thin-bladed desperation in the voice that cut through the layers in Jack's brain. His senses began to reassert themselves. He smelled the flinty dryness of the stone and caught the sharp ammonia whiff of urine. His vision blurred into focus. He saw the rock, his hands—they were distorted, as if seen through rounded glass.

The cavern lured him back. He pulled against it, whipping his head around in the direction of the voice.

The eyes of a madman looked into his. A seer, blue-eyed, hollow-cheeked, lips as dry as bone. Bound to his stone, the ropes had shaped his body like bread set to bake in a mold. Two mighty coils crossed his chest, and Jack could see how his rib cage had developed around the rope. The normal curve of chest wasn't there. There were two deep depressions where the ribs had been unable to grow normally. The sight was appalling. What about the organs underneath—the heart, the lungs—were they misshapen too?

Young boys, Stillfox had said. The seers were bound before they were full grown.

"Do what you were born for."

No. The eyes of the seer weren't mad. Desperate, yes, but not mad. The man was calling for his own destruction.

Jack senses sharpened like crystal. He saw where the rope cut through skin. He saw open sores, infection, mal-formed limbs, and atrophied muscles. He smelled decay. This was what Larn was made of. The mighty rhythm of the cavern was all for this.

And it was time to bring it to an end.

Jack turned back to the wall. No warm welcome this time: the rock was cool to the touch. He spread his palms fully and concentrated on the pulse in the stone. He smiled. The cavern had done the work for him: to entice him in it had to give him the key. His heart now matched the beat of the core. Jack drew upon his power. He tasted the metal on his tongue, felt the telltale pain in his head. The bands of muscle around his stomach contracted in perfect time, and the sorcery left his mouth with a vengeance.

The power rose up: up above the cavern, high above the island, soaring far into the night. Up and up it went, the sheer force of it pulling the ocean onto the shore, and dragging the clouds into lines. Jack felt the terrible suction it created, fought against the void it left behind. Everything—his blood, his breath, the skin on his back—strove to soar upward with the force.

Reaching the point where the heavens met the sky, the power slowed and began to gain weight. It collapsed in on itself: condensing, thickening, doubling down, gaining intent and body and mass. Jack knew without thought what he had to do, he knew without doubt what he was born for. Everything snapped into place within the space of an eyeblink and Jack became master of Larn. Working from memories older than himself, using strength offered up by the seers, he shaped a custom-made weapon to destroy the cavern's heart, and blasted it down to the source.

This time the power didn't flow through the rock. It tore right through it.

Down the power went. Heavier than metal, faster than a high storm, it smashed through the cavern like a message from the gods. Jack sent it plunging through rock and soil and minerals, down toward the core. Down to the dark primeval mass that formed the heart of Larn. The two forces met: one ancient beyond telling, one untried and blinding and raw. They were matched only for a quarter second, and then the old world gave way to the new.

In the flashing brightness of an instant, Jack's power destroyed the cavern's flow.

A single scream rose high from the seers, and then a wave of hot air ripped through the hall of seering.

A low rumbling rose from beneath the stone. The cavern began to tremble. Walls began to crack. The ground shook, rocks plummeted from the ceiling. Jack was dazed. He lay against a seer stone as the light in the cavern began to fade. Fissures formed in the floor, and dust flying from them choked the air. The whole thing was collapsing. All the seers would die. There was no other way: they were never meant to be saved.

Jack didn't have the energy to move. Chunks of rock crashed around him. Seers keened their death songs as the walls began to give way. The entire cavern began to churn: rolling, fracturing, falling in upon itself. A rock grazed Jack's thigh, and another hit his chest. The dust made it impossible to breathe. And then, in the middle of the madness there was Tawl. Blood-soaked, bloody-eyed, badly limping Tawl.

He grinned. "I thought I'd find you lying down." Pushing the rocks from Jack's body, he lifted him from the ground.

Tawl half-dragged, half-carried him from the chamber and up through the maze of buckling corridors toward the surface. They ran ahead of collapsing walls, dodged falling stonework, skimmed over broken paths, and used up two lifetimes' worth of luck in one night.

Twenty-two

Maybor woke before dawn. He never slept well anymore. His dreams led him down the same path every night, and every morning he awoke with the same image tearing away at his soul: Melli kicking and screaming to distract the guard's attention while he ran away from the courtyard. How could a man sleep knowing that his brave and beautiful daughter was being held by a monster? And that he might have done something to prevent it, if only he'd been daring enough to try?

Melli wasn't dead. Maybor had to think that to keep his sanity. There had been no word of her for months. Occasionally reports would come in from palace servants, who told of a mysterious woman being held in the east wing under lock and key. It hadn't taken Maybor long to convince himself that the woman was his daughter: he *needed* something to believe in.

"There's a commotion going on at the south gate, m'lord," said Grift, entering the tent. "Looks like they're going to open it."

"Well, dammit, man! Don't just stand there, help me dress." Ever since Grift had recovered from his injuries, he had acted as Maybor's equerry. The man was slow about his work, inclined to drink and gamble, and was full of the worst advice about women that Maybor had ever heard! Court ladies fancying field hands, indeed!

What woman would want a field hand when she could
have a mighty lord? It was insanity! In fact, the only
reason why Maybor kept the guard around was to keep
track of Melli's condition. The man knew about pregnancy and women's complaints, and whenever Maybor
wanted to know how close Melli was to term, or how she
would be feeling, all he had to do was ask Grift. The guard
always began his reply with: "The Lady Melliandra is as
healthy as a packhorse, and I guarantee you she'll be doing
just fine." To Maybor those words were more precious
than gold and made enduring the man's incompetence
worthwhile.

Maybor picked out a fine scarlet tunic to wear
beneath his breastplate. It seemed that today they would
finally get a chance to fight Bren's army man-to-man.
About time, too. Those blackhelms had spent the last
two months hiding behind the city walls like nuns in a
convent.

"Full armor," he said to Grift, who was busy putting a
shine to the breastplate with a gob of spit. He wasn't
going to sit in the tent all day. He was going to ride out
and meet the enemy. This might be their one chance of
breaking Bren's defenses. Oh, the blackhelms were probably up to something, but whatever it was, it would make
them vulnerable.

Maybor strapped on his shin plates, grabbed hold of
his helmet, and walked out into the field. It was cold,
barely light; an icy wind that spoke of snow was blowing
down from the mountains. Lord Besik, leader of the
Highwall forces, was standing outside the command tent
surrounded by his military aides. A man to be reckoned
with both physically and mentally, he spied Maybor and
hailed him over.

The two men clasped hands. "Well met, friend," said
Besik. "What do you think of this?" He indicated the
south gate, which was slowly being drawn open.

Maybor liked Besik. The man didn't mince words, he

was bad tempered but even-handed, and he always listened carefully to advice. "Perhaps the blackhelms are bored with waiting. Perhaps they're desperate for food and supplies." Maybor shrugged. "But it's more likely to be a trap."

Besik sighed heavily. "You're right. But we've still got to deal with it. I've positioned a line of crossbowmen in the trench—they'll be firing quarrels so that should be enough to stop the first wave of troops. If the blackhelms are still coming, we'll send out the light cavalry and back them up with mounted archers."

"Let's play it safe," said Maybor. "Cover both flanks with foot archers and send out two parties of heavily armed horsemen, one to the eastern plains and one to the base of the foothills."

Besik looked at him sharply. "There's been no word from reconnaissance."

"Men with slit throats make bad messengers."

Besik nodded. "Very well. Caution it is."

Maybor mounted his horse. He felt more alive than he had in months. Finally to be doing something physical, to be taking action instead of planning, to fight instead of strategize. Patience was needed in a siege, and that was one quality that he had never been endowed with. He hated sieges. A good and bloody battle was long overdue. It frustrated him to think that Melli was less than a league away from where he stood, yet he was powerless to help her. They'd tried things, of course: blasting the northern wall, poisoning the lake, sending divers to access tunnels under the water level. But nothing had seemed to work: the trebuchet had been set alight, the poison dissipated too quickly because of the sheer size of the lake, and the divers had never returned to shore.

But now, today, there was a real battle to be met. The portcullis over the south gate was fully raised and a legion of mounted blackhelms rode out of the city of Bren.

The ground shook with their thunder. Their horses

were dark, their colors were midnight blue, and their helmets were blackened steel. Maybor watched them for a moment. Kylock had sent out Bren's best: the duke's guard, personally trained and handpicked by the now deceased duke. Banners waving, weapons glinting, they were a beauty to behold. And then the Wall's bowmen took aim. Their mighty four-sided arrowheads were enough to stop a horse. The quarrels pierced breastplates, helmets, even shields. Maybor clearly heard the release cry, he heard the soft *thuc* of the bows and the air-skimming *swish* of the bolts.

The quarrels slammed into the blackhelms. Horses reared, squealing in terror; men fell and were crushed beneath their hooves. From his position on the rise, Maybor saw everything clearly. The first line of blackhelms fell like flies. Still they kept coming, spilling out of the gate by the hundreds. The crossbowmen cocked their bows. Moments later they released. The second line of blackhelms fell as easily as the first.

Watching them fall, a dark warning sounded in Maybor's brain. Something wasn't right. Behind the second line of blackhelms were badly equipped, poorly armed mercenaries. Not for them the midnight blue and horses that shone like steel. The blackhelms weren't out in force—there were only two lines to fool the eye. Kylock was holding the elite troops back, saving them—but for what?

Even as Maybor urged his horse forward, Besik gave the order to charge. The Highwall cavalry began to advance. Clad in silver and maroon, they rode down the hillside to join the battle. The crossbowmen in the trenches shifted their positions to the flank and were backed up by mounted archers. A massive half-circle of Highwall forces began to come together around the south gate. Maybor was worried. Something was wrong. He had to make it to Besik.

The sun appeared over the eastern horizon. It sent

pale rays slanting across the battlefield and onto the mountains. The shadows of troops and horses were grotesquely long. Besik rode down the rise, shouting orders to the foot soldiers. The cavalry of Bren and Highwall met. The maroon and silver began cutting a swath into the enemy lines. Bren's mercenaries were no match for the Wall. Half of the blackhelms were down, and those who'd survived the crossbow fire could be seen making their way back to the gate.

Maybor raised his hand to shield his eyes from the sun. He was halfway down the hillside, on his way to confer with Besik, but as he caught a glimpse of the courtyard that lay beyond the gate, he stopped in his tracks. He shifted his position back a few feet and to the left. Blackhelms, thousands of them, were waiting behind the gate.

Waiting for what? Maybor kicked his horse into a gallop. Kylock had lured Highwall into a battle, forced them to train their best resources upon the gate, and fooled them into thinking they'd be doing battle with the duke's guard, when in reality they were fighting untrained, badly equipped mercenaries. Now it seemed that Kylock had every intention of bringing out the duke's guard, but not until . . .

A high clarion call sounded on the westerly wind. Maybor was now only a short distance from Besik. The two men turned to the west at exactly the same instant. The mountains were banked by a shallow range of foothills. Above the foothills, lit brilliantly by a cruel morning sun, emerged the kingdoms' army. Formed into tight, orderly columns, their armor flashed in the sunlight with all the arrogance of a perfectly worded threat.

For half a second, perhaps less, Maybor thrilled at the sight. The kingdoms: his homeland, his troops, his country's colors of blue and gold. And then a deep weight fell upon his heart. They hadn't come to save him. They'd come to destroy him. He was a traitor in their eyes— backing his daughter instead of his king.

Instead of his sons.

Maybor sucked in a thin breath and closed his eyes. His sons. The pain in his old heart increased with a dull and blinding ache. Kedrac would be leading the kingdoms' forces. Son fighting father, father fighting son. Maybor shook his head slowly. His hands crept down to feel the warmth of his horse's neck. He was so cold. How had it come to this? He couldn't blame Kedrac; he was doing what any young grasping nobleman would do: standing beside his king. He had chosen country over family. And growing up with a father who had always put ambition first, his decision was hardly surprising.

"There, there, Lady," murmured Maybor to his horse. His hands shook as he smoothed down her mane. There was a lump in his throat that wouldn't be swallowed and an ache in his heart that he knew wouldn't go. Kedrac was so young, so ambitious, who would condemn him for repeating his father's mistakes?

It had taken Maybor a quarter of a century to learn the importance of his family. Not until he lost Melliandra did he realize that his children were all he had. He cursed himself for not being a better father. He should have cared for his children more and hugged them harder and spoken words of love, not pride.

Maybor looked down from the foothills to the Highwall camp. Besik was looking at him. The commander of the Highwall forces trotted his horse over to Maybor's side.

"I will understand if you go now," he said.

Maybor reached out and grasped Besik's arm. He was a good man, born of a time when loyalty and codes of honor were always respected on the field. "No, my lord," Maybor said, deliberately addressing him as a superior. "My place is here, my loyalty is here. It is only my heart that is divided."

Besik looked at him carefully a moment. He nodded once. "I am glad you will fight at my side."

Maybor bowed his head. He was almost crushed by

the weight upon his heart. With a great effort, he raised up his chin. When he spoke his voice was strong and competent. "Bren and the kingdoms will work together to try and flank us. We need to send a battalion to watch the two eastern gates. I expect they're probably being opened as we speak. We need to recall the company that was sent to the foothills earlier—judging from the size of the kingdoms' army, they won't stand a chance without backup. . . . "

Baralis lay in the dark. Any light was a torture to him. The candles had long been snuffed, the shutters were tightly drawn, even the fire was kept banked and shielded, lest its flames cast their light into the room.

The temple had fallen.

Larn was gone, destroyed, its power broken by the baker's boy. The most ancient magic in the Known Lands had passed from the world last night.

Baralis didn't move. He didn't dare. Pain tore at his chest with every breath, spasms ripped across his forehead with each thought. The storm he'd created, the mighty, tide-turning storm, had proven useless. And now he was left paying the price.

If only he'd known they would choose to set themselves adrift! But who could have predicted such madness? If he'd known he would have expended less energy against the ship and saved his strength for the boat. Instead, he had weakened *The Fishy Few* to the point where one more blow would have smashed it to pieces. The mainmast was set to fall, and yet the baker's boy had picked that moment to abandon the ship, so Baralis had been forced to abandon it, too. His strength rapidly depleting, he'd had to start a whole new attack upon the rowboat. He had just enough power left to draw the one mighty wave that had been intended for *The Fishy Few*. He did it, watched the wave crash against the boat, saw the boat begin to break up, and spied Jack and the knight being dragged below the water. He thought they were as good as dead!

They *should* have been dead. With his last breath of consciousness, Baralis had sped to Larn and told the priests that the threat had been removed. He believed it had. For twenty-four hours he believed it had. Then it was too late. He was too weak to move let alone perform a drawing. The priests at Larn had been blind, sitting targets.

Oh, the pain was intolerable! Fueled by knowledge of his failure, it ate away at his soul. He had made the worst mistake of his life. A mistake of such enormity that it would haunt him for the rest of his days.

But it would not stop him. No. He wouldn't let it. Larn was just one step in the dance, and the music still played on.

The baker's boy was just that—a boy. Naïve, inexperienced, unable to control his powers: he was a force, but not one that couldn't be reckoned with. Baralis began to feel calmer. After all, things were still moving in his favor. Right now, as he lay here in his bed, Kylock was directing the armies of Bren and the kingdoms to victory. The Wall didn't stand a chance; they were out-manned, outmaneuvered and out of luck. Annis would soon find itself with neither neighbors nor friends, and come spring it would fall to the empire. Kylock was the most brilliant military strategist of his generation. No one could stop his advance.

The seers' prophecies would be missed, but they wouldn't make a difference in the end. By predicting the exact date of the winter storms, they had already performed their greatest feat. Baralis relaxed beneath the heavy covers on his bed. Yes, Larn was gone, but it had tilted the balance in their favor first.

As for Jack, well, he would doubtless head back to Bren now. In fact, by letting out the rumor that Maybor's daughter was alive, Baralis could ensure that he did. Jack and the knight were both close with Melliandra; they would come to her rescue in an instant. Not that Baralis had any intention of allowing them to get to Bren. Skaythe should have recovered from his injury and be in Rorn by now: he could track them north. He wasn't enough, though. He had already failed once, and Baralis knew better than to rely solely upon him again.

Who else could he get to deal with Jack and the knight? Baralis thought only for a moment. Tyren. Tyren would do it. The head of the knights had men along the eastern coast and an intelligence network that was second only to the archbishop of Rorn's. He could arrange to have the two fugitives tracked and caught. It was perfect. The knight was a wanted murderer, he had disgraced and disowned the knighthood—it was Tyren's duty to see him brought to justice. And if the knight and his companion happened to meet with a nasty accident along the way, then that would be most unfortunate.

"Crope," called Baralis.

"Yes, master?" Crope had been sitting in the dark waiting patiently for his master to stir.

"Is Tyren amongst the kingdoms' army?"

"Yes, master. He's brought a cohort of knights to the field."

"Good." Baralis risked moving a little to face his servant. Pain raked down his side. "As soon as he enters the city, send a message to him saying I will see him tomorrow."

"Yes, master." Crope sounded faintly distracted. His beloved wooden box was in his lap. "You slept a long time, master. Said things in your sleep."

"What things?"

Crope turned the wooden box around in his hands. "About Larn. Said it was gone."

"Yes. Yes, the temple there has been destroyed. What is it to you?" Baralis was getting impatient. He needed to rest before his meeting tomorrow with Tyren.

Crope slipped the little box back into his tunic. "Nothing, master. Nothing."

"Here, drink this." Tawl offered Jack a cup of something hot.

Jack took it from him. He had been awake only seconds and was still in a half-dazed state. "What is it?"

"Rainwater holk."

"Well, I see the rain, but where—"

"I have my ways." Tawl smiled. He looked terrible. He had two black eyes, a swollen lip, a huge purple bruise on his left cheekbone, and a bloody gash on the right.

"Do those ways include food?"

Tawl held out something vaguely fish-shaped. "They do. Here, take it."

"No, thanks. If that's a fish, it looks like it hasn't seen the sea in a long time."

"You could be right. An old woman gave it to me. She's got a basketful of them." Tawl swallowed the thing whole. "Hmm. I think I'll go back for more."

"I'll come with you," Jack said. He remembered the old woman rocking in her chair from the night before, and he wanted to see if it was the same one who had given Tawl the fish. He had a feeling it would be. How many old women could there be on an island this size?

Getting up off the ground caused all sorts of problems. Aches, pains, blurred vision, buckling legs, and dizziness. In the end Tawl had to heave him up like a sack of grain. Part of Jack wanted to laugh. He and Tawl must look quite a sight—like a pair of wounded drunks.

They were, as far as Jack could tell, somewhere in the cluster of shacks and lean-tos that lay behind the temple. A roof stretched over their heads, supported by two walls, not four. Ahead of them lay a similar structure, and beyond that there was nothing except sky. Jack didn't remember getting here. But then, there were a lot of things he didn't remember. A lot of things he didn't *want* to remember.

Tawl had a bad limp, yet he still managed to lend his strength to Jack. Together they limped, hobbled, and dragged their way toward the temple. Priests in brown cassocks crossed themselves as they passed. Wild-eyed men stared at them, and grossly disfigured women scuttled away like rats. No one challenged them.

The rain drizzled softly. There was no wind. As Jack walked he became aware of the hollowness of the place. There was nothing: no rhythm, no inner warmth. Larn was just an empty shell.

It beat inside, though. Jack could feel it in his heart. He had been changed, his whole being now beat in time with the ghost of the island. Faster and more urgent, it controlled his heart, his blood, his lungs. His body wasn't used to it: it fought and strained and sweated. Jack felt as if he was developing a fever—sweating, shaking, aches— yet it wasn't quite the same. It was his body coming to terms with being thrown out of kilter.

"Jack, are you all right?"

"I'm fine. Just feeling . . . " The words died on his tongue as he looked up at the temple of Larn. It was in ruins. The entire east side had collapsed. Massive granite slabs lay piled on top of each other like logs on a fire. Whole walls had fallen in, leaving doorframes standing like gravestones. Jack shuddered. He had done this.

"The temple was built around the cavern," said Tawl. "When that collapsed, it brought everything down with it."

Jack shook his head. He could think of nothing to say. Beneath the rubble, beneath the granite blocks and the dust and the rock, the seers lay dead. Bound to their stones, unable to save themselves, they had been crushed by the very temple they served. It was an appalling way to die. The seers had been as helpless as newborn lambs.

"Everything comes with a price," whispered Jack. "Everything."

"I know, Jack. I know." Tawl's voice was soft, close to breaking. "All you can do is learn to live with it."

Hearing the knight speak, Jack knew he wasn't alone. He wasn't the only one who had a past filled with regrets, uncertainty, and guilt.

"He! He! He!" A high, cackling voice broke the silence. "It's gone now. No coming back. *He! He! He!"*

On the west side of the temple, sitting on the bottom step, was an old woman. A basket by her feet, a thin shawl around her shoulders, she slumped oddly to her right. Jack moved toward her. It was the same woman who had shown them the way in last night, perhaps even unlocked the door. As he drew nearer, he saw that the right side of her face was slack. She was still laughing away, but only the left half of her mouth opened and only her left eye blinked. Her right eye was closed. Jack's gaze fell down to her lap, where her right hand emerged from the shawl. Curled up in a fist, it was brown and shriveled like a corpse. The fingernails were long and curved and dug into the dried-out flesh of her wrist.

The old woman looked straight at Jack. "Did what she wanted, didn't you?"

"Who? Who wanted me to do this?"

The old woman rocked back and forth on the step. "She did."

Jack was trembling. "Who's she?" The woman didn't answer. Jack ran to her. He put his hands on her shoulders *"Who's she?"*

The woman just rocked and cackled.

Jack began to shake her. She knew something. Something about him, about why he had to come here, what it all meant. He had to know what she knew. He would shake the answers out of her.

"Jack! Leave her alone." It was Tawl, placing a restraining hand on his arm. "Come away."

Jack stopped. He was out of breath. The old woman looked frightened. He looked into her good eye. It was a bright, watery gray. "Please, *please*, tell me what you know. Why did you help us? Why did you show us the way?"

The old woman began to rock back and forth again. Her gaze shifted out to sea, focusing far away on the horizon.

Realizing he would get no answers, Jack turned away from her. "Let's get off this island," he said to Tawl.

Together they rounded what was left of the temple's back wall. Just as they fell under the shadows of the west face, the woman's voice rang out one last time:

"He! He! He! The seers knew. They wanted to die. That's why they didn't tell. *He! He! He!"*

They found two skiffs on the island's north beach. Tawl wanted to carry one of them overland to the southern shore, but Jack just wanted to be off, even if it meant extra rowing.

His mind was an ants' nest of emotions, suspicions, and thoughts. Somewhere, somehow everything was connected: the old woman, Larn, Captain Quain's story, the past, the present, the future. He needed to find the thread that ran through them, the one thing that joined him to the seers and Marod's prophecy. If only he didn't feel so tired and heavy-headed. He needed sleep as much as answers.

Being on the skiff didn't help. The water was calm, but even the slightest swell sent his stomach reeling. The rain was good, though. Cool and fresh on his hot, shaking skin.

After a while, Tawl took the oars from him and rowed on his own. He looked worried. Jack began to drift in and out of consciousness. After a while, a thought occurred in his bleary brain. "What about *The Fishy Few*, Tawl? What if they didn't wait?"

"They'll be there," said Tawl. "Unless the ship sank to the bottom of the ocean, they'll be there."

Besik looked at Maybor. "If we don't withdraw to the east now, they'll have us flanked within the hour."

Maybor was sweating. Blood pumped wildly in his ears. Although Besik shouted, he could barely hear him. The sounds of battle were deafening. Blades clashing, hooves pounding, drums beating, screaming—it was enough to drive a man insane. The sun had gone in and thick dark clouds had come down from the mountains, bringing the sky that much nearer to the earth. Maybor felt trapped: everything was closing in on them.

He'd just come from leading a charge on the east gate. It had hardly any effect on the blackhelms: they just kept pouring out. Nothing could stop them. The Wall was outnumbered three to one. Kylock's Royal Guard were converging upon them from the west, to the north were Bren's mercenaries, and to the east the blackhelms were working to cut off Highwall's only escape route. With the mountains behind them, they'd soon have nowhere to go.

Maybor took a swig of brandy from his flask. Looking down at the battlefield, it was easy to see the maroon and silver of the Wall. A circle of black and blue was closing around them. They'd be cut off within minutes. Despite what Besik said, Maybor had a feeling it was already too late.

"They'll be expecting us to make a run to the south-east."

Besik nodded. "I know, but we haven't got a choice. We can't go south. Look at those clouds gathering in the west. The winter storms are coming. We withdraw to the mountains and we'll all be dead within three days."

"We won't even make it to the east." Maybor was growing impatient. Time was running out. "Our men are tired. They've been fighting solidly for four hours. The blackhelms are just getting started—they're fresh, eager, and they're the most highly trained soldiers in the north. Why do you think Kylock is sending them through the east gate, not the south or the west?" He answered his own question. "Because they're there to slaughter us the moment we withdraw."

"Don't you think I know that, Maybor? Don't you think I've taken that into consideration? To me it's a choice between the southern mountains or the blackhelms, and I'll tell you now, I'll take dying from battle wounds over dying from exposure any day of the week." Besik was shaking. Deep lines of tension creased across his brows.

Maybor offered him his flask. "You're a brave man, Besik."

Besik took the flask. "This is what we'll do. I'll have Hamrin sound the retreat. Bowmen, heavy cavalry, and two battalions of foot soldiers will clear a path to the southeast. The light cavalry and the remaining foot soldiers will bring up the rear. As they're pulling back, I'll have them flank out to the south. That way, we won't risk being cut off from the mountains as well as the east."

It was a good plan. A fair plan. Once again, Maybor found himself admiring Besik: he always listened, always considered. Always gave his best. "I'll take the southern forces."

"It's a dangerous command. You'll be the last on the field."

"Don't you think I know that, Besik?" said Maybor softly.

Besik smiled at the irony. His once jet-black hair was shot with gray. He wore the same clothes as his soldiers except for his one vanity of a beaten-silver belt. "The south is yours. I'll lead the east."

The two men clasped hands and minutes later the retreat was sounded.

Maybor rode down onto the field. The noise at

battle-level was overpowering: it cut through thought, making it impossible to concentrate. The ground had been churned to mud. Red mud. Men and horses lay dead in it, their bodies missing limbs, hands, even heads. Maybor knew better than to look at the corpses—he'd mastered soldier's blindness in his youth. The living were what counted.

Already the retreat had started. The maroon-and-silver were slowly edging back. The kingdoms pressed against them from one side, the blackhelms from the other. Only the middle of Bren's forces—made up of mercenaries, untrained, and partially trained men—was weak. Maybor had to admit that Kylock was a clever strategist: he had made the middle weak on purpose, to encourage the Wall forces to come forward. The nearer they got to the city, the easier they were to outflank.

Maybor began barking out orders to the men. The foot soldiers would retreat ahead of the cavalry, and he wanted to give them a good head start. Besik was over on the east side of the field, claiming the majority of the men for the eastern assault. It wasn't going to be a simple withdrawal; the commander of the Highwall forces was going to have to blaze a path through the duke's guard. Maybor wished him luck.

The minute the foot soldiers withdrew from the front line, the Wall cavalry began to break up. The blue-and-gold of the kingdoms was pressing hard from the west. They were trying to force the Wall east. Maybor, sweating, tired, and feeling very old, sent a silent prayer to Borc for protection. Not for himself, but for Besik: he was leading two-thirds of the Highwall forces into territory marked for slaughter.

Maybor could no longer see what was going on in the east. Already the division between his troops and Besik's troops had started. And already a company of blackhelms were riding in from the north, intent on driving a wedge into the breach.

Looking to the south, back over what little remained of the Highwall camp, and the foothills and mountains that lay beyond, Maybor checked on the progress of the retreating foot soldiers. The men were running for their lives. They had just reached the first line of foothills beyond the camp. Good. It was time to give the order to the cavalry. As Maybor swung back on his horse, he caught a glimpse of blue and gold in the southwest. The kingdoms' forces were closing in.

Maybor gave the order to the horn-blower. Three notes sounded: two high and short, one low and long.

It was during the last note that Maybor spotted his son.

Midway down the western slope, high atop a chestnut stallion, sat Kedrac directing his troops. His horse was decked in blue and gold, but his colors were Maybor's own. Red and silver. The colors of Maybor's coat of arms. The colors of the Eastlands.

Maybor felt a terrible, crushing pain in his heart. Pride was mingled with the suffering. *His* son was leader of the kingdoms' forces.

Kedrac looked magnificent: young, determined, in control. A score of men surrounded him like courtiers around a king.

Then, as Maybor watched, Kedrac raised his hand. Maybor went cold. His son was looking straight at him. The gesture was for him alone. They stood perhaps a third of a league apart—the only two men on the battle-field wearing red and silver—and stared at each other. Maybor felt his heart would break. His son wasn't wearing the family colors out of pride, but rather as a slap in the face. A cruel taunt to a father he considered a traitor.

Maybor turned away. He didn't need to look at Kedrac to know what his next order would be.

The final retreat was underway. Bloody, mud-smeared chaos reigned. The Highwall cavalry were pulling back fast, but Bren's mercenaries and the Royal Guard were coming after them. Hundreds of men were going down, arrows and blades in their backs. The air was filled with their screams. Maybor shook his head. The retreat losses were going to be heavy. They'd lose hundreds more lives than they saved.

The entire battlefield was moving to the south. All of Bren's forces were charging after the Wall. Out of the corner of his eye, Maybor spotted a company of heavily armed knights swiftly descending down Kedrac's command slope. He watched them for a moment, his face grim. Then, spinning around, he waited until the first line of Highwall cavalry drew abreast of him and kicked his horse into a gallop.

"To the mountains!" he cried, filled with a mad rush of exhilaration. So his son wanted him dead, eh? Well, he'd just have to see about that.

Twenty-three

The journey back to Rorn took six days. The main-mast of the ship was too weak to bear a topsail, so they had to rely on the mainsail to bring them home.

It had been a calm voyage. A time of rest. The winds were gentle upon the ship, the sea itself almost concilia-tory. The days were short, but the sunsets were long, and the nights were spanned by stars. *The Fishy Few* creaked and listed from wave to wave, and the crew cosseted her all the way.

During five of the six days, Jack was abed with fever. Fyler and, surprisingly, Captain Quain looked after him day and night. Tawl himself was out of the reckoning for the first two days, whilst his various cuts, bruises, gouges, and swellings were seen to by the crew. Fyler was the ship's unofficial surgeon, and never had Tawl come across a more enthusiastic—and thereby dangerous—amateur. Sometimes Tawl got the feeling he was being stitched just for the sake of it. The stitching wasn't as bad as the raw fish poultices, though, and not nearly as painful as the cauterizing. In fact, Fyler's only saving grace as a surgeon was his heavy reliance on hot rum tod-dies as painkillers.

Indeed, Tawl had spent much of the past six days in a toddy-induced stupor. It was, he found, the perfect anti-dote to Larn.

The island was having a more lasting effect upon Jack. It had done something to him: in the hours between destroying the seers' cavern and waking up the following morning, Jack had aged five years. His hair had lost its brightness and there were strands of gray around his temples. But that wasn't the worst. Deep lines now cut into his face, across his brow, along his cheeks, and down to his mouth.

Tawl hadn't said anything to him. There were no mirrors on the ship, but they'd be docking in Rorn within an hour, and so he'd find out soon enough. Tawl smiled, bringing his hand up to feel his own face. It was a mass of stitches and swellings. Neither of them was a pretty sight now.

Still, they'd gotten off lightly. They were lucky to be alive. Tawl had no idea what happened at the cavern, what Jack had gone through, but he'd sensed the power of the place, felt it throbbing through his bones. Whatever sorcery had been there was mighty beyond telling, and it was hardly surprising it had taken a toll.

Tawl had expected to feel relief, even perhaps satisfaction, at its fall. In reality it just left him feeling empty. The seers were dead, the cavern had been destroyed, yet many of the priests had survived—they were the real evil on Larn. Ancient magic had never tied anyone to a stone.

"Rorn looks good from here."

Tawl turned around to see Jack coming to join him on the foredeck. Once again, Tawl had to hide his surprise over the change in Jack's appearance. He still hadn't got used to it . "How are you feeling?"

"Not bad, really. I think I'm becoming immune to rum."

"You're a stronger man than me, then. Four of Fyler's toddies and I'm away licking the deck."

Jack smiled. His face was pale and drawn. The fever had left him two days ago, and Fyler had only allowed him up yesterday. "We've a long way to go yet, haven't we?"

Tawl watched the white spires of Rorn grow larger on the horizon. "We'll be in Bren before you know."

The Fishy Few glided into the dock, pulled by two heavy rowing craft. Jack and Tawl were joined by Carver and Captain Quain. All four men stood on the foredeck and watched as the ship was drawn past lines of fishing boats and caravels to its berth along the wharf. Seagulls dipped and looped in the blue sky, and the breeze carried messages from Rorn.

As they drew nearer, Tawl raised a hand to shade his eyes and looked out at the quayside. Two figures waited on the dock. Tawl recognized Nabber straightaway—the bulging tunic, the pack slung over the shoulder, the impossibly skinny legs—but the second one he couldn't make out.

Carver had a spyglass to his eye. "We've got one waiting for us, Captain. A bit raggedy, she is, but a live one just the same."

Quain glanced at Tawl, noted where he was looking, and said, "I don't think she's waiting for us, Carver. Why don't you give the glass to Tawl?"

"Here you go, mate," said Carver, handing over the spyglass. "She's standing next to that young lad on the quay. Pimps get younger by the day."

Tawl looked through the glass. He couldn't help but smile as he spied Nabber. The young pocket did not look happy. The girl who stood beside him was cleaning his face and neck with a rag. The girl herself was pitifully thin. Her hair was shorn short, and if it wasn't for the fact that she was wearing a dress, she could have been mistaken for a boy. As Tawl watched, she turned to face the ship. Tawl caught his breath. It was Megan. *His* Megan.

He brought down the glass. What had happened to her? Where were her bonny curls and rosy cheeks? Her plump lips, her curves, her sparkling eyes? Tawl felt a cold dread steal over him. He remembered the last time he'd disembarked *The Fishy Few*, running down the gangplank and heading straight for the whoring quarter, hoping to spend the night with Megan. Only she hadn't been there. Her room was empty, her possessions in disarray. He'd just accepted that she'd gone. What if he'd been wrong? What if she'd been in danger, and he'd just carried on?

Gradually the ship drew level with the wharf. The two figures on the quay began to move down the wooden walkway. Tawl could see them clearly now. Megan was dressed very prettily in a pink skirt and bodice that, judging from the way it gleamed in the sunlight, could only be silk. A woolen shawl lay across her shoulders, and every so often Nabber would reach up and pull it close against her arms. The two walked hand in hand.

"Whoa! Tawl!" shouted Nabber, approaching the docking ship. "I've brought a friend to see you."

Tawl looked down at Megan. Even from this distance, he could see he had been wrong: her eyes still sparkled. She didn't say anything, but she smiled. It was a smile of welcome and warmth and friendship, and it filled Tawl's heart with a sharp, aching joy.

He was down the gangplank before the mooring ropes had been secured. He raced along the walkway and into Megan's arms. She was so thin, so frail, he was frightened he might crush her. Her cheeks were wet with tears, and she shook like a newborn colt. "Tawl, I'm so glad," she murmured, resting her head against his shoulder. "I'm so glad you're here."

The crew cheered. Tawl looked up to see all twelve of them lined up along the ship's railings, grinning. He couldn't help but laugh at the sight of them. They were good men. He raised his arm and waved. After a second, Megan waved, too, and the crew went wild· yelling, throwing kisses, and asking her if she had any friends.

Shaking his head, unable to stop smiling, Tawl put his arm out for Nabber. The pocket slid under his arm and against his chest.

"If you don't mind me saying so, Tawl, you look a bit rough."

Tawl burst out laughing again. He squeezed the boy hard. "If you don't mind *me* saying, Nabber. I think you could do with a little tact."

Jack was saying his farewells to the crew. Tawl watched as he exchanged a few words with the captain and then made his way down the gangplank. He had a strange look on his face.

"Hey! Jack!" cried Nabber, disengaging himself from Tawl and running up to meet him. Jack hugged the boy.

Tawl was standing with his arm around Megan, waiting for Nabber to put his foot in it. He didn't have to wait long.

"Borc's kneecaps, Jack! What happened to you? Tawl looks bad, but you look awful. Is that gray in your hair, or wet paint?"

Jack raised a hand to his hair. "Gray?"

"Just around the edges, mind."

Jack looked at Nabber a moment and then laughed. "Well, if a few gray hairs are all I've got to show for Larn, then I didn't come off too badly."

Tawl breathed a sigh of relief. He beckoned Jack over to meet Megan. As he introduced her to Jack, he couldn't help wondering what she had gone through. Dark circles ringed her eyes and her cheeks were empty hollows.

"Pleased to meet you, Jack," she said. Her voice was thinner than he remembered.

Jack bowed and took her hand. Tawl smiled at him, pleased that he greeted her as if she were a highborn lady.

After a moment, Nabber padded up from behind to join them. "I've just had a quick word with the good captain. Told him we'd be back later with the payment."

"You've managed to raise it?" said Jack.

"Of course I have," said Nabber, instantly indignant. "What d'you think I am, a bungling amateur? You two aren't the only ones who have been up to stuff, you know. I've been busy, too. Having meetings, rescuing damsels, acquiring the loot. Right put upon, I've been. Right put upon."

Tawl, guessing Nabber's feelings had been hurt by being left in Rorn, said, "That's why we left you here, Nabber. Because we knew we could rely on you to take care of business."

"Take care of business, my earlobes! Stranded, I was. Left to fend for myself without so much as a word of warning or thanks. You two should count yourselves lucky that I'm here today. Mortally insulted me and I'm still paying the bills!"

Tawl grabbed hold of Nabber's arm. He began steering him along toward the quay. "Why don't we go to the Rose and Crown, have a hot meal, and you can tell us all you've gone through?"

Nabber snorted. "I suppose I'll be paying for that, too."

"Your Eminence, word has just come in from the north. Highwall's armies were defeated six days ago on the southern plains of Bren."

Tavalisk put down the asparagus that had just been aimed at his throat. "How did this happen? Bren's armies alone couldn't possibly have been enough to rout the Wall."

"The kingdoms' forces moved across the mountains last week, Your Eminence. They arrived in Bren just ahead of the winter storms."

"So that was what Kylock was waiting for all this time. The winter storms." Tavalisk licked the asparagus butter from his fingers. This was the worst news that Gamil had ever brought him. The northern empire was no longer a threat. It was a reality. Baralis and Kylock had effectively conquered the north. "Tell me, was it a massacre?"

"Yes, Your Eminence. Apparently the Wall was surrounded on three sides. They tried to withdraw to the east, but they didn't make it. Bren's blackhelms slaughtered them. By all accounts it was a bloodbath. No prisoners were taken."

"Maybor and Besik?"

"Lord Besik went down with his men. There's no word on Lord Maybor. There's a rumor that he led a third of the Highwall army into the mountains, but from what I can ascertain, most of their number died. They were the last to withdraw from the field."

"Yes. That would do it." Tavalisk was distressed, but not about to betray that fact to Gamil. Ever since that unfortunate incident last week with the young pickpocket, the archbishop found himself trusting Gamil less and less. His aide was obviously up to something of a dubious nature, or he wouldn't have been successfully blackmailed by a street urchin. And, more importantly, there was now a remote possibility that the man knew about his treasure trove.

Tavalisk picked an asparagus spear from the tray. He bent it until it snapped. As soon as that pesky little pocket left Rorn, he'd arrange to have his savings moved. Might even split it—half in the city, half outside. The way things were looking in the north at the moment, a man couldn't be too careful where his assets were concerned. Especially when those assets were hard gold.

"How are Camlee and Ness taking the news of Highwall's defeat?"

"Badly, Your Eminence. Ness is but three weeks hard march from Bren. It doesn't take a genius to see where Kylock's eye will fall next."

Tavalisk waved an asparagus stalk at Gamil. "Hmm. You're probably right. Kylock will be hoping that the mountain storms keep Annis on ice all winter. And now he's got his kingdoms' army with him, he'll be loathe to sit around and do nothing. There's no one more restless than a newly crowned king."

"He is in a very strong position, Your Eminence."

"Gamil, if I'd wanted someone to state the obvious, I could have brought in a copper-polisher. He might be ill-informed, but at least he's sure to see everything in front of his face." The archbishop slipped the top half of the asparagus in his mouth. He never ate the bottoms. It was an act of kindness, for he always sent the remainders to the poor.

"Come spring Kylock will have problems, though, Your Eminence. He'll have to cross the mountains and claim Highwall, keep Halcus subdued, and defeat Annis."

"He'll be stronger by spring, Gamil. Only half the troops in Bren are fully trained at the moment. There's all sorts: mercenaries, farmers, conscripts. If the man's got any sense at all, he'll spend the winter making sure they're fully trained for the spring."

"What of the invasion of Ness, Your Eminence?"

"The blackhelms and kingdoms' forces can take care of that. Ness can't be expected to put up much of a fight."

"But won't the south help the city?"

Tavalisk considered the asparagus: green, glossy with butter, scenting the air with the faint tang of sweat. With their furtive little spearheads, they were the perfect vegetable to scheme over. "The official line should be that the south is not prepared to help Ness at all."

"And the unofficial line, Your Eminence?"

"We need to give Bren the impression that we're wiping our hands of Ness, that way they'll be more likely to send out less troops and be less prepared. Only when they look set to conquer that wretched sheep-bound city will the south make its move. I say we arm Camlee in secret, mind our own business until the last possible moment, and then take young Kylock by surprise."

"Your Eminence is wise indeed."

Tavalisk beamed. He was still the chosen one, after all. Marod had certainly picked well when he'd picked him. "Any more news, Gamil?"

"*The Fishy Few* was spotted in the east bay this morning, Your Eminence. She's probably already docked by now."

"Hmm. I think it's best if we let the knight and his friends go. Wouldn't want to waste my time with such trivial matters as torturing commoners—not at the moment, anyway."

Gamil was quick to bow. "Your Eminence is quite right. Let us concentrate on more important matters."

He'd certainly changed his tune. What *did* the pocket have on him? "That's all for now, Gamil. After you've done me a little favor, you can go." It was, Tavalisk considered, exactly the right time to put Gamil in his place.

"What favor, Your Eminence?"

"I'd like you to make me a written list of all your intelligence sources."

"All of them?"

"Yes. From the richest merchant down to the lowliest scullery boy."

Gamil looked worried. "But, Your Eminence, that would take all day."

Tavalisk faked a yawn. "I'm prepared to wait."

"So the archbishop's chief aide was working for Larn?"

"That's right, Tawl. The Old Man was spot on."

"What is the man's name?"

"Gamil."

Tawl sat back in his chair. They were gathered around a small circular table in the Rose and Crown. The remainders of a roast pork dinner lay congealing on platters, and Nabber was just finishing off the last of the pie. The place was quiet and warm. The tavern-keeper had just put more logs on the fire, and the tavern-maid kept coming by to top up the ale.

Gamil. It was the name they had given him all those months ago at Larn. The man he'd delivered a letter to on their behalf. Tawl remembered his face clearly, remembered his surprise at seeing who was waiting outside his door. The man was just another self-serving coward—he and the archbishop deserved each other. Tawl rubbed his aching forehead. "Everything is connected in the end."

Jack looked up. During the telling of Nabber's and Megan's stories he hadn't said a word. "What's connected?"

Tawl had dropped the comment casually, yet Jack's manner was anything but casual. Tawl shrugged. "You know: Larn, Rorn, Bren. Even you and Melli—the way you both came from the kingdoms."

"Larn, Rorn, Bren, and the kingdoms," repeated Jack. He had been acting strangely since he got off the ship. Distracted and introverted, he had kept his distance from them all. Tawl wondered what was going on in his mind.

"Why don't you get some rest?" Tawl said. "Nabber's taken three rooms for the night." As he spoke, he shot a quick glance at Nabber.

Nabber nodded. He stood up, walked over to where Jack sat, and pulled on his arm. "Come on, Jack. I'll take you upstairs. You can have the room with the bed. Two golds extra it cost me."

Jack allowed himself to be led away. Tawl watched him go.

"You are worried about your friend?" Megan drew her chair closer to his.

"Yes. We've all been through a lot." Tawl took hold of Megan's hand and kissed it. "But none as much as you." Her smile was so sweet, it pained his heart to see it.

She raised her finger to his lips. "Don't blame yourself, Tawl. You can't go through life protecting everyone you care for. It just can't be done."

Tawl shook his head. "Megan, I—"

"You care too much, Tawl. You always live for others, never for yourself."

"If I'd known you were in danger, I would have come."

Megan ran her finger down his cheek. She smiled softly. "Don't you think I know that, Tawl?"

She was so beautiful. More beautiful now than she had ever been. The bright curls she had lost were nothing compared to the sparkle in her eyes. He reached over and kissed her on the lips. "I have so much to thank you for."

"You don't owe me thanks, Tawl. You've been so hard on yourself for so long that you expect others to be, too. Telling you that my imprisonment wasn't your fault isn't a favor. It's the truth. The archbishop threw me in a dungeon, not you."

"But—"

"Tawl, you *cared*. If you'd known, you would have been there." Megan's deep green eyes looked straight into his. "That's enough for me."

It *was* enough. She wasn't lying to spare his feelings. She was speaking the truth. Tawl felt a subtle shifting in his heart. A lightening. Perhaps there was something to what she said. Perhaps sometimes caring could be enough.

Megan was smiling like a wily fox. "Now, tell me about the woman you love."

Tawl didn't bother to hide his surprise. He did take a deep draught of ale, though, to give himself a moment to think. "What makes you say that?"

"Your kiss. It was sweet rather than passionate."

What was it about this woman? How could she know so much?

Megan laughed. "You look quite indignant. I didn't mean to offend you."

No. She meant to let him off lightly. By bringing the subject up, she was relinquishing all claims on him, telling him he was free to leave. "You are a remarkable woman."

"I'm glad you've found someone to love."

Tawl took both her hands in his. "Wasn't it you who told me it's love, not achievement, that will rid me of my demons?"

Megan rested her head upon his shoulder. "You still have a fair distance to go."

Jack lay on the bed but didn't sleep. His head was bursting. His senses were overpowering him. He felt the rough wool of the blanket scratching his wrists, felt a droplet of sweat run along his cheek. He saw the air swirl and thicken in front of the fire, and the ceiling bear the strain of footsteps above. He heard everything: moths beating their wings against the shutter, worms burrowing into the wood, a man in the next room snoring, and the tide pushing its way to the shore.

Voices. He heard voices, too.

Fyler's last words: *"I've never seen the captain care for anyone the way he cared for you on the voyage home. Treated you like a son, he did."*

Quain's last words: *"Jack, next time you're in Rorn be sure to come and see me. We've got a lot in common, you and I."*

Tawl in the tavern: *"Everything is connected in the end."*

Voices, hundreds of them, buzzed across his mind like flies around a joint. Why wouldn't they leave him in peace?

Jack tossed and turned in the bed. The blankets beneath him were wet with sweat. Outside someone was walking down the street—their footsteps pattered in time with his heart. Like a guard listening for intruders, Jack strained his ears to hear more. The fire crackled, the moths flew, the man in the next room snored, and the sea lapped against the shore—all in time with Larn.

Jack couldn't bear it. He felt as if he were going mad. Larn was squeezing him from all sides.

"Did what she wanted, didn't you?"

The voices grew loud again. Taunting, arbitrary, lashing against his soul.

Stillfox sitting by the fire: *"I heard a tale about a girl who came from Larn once. Her mother was a servant to the priests."*

Falk talking about his mother: *"It seems to me that she might have kept her past a secret to protect you."*

Quain before the storm: *"She was adrift on a skiff with neither sails nor oars to get her moving."*

Jack clamped his hands to his ears. The voices still wouldn't stop.

Stillfox again: *"It was her mother—a woman so badly deformed that she could use no muscles on the right side of her face, nor lift her right arm—who saved her. With her help the girl was cast adrift on a small boat in the treacherous waters that surround the island."*

Master Frallit: *"She was a foreign whore at that."*

His mother on the castle battlements each morning: *"Keep your head low, Jack, you might be spotted."*

Jack felt as if he were suffocating. He was being crushed by the weight of the voices. The words were heavy, penetrating, persistent. They would give him no peace. Sweat dripped from his nose and into his mouth. It tasted of the sea.

Stillfox: *"She swore a terrible oath that one day she would destroy Larn."*

Quain: *"She was running away."*

Falk: *"Perhaps she was afraid for you more than herself."*

"STOP!"

Jack sat up. His ears were ringing. His heart was racing. The blankets were ropes binding him to the bed. He tore them from his body. He had to get away.

The coolness of the wooden floor was a blessing. He dressed quickly, pausing only to splash water on his face. He took the stairs three at a time, and if a door wouldn't open, he forced it. People tried to stop him, but he shook them off. Their voices were no different than the ones in his head.

At last he was outside. Taking a calming breath of the night air, he willed the madness to recede. The voices faded to whispers, to senseless humming, and then to nothing. Jack felt drained. His feet found their own way along the streets.

Prostitutes called to him, drunken men appraised him, old women crossed the street when he passed. The stars were out tonight. They glittered in time to Larn. Jack quickened his pace. No matter how fast he walked, Larn was inside him. No matter how hard he tried, things would never be the same.

Down toward the sea he walked. Across half a league of seafront, along the eastern quay, between row upon row of fishing boats, and up the gangway to *The Fishy Few*. Until he got there, Jack didn't even know where he was going, but as soon as he saw the hull of the ship, he knew he'd come to the right place.

"Who goes there? Disturb this ship at your peril."

"Carver. It's me, Jack. I've come to see the captain."

"Well, you're in luck. He hasn't left yet. He's still in his cabin, making a log of the voyage." Carver let him board the ship. "Hey! You best not be proposing to go on another journey, matey. Because if you are, I'll throw you overboard right here and now. Ain't never sailing to Larn again. And I'm prepared to commit murder to keep it that way."

"It's all right, Carver. Larn is just another barren island in the middle of the sea." Even as Jack said it, he didn't believe it. How could he? Larn beat in his heart and in his soul.

"Hmm. Just you watch it, matey."

"I will, Carver. I will."

Jack went belowdecks. The wood of the ship smelled sharp and confining. The low ceilings cut down the size of the night. The captain's door was closed.

Jack didn't knock. He pushed.

The captain was sitting at his desk, scribing in a ledger. He didn't look up. "Come in. Sit down. I've filled you a glass."

Jack stepped into the room. It was warm, but not too warm. Bright, but not dazzling. On the table lay two glasses: one was full to the rim, the other was short of the mark.

Quain swung around to face him. "I thought you'd be here by now."

Jack sat. "You knew I would come?"

"Well, I had an inkling you might."

"And if I hadn't?'

"Then I'd have the second glass all to myself." The captain smiled softly. "I'm rather fond of arrangements where I get to win either way."

Jack took hold of the full glass. It was smooth and heavy in his hand. "What became of the girl from Larn?"

The captain spoke straightaway, as if he'd been expecting the question all night. "After *The Bountiful Breeze* docked, I took her home with me. She was still ill, and my mother and I looked after her for several weeks. I've never seen a woman so determined to get well—she near as willed herself to health. The day she was strong enough to walk was the day she left the city. There was no stopping her. She was afraid of Larn, afraid the priests would track her down and kill her. Though it broke my heart to do it, I gave her my savings and let her go."

Jack felt as if the night itself was spinning, and he and Quain were the only stationary points. "Where did she go?"

"She wouldn't tell me. She didn't want to put me at risk." Quain spoke in a whisper. "I think she headed north."

"What did she look like?"

"Dark hair. Blue eyes, small bones, a heart-shaped face. Simply beautiful."

Spinning. Everything was spinning. Jack heard the air rush past his ears. "What was her name?"

"Aneska."

And then it all stopped. Dead.

Quain brought the rum glass to his lips. He swallowed and then looked straight at Jack. "The day she left Rorn she said she must go by a different name. A name that would go unremarked in every city in the Known Lands. I said she should call herself Lucy. Whether or not she took my suggestion, I'll never know."

All the time that Quain was speaking, Jack hadn't taken a breath. He took one now, and the air crackled all the way down to his lungs. He was out of the chair before he knew it. He had to touch the captain and prove to himself that the man and his words were real. Quain was warm and smelled of rum: solid as the old sea dog he was. Jack knew he spoke the truth.

A tightness formed in Jack's chest. He felt a world of new emotions pushing against his heart, causing it to ache with a sharp-sweet pain. There was relief, wonder, excitement, joy, and most of all there was sadness. *How she must have suffered*, he thought. *How well she had hidden both her past and her fears*.

Jack was grateful, too. Grateful that the man before him had been the one to reveal the truth. Coming to kneel at the captain's feet, Jack said, "She did take your name. She called herself Lucy."

Quain's hand came to rest upon his shoulder. "Aye. You're her lad. I knew it the moment I set my eyes upon you." There was longing in his voice as he spoke. "She was a brave lass."

Jack nestled close to him. Finally there were answers. He knew why his mother had changed her name, why she climbed the battlements every morning to search the faces of strangers, and why she lied about her past. Fear had been the one defining force in his mother's life, and Larn had been the cause of it.

She lived *with* fear, but she lived *for* vengeance. The oath she swore to destroy the temple was so strong it had outlived her. Perhaps it had even destroyed her. Still, her work was done now: Larn was gone and she could rest easy in her grave.

Jack looked up at Quain. "Why did you wait to tell me this? I might never have come to you."

"Jack, I know the sea. It can lull a man as surely as if he were a baby in a crib. When your eyes can't see the shore and your feet can't feel the earth, the only thing that matters is the journey itself. A man needs to get back on dry land again before he can see things in their proper perspective. I figured it would be the same with you. A few hours on solid earth and you'd work it out on your own."

"But there are still some things I don't understand."

"I've told you all I know." Quain patted Jack's shoulder. "Pour us some more rum, lad. It's time we toasted your mother's memory—questions without answers can wait until tomorrow."

Jack stood up, filled both glasses to the brim, and handed one to the captain. Quain was right: tonight should be a celebration.

So that evening aboard *The Fishy Few* two men toasted and drank, swapped stories and histories, and laughed and wept until dawn.

Twenty-four

*I*t was dawn. The light coming in from the shutters was steaming with mist from the lake. It was bitterly cold. Melli didn't think she had ever been so cold in her life. The winters at Castle Harvell were nothing compared to this. The storm had raged for six days. Today the sky was clear.

Ice had formed on the damp northern wall of her room. The cup of water by her bed was frozen. Her breath plumed white in front of her face and beneath the covers; her body wouldn't stop shaking. Freezing gusts of air frisked around the room. Cold blasts from the chimney fought with thin drafts from the windows, lifting curtains, rattling furniture, and sweeping the dust from under the bed.

Melli was nose-deep in covers. She badly wanted to relieve herself, but she knew from experience just how cold it was out there. Besides, her waterglass wouldn't be the only thing that was frozen, and she didn't fancy peeing over a thin layer of ice. She'd wait until the guards brought her a new pot.

It was actually colder now than during the storm. Oh, the wind had blown up a terrible fuss, sending snowflakes flurrying down the chimney and breaking the catches on the metal shutters as easily as if they were wood. But at least while the air was moving it was too busy to freeze your toes.

And your nose and your cheeks and your eyelids. Could one's eyelids freeze? she wondered. Might they just seize up, leaving one's sights caught in midblink? Alarmed by this thought, Melli pulled the blankets up right over her face. Better to suffocate than risk freezing eyelids.

It was really quite amazing how much warmer it was beneath the covers. Her little pot-belly was as good as a stove. Nearly seven months now, she guessed—keeping track of time had never been one of her strong points. She'd always had servants to do that for her.

No servants now, though. She had two, sometimes three, guards and old no-teeth herself, Mistress Greal. Metal-helmed, foul-smelling, and blade-brandishing as the guards were, Melli infinitely preferred them to Mistress Greal. The guards were silent, courteous—if you could call a man pointing a spike at your throat courteous—and blissfully disinterested. Mistress Greal, however, was like a dog who'd got a bone and wouldn't let go. She sneered, prodded, insulted, and was constantly on the lookout for some other luxury to take away. It seemed that candles, heat, floor mats, supper, and fresh water just weren't enough. Now Melli had to wear the same clothes for weeks on end, wash in freezing lake water, gnaw bones that looked like they'd been chewed on by packs of dogs, and sleep under blankets coarse enough to try a saint.

Melli had found she could adapt to anything that Mistress Greal threw at her. Despite everything her pregnancy was going well, and except for a little swelling in her ankles and a back that constantly ached, she was actually growing stronger by the day. Weeks merged into months and autumn gave way to winter, but every time she felt a tiny shift within her stomach it gave her reason to carry on.

Melli liked being pregnant. It meant she wasn't alone. She hugged her belly and talked to her child and promised him or her that she'd escape before it was born. It wasn't an idle promise, either. She knew exactly what Kylock wanted from her and she wasn't prepared to give it. She wasn't going to let Kylock use her body to wash his sins away. What he had done could never be forgiven. Seven days ago he had ordered the massacre of five thousand men. The Highwall army was beaten, and he could have disarmed or imprisoned them. But no, their throats had been slit, their bodies mutilated, and their remains left to freeze upon the southeastern plains of Bren.

Kylock was a monster and he should have been strangled at birth. Melli was sick of playing his twisted games of sin and repentance, sick of being the apple of such a distorted eye. She was going to escape. She knew her child was marked for death: Baralis would never allow Bren's rightful heir to live past the birthing. Kylock wasn't interested in the child—he wanted her—but she was damned if she was going to wait around for the next two months and then just deliver herself up like a gamebird on a platter. She would be no one's rite of absolution.

A sound came from behind the door. Melli pulled back the covers in time to see Mistress Greal make her entrance. The good lady was dressing like a queen these days: furs, brocaded silks, gold chains around her scrawny neck. She probably looted the chambers of all the noblemen Kylock had tortured then killed. Anyone in the city who spoke a word against Kylock was likely to end up dead.

"Any news of my father?" demanded Melli.

"M'lady," countered Mistress Greal sharply. "Any news of my father, *m'lady*." She took off a glove and stuck one of her bony fingers in the air. "Colder, but not as drafty."

"Why don't you just knock down the wall and throw me in the lake? Seeing as you're so intent on freezing me to death."

Mistress Greal shrugged. "You'd be going the same way as your father, then."

"Have they found his body"—Melli grit her teeth—"m'lady?"

"After the storm that just passed, do you really think they need to look? Your father might have run like a coward from the battle, but the mountains would have got him in the end. After all, he was hardly in his prime."

Melli ignored the speculation and jibes. They hadn't found his body, so that meant there was still a chance he was alive. "How many other men are unaccounted for?"

Mistress Greal approached the bed. "Nosy, aren't we?"

"You mean you don't know."

"There's nothing that goes on in Bren that I don't know about, missy. Nothing."

"Has my brother asked to see me?" Melli knew her brother was in the city, but did he know that she was?

"The king has told him you're dead. You died of a fever three months back. No one knows you're here, missy. And no one cares." Mistress Greal spoke with relish. "Anyway I'd hardly set store by that brother of yours. I heard he sent his special guard onto the field to kill your father."

"You're lying." Melli wanted to slap Mistress Greal's toothless face. She wanted to tear her hair from its roots and ram her head into the chamberpot. Melli had tried the slapping thing before, though, and it had taken Mistress Greal less than a second to call the guards.

"Ask the king next time he comes—see if I'm lying then."

Melli rested her head against the pillows. She couldn't bear it to be true. How must her father have felt knowing Kedrac had sent men to murder him? The fact they fought against each other was bad enough, but this . . . The only thing Maybor had lived for was his sons.

No. That wasn't entirely true. Maybor loved her as

well. It had just taken him many years to show it, that was all.

"Maybor was seen riding away from the battle?" Melli had already asked this days ago, but right now she needed reassurance.

Mistress Greal smiled. "Your father is the sort of coward who likes to hit defenseless women. First sign of real danger, though, and he's off faster than you can call him a drunken bastard."

Melli was out of the bed in an instant. As always, her increased weight was a shock. She grew heavier by the day. But no slower. Her arms were around Mistress Greal's throat before the woman could take a breath. Mistress Greal elbowed Melli in the chest.

"Guards!" she screamed, aiming her other elbow for Melli's stomach. Melli grabbed her wrist. Mistress Greal's hand slipped away and Melli was left holding her glove.

The guards came in, spears pointing. Melli backed away, one arm up in submission, one arm behind her back, tucking the glove into the waistband of her skirt. At least one hand wouldn't be blue with cold tonight.

"You little bitch!" Mistress Greal stepped forward and slapped Melli on the cheek. "Get on the bed." And then to the guards: "No food for her today."

"But, m'lady, the king said the girl was to be fed proper."

Mistress Greal looked at the guard. Melli was gratified to see she had two nasty-looking red marks on either side of her neck. "Give her your slops, if you must. But nothing more." With that, she turned on her heels and left the room.

Melli breathed a sigh of relief. "Thank you," she said to the guard.

The guard nodded. He was young, with a bad complexion and brown hair. "Was nothing, miss." He and his companion left the room. The lock turned, the bolt was drawn, and Melli was left alone once more.

She pulled Mistress Greal's glove from her skirt. It was her prize. Soft brown pigskin lined with rabbit hair, it was shaped for a large left hand. Melli put it on. The fit didn't matter. The *fact* of the thing did. She was going to escape from here somehow, and she'd need a weapon and some warm clothing when she did. Melli held her gloved hand up to the light. It wasn't a bad start.

"So you've finally decided to join us, then," said Tawl, hand on hips, looking like a cross between a riled fishwife and an impatient merchant. He had a new tunic on, and it was colored a little more brightly than the usual one he wore. But then everything looked brighter today.

Jack was hung over. His mouth was as dry as a bag of grain and his head felt as heavy as a stone. "I spent the night with the captain. Had a few drinks, fell asleep at dawn, next thing I know it's midmorning."

"You know we're leaving Rorn today?"

Jack looked around. Only a minute earlier he had practically walked into Tawl, Nabber, and Megan on the steps of the Rose and Crown. "Where are the horses?"

"Nabber sold them. We'll pick up some more in Marls."

"Marls?"

"We're sailing there today. I'm not risking going back up the peninsula. Baralis will be expecting us to go that way."

Jack wished his head felt clearer and that the sun wasn't shining so brightly. He couldn't think of any objection to Tawl's plan, so he clapped Nabber on the shoulder, and said, "Marls, it is, then."

Giving him a strange look, Tawl said, "What happened to you last night?"

"I finally learnt the truth."

No one spoke after that: the words seemed to carry a charm that held the tongues of all who heard them. Tawl nodded once, as if he had received exactly the answer he had expected, and Nabber simply smiled, his gaze firmly on the crowd.

They made their way down to the harbor in silence. Tawl and Megan were arm in arm, Nabber was some distance behind them—doubtless engaged in some last-minute withdrawals—and Jack walked a few steps ahead.

Jack was trying to come to terms with what had happened last night. His hangover was not making it easy. He and Quain had finished off a bottle and a half of rum. They'd told tales, sang songs, and then fallen asleep. Or at least Jack did. He woke up the next morning to find himself covered with warm blankets and Quain sitting in the corner, watching. "You're so like her," he said. "Just to see you fills my heart with joy."

Jack looked up at the bright morning sky. Quain had obviously been in love with his mother. He had helped her selflessly, saved her life, given her his savings, and ultimately let her go. Thirty years had passed and he still remembered her with all the bright intensity of youth.

What had she been like then? Jack wondered. Above all else she must have been brave. A young girl traveling the length of the Known Lands on her own was unheard of. And she had done no half-measure, either. She'd headed to the farthest possible point from Larn: to the Four Kingdoms. Jack felt a cold chill chase down his spine. What fear she must have felt to cross a continent.

She had never shown any of it to him, though. Nine years they'd had together, and not once in that time had he seen her cry or look afraid.

Larn was gone now, but it would never be forgotten. It was inside him, and as he thought about it now, he realized that it might have always been there. Jack recalled the moment when he had first touched the rock in the cavern; he remembered the smell, the sight, and the feel of it. It was just like coming home. His mother's home, the place that made her who she was.

Jack stopped in his tracks. The old woman who had sat and rocked and shown them the way was his grandmother. Stillfox had said the girl from Larn's mother was deformed, unable to use her right arm or the muscles on the right side of her face. It was her. Jack recalled her right hand, curled up like the skeleton of a dead bird. Somehow she had known he was coming and helped him.

The seers had helped him, too. That last day, they must have known he was on the island, yet they held their tongues. Wishing for death.

"Are you all right, Jack?" It was Tawl.

"I'm fine, really. Just tired."

"You look pale. The ship's at the end of the quay. Once we've boarded, you should get some rest."

"What ship?" Jack hadn't been paying much attention to where they were walking. But now, looking around, he saw they were in a different section of the harbor from where *The Fishy Few* docked.

"*Shrimp Scourer*. Over there." Tawl pointed to a small, single-masted caravel. "Quain recommended it to me. They should be expecting us."

Jack nodded and walked on. The sea was gray and calm, the wind fair, and the sky clear except for a band of streaky clouds to the east. It was a fine day. In the kingdoms at this time of year it would be cold, dark, and frosty. Jack wondered if his mother had ever gotten used to the difference in climate. She had never liked the cold; her winters were spent inside by the fire, sitting so close she'd scorch her cheeks. Her self-imposed exile must have been hard for her to bear.

Reaching the boat, Jack waited for Tawl to say goodbye to Megan. Nabber had appeared out of nowhere, and by the looks of things, he and Tawl were arguing over the contents of his sack.

"All of it?" squawked Nabber.

"Yes," said Tawl. "We can pick up some more cash in Marls."

"You mean *I* can pick up—"

"Stop," said Megan. "I don't want your money, Nabber. You've already bought me these lovely clothes. I wouldn't ask you for anything more."

Nabber hung his head low. "I could give you half."

Tawl gave himself away by laughing. "Make it three quarters."

"Two thirds."

"Done. Now hand it over."

While Nabber counted out the money, Tawl took Megan's hand in his. Jack, wanting to give them privacy, stepped onto the *Shrimp Scourer*'s gangplank.

A small, swarthy man cut across the deck. "Friends of Captain Quain?" he asked.

Jack nodded.

The sailor waved him aboard. He was dressed in a brightly embroidered waistcoat and bloodred britches. "Perfect day for setting sail," he said, holding out his hand to be clasped. "I'm Balvay of Marls, first mate, ship's outfitter, and son of Nollisk."

Jack took his hand. "I'm Jack of the Four Kingdoms." He hesitated for a moment and then added: "And Larn. My mother's family hails from Larn."

The words were strange upon his tongue, but they rang with the clear note of truth. At last he had found half of himself. He had origins and history and family still alive. "Yes, my mother came from Larn," he repeated, just for the sake of it.

Baralis stood on Bren's battlements and looked out upon a field of frozen corpses. Snow had drifted against the dead, forming a landscape of white limbs and white bodies reaching up from icy graves. Dark little figures, quick-moving like ants, could be seen scurrying between the mounds. The storm had delayed the looting, and only now were people venturing from the city in search of spoils.

"The bodies need to be disposed of," Baralis said to Kylock.

"Why? They won't start to stink until spring." Kylock raised a gloved hand to his cheek. "Besides, they serve me better here, where everyone can see them, than smoking poorly on a pyre with little flame."

This statement annoyed Baralis. Kylock was far too arrogant for his liking. His temper engaged, he swiftly turned to the subject that irked him the most. "The girl should be moved from the palace before Kedrac discovers she's here."

"I wondered how long it would take you to get around to Melliandra, Baralis. Quicker than normal today." Kylock leant against the wall. He gazed out at the southern plains. "There's no need to move her. In two days time Kedrac will be leaving the city."

"He'll head up the force bound for Ness?"

"No. Not Ness." Kedrac turned to look at Baralis. "Camlee."

"An attack on Camlee will be seen as an attack on the south."

"I've seen it on a map, Baralis, and it's north enough for me."

Baralis took a settling breath. Kylock was ravenous for victory, but not for power. The two were very different. Kylock would take Camlee because he could, because he enjoyed all the bloodiness and passion that went with conquering, not because he wanted to rule its people. He didn't care a jot about the cities he defeated—he agreed to leave Helch in the hands of Tyren! No, he wanted only the thrill of the rout. The delights of political dominance, exploitation, and control—where the *real* power lay— were concepts too subtle to catch the young king's eye. All that might well change over time, but for now it meant Baralis could use the king's ambitions to fulfill his own.

"Camlee would be quite a prize."

"It will be so easy to take it, Baralis. Everyone will assume we're heading for Ness. We'll even encourage them to believe it—we'll set a course due east and only turn south at the last possible moment."

"What about Ness?"

Kylock waved a negligent hand. "Ness is nothing. A trumped-up sheep market. They have no battlements to speak of, no army, no decent leadership. Their only defense is the hillsides that surround them. We can leave them until after Camlee has fallen."

Kylock was right, but not for the reasons he thought. Given a chance the south would rally around Camlee—it was one of their own, a close relative, and they would defend it if they had to. Ness, however, was a distant cousin. The south would care little for its fate. By choosing to attack Camlee first, Kylock would take the south by surprise, thereby robbing them of the chance to arm in secret.

"The south won't do anything if Camlee is taken quickly," said Kylock. "Valdis will be to the south, Bren to the north, and by the time I've finished, Ness will be to the east. Camlee will be surrounded by cities loyal to me."

"The weather in Camlee will be more favorable at this time of year," murmured Baralis. He found himself liking Kylock's plan more by the minute.

"Yes, I've considered that; it will be a lot warmer than in Ness. Supplies will be easy to come by, too. We'll raid villages along the way for anything we need. I'll give Kedrac free reign to do whatever he pleases."

"What forces will he take with him?"

"All the kingdoms' forces—hardly any of them were wounded in last week's battle—all the blackhelms fit to fight and a dozen mounted cohorts of knights. That should be almost nine thousand men in total—more than enough. Camlee is an old city, it lives off old victories and defends itself with old battlements. The empire's forces will prove more than enough for them."

The empire. It was the first time Baralis had heard Kylock speak its name. It was a real living thing now. The kingdoms, Bren, Halcus, and soon there would be Camlee and Ness. After winter they would claim Highwall, and Annis would surely follow. The northern empire was coming to pass.

Baralis brought himself down. He didn't like to spend too much time in self-congratulation. Details were everything. "And what of Bren's defenses? There is always a chance the passes might clear, enabling Annis to send a force over the Divide."

Kylock was already ahead of him. "The wounded blackhelms number approximately two thousand—half of them can be expected to recover to fighting fitness. Those who cannot fight will train. I want every man in the city—free lances, mercenaries, barrow-boys, and farmers to be fully equipped and ready to fight within a month. I've already given orders to every blacksmith in the city to prepare the necessary armor and weapons."

"Tell them to make the blackened helmets first." Baralis moved closer to Kylock. "Men in the north have come to fear the blackhelms. The sight of, say, five thousand men wearing the telltale blackened helmets might seriously discourage an invading force."

Kylock smiled. "Baralis, as always you can refine even the best of plans."

"It shouldn't be too hard to hold off a siege for a month or so. Bren's defenses are second to none," Baralis said.

"Yes. We have the old duke to thank for that." Kylock began to walk toward the gatehouse door. "Oh, by the way, we shouldn't have to worry about Maybor. I sent out a force to patrol the base of the southern mountains. If he's alive and he's got men, he won't be coming down."

The cold was a disease. It blighted thought, movement, speech, and even sanity. It blighted a man's soul. The air was still at last, but the stillness came with a price. The temperature had dropped sharply overnight, and daylight had done little to raise it. The snow was beginning to freeze over; it had lost its graininess and was becoming like a solid wall around them. Yesterday water had trickled down from the rocks; today, in its place were spikes of glistening ice.

Maybor didn't want to breathe. He could feel the freezing air stealing its way into his lungs. Slowly, it was killing him.

Already he had lost all sensation in three fingers on his left hand, two on his right. He could still grip a sword, but never again would he wield one. At the moment, his main priority was keeping his remaining fingers sound. Both hands were inside his tunic, against a layer of scarlet silk.

Two hundred men pressed against the hard spine of a mountain in full winter. Many of the horses were dead. One was being cooked now. The men had long given up caring about the dangers of smoke.

Four days ago they had located a large but shallow depression in the rock face. Not deep enough to be named a cavern, they had taken it nonetheless. Snow had gathered and drifted, and the men who could worked to keep it building at the mouth of the recess. The snow wall had reached its limit. It now spanned perhaps a quarter of the opening, and that was as high as it would go without collapsing. Currently a group of men were in the back of the depression, seeing if they could loosen any rocks and roll them over to support the wall. Maybor had seen the size of those rocks. They wouldn't get anywhere with them. The freezing wind would have to be endured.

Or would it? Maybor made a mental note to ask Grift to pull together all the extra breastplates and shields—they could be used to add strength to the wall.

"Five more men have died since noon, m'lord," said a young man coming to crouch beside Maybor.

"Strip them before their clothing freezes to their bodies."

"But, m'lord, the men—"

"Do it!" hissed Maybor. "Would you have us all freeze out of respect for the dead?"

The man walked away, head down.

Maybor knew what all the men were thinking: better to have died on the field than on a frozen mountainside. No one had dared say it, but he could see it in their eyes. They wished they had never withdrawn. Maybor's damaged right hand curled into a fair likeness of a fist. Well, damn them all! He'd make sure they survived now just to spite them.

Twenty-five

*A*ll things considered, Marls was a very strange place.
It shouldn't have been—after all it was only seven days
sail from Rorn—but it was nevertheless.

The buildings had more curves than angles, but the
streets were as straight as reeds. The sun wasn't shining,
but it was warm, and it wasn't raining, but it was wet.
The women wore bulky, shapeless dresses that were slit
up the sides to their thighs. The men wore hats, which
they constantly pulled down over their ears, whilst smiling all the while revealing stupendously bad teeth. There
were no children to speak of. Probably kept them in the
dungeons till they were old enough to earn a living,
thought Nabber spitefully.

Nabber was, he admitted to himself, disinclined to like
Marls—it being Rorn's greatest trading rival and so on—
but even he had to admit that it was *interesting*. And not
just in your common-or-garden interesting buildings and
people way. No. Marls was interesting in a fiscal way.
Very interesting indeed.

They'd just gotten into the harbor this morning, and
already Nabber had quite a stash going—a good one, too.
A little heavy on the silver, perhaps, but with a fair
amount of precious stones to make up for the lack of
gold.

Tawl had gone looking for errant knights. The captain

of the *Shrimp Scourer*—a wide man name o' Fermcatch—
had said that Marls had recently been inundated with
knights looking to gain passage to the Far South.
Apparently they'd been leaving the knighthood in droves
since old Tyren had got them fighting Kylock's battles in
the north. Anyway, the moment the ship docked, Tawl
had gone in search of a certain establishment where it
was rumored that knights could be found. Nabber had
the distinct feeling that if Tawl did find any knights, he'd
find trouble as well.

Which was why he was currently on the way to the
Seaman's Fancy himself. Tawl might be brave and lethal
with a sword, but he lost all his good sense when the
name Tyren was mentioned. He had a soft spot as big as
a turnip patch for the leader of the knights. Wouldn't
hear a word against him, and Nabber knew more than
anyone that the man was as good as a rogue.

"'Scuse me, sir," said Nabber, tapping a passerby on
the shoulder and casually pocketing him while he did so.
"Could you tell me the quickest way to the Seaman's
Fancy?"

"No," said the stranger. "You are too young to be
drinking. Go home and learn your prayers."

"Aah, well, I'd be there now, sir, if it wasn't for the
fact that my mother's taken my prayer book with her to
the Seaman's Fancy."

"The only women in the Seaman's Fancy are prostitutes."

"All the more reason for me to pray for her, then."

The man tugged on the earflaps of his hat. He was
beaten—and he knew it. "Straight down this road. Turn
left at Pickling Street, left again at Salting Street, right on
Preserve. You can't miss it."

"Thank you for your kindness, sir," said Nabber,
bowing and walking away. "I'll be sure to mention you in
my prayers."

Nabber followed the man's directions. He still didn't

like Marls, but its people were definitely a challenge to his wits.

The journey *here*, however, had been a challenge to his guts. Never sailed in his life before. Never wanted to. First couple of days were murder. He tried everything from sitting blindfolded in the crow's nest to crouching barefoot in the hold. Nothing worked on his seasickness until Captain Fermcatch—a man who was as good as he was hairy—suggested that Nabber take the wheel. Well, after that it was plain sailing all the way. Being in charge made all the difference. Took to it like a fish to water. Might even be a sailor himself one day. A pirate! That's what he'd be. A pocketer of the high seas.

Yes, there was a lot to be said for sailing. For one thing, it was most definitely better than riding. Tawl had said that they would only spend one night in Marls and ride north first thing tomorrow. Nabber wasn't looking forward to that at all. Riding meant horses, and horses meant grief. In fact, that was where Jack was now—out finding two nags worthy of purchase. They were all supposed to meet up later by the quay, buy the nags in question, exchange any information they'd managed to glean about the war, and then find a place to stay.

"'Scuse me, madam," said Nabber, stopping yet another person. No pocketing this time—the woman only looked good for a few coppers. "Is this Preserve Street?" Nabber couldn't read, so he was forced to rely on the kindness of strangers.

"This is indeed Preserve," said the woman, "but a boy as young as you should be home learning his prayers."

Nabber bowed and walked on. Very strange place, Marls.

The Seaman's Fancy was not as much a building as it was a door. Nabber would have walked right past it if it hadn't been for the smell of ale and sailors wafting from around the frame. The building the door was located in was derelict; the shutters had been torn from the windows, the paint long peeled, the top floor was open to the skies, and the lower masonry looked fit to crumble. The only part of the building that was in any state of repair was the door: blue for the sea, bloodstained from squabbling sailors, and emblazoned with a crude likeness of a naked woman to attract the fancy of passersby.

Knocking didn't seem in order, so Nabber walked right in. He found himself on a badly lit staircase leading down. Fatty, acrid tallow smoke wafted from below. Nabber descended with caution.

He emerged in the corner of a low-ceilinged cellar. The place was sparsely furnished with a handful of upturned beer barrels and three-legged stools. The cobblestone floor was damp and the wood-braced walls were sprouting. The few customers there were looked dangerous. Nabber spotted Tawl straightaway. He was talking to a large, dark-haired man. Neither man seemed especially agitated, so Nabber took a seat near the bar and prepared to bide his time.

"Yes," Gravia said, his voice low and harsh. "There was a battalion of knights on the field. Tyren accompanied Kedrac to Bren."

Tawl's lips felt dry. He licked them. "Did they take part in the slaughter?"

Gravia's expression didn't falter. "Why do you think I'm here today?"

So they had. Tawl leant back against the wall and regarded his old friend Gravia. He hardly looked a day older than when Tawl had seen him last; the dark hair was as glossy as ever, the handsome, angular face still smooth.

Nearly seven years ago they'd parted. Valdis had enjoyed a warm spring that year. The world was full of hope and he and Gravia were full of dreams. They had plans to meet up in summer and travel together to the Far South in search of holy relics or a burning cause. They never made it. The trip home changed everything. One sight of the burnt cottage and all promises were sundered.

Now this man, this knight whom Tawl respected as a peer and loved as a friend, sat across the table and told him he was leaving the order.

Tawl had spent three years at Gravia's side. He knew him well. Of all the knights that gained the second circle that fateful spring, no one was more dedicated than him. To find him here, in this seedy tavern, arranging swift passage to Leiss, was a profound shock to Tawl. It made his heart ache.

Tawl glanced at Gravia's right arm. His circles were well covered, just like his own. "Will you ever come back?" he asked.

A bitter smile flashed across Gravia's face. "No. As long as Tyren is head of the order, I will not count myself a knight. I was there in Halcus when Kylock ordered the slaughter of innocent women and children—Tyren didn't raise a finger to stop him."

Tawl looked into Gravia's dark brown eyes. "I can't believe that of Tyren."

"You've spent the last six years with your head in the sand. You don't know what he's capable of."

Hearing Gravia's words brought back an echo of another similar conversation, many weeks old. *"Tyren's a bad man, Tawl,"* Nabber had said the night an expertly aimed arrow sent them traveling through the night. Tawl swallowed hard. It wasn't true. It couldn't be. Angry at himself for doubting Tyren for even an instant, he cried, "Tyren was always a friend to me."

Gravia made a hard little sound in his throat. *"Friend.* He was never your friend, Tawl."

"He brought me to Valdis, gave me free training. He saved my life."

"After all these years you still don't know?" Gravia shook his head. The edge in his voice changed the nature of the air between them. It became clear, taut, charged like before a storm. "No one ever told you?"

Tawl brought his whole body forward. "Told me what?"

"Told you that Tyren sold your services to the man with the most gold." Gravia, seeming to regret his harsh words, put a hand on Tawl's arm.

Tawl shook it off. "What do you mean?"

"I mean the only reason why Tyren sent you to Bevlin was because he was paid handsomely to do so. Bevlin tried for months to get Tyren to send him a knight. Tyren refused until Bevlin offered him gold." Gravia sighed. All the force in his large and well-toned body ebbed away, leaving a tired and disillusioned man in its wake. "Tyren never believed in the wiseman's cause. He never believed in you. Gold was—and *is*—his only motive."

"You're lying."

"No, Tawl. What do you think I did that spring we parted? Tyren sent me to Bevlin to pick up the payment. Five hundred pieces of gold I carried home."

Tawl closed his eyes. Gravia's words were blades in his heart. Everything he held dear was a sham. Seven years he had lived with the pain of losing his family, and during that time his one, his only, comfort was knowing that Tyren had believed in him. Only now there was no belief—just a dirty little transaction where his services were bought and sold.

Slowly he began to shake his head. "No. Not this." The pressure in his chest was unbearable. He dug his fingertips into the wood of the table. "Dear God, not this." A lump formed in his throat, cutting down his words to a rasped whisper. Everything was tainted now. Every action he had taken since his sisters' deaths had been paid for with gold. He felt dirty, violated. Dropping his head to the table, Tawl tried hard to stop his shoulders from shaking.

"Get away from him, you!" shrieked a familiar voice. "You leave him alone. Go tell your lies to someone else."

Tawl looked up to see Nabber pulling at Gravia's arm. "Stop it, Nabber," he said.

Gravia stood up. "I'm sorry, Tawl. As Borc is my witness, I never meant to hurt you."

Tawl swallowed hard. "Gravia, I think Nabber's right. You'd better go."

"But—"

"You knew. You knew and you never told me. We were like brothers—you and I." As soon as the words were out, Tawl regretted them. The pain on Gravia's face was unmistakable. The deed of seven years back was like a dying man's curse: it corrupted beyond the grave. Gravia was young, they both were, and together they had looked up to Tyren as if he were a god.

"Gravia, I'm—" The words died on Tawl's lips. Gravia was already on the other side of the room, climbing the stairs.

Tawl watched him go.

Old pain merged with new pain and settled close against his heart. He would never see his friend again. Tawl sighed. He felt very tired. He had made a bad thing worse. He'd not only lost Tyren today, but he'd lost Gravia as well.

There was no end to what a man could bear.

After a moment, he stood up. "Come on, Nabber. Let's go." There was only one thing left to him now: traveling to Bren to rescue Melli.

Tavalisk had just come from supervising the packing of his stash. It was all due to be removed tomorrow: half was going to a little town just south of Rorn, and half was going to a house on Kirtish Street. The archbishop's mind, while not totally at ease, was now in midrepose. No one would get their greasy little hands on his treasures after tomorrow. No one.

Browsing through room after room of gems, holy icons, and gold had calmed Tavalisk considerably. If things did come to the worst—and the way things looked in the north at the moment they certainly might—he at least could be assured of a comfortable retirement. Kylock and Baralis were dangerous men individually, but together they were proving unstoppable. At the moment their empire was restricted to the north, but who could tell what would happen after spring. Once they took Ness it would be so easy for them to turn their sights south to Camlee.

Oh, the south would arm Camlee—eventually—but cities like Marls, Toolay, and Falport simply didn't realize just how great a threat Kylock's armies could be. The south had spent centuries scorning the north. It was considered backward, its people barbarians, its cities primitive citadels, and its policies no concern of the south. Tavalisk rubbed his chubby chin. Such thinking could well seal their fate.

A dozen roasted sheeps' hearts were slowly congealing on a platter. Tavalisk pushed them aside. He didn't have the stomach for them.

The archbishop crossed over to the windows and made sure there was no light peeping through. Next, he walked to the door and turned the key. He had brought back only one box from his hideaway, and he opened it now in the safety of a locked and shuttered room. He couldn't risk anyone else moving it. Its contents were more precious and damning than gold.

Off came the lid. Books, scrolls, and manuscripts gleamed dully like old skin. The smell fluttered, as if on moth's wings, straight up to the archbishop's nose. Memories scurried across his consciousness the moment the scent was named. Rapascus. These papers were his lifework. The lifework of the greatest religious scholar of the last five hundred years.

All miscredited to a young, aspiring clergyman known as Father Tavalisk.

*

Tavalisk remembered the journey across the Northern Ranges. It was early spring. Cold winds blew from the west and the snow was wet underfoot. The caravan he traveled with was poorly equipped and they had to stop every few minutes to clear paths. Altogether the crossing took them a month. In summer it would have taken a week. Tavalisk, who had paid the minstrels well for the privilege of joining their wagon train, spent most of his time in the back of his covered cart, reading all the papers he had stolen.

By the time they made it to Lairston, he knew Rapascus' lifework as well as if it were his own. The great wiseman was dead, his house had been burnt to the ground, there was nothing left of him but his books. And once the word got out, everyone would assume those books had perished with him. Indeed, Tavalisk intended to be the first to spread the word. He'd already practiced his lie: "Such a tragedy. Rapascus spent the last twenty years in mystical research, and it was all consumed by the flames. Nothing was saved."

Then, if the question happened to arise as to what business *he* had with the great man, he would shrug humbly and say, "Oh nothing. I am engaged in a little religious work, and I sought Rapascus' opinion."

Three nights Tavalisk spent in Lairston preparing his tale. On the third night he met Baralis.

Lairston nestled at the foot of the Northern Ranges. It was a small mining town, boasting a handful of inns and a blacksmith. Situated directly below one of the few passes to the north, it did a fair business in travel. Tavalisk was eating alone in the dining hall of the Last Refuge when in walked a man from the cold. The wind swept ahead of him and the snow flurried behind. Tall and striking, dressed in black, he waited less than a minute to be served. The tavern-maid, a silly girl with a conspicuous bosom and eyes inclined to wink, showed the stranger to a seat next to the fire. Tavalisk was sitting on the other side of the great hearth and listened as the man requested dinner and a room.

"Have you come to take the pass, sir?" asked the tavern-maid.

The man nodded.

The girl waved an arm Tavalisk's way. "This gentleman has just come down from the mountain. He says conditions in the pass are bad." With that, she left them, bobbing a crude curtsey and promising to be back.

The stranger stripped off his gloves. Tavalisk noticed his hands were scarred, the skin warped and reddened around the knuckles. They sat in silence, the fire cracking between them, the candlelight flickering above. A vague feeling of unease came over Tavalisk as he sat watching the stranger. The silence they shared had a predatory feel, and after a few minutes Tavalisk felt *compelled* to speak.

"The snow is soft and the winds are high. It's not a good time to take the pass."

The man raised his gaze from the fire. Tavalisk had never seen eyes as cold as those: they were ice formed over granite. The stranger stretched half a lip. "But you took it all the same."

"I had no choice. I need to get home as soon as possible."

"And where is home?"

Tavalisk felt a slight pain in his head. Somehow the stranger had managed to take control of the conversation. "Home is . . . " Tavalisk paused, considering. Home wasn't Silbur anymore, so where was it? Where would he go? Somewhere far away. He and Venesay had once visited Rorn. Tavalisk remembered it well; it was a city burgeoning with new wealth and trade. Its streets teemed with people and its temples were decked in gold. The perfect place to make himself anew. "Rorn," he said. "My home is Rorn."

The man made a minute gesture with his finger, and Tavalisk knew he hadn't been believed. "Where do you come from?" Tavalisk said, trying to shake off his feeling of unease.

"Leiss, Hanatta. Silbur."

The last word was spoken with telling emphasis and Tavalisk felt himself blushing. He was saved by the reappearance of the tavern-maid. The girl held a tray full of food just below her bosom. She fussed, smiled, served, and then reluctantly left.

The stranger wiped the froth from his ale. "What business did you have in the north?"

Tavalisk wasn't used to feeling cowed and he disliked the sensation very much. He cleared his throat. "I am a religious scholar. I was visiting with the great mystic Rapascus." As he spoke, his confidence grew. It was time to try out his lies. "Unfortunately a terrible tragedy occurred and the great man died. His home and his works were destroyed."

"Then you have saved me a journey, my friend. For I, too, was to visit Rapascus."

Tavalisk drew in a quick breath. This was the man whom Rapascus had invited to take his place. The brilliant scholar from Silbur.

"Tavalisk, I believe," said the stranger.

"And you would be Baralis," said Tavalisk.

The one called Baralis turned to his dinner and broke both wing bones of his fowl. "Rapascus wrote of you in his letters. He never mentioned you were interested in religious research. But then you and he must have had a lot to talk about, as that was his greatest area of interest, too."

Tavalisk loosened the collar of his tunic. He suddenly felt rather hot. "Oh, he dabbled in religion, but his true love was mysticism: arcane ceremonies, inexplicable phenomena, sorcery."

"You are mistaken, my friend," said Baralis in a light but pointed tone. "In one of the first letters Rapascus ever sent to me, he told of how close he was to completing a reinterpretation of the classic religious texts. Borc was revealed to him in a new but beneficent light, and he had spent years styling that revelation into words."

"Well, whatever he did has gone up in smoke, so we'll never know the truth of it." Tavalisk decided it was time to retreat. He stood up.

"Tell me, my friend," said Baralis, just as Tavalisk's foot touched the stair. "Do you intend to publish your work?"

At that moment Tavalisk knew that Baralis had not been fooled. He had seen through his lies as surely as a nightfeeder sees through the dark. Tavalisk's first instinct was to get away. Leave now, with the silent, accusing manuscripts in tow. He mumbled, "Possibly. It's too early to tell," as he took the stairs two at a time.

Baralis' voice reached the top before he did. "I shall watch out for you, my friend," he said. "I'll be most interested to see just how far you go."

Tavalisk didn't leave that night, he left just before dawn the following morning. The tavern-maid took care of the bill. "Oh, I nearly forgot, sir," she said as she handed Tavalisk the change. "That handsome gentleman from last night asked me to send you his regards. He said he had a feeling you'd be making an early start."

Tavalisk glanced around the room. There was no sign of the man. It was time to get going. He sorted through the copper pennies. "Here," he said to the girl, handing her four of them. "Give these to the stableboy. I've a chest in my room that needs to be brought down."

The girl and her bosom simpered simultaneously. She shook her head and raised a flattened palm. "Oh, the stableboy's already been paid for the job, sir. That nice gentleman thought you'd be traveling with a heavy trunk."

Tavalisk couldn't leave Lairston fast enough. He paid the wagon master to take the whip to his horses and wouldn't hear of stopping, even for food.

Two weeks later he reached Ness. His neck was badly cramped from constantly looking over his shoulder, and his fingernails were bitten to the quick. Time and the warm climes of the south eventually cured him of his watchfulness, and by the time he arrived in Rorn he had shaken off all his doubts. Baralis might indeed know that he was in possession of Rapascus' lifework, but he was just one man with no proof. It would be the word of a suspected sorcerer against the word of a man of God.

And that was what Tavalisk styled himself on coming to Rorn: a man of God. It was his last and final incarnation: Brother Tavalisk, classic scholar, man of letters. Visionary.

Working out of a small basement located beneath a fishmonger, it took Tavalisk two years to transcribe Rapascus' work into his own hand. During the last few months, he distributed a series of religious pamphlets as a taste of what was to come. Even before he published the first of his masterworks, his name was made. Rorn, with its growing merchant classes, its new-found sophistication, and its burgeoning sense of pride, was ripe for the taking. It was hungry for new ideas, new leaders, and new blood. Successful in its own right, it was ready to step out from Silbur's shadow and find a sun of its own.

It was so easy. With the pamphlets he gained disciples, with the masterworks he gained a city. He was feted by everyone: the merchant classes loved his position on wealth, the intellectuals loved his subtle attacks on religious traditionalism, and the lower classes loved his wit.

Only the Church hated him. And that was, for their part, the worst thing they could possibly do. At that time in Rorn clergymen were looked upon as Silbur's spies. Silbur itself was eyed with growing resentment by the people of Rorn. What business did that old, decaying city have telling them how to live their lives? Rorn was vital, new, flourishing. Silbur was as bloodless as old bones.

Tavalisk became a champion of this movement. He nudged, he stirred, he inflamed. Each night he rifled through Rapascus' works, looking for more fuel for the fire. Pamphlet after pamphlet he published. His fame spread, his following grew. He couldn't leave the cellar without being mobbed.

Then the old archbishop died and everything came to a head. Silbur sent a replacement out straightaway—it was a grave error in judgment. They acted rashly because they were afraid their influence was waning in Rorn, and they felt a flex of holy muscle was in order. The man they sent was unknown to the good people of Rorn—he was a dour-faced authoritarian who originally hailed from Lanholt—and the city forcefully rejected him. During his welcoming parade, he was dragged from his horse and stabbed in the back countless times.

It was a sight Tavalisk never forgot. It demonstrated exactly what the people of this fair city were capable of: brutal, daylight murder.

After that Silbur became cautious. Fearing that they might lose influence over Rorn altogether, that a dangerous fracturing might occur in the Church and the city might simply declare itself a religious power in its own right, Silbur agreed to let the city choose its own archbishop. Well, not the city itself exactly, rather the holy synod, but by that time Tavalisk was so powerful with the merchants and the masses that the clergy dared not pick another. Apparently Tavalisk was not the only one who never forgot the sight of the newly appointed archbishop lying in a pool of his own blood. After all, clergymen were notorious cowards.

Within a month Tavalisk was ensconced in the holy see of Rorn. He was the most popular archbishop in over a thousand years. Silbur hated him, the local clergy despised him, and He Who Is Most Holy had tried, unsuccessfully, to excommunicate him. The citizens of Rorn adored him: he had brought the Church to heel.

He was young, brilliant, rebellious—a man of the people. He grew with the city; as it prospered, so did he.

Months, years, decades passed. Rorn became the greatest trading city in the Known Lands and Tavalisk became the most influential holy leader. His power was immeasurable, his influence still great enough to cower Silbur. No one dared challenge him, not He Who Is Most Holy, not even the old duke himself. He was the unofficial head of the Church in the east, and was as good as a king in his adopted home of Rorn.

Tavalisk laid a hand upon Rapascus' manuscripts. He could trust no one with the task of moving these. Their discovery would ruin him. All the provocative theories, all the blinding insights, the subtle reinvention of the Church: none of it was his. And these documents alone could prove it.

Tavalisk dragged the chest across the room. It was time do what should have been done long ago. Picking a scroll at random, he threw it onto the fire. It crackled, caught, and blackened in an instant, giving off a thin plume of musky smoke. Tavalisk tossed in another straight after it, and another after that. Soon the fireplace was raging like a makeshift hell. The sight was comforting, to say the least. Now only he and Baralis would ever know the truth.

Twenty-six

Melli was huddled in a corner. She had two blankets to keep her warm, but it was still barely enough—even now, after Kylock had ordered Mistress Greal to have the shutters sealed and thick velvet curtains hung to keep out the drafts. No fire, though. That in itself was telling. Kylock was obviously worried that she might try to set either the palace or him alight. And he was right: she would.

Melli wasn't at all sure if she liked the new refinements to her room. With the shutters closed, the light came in stingy slivers, banding the room like the markings on a tourney field. Melli had developed a certain superstition concerning the slow-moving lines and never liked to cross them. She was obviously going quite mad cooped up in here. Not crossing lines, indeed!

The problem was that when there was nothing else to do, little things began to occupy, then niggle, the mind. Those new curtains, for instance. Melli was quite sure—but not positive—that they were the same ones that used to hang in the duke's bedchamber. Her wedding night was one of the few times she had been in that chamber, but minor details had a way of staying with her. Strange to think that whilst being held at knife-point, her gaze had wandered to the furnishings. Well, eyes had to look somewhere, and better the curtains than the knife. Anyway, the point was Melli believed that the curtains were one and the same, and she was now concerned with deciding if it was a bad omen or a good one.

The duke had died in sight of those curtains, but she, herself, had survived. Melli now knew that she had never really loved the duke; she was flattered by his attention, impressed by his power, and drawn along by the sheer force of his will. She had desperately wanted to be loved for herself, and the moment she thought that was so, she swooned like a lovesick maiden. She had no experience of love, nothing to judge it against. The duke was the first person to woo her. He gave her exotic, eloquent gifts and filled her head with praise. He loved her spirit and acknowledged her intelligence by promising her equal say. All this coming from the most powerful leader in the north. Her vanity wasn't just flattered, it was overwhelmed.

She hadn't been in love with the duke, she'd been in love with his vision of *her*.

Her feelings for Tawl had put everything in perspective. When you really loved someone, their absence didn't make you feel numb, it tore away at your heart. The duke's death had been a shock, nothing more. It had left her cold, frightened, and bemused. She had hardly spared him a thought in months, and if it wasn't for those green velvet curtains, she wouldn't be thinking of him now.

Melli shrugged. Perhaps she was hard-hearted, but having endured over four months of imprisonment and persecution and abuse, she was inclined to think her husband got off lightly.

The curtains *were* a good omen, she decided. They weren't red, and that in itself was a blessing, but more importantly than that, they were the curtains that had swished on the breeze as Tawl raced in to save her life. With luck they just might swish again.

Not that she was content to count on luck. Melli stood up. Her knees cracked like an old woman's and her back protested like an old man. Her body was now heavy with pregnancy and every movement she made was a challenge to her spine, her joints, and her hips. Swollen-ankled, belly cupped, Melli made her way toward her secret stash. She crossed two light lines just to spite herself and paused to put her ear to the door for safety's sake.

Her collection, as she liked to call it, was hidden in the space between the large linen chest and the wall. It had started with Mistress Greal's left glove and now had grown to another left glove—courtesy of Kylock this time—a glass goblet, a candle, a belt and buckle, and a handful of old bones. Melli wasn't entirely sure that all of them would prove useful, but she cherished them all the same. Turn Kylock's glove inside-out and it would do for her right hand. The belt could tie someone up. The candle was a problem—she needed a flint to light it—but the goblet was a weapon in the making.

It was easy to acquire things. The secret was to push them discreetly from the line of view while the other person's attention was occupied elsewhere. Both Kylock and Mistress Greal made a point of scanning the room before they left, checking that nothing had been left behind. If they didn't see anything, then that was that. After all, a king could hardly be expected to remember a candle or a glass.

Now all Melli needed was a knife. Kylock always had one hung at his hip, but so far that's where it stayed: he preferred using hot wax and thin rope on her. She might have to do something to provoke him into drawing his blade—either that or steal it right from his thigh. Whatever she did, it must be done soon. As best she could work out, she was drawing close to her final month of pregnancy, and the way her belly was expanding she doubted whether she'd be able to make it across the room, much less escape from the castle, once the last few weeks were upon her.

Melli returned her collection to its hiding place, careful to ensure that the chest was in exactly the same position as when she'd started. Mistress Greal would be along soon, and she had eyes like a hungry cat.

Making her way back to the corner, Melli pulled her blankets close around her. Soon, very soon, she would make her escape.

The weather grew progressively worse as they rode east then north from Marls. First the wind sent clouds scudding across the sky, and then the clouds ganged up and styled themselves a storm. Midday became as dark as twilight, rain struck in small but dense patches, the ground underfoot softened to mud and the air blasted against their faces like a gale.

The horses weren't happy; the riders weren't happy. Wet clothes, wet food, no fires at night, no rest, no warmth, no give.

The terrain itself proved easy enough to maneuver. Farmland for the most part, it was flat or rolling: pastures, meadows, and plowed fields broken up by hedgerows and low, grassy hills. The rain had plumped and greened the earth, and the landscape had the look of spring.

As the days went by the weather became colder, and Tawl realized spring was only an illusion. The journey was hard on all of them, especially Nabber. The young pocket had caught a chill and spent a lot of his time sleeping at Tawl's back. Tawl knew he was setting a hard pace, but he just couldn't bear to slow down.

Slowing down meant time to think, time to dwell on what Gravia had told him in that squalid little tavern in Marls. Tawl wished the conversation had never taken place, that he'd never learnt the truth about Tyren. But he had. So the best he could do was ride fast and furious and create the illusion it was all in the past.

It was getting harder, though. Every step his horse took brought him a step nearer to Valdis. They rode in its shadow now. Tawl could feel its presence pushing against his left cheek, like heat given off by a fire. They were perhaps fifty leagues southeast of the city. Tomorrow they would draw parallel to it. The only thing that stood between them was a thick stretch of forest known as the Gandt. Tawl remembered it well. He had trained, fought, hunted by day, and tracked stars by night, all within its leafy bounds. He'd got blind drunk on more than one occasion, too. He and Gravia would place bets on who could drink the most. Gravia always won. He won at everything except swordplay. Tawl beat him hands down at that.

They were such good days. Rivalry was fierce but never bitter. Fights were fought hard but without grudges, and friendships were slow to form but long to last. Above everything there was Tyren: father, mentor, hero, and god. He was the ideal that they all strove for, the man they most wanted to impress. Tawl would have done anything for him. Would have laid down his life.

And now he'd found he'd laid down his soul, instead.

All those years he'd spent believing that Tyren saved him when really he had been bought and sold. The most precious and enduring image in Tawl's life had been shattered, and it left a dangerous hollow that was filling up with rage.

The last six years of his life had been based on a lie, and Tyren had been the master of the sham.

"Tawl!" called Jack. "Let's stop. Nabber's not looking too good."

Tawl glanced to the northwest. They were so close to Valdis now he didn't want to stop. "Just for five minutes," he cried, pulling at the reins. "Then I want to get going again."

Jack did not look pleased. He had changed a lot since Larn. He had become more confident, more aggressive, less willing to follow, more to lead.

They stopped by a small glade of trees. To the east there was farmland, to the west was the dark, far-ranging form of the Gandt. It was not raining, but a shower had passed by minutes earlier and everything was wet and dripping.

Jack lifted Nabber down from Tawl's horse. He placed his bedroll down on the ground and urged the boy to rest. He then turned to Tawl. "Over there," he hissed, indicating a spot where Nabber wouldn't be able to over-hear them.

Tawl jumped from his horse and prepared to do battle.

"This pace is too hard on the boy," said Jack.

"You mean it's too hard on you."

Jack gave Tawl a hard look. "What happened to you in Marls?"

"It's none of your business, Jack."

"It is my business when we're up before dawn every morning and ride well past sundown every night. I want to get to Bren as fast as you do, but this isn't the way to do it. Nabber needs rest. He needs a warm bed and a hot meal. I say we stop overnight at the next village we come to. If Melli *is* alive, she'll be all right an extra day. And if she's dead, there's no hurry."

Jack's cool assessment of the situation annoyed Tawl. "Who are you to say—"

"I'm the one who'll deal with Baralis and Kylock. Not you, Tawl. Me."

"And who will cut you a path?" Tawl was shaking now. "Or do you expect the guards to just lay down their arms the minute you walk in the palace?"

"I expect you to be by my side, Tawl."

The expression on Jack's face killed Tawl's anger dead. Some things were too important to fight over. Running his hands through his hair, Tawl took a deep breath. "I'm sorry, Jack. You're right, I haven't been thinking straight since Marls. I talked to an old friend while I was there and he told me someone . . . " Tawl struggled to find the words, "someone I cared about had lied to me."

"Tyren?"

Either Jack was quick or he'd been talking to Nabber. "Yes, Tyren."

"People lie all the time, Tawl." There was a trace of bitterness in Jack's voice, "All the time and for all sorts of reasons."

Tawl nodded slowly. He was right.

The wind suddenly picked up. It was coming from the west, and for a moment Tawl thought he heard a high sound, like a cry. It was gone before he could place it. "Let's go," he said. "We'll ride until the next village."

Jack didn't object and Tawl guessed he hadn't been the only one to hear the noise.

Protesting vociferously despite his cold, Nabber was placed on Tawl's horse. Jack worked quickly to secure his pack, then they turned onto the cow path and rode north.

An unspoken assent between Jack and Tawl caused them both to steadily pick up their pace. Before long they were cantering down the narrow trail, heads brushing against bare branches, mud flying in their wake. Tawl was concentrating, listening for the slightest sound. A pair of geese took noisily to the air as they passed, somewhere over the hill a lone dog was barking, then the rain started to fall, blotting everything out.

Tawl was nervous. The path they were on dipped and twisted, and the way ahead wasn't clear. The farther they went, the nearer the dark expanse of the Gandt came. It seemed to be reaching out toward the path, closing in on them. Tawl broke into a gallop.

At first he thought it was Jack at his heels, but the rhythm of pounding hooves became too complex for just one horse. Then, out of the corner of his eye, Tawl spotted a fast-moving form emerging from the Gandt.

"Hang on, Nabber," he cried. And then to Jack, "Break to the east on my say-so." Tawl dug heels into horseflesh and gave his gelding the reins.

There were more forms now. At full gallop they cleared the forest, cutting a slanting path toward the trail. Tawl recognized the colors: yellow and black. They were knights, and they were trying to head Jack and Tawl off.

With fresh, specially trained horses beneath them they'd be able to do it, too. Tawl knew his own horse didn't have much fight left in him. Two to carry, a week of solid riding, the poor old gelding must be on its last legs.

The riders were drawing level with the road. Tawl could see their faces, but it was to their weapons his eyes were drawn. They were wielding triple-edged spears. Tawl had trained with such a spear, he knew exactly what damage they could do. The leading two-edged blade slipped in first, and the matching barbs went in after. Once the head was pulled out, it tore a man apart.

Tawl switched his gaze forward. The road swung to the west up ahead. If Tawl and Jack followed it, it would lead them right into the knights' path. It was too early to break east, though. Best to wait until the last possible moment. Tawl risked a second glance at the riders. Their heads might be bare, but metal gleamed beneath their colors. They were wearing breastplates on their upper bodies, chain mail on the lower. Fighting was out of the question—he and Jack wouldn't stand a chance.

The bend was coming up fast. Tawl could see the knights beginning to rein in their horses. He counted— *one, two . . . three*—then cried, "Now, Jack. *Now!*"

Tawl pulled on the right rein. The gelding's head whipped to the east. Nabber dug his fingers into Tawl's side as the beast changed its course in midstride. The path was bounded by a ditch, and the gelding barely had time to find its feet before it was forced to leap across the trench. The horse hit the soft muddy bank. It struggled for its footing. Jack's horse cleared the trench easily, and he rode ahead into the plowed field. Behind them, Tawl could hear the knights crying out to each other, switching their plan from a blockade to a chase.

Tawl guided his horse farther along the ditch, until they reached a section where the bank wasn't as steep. The gelding scrambled up and onto the field. Jack was way ahead of them, setting a course for a wooded copse on the other side of the hedgerow. The rain had stopped now, but the field was heavily waterlogged, with pools of water lying between the furrows. The water made the gelding skittish; it was a city horse, unused to country conditions, and although Tawl encouraged it to run straight through the pools, it preferred to jump them.

The knights were gaining on them. Their blinkered mounts were trained for the chase and bred for speed alone. Swinging his head back, Tawl saw that not all the knights were following his path; some had veered off to the north, and others had come to a standstill. Tawl caught his breath. The men who'd come to a dead stop were dismounting their horses. Marksmen.

Tawl immediately switched his riding to a zigzag pattern. It slowed him down, but he'd rather take a spear in his gut than risk an arrow in Nabber's back. Jack was too far ahead to warn, but not far enough to be dismissed from a marksman's sight. He was almost upon the copse now—if he made it there, he'd be safe.

An arrow whirred past Tawl's knee. They were aiming low. Too low to bring down a man. Tawl looked ahead just in time to see Jack's horse collapse beneath him. Jack was propelled forward, headfirst into the hedgerow.

In that moment, Tawl realized the knights weren't interested in killing—they wanted to capture them. Valdis' marksmen were the best in the Known Lands, and when they brought a horse down rather than its rider it was with intent. The triple-edged spears, too—they were heavy enough to stop a horse in its tracks. A lighter one would do for a man.

"Nabber," shouted Tawl, "put your left hand straight up in the air." They couldn't outrun the knights. Jack was down, the gelding couldn't keep up the pace much longer. It was only a matter of minutes before they were caught. It was better to surrender now, while Jack was the only one down, than keep on running and risk arrow nicks and broken bones from falls. It was time to cut their losses.

Nabber did as he was told, and Tawl gradually slowed down his horse. He knew the knights would stop firing once they saw the signal: Valdis' code of honor would prevail. Tawl turned to meet his pursuers. Four men rode forward to meet him.

"Off the horse. Now!" said the man in front.

Tawl reached for Nabber's hand and squeezed it. "We'll be all right," he whispered. Jumping down into the mud, he lifted Nabber from the gelding. The boy's body was stiff and cold.

The knights withdrew their spears. One man came forward and frisked them for weapons.

The two riders who had headed north were making their way toward Jack. Tawl had no way of knowing what, if anything, Jack was planning. "Jack," he shouted, "I've surrendered. Come peacefully." Tawl had seen what Jack was capable of, and this wasn't the time for a replay of Larn. These men had acted honorably and they would receive honor in return.

Tawl watched the hedgerow. He saw the riders approach, heard them shout out, and then spied Jack slowly emerging from the bushes. His face was covered in blood and he was limping. His hands were above his head. Good. He had heard and understood the warning. No sorcery. Not on the knights.

Tawl watched Jack for a moment, satisfying himself that he would be all right, and then spun around to face the leader. *"Es nil hesrl,"* he said: I am not worthy. It was the traditional greeting at Valdis, and somehow, despite everything—despite Tyren's betrayal and the knighthood's decline—it seemed the right thing to say. These men were his brethren.

The leader appeared surprised to hear the words. He glanced at his companion before speaking. "I am not your judge, Tawl of the Lowlands," he said. "Tyren claims that privilege in Bren."

Skaythe watched the party ride away. Ten knights, four of them marksmen, three hostages, thirteen horses, two mules, and enough supplies to provision a journey to Bren.

So Baralis hadn't relied on him alone.

Skaythe returned his bow to its sheath. The rain had done it no favors and it would have to be waxed and then restrung. A good shot at this distance, with a damp string and the air heavy with rain, would be nearly impossible. The Valdis marksmen were no better than he—just a whole lot closer.

It had been an interesting scene to watch. It had taught him a little more about his mark. Tawl was not stupid; he knew when to quit. The knights had outrun and outnumbered him, his friend was down and his horse was less than a barn's length from collapse. The man was no fool, but he wasn't a hero, either. Skaythe shook his head. Most definitely not a hero. Heroes don't smash their opponent's brains out when they're no longer capable of fighting. They don't keep on beating a man long after the fight is over. And they don't kill from lack of control.

Blayze died by Tawl's hand. It was an unnecessary death, and one Skaythe intended to vindicate.

Skaythe rubbed his aching shoulder. The damp brought out the worst in that, too. Tawl had a lot to answer for.

After the duel on the cliffs north of Toolay, it had taken Skaythe two weeks to recover from his injury. He had found an old woman in a small village to tend to the wound. A lot of blood was lost, the shoulder blade had been grazed, and there had been some minor muscle damage. The old hag had done a fair stitching, but she hadn't used a clean knife and infection had set in. He lost a week to fever, and another to poor health. When he finally mounted a horse again, he had to ride slowly with many rests. He eventually arrived in Rorn only to find no trace of the knight or his companions. By making inquiries at the harbor he'd discovered that the knight had sailed to Marls two days earlier. Skaythe promptly followed.

The week aboard ship had been good for him. It gave

him a chance to finally recuperate. His shoulder had stiffened during the ride to Rorn and the voyage gave him the time to work the suppleness back. He exercised and massaged, gradually extending his range of movements. By the time he landed in Marls his shoulder was strong enough to hold a bow for the draw.

During the journey north, he had taken a few practice shots. He had lost both distance and accuracy, but even then he could still outshoot Valdis' best. A few weeks of rest and he would be back to fighting form. The problem was the riding. The knight had set a grueling pace from Marls, and Skaythe was forced to better it to catch up. Long hours in the saddle, combined with sudden downpours and biting winds, had started the stiffening process once more.

A few more weeks of these sorts of conditions and his shoulder would be back where it started. But Skaythe had no choice—especially now—he had to follow Tawl. The knight's life was his for the taking and no one else was going to get there first.

Skaythe mounted his horse. Perhaps it was a good thing that the knights had captured Tawl. It would slow the pace down and make him easier to track. Warning arrows were out of the question now, though. With four trained marksmen in the party, Skaythe had no intention of giving away his presence. Skaythe kicked his horse forward. Next time he came for Tawl, the strike would be unannounced.

Tawl leant back against the tree he had been bound to. Glancing over at Jack, he hissed, "Are you all right?"

Jack nodded. "My head's splitting, but I'm sort of used to that by now."

It was dark. They had traveled north all day. With one hand tied behind their backs and both feet tied to the stirrups, it hadn't been an easy ride. Nabber fared better over the back of the mule.

The knights had just made camp. They were well

organized. A fire was started within minutes, and holk and drymeat porridge were set to boil. The horses had been fed, watered, and brushed. A watch was currently circling the camp, bows at the ready to bring down intruders or game. Waterskins had been filled, breast-plates loosened, muscles massaged, and brandy passed from hand to hand. Even the captives had been seen to. Jack's wound had been tended, Nabber had been given herb tea for his cold, all their bindings had been loos-ened, and they had been retied, with care, to three separate trees. Later there would be food.

Tawl had watched all the activity with a certain admi-ration. These men worked well together. They carried out their various jobs with little need for orders. They were efficient, but not unkind, and relied upon each other heavily. Tawl recognized just two of them. Andris, who seemed to be second-in-command, had been a circle below him at Valdis, and Borlin, who was one of the four marksmen and the oldest knight in the group, had first taught him how to use a bow.

It was Borlin who walked toward them now: heavyset, short for a knight, with arms as thick as his thighs, and the grin of an old campaigner stretching his blue-veined face. He waggled a bow-callused finger. "No talking between the prisoners. You know that, Tawl."

"I was just testing your memory, Borlin. After all, it's got to be thirty years since you learnt that rule."

"You calling me old, boy?"

"I'm not calling you a spring chicken."

The sound of Borlin's laughter brought back vivid memories for Tawl. The low, gurgling laugh had been something of a phenomenon at Valdis. People used to say it sounded like a barrel full of rocks rolling down a hill.

"Got yourself in a bit of a mess, haven't you, Tawl?" he said. "Word is you murdered Catherine of Bren."

"Word is the knights stood by and watched women and children being slaughtered in Halcus."

Borlin's face hardened in an instant. "You weren't in Halcus, Tawl."

"No, but a friend of mine was—a good man who couldn't bear it any longer. He headed south and took a boat to Leiss."

"A deserter."

"No," Tawl shook his head. "Not a deserter. A man who remembers what Valdis once stood for."

Borlin turned and began to walk away.

"Is that how you manage to live with yourself, Borlin?" Tawl shouted after him. "You just turn the other cheek?"

Tawl's chest strained against the bindings. He was shaking, and behind his back his hands were balled into fists. A handful of the knights were staring at him.

"Why did you say all that?" whispered Jack.

"Because it needs to be said. These are good men following a bad leader, and in their hearts they know it. But no one dares speak it out loud." Tawl's thoughts turned to Gravia. Perhaps he shouldn't have sailed to Leiss: the knights would have listened to him. He wasn't an outcast and a suspected murderer.

"Tyren can't be the only one to blame," Jack said. "He must have found knights willing to carry out his orders."

Tawl shook his head. "You don't understand. The knights are sworn to obey Tyren. It's not a matter of which knights are good and which are bad. They don't have a choice. Disobey Tyren and they break their oath. Most knights would rather die than do that." Try as he might, Tawl could not keep the bitterness out of his voice as he spoke. He had broken his own oath in front of the entire city of Bren.

Jack gave him a long, appraising look, and then said, "The knight who cut me from the horse said that Kylock's forces were on the move again. They're heading to Ness."

Tawl exhaled softly. Jack was right: it was a good time to change the subject. With an effort, he switched his mind to the topic of Kylock. "He's wasted no time."

"We can't either. We've got to escape—"

"No." Before Jack had finished speaking, the word was out. "There's no need to escape just yet. We're heading north. The knights are setting a good pace. We can afford to bide our time for a few days."

Jack flashed him a hard look. "What are you up to, Tawl? Why didn't you want me to do anything in the field?"

"I don't want you using sorcery on these men, Jack. They don't deserve it."

"Neither did the seers."

Tawl slumped against the tree trunk. There was no possible reply. Jack was focused on what he had to do, and that was the way it should be. But there was something else here, something that had nothing to do with Jack but everything to do with him. He was Tawl, Knight of Valdis, and no amount of vows, denials, or dishonor could change it. The circles would be with him for life.

Tyren was forcing knights into making a terrible choice: stay in the knighthood and be used as Kylock's mercenaries, or desert like cowards in a cloud of secrecy and shame. To men who prized honor and loyalty above anything else, it was a hard decision to make. They were damned either way.

Tawl watched the knights gathering around the campfire. They were settling down, pouring cups of holk, exchanging jokes, rolling out their bedrolls for the night. One man was humming a tune, another was mending his leathers. Good men following a bad leader.

"Andris!" shouted Tawl toward the fair-haired man who was busy stripping branches for the fire. "Come over here and loosen my bindings."

It was time someone gave these men another choice.

Twenty-seven

*I*t was early morning, an hour or two before dawn, and Mistress Greal was up and about doing a discreet spot of scavenging.

The nobles' quarters in the east wing of the palace were her looting ground. A dark and chilly place. A closed-door, silk-carpeted, rat-rustling sort of place, where fortunes lay around for the taking.

King Kylock—Borc bless his dark little soul—was having so many of the old nobles impaled, beheaded, and poisoned that it was impossible to keep track of the deaths. Unless one kept a little notebook, of course. Mistress Greal patted her bony bodice, where a softly bound book served to cushion her carcass. *"Keep records,"* her father always said, *"you never know when they might come in handy."*

Death was a great liberator of wealth. And messy, furtive assassinations made that wealth much easier to purloin. A lot of times wives couldn't be sure that their husbands were dead—one beheaded corpse floating belly-up on a lake looks much like another. When there was no body to speak of, children preferred to believe that their fathers were imprisoned, not dead, and when all one had to go on was a few bloodstained sheets, it was easy to assume one's errant brother had taken yet another virgin to bed.

Rumors abounded about the assassinations, but no one knew for sure. Kylock had a talent for disfiguring the corpses. Fingers, moles, birthmarks, double chins, battle-scars, and manhoods of significant size were all sliced off with surgeonlike skill. Mistress Greal had seen her king in action: Kylock was entranced at such times. Blind to the world, he saw only the bodies in front of him and the razor-keen edge of his blade. He spent hours down in the castle dungeons, eyes glazed over, knife in hand, lips moving without making a sound.

Feeling suddenly chill, Mistress Greal pulled her shawl close about her shoulders. The brief pulling action caused a sharp cramp in her damaged left wrist, and she quickly released her hold on the fabric. Ever since Maybor had broken the bones two years back in Duvitt, she had problems with certain hand and wrist movements. It was inconvenient, but not a great obstacle: luckily her money-grabbing right hand was as nimble as ever.

She soon came upon the door that marked her destination. Pushing gently upon the honey-colored wood, she let herself into the chamber of Lord Bathroy, one-time close advisor to the duke, now a faceless corpse rotting in a shallow grave. A week ago he had made the mistake of openly criticizing Kylock—blasting his decision to massacre all of Highwall's troops—and had been taken into custody, tortured, then killed. These days, fewer and fewer people dared to speak up against the notoriously unstable king. The candle Mistress Greal carried gave off just enough light to set the deceased lord's silken tapestries gleaming. She smiled with satisfaction. Kylock's madness was her gain.

Mistress Greal quickly set about piling various items into her large woolen sack. Clever as well as fast, she never took too much: a gold goblet here, an embroidered tunic there. Nothing in sufficient quantity to be missed. Lord Bathroy's family might be unsure of his status at the moment, but once he'd been gone a month, they'd have the Church declare him dead and be round within an eye-blink to split the spoils.

Once the sack was heavy enough for her liking, Mistress Greal took her leave and headed toward the next chamber on her list.

Her dear but rather silly sister, Madame Thornypurse, would sell the scavenged goods at market. Sadly, the brotheling business had taken a decided turn for the worse since the Highwall army had been defeated. The night following the battle all the troops in the city had gone on a raping spree; their blood was hot with victory, and with no enemy women to ravish, they turned instead to Bren's whores. No brothel was left untouched, no streetwalker overlooked, and not so much as a copper penny to show for it! Kylock had done nothing. It was well known he had no love for women, and he simply let his men do their worst.

Things had hardly been better since. Once the men realized they could get away with their behavior, they simply took women at will. Madame Thornypurse had hoped for an improvement once the siege army left for Ness, but that was two weeks ago now, and chaos still reigned in the city. If you were a member of Kylock's army, then you were free to do as you pleased.

It didn't help matters that the city was now rumored to be riddled with Kylock's spies and informants. Everyone was under suspicion of dissension: guildsmen, merchants, petty gentry, and great lords. Men were so nervous of being accused of treachery against the king that they preferred to stay home at night and talk to their wives. Dull evenings were nothing compared to the threat of a public hanging.

Mistress Greal didn't really care what happened in the outside world. The palace was her home now. She knew its every nook and cranny. All the servants feared her, the noblemen regarded her with wary distaste, and Baralis

and King Kylock treated her as if she didn't exist. All of
which suited Mistress Greal very nicely, indeed. She was
queen bee in this domain.

There was no need for her to resort to her old plan of
blackmail now. She was making an excellent living from
her predawn excursions, and as long as she continued to
make herself useful, she would be able to carry on.
Besides, blackmailing Baralis would not be a smart move.
Now that Mistress Greal knew him better, she realized
that if she ever tried to use her knowledge of the duke's
murder against him, he'd kill her where she stood. The
man had too much to lose.

Mistress Greal approached the second door of the
morning. The door to the very rich and now very dead,
ex-chancellor, Lord Gantry's chambers. Why risk her
life with blackmail when there were so many safer ways to
make money?

Just as she was about to turn the handle, she heard a
noise coming from the other side. Strange, just yesterday
she had seen Crope carrying Lord Gantry's body down to
the lake. So who would be in his chamber now? His wife
had apartments of her own. Putting a bat ear to the wood,
Mistress Greal took a thin listening breath.

A vague mumbling could be heard. There was something familiar about the voice . . . Mistress Greal sucked
in the sound like a leech siphoning blood . . . it was
Crope!

She flung open the door. "What are you doing in here,
you hapless imbecile?"

Crope was sitting by the great lord's desk. By his side
was a bamboo cage, and on his wrist perched a bright
green bird with a hook-shaped beak. Crope looked decidedly guilty. "I was feeding the birdie, miss. It must be
hungry now it's on its own."

"Well, don't just sit there looking at me," said Mistress
Greal. "Put that ugly green thing back in its cage and
leave this room at once."

The bird squawked loudly.

Crope stood up and began fumbling with certain items on the desk, stuffing them into a little painted box.

Mistress Greal came forward and clamped down a proprietorial hand on the box. "You leave this stuff alone, you great big robber. These things aren't yours."

Crope became immediately agitated. "They's mine, miss. I swears it." He pried Mistress Greal's hand from the box and hugged it tight to his chest. "I swears it."

Mistress Greal snatched the box from him. Crope struggled to stop her, and the box went flying into the air. The lid came off and the contents spilled over the desk. Crope issued a low whine and scrambled to gather the contents together.

No one had a faster eye than Mistress Greal. Even before Crope made it to the box, she had taken a visual inventory of the contents: two baby teeth, a length of string, a butterfly cocoon, a lock of hair tied with a blue ribbon, several pieces of amber, some cheap jewelry, and an ancient-looking letter sealed with wax.

Mistress Greal reached for the letter. As she did so, her eye skimmed across the jewelry. Three brass owls hung from a brass chain. Mistress Greal felt her heart drop toward her belly. Tiny onyx eyes, painted yellow beaks, the owl in the center a little bigger than the other two: it was the very necklace she had given her niece five years ago. The same one that Madame Thornypurse swore Corsella was wearing the night she went missing. Mistress Greal remembered it well. She had commissioned its making, switching her order from gold to brass when the price quoted proved too high.

Crope went for the necklace.

Mistress Greal reached it first. "Where did you get this?" she demanded.

"It's mine."

"No, it's not. Now where did you get it?" Mistress Greal was shaking. She wrapped the chain around her fist and brandished it at Crope. "If you don't tell me right now, I'll let everyone know I found you thieving. They'll lock you in a dungeon and keep you there for life."

Her words had a profound effect on Crope. He brought both hands to his head and pressed them against his ears. "No. Not lock up Crope," he mumbled, shaking his head. "Not lock him up."

Mistress Greal sniffed victory. "Yes. Lock him up and throw away the key. Lock him up so deep he'll never see the sun again. Now, tell me where you got it."

"I didn't steal it," screamed Crope. He was shaking his head furiously. "Master said I could have it. I asked him, I swear."

"*Stop it!*" shouted Mistress Greal. Crope's wailings were fraying her nerves. "You got the necklace from Baralis—so who did he get it from?"

Crope stopped whimpering the moment the question left her lips. "Don't know where master got it from." With that said, he pressed his lips tightly together and dropped his gaze to the floor.

"Hmm." Mistress Greal regarded Crope for an instant. The lumbering idiot had clammed up. She knew she wouldn't get anything else out of him. He was protecting his master. "Go on," she said. "Get going. Take your stuff with you."

Crope moved swiftly to put the last of his things in his box. The green bird was pecking its way through a fine silk curtain, and the huge servant lifted it up and returned it to its cage.

"If you want to keep coming here to feed that thing," said Mistress Greal, "you'd better not mention our little chat to your master. Understand?"

Crope nodded and left.

As soon as he was gone, Mistress Greal brought the necklace to her lips and kissed it. Tiny acid tears trickled down her cheek. Crope had gotten this from his master, who in turn must have taken it from Corsella's throat. In Mistress Greal's mind that meant only one thing: Baralis had murdered her niece.

"Tyren sold my services, just the way he sold yours. Five hundred pieces of gold."

"Why should we believe you, Tawl?" said Crayne, the leader. "You forsook your oath and then you murdered Catherine of Bren."

"Who had the most to gain from Catherine's murder?" said Jack, speaking up for the first time. "Kylock, that's who. Tawl didn't gain a city. Tawl didn't gain an army. He didn't poison Catherine, either. You all know that— poison is a coward's weapon. And I defy anyone here to call Tawl a coward."

Silence followed Jack's words. Out of the corner of his eye, Jack spotted Tawl about to speak, and with a small movement of his hand, he waved him down. Let the knights think about what he'd said for a while.

Slowly, the men began to move away from the camp-fire. Their faces were hard to read in the pale dawn light. Their movements were subdued. Still no one spoke.

They had been traveling north with the knights for eight days now. Every time they stopped—for water, to rest the horses, to bring down game, or to sleep—Tawl would go to work on them, slowly chipping away at Tyren's leadership. He had been subtle at first, asking what role each of them had played in the capture of Halcus, mentioning the decline of the knighthood's reputation, and bringing up the growing number of deserters. At first the men had ignored him, but as the days wore on, Tawl provoked them more and more. Now, having just told them how Tyren forced Bevlin to pay for the knighthood's services, Tawl had finally said something they couldn't ignore.

"Give them time, Tawl," said Jack, after all the knights had walked away. "You're not going to change their opinions that fast. They've spent too long following Tyren to be converted overnight."

Tawl's blue eyes were unusually dark. "I've got to keep trying, Jack. I've got to make these men see the truth."

There was a raw edge to Tawl's voice that made Jack sad. "Why is it so important? We don't need these men. We could escape tonight—you, me, and Nabber."

Tawl shook his head. "No, Jack. I don't want to betray their trust. They've treated us well—they let us ride freely during the day and don't bind us at night. They're men of honor . . . " he hesitated, his gaze lingering over the dying fire ". . . and I was one of them once."

That was it. Tawl was one of them. He was a knight, and having traveled with him for many months now, Jack knew just how deep his circles went.

"If I could just get them to believe what I've told them." Tawl was speaking more to himself than Jack. "If I could just make them see that there *is* another choice."

"What is that choice, Tawl?" Jack's voice was harder than he had intended.

The knight didn't seem to notice. He smiled, a little sadly, and said, "I'm not sure yet. I just know following Tyren isn't right."

Looking into Tawl's eyes, Jack saw a man who was hurt and confused. After a moment he stood up. It was an hour after first light and the knights were preparing to break camp. Leaving Tawl to dampen the fire, Jack crossed over to where Andris was saddling his horse. Of all the knights in the party, Andris was the one who was the most sympathetic to them: Tawl had been a year above him at Valdis, and Jack got the impression that Andris had once looked up to the older knight.

"It's getting colder all the time," said Jack, stroking Andris' horse. "I saw snow on the far hills yesterday."

"We'll reach those hills by the end of the day." Andris bent down to buckle the girth. He had long, light brown hair and fine northern features. A jagged scar ran from just below his left eye down to his neck. "This time tomorrow we'll all be stiff with cold."

"I don't mind snow and ice. It's the wind that sets me shivering."

"Aye. I know all about the wind. I'm originally from eastern Halcus, and they have winds there that can blow the sense right from a man's head."

"I know," said Jack. Andris looked up at him, and he continued speaking: "I traveled through eastern Halcus in midwinter, and I might not have lost my senses, but I lost a good layer of skin. The wind was a demon."

"You from the kingdoms?"

"Yes, Harvell. I spent some time in Halcus, though. It's a beautiful place in spring." As he spoke, Jack remembered the morning he and Tarissa had run off to the little pool ringed with daffodils. It seemed a lifetime ago now.

"What was your business there?" Andris began to brush out his filly's mane. Jack noticed the tip of his left index finger was missing.

"I had no business, really. I was running away. I found people in Halcus who were willing to take me in. Good people." Jack took a deep breath. "And some bad ones as well."

Andris stopped what he was doing. "What did you come over here to say to me, Jack? I don't think you really want to stand here and chat about Halcus."

Jack respected the man's directness. It was time to come clean. "I came to tell you about Tawl."

"What about him?"

"He didn't forsake the knighthood, not really. Not in his heart. Even now he's still doing Bevlin's work. We just came from Larn—we destroyed the temple there. No more stones, no more bindings, no more lives served up to God."

Andris shook his head. "Larn is an old wives' tale. There's no such place."

"I've been to the island. I've seen the seers with my own eyes. My mother was born there." Jack's voice was grim. "Don't tell me it doesn't exist. Go ask Crayne or Borlin; they'll know about it." Jack was taking a guess that the two eldest knights in the party would have heard of Larn; their timeworn, deeply lined faces told of count-less sights seen and dark tales told around campfires at dusk.

Andris looked around the camp. The fire was dead, the bedrolls were up, most of the knights were already on their horses. His gaze returned to Jack. "Why are you telling me this?"

"I'm telling you because I know Tawl wouldn't. He'd never speak out for himself. He's too modest for that. You were with him at Valdis—you know what I'm saying is true."

Andris mounted his horse. "So what's your point?"

"My point is this: Tawl's not a liar, he's not a mur-derer, he's the bravest man I've ever met. The knighthood is part of his soul. I've been with him for months now, and up until twelve days ago he refused to hear a bad word said against Tyren. He loved the man like a father. And now he's learnt the truth he feels betrayed. He's hurting inside. I know how he feels, and I think you do, too. Tyren's betrayed all of you."

A second or two passed. Andris looked down at Jack, his gray northern eyes the same color as the sky. Kicking his horse forward, he said, "I'll talk to the others at midday."

They made good time that morning. It was cold enough to harden the mud, and as the temperature dropped so did the wind. The mountains were close now. The party was to the southwest of them, their peaks shrouded in mist.

The farther north they traveled, the more excited Jack became. A subtle pressure had started building in his stomach the moment he landed in Marls. Every day the knot grew a little tighter. He felt as if he was being reeled in, pulled forward to Bren, to Baralis. To Kylock. Things were different now. Learning about his mother's identity had made him stronger. It was as if he had claimed her strength along with her true name: Aneska. It was a charm to ward off evil. Whatever happened in the coming weeks, nothing could take that away from him. He knew who he was, where he had come from, and what he was fated to do.

There were still things he didn't know or understand: who his father was, why he had to destroy more than just Larn, and what the link was between Marod's prophecy and his mother. He could live without those answers, though. For the time being at least.

Now, today, and every day until they reached Bren, he had to prepare himself to face Kylock. The king had to die. There was no other alternative. The northern empire would crumble without a leader. Baralis, with all his cunning and special skills, wouldn't be able to hold it together once his figurehead was gone. Kylock had the birthright to rule the kingdoms and the marriage right to rule Bren. If he was assassinated, the two powers would spring apart like a severed bowstring. There was no natural connection between them, no history to bind them close: Kylock was the only link. If he was murdered, Bren and the kingdoms would stand alone once more, and the empire they held between them would disintegrate into its separate parts.

Jack had thought long and hard about what he would do when he finally arrived in Bren. There was no need to deal with Baralis, no need to wage a war. Kylock's death was all that counted.

And he, Jack of the Four Kingdoms and Larn, former baker's boy and scribe, was the one man who could bring it about. He and Kylock were connected, and the time was coming close to sever the thread.

Tawl had his own concerns: the knighthood, Melli,

and whatever ghosts lay in his past. Jack would help him as far as he could, but there was a limit—a point when only he and Kylock mattered—and the nearer they got to Bren, the closer that limit came.

Jack glanced over at Tawl. The knight was riding close to Nabber's mule. He caught Jack's gaze and offered a silent salute. Jack saluted back. They both knew the way things were.

Midday came, cloudy and cold with gentle but bitter winds. Crayne decided to stop along the banks of a slow-moving stream. "When it's as cold as this," he said, in his blunt, soldier's voice, "there's little point looking for tree cover."

All morning they had been traveling through snatches of woodland separated by grassy hills and valleys. Everywhere Jack looked there was water: streams, pools, scampering brooks. Some of the smaller pools were just starting to frost over, and greasy plates of ice could be seen floating around their edges. For the most part the water was flowing free and the sound of it rushing, tinkling, and dripping filled the midday air.

Jack watched as Andris approached Crayne. The two men exchanged a few words. Crayne then beckoned Borlin over. Although he was some distance from the three men, Jack could see Andris' lips shaping the word *Larn*. Borlin nodded. More words were exchanged. Two other knights came over to join them.

Jack rode over to Tawl and Nabber.

"What's going on, Jack?" asked Tawl, lifting Nabber down from his mule. "What did you say to Andris earlier?"

"The truth. I told him we destroyed the temple at Larn."

"You destroyed the temple, Jack. Not me."

"No. We both did."

Tawl didn't reply. He turned to Nabber and said, "Open up," and peered down the pocket's throat. Next he felt for lumps under his jawline and then clamped a palm over his brow. He seemed pleased with what he found. "You're getting better."

"How come I don't feel no better, then?"

Tawl smiled. "Because I didn't put any brandy in your holk this morning. Now go and lie down for a while. Take my extra blanket and make sure you cover yourself well. I'll be over with some hot food soon."

Nabber looked at Tawl and then Jack. "I know when I'm not wanted. I might be sick, but I'm not stupid." He began to walk toward the water's edge. "Make sure you bring me plenty of cheese."

As soon as he was out of earshot, Tawl said, "Jack, I don't need you to fight my battles for me. I can deal with these men on my own."

"I know you can, Tawl. But we haven't got much time. If they're not going to help us, then we have to escape."

"You think I'm holding you up." It was not a question.

"That's not why I spoke to Andris."

Tawl managed half a smile. He brought up his hand and laid it on Jack's shoulder. "I know."

The two men looked over toward Andris. All the knights had gathered around him, and judging from the amount of noise they were making, a heated discussion was taking place.

Tawl took a step forward. "I'll go and talk to them."

"No," said Jack. "Let them come to you." He reached over and took his flask from his pack. "Come on, let's get some water."

Tawl followed him down to the edge of the stream. Nabber was close by. Bundled in a heavy blanket, he was leaning over the water looking for skimmers. "Where does all this water come from, Tawl?" he said, holding a pebble up to the light. "Ain't seen so much wet stuff since we took our leave of Marls."

"It runs down off the Divide," said Tawl, dipping his

flask in the stream. "All these little streams eventually run into the Silbur."

"Is the river close by?" asked Jack. Everyone in the Known Lands had heard of the mighty River Silbur.

Tawl shrugged. "About five leagues west of us. It runs along the base of the foothills. Its current is so strong it actually cuts a path through the Divide."

"It runs through the mountains?"

"Yes. A hundred leagues south of Valdis." Tawl put the cap on his flask. "Tomorrow we should pass close to Lake Ormon. It's the deepest lake in the Known Lands. It's where the River Viralay joins the Silbur. The Viralay flows northward through the mountains until it hits the lake." As he spoke Tawl's voice grew quieter. His eyes focused on a distant point across the stream. "I followed the Viralay's path my first year at Valdis. I had to make it to the mountain shrine to gain my first circle. I'll never forget my first sight of the falls."

"The falls?"

"The Faldara Falls. The Viralay drops down from the mountains and into Lake Ormon. It's the place where Valdis . . . " Tawl's voice trailed away. He was crouching by the water's edge, and he began to rock back and forth on the balls of his feet. Abruptly he stood up.

A warning pulse beat in Jack's temple. "What happened at the Faldara Falls?" he cried, suddenly afraid. Something dangerous and unnamable shone in Tawl's eyes.

The knight began to walk back to the campsite. "Valdis earned the faith of his first followers."

Kylock dropped his gaze to Melli's stomach. "How much longer?" He was so close Melli could smell him. A faint sulfurous odor escaped from his lips.

"Five weeks," she lied. It was more like three.

Kylock made a small clicking noise with his tongue and turned his back on her. He had let himself into her chamber only a few minutes earlier. Melli had been almost glad of his arrival. Mistress Greal had failed to make her daily visit, and Melli found she missed the usual clashing of tongues.

Melli moved closer to Kylock. She had her eye on his knife. She was determined to have it in her stash before the visit was through. "Does five weeks fail to meet with your approval, sire?"

The clicking sound came again. Kylock swept around to face her. "Women are such lying whores." He grabbed her by the throat. "Tell me the truth this time. How much longer before you give birth?"

Melli felt the baby kicking. She tried to take a breath, but Kylock's thumb was pressed against her windpipe. Even though she had witnessed Kylock's mood swings many times before, they never failed to frighten her. She knew her best course of action would be to placate him: to beg, to apologize, to admit her guilt. He liked to see her sorry. Her mind was on his knife, though. She could feel it pressing against her side.

Moving her right hand down toward his hip, Melli grasped hold of the hilt. As her fingers closed around the leather binding, she raised her left heel and stamped down hard on Kylock's foot. He jerked back, and Melli pulled the knife from its sheath.

Before she'd had a chance to hide the knife behind her back, Kylock's fist smashed into her face. Pain exploded in her jaw. Her vision blurred. Without thinking, she brought the knife forward and slashed at Kylock's arm. The blade cut through linen and flesh. Even as the blood welled from the cut, Melli knew she'd made a terrible mistake.

Kylock looked down at his arm and then up at her. A faint smile was on his lips. He shook his head. "You shouldn't have done that, Melliandra."

Melli was scared now. Everything was happening too fast. She brought her left hand down to protect her stomach, and then dropped her knife hand down to her side. "I'm sorry. I don't know what I was doing."

"Oh, I think you did. I think you knew exactly what you were doing." Kylock lunged for the knife. Instinct made Melli raise the blade. The edge cut deep into Kylock's palm. Blood poured from the gash.

"Get away from me!" she cried.

Kylock did as he was told. Very slowly he began to back away.

Melli's heart was beating fast. The knife shook in her hand. She tried to calm herself; she was in charge, she had the knife, Kylock would do what *she* wanted. Then she looked into his eyes.

They were as blank as stone.

Melli dropped the knife. With both hands she hugged her belly. *No, Borc. No,* she mouthed. She had seen that look before. The day Jack turned and faced the mercenaries his eyes had looked exactly the same.

A metallic taste reached her lips. A warm breeze touched her cheek. The light went out. And then a band of solid air hit her full in the stomach. It was like being smashed with a metal bar. She was lifted off her feet and slammed against the chamber wall. Her back cracked. Her head hit stone. Something warm gushed down her thigh.

Melli slumped to the floor. The chamber around her was moving. Her face was burning up. Her skirt and legs were wet. Kylock stood above her, smiling.

"That should teach you not to lie."

Melli barely heard him. She barely saw him walk away. Deep, heaving contractions gripped her stomach. A terrible, cold fear gripped her soul. The one arm she was capable of moving came up around her belly. And the baby within shifted downward like a dead weight.

Oh, no. Please. NO!

The night was filled with pain. Her own screams filtered down to her through layer upon layer of suffering.

Everything was red. She opened her eyes, she closed her eyes, and all she saw was red.

Her body stopped being hers and became an instrument of the child. Violent, sickening contractions tore through her abdomen. Hot blood-flushes plumed up her neck and face. Her chest was a clawing hollow; it was as if her heart and her lungs didn't exist. The muscles in her stomach were taut with straining, like ropes lashed around her belly. The center of the pain was lower, deeper, nestled between her hips. Flesh, muscle, and ligaments were stretched to the tearing point. Melli felt as if she was being split in two.

And then there were the other pains. Little separate pockets lurking within the whole. Right arm throbbing, dead at the wrist. Head pounding against the stone. A knifing sting in the back, and the skin on her face scalding in the cool air.

At first there was no one. Melli was alone in the red-tinged darkness, screaming. Then came men with lights. A cushion was placed beneath her head, a blanket over her belly. Something warm dripped between her lips and she heard the tear of fabric as her dress was slit. Melli looked up. The figures looked like ghosts around a grave. Three of them now—the last one an avenging spirit who banished the other two.

Melli felt a slap upon her cheek.

"Take a grip of yourself, you little slut." The figure dumped a cup of cold water over Melli's face. "And stop that infernal screaming."

Melli stopped screaming and started choking. Water splashed down her throat and into her windpipe. She raised her head up from the cushion to clear her lungs. Pain splintered her spine.

"Stay where you are, missy. You're not moving anywhere."

Melli actually laughed. Move? Mistress Greal was being overly optimistic.

If Mistress Greal slapped, kicked, or drenched her again, Melli didn't feel it. A massive, muscle-tensing spasm racked her body. Her chest was a vacuum threatening to collapse. Spirals of pain caught her in their snare. She felt as if a sharp-toothed dog was tearing away at her abdomen.

Above her the light source bobbed and swayed. Mistress Greal's toothless face glowed like an apparition. Spiny claws fingered Melli's belly, prodding, pushing, scratching.

"Bite on this." Something hard and thumb-sized was thrust into Melli's mouth. Rough and wooden, its needle edges tore at her gums. Melli bit down on it anyway. Bit down hard and fast, puncturing the wood with flinty, saliva-glazed teeth.

Another spasm hit. It wrenched the middle of her being, twisting muscles and organs and flesh. Melli tasted blood. She smelled her child. It was on its way.

Melli prayed to Borc. She prayed for her father's luck.

"What did you do to her?" Baralis willed himself to stay calm. He reminded himself he was addressing his king. "What happened, sire?"

Kylock was lounging on a cushioned bench in his chambers. His face was pale, his eyes unnaturally bright. A young girl sat cowering in a chair in the corner. Her pale hair was down around her shoulders and she was wearing a linen nightgown. Baralis noticed that both her arms were behind her back.

A jeweled goblet full of wine rested in Kylock's hand. "Nothing happened that you need worry yourself over, Baralis. I merely taught the Lady Melliandra a lesson."

Baralis' glance flickered over to the girl. Kylock noticed the object of his gaze. "Don't worry yourself so, my dear chancellor. Our little friend here will tell no tales." Kylock favored the girl with a patron's smile. "Not after tonight, eh?"

Baralis walked over to the chest against the wall. Two flagons of wine rested there. He took the caps off both of them and inhaled their fumes deeply.

"Testing for poison, Baralis?"

"Yes, sire. I have a nose for such things," lied Baralis. He was testing for traces of *ivysh*. Kylock had drawn power this night, and Baralis needed to know how he had managed it. The almost imperceptible odor of sulfur met his nostrils. *Ivysh* was present. Kylock was still drinking tainted wine, which meant that once again he had managed to break free from the restraints of the drug. It shouldn't be possible.

Baralis turned back to Kylock. "How are you feeling, sire? Are you weak, tired?"

Kylock raised an eyebrow. "Since when did you become my doctor, Baralis? You will have me urinating in a glass next." He downed his cup of wine and slammed it onto the table. "I've never felt better."

Baralis sucked in his breath. Kylock had just drawn enough sorcery to shake the whole north wing and he'd never felt better? He should be physically drained, close to collapse, and yet here he sat, confident and relaxed, a girl waiting close by to see to his pleasures. "You know what you did tonight?"

"Quite a surprise, wasn't it? The lady in question was swept off her feet." Kylock stood up. "Now, if you'll excuse me, Baralis. My little friend and I have business to attend to."

Baralis bowed to Kylock and inclined his head to the girl. Her pretty face would never see the light of day again.

Once the door was closed behind him, Baralis cut a path to the north wing. He was anxious to see what damage Kylock had done. As he walked, he wondered whether he should increase the king's intake of *ivysh* one more time. Already he was taking three times the normal dose, but it was having less and less effect. Kylock was building an immunity to it. Baralis shook his head. First the wedding night, now this.

Kylock was growing stronger, and the one weapon Baralis could use against him had been blunted by too many strikes.

Increasing the level of *ivysh* might prove dangerous. Nerve and brain damage could occur at higher doses. Baralis had already considered ways to bring about just such an effect—he had plans to rule the empire through a weak-chinned, weak-minded king—but not now, though. It was too early in the game for that. He needed Kylock strong. He needed his expertise, his military genius, his talent for getting the best out of his troops. He needed him to stabilize the empire. Annis, Highwall, Camlee, and Ness—they all must be brought into the fold. Then and only then would Kylock's wits become expendable.

Up until that point his power had to be contained. It was too dangerous to leave the king to his own devices. He was irrational, unpredictable, and he couldn't be relied upon to control the power inside.

More *ivysh* was unfortunately in order; there was no other alternative. He would just have to watch Kylock closely.

Baralis climbed the stairs up to Melliandra's chamber. There was a long, hard winter ahead.

The two guards let him pass without a word. Their faces were strained and they both smelled of ale. As Baralis entered the chamber, he felt the waves of the drawing ripple over him. It was strong and, unlike the wedding night, when there had been no definite target, an attempt had been made to focus it. Kylock was learning new tricks.

Though he hadn't mastered them yet. Melliandra would be dead if he had. Instead she was lying on the stone floor, head propped up by pillows, legs thrown apart, bit between her teeth, about to give birth to the duke's only heir. Her face was burnt, her right arm looked as if it was broken, but all things considered the girl had gotten off lightly.

Having seen enough, Baralis turned away. He had no desire to see the child being born. Such matters were distasteful to him. With a crook of his finger, he beckoned the Greal woman over. Briefly, he considered taking the newborn for his own purposes, but the memory of six men, two with their arms burnt black to the elbow, chased the desire away. Baralis valued his body too highly to risk losing it on a single, magnificent unleashing.

"As soon as the baby is born, take it away and smother it. Destroy the body when you're done."

The woman didn't blink an eye. "And the girl?"

"Leave her. She is nothing without the child." Baralis made his way toward the door. "Let the king do with her what he wants."

It was midnight, but the snow and moon mustered enough light to show a way in the dark. Most of the men were on foot, so the trail was easy to follow. All but a dozen of the horses were dead. There hadn't been enough room for them in the cavern and they had died off one by one. Half of the men were dead, too. They were down to a hundred now.

Maybor was riding one of the last remaining horses. He was bundled up well and the night, though cold, was mild compared to most. Maybor knew he was in a bad state. Frostbite had taken his toes and his left hand. Lung fever had set into his chest. All his life he had been a lucky man, yet tonight, here on the eastern side of the Divide, with the wind blowing northward and the frost coming down from above, Maybor was overcome with the sudden feeling that he'd just seen the last of his luck.

He shivered violently, his teeth clicking together and his shoulders arching upward.

"Come on, lads, let's go," he said, speaking only to

hear the sound of his own voice. He kicked his horse forward, eager to leave all misgivings behind.

They didn't have much time left: a hard freeze or a sudden storm and they'd be at the devil's side before they knew it. So they were coming down the mountain while they still could.

They weren't traveling north toward Bren—Kylock was patrolling the northern foothills and they'd be picked off by marksmen as soon as they came within range— they were heading to Camlee, instead.

Southeast along the divide, traveling both day and night, they skirted the great peaks, gradually winding their way down to the foothills north of Camlee. For the most part conditions in the mountains had been in their favor: the air was clear but cold, snowfall light, and once they'd turned south, the northern winds were behind them. Underfoot the snow was hard, frozen, and the farther they descended the lighter the coverage became. All the men were wrapped up well now, dead men's clothes on their backs, dead men's boots on their feet. No more limbs would be lost to the cold.

Maybor had grown to respect the quiet determined men of Highwall. He joined in their somber songs of mourning and listened to their fireside tales of war. They were proud men, and they bitterly regretted not being there to die by their leader's side. Maybor thought them very young and naïve, yet he loved them all the same. They were his boys now. And he wouldn't let their retreat from Kylock's forces be in vain. He was old, his life long, but they were young and had many battles left to fight. He would bring them down from the mountain and see them safe into Camlee territory. From there they could find glory on their own.

Maybor guided his horse around a curve in the path. No, he didn't feel lucky anymore, so he would have to save these hundred men on nothing more than guts.

Twenty-eight

*I*t was warm inside the pit. Warm and quiet and dark, with blankets layered high to keep out sights, sounds, and drafts. The pit was safe. It fit her form like a coffin, and like a coffin it offered peace. She didn't want to rise, didn't ever want to wake up again. Sleep was her dark pit, and with instincts so potent they pervaded her dreams, Melli knew that's where she should stay.

To awaken meant the death of her soul.

Dreaming was the only way to keep it alive. Nothing could be taken from her while she was here in the pit. It was getting harder and harder to stay, though. Little discomforts began to niggle away at her: the pit was growing horns. Pain pricked at her arm, head, and back. Dryness tickled her throat. An aching softness lay between her legs and her stomach felt strangely hollow. Melli tried to burrow deeper, tried to gaze downward instead of up, but the walls of the pit began to close in on her, and the floor rose up and squeezed her out.

She opened her eyes. Bright bands of sunlight sliced the room. Melli blinked, trying to make sense of the shadows and forms, forcing her mind into focus. She was looking at the ceiling: curved stone, wooden beams, damp patches where the rain came through. In the same way Melli knew she shouldn't wake up, she also knew she shouldn't look down. Her eyes moved ahead of her brain, however, and her gaze arched a quarter circle to the floor.

She was lying in a pool of dried blood. Her dress, her legs, and the surrounding stone were sticky with wine-dark stains. Melli was aware of a feathering sensation in her head: a lightness, a ripple across her thoughts. All pain had left her. The slate was clean. A tiny dark spot was all that was left, and as she raised her gaze to her stomach, the spot hardened to lead in her throat.

Her belly was a slack curve. The gleaming roundness had gone.

Melli's body began to convulse. Her spine jerked against the stone floor. Dry sobs pumped up from her chest to her lips. Her mouth opened and closed, opened and closed, with only a soft choking noise to show for it. She was empty. *Empty*. Her baby had gone. They had forced it from her and taken it away.

"You're not really going to do this, Tawl?" said Jack. "The water temperature alone could kill you."

Tawl looked at him in what Jack had come to recognize as his hard-headed way. "It's too late to go back now."

They were walking up a winding mountain path, their horses trailing behind them. Rocks, tufts of dry grass, and thorny yellow bushes marked their way. Lake Ormon lay below them, its deep green water as glassy as a jewel. The sky was pale and cloudless, the sun already on its way to the west. They had spent the last four hours edging the lake, and for four hours before that they were riding along the Silbur's bank. Darkness was two hours away at the most.

Crayne was leading the way. Nabber and Borlin were bringing up the rear. A small mountain village was their destination, a sheep herding village that lay in the same high valley as the Faldara Falls. Tawl was going to jump into the River Viralay and go over the falls to the lake. "Valdis did it," he explained, "to gain the faith of the villagers. Over the centuries a handful of others have followed his lead, seeking to prove their worth, or their faith. Or both."

Jack thought it was madness. Like every child, he had heard the tale of Borc freezing the waterfall, but he never thought it was true. And he couldn't believe that they were actually hiking up to that same waterfall now.

"There must be an easier way to make the men believe in you." Jack wiped the sweat from his brow. It was cold, but the path was steep. "I can't see a dead man inspiring much faith."

Tawl shrugged. "The knights respect the falls. If I back out now, they will say I have no faith."

"Why did you offer to do it? No one forced your hand."

"You heard them, Jack. They don't believe what I say. They still think I'm a murderer, a liar. A man who has forsaken his oath."

"They were beginning to listen to us. Andris and the younger ones are on our side."

Tawl started shaking his head even before Jack stopped speaking. "Crayne, Borlin, the others—they'll never listen. They understand courage and strength and faith. Words mean nothing to them. Actions are the only way to judge a man."

"You've taken actions enough," said Jack. Frustration over Tawl's stubbornness was making him lose his temper. "You've got nothing to prove to these men. *Nothing.*"

"You don't understand, Jack. You're not a knight. You don't bear the circles. You've never lived your life for one thing only to find corruption at the very heart of it."

"I understand revenge."

Tawl looked at Jack. He ran his fingers through his hair. When he spoke, the tension had drained from his voice. "I won't lie to you, Jack. Part of this is revenge. I'm only human; I hurt, I feel betrayed, but most of all I feel lost."

"And what about Melli?" said Jack quickly, grasping for anything that would make Tawl listen to reason. "How *lost* will she feel if you don't survive?"

Tawl closed his eyes. When he opened them a moment later, they were infinitely brighter and darker than before. A soft sound, like the cry of a wounded animal, escaped from his lips. Hearing it, Jack wished he had never asked the question. Seconds passed. Tawl's face fell under the shadow of a nearby pine. He gripped the reins of his horse so tightly that white bands of flesh swelled to either side of the leather. When he spoke his voice was so low that Jack had to strain to hear it. "If I don't make it over the falls, Jack, you must take my place. You must protect Melli for me. She must be kept safe."

Jack nodded once. Briefly he met Tawl's gaze and then looked away. He felt ashamed. There was a lifetime's worth of anguish shining softly in the knight's blue eyes. "I'm sorry, Tawl. I shouldn't have mentioned Melli."

Tawl seemed not to be listening; he adjusted his horse's bit and then smoothed down its mane. After a moment he patted the old horse gently and said, "Melli is everything to me, Jack. But since we left Marls, saving her no longer seems enough. I must be *worthy* of her, too. I can't bring all my failures back with me and expect her to love me all the same. She deserves better than that." Tawl made a small, helpless gesture with his hand. "If I don't take this jump, I will have failed Melli as well as myself."

Jack knew he spoke the truth. The falls were a personal ordeal for Tawl—they weren't just about winning over the knights, they were about testing his own worth. "What will happen if you do succeed?"

Tawl shrugged. "I don't really know—I haven't got a plan. I just know that I want to replace something in the knighthood that has been lost." Tawl paused a moment before adding, "And perhaps something in myself, too."

As if embarrassed by this admission, Tawl rushed on. "With the knighthood corrupt there's nothing to look up to anymore. There's no ideal—there's just men, merchants, and mercenaries. To say you were a knight used to mean something; strangers would trust you, old ladies would invite you into their homes. People were never afraid to ask for your help. Now, if you're a knight in the north you're branded a mercenary, and if you're a knight in the south you're a fugitive."

Tawl stopped a moment and gazed out over the lake. "I want the ideal back. I want it for the knights who have deserted and all those who are *thinking* about desertion. I want it for these men here and I want it for myself."

Jack had never heard Tawl speak so long and passionately, and he began to understand just how deep his feelings ran. Nothing short of drugging and binding would stop him from taking the jump. Some things *were* madness—helping a golden-haired stranger escape from the guards, entering the temple at Larn with only a handful of rocks as a weapon, setting a rowboat down in a storm—and perhaps it was that element of madness that helped them get so far.

They'd been acting on faith all along: faith in Marod's prophecy, and in each other, and the belief it could all be done. Jack tugged his horse away from a snatch of grass and made his way up the trail. Could he really blame Tawl for taking one more leap?

The men formed a crescent around the bank. They were silent, faces grave, weapons unsheathed, arms bared to reveal their circles.

Tawl looked at them, meeting their gazes one at a time, making a connection with all who were there. The knights regarded him with grim respect: the falls were the ultimate test of a knight. Not of his training, or his skills, but of his courage and his heart. Believe in something enough to ride the river down to the lake and you might not be a good man, might not be a bad man, but at least you had the strength of your convictions.

And to Tawl that was what it was all about: showing these knights that he believed in himself.

He took a step back toward the edge. Jack raised his hand—in farewell or warning, Tawl didn't know. Seeing him from this distance, Tawl realized just how much Jack had changed. He was so much older now.

Nabber was looking down at the ground. Dark brown hair falling over his eyes, shoulders slumped, hands clasped into tight knots by his sides—he didn't like this one little bit. Tawl wanted to say something to him, to reassure him, but false promises had no place at the falls. As he looked on, Jack put his arm around the pocket. That would have to do.

Tawl turned to face the river. The Viralay belonged to the mountains. It flowed through valleys and clefts and hollows, gathering mass during the spring thaw, running low in midwinter. It was low now, down to two-thirds of its normal level. Low, cold, and slow-moving until it came to the twist before the drop. Tawl looked along its length: it ran straight, right up to the end, and then a sharp outcropping of rocks changed its course, bending the river into the shade of overhanging cliffs, concealing the drop from all who stood on the bank.

No one would see him go over the edge. They would wait until he was out of sight and then make their way down the path to the lake. He was on his own once he disappeared behind the bend. It had taken the party almost an hour to climb up here. It would take them at least half of that to come down: by that time he would be saved or damned.

Tawl took off his leather tunic and his heavy boots. He unhooked his sword and laid it on the ground. Reaching for his knife, he went to discard that, too, and then thought better of it. He replaced it in its scabbard.

He didn't turn to look at the knights. He looked only at

the water. With the words *"Es nil hesrl"* on his lips, he jumped into the river.

The shock of the cold hit him straightaway. The water was only a few degrees above freezing. He had minutes before his body started to numb. He felt the water soaking his undershirt and his britches, settling against his skin.

The current took him, dragging his body away from the bank, tugging his torso under. Water splashed, then covered his face. Tawl looked up through the wetness to the bank. The knights' figures rippled above, green-hazed, distorted, like a coven of witches. The water was too cold to bear and Tawl closed his eyes. Moss-green light filtered through the lids. He raised his neck out of the water and took a gasp of air. The current snatched him back before he'd finished.

He felt himself moving downward and along, his speed quickening. Arms and legs moved rapidly at first, working to counteract the current's pull, buoying, steering, keeping him afloat. It was so cold, though. Freezing. Tawl started to shiver. His instinct was to curl up, to bundle his body into a warming ball. He fought his desire for warmth, forcing his feet to keep kicking and his arms to stay straightened out.

The shivering changed to shaking as he rounded the bend. The current was strong now; it was an icy band around his waist. It wanted him under. Tawl flexed his shoulder muscles and sent his arms beating against the water. His face broke the surface. The air was warm on his forehead, hot in his lungs. He took two mighty breaths and then the current was at him once more. As he was sucked under, he risked opening his eyes again. Everything was green—above and below—green flecks floated on the surface, fragments of plant life swirled beneath.

Suddenly his body was yanked around. His shin hit something hard. Tawl was glad of the pain. His mind was growing torpid, and anything that helped him fight the numbing cold was welcome. In water near freezing, losing consciousness was the greatest danger. He had to stay alert.

The end was just ahead of him now. The various eddies within the river were streamlining, giving way to the overpowering pull of the falls. Tawl felt as if his whole body was being sucked forward. Feeling the beginnings of panic, he opened his eyes, trying to orientate himself. The green flecks on the surface had stretched to lines. He was moving quickly now. He spotted the cut-off point ahead. The water ended abruptly, leaving only the green-gray sky.

He needed to take a breath. His arms were slow to respond. He had no sensation in his fingers. Stretching his neck up as far as it would go, he propelled his elbows backward. Up he went, through the mineral-heavy froth, up to the surface. He took a mariner's breath. A deep, lung-stretching, water-chasing gulp. The river water slid along his tongue. It tasted of copper and cloves.

There was a lot of white in the green now. The rocks bounced the water into a surface frenzy. Below, the current remained unaffected, the foam nothing more than a sideshow.

Tawl had stopped moving his arms and legs; he didn't want to exert himself. His last breath had to take him over the falls.

He was fully under now. The current had flipped him over onto his back and swung him around feet-first. Panic had fallen from him. Calmness remained. Whatever happened now was just water over the falls. Melli could survive without him, the knighthood would go on, Jack was capable of reaching Kylock on his own, and whoever prevailed in the end would find their triumph only fleeting.

A sucking rush filled Tawl's ears. The drop was a void that pulled him in. His body careened forward, buffeted by the current. Hard, driving water surged between him and the sky. A blink revealed the gray-green and then the world turned inside out.

Down he went, reality dropping from beneath him. The current was gone, replaced by crashing water and damning gravity. Wind ripped along his body, pushing on the soles of his feet. The wind blew upward, but the water plunged him down.

The light was beautiful, radiant, a many-hued green. The water glittered around him in tiny, dazzling drops.

He was so cold. So very cold.

And then he crashed into the water below.

His body slammed into the lake. The jolt was shocking. His wrists bent backward, his teeth smashed together. Downward he speared, the water from the falls ramming him under.

The greenness became thicker, heavier. Colder. The light grew dim. Down and down he went, leaving it all behind.

The water was a heavy cloak about his shoulders. The coldness was a drug that made him sleep. Descending ever deeper, he gave in to the icy darkness, leaving all thoughts, dreams, and oaths silently behind. Air no longer had any business in his lungs, and the future had lost its hold upon his heart.

Tawl glided into Lake Ormon's depths, memories racing ahead of him like torches to light the way. Sara and Anna were there, arms open in welcome, leafy tendrils trailing from their hair. His mother flitted past, not pregnant anymore, but young and beautiful, a smile just for him upon her lips. Bevlin was there, too: age wrinkles and water wrinkles vying to line his face. Their welcomes were a rite of passage. He was finally being allowed home to the cottage by the marsh.

Tawl's chest was tight with joy. This was all he had ever wanted.

As he reached out to Sara, a dark green shadow caught

his eye. Two shades short of black, it hovered behind his family like an armed man ready to strike. Tawl screamed a warning, but it was drowned out by the pressure rush. The dark shadow showed its carrion teeth and Tawl's family sped away, disappearing into the darkness like ghosts before the dawn. The creature raised an armlike limb, and even before Tawl's eyes focused he knew what was branded upon the flesh: the mark of Valdis. Three circles. Everything began and ended with them.

Tawl looked more closely at the shadow. A tremor of recognition passed along his spine. It wasn't a random monster conjured up out of the depths, it was his *own* demon.

He had brought it down with him.

And with him it would stay until the very end.

Unless.

Tawl began to kick his feet, beating at the water with sheer willpower alone. Up came his hands, over his head, fingers pointing skyward to the world of light above. His life was far from finished, his fate far from complete, and as he rose toward the surface, he knew what he must do.

Tavalisk was eating pansies. Purple ones.

Flowers, his cook said, were good for the digestion, the hiccups, and for garnishing a platter. The pansies in question were here in their garnishing capacity, but, due to the unsavory nature of the main dish—eels baked in a casing of pig's intestines—the archbishop had promoted them to food. At this point he wasn't entirely sure that he found them appetizing—they had the texture of damp velvet and the taste of cheap perfume—but they were a definite improvement on the eels.

He was just considering having his cook fry a few for him when in bounded Gamil. The guilty expression that was so often upon his face of late had been replaced with a sort of stricken death mask.

"You're looking remarkably well today, Gamil. That

glazed expression is really most becoming." The archbishop rose from his chair. "Would you care to try a
pansy?"

"Kylock's forces are on their way to Camlee, Your
Eminence."

The pansy fluttered to the floor. The archbishop sent
out a hand to steady himself against his desk. His heart
started pattering like hailstones against a shutter. "Not
Ness?"

Gamil shook his head. "They turned at Lake Herry."

Tavalisk closed his eyes. Of course they turned. Why
hadn't he thought of it sooner? He knew Baralis, and had
learned not to underestimate Kylock, so why had this
latest strategy passed him by? Unsure that his legs could
carry him any longer, Tavalisk sat down. He slumped
heavily in his chair, his many rolls of fat gathering around
him like worker bees. For the first time in years, he actually felt afraid. Events were getting out of hand. The
northern empire was no longer a vague possibility; it was
here, on their doorsteps, about to pry its way in.

Camlee. Gateway to the south. Kylock had redrawn
his boundaries, and might do it yet again.

Tavalisk spread his chubby fingers out upon the desk.
"When will Kylock's forces arrive in Camlee?"

"My news is late, Your Eminence. It is possible they
are only a week away now."

"And what numbers have been sent?"

"Conservative estimates say six thousand, Your
Eminence, but eyewitnesses have reported close to nine.
All the villages en route have been pillaged then burned.
The army is like a plague of locusts, leaving nothing but
destruction in its wake."

A tiny wheezing sound escaped from the archbishop's
lips. "Is Kylock leading them himself?"

"No. Maybor's firstborn, Kedrac, is in command. He
led the kingdoms' forces to victory in Halcus. He battles
in Kylock's image."

"What about Tyren and his branded cohorts? Are they on their way to knife their neighbors in the side?"

"There *are* a battalion of knights in the army, Your Eminence. But Tyren himself is still in Bren. Since Highwall has been routed, he has set up camp outside the city and is currently in negotiations with Kylock."

"If I know Tyren he'll be after first spoils. He was granted them in Helch, and he's probably hoping to secure them in Highwall after spring thaw." The archbishop drew sweaty circles on the surface of his desk—then wiped them out. "Tyren is just a greedy little pawn. Baralis and Kylock are using him as surely as they use the boot leather on their feet."

"First spoils in Highwall would be quite a prize, Your Eminence. Tyren is more a knight than a pawn."

"Knights! Pawns! Spare me the chess metaphors, Gamil. You're a servant, not a wandering minstrel." Tavalisk drummed on the desk. He was beginning to feel a little hysterical. "I need facts. *Facts.* Have any of our supplies reached Camlee yet? How are the city's armaments? How long could they hold out for?"

"Some of our supplies have reached the city, Your Eminence: food, armaments and the like. No manpower has been sent, though. No one thought the attack would come quite so soon." Gamil fingered the fastenings on his tunic. "As for the city itself, it will be caught almost entirely off guard. They've had no time to prepare, their battlements are run-down, and their army consists mainly of conscripts. I would say they can hold out a month at the most."

Tavalisk slumped back in his chair. Kylock was going to get away with it. He was going to steal Camlee from under their very noses. There was literally no way to stop him. The south would send mercenaries and supplies, but they wouldn't risk sending their armies. The southern cities were notoriously self-serving, and they'd rather hold out and save their own necks than band together and save everyone else's. Besides, Camlee was in a peculiar position: southerners regarded it as the north, and northerners swore it was in the south.

Kylock had chosen both time and destination well.

Tavalisk had hoped that a show of southern solidarity might have put him off, but now he realized the new king would have seen it for what it was: a show. Solidarity was one thing. Force was quite another.

From his own point of view his hands were tied. The good people of Rorn loved him—today—but if he as much as hinted that he wanted to embroil the city in a disabling foreign war, he'd be kicked out of office before he could say the words: *We might be next.* The other southern leaders would be in the exact same predicament.

Gamil mustered a polite cough. "What instructions does Your Eminence have?"

Instructions? Tavalisk felt an unfamiliar vacuum in his thoughts. He *had* no instructions. For seventeen years he had been archbishop of Rorn, and not once in all that time had ideas failed him. He schemed as naturally as others breathed. There was always a plot, a maneuver, a tricky little bluff. But now there was nothing. He couldn't come up with any way to prevent Kylock from getting his claws into Camlee.

He, the chosen one, had no strategies left.

The sun disappeared behind a cloud and a gray shadow passed over the room. Tavalisk shuddered. Was this the beginning of the end?

Something sharp jabbed against his throat.

"Get up."

Another jab, followed by a kick, then something warm landed on his cheek. Tawl opened his eyes in time to see Skaythe wiping the spittle from his lips.

"Get up, you bastard."

Memories and senses worked quickly to shape Tawl's world. He was lying on a grassy bank, cold, wet, shivering.

Lake Ormon lapped against his ankles, and a bloodied knife was pointed at his throat. He must have passed out after dragging himself from the water. But for how long? He glanced around. The sky was a fly's wing darker than when he'd seen it last. Ten, perhaps twenty minutes, then. So that meant Jack and the knights would be about halfway down the path.

A subtle flexing of his muscles revealed that stalling was in order: it was going to take him some time to regain his strength and increase his body temperature. Weak and disorientated, Tawl fell back on his knighthood training, recalling techniques, both physical and mental, to ready his body for action. Rhythmically tensing the muscles in his lower body to encourage the blood flow, Tawl concentrated hard on his heart, overriding its natural pacing, forcing it to pump harder. All the while he took quick, deep breaths, filling his lungs with air. Tilting his hip a fraction, he felt for the weight of his knife.

"Come on. Draw it." Skaythe aimed a kick at Tawl's knife belt. "Get up and draw your blade."

Tawl was instantly on guard. Skaythe was quick.

"I figure we'll be evenly matched," said Skaythe, backing away a fraction. "Me with my bad leg and shoulder and you"—he shrugged— "with your little chill."

While he was speaking, Tawl was working to pump blood into his blue-tinged limbs. His heart rate had increased, but he still felt physically drained—he needed more time. Rising to a sitting position, he said, "I'm sorry about what happened to Blayze. I should have stopped at victory."

"Yes, you should have." Skaythe moved close and slapped him across his face. "Now, get up!"

Tawl had said the apology merely as a stall, but as he spoke the words he realized that he meant it. He had done some terrible things in his life and had many burdens to bear. Sometimes he made bad choices, sometimes he was given no choice at all. But today, in the green depths of

Lake Ormon, he had finally made the *right* choice. He chose redemption. His path was clear now; his fate cut two ways. On one side was Melli and his oath to protect her, and on the other side was Valdis and his obligation to his brethren.

Saving Melli was for himself.

Saving the knighthood was for his family.

Nine years ago he had walked out on his sisters, abandoning them for all the glory that lay beyond Valdis' gates. Only there was no glory, and its absence made his sisters' deaths meaningless. *He had deserted his family for a sham*—that was his demon, it was what he had seen in the icy water. It was the monster with teeth that bit beyond the grave.

And the only way to stop them biting was to make the knighthood glorious once more. For Anna, for Sara, for the baby.

Tawl stood up. He had not chosen redemption to be waylaid so early in the game. His time was far from up, and he couldn't allow one man's vengeance to get in the way of his fate.

He drew his knife. His legs were weak, his muscles aching, his sense of balance slightly off kilter. Even as Tawl made a mental inventory of his physical state, his body took a fighter's stance: legs apart, knees slightly bent, knife hand close to the waist, blade facing up.

"Skaythe," he said, gently settling himself on the balls of his feet, "I would prefer not to kill a man this day. I offer you a choice: put down your weapon, accept my shame as an apology, and walk away from this fight. Or die here, by my hand, and I'll send your soul straight to hell and your blood dripping into the lake."

Skaythe brought his blade up. "How can I accept a choice from a man who failed to offer my brother one?" He lunged forward, slashing diagonally with his knife.

Tawl was forced to jump back. The impact of landing nearly buckled his legs. He scored a wide half-circle with

his knife, forcing Skaythe to stay put for a critical second
while he righted himself. An instant later, Skaythe was
upon him, edging him back toward the lake. Tawl felt
water creeping around his ankles. Cursing his aching
muscles, he tried to dodge Skaythe's blade. The man was
tenacious, though, and matched him feint for feint.

Noticing that he favored his left leg, Tawl sprang to
Skaythe's right, trying to throw him off balance. Skaythe
was obviously used to compensating for his lameness, for
he immediately shifted side-on, bringing his left foot
behind him to support his weight. Tawl stepped farther
back into the water. In his current condition there was no
way he could beat Skaythe fair and square. The man was
faster, stronger, and more alert. Alternative tactics were
called for.

The water was his only advantage. Lake Ormon
favored its own, and after what had happened earlier,
Tawl knew he was counted amongst them. He had been
down to its slow-pumping heart, had seen its secret green
caverns. It was his territory now.

Tawl made Skaythe come in after him. Every step
sideways was also a step back. Knee-deep now, Skaythe
was forced to pay more attention to his footing; one slip of
his right foot and the lake would have him. Tawl edged
out into the water, sweeping his knife in defense while
feeling for the lakebed with his toes.

The shelf was starting to slope sharply. Tawl sent out
his foot, but could find no hardness to rest upon. He was
standing a foot-length away from the point where the
shelf became a drop. He moved to his right. Skaythe
moved forward. Tawl deliberately let down his guard,
leaving his torso open to an attack. Skaythe seized the
opportunity, lunging at the unguarded flesh. Tawl felt a
slicing sting in his chest—he ignored it. Again he moved
to his right, forcing Skaythe to turn his back on the ledge.
Their positions were reversed now.

Tawl gritted his teeth and sprang out of the water

straight toward Skaythe. He hit him full in the chest. Skaythe's knife was up, but Tawl's momentum forced him to step back. Trying to steady himself with his strong left foot, he sent out his right behind him. The minute difference in length between his legs meant Skaythe was accustomed to judging distances with his left. His right leg was used to feeling no ground beneath it because it was the shorter of the two.

He stepped back, assuming the lakebed was just a fraction below his foot. The lake sucked him under. Tawl saw Skaythe trying to pivot his weight forward, but he had moved too quickly and tried to compensate too late.

Tawl took a step back toward the bank. Bringing his knife forward, he watched as Skaythe struggled to find a foothold on the shelf. He was panicking, gulping in water, flaying his arms around wildly. When he finally managed to balance himself, Tawl would slip in with his knife.

The lake would take a life today after all.

Tawl closed his eyes for a moment. He felt very weak. He wanted to sleep in soft blankets by a blazing fire and dream about his sisters till dawn. Despite his threat to Skaythe, he didn't want to kill him: not here, not now, not like this. He had been given a gift today, and it was only fitting he gave one back.

Tawl dropped his knife. It splashed against the surface, flashed once in the dimming light, and was lost to the water's keeping. Turning, Tawl began wading his way back to the bank. Skaythe could live to fight another day.

Just as he drew near the water's edge, Tawl heard splashing behind him. He spun around. Skaythe was running forward, knife in hand, lips moving in silent fury.

Tawl had a fraction of a second to register disappointment, and then Skaythe stopped in his tracks. He staggered backward and plunged into the water, an arrow quivering in his heart.

The pain in Tawl's chest suddenly reasserted itself. He felt dizzy and lightheaded. He needed to get to the shore. Forcing himself to keep wading, Tawl started to blank out: the world grew dark around the edges and the lake rose up to meet his face. And then Jack was there, pulling him out of the water, carrying him to the shore. The knights were waiting on the bank. Nabber came dashing forward; Borlin was putting away his bow. Everyone gathered around, touching, smiling, caring. Tawl wanted to say something, to explain what had happened, to tell them he was all right, but his heart was too heavy with love and pain to do anything more than give thanks.

Twenty-nine

*T*yren leant forward. His leathers were so well beaten they didn't make a noise. "I can help you take Camlee within a month."

Baralis waited for the man to explain himself, but Tyren's lips were pressed into a tantalizing line. The leader of the knighthood stroked his sleek beard; his eyes never leaving Baralis for an instant. Tyren was one of the few men Baralis had ever met who was not afraid of silences. He was willing to let them linger—no matter how strained or awkward—in order to compel his opponent into speaking.

Baralis took a thin breath. "How can you help us take Camlee?"

Tyren smiled. He moved his hand from his beard to his temple and smoothed back a lock of gleaming hair. "Let's first talk about *why* rather than how."

So the negotiation had started. Tyren had certainly taken his time. He had been in the city for weeks now, and had even gone so far as to set up camp outside the gates, but up until today there had been no whiff of deals. He had been playing a waiting game, and now Baralis realized what he was waiting for. Word had come today that the empire's forces had finally reached Camlee.

Baralis crossed over to his desk and poured two cups of wine. They were sitting in a silk merchant's house in the

south side of the city. The good merchant himself was
out—probably off spending the fifty golds that had
bought the use of his home and his silence. Even though
there was less need for secrecy now than when he and
Tyren had first met, Baralis preferred to be discreet all
the same. There was no need to involve Kylock in this
particular negotiation.

Sitting back in his chair, Baralis said, "What exactly do
you want, Tyren?"

Tyren slid his hand along his thigh. Finely manicured
fingers rested upon a block of solid muscle. "I want first
spoils in Highwall."

Baralis had expected no less. "And?"

"Free rein in Camlee when it's taken." Tyren's tone
was carefully modulated. He always worked hard on his
voice. "After a slow start, the conversions in Helch are
going well. I want to move forward quickly while Valdis'
successes are still fresh. Of course, I'll require the same
latitude in Camlee that you so kindly allowed me in
Helch."

He meant he wanted to be free to persecute the people
of Camlee without fear of repercussions from Kylock.
Baralis brought his goblet up to his lips to hide a smile.
Tyren was trying to steal religious power from Silbur
and keep it for Valdis and himself. With religious power
went taxes, property, Church land, and gold.

Tyren was being greedy.

Baralis decided it was time to make the man show his
hand. "You ask a lot, my friend. What would you give in
return?"

A calculated pause followed. Tyren liked to build tension, to create drama by speaking only when he was
ready, and to force people to wait upon his every word. It
was yet another use he had for silence.

After a moment he inclined his head. Dark skin, dark
eyes, and dark hair caught the light. "I have three thousand knights in Valdis. On my word they will move north

toward Camlee." Tyren made a small gesture with his hand. "They will not only bring extra manpower to the siege, but they will also provide access to the tunnels."

"Tunnels?"

"Camlee is an old city built by an old king. There are ancient ways under the wall—passages that not even their generals know about—and one of my knights can supply you with their locations. His father was a stonemason in Camlee. He knows all the secrets of the guild."

Baralis took a draught of his wine. He was going to give Tyren what he wanted. The empire's forces could take Camlee on their own, but cold-weather sieges could be long and unpleasant affairs. Bren was vulnerable at the moment; Annis could decide to cross the mountains in defiance of the snow. And if they did, they'd find a city seriously undermanned. The sooner Camlee was defeated the better.

Baralis turned his head, smiling softly into the shadows. The sooner Camlee fell, the sooner Rorn and Rorn's archbishop would fall. Twenty years ago, Tavalisk had murdered a man, then taken credit for his work, and punishment was long overdue.

"I think we have an agreement, my friend," said Baralis, raising his cup. Highwall's coffers were nothing to him. Camlee's people even less. Tyren could do whatever he wanted in both the north and south as long as he didn't raise his sights above religion and gold.

Tyren was not a fool. He didn't permit himself to look even a little smug. He stood and bowed. "I am well pleased, Baralis. I will send a messenger to Valdis today."

Baralis opened the door to him. "It is always a pleasure, Tyren."

The wind was blowing straight from the mountains and the sky looked ready for snow. Jack couldn't get warm no matter what he tried. Cold air gusted beneath his cloak despite the fact he was sitting on the hem, and his toes were numb even though his boots were lined with wool. Riding a horse all day through banks of freezing fog was not a pleasant experience.

But it was a necessary one. Up before dawn every day, riding past dark each night. When Tawl wasn't driving the men forward, Jack was. They had to get to Bren. Four days ago, when they had ridden through a mountain village west of Camlee, the villagers told them that the empire's forces were about to lay siege to the city. The skin on Jack's neck prickled when he heard the news. Kylock was moving fast. He wasn't content to sit out the winter; he wanted another victory under his belt.

The knights had taken the news of the siege badly. Camlee was Valdis' closest neighbor, and all the men in the party knew people in the city—some even had family there. They were anxious to discover if Tyren had sent any knights along with the siege force, but the route they were taking at the moment kept them away from villages and towns.

Ever since they'd learnt the empire's forces were in the vicinity, they had taken to riding along the foothills of the Divide. No one wanted to risk a chance encounter with a battalion of blackhelms, so they took a longer and more arduous path. The past four days had been hard going. The temperature dropped to below freezing at night and hardly rose significantly during the day. The knights still kept on the lookout for villages, but they hadn't seen a single hut since Camlee.

Things had changed since the day at the lake. Tawl's leap had transformed the party. The knights were his now. There were no more questions, no more doubts, nothing except respect and something close to veneration. Tawl had emerged from the lake a different person. His blue eyes were bright with purpose, his voice strong and clear. He was full of strength and light; it was as if the falls had renewed his soul.

Tawl had offered the knights a chance for honor by

rescuing a highborn lady from her captor, and the knights seemed glad to take it. There was not a knight alive who would hesitate at saving a damsel in distress. Tyren was a more delicate subject. Tawl did not want to push the men into doing anything they weren't comfortable with. He gave them time and space to reach their own decisions, and judging from the gradual shift in opinions that was taking place within the party, it was the wisest thing he could have done.

Jack was pleased that Tawl had managed to win the loyalty of the knights, but he felt a certain sadness, too. He and Tawl were moving apart; they had different motives, different goals, different fates. Bren would mark the end of their partnership. From there they would go their separate ways.

"Smoke ahead!" cried Andris.

Jack looked up. He had been drifting off into the future and was glad of the chance to get back to the present. In the distance, in a cleft between two hills, a silvery stream of smoke could be seen rising against the gray sky. As his gaze focused, Jack could see that there was more than one plume: it had to mean there was a village ahead.

The party was excited by the sighting, and everyone spurred their horses on. It was well past midday, and thoughts of a hot meal and a warm bed for the night were uppermost in Jack's mind.

It took them longer than they thought to reach the village. They had to cross a snowbound valley where the deep drifts and a frozen pond forced them to dismount their horses. Snow started falling when they were halfway across, and the wind from the mountains whipped it into a flurry, making it difficult to see anything. By the time they approached the two hills it was already growing dark.

Crayne sent Andris and Mafrey ahead to scout the village. Although it was far to the west of the army's path, Crayne was taking no chances. The party gathered in the lee of the hill and waited for the two men to return. The snowfall grew steadily heavier, and the temperature began to drop for the night. The men huddled close, their breath crystallizing in the darkening air, their cloaks white with snow.

Tawl, Crayne, and Borlin were speaking in hushed voices. Jack could see them glancing toward the path that led between the hills. Andris and Mafrey should have been back by now. After a moment, Crayne nodded. "Let's follow them in," he cried.

Jack kicked his horse forward, steering toward Nabber and his mule. Tawl had a similar instinct and held back until Nabber drew level. Together they picked a route along the base of the hill until they crossed the path leading into the village.

"Do you think Andris and Mafrey have been attacked?" shouted Jack above the roar of the wind.

"I don't know," Tawl said. "The villagers may have spotted them and assumed they were part of Kylock's forces." With his right hand he made a small gesture down toward his scabbard.

Jack nodded. Tawl was warning him to be ready with his sword.

The snow was falling so fast that hoofprints were covered within minutes; there was no sign of Andris and Mafrey's passing. As they rode through the narrow pass, a subtle change began to take place within the party: everyone sat forward on their horses, Borlin and the archers slung their quivers over their backs, Crayne took his spear from its horn, and all but the thinnest gloves were stripped off.

Sharply slanted roofs came into view above the hill line—a few at first, and then more. The village was bigger than they thought. Pale strips of light escaped from shutters and the smell of woodsmoke was carried on the wind.

They rounded a snowy crag and came face-to-face with a band of armed men. Andris and Mafrey rode in the middle. Borlin's bow was out of its sheath in an instant.

"Don't shoot!" cried Andris.

Crayne raised an open palm, halting his archers. His glance took in the half-dozen mounted men. "Release my brethren, or be shot where you stand." The steel in his voice cut straight through the snow.

Andris urged his horse forward. "They haven't captured us, Crayne. They're just escorting us back."

"They're Highwall men," hissed Tawl to Jack. "Silver and maroon."

Highwall? What business did the Wall have seventy leagues northwest of Camlee? Jack moved ahead of Tawl. Crayne was speaking to one of the armed band and he wanted to hear what was being said.

"Yes," said Crayne, "Tawl of the Lowlands and Jack of the Four Kingdoms."

The man nodded. "Come with us."

Jack shot a glance at Tawl. The knight shrugged: he had no idea what was going on, either. The party began to move forward. Crayne still held on to his spear, but he seemed content to follow the men. The path began to widen out and the village soon came into view.

Nestled between two hills, it was saved from the bite of the wind. Thickly timbered cabins dotted the slopes, and three-story houses clustered in the valley. All the buildings had eaves and pointing roofs. There was one road: it ran from east to west along the center of the valley, tapering off abruptly when it reached a huge, fenced enclosure full of sheep. Jack didn't think he'd ever seen so many sheep in his life. There were thousands of them, their backs daubed with red and blue markings.

The armed men led them to the largest building in sight. A sign creaked over the door, but Jack couldn't read what it said.

As soon as they came to a standstill, Crayne beckoned Jack and Tawl over "There's a man inside who wants to speak to both of you."

"Who?"

Crayne shook his head. "They wouldn't say. I think we should all go in together."

"I agree," said Tawl. "Where did these men come from?"

"Bren. They escaped from the battlefield."

"They were lucky not to be picked up by Kylock's forces," said Jack.

"They probably stayed close to the mountains." Crayne jumped from his horse, signaling the rest of the party to do likewise. He looked over at the tavern and then back to Jack and Tawl. "I don't expect any trouble in here, but the first sign of anything strange and we're all coming out. Is that clear?"

Jack nodded. He didn't feel in any danger. Almost without being aware of what he was doing, he had sniffed for sorcery in the air. Nothing sinister was lying in wait for them. He walked forward toward the tavern door, the armed men moving ahead of him, Tawl and Crayne behind.

After the freezing cold darkness of the night, the tavern's warmth and brightness were shocking. Jack was dazzled by the light, his senses overpowered by the smells, sights, and sounds. The aroma of roasted meat and onions wafted through the low-ceilinged room. The place was packed with men wearing maroon and silver. Gaunt-faced, hollow-eyed, they fell silent as Jack moved amongst them.

"Up here," said the one who was leading the way.

Jack followed him to the back of the tavern and up a flight of narrow stairs. Tawl was at his heels. They came to a curved oak door. Two men guarded the way.

The taller man held out a restraining arm. "Wait here." He went inside the room. After a moment he came out with another man.

"Jack, Tawl, come inside."

It took Jack a moment to recognize the figure in front

of him. It was Grift. His voice was the same as ever, but the face and body were changed beyond recognition. He had lost a great amount of weight. His double chin had gone, his once chubby cheeks were now slack, and dark circles ringed his eyes. "Come on," he said. "Lord Maybor's waiting for you."

Melli lay on the bed and held the pillow to her stomach. Sometimes, if she closed her eyes tight enough and hugged the pillow hard enough, she could imagine her baby was still there. Other times she fell asleep with the pillow beneath her, and in the morning when she awoke there was a moment of pure joy. Those were the moments she lived for; those fragments of seconds, those blinks of an eye, when the past eight days were lost inside her mind.

Tonight there was no forgetting. The pillow was just a pillow, her belly just a curve, time was too rigid to be changed and her mind too sharp to let go. There was nothing except the emptiness in her stomach and the terrible, aching soreness in her breasts.

Milk soaked through her bodice. Sticky, slow to dry, it seeped from her breasts, running down along her rib cage, forming dark stains on the fabric of her dress. Melli couldn't bear it. She reeked like a wet nurse.

In one quick movement, she made a fist and slammed it into the pillow. She felt the blow in her stomach and didn't care. Again and again she brought down her fist, pummeling the soft fabric with all her might. Nothing mattered anymore. Nothing.

Bringing up her second fist, she struck the pillow as hard as she could. *Crack!* A blinding pain coursed up her arm. Melli's face crumpled and quick tears flared. She slumped against the bed, cradling her broken arm against her chest. She had forgotten how fragile it was. Now she had rebroken it before it had a chance to heal.

When the pain subsided to a dull throb, Melli ran her

fingers over the bone. An uneven swelling jutted out against the skin of her forearm. It was too dark to see anything except the outline, so she wouldn't be able to do anything until first light. She had made a halfhearted attempt to reset the bone a few days earlier, but she didn't know the first thing about physicianing, and the pain she experienced trying to force the bones to meet smoothly had been frightening enough to make her give up. Tomorrow she would try and fix a splint.

Melli knew she wouldn't get any help from Mistress Greal or Kylock—she hadn't seen either of those two since the night she had given birth—but the guards outside the door might be persuaded to cut her a length of wood. She would ask them when they brought her breakfast in the morning.

Melli stopped herself in the midst of her planning. Here she was, thinking how to fix her arm with as little discomfort as possible, while her baby was dead—torn away from her before it had taken its first breath. She hadn't even seen its face, didn't know if it was a boy or a girl. Suddenly, every thought she spent on her own survival seemed like a betrayal. *Her* life was carrying on, and more than just allowing it to, she was actively protecting it.

A dark shroud fell over Melli's thoughts. Guilt and shame were its rough-woven fabric. Was it wrong for her to want to survive? Was she being callous and self-centered by thinking of herself?

Keys jangled on the other side of the door. A sliver of light stole across the floor. The door opened and light flooded in. Kylock stepped into the room bearing an oil lamp in front of him.

Melli sat up on the bed. Her right arm fell to her lap with a sharp, streaking pain. Seeing Kylock's shadowed face in the doorway banished all doubts from her mind. She had to survive. Give up now and she would be used as a depository for all of Kylock's sins. He wasn't going to renew himself by coupling with her. He had done too many things, sanctioned too many deaths, set her brother against her father, and allowed Baralis to murder her child: he couldn't be allowed to wash himself clean.

Taking a deep breath of light-filled air, Melli leant forward and said, "Go away. You seek me out too soon, my lord."

Surprise flitted across Kylock's face. He put the lamp down on the table and walked toward the bed.

Melli brought her hand up to halt him. "Come no nearer. I am not ready for you yet."

"Oh, but you are." Kylock's voice was seductive, his movements as careful as a lover's. His gaze lingered over the damp patches of milk on her bodice. "I've given you a week, there's no need for more time."

Melli crossed her hands high on her chest, covering up the stains. Her breasts ached with a dull, sickening pain. "I need longer," she said, scouring her thoughts for a plausible reason. She wanted to shock him, to throw him off guard. "You can't come near me yet. I haven't healed inside. You wanted me clean and pure, but right now I'm filthy with old blood and old scars. You must wait until I am fully mended, or risk failure and infection if you don't." Melli relished every word she was saying. For the first time in many months she felt her old power returning. She was Maybor's daughter: confident and in command.

Kylock recognized it, too: she could see it in his eyes. He believed her.

"I will give you another week."

"No. I need ten days." Melli tilted her chin upward and fixed him with her dark blue eyes. She had no reason for naming ten days—it was just another way to reassert her power.

"Very well. Ten." Kylock didn't seem annoyed; if anything he seemed excited.

Melli was repulsed. "Please go now. I need to rest."

Kylock stood over the bed, looking at her through black-banded eyes, a trace of a smile upon his lips. After a moment he turned and left.

As soon as the door closed behind him, Melli fell back amongst the covers. She was physically and emotionally drained. Shaking from head to foot, pain snaking down her arm, she drew the sheets up to her neck and immediately began to fall asleep. Just as she was about to slide into the blissful darkness, a thought drifted down from above: she hadn't asked Kylock what had happened to her baby. It had not occurred to her once.

Grift ushered them into a small, hot room. A mighty fire blazed high in the hearth and the windows had been hung with woolen blankets. A low pallet lay in the corner and upon it rested a man. A soft, rasping sound escaped from his lips and his chest rose and fell very fast.

"Jack, Tawl," murmured the man. "Come close so I can see you."

Jack crossed the room and knelt beside the pallet. Blue eyes the same color as Melli's looked up at him from a face slick with sweat.

"It is you," he said, shutting his eyes for a moment. "They told me it was."

Jack searched the man's face for signs of the old Maybor. His full lips were shrunk to lines, his red jowls now pale. There was so little of the man left that Jack could hardly bear to look at him. Grift stepped forward and dabbed Maybor's brow, and as he drew back with the cloth, he nudged Maybor's hair into place. That small gesture made Jack look again—not just at Maybor's face, but the whole man.

His hair was shiny and beautifully brushed, his chin shaven smooth, fine red silk was wrapped around his shoulders, and the smell of fragrance escaped from beneath the sheets. Jack smiled softly. There was more of Maybor left than he thought.

"You escaped from Kylock's forces at Bren?" Tawl came and knelt by Jack's side.

Maybor nodded. "We stayed in the mountains for a few weeks and then made our way down." He spoke so softly that Jack and Tawl had to lean forward to hear him.

"How many men are here with you?"

"Eighty survived. I lost more than that number in the mountains." Maybor began to cough. His whole body jerked with each strained rasp of his throat. A hand came up from under the sheets; the skin was black and shiny, the fingers curled into a misshapen fist.

Jack had to look away. Tawl's eyes met his. They both knew Maybor was dying.

Grift came over with a cloth for Maybor to spit into. The guard was careful to fold it well before taking it away.

After a moment Maybor's cough subsided. When he spoke, each phrase was punctuated with a wheezing breath. "There's ten horses as well. The villages will sell us some. I had one of the men count them—said there's eighteen horses and double that in ponies."

Jack was beginning to understand what he had in mind. "What state are the men in?" he asked.

Maybor made a small gesture with his ruined hand while he cleared his throat. "They're young. A few lost fingers and toes, but most of them are fine." He leant a fraction forward. "Take them with you, Jack. They're good lads who need a chance to fight. I thought I was doing the right thing by leading them off the field, but now I know it was wrong. I stopped them from being soldiers and made them men, instead."

Jack didn't hesitate. "If they're willing and able they can come with us. We need all the help we can get."

"They know some fine songs, Jack," said Maybor, swallowing hard. "And they're not afraid of long hours on the move."

After Maybor had finished speaking, his facial muscles relaxed and his eyes started to close. Tawl touched him lightly on the chest. "What was the last thing you heard about Melli?"

"She's alive. I'll swear to it." Maybor's eyes sprung open and his voice rang clear. He looked first to Tawl and then to Jack. "You've got to save her. Promise me you'll save her."

Tawl reached forward and took Maybor's hand. He ran his fingers over flesh that had died on the bone. "I promise you I'll try." His words were as gentle as a kiss.

Jack brought his hand to rest on top of Tawl's. He looked straight into Maybor's shining eyes. "I promise I will not rest until she's safe."

Maybor nodded slowly. His body seemed to diminish, growing smaller and less substantial. He settled back against the pillows and said, in a voice that faded with every word, "You should have seen her when the guards came to the cellar, Jack. She was so beautiful, kicking up a holy storm—for me. Just for me."

Grift came forward and stroked back his hair. The guard's hand shook as he smoothed the lustrous gray locks.

Jack took Maybor's hand and placed it against his side. "Melli loved you very much."

"Did she?" Weak though Maybor was, there was an urgency in those two words that spoke of bright, rekindled hope. "Tell her I loved her more than she knew. Tell her I'm sorry I failed."

Jack shook his head. A hard lump was rising in his throat. "You didn't fail."

"I failed all of my children. All of them." Maybor's voice was a thin line receding into the distance. "I was too selfish, too ambitious, to see them for . . . " His last words were stolen by a series of choking coughs.

Grift took Jack's arm. "Go. I'll be out later."

Jack and Tawl moved toward the door. The sound of

Maybor's coughing followed them out of the room.

They waited outside the door in silence until the coughing tapered off. After a few minutes, Grift emerged. He looked tired and pale. "Lord Maybor's sleeping now," he said. "Come on, let's find you both a drink."

Grift led them down into the tavern. Once again the room fell silent, but this time all eyes were on Grift.

"He's sleeping," he said to the men, making a calming gesture with his hands.

Hearing this, the men nodded and whispered and turned back to their business, more than a few of them calling for more ale.

Grift led Jack and Tawl to a table near the door. Crayne and the other knights were sitting close by; they all had bowls filled with hot food in front of them and mugs full of beer in their hands.

Seeing them settling down, Nabber left the knights' table and came to sit at Tawl's side. Grift seemed surprised to see the young pocket and rubbed the boy's hair affectionately. "Well, I would never have thought I'd find you in the mountains, Nabber," he said.

"Never thought I'd find you here, either, Grift. Especially after you telling me that mountain girls were sour tempered and prone to the ghones."

Jack didn't expect Grift to laugh, but he did. A warm, hearty laugh that brought back memories so sharp that Jack wanted to cry. All those winter nights spent in the servants' hall listening to Grift holding court while marveling at how he held his ale. Everything had changed so much from those innocent days: Grift had changed, Tawl had changed, Maybor lay dying, and Melli was imprisoned in Bren. Anger pushed Jack's memories back, squeezing them into a long gone past. Baralis had a lot to answer for.

"Lord Maybor saved my life," said Grift. He leant over the table, resting his chin in his cupped palm. "He dragged me out of Bren when I was so sick I could hardly walk. He could have left me in the wine cellar and gone under the wall on his own, but he didn't."

Jack put an arm around Grift's shoulders. Why was everyone who once looked so strong now so frail? "What happened to Bodger?"

"I don't know. They took him with the Lady Melliandra." Grift shook his head. "He's just a young one, really. Wouldn't know what to do without me around to tell him."

"People find all sorts of strength inside themselves when they need to," Jack said.

"Aye, lad, you're right there. Take Lord Maybor. The man's been running a high fever these past couple of days, yet nothing was going to stop him from bringing us down that mountain. Determination alone kept him sitting on that horse. All the men resented him at first, but once they saw for themselves what he was made of, everything changed. They'd do anything for him now."

"Maybor wants us to take them to Bren," said Tawl.

"He feels he wronged them by withdrawing to the mountains. He wants to give them a chance to fight."

"What happened at the battle?" asked Jack. Someone had brought a flagon of ale and he began to pour it into four mugs.

"Highwall was flanked then slaughtered. Besik led two-thirds of the men to the east; Maybor led a third to the south. It was chaos. Men being slaughtered, arrows flying, blood everywhere—I'll never forget it till the end of my days." Grift downed his ale. "The bloodshed wasn't the worst thing, though."

"Why? What else happened?"

"Kedrac sent men to slay his own father. He was commanding the kingdoms' army, and as soon as he spotted Maybor on the field, he ordered the Royal Guard to go after him."

Baralis again. Setting father against son. There were so many tragedies, not just of cities and armies, but more intimate ones as well: ideals shattered, loves lost, families torn apart. Jack couldn't begin to imagine how Maybor must have felt knowing his son wanted him dead. How had he survived the long weeks since the battle with such a betrayal lying heavy on his heart? Jack's memory of Maybor was of a brash and vital man who always wanted the best for his children—even if they didn't want it themselves. A father who showed his love through pride. How did such a man cope with the treachery of his first-born son?

No one spoke for a while after that. Tawl, Grift, Nabber, and Jack downed the last of their ale in silence. Words seemed far too slender to span all the tragedies of life.

Maybor was very warm and his bones ached little now. Strange, but he could still feel the fingers that had been destroyed by the frost. In a way he felt them the most.

All the things he had lost he felt the most.

Melli, Kedrac, his two youngest boys: if he thought very hard he could conjure them up. If he thought even harder he could imagine their forgiveness.

Sleep tugged him downward, though, and he knew it was time to go. With one last great effort, he turned his head so that it lay perfectly straight on the pillow—no one would catch *him* drooling like an invalid—and brought his hands to rest at either side of his body. *Stately,* he told himself. *Like a king.*

With eyes already closed and strength drained by his exertions, the natural thing to do was to follow the darkened curve. A little bit frightened and very much tired, Maybor let his mind be carried off to sleep.

Later, much later, when Jack was asleep in the tavern kitchen, his body pressed close to the stove, he was awakened by a strange noise. At first he thought it was the wolves howling, and then perhaps the wind. But as his senses came around, he realized that it was the sound of men singing. Low, throaty notes were followed by long pauses and hoarse cries. Someone was keeping a primitive beat, and above it all, one voice soared high and clear.

Jack felt a wave of cold air roll over his body. It was a death song. The Highwall troops were singing for Maybor.

He opened his eyes, and in the dimming light of a long-lit fire, he locked gazes with Tawl. The knight's expression was solemn, his eyes midnight dark.

"Jack," he murmured, "you and I have a lot of fighting to do."

Jack nodded. He knew how Tawl was feeling, and felt exactly the same way, too: Baralis had finally taken one of their own.

Thirty

Jack awoke to a sinking sensation in his stomach. The events of the night before came back to him in a vivid rush. He remembered falling asleep to the sound of mourning, drifting off as the men of Highwall sang for Maybor's soul. They keened until dawn; Jack knew it because he had heard them in his dreams.

Now he awoke to a different sound, one that pulled at his senses with all the power of the past. It was the sound of the kitchen: scraping, chopping, pots rattling, brooms sweeping, fat sizzling, and chickens clucking. It was like being at Castle Harvell all over again. Jack opened his eyes. A large white-clad woman hovered over him.

"About time, too," she said. "Wake your friends up and get from under my feet. Sleeping by my oven, indeed! What was Master Tallyrod thinking? Haven't I got enough to cope with already? There's so many men sleeping in the tavern hall I swear I haven't seen a floorboard in a week. And I know Ginty hasn't. That girl's so busy flirting with every man in a maroon coat that she's just plain forgotten what a floor looks like."

Jack smiled up at the woman. "I'm sorry. If there's anything I can do to help?"

"Take those men out from under my feet and I'll be your friend for life. Might even treat you to a nip of my special brew."

"You've got a deal." He stood up and shook Tawl, Nabber, and Andris awake. The other knights were sleeping in the stables.

The white-clad woman was as good as her word—better, even. By the time everyone had wiped the sleep from their eyes, buckled their belts, and rolled up their packs, the kitchen mistress had laid out a breakfast feast: warm bread, cold chicken, damp cheese, and special brew. Her one stipulation was that the feast be eaten in the hall. Jack had picked up his platter to follow the others when she put a hand on his arm.

"Now, if you can just get rid of those maroons for me."

Jack laughed. The kitchen mistress' kindness filled him with a simple joy. There were so many good people in the world, and so much more than vengeance worth fighting for.

The kitchen mistress kissed Jack firmly on the cheek. "Hold on a minute while I find a little extra chicken for your plate." She dashed off to the larder and came back wielding a pair of matching drumsticks, which she promptly deposited on Jack's plate. "There. That should keep you going through the day."

Jack put down his plate and gave the woman a big hug. "I'll be taking those maroons out of your way."

"Aye, lad. Be sure to leave me a couple, though. A woman needs someone to cook for."

The main hall was cold. The men of Highwall had mourned until the embers had died in the hearth, and no one wanted to be the first to bring a new flame to the fire.

Jack and Tawl ate in silence. The atmosphere in the room was subdued; the men were gaunt-faced, pale, tired. The rest of the knights came in from the stables, and Crayne came to sit at Jack's side.

"What's happening?" he whispered.

"Maybor's dead. He asked us to use his troops."

Crayne glanced around the room. "These men are in no fit state to travel today. They're exhausted."

Jack nodded. "They'll have to follow us. It will take them a full day to get enough mounts together, and we can't afford to wait that long."

Tawl looked up from his breakfast. "They can ride behind us to Bren. Once there, they can lie low on the eastern plains until we need them."

"Tyren's camped outside the city," said Crayne.

"East or south?"

"South, a full league from the gate." Unblinking, Crayne looked straight into Tawl's eyes.

The two regarded each other for a long moment, and then Tawl's hand came up to rest on Crayne's shoulder. When he spoke, his voice was oddly strained. "How many men has he got with him?"

Crayne shook his head. "I can't be sure. Could be three hundred, could be more."

Suddenly Jack realized what had passed between them: by giving Tawl privileged information about Tyren's camp, Crayne had denounced Tyren as his leader. His acceptance of Tawl was now complete.

The two men carried on talking as if nothing had happened. When Jack glanced at Tawl next, the knight was looking at the Highwall troops with renewed interest. Jack got the distinct feeling he was doing a head count.

Crayne and Tawl were now fighting men once more, discussing strategies, weaponry, and numbers. Deciding the best way to take Tyren's camp.

"Our priority is to get inside the palace," Jack reminded them. Tawl had long had his own agenda with the knighthood, but since he'd taken the leap over the falls it had turned into a burning cause. Whatever it was, Jack couldn't allow it to interfere with saving Melli and eliminating Kylock.

Tawl gave Jack a pointed glance. "Don't worry," he said. "I know what my priorities are."

Crayne and Andris exchanged looks.

Nabber, whom no one had noticed wandering off, came bounding back to the table. "Grift's upstairs, Tawl. He wants to talk to you and Jack."

Jack stood up, and after a moment Tawl followed him. Together they climbed the stairs. As they reached the top step, Tawl pulled Jack aside. "Look," he said, "I know what we've got to do. I know what *you've* got to do, I know what *I've* got to do. Marod's prophecy and my oath to the duke come first—don't doubt that—but I just want you to know that I will try to rid the knighthood of Tyren. I haven't got a choice. As long as there's blood in my body I'll do it."

"What happened at Lake Ormon, Tawl?" Jack spoke softly. He respected Tawl's determination, but he needed to know the reason behind it.

Tawl stared at the floor. His chest rose and fell many times before he spoke. "I found what I've spent the last six years searching for: a chance to make up for the past. I caused the death of my family, Jack. Two sisters, two beautiful golden-haired sisters and a chubby little baby who always looked up at the sound of my name." Tawl's voice began to break. "I abandoned them—just left them, just took off and left them."

He ran his hand over his face. A minute passed in silence as he tried to control his emotions, and when he finally spoke again his voice was altogether different from before. "They were helpless without me, Jack. Helpless. I should have known better. I was *old* enough to know better. I knew the hands I left them in weren't safe."

A tight coil of self-accusation lay just below the knight's words and Jack knew that he was out of his depth. Tawl's pain was something he could neither begin to understand nor measure. Touching Tawl's arm lightly, he said, "I won't stop you from doing what you have to."

Tawl's eyes were bright. A muscle in his cheek was pumping hard. "That's all I'll ever ask from you, Jack."

Jack smiled. He wished very much he had more to give. "Come on," he said, laying a hand on Tawl's back. "Let's go and see Maybor one last time."

Grift was waiting for them outside the door. Seeing him in the harsh morning light, Jack was once again shocked at how much he had changed. The once portly guard was as lean as a pick. It was a day for touching and being touched, and Jack came forward and wrapped his arms around Grift's shoulders.

"He died without pain, you know. Just slipped away in his sleep." A huge tear slid down Grift's cheek. "He was a brave man. Some will try and tell you he was vain, others will say he was a devil, but don't ever listen to them. You go to the Lady Melliandra and tell her her father was a hero. That's the truth, and every man under this roof will tell you the same."

"I know, Grift. I know."

Grift opened the door to Maybor's room and let them in. The sheets had been changed on the pallet, and Maybor's body rested on top of them, his arms folded over his chest, a red silk robe draped across his torso. His face had lost its color, but his hair was still shiny and the skin on his cheeks looked newly shaved.

"Here." Grift handed Jack a small cloth bag. "That's the rings and the torc he wore for battle. He wants them to go to the villages to help pay for the horses and the lodgings. He signed them a note, too. Promising payment in full from his son."

Jack slipped the bag into his tunic. "Do you think Kedrac will honor it?"

"I doubt it, but that's not important. Maybor died believing he would, and that's what counts."

"But surely after what happened at the battle—"

"No. Maybor was adamant his son would honor his memory—by leaving this note he's offering Kedrac a chance to be forgiven. He doesn't want his son to go through life thinking his father went to his grave hating him." There was more than a touch of pride in Grift's voice, and Jack realized that the castle guard must have grown close to Maybor. "I know Kedrac," he continued, "and he may be headstrong and impressionable now, but one day he'll be sorry for what he did. And by giving him a chance to pay the villagers and the tavern-keeper, Maybor is offering him a way to make amends when that day comes."

Jack tried to think of a suitable reply, but he searched for words in vain. He had little to say on the subject of fathers.

Strangely it was Tawl who spoke. His voice hadn't recovered from his confession on the stairs, and his tone was rough and low. "Maybor was a good man to think of his son. Not all fathers would care enough to spare their sons from guilt."

Tawl's face was grim. Jack wondered what else lay in his past besides the death of his sisters. Why weren't his father and mother there to help him? Why were there always so many layers of grief and pain hidden within families?

Grift came forward to usher them from the room. "You'll be leaving today?"

"Yes," said Jack. "We'll meet next in Bren."

Grift nodded. He seemed very old to Jack all of a sudden. Old and small. "May Borc bless your journey," he said.

"And yours, Grift."

Just as he walked through the doorway, Tawl turned and said, "I want to be able to give Melli something of her father's."

Without a word, Grift moved over to Maybor's body and cut off a lock of his hair. He bound it with a strip of silk from his tunic and handed it to Tawl. Silver hair, red silk—it was Maybor through and through.

Baralis was worried about Skaythe. The man had not responded to his sending. It had been over a week now since their last communication, and Baralis was beginning to think that something had happened to him.

After all, no one could ignore him for that long. Certainly not a man like Skaythe.

Measuring a thumbnail of the mind-freeing drug into the palm of his hand, Baralis swallowed it dry. Only when the bitter taste of the drug had gone from his tongue did he see fit to take a sip of wine. Such small acts of willpower had helped make him who he was today.

Baralis raised his hand, and Crope, who was busy sealing the shutter cracks with carded wool, came over and saw to the fire. By the time the flame was high, Baralis was ready with the compound. Blood, leaf, and drug moved within a copper bowl, swirling in time with the motion of his palms. From his heavily cushioned chair, he inhaled the toxic fumes. As always there was a brief instant when his body fought him tooth and nail. The physical world detested relinquishing its mastery to the dark.

Baralis' thoughts shifted out of place. His point of consciousness rose above his body, as insubstantial and weightless as pollen on the breeze. Up and up he went, passing through stone as if it were water, and water as if it were air. He skimmed the great lake to gain momentum and circled the city to catch the scent. Skaythe's responses to his sending had left a trail, a trace of sorcery that could be followed like a thread through a maze. Baralis sniffed him out, then tracked him down: Skaythe would not ignore him tonight.

South he went, high above the mountains, well above the clouds. The moon shed light but not warmth on his back, and the stars glinted like beacons upon his soul. They would have him for their own if they could. Not tonight, though. Not ever if he had his way.

Skaythe had left a tenuous trail. Weak to begin with, the past ten days had reduced it to a broken line. Baralis was a hound on the scent of blood, and then a scholar making guesses. The last time he had heard from Skaythe was after Valdis had captured the baker's boy and the renegade knight. Skaythe had intended to follow them north and, as soon as he had a chance, assassinate both of the fugitives. That was what the man had said, anyway. Baralis was beginning to suspect that Skaythe had a drama of his own to play.

Still, no matter what happened to Skaythe, Baralis knew he could count on the knighthood to bring the fugitives to Bren. At least Tyren would not fail him.

Baralis continued soaring southward along the Divide. Gradually he began to make his way down. The peaks were like spearheads below him, the stars like pinheads above. The trail was stronger now, and he followed it lower, the cold mountain mist brushing against his mind. Eventually he came to the area where Skaythe had last communicated with him. It was an exposed hillside at the foot of the Divide. There was nothing to tell of his passing. No sign of anything amiss.

Gathering his wits and his perceptions about him, Baralis *pulled in* the air to the north. He was searching for a physical trail now. The vestiges of sorcery would be too weak to track. Slowly, Baralis began to make his way northward again. This time he used all his senses, spotting signs of campfires well dampened, sighting paths most likely to be taken, catching whiffs of old horse dung on the breeze.

Just as he approached the cool depths of Lake Ormon, Baralis felt a glimmer of Skaythe again. A tiny speck long stale. Swooping down to the mineral-green surface of the lake, he tried to hone in on the scent. It was as if the power was dissolved into the water itself. Puzzled, Baralis spread himself out and skirted along the waterline.

He could feel himself weakening. He had been out too long and his body was calling him back. Ignoring the warnings, he carried on, plunging in and out of the water, tearing through dried reed beds and leafless shrubs, racing along the shore. The trail went no farther than the lake, so the answers had to be here for the finding.

Finally he came to a grassy bank. The scent was a fraction stronger and Baralis tracked it down. At the water's edge, under the shade of an old mountain ash, half in, half out of the water, lay the partially frozen body of Skaythe. Dead. An arrow in his heart.

It seemed Skaythe had drawn his power at the moment of death, and with neither the time nor strength to send it further, the icy water of Lake Ormon had claimed it for its own. Death drawings had a way of lingering long after the corpse was cold, working their quiet intent until their potency was lost to time. This one was weaker, but no different, than most.

A sharp spasm racked through Baralis' thoughts. He didn't have much time now. His flesh was cold and soulless and it couldn't survive much longer without a mind to give it meaning.

Just as he turned to go, Baralis took a quick glance at the arrow in Skaythe's heart. A dark thrill passed over him. It wasn't just any arrow: the yellow-and-black fletchings were an emblem of Valdis. The knights sent to capture Jack and Tawl had shot down Skaythe.

It could be a random shooting of an intruder, but why then was the body in the lake and not on a hillside near a camp? Baralis gave in to the pull of his blood and began the journey back to Bren. He had no eyes for the moon or the clouds or the stars, no thoughts to spare on the firmament. He saw only the yellow-and-black fletchings of an arrow loosed by Valdis. What possible reason could the knighthood have for coming to the defense of Jack and Tawl?

Tavalisk was studying. It was making him hungry, irritable, and sore. He had craned his neck over so many books now that it clicked whenever he moved. Sounded like a damn cricket in his collar!

Slamming his current book closed, Tavalisk pulled on the bell rope. It was time for a stiff but sweet drink, a large dinner, and his daily dose of Gamil. Studying was for lesser mortals, and as archbishop it was his moral obligation to free up his mind for higher pursuits. Which meant he might just ask Gamil to do his research for him.

After a commendably short period of time, his aide appeared at the door. Not only had he been speedy, but he had also been resourceful. He came bearing a platter of hot food.

"Aah, Gamil. Come in, come in. Just the man I was hoping for. Bring that tray straight over here." Tavalisk patted the desktop. "Any wine on you, by the way?"

"Alas no, Your Eminence. I only have one pair of hands."

"Hmm, you really should look into that." Tavalisk took a duck egg from the platter. "Any news of Kylock's army?"

"They reached Camlee four days ago, Your Eminence. I received a message on the leg of a bird that stated the army attacked the moment it arrived."

"Camlee won't be able to hold up to a full-scale army for very long. I'll give them six weeks at the most."

"Less, perhaps, if Valdis sends troops from the south."

The duck egg turned to sawdust in the archbishop's mouth. Of course Tyren would send troops from Valdis. Why hadn't he thought of it sooner? He spat out the egg into a cloth. "This is ill news."

"There's more, Your Eminence," said Gamil with a touch of relish. "All the towns and villages between Bren and Camlee have been ravished. Kylock's forces seized all their livestock and grain for army supplies. The reports I've received tell of people being killed by the thousands, of villages being burnt to the ground, and women raped and defiled. It sounds as if Kylock is allowing Kedrac free rein to do whatever he pleases."

"No. Not free rein, Gamil. Kylock will be actively

encouraging Kedrac to ravish the northeast. The young king knows the value of fear." Tavalisk was looking around for a drink. There was nothing on his desk except a jug of water. It would have to do.

"Fear, Your Eminence?"

"Yes. Word will spread that Kylock's forces are brutal and merciless. People will soon surrender to him rather than risk his wrath. At the end of the day, an occupied town is better than no town at all." Tavalisk drank his water. It tasted quite strange without a decent measure of wine. "Of course, the other thing fear is good for is keeping conquered cities in line. A man's not going to risk revolt if he thinks his wife and children might be killed."

"Your Eminence is most wise."

Tavalisk glanced up at his aide. There was no sign of irony on his face. He made a quick decision. "Maybe not as wise as I thought, Gamil."

"How so, Your Eminence?"

"You know Marod's prophecy, the one that starts with men of honor?"

"Certainly, Your Eminence. The verse that names you as the chosen one?"

Tavalisk waved an arm. "Yes. Yes. That's it. Recently I've been wondering about the authenticity of the verse. Its origin, its wording, and so forth." The archbishop took a pause. This sort of thing wasn't easy for him. "I'm beginning to think that I might have been wrong. Only thinking, mind."

"Why, Your Eminence?"

"This business with Kylock is getting out of hand. He's becoming too strong, too powerful. Short of a knife in his heart, I don't think there's any way to stop him. The other southern cities will never join forces with Rorn to defeat him—they're too busy thinking about their own personal interests. They're not going to take action until he's right on their doorsteps. And by then it will be too late." Tavalisk's chubby cheeks were quivering. "Our only hope is that Kylock will draw the line at Camlee."

"I think he will for the time being, Your Eminence. After all, he'll have Highwall and Annis to take care of once spring comes."

"Time being! Time being! What about time coming? What about all the years ahead? What about ten, twenty, *thirty* years of springs? Kylock is young—he has a lifetime ahead of him. He could take over the entire continent before he finds his grave."

Gamil was looking worried. It was unusual for Tavalisk to become so animated. "What can we do about it, Your Eminence?"

The archbishop let out a heavy sigh. "We must do whatever is expedient. Rorn must survive intact, that much is certain, but how such a thing will be managed is anything but clear. Up until now it was my natural inclination—and my Marod-given duty—to fight Kylock's forces. However, I'm beginning to suspect that such a course of action may not be in Rorn's best interest."

"An occupied town is better than no town at all?"

"Exactly. If I stick my head up and openly oppose Kylock, who knows what he will do to Rorn?" Tavalisk was thinking more of himself than Rorn at this point, but he knew it was prudent to link the two. "Now, say I *am* the chosen one in Marod's prophecy, then ultimately I can be sure of prevailing. But if I'm not, then I risk ruining Rorn's livelihood in the pursuit of a misdirected dream."

"Aah," said Gamil slowly, "I see Your Eminence's dilemma."

"It is Rorn's dilemma, too," reprimanded Tavalisk. He would not have his fate separated from Rorn. They were one and the same. "So, I need to know for sure if I am the chosen one. And that's where you come in, Gamil. I want you to discover all you can about Marod and his prophesying, and find out just how accurate he is. I need to know if I am reading things right."

Gamil bowed. "I would be honored to do such a task, Your Eminence."

"Good. You can start today." Tavalisk pushed all the various charts, manuscripts, and books on his desk over toward Gamil. "Here. These should be enough to be getting along with."

They rode north through the day and much of the night. Maybor's death had given them a new impetus. It made them realize they weren't playing a game. Real people were dying. The little village in the valley was full of men, women, and children whose lives would soon be shattered. Kylock's forces would take whatever they wanted and tear the rest apart. Nothing was safe from them now.

Jack's blood itched. He felt it coursing through his heart, ribboning along his cheeks. His desire to get to Kylock was becoming a physical need; he had to see him face-to-face and, with his own hands, destroy him.

Jack rode at the head of the party—he couldn't bear to be at the back. Maybor had died and that meant Melli could die, too. They weren't immortals anymore. None of them.

They had to get to Bren before it was too late.

Their route brought them down from the foothills and onto the plains. They rode through frost-tipped fields and white-green meadows, along frozen mud roads and cattle paths thick with dung. The land was quiet, deserted, the smell of burning lingered in the air. Occasionally they would catch glimpses of farms and villages, their charred timbers black against the icy landscape. They were traveling in Kedrac's wake.

Eventually they fell upon the army's path. Thousands upon thousands of footprints stamped in the light snow. Debris lay on both sides of the path: pots, pans, fragments of tunics, sandals, boxes, jewelry—scraps of people's lives, plundered then discarded.

Two hours after finding the path, they came upon a camp. The smell warned them away. Tawl wanted to ride around it, but Crayne insisted they stop and investigate. There was the usual wreckage—burnt ground, hacked trees, decaying food, and human waste—but at the back, in a shallow ditch hidden by a cluster of bushes, lay the bodies of thirty women. Their naked limbs were smeared with blood, ice, and mud. Their hair had been shorn from their heads, their breasts sliced open, and their sexual organs were black with clotted blood.

Every man in the party crossed themselves. Borlin took his shield from his horse and, using it as a spade, began to dig up the frozen earth. Crayne joined in, then Andris and the rest.

Their journey was halted for an hour whilst they covered the bodies with soil. None of the knights spoke, but their faces gave it all away. At the shore of Lake Ormon they had taken Tawl into their hearts, and now, today, they finally rejected Tyren. No one dared say it, yet all of them knew: there were knights in the party that had camped here.

They rode faster after that. They wanted the campsite well behind them.

The moon was a fitful splinter that peeked out from behind heavy clouds. A fair breeze was blowing and there was an occasional speckling of snow. After the freezing, windy conditions in the foothills, the plains seemed almost mild. The horses were put under less strain so they could ride longer between rests. Jack set a hard pace, but the knights were always just one step behind.

North and west they rode, changing course as the land permitted. The mountains of the Divide were shrouded in gray mist, and as the night wore on the mist stole across the foothills and down onto the plains, making the horses nervous and dampening everyone's gear and cloaks. Jack slowed his horse down to a trot and looked for a place to make camp.

In the dark band between mist and cloud, time and distance were difficult to judge. Jack had no idea how long or far they traveled before finding a place to stop. Grass for the horses wasn't a problem as they had picked up grain in the village, but tree cover was important and fresh water a must. Finally they came upon a knot of gnarled oaks; not quite a wood, larger than a grove, Borlin called it a *bosk*.

A narrow stream threaded its way through the trees, and Jack led his horse to drink. By the time he'd unbuckled the saddle, the knights were already building a fire. Jack liked to watch the knights make camp: they could strip branches with lightning speed and cook up something hot within minutes.

After everyone had eaten their fill, they sat around the fire, pulling their blankets close to keep out the mist and taking swigs of brandy from a flask.

"How far are we from Bren?" asked Jack, passing the flask on to Nabber.

"Eight days of hard riding. Seven, if we flog the horses." Crayne poked the fire with a stick. He was a well-built man, with a streak of gray in his dark brown hair and a glint of green in his eyes. Next to Borlin, he was the oldest in the company. "The approach to the city will slow us down. We'll have to keep an eye out for scouts. If anyone stops us, we'll have to maintain we're on Tyren's business."

"And what if we're stopped by knights?"

Crayne looked to Borlin, then Tawl, before he answered. "We'll have to kill them. We can't risk Tyren's men stopping us before we enter the city. Once word gets out that you and Tawl haven't been captured, then Tyren will come after us, Baralis will move the Lady Melliandra to someplace where we'll never find her, and Kylock will ring the city with whatever's left of his forces. Secrecy is the most important consideration if we're going to gain access to the palace."

As Crayne spoke, Jack got the distinct impression that he had talked to Tawl at some point today. His priorities had shifted from the knighthood to the palace. Jack made a mental note to thank Tawl later. It was good to have someone to depend on.

"How can we be sure where the Lady Melliandra is being held?" asked Andris.

Tawl shrugged. He had just wrestled the brandy flask off Nabber. "Once we're in the city, we'll have to split up, ask around, find out whatever we can. Someone will know where she is."

"If she is in the palace, how are we going to get to her?"

Nabber snatched the brandy flask back. "That's where I come in, Andris. I know that palace like the moles on my feet. I'll have us in there before you can strap on a breastplate." The word breastplate came out as *bwestfate*. Nabber had drunk more than his share.

Tawl handed him his water flask. "Drink all of this . . . Now!" he boomed when Nabber hesitated.

Borlin reached in his pack. "Here," he said, handing a loaf of bread around the fire. "Make him eat this as well."

"So," said Crayne, ignoring the drunken pocket. "We can gain access to the palace. We can probably get into the city—though some of us will have to go on foot to draw less attention—but what do we do once we've got the Lady Melliandra?"

"We lie low until nightfall," said Tawl, "smuggle ourselves under the wall, and then ride east to meet up with Maybor's men. Once they've arrived, we head to the south of the city and take over Tyren's camp." His words met with nods of approval from the men. Tawl seemed relieved.

Jack coughed to gain everyone's attention. "Once you've got Melli from the palace, I'll be going in to take Kylock. I won't ask anyone to follow me, and"—he looked straight at Tawl—"I don't want anyone coming back to rescue me if I don't come out. I expect you to go after Tyren."

The mist swirled around the fire, hissing when it came close to the flames. The knights were silent, waiting for Tawl's reply.

Tawl's gaze did not leave Jack's for an instant. They both knew how much was being offered. Finally he spoke: "You're a good friend, Jack. I will promise to do as you ask, though my heart might lead me astray."

Sleep was slow to come that night. Jack tossed and turned until dawn, visions of Maybor on his deathbed and the thirty women in the ditch flitting through his dreams. The knights were restless, too. Jack suspected they were thinking about Tyren and how they would soon betray him. There would be no turning back if they failed.

The night was long, the mist icy cold, and the earth beneath their blankets as hard as stone. When dawn finally showed itself as a pink tinge in the east, the party was already awake. With breaths whitening in the freezing air, and joints cracking as they rose, they collected their belongings and kicked out the fire, and headed north toward Bren.

Thirty-one

Baralis decided it was time to visit the fair Melliandra. He had just come from a meeting with Kylock, and from what he had managed to ascertain, the girl was playing games with him. The king was needed in Camlee. Kedrac was a good leader, but he didn't come close to Kylock, and for victory to be both swift and assured, Baralis knew Kylock should be there. However, Maybor's daughter had Kylock wrapped around her little finger, and he was now delaying his departure for Camlee, waiting for her to be *ready*.

Baralis didn't know or care what ready meant, but he could spot delay tactics a league away, and he knew the girl was bluffing. Which was the main reason he was going to see her: no one put pay to *his* plans.

The other reason was less substantial, but just as compelling all the same.

Baralis lit an oil lamp and, checking the fold of his robe for his copper sigiling knife, left his chambers in the dark behind him. Through corridors that were always deserted, up stairs that hadn't been swept in a year, Baralis traveled, hands curled up beneath his robes, feet making no sound to tell of his passing.

He rounded a corner and came face-to-face with Mistress Greal. Meeting her thus, Baralis realized he hadn't seen her since the night of the birthing. Over two weeks ago now.

Mistress Greal seemed surprised to see him. In her hand she had a small bowl of steaming water and in the other a lambswool blanket. "Just off to bed for the night, my lord," she said, raising the water.

"A little early for a night creature such as yourself." Baralis didn't like the look on the woman's face.

Mistress Greal attempted a simper. "Must get my beauty sleep, my lord." She bobbed a quick curtsey and scurried off.

Baralis opened his mouth to command her to stop, but the knife pressed a reminder against his thigh: he had more important things to take care of at the moment. The toothless hag was probably up to no good, but she'd had free run of the palace for the last five months, so stopping her here and now wouldn't serve much purpose. Baralis turned back to his business.

A few minutes later he climbed up the stairs to Melliandra's chamber. Situated in an unused annex just off the nobles' quarters, no one had occasion to come here. The two guards stood up when they saw him appear. Baralis could tell immediately that they had been drinking. Normally such petty transgressions wouldn't concern him, but a certain worry that had grown within his mind this past week caused him to take the men to task.

"You," he said, pointing his finger at the nearest guard. "Drink once more whilst you're on duty and I will have your fingers chopped off one by one." And then to the other man: "Seeing as you are the oldest here—and so responsible for your companion's behavior as well as your own—I will have your arms hacked off at the elbow." Both men stared at him, their eyes large with terror. "Is that clear?"

The older of the two men nodded. He began to speak.

Baralis cut him short. "No excuses. No promises. Just do as I say." Much eager nodding followed. Baralis was well pleased. "Good. Now, I want you to wait at the bottom of the stairs until I call you." The guards hesitated. *"Go!"*

Baralis watched them scurry away. When their footsteps had receded to dim patters, he took out his knife. Copper hilt, copper blade, good for little except show, it wasn't designed to slice flesh or spear meat or cut rope. It was used for scoring wood and designed for making sigils.

Sigils were warding signs marked upon doors. When scored properly, using the correct blade and the correct sequence of angles, the sigil acted as a gatekeeper. A silken thread of sorcery linked the sigil to its maker, and the slightest pull on the thread was a warning the link had been breached. Baralis had scored such markings upon the door to his own chambers in Castle Harvell. He always knew the moment anyone crossed *his* threshold and, having thought long and hard about the Valdis arrow in Skaythe's heart, he intended to have a similar arrangement here.

Placing the oil lamp down on the stone, Baralis warmed the blade in the flame. The incident at Lake Ormon had troubled him for a week now. He couldn't be certain what it meant; it might have just been an offhand killing, or it might be a sign that the knights were now in league with Jack and Tawl. At times like this, Baralis was always inclined toward caution. By his reckoning, the party should be arriving in Bren in the next few days, and if there was even a remote chance they might be free to try something, Baralis planned to make sure they would fail.

The baker's boy had to be killed. He had already destroyed Larn. He could not be allowed to destroy the empire as well.

And as for the knight—well, he had to be tried and hung for Catherine's murder. Justice was long overdue.

Baralis lifted the knife from the flame. The blade was beginning to darken and the hilt had grown hot in his palm. Bringing the tip up to the banded wooden surface of the door, Baralis began to utter the appropriate words of warding. His saliva thickened with sorcery as the chant escaped from his lips. The heated blade scored a mark three hairs deep in the wood.

The signs etched weren't as important as the angle of the blade. It was the bevel of the mark that made the sigil dance. Runes, stars, and other devices worked more as a physical deterrent rather than a magical one. Superstition alone kept most people from crossing a warded door. On first sight, though, no one would be able to tell this door was warded. Baralis made the sigil follow the grain of the wood, veering off at angles only when necessary. To a casual glance the door would look normal.

Which was exactly how Baralis wanted it. Just in case.

"We'll meet outside the Brimming Bucket at midnight," said Crayne. He made a point of meeting everyone's eyes. "If either party gets delayed or caught, or if the others don't turn up, then we continue on without them. Understood?"

Jack nodded along with the rest. They were on a dark street corner in the east side of Bren: to the left lay a cobbler's shop, to the right a dimly lit tavern with saffron-yellow shutters. It was early evening. They had passed the gate less than a quarter of an hour ago.

It had taken them seven days of hard riding to reach the city. Seven days of freezing sleet, driving winds, and morning fog. They stopped only when the horses needed rest and rode five hours past sunset every night. Burnt villages and farms dotted the horizon, and corpses and refuse littered the fields. They followed Kedrac's path all the way; it was the fastest road to Bren.

When they finally drew near the city this morning, they made a small detour north to the village of Fair Oaks. This was the place where they had arranged to meet Maybor's troops. The Highwall men would be two or three days behind them, so Crayne dropped Follis and

Mafrey off in the village to wait for their arrival. The remaining men had split into two groups. Jack, Tawl, Nabber, Crayne, and Borlin were in the first group. Andris led the others in the second. The job of the first group was to go into the city and find out all they could about Melli's whereabouts and security arrangements in the palace. Later they would meet up with the second group and decide upon a definite course of action.

No one had challenged them so far. The run up to the city had been without incident, and Jack and his party had met no problems at the gate. They had left half of their horses in Fair Oaks, and only Borlin and Nabber had been mounted when they approached the wall. Both knights had pared down their armor and weapons, and they had their circles well covered. Jack still thought they could be spotted a league away, but knights were currently welcome in Bren, and the gatekeeper hadn't batted an eye.

Tawl was the only one who caused them problems. A lot of people in the city knew what he looked like, and there weren't many men who could match his size and golden hair. He had claimed Nabber as his son, donned a felt hat, rubbed ash into his seven-day beard, and took to leaning against his horse as if he were half lame. Jack wanted to laugh when he saw him—up to that point Tawl had never looked anything less than dignified. Now, with a felt hat flopping around his ears and a fake limp dragging at his foot, he looked like an unusually large village idiot.

The disguise had worked, though. The gatekeeper had addressed his questions to the bright-looking son rather than the dim-looking father and, hearing nothing amiss, had let them pass.

The gate was heavily guarded. A dozen blackhelms stood on either side of it, and two dozen more manned the wall. When they entered the city it was the same: black-helms on every other corner, blackhelms keeping watch from the battlements. Tawl said, and Crayne agreed, that not all of the men could be fully trained, as Kedrac would have taken the best to Camlee. Still, there were enough of them to intimidate no matter what their weapons skills were, and as Jack made his way across the city, his heart was pounding fast inside his chest.

He, Tawl, and Nabber had split up from Crayne and Borlin; four grown men walking around the city together might attract unwanted attention from the blackhelms. They would meet four and a half hours later at a tavern of Nabber's choosing. Andris and the men in the second party planned to enter the city two hours before the gate was closed for the night. Their job was to acquire supplies and find lodging.

"Where should we start?" said Tawl. The brim of the felt hat cast his eyes in deep shadow. Which was just as well, thought Jack, for Tawl was constantly looking from side to side to check for blackhelms.

"Let's try and find out what happened to Lord Cravin." Jack was standing with his hands thrust into his tunic to stop them from going numb. Bren was a full winter colder than when he'd been there last. "I say we skirt close to his townhouse. Talk to a few street traders, maybe go into a couple of taverns."

Jack and Tawl both looked to Nabber. As acknowledged master of city life, any objections he could raise were invaluable. Like a true expert, Nabber knew his worth. He sucked in his breath, then let it out with a series of cheek-puffing motions. "I say Jack's got a plan. I'll hang back a bit from you two. Keep an eye out for trouble. Raise the cry if it's needed. No one will pay any attention to a boy like myself. I'll be as good as invisible."

"Sounds good to me, Nabber," said Jack. "Let's go."

They didn't have far to walk. Lord Cravin's townhouse was less than a league from the east wall. On Nabber's advice, they decided not to pass too close to the building and kept a few streets south of it at all times. Coming upon a small square where market traders were packing away their goods for the night, Jack veered off into the pathway between the stalls. A light drizzle had just started up, and the men and women who were closing shop worked quickly to prevent their wares from being soaked.

Spying a pastry seller, Jack darted around the various fruit sellers and vintners and approached the coarse wooden stall. A tiny, bald man was busy placing sweet rolls onto a covered tray. Without looking up, he said, "No handouts here, my friend. The stale stuff goes to the wife's pigs."

"They must be happy pigs."

"Aye. The wife cares for those pigs like they were her children. She'd have the skin off my back if I didn't come home with the leftover pastries."

"How's business lately?" Jack spotted Tawl drawing close and waved him back with a small movement of his wrist.

The pastry seller still hadn't looked up. He started on his second tray. "Things have begun to pick up some since they opened the gates to trade. No one's got much money, though. Grain's running out, too. It won't be long before I've got nothing left to bake with except fresh air."

"Some say things were better under the duke."

The pastry seller's hand hovered above a pastry. It was shaking. "I'm not one of those," he said.

Jack nodded slowly. The man thought he was a troublemaker. Well, it wouldn't do him any harm to act like one. "'Course with all the goings-on at the palace, the king hasn't got much time for city affairs."

"I don't know anything about goings-on at the palace. I hear rumors like the rest, but I pay them no heed." The pastry seller had stopped placing the pastries on the tray and simply threw them on, instead. He dumped the trays on his cart and took hold of the yoke. "I've got to be off now. Can't keep the wife waiting."

Jack caught the man's arm and squeezed it. "What

rumors do you hear?" The pastry seller was as small as a child. His bones were as thin as sticks. Jack felt sorry for him, but he had no choice: time was running out.

"I hear that Kylock's killing off all the nobles who oppose him. That Lord Baralis is a demon who eats babies, and that the entire palace is being run by a mad woman with no teeth." Although scared, the pastry seller seemed to find satisfaction in uttering the last words. He yanked at his arm, and Jack let it go.

"Is Lord Cravin one of those who Kylock has killed?"

The pastry seller hooked the yoke of his cart over his shoulders. "He was hung months back now. Hung, quartered, and set to rot on the walls." He began to move away, his cart trundling after him.

Jack was about to let the man go when, as an afterthought, he shouted, "What's the name of the woman who runs the palace?"

"Mistress Greal," cried the pastry seller. "Her sister owns a brothel on the south side of the city."

"And the sister's name?"

"Can't recall." The pastry seller's voice was lost beneath the creaking of his cart for a moment. "Thorny something, perhaps."

Jack turned away. He felt disappointed. The man had told him nothing useful. Lord Cravin was dead, so that ruled out going to him for information. Now all they had to go on was some half-remembered brothel-keeper's name in a city full of brothels.

With heavy steps he returned to Tawl. The drizzle had thickened to snow. The soft flakes clung to Jack's hair and dripped down his collar when they melted. Tawl was silent while Jack told him what the pastry seller said. At the end, however, when the name of the brothel-keeper was mentioned, Tawl's eyes narrowed to slits.

"Thorny, you said?"

Jack nodded.

"Thornypurse." Tawl made the word sound like a

curse. Despite the flapping felt hat, he suddenly looked like a man whom no one would want to cross.

"You know who she is?"

"She nearly killed me." Tawl swiveled around, and seeing Nabber lurking on the opposite side of the square, he beckoned him over.

Nabber ran through the slush and dirt with a dancer's grace. "What is it?" he said, skidding to a showy halt.

"We're going to pay a visit on an old friend, and I think you'll want to come along for the ride."

The clawing noise outside the door went on for a few minutes. It sounded like rats. Only higher.

Melli scratched her arm. She had just taken the splint off because the skin underneath was itching so much. In the pale light that seeped under the door, she could see the uneven line of her forearm. A knot of bone pushed against the skin. The break was rehealing, but it wasn't a clean join, and Melli knew her left arm would never be the same again. If a surgeon could only get to it, he might be able to limit the damage, but every day that passed lessened her chances of having the bone reset.

In her head she counted the number of days that had passed since she put Kylock off. Eight. When he finally came to her in two nights time, she had another plan ready to postpone him further. For a week now she had been saving odd scraps of food, nothing much—an apple here, a sliver of chicken fat there—but enough to fester along nicely under the bed. The day that Kylock was due, she was going to rub the moldy meat and vegetables over her clothes and thighs. If the smell alone failed to put him off, then Melli intended to claim the ghones or worse.

It wasn't at all ladylike, but then Kylock was no gentleman.

Melli was rather pleased with her plan, and as no one entered her chamber these days except the guards, there was little chance of discovery.

The scratching on the door stopped abruptly. Melli's abdomen squeezed a ghost contraction. Since the baby was born, she always felt fear first in her belly. All was quiet for a few seconds, but shadows bobbed under the door with the light, and Melli could tell someone was moving on the other side. Was it Kylock? or Mistress Greal? Melli shot her good arm out to feel for the splint. Once she had it in hand, she began the lengthy and awkward process of rebinding it to her arm. She felt vulnerable with the damaged bone on show.

Biting one end of the bandage with her teeth, Melli wrapped the other round with her right hand. She had to move slowly, for the slightest sudden movement might cause the bone to break.

"Playing doctor, I see."

Melli looked up. Baralis stood in the doorway. She hadn't heard him enter.

He brought the light forward. "Has no one tended to your arm?"

"Has no one cut your throat yet?"

Baralis' laughter was surprisingly warm. "Such a proud little girl. I would have thought five months of captivity might have blunted your sharp little tongue."

Listening to his rich, cultured voice brought back glimpses of the past to Melli: fingers running down her spine, a breath taken deeply, a scent so heady it drew her in. This was, she realized, the first time they had been alone together since the day at Castle Harvell when he'd moved her to a storeroom for safekeeping. Years ago now, yet why did she remember it like yesterday? Her stomach sent her a warning, but the blood in her head pumped fast, as if she were drunk.

Forcing herself to stay calm, Melli continued to bind the splint to her arm.

"Here." Baralis was beside her before she knew it. "Let me take a look at the bone."

She pulled away from his touch. Another memory,

older, fainter, chased up her nostrils along with his scent. A hand upon a silk dress—a child's dress. The stiff fabric had been out of fashion for ten years.

"Not afraid of being touched, are we?" Baralis' voice was mocking. "Don't worry, I'm not Kylock. I'm not about to please myself with petty torture."

"No. You have a taste for far worse." Melli was shaking. The ghost contractions pumped away at her empty belly. "What did you do to my baby?"

Baralis took hold of her arm. The bindings came apart and the splint fell to the bed. "You know what I did. He's dead."

He. Melli closed her eyes. She'd had a son. Learning that one small fact was like losing the baby all over again. The pain of the first morning flooded back; her throat tightened and her stomach snatched itself in. Her breasts—dry of milk these past two days—ached with a sharp, sickening pain. She fought the desire to wrench herself away. Baralis had hold of her arm and one pull could break it.

Baralis ran his thumb over the lump of bone. His nails were smoothly filed, but there was something appalling about them: they were too large for the thin, bloodless fingers they capped. The lack of such a basic human proportion unnerved Melli. It turned Baralis into a monster.

His touch became a caress. "Such a nasty join, such an unsightly little bulge—it all but ruins the perfect line of your arm."

Melli's chest was heaving. Her throat had tightened to a pinpoint and airflow to her lungs was constricted like sand in a glass. Tears streamed down her cheeks. "How did my baby die?"

Baralis tapped the bone. *Tht. Tht. Tht. Tht.* "I don't think, my dear Melli, that you are in any position to ask questions." Baralis' gray eyes met hers. He pressed his thumb against the bulge. "Do you?"

"What do you want?" To Melli her voice sounded high, almost hysterical.

"Aah." Baralis let up the pressure. On the underside of her arm, his fingers nuzzled her flesh. "Ladies who play games should expect them in return." His fingers traveled up her arm and then along the bodice of her dress. The palm of his hand came to rest against her belly. "And games always end with a loser."

Like a drug, Baralis' scent heightened her senses. Even through the fabric of her dress, Melli could feel the rough texture of his palm. His touch was firm and cool. Slowly Melli's body began to relax; her throat widened, letting in air, and her stomach settled down beneath his hand.

"Good, good," said Baralis. "Now listen very carefully. I don't know what you've said or done to Kylock, but I do know that you're playing him for a fool. When he comes to you next, I expect you to be more than accommodating."

Melli had a dim feeling she'd been through this before with Baralis. Him touching her, telling her what she would do. Even the sensations were the same: attraction, confusion, a vague thickening of her thoughts. What was he doing to her?

His hand was no longer on her arm, so Melli pulled away from him. As she moved, she caught a whiff of his breath. She paused a moment, waiting to feel his fingers trailing down her spine, before she realized it was a memory. Why did she feel so attracted to him? She didn't understand.

Clenching her teeth together and contracting the muscles in her neck and jaw, Melli forced herself to think clearly. It was so hard, though: her thoughts were heavy and her body was slow to move. She pressed the thumbnail of her good hand into the soft flesh of her index finger. The pain sent a shock wave through her head, and in the moment of vivid clarity that followed she managed to stand free from the bed.

He followed her up, and as she tried to back away from him, he matched her step for step. Finally she could go no farther, her calves pressed against the chest by the wall.

"You disappoint me, Melli," he said. "I so much wanted to keep things pleasant between us."

Gone. The muddling of her thoughts cleared in an instant; the hot pulsing in her temples stopped as quickly as it started. In the cold, pain-filled world that emerged, Baralis looked like a sharp-edged, sharp-eyed demon. He wasn't a mysterious lover come to woo her: he was a man prepared to use all his powers to get what he wanted. She felt attracted to him because he *willed* it. Just like the time at the storeroom, only she hadn't realized it then. Foolishly, she had flattered herself into thinking he felt something for her, but looking at him now—his face cast with shadows from the lamp behind his back—she realized Baralis felt nothing for anyone except himself.

He didn't have a sensuous nerve in his body. He found his pleasure exclusively in control.

The myth of the powerful man succumbing to her charms died. Melli was left feeling naïve and angry: Baralis had manipulated her with the force of his will not once but twice, maybe even three times, if the vague childhood memory was to be relied upon. He had pried his way into her brain and made himself master of her thoughts. It was a kind of rape, an invasion of the most intimate sort, and he did it without blinking an eye.

Baralis made a grab for her arm. Melli jerked backward. Her knees collapsed and she landed in a sitting position on the chest. In the second it took to settle herself, Baralis seized hold of her wrist. Straightaway his fingers slid to the break.

"Such a foolish, headstrong girl," he said, stroking the lump of broken bone. "You should learn to be better behaved."

Melli's right hand was trailing over the side of the chest. Very slowly, she moved it around to the back. In the space between the chest and the wall lay the supplies she had stocked for her escape. To distract Baralis' atten-tion, she kept him talking. "What will you do if I turn Kylock away?"

A push upon the bone. "Oh, you won't turn him away, my dear. You most certainly won't do that."

Melli stretched her hand down along the back of the chest. Tilting backward to increase her reach, she said, "Why wouldn't I?"

"Because I will have to punish you if you do."

Melli's hand closed around the cool stem of the glass. "Really. And what will that punishment be?"

"Warning *and* punishment, I think." Baralis clasped her forearm just below the elbow, and with his other hand grabbed her wrist. He meant to break the bone.

Panicking, Melli raised the glass. She smashed it against the wall, sending splinters flashing into the air. The fragment that remained in her fist she thrust straight for Baralis' face. Dropping her arm, Baralis jumped back. The shard of glass caught his chin, drawing blood. Melli saw his lips move.

The smell of metal in a furnace filled the room.

"*No!*" she screamed. "Hurt me now and Kylock will destroy you."

Baralis closed his lips.

She held the glass out before her like a shield. "He thinks I am his one chance of redemption. Take that away from him and he will never forgive you. *Never.*"

Baralis formed a fist to wipe the blood from his chin. His eyes were as dark as slate. "You have just made a fatal mistake, Melliandra. Do you really think you can hold me for ransom? I have shaped men and countries, lives and fates. I have changed lineages of kings and signed death warrants for dukes, and no silly little girl from a family filled with fools is going to get in my way."

Baralis was shaking now. His beautiful voice was honed sharp like a blade and each word was a cutting blow. "Don't think for one moment you can get the better of me. Don't even think it in your dreams. Take me on and I will win every time. I know of nothing but victory: it is what I live for. And you, my dear Melliandra, with your proud, flaunting ways and your fast-working tongue, are nowhere near a match for me."

He took a step toward her. Melli raised the glass. Baralis smiled, and Melli suddenly felt like a child with a child's toy.

"So you think I can't harm you, eh? I could kill you now in a hundred different ways and Kylock would never know who did it. I could stop your heart, or harden your liver, or clot the blood in your brain. I could block the air in your lungs, or halt the juice in your belly, or prevent the poison in your kidneys from getting out. There is nothing I couldn't do to your body." Baralis waved a dismissive hand at the glass. "That, my dear Melliandra, has just cost you your life. If you refuse Kylock again, then I will design a death so slow and painful you will beg for the end to come. Accommodate his wishes, however, and I will kill you with one clean blow. The choice is yours."

Baralis looked at Melli a few seconds longer, and then turned and walked away.

The second the door closed behind him, Melli dropped the glass. The shard had cut a deep pit in her palm, and she hadn't even felt it. Cradling her left arm, she lifted herself off the chest and made her way over to the bed. Settling amidst the covers, hugging her frail limb close, Melli gave way to the blinding tension that had been building inside of her and cried herself into a frenzy.

She was tired of being strong, sick of being on her own, incensed by all the waiting. Where was Tawl when she needed him? Why hadn't he come to save her?

As a rule, Madame Thornypurse always closed early on nights when the pits were covered. No matches meant no spectators, and no spectators meant no loot. Heavy sleet, rain, or snow didn't prevent the matches from being fought—a desperate man would fight under any conditions—but it did make it hard to keep the torches lit. A fight in the dark was as good as no fight at all to the bloodthirsty men of Bren.

Still, even though tonight was deemed too wet to fight, Madame Thornypurse was enjoying a rare boom in business. Tomorrow morning a large portion of the new recruits were going on a four-day training expedition north of the city, and they were out in search of a little feminine comfort before they left.

Of course, they didn't pay well—these days no one did—but a bucketful of coppers was better than nothing at all. Things had settled down a bit compared to right after the victory over Highwall, but there was still little profit in whoring. Which meant that Madame Thornypurse had to take anything she could get.

A sharp rapping came at the door. Madame Thornypurse was in the process of rubbing rat oil into her scrawny neck, so she sent Franny to see who it was. Half a minute later Franny returned. "Two gentlemen to see you," she said.

Madame Thornypurse put the lid firmly on the rat oil—on cold nights such as these it could get cloudy unless it was well covered. "What's the look of them?"

"One looks a bit simple, but the other's quite handsome. Both big, they are."

Madame Thornypurse peeked her coifed and powdered head around the corner into the main room. Half a dozen blackhelms were currently lounging beside her girls. Her practiced eye knew immediately that the men had reached the stage where no more money would be spent: they were too drunk to eat, drink, or wench. A few customers more would not go amiss. Gathering her second-best shawl about her, Madame Thornypurse made for the door.

"Gentlemen, gentlemen. Come out of the cold." She held a hand out for kissing. Neither man took her up. "I have a warm fire, strong ale, and the best girls in town."

The stupid-looking man in the felt hat lunged forward. Clasping a hand over her mouth, he yanked her out onto the street. Madame Thornypurse tried to scream, but her lips were pressed tight against her gums. The second man slammed the door shut, and then Madame Thornypurse was dragged into the alley at the side of the building.

Her first thought was for her shoes: silk—the slush would ruin them. Her second thought was for her complexion: the freezing cold would dry out her skin. Only when these considerations had whipped through her mind did she actually begin to panic. She might be robbed, raped, killed, or maimed!

The felt-hat man drew a knife. Raising it to her recently oiled throat, he said, "One scream from you and you're dead."

Madame Thornypurse nodded vigorously. Her eyes flicked to the front of the building. Surely Franny would notice she'd gone?

"Now," said the felt-hat man, easing up his hold on her mouth. "Tell me what you know about Melliandra."

Madame Thornypurse's hearing was nowhere near as good as her sister's, but she was certain she heard screaming from inside the building. Screaming and the sound of furniture being upturned. "What are you doing?" she cried.

The knife came closer. "You didn't answer my question."

The lights in the brothel started to go out. Smoke, lots of it, began billowing from the spaces beneath the shutters. Madame Thornypurse's knees buckled under her. Her business was under attack! The strong arm of the man stopped her from falling to the ground. Even in her distraught state, Madame Thornypurse could appreciate the man's firm grip. She tried a little feminine wheedling.

"Sir, if you could only tell me what exactly you want to know, I'll be more than pleased to help you." She finished her request with what she hoped was a beguiling smile.

"Listen very carefully, woman. I need to know where Baralis is keeping the Lady Melliandra. I've had it on good information that your sister runs the palace, and if you don't tell me everything you know in the next thirty seconds, then my boy inside the building is going to stop smoking your customers out and he's going to start burning, instead. Is that clear?"

As the man was speaking, the light from the building across the way caught his face. Madame Thornypurse recognized his features at once: it was Tawl, the duke's champion. Strange, but his voice wasn't at all as she remembered it. He sounded a lot more dangerous now.

The second man was standing at the corner of the building, keeping an eye on the front. People were running past the alleyway, screaming about ghosts and smoke. So much for the blackhelms!

Madame Thornypurse was, above all, a practical woman. She had no intention of having her throat cut in a heroic attempt to guard her sister's secrets. If the man wanted information, then that was what he was going to get. "Come to think of it, I *have* heard a few things," she said with a teasing pucker of her lips. Madame Thornypurse prided herself on being able to flirt with anyone—even potential murderers. "You know, one or two things here and there."

"What things?"

"Well, Lord Baralis charged my sister with looking after the little bitch. First they held her in one of the northern turrets, then there was some sort of incident with fire, so they moved her to an annex not far from the nobles' quarters. Too good for her sorts by far, I'd say."

Tawl relaxed and lowered his blade. He took several deep breaths. "Has she been moved since then?"

"I don't know. I haven't seen my sister for over two weeks now. Bit strange it is, as she usually pops in at least once a week with—" Madame Thornypurse caught herself. She wasn't about to tell him about Mistress Greal's penchant for smuggling dead noblemen's valuables away from the palace and then selling them for a tidy profit. "—kitchen scraps for the hens."

"Has anything happened in the palace these past couple of weeks to stop her from coming to see you?"

Madame Thornypurse patted the hair around the nape of her neck. "Can't say. But last time I saw my sister she mentioned that the little bitch was near her time."

Beneath the rim of the felt hat, Tawl's face visibly hardened. "Go on," he said. "Get back to your business. One word to anyone about what happened here tonight, and I'll personally return to burn the place down—and I won't come knocking first. Now get out of my sight."

Madame Thornypurse never moved faster in her life. Her second-best shawl went flying to the mud and her skirts flew up around her knees. She ran past the second man and up the stairs to her door. A steady stream of smoke billowed out of the building, and after gritting her teeth and calculating the smoke-resisting capabilities of rat oil, Madame Thornypurse ran straight into the flow.

As she raced toward the shutters in the main room, she came face-to-face with a small, masked demon. Black from head to foot, reaching only to her shoulder, the demon was carrying a bulky sack in one hand and a handful of smoking reeds in another. Catching sight of her, the demon raised the reeds in greeting. Madame Thornypurse took a deep startled breath, inhaled two lungfuls of smoke, and promptly keeled over onto the floor.

"You should have seen 'em run, Borlin. The old fearless blackhelms took one look at me and scaddled for their lives. Thought I was the grim reaper." Nabber bent his head to take a drink of his ale and a small landslide of soot skidded onto the floor. "'Course, blocking off the chimney was the worst. That roof was as slippery as a tinker's tongue—nearly fell to my death, I did. Worth it, though. That place filled up so fast that by the time I'd squeezed through the back window, I couldn't see my hands in front of my face. Hardly needed the reeds."

"You weren't supposed to show yourself," said Tawl. He was leaning against an old upturned dyeing vat, and he did not look pleased. "I told you not to go into the main room."

"I had to get some loot, Tawl. It was only fair: last time I met the rat woman she robbed me of my contingency." Nabber smiled, encouraging Tawl to forgive him.

Tawl didn't return the smile. Since he'd questioned Madame Thornypurse about Melli he hadn't smiled once.

They were sitting around a pressing slab in a derelict dyemaker's shop. As planned, they had met up with the others earlier outside of the Brimming Bucket. Andris and his men had made it through the gate successfully, and they had spent their time scouting around the city for a safe place to hole up. They had managed to lay their hands on ale, fresh food, hay, and candles, and everyone had enjoyed their best meal in days. No one wanted to risk lighting a fire, so the place was bitterly cold, but the two candles on the granite slab gave a cozy feel to the room, and the brandy in their bellies warmed like a well-stoked hearth.

The dyemaker's shop was one in a row of disused, rundown businesses located in a pitch-black street in the southeast of the city. The roof leaked, and all the wooden surfaces were damp; there were no doors, no shutters, few floorboards, and a lot of drafts. The one room that had no windows to speak of was the storage bay. Half above-, half belowground, the large, low-ceilinged room was where Andris had made his camp.

"I say we go in tonight," said Tawl, bringing the conversation around to the one topic that was on everyone's mind. "We know for sure Melli's there now, so there's nothing to stop us from moving ahead. The blackhelms aren't expecting any trouble—as far as they're concerned they thrashed the enemy eight weeks ago. They won't be on their guard."

As he spoke, Jack noticed that Tawl was the only man in the room who was not sitting down. He hadn't eaten his food, either. It lay untouched on a cloth on the floor.

Crayne shook his head. "No, Tawl. I say we wait. We're all bone weary; we've had seven days in the saddle without one good night's sleep between us. We need to rest."

"Crayne's right, Tawl," said Borlin, picking his huge teeth with a chicken bone. "We've been up since before dawn this morning. If we go in tonight none of us will be at our best—you know that." Borlin waited for Tawl to acknowledge the truth of what he was saying. A mere tightening of lip was all the response he got. Borlin wasn't put off. "Besides, if we wait until tomorrow night, there's a chance there'll be fewer trained men in the palace."

"Why? What have you heard?"

Borlin let Crayne answer the question. "You were right about the blackhelms, Tawl. They all went south to Camlee with Kedrac. The ones left in the city are a mixture of mercenaries, new recruits, farmers, and fortune hunters. Kylock's ordered a four-day training exercise for them just north of the city. They leave in the morning."

"A training mission like that won't affect the palace guard count."

"I think it will." Crayne's voice was firm. The candlelight brought out the gray in his hair and threw deep shadows across his face. Jack realized he had never seen Crayne laugh or share a joke with anyone: the leader of the knights was a serious man.

Crayne continued, his eyes focused steadily on Tawl.

"Who are the best-trained men in the city now that Kedrac has taken the blackhelms?" He answered his own question. "The palace guards, that's who. Kylock is going to need highly skilled men to train these upstart black-helms, so he's bound to send some of the best guards from the palace on the training mission."

Behind Crayne, one of the horses nickered softly. They had brought six mounts to the city between them, and Andris had laid a makeshift ramp down to the storage bay so their presence could be concealed.

Before Tawl had a chance to say anything, Borlin spoke up again. "There's things we'll need to purchase tomorrow," he said. "New bridles, stirrup straps, sad-dles. At the moment the horses are a dead giveaway. Everything on them is yellow and black. If one of us is going to wait outside the palace with them, then their tack needs to be changed."

Everyone grunted in agreement with this. "Same with us, too," continued Borlin. "We took a big chance coming into the city looking the way we do. We all need to get some discreet clothes, and you and Jack need some chain mail for under your tunics."

Tawl looked at Jack. "What do you think? Should we wait until tomorrow night?"

Up until now, Jack had just been an observer at the meeting. The knighthood was a closed rank and he was just an inexperienced outsider. He knew nothing of tac-tics and predawn raids. He wasn't a fighter—though he *could* fight—he was someone with one specific job to do. He had to murder Kylock. Up to this point, Jack had deliberately pushed the details to the back of his mind; details were the things that frightened him, the things that made the whole situation seem real. And hopeless.

What Crayne and Borlin said made good sense, and Jack agreed with them, but they hadn't come up with the real reason why they shouldn't enter the palace tonight. Only *he* knew that.

He wasn't ready.

The journey here had been one mad, breathless gallop, and Jack hadn't had a moment to think. He rode, he slept, he rode some more. Always there was the knowledge he was drawing closer to Bren, but never once had he stopped to consider what he would do once he arrived. He needed tonight to prepare himself. Not for the details—there was no way to plan for the unknown—but the *reality* of the situation. It was time he came to terms with what had to be done. The responsibility was his alone.

"I say we go in tomorrow night," he said.

Tawl looked down, disappointed, but the faces of the other men visibly relaxed, and Jack realized he had misjudged them. They didn't think he was an inexperienced outsider after all: they would have moved tonight on his say-so. It was a sobering thought, and as the night drew on and plans were made, refined, and then finalized, it became the first of many.

Thirty-two

*T*hey left the dyemaker's shop at midnight: Jack, Tawl, Crayne, Nabber, and Hervo who, besides Borlin, was the best marksman in the party. By turns, it had been sleeting, raining, spitting, and drizzling all day, and the streets were thick with sludge. Like they did when they entered the city, they had split up into groups to avoid any unwanted attention. Andris was head of the second group, Borlin head of the third.

Only half an hour before, Jack had put chain mail on for the first time in his life. It was heavy, confining and it itched like mad. It was like wearing a rack of cutlery next to your skin. Tawl said it would have helped if the mail had been custom-made, but personally Jack couldn't see it: if anything, it was a relief that the metal rings ended at his stomach, not his vitals.

Nabber had been forced into wearing mail, too, and was currently walking with an exaggerated stagger. "It'll be wet in the dungeons," he said, holding his palms up to catch the rain. "All the water that can't find its way *around* the palace ends up running through it."

"That's good," murmured Tawl. "No guards will want to be down there if it's running with water."

Hervo grunted. Like Borlin, he wasn't a large man, but his arms were as thick as a butcher's block and his eyes were as sharp as a cleaver. He was carrying his bow in an oilskin bag under his arm, and his arrows were tucked into his tunic. Jack had watched Hervo preparing himself earlier: he had kissed each arrow before putting them into his quiver. Crayne said he had chosen Hervo because although he was first and foremost an archer, he was also an expert with the long-knife.

Crayne himself was a study in concealed weaponry. Subtle but deadly bulges broke the line of his tunic, his britches, his sleeves, and his boots. Knives, throwing spears, a sword, a small crowbar, and a coil of metal rope were just the items that Jack had spotted. The leader of the party was quiet as they walked through the city, his face drawn into hard-earned lines, his gaze never resting in one place. On the few occasions he did speak, it was to whisper terse, one-line orders in a voice well used to command.

Tawl seemed content to let him take the lead. Whether that would remain the case when they were actually in the palace was another matter entirely. Jack couldn't imagine Tawl even *listening* to orders once he caught sight of Melli.

"Are you sure you know how to get to the nobles' quarters?" asked Tawl for what must have been the fourth time that day.

"'Course I do," said Nabber with an indignant squeak. "I even think I know the annex old Thornydraws mentioned. There's quite a few areas leading from the nobles' quarters, but if I remember rightly, only one of them is out of the way enough to conceal furtive comings and goings."

Tawl was quiet after that. The remark Madame Thornypurse made about Melli being near her time had affected him deeply. Jack had seen it last night in the alley, and he saw it now as they made their way across the city. The knight's face was a shield of taut flesh, and on both sides of his body, his hands were curled into fists.

Like Tawl, Jack had chosen not to load himself down

with weapons. A sword and two knives, one concealed. Jack had strapped his second knife against the lining of his boot. He could feel it there now, the covered blade pressing into his skin with every step forward.

"Andris will be starting out any minute now," said Crayne. "He should be less than an hour behind us."

"Aye, he'll keep good time," said Hervo in his soft, drawling voice. "It's Borlin who'll be dashing ahead of the game. He hates to be kept waiting." Hervo laughed softly and even Crayne managed a smile. Obviously a tale or two there, thought Jack.

Borlin and the other two men in his group would bring the horses across the city. Two archers and one swordsman, their job was to wait at the entrance to the tunnels—the swordsman with the horses and the archers concealed at shooting distance—and provide cover for the escape. Andris, Gervhay, and the last archer were to wait on a prearranged street corner near the palace until Nabber appeared, gain access to the tunnels, and follow Crayne's party up through the palace, covering their backs, keeping the escape route clear and watching out for trouble.

That was the plan. Everyone knew it, most of the night had been spent in fine-tuning and coming up with various contingencies, and now they were about to put it into action.

They made good time crossing the city. There were fewer blackhelms to avoid than the night before, and the bad weather and the lateness of hour combined to make the streets almost deserted. Nabber was in charge of choosing the route, and Jack had to admit it was a good one: dark alleyways, sleazy back streets, deserted court-yards. The pocket knew his stuff. Earlier Jack had pulled Nabber aside and asked him where Baralis and Kylock's chambers might be located. Nabber, always pleased to show off his knowledge, had told him the exact location of Baralis' chambers and the possible location of

Kylock's—the old duke's quarters. Jack had asked Nabber not to mention this to the others, and the pocket had sworn an oath to that effect, spitting upon his palms and calling upon Borc to strike him down with the ghones if he broke it.

Jack didn't so much mind the others knowing, it was more that he didn't want to distract them from their mission. They had enough to deal with already. His plan was simply to slip away once Melli was safely in hand.

"Almost here now," said Nabber with a theatrical whisper. "Remember, it'll be wet down here, so hold all your necessaries above your heads."

They came to a halt at the end of an alleyway. The two walls to either side were running with water, and the eaves of overhanging buildings were sending streams of run-off pouring onto the road. It was very dark. The surface of the road was more dirt than cobbles, and it was heavily cambered.

"Are you sure Andris will be able to find this place?" The dark form that was Crayne's head moved from side to side. "It's further out of the way than I thought."

"No problem," said Nabber. "He knows where Cabling Street is, and as long as he makes it there, I'll find him." As he spoke, Nabber handed his sack to Tawl. Inside were two oil lamps, and Tawl set about lighting them. Nabber crouched down and started brushing away the dirt near the wall. "The drain's here, I know it," he murmured. "Must have got clogged up. Here, Jack, give me a hand."

Jack knelt down beside him and thrust his fingers into the mud. After a moment, he felt the cold hardness of metal. By this time Tawl had the lamps lit and everyone helped to clear the drain. "How far are we from the palace?" asked Jack, trying to pry the drain grille open.

"Not far at all. Less than a quarter league due east." With his little finger, Nabber cleared the mud from around the edge of the drain. "Got the bar, Crayne?" he said. "This is going to need a good wrenching. Last time I was here, all of this dirt was on the other side of the alley. Must have moved south for the winter like the birds."

Crayne whipped out the contents of one of his bulges and went to work. Jack and Tawl helped him get a grip, Nabber supervised, and Hervo stood watch at the end of the alley. After a while the grille was loosened, and Crayne managed to pry it open. Everyone was soaked and muddy. Crayne took a hand of mud and rubbed it into his face. He ordered everyone else to do likewise. "Once we hit the palace, it's lamps out. Understood?" He waited for each of them to nod. "You go first, Jack. After that it's Nabber, me, then Tawl. Hervo, you're bringing up the rear."

Tawl held the lamp out while Jack lowered himself into the murky darkness of the drain. A sharp, rotting smell wafted upward. Jack felt a cold stream of air whipping around his ankles. He gripped the ground to either side of the drain more firmly and lowered himself deeper. His feet plunged into icy water, sending a shock wave coursing up his spine. Feet, ankles, calves, knees, thighs were all engulfed by the freezing flow. Jack didn't want to release his grip. He still couldn't feel the bottom with his feet.

"Go on, Jack," cried Nabber. "It can't be much deeper."

Jack took a deep breath and let go. He dropped less than a hand's length before hitting the bottom. His feet landed in a thick layer of mud. Reaching up, he took the lamp from Tawl, and then stepped away to give Nabber room to be lowered. The lantern revealed a roughly circular passage. Stone slabs lined the walls and ceilings, and earth and roots had forced their way through the masonry, splitting stones, and providing runways for seeping mud and rainwater.

The water level reached Jack's hips, and already he

could feel his toes numbing. The water itself was dark brown and thick with mud and refuse. As Jack moved away from the opening, the mud on the bottom sucked at his feet, turning every step into a struggle of balance and coordination. Pull too slowly and he wouldn't be able to break free from the bottom, pull too fast and he could go splashing head-first into the water. And from the smell of it, he most definitely didn't want that to happen.

By the time the others were down, Jack was shaking from head to foot. It was freezing. Nabber's teeth were chattering loudly—he was up to his chest in water—and even Tawl was showing signs of the cold, crossing his arms over his chest to stop himself from shivering. Hervo held his bow and quiver above his head, and Crayne's many bulges had apparently moved upward toward his neck.

"Let's go," he said.

"Right," said Nabber in Jack's ear. "We wade down here a while till we come to the first passage on the left."

Jack nodded and began to make his way forward. Each step was a fight against the suction of the mud and the numbness of his limbs. The surface of the water was thick with grease. White gobs of animal fat bobbed up and down with each ripple. Jack felt top-heavy and awkward. He took great lurching steps like a drunkard. Below the water he was almost weightless, but above his chest was artificially heavy due to the chain mail.

The sound of water dripping was everywhere. Echoes seemed louder than the noises they mimicked, and the wind howled through the tunnels like a wolf.

The light from the lantern bounced off the moss-covered walls, picking up a green glow. Jack's hand was shaking and the lantern shook with it, sending quick shadows and light flashes careening from ceiling to water.

"Here!" cried Nabber. "Turn left."

Jack had been lost in his own thoughts, hypnotized by

the light. He had stepped right past the turnoff. Backtracking a few steps, he was aware that the numbness in his limbs was moving upward. He suddenly realized that the journey was a lot harder on Nabber: half his chest was submerged in the freezing water. Once the pocket had guided them to the palace and shown them the way up to the nobles' quarters, he had to come back through the drains for Andris.

Jack sped his pace up after that. He found that a light running step actually stopped his feet from miring in the mud. It got his blood pumping, too, and helped stop the numbness from spreading up his legs. The water in the second tunnel was a fraction lower than the first, and as they made their way along it, the level dropped even farther.

Suddenly Jack's foot hit stone. He stopped dead, raising his hand to halt the others. "There's something blocking the way."

"It's all right, Jack," came Nabber's breathless voice from behind. "It should be the steps leading up to the dungeons."

Jack brought his lantern forward. It was impossible to see anything below the surface. He moved his foot upward, grazing the stone with his toes until he found a ledge. Nabber was right, it was a step. A step tall enough for giants. Jack hauled his tired body up through the water, swinging around after each step to lend a hand to Nabber.

"We're here now," said Nabber, as Jack dragged him up the last step. "We're in the palace."

As soon as Nabber said those words, Jack realized that he hadn't done nearly enough to prepare himself. One night was nothing. Somewhere above him lay Baralis and Kylock, and somehow, tonight, he was supposed to destroy them. The full enormity of the task hit him like a dead weight. He felt like he'd been punched in the stomach. How could he possibly get to Kylock? And once there, how could he destroy him? He didn't know the answers. All he knew was that he had to try.

Melli had pulled the curtains back and opened the shutters. The window was, she judged, large enough for her to squeeze through. It was high, though, and she dragged the chest across the room to give herself something to stand on. The splint was back against the broken bone, and as she worked the chest from its position against the back wall, her left arm trailed at her side. Sweat poured down her forehead, dripping off the end of her nose and soaking the neckline of her dress.

The chest was made of oak a wrist thick, and it was large enough to store a sheep. It took Melli many minutes and many rests to position it below the window.

Sleet drifted down through the open shutters, landing on Melli's face as she pulled herself up. The stones forming the wall had been smoothed only to man height, and the masonry around the window was coarse and unfinished. Melli made a grab for the stone frame, and she felt a quick burn on her wrist as her skin brushed against the rough surface. "Damn," she hissed. It was too dark to tell if there was blood.

Melli had taught herself to ignore pains a lot more serious than a scraped wrist, and she didn't miss a beat. Standing on her tiptoes, she leant out of the window and looked down to the world below. The cold air made Melli's eyes sting, and she could see nothing at first but a black pit. Then, as she blinked away the tears, she began to pick out a few details: light escaping from shutters, stretches of white snow nestling between eaves, the wet sheen of the courtyard below. Melli leant out a fraction farther so she could see what lay directly beneath the window. It was a dead drop: no ledges, no broken levels, no low roofs.

A dull wave of disappointment washed over her. She was very high up, higher than she had thought, and there was no possible way to escape. She could jump, of course, but even now, with Baralis' fatal promises still ringing in her ears, suicide was not an option. Maybor's daughter had more courage than that.

She had hoped for a little luck, though—just a smidgen of her father's famous luck. It wasn't to be. Melli took one final look at the drop and then stepped down from the chest. Maybe it was a good thing; if her father was still alive, freezing up on a mountain, then he needed to keep all the luck for himself. She couldn't begrudge him that.

Melli didn't bother hauling the chest back to its usual place. That sort of thing didn't matter anymore. Tomorrow Kylock would come for her and nothing would ever matter again.

The darkness underneath the palace was alive with noises. Water dripped, rats scuttled, wood creaked, and drafts whistled around corners and along the walls. With the lamps out it was impossible to see anything except the occasional glint of wetness and the whites of each others' eyes.

Time was difficult to judge and distance impossible. All Jack knew was that he was soaking wet and chilled to the bone. His heart was racing fast despite the fact that he had stopped running what seemed like a very long time ago, and his stomach had contracted into a tight ball.

"Mind the wood brace straight ahead," hissed Nabber. He was leading now, and Jack could only wonder how he managed to find his way in the dark. After they'd all dodged around the wood brace and taken a few steps up out of knee-deep water, Nabber called a halt. "Not much further now," he said. "Once we go through the passage to the left, we'll be in the part of the cellar they use for storing foodstuffs and the like. There's not much chance of anyone being around at this time o' night, but you can never tell."

"Hervo, ready with your bow," said Crayne. "First sign of light and we move against the walls."

"How do we get to the nobles' quarters from here?" Tawl asked, his voice low and urgent.

"I'm going to show you," replied Nabber.

"No. You go no further than here. I want you back waiting for Andris."

"But—"

"No buts, Nabber. Not this time. And when you've brought Andris this far, you turn back again and get the hell out of here. I expect to find you waiting for me at the hideout when I return. Is that clear?"

A small disgruntled noise emanated from the dark shadow that was Nabber.

"Now give me the directions."

A long pause followed and then Nabber reluctantly reeled off the directions. Jack didn't bother to listen to them: he was too keyed up to remember anything. All he could think about was Kylock. He could *feel* him now— he was sure of it. Kylock's presence pulled at his blood, forcing it to the surface in a hot, dizzying blush. His heart told him that Baralis didn't matter: his blood ran only for Kylock.

Jack didn't even notice when Nabber stopped speaking. A hand on his arm made him jump.

"Jack? Are you all right?" It was Tawl. "Come on, we've got to get going."

"Nabber—"

"Bye, Jack. Good luck and all that. See you back at the hideout." Nabber's voice faded into the distance.

Jack wanted to say something—to thank him, to warn him to be careful—but his mind couldn't find the words.

"Weapons out now, everyone," said Crayne as soon as Nabber was out of hearing range. "Hervo, you come forward and lead. Jack, fall in line right behind him."

Jack slid his sword from its sheath. He was grateful

that Hervo was leading the way; he didn't want the others knowing he hadn't listened to a word Nabber said.

A dim glint of light shone down the passage, brightening the farther they went. Gradually a world began to emerge from the darkness: stone barreled ceilings, storage barrels stacked high, elaborately carved doorways leading back into darkness, and stairs leading up to the light.

A soft noise sounded to the left. A shadow that had been static started to move across the wall. Hervo brought arrow to bow and shot into the dark corner. A startled intake of breath was followed by a dull thud. Hervo already had a second arrow nocked. He aimed but didn't shoot.

Tawl sprang ahead, sword out before him. After a moment his voice came from the shadows. "He's dead. Looks like a servant."

Crayne glanced at Hervo. "It must be two hours past midnight now."

Hervo nodded. "If he was a servant, then he must have been a crooked one. No decent man's up at this hour."

"Jack, come and give me a hand with the body," called Tawl.

Jack's eyes were finally growing accustomed to the dim light. He found Tawl in the corner crouching down next to a man with an arrow in his gut. Together they dragged the body behind a row of beer barrels. A line of blood dripped down the man's britches and onto the floor, but there was nothing they could do about that.

As they shifted the barrels to better conceal the body, Jack felt Tawl's hand brush against his cheek. "I thought so," he whispered. "You're burning up. What's the matter?"

Jack shook his head. How could he tell Tawl that Kylock's presence was sucking his blood to the surface? "It's all right, I'm not sick," he said. "Just on edge."

Tawl grabbed his shoulders and studied his face for a minute. Finally he said, "Be careful."

"You two, hurry up," hissed Crayne. Jack was grateful for the distraction: Tawl looked worried, and that made him worried, too.

It took them a while to find the concealed door leading up into the palace's secret passageways. It was at the back of a shadowed recess and looked more like a wood panel than a door. The entrance was extremely narrow—not more than the length of a man's forearm—and Jack had to turn side-on to squeeze through. Once inside, the passage grew only slightly wider. Crayne passed along a lit lantern. In the confined space, the oil smoke was noxious and Jack had to hold the lamp out at arm's length to stop himself from coughing.

"These passages were built to be undetectable from outside," said Crayne, glancing around. "They're so narrow that anyone looking would just think they're a thick wall, nothing more." He waited until Tawl had closed the door behind him. "Right. Let's get a move on."

Jack saw a rat scuttle across his path. The shock nearly made him drop the lantern.

"Easy, lad," said Crayne.

Jack shunted along the wall, taking turns when Crayne indicated. His fingertips trailed over soft mosses, cobwebs, and cold trickles of water. The air in the passage was thin and it had to be taken in quick breaths to satisfy the lungs. They came upon a flight of steep steps and Jack's heart thumped hard as he took them. As always these days, the rhythm was straight from Larn. What had started two months ago as something frightening now became a comfort to him. It was almost as if it were beating to keep him safe.

"Sharp right at the top," warned Crayne. Somewhere along the line, the leader of the party had figured out that Jack didn't know the way.

Jack took the right, then flew up another flight of stairs that ended in a wooden panel. A gentle press on the panel sent it swinging forward. A heavy brocade curtain flapped against Jack's face. On the other side of the panel was a thin brick facing that had been cut to mimic the exact lines of the wall.

Pushing through the curtain, Jack came face-to-face with a guard. Not pausing to think, he swung the oil lamp straight for the man's eyes. The man brought up his hands to stop himself from being burnt, and Jack sent a clean slice to his gut. Wrenching his sword free of the guard's stomach, Jack stepped to the side as the man fell forward. Blood pumped from the gash.

Crayne pushed past Jack, swinging around to take in both sides of the corridor. "Guards always come in pairs," he said. "Hervo, cover us while we put the body in the passage."

Jack bent down and wiped his blade against the guard's shoulder. As he stood up to make way for Tawl, he felt a quick thrill of dizziness pass over his body: Kylock was very close now.

Tawl and Crayne hauled the guard into the passage while Hervo checked the corridor ahead. No second guard appeared. Jack caught a tense glance passing between Hervo and Crayne.

As soon as the body was out of sight, they headed eastward down the corridor. On the long stretches, Hervo would take the lead—his bow could bring a man down at any distance—but as soon as they neared a turning, Hervo dropped back and Tawl and Crayne came forward. An armed man waiting around a corner could cut down a marksman in an instant.

Along the way they killed two more guards and one doddering nobleman in his nightshirt. Hervo took the guards with his bow, and Crayne used metal wire to silence then kill the old man, who had surprised everyone by emerging into the corridor just behind Tawl. They were in the heart of the nobles' quarters now, and Jack could feel the blood swelling across his cheeks. They passed one corridor that was well-lit with torches and well-insulated with carpets, and Jack knew, he just *knew*, that down there lay Kylock's chambers. His blood expanded like mercury in a glass, making his head feel ready to burst.

Later, he told himself, *later*. Melli had to come first.

Finally they reached the point where Nabber's instructions ran out. A stone gallery led to the left of them, curtained stairs straight ahead, and to the right ran an unlit passage. Everyone was tense; the slightest noise brought up blades and the merest flicker of a shadow nocked Hervo's bow.

Tawl made a brief sally into all three areas. No one said a word while he was gone. Back-to-back they formed a triangle and waited for him to return. Seconds took on the feel of minutes, and minutes themselves became *hours*.

"I think it's up here," hissed Tawl, emerging from behind the curtain. "The masonry's less ornate, and the color of the stone flags changes at the base of the first step—it looks like the stairs were built later."

Crayne nodded. "Then there's a good chance it leads to the annex." He swung around to face Jack. "You go with Tawl. Hervo and I will stay here and keep the retreat clear."

Jack hadn't expected this. He thought they'd all go up together.

His surprise must have shown on his face, for Crayne quickly added, "Look, if there's anything up there you can't handle, just shout out and I'll be up those stairs before you know it."

Jack took a quick breath before he said, "It wasn't me I was thinking about."

Crayne gave him a sharp look. "It goes the other way, too, Jack. I'm counting on you and Tawl to get back here as quickly as possible." His voice was level, but as he spoke his gaze scanned all four passages. "Besides, someone's got to stay here to keep an eye out for Andris. Otherwise there'd be no way of telling which way we'd gone."

Tawl came to stand by Jack's side. He looked first at Crayne and then Hervo, clasping each man's hand in turn. "Keep yourselves safe. We'll be back as soon as we can."

"Until later, my brother," said Crayne. It was the first time Jack had heard him use the knight's formal address to Tawl.

Tawl looked at Crayne for a moment, his expression showing many things, but most of all respect. Crayne nodded almost imperceptibly and Tawl turned and walked away.

Jack reached forward and clasped hands with both knights. He had already made the mistake of letting Nabber out of his sight without a word of thanks, and he was determined it wouldn't happen again. "I want to thank you—"

Crayne cut him short with a wave of his sword. "Wait until we're safe, Jack, and thank us then."

"Aye, lad," echoed Hervo in his soft, lilting voice. "Until we're all safe."

The stairs wound upward, broke for a small landing, and then continued on. Occasionally there were passages and doors leading off, but thick layers of dust spoke of no one's passing, and they hurried by them without a word. The stairs themselves were clean. Tawl took every step carefully now, and Jack followed his lead. Leather soles padding softly against the stone were the only noise they made.

The farther away from the nobles' quarters they traveled, the cooler Jack's face became. His blood was not pushing for the surface anymore, but his heart still raced and his stomach felt like a spiked lead ball.

"Ha! Ha! Ha!"

The sound of laughter made the spikes dig deep. Jack glanced at Tawl. He had heard it, too. They rounded a few more steps and then the laughter came again. Nearer this time. Tawl raised his sword, beckoning Jack to his side, and they took the next few steps in unison.

The light grew brighter, the noises became louder, and abruptly the stairs ended in a rectangular hall. Two guards were sitting on the floor, between them lay plates full of food, several lit candles, and a set of gaming pieces. For a fraction of a second the two men looked up, startled expressions frozen on their faces, and then they whipped out their swords.

Wooden chips scattered as they rose to their feet. Tawl lunged forward and sliced the smaller of the two in the thigh. His companion made a broad defensive sweep with his sword and Tawl was forced back. Jack slid into the space that opened up at the side and attacked the injured guard's flank. Feeling a sharp jab in his side, Jack stumbled back, winded. Tawl locked swords with the big man, metal screaming to a halt. Somehow, Tawl had managed to draw his short-knife with his left hand, and he used it now—slashing at his opponent's sword arm—to break the deadlock. As a reflex action to the attack, the guard withdrew his sword. Tawl allowed him no space and jumped forward as he stepped back, spearing the man's chest with his blade.

Jack was fending off an attack from the injured guard when Tawl came from behind and stabbed the man in the back. The man cried out and fell hard onto the stone floor, bones cracking as he landed. Tawl ran his sword through both men again, aiming for the heart each time. Sweat was pouring off his brow and his breath came short and ragged.

"Are you all right?" he asked, wiping a blood smear from below his eye.

Jack nodded. "The chain mail stopped the edge from

getting through. I think I'll end up with a few bruised ribs—that's all." Jack was in a lot of pain, but now wasn't the time to mention it.

"Who's there?" came a small, muffled voice.

Jack and Tawl glanced at each other.

Tawl rushed over to the door that lay opposite the stairs. "Melli, is that you?"

"Yes, it's me!"

Hearing those words, Tawl closed his eyes. A look close to hunger crossed over his face, and his lips mouthed something that Jack could only guess was thanks. He pushed hard against the door. It didn't give. "Stand back!" he cried. Taking a brief run-up, he slammed his shoulder into the door. The lock gave way and the door swung open.

Jack felt a faint *shearing* sensation ripple through his body. It was as if something passed through him like a ghost. But then Melli was there standing on the threshold, and the sight of her was enough to make Jack forget the feeling the moment it passed.

She was so thin—like a child—her blue eyes huge in a face smaller and paler than he remembered.

Tawl swept forward and grabbed her. He took her in his arms and held her tight against his chest. Jack was reminded of how injured men press their fists against a wound to make the bleeding stop. Tawl was like that—an injured man. His shoulders were shaking and his hands jerked up and down, stroking Melli's hair, her back, her cheeks, her neck. He couldn't stop touching her. When she pulled away to greet Jack, he didn't want to let her go. He clasped at the fabric of her dress as if that alone would hold her.

Gently, Melli disengaged herself from his grip and turned to face Jack.

Seeing her full-on for the first time, Jack knew that Melli was no longer pregnant. "What happened?" he said.

Melli looked at him through eyes as dull as etched glass. "Baralis murdered my baby."

Baralis' eyes opened the moment the sigil danced. A wave of tiny prickles jigged their way across his brain. The door was open. The sigil had been broken.

Day or night, Baralis always knew what time it was, and he knew now that it was far too late for the guards or Mistress Greal to be paying Melliandra a visit. He got out of bed and dressed, pausing a second to strike a flame. He had no need for light, but he felt naked without a shadow trailing after him. Crossing the room, he called for Crope, but impatience placed his hand upon the door, and he made his way through the palace on his own.

Tawl refused to go until he had bound Melli's splint properly to her arm. "I don't want to risk it breaking during the escape," he said. With great tenderness, he unwound the bandage and lifted off the wooden brace.

Jack took a sharp intake of breath. Melli's forearm was badly disfigured; the bones met at a slight angle and a lump had formed at the join.

"Who did this to you?" asked Tawl.

Melli looked down. "Kylock. The night I had my baby. It came early—two weeks before its time." Melli's voice was so low Jack had to strain to hear the words. "It was a boy. Baralis said it was a boy."

For an instant a look of raw anguish flitted across Tawl's face. Just as quickly the expression was gone, leaving only hard lines in its wake.

Jack leant forward and kissed Melli's hand: there was nothing he could say to her to make up for the loss of a child. As he straightened himself up, a sharp spasm ripped through his stomach. Pressure in his temples blinded him for an instant. *It's just the effects of the sword wound,* he told himself, trying hard to mask the pain.

"Right," said Tawl, tying the ends of Melli's bandages

together. "That should do it until we get to the hideout. Borlin can see to it then." He forced his face into a grim smile. "He's a genius with broken bones—he's caused enough of them in his time."

Melli returned the smile—probably just for Tawl's sake.

"Are you all right to walk?" asked Jack. His own pain had gone now, but a soft buzzing still sounded in his head.

She nodded. "I'm fine."

"Let's go, then." Jack's mind was already moving ahead. He would go as far as the passage entrance with Tawl and Melli, then strike off on his own. Kylock was his priority now.

Tawl took Melli's hand and they headed for the stairs behind him. They moved fast, anxious to get back to Crayne, eager to be gone from the palace. Gaining momentum as they traveled downward, they took the stairs two at a time, and by the time they reached the bottom all three of them were out of breath.

Jack saw Crayne's body before he smelled the sorcery. He pushed back the curtain and saw Crayne lying face-up in a pool of blood. He had no eyes, just hollow sockets filled with blood. Hervo was sitting, slumped, against the wall. His head was tipped forward, so Jack couldn't see his face, but a stream of thick red mucus was dripping from his nose. His right fist was curled around an arrow, and his bow lay to the left of him; the string still quivering.

Jack cursed his own stupidity. This was what he felt before when he held Melli's hand. He should have guessed. Should have known.

In the quarter-second it took him to realize all this, Tawl and Melli emerged from the staircase behind him and Baralis stepped out of the shadows in front.

Too late. Jack could taste the drawing on Baralis' lips. He could feel the power building.

Time slowed, then thickened.

He heard a voice screaming *"GO!"* and hardly recognized it as his own. He pushed something soft with all his might—Tawl, Melli—he didn't know who, then dove in the opposite direction. As he moved through the air his mind worked with his gut to form a drawing. He could see Baralis' power now. See it coming for him—scorching, crackling, dagger-smooth, dagger-sharp—blistering the air with its hot metal fury.

Too late. There was no time, only hair-thin slices of seconds. Baralis had begun his drawing before he'd reached the last step. A nauseating pulse swelled through Jack's body. The walls of his stomach snatched shut. He felt himself falling. Up came his hands to break his fall.

And then Baralis' drawing hit him full-on. A sizzling pain ripped through him. His limbs, his belly, and his face were slashed by scalding blades. His skin was slit open in a thousand needle cuts and white-hot fire raced toward his heart. Jack's body convulsed. A mighty spasm tore through his chest and then there was nothing more.

Too late.

Thirty-three

*T*awl was racing for Baralis when Jack went down. Melli in one hand, sword in the other, Tawl tried to cross the distance between them. Still righting himself from Jack's mighty push, Tawl's feet only had time to make three steps forward before the drawing hit.

The air roiled, whitened, then blasted into Jack. Tawl felt hot gusts whip over his face, burning his skin, sucking the air from his lungs, blinding him like a glance into the sun. There was a scintilla of an instant when he managed to step in front of Melli, but she had already taken the front of the blast and her scream was like a tear in his soul.

Jack was a moving blaze of white light, his body convulsing on the floor, his limbs engulfed by crackling fire. Then everything stopped.

There was a moment of pure calm. Jack's body slumped against the stone flags. Baralis was a sliver of darkness standing over it. Melli's head came to rest upon the back of Tawl's shoulder. And Tawl, suddenly realizing that the hilt of his blade was searing his palm, released his hold on the weapon. The sword clattered to the floor, shattering the calm like a church bell at daybreak.

Baralis collapsed. His body crumpled inward then downward and he landed in an angular heap, his cloak spreading out around him like a black fan. A huge giant of a man came running out of nowhere, sobbing and muttering to himself and shaking his head wildly. He ignored Tawl and Melli and made straight for Baralis' side.

"Come on, Tawl. Let's go," cried Melli.

Tawl went to pick up his sword. He was going to finish off Baralis once and for all.

"*No!*" screamed Melli. "Don't go near him. You don't know what he's capable of—even now." She tugged at his arm, and Tawl turned around to look at her. The skin on her face was red and wet, the result of the drawing. The fear in her eyes was as raw as an exposed nerve. "Please, Tawl. Let's get out of here while we can."

Shouts sounded in the distance. Two armed guards came running down the far gallery, weapons held out before them. Tawl picked up his blade. It was still hot, but no longer burning. He glanced over to Jack's body— his chest wasn't moving, there was no sign of life. Melli was right: they had to get away before half the palace guards came after them. Jack couldn't be helped now.

It was so very hard to turn away, though. The idea of carrying Jack's body back with him flashed through Tawl's mind. Perhaps he wasn't dead, just very still.

"Tawl! The guards!" Melli was frantic now. Blood and tears coated her cheeks. Her whole body was trembling. The front of her dress was scorched black, and as she pulled him forward, Tawl could see where the drawing had singed all the hairs on her arm.

Tawl knew he had to get Melli to safety. More than his oath, she was half the bargain he had made with himself in the cold, green depths of Lake Ormon. Saving her was the first part of saving himself.

There was no time to carry a body. It would slow them down too much. The guards were nearly on top of them, and by the sounds of things there were more on the way. Tawl clasped hold of Melli's hand and they ran down the corridor, the guards chasing after them.

Tears stung the raw flesh of Tawl's cheeks as he ran.

Hervo, Crayne, Jack: Baralis had taken them all. Friends, brothers, good men who had followed him into danger with no thought for themselves. Hervo and Crayne weren't on a quest, they weren't bound by an ancient prophecy; they had simply *believed* in him. The image of Crayne's eyeless body flickered across Tawl's thoughts. He felt a tight, angry pain in his chest. What had Baralis done to him?

Anger burned into rage and, as Tawl sped along the corridors with Melli at his side, he knew that Baralis, Kylock, and Tyren all had to be destroyed.

The guards were catching up. Any second now Tawl knew he would have to turn and fight. He could take two men on his own, but he was afraid that Melli might be injured in the fray. Tawl was just about to order her to run ahead, when, like a gift from the gods, Andris appeared before him. The tall fair-haired knight had two other men with him, their weapons were drawn, and after the briefest of acknowledgments, they stepped in to cut down the guards at their heels.

The knights hacked at the guards with all the speed and enthusiasm of troops new to the battle. Tawl caught his breath for a moment. Melli was at his side, and although he was still holding her hand, he reached up and brushed her cheek with his sword arm. He couldn't touch her enough.

Smiling up at him, she said, "I'd almost given up hope."

He kissed her, then. Blistered lips on blistered lips, tear-wet noses touching, eyes open to see one another, frightened that if they closed them the other person might disappear. Tawl knew then that it wasn't just about saving himself. It was about love as well. Melli was more than half a bargain: she was the woman he loved. And perhaps, Borc willing, at the end of everything there might be a way for them to be together. If it all turned out all right.

"Where's Crayne and the others?" It was Andris. He was wiping his blade against his leg. The two guards were down. One of the other knights, Gervhay, the youngest, had his bow strung, ready to pick off anyone who came down the corridor.

Tawl looked down at the floor. The end was a long way off: too long to even think about. "They're dead. Baralis killed them."

Andris nodded. Tawl knew he had been expecting just such an answer. *"Thes ve esrl,"* he said.

Tawl, Gervhay, and Corvis repeated it. They *were* worthy.

There was no time to mourn. Andris barked an order and everyone began to run down the corridor toward the tunnel entrance. Faces were grim, grips were tight, and when anyone crossed their path they were hewn down within seconds. Gervhay's arrows never missed, Andris' blade dealt only mortal blows, and Corvis' long-knife found heart after beating heart. Blood covered them and dried on them, filling their nostrils with its life-stealing scent. Everything was smeared red: the walls, the shadows, the guards, their sight. Nothing was untouched by the taint.

Finally they reached the passage entrance. Their pursuers were all dead or dying, and Andris raised the curtain that covered the panel.

That was when Tawl heard it.

He was bringing up the rear, trailing behind the rest, spearing bodies with his sword, ensuring that no one was left alive to report which way they headed, when an unmistakable sound rang out in the distance.

As soon as he heard the noise, he looked to Melli. Andris had just beckoned her forward and she was about to squeeze her body into the tunnel. She didn't look up at the sound. None of them did.

Tawl made a quick decision. He waited until all four of them were in the tunnel before approaching the entrance.

"I want you to go on ahead. Get out of here. Go straight to the hideout and wait for me."

Andris shook his head. "No, Tawl. We go together."

"There's something here I've got to look into. I'll just be a few extra minutes, that's all."

"Tawl, don't leave me. Not now." It was Melli, calling from the shadows of the passageway. She sounded afraid.

He reached out a hand, feeling for her touch. "As Borc is my witness, I swear I won't do anything foolish. I'll be back by your side before the night is through."

Melli's fingers clasped his. "I love you," she said.

Despite everything that had happened that night — despite the blood, the carnage, the loss of his friends—the moment Melli said those words Tawl felt a joy so intense he thought his heart would break. He reached up and kissed her hand. "I love you," he said softly into the darkness. "I promise you I will return."

Letting go of her hand was the hardest thing he had ever done in his life. His soul, his heart, his muscles, and his mind did not want to let her go, but he had just heard the sound of a baby crying and he knew he must follow his oath.

"Ssh for Nanny Greal, my little one. Ssh for Nanny Greal." Mistress Greal held the baby to her and rocked it gently against her bony breast. Every now and then she would make cooing noises and offer her finger up for sucking.

Little Herbert—named after Mistress Greal and Madame Thornypurse's father, Herbert Skinflynt Greal—had never cried before at night. He was so weak that he slept most of the time, and the few hours a day he was awake he was as quiet as a lamb. He was the tiniest baby Mistress Greal had ever seen. Even now, three weeks after his birth, he hardly weighed a thing. His fists were as light as dandelions and his precious little head felt like a pincushion in her hand. He was early, that was the problem. Pushed out before his time by his tart of a mother, Melli, who didn't have the backbone to carry him to term.

Herbert shifted in Mistress Greal's arms, opened his blue eyes wide, and began to bellow at the top of his lungs.

"Ssh, my little one. Ssh." Mistress Greal rocked, cooed, squeezed, cradled and, when that didn't work, panicked. It was the wee hours of the morning and sound could travel a long way in the stone-cold silence before dawn. Mistress Greal carried the baby across the room, opened the wardrobe, stepped inside, and drew the door shut behind her.

The baby reacted to the changes in light and warmth by crying louder.

Mistress Greal bounced little Herbert tenderly in her arms. "Ssh, Nanny Greal won't hurt you. No, not Nanny Greal. Nanny Greal loves little Herby. Yes, she does. Yes, she does." The words began to have a calming effect on the baby, and Mistress Greal carried on talking whilst he drifted off to sleep.

Standing in the dark, back pressed up against her winter robes, legs aching from lack of movement, baby sucking on her thumb, Mistress Greal felt a protective tightening in her chest. Herby was hers now and no one could take him away.

She hadn't meant to love him. She had taken him purely for spite. Baralis had murdered her beloved niece, Corsella, and that meant he had to pay. Mistress Greal had simply taken something to use as a weapon against him. Little Herbert was more dangerous than any army: he was the true heir to Bren—he had the birthmark of the Hawk on his left ankle to prove it. All Mistress Greal had to do was let the word out that the baby was alive, well, and legitimate, and the good people of Bren would rebel against Kylock. They would take the duke's son over a foreign tyrant any day of the week. Baralis would find himself thrown out of the city, and if things went right, hounded until death.

That was the plan, anyway: revenge. But something had happened to Mistress Greal when she held the tiny newborn baby in her hands, and now Baralis and his schemes didn't seem nearly so important.

The baby was so frail, that was what had got her started. He needed care day and night, needed feeding through a dripping cloth and massaging with warm oil. He was helpless without her. All he could do was lie on his blanket and kick his tiny fists and feet. Mistress Greal had never been married, never had a child of her own, never knew what it felt like to have someone entirely dependent on her. The baby loved her, trusted her—she was the only person who mattered in its short and innocent life. The baby wasn't weaseling, ungrateful, or money-grabbing; he wasn't out to fleece her of her loot, or rob her of her business. He just wanted to feel her arms around him and suck on her thumb.

Gradually, over the course of a few days, Mistress Greal found herself in the unheard-of situation of wanting to *give*: her time, love, money, protection. Nothing was too much when it came to keeping Herbert safe.

Baralis was a murderer: he had killed the baby's father and half-sister. To try and take him on was more than foolish, it was suicide. She would only put herself and the baby at risk. The best thing she could do would be to steal away from the palace, leave the city, travel back to the kingdoms, and never let a living person know the true identity of her baby. Mistress Greal brushed Herbert's baby curls with her hand. Tomorrow she would go and see her sister and make arrangements to liquidate her assets. Tonight had proven that it was much too dangerous to keep the baby in the palace. He couldn't be blamed for crying, but he couldn't be stopped, either. It was time to take him far away from danger.

Mistress Greal pushed her elbow against the wardrobe

door and stepped out once more into the light and warmth of her chamber. It was very late now and she wanted to get a few hours sleep before dawn.

Just as she was about to lay Herbert down in the shallow chest that had become his crib, the bones in Mistress Greal's wrist snapped into a cramp. The sharp pain caused her to release her grip on Herbert's legs and sent the baby's bottom thumping down onto the blanketed base of the chest. It wasn't a hard blow, but it was enough to wake up the baby and set him off in an indignant bawl.

Mistress Greal was frantic. "Ssh. Ssh," she cried, picking him up again and rocking him to and fro. "Come on, my little Herbert. Ssh for Nanny Greal."

Tawl was about to give up, when he heard the baby crying again. Very close now. He stopped in his tracks and tried to pinpoint the sound. Ahead, to the left and down a level. Checking the corridors to either side for guards, he made his way forward.

As far as he could tell he was no longer in the main part of the nobles' quarters; there were fewer lit torches on the walls, no hanging tapestries, and no stationed guards. Occasionally he would hear footsteps sounding in the distance, but no one appeared to be heading his way. Tawl was grateful for the opportunity to catch his breath, but he was taking no chances, and paused constantly to check his back. Dim light was a definite advantage, and he had taken to extinguishing the odd torch here and there to add to the gloom.

Coming upon a short flight of stairs, he headed downward. The crying had stopped now, but Tawl guessed he was very close to the source, and when the stairs ended in a circular gallery, he made straight for the door on the left.

Putting his ear to the wood, he heard a woman's voice. She was speaking in the peculiar, singsong tones that mothers use on their babies. Tawl took a settling breath.

He knew it was quite possible that the baby within might be someone other than Melli's, but he had to know for sure. He had sworn an oath to the duke to protect his wife *and* his heirs, and if there was even a remote possibility that his son still lived, then Tawl was honor-bound to protect him.

Gently, Tawl tested the door. It was bolted on the other side. He hadn't wanted to go barging in, but there was nothing else for it. Pivoting on one leg, he aimed a kick at the center of the door.

The door swung back. The woman screamed. The baby started to cry.

Raising his sword arm in a gesture of no contest, Tawl entered the room. Immediately the woman sprang at him. She had a knife in her hand and stabbed straight at his chest. Tawl brought down his arm to block the blow and caught the full impact of the blade just below his shoulder. Pain shot along his upper arm, bringing sharp tears to his eyes. Anger made him lash out with his fist, and he clipped the woman's lower jaw. She went reeling backward, flaying out her arms to break her fall. She landed in the corner by the baby.

Tawl immediately rushed to her aid. The woman still had hold of her knife and stabbed at the air between them. "Keep away from me and my baby," she cried.

Tawl backed away. His arm was bleeding badly and he clamped his palm over the wound. "Your baby?" The woman looked far too old to be the mother of a young child.

"My daughter's baby," replied the woman. "Now get out of here before I call the guard."

Ignoring the threat, Tawl peered into the chest. The baby was tiny, no more than a newborn. Its little hands were curled into fists and it was crying with a sort of amazed abandon, as if it were surprised by how much noise it could make. Tawl raised the tip of his sword toward the woman. "Make it stop crying."

As the woman scrambled up, he cut across the room and closed the door. Tearing off a strip of fabric from his tunic, he attempted to bind his wound. It wasn't easy; there was a lot of blood and he had to use his left hand to tie the knot. He fastened it as tight as he could bear, and then pushed his fist into the center of the bloody rag. The pain forced his eyes closed for an instant before subsiding to a biting ache.

Holding his fist firm, he turned to look at the woman. She had the baby in her arms and was calming it with a stream of mother's talk. Tawl thought the woman had rather a sharp and grating voice, but the baby responded to the sound, and his cries soon gave way to gurgles.

"Bring it over here so I can look at it," he said.

The woman snatched the baby to her chest.

Tawl suddenly felt very weary. It had been a long hard day and he just wanted it to end. "Lady, I have no wish to harm you or your baby, but I do need to take a look at the child." As he spoke, he sheathed his sword—his right arm was too weak to wield it, and his left arm was not trained for heavy weapons. He pulled out his long-knife instead. "Now bring it here."

The woman's eyes flicked to the long-knife. "Who are you?"

Tawl was losing patience. He crossed the room. "Give me the baby."

"I'll scream."

"I don't think you will."

The woman gave him a sharp look and offered the baby forward.

Tawl watched her carefully. He had seen how fast she was with a knife. He decided to take no chances. "Lay it on the bed. Strip its clothes off."

The woman did as she was told, leaving only the nappy and woolen bedsocks on the baby. "Stand over in the corner while I take a look at it," said Tawl, pointing the blade of the long-knife at her chest. She hesitated. *"Go!"*

Tawl moved to the opposite side of the bed so he could keep an eye on the woman. He reached out and touched the baby. It was still awake and it looked up at Tawl with unfocused blue eyes. Eyes the color and shape of Melli's. "How old is"—Tawl couldn't tell if it was a boy or a girl—"it?"

"My daughter birthed it nine weeks ago now. She's sick so I'm looking after it for her."

The woman was lying to the wrong person. Tawl knew all about babies; he had raised a newborn single-handedly after his mother died. The child before him wasn't big enough to be nine weeks old. Gently, he rolled the baby onto its stomach, checking for any birthmarks. He had heard once, long ago, that babies born into the house of Bren had the mark of the hawk upon them. The baby's back was spotless.

"Take off its nappy and bedsocks."

Out of the corner of his eye, Tawl saw the woman raise her knife. Suddenly, he'd had enough. The baby wasn't hers or her daughter's. It had eyes and hair the color of Melli's and it was tiny enough for a newborn. He bent down and scooped the baby up in his injured arm. Pain clawed down his shoulder. He ignored it.

"Don't take him," cried the woman. She hovered forward with her knife, but Tawl's knife hand was free and he forced her back with warning circles.

"Get me a blanket."

The woman grabbed the blanket off the bed. "Please don't take him. *Please*."

"Lady, he's not your baby. We both know that." Tawl neither liked nor trusted the woman, but he could tell she cared about the baby. "Why don't you tell me the truth? I'm not going to harm you."

"But you'll take the baby?"

"Yes. I'm taking it now whatever you say." Tawl took the blanket from the woman. She made no attempt to stab him. He tried his best to tuck the blanket around the baby, but it was difficult with only one hand. To keep the baby calm, he rocked his chest back and forward.

"You know about babies?" she said.

"Yes. I raised one. Long ago now." Tawl sensed the woman was relaxing and began to relax a little himself. "Help me pull the blanket around him. He's getting cold."

He watched as the woman decided whether or not to put down her knife. "Who are you?"

Tawl was about to ignore the question, as he had the first time, but for some reason, he decided to take a risk. He needed to find out the truth. Looking straight into her eyes, he said, "I'm Tawl, duke's champion. Before an entire city I swore an oath to protect the duke and his heirs."

The woman's gaze dropped to the baby. She tucked the blanket around his body, making sure his little arms were well covered. "You think this baby is his son?"

"I believe so, but only you can tell me for sure." Tawl's voice was gentle. "I won't condemn you for taking him. How could I? You saved his life. I owe you a debt that can never be repaid, and I will be forever grateful to you, but please, *please*, tell me the truth."

A few moments of silence followed. The woman stroked the baby's head. Abruptly, she looked up. "If I tell you everything will you take me with you? The baby loves me, you see. I'm all he knows. I'm like a mother to him—he might be frightened without me."

Tawl dropped the long-knife on the bed. Reaching up, he placed his hand over the woman's bony, misshapen wrist. "I promise I'll take you with me. I know you love him—I can see that. Now please, tell me what happened."

In a gesture of trust, Tawl handed the baby back.

The woman was shaking. Teardrops turned her eyelashes into spikes. "Come to Nanny Greal," she cooed. "There's a good boy." Settling herself down on the edge of the bed, she uncovered the baby's left foot and pulled off his sock. A pink mark, small as a thumbnail, rested in the chubby fold of flesh just above his ankle. The mark of the Hawk.

"Baralis ordered me to take the baby away and kill it," said the woman quietly. "I would have done it, too, if it hadn't been for Corsella."

"Corsella? Thornypurse's daughter?"

The woman looked up. "Yes, she's my niece. Did you know her?"

"She took me in when I first arrived in Bren."

"Good girl. Heart of gold. Beautiful, too."

Tawl didn't have quite the same opinion of the girl, but now wasn't the time to dispute it. "What did Baralis do to her?"

"He murdered her. Crope had her necklace in a box, said his master let him have it."

Tawl sat on the bed next to the woman. Together, they stroked the baby. "I'm sorry," he said, feeling guilty at how roughly he'd treated Madame Thornypurse. "I didn't know."

"Nothing for you to be sorry for. Baralis has done just as bad to you."

"What do you mean?"

"He was the one who plotted the duke's murder. I was listening in when he got that man Traff to do it. Heard everything, I did."

Tawl's head was reeling. "Where was this?"

"At my sister's place, of course. Traff was staying there and Baralis paid him a visit. Told him about the secret passageways and the like. Promised him Melliandra all for himself."

"And you heard all this?"

The woman nodded. "Word for word."

"What else do you know about Baralis?"

"Plenty. I keep a notebook of all the nobles he and Kylock have had killed. Kylock maims the bodies so they can't be recognized, and then throws them into the lake. The official word is that they all go missing."

"Do you have that book with you now?"

The woman patted her side. "Never without it. Some of the richest and most respected noblemen in Bren are listed in it."

Tawl was beginning to realize how valuable Nanny Greal could be. The things she knew about Baralis and Kylock could turn the city upside down. "I think we'd better get going," he said. "I'll watch the baby while you get your belongings together. Only take things you can carry on your back. You'll need both hands free for the baby."

As she rummaged around in her wardrobe, Tawl took the baby in his arms. Melli's baby. It was perfect: a tiny, tough-looking thing with eyes as large as pancakes. Tawl hugged it to him, enjoying the feel of its warm little body pressed against his. "What were you going to do with him?" he asked the woman.

"Take him far away. Make sure no one ever knew who he was." She smiled at Tawl—an unpleasant sight, for she had lost both her front teeth. "You're good with him, I see."

"He's beautiful." Tawl looked up at the woman. "You did the right thing, you know. Baralis would have found out sooner or later. He would have tracked you down and killed you both."

"Aye. You're probably right." The woman fastened her cloak and came over for the baby. "So where will you take us?"

"Outside of the city, until it's safe to come back." Tawl handed over the baby. His sword arm had stopped bleeding, but a sharp spasm coursed down his shoulder as he held the baby out.

"I can't see that it will ever be safe to come back."

"Oh, it will," said Tawl. "It will."

Mistress Greal, or Nanny Greal as she now preferred to call herself, showed Tawl a back way down to the servants' chapel. The palace guards were out in full force now, but they were concentrating their efforts in the nobles' quarters, and apart from one lone guard Tawl dispatched with his long-knife, and a young scullery maid who looked so terrified at the sight of Nanny Greal that Tawl simply let her go, they met no one along the way.

Nanny Greal hugged little Herbert tight as she followed Tawl down through the palace. She liked the golden-haired knight a lot: he was handsome, honorable, gentle, and most of all she believed him when he said he'd protect little Herbert with his life. She hadn't meant to go with him, not at all, but seeing him handle the baby—big hands gently cupping Herbert's soft, vulnerable head—she knew she could trust him. He had a good heart, and that was something Nanny Greal hadn't seen in anyone in a long time.

He was right about Baralis, too. The man *would* find out that the baby was alive—there was nothing he couldn't do. And nothing he wouldn't stop at to get what he wanted.

Yes, she thought, *it's for the best. Keeping little Herbert safe is all that matters now.*

They entered the servants' chapel, and Tawl set about pulling the center panel off the wall. It had been nailed down, and Tawl had to use the blade of his sword to pry it open.

Soon they were in a pitch-black passageway, wading through ankle-deep water, then knee-deep water, then water that came up to Nanny Greal's chest. Tawl took the baby then, holding it high atop his shoulder, pausing whenever they came to a tricky bit to lend Nanny Greal a hand. The farther they went, the colder it got, but the warmer it felt in Nanny Greal's heart. Little Herbert was in safe hands, kind hands, hands that would never harm him. Nanny Greal smiled a satisfied toothless smile. For the first time in her fifty-year lifespan, she didn't care a jot about herself.

*

"Here, my lady, drink this; it well help you relax." Melli took the bowl of holk from Borlin, even sipped it, but she knew she wouldn't relax. How could she rest until she knew Tawl was safe?

Pulling the blanket close around her body, Melli closed her eyes for a few minutes. She couldn't believe that she was free. Baralis' threats had no power to harm her, Mistress Greal could no longer terrorize her, and Kylock could never use her to wash away his sins. Safe at last. Luck had waited until the last minute—as luck always does—and whisked her away from the palace in the company of six gallant knights.

Why then didn't she feel happy? Why did she just feel hollow and ready to cry?

The time after Tawl had left her had passed in a series of flashes: freezing water, tense faces, strung arrows, and galloping horses. The escape had gone smoothly. They emerged into a dark alleyway and were met by a man who was holding horses ready. He introduced himself as Borlin, whisked her onto the back of his horse, and together they rode across the city in the rain. They met up with the others later at the hideout.

Nabber was there. He greeted her with a great big smile and then looked over her shoulder for Tawl. The smile slid off his face when Borlin said, "Tawl went off on his own for a bit, lad. He'll be back later—wait and see."

And that's what everyone did: wait. They sat around, one candle lighting the space between them, and listened for the sound of Tawl's approach.

The knights' kindness brought a lump to Melli's throat. In hushed voices they asked her how she felt, gently touching her brow, rubbing salve into the burns, tracing concerned fingers along the line of her arm. Borlin wanted to reset the bone then and there, but Melli was reluctant to take a painkilling drug in case it dulled her wits or sent her to sleep, so she put the operation off until morning. She wanted to be alert when Tawl returned.

Neither Nabber nor the knights asked her about what had happened in the palace. Melli was grateful for that. She didn't want to think about her last sight of Jack. He had saved both her and Tawl—that much was clear—but how he had done it she didn't really know. Everything had happened so fast. There was a bolt of blinding light, a wave of scorching air, and then . . .

Melli brought her hand to her face. Hot tears spilled down her cheeks. Jack was dead. He had died saving *her*. She remembered the moment they first met, when she was attacked on Harvell's east road—he came to her rescue then. There were so many times after that as well: the dungeons, the forest, Cravin's townhouse in Bren. He was always saving her. Now he couldn't save her anymore.

"There, my lady." Borlin was beside her, stroking her hair, his gruff voice as soft as he could make it. "Don't take on. Tawl will be back soon."

But Jack won't, Melli wanted to say. *And neither will your two brethren. Baralis has taken them all.* Instead she said nothing, and let herself be comforted by Borlin until the tears went away.

A sharp noise awakened her. Surprised that she had fallen asleep, even more surprised that she had been sleeping against Borlin's chest, Melli sprang to her feet. Two of the knights had gone to investigate the noise; the others were looking in the direction of the stairs. Nabber was standing by the bottom step, swaying impatiently from side to side. Melli came and stood by him, bringing her good arm up around his shoulders.

The two knights came back first. Melli let out a sigh of disappointment, then, just as she sucked in another breath, Tawl appeared at the top of the stairs, covered in blood, soaked to the bone, a makeshift bandage around his upper arm. She rushed forward, pushing past the knights to get to him. But then, suddenly, she stopped in her tracks.

Mistress Greal was walking in Tawl's shadow. In her arms she was carrying some sort of bundle.

Melli's stomach quickly turned. She looked at Tawl; he was smiling. She looked at the two knights; they were smiling. Didn't they know who this woman was? Didn't they know it was a trap?

Tawl whispered something to Mistress Greal, and the woman stepped forward. Melli readied herself to attack her. These men here might not know who the woman was, but *she* did, and with bare hands she was going to kill her. Mistress Greal held out her bundle—she obviously meant to throw it. Melli was poised for the block.

Mistress Greal looked confused. "Don't you want to take him?" she said.

Melli glanced at Tawl. He made an encouraging gesture with his hands. Melli felt like she was going mad. The woman had bewitched him.

And then a sound came from the bundle. A tiny gurgling noise.

Melli's heart stopped beating. The hairs on her arms prickled. Her entire body swayed forward. She didn't dare hope, didn't dare think.

Everyone was looking at her now. "Take him, Melli," murmured Tawl.

The room began to blank out. Sides and edges faded into shadow and all that remained was the bundle in Mistress Greal's arms. Melli took a step toward it. The blanket moved. The corner of the fabric fell away and a fierce little fist came into view. A quick breath escaped from Melli's lips. Her heart pumped wildly in her chest. She leapt toward the bundle, arms outstretched, hands cupped ready, tears streaming down her face. Mistress Greal handed the warm and shifting bundle to her. Slowly, carefully, Melli took it into her arms. It was lighter than she had expected—so light it made her heart ache. She hugged it against her chest and peered down into the calm blue eyes of her baby. *Her* baby.

The clawing hollow in Melli's stomach snapped closed. She felt complete.

Looking up through a blur of tears, she searched out Tawl's face. This was what he had gone back for: he had gone back to find her baby. "Thank you," she whispered softly, hugging her baby tight. "With all my heart and soul, I thank you."

Thirty-four

Stop calling him Herbert. He isn't Herbert."

"What is he, then?" Nanny Greal cooed down at the baby. Much to Melli's annoyance, he stopped crying immediately and gurgled up at Nanny Greal.

"He's . . . " To Melli's further annoyance, she couldn't think of a suitable name. Garon, after his father? No, it sounded too challenging; she wanted her son to have a gentle name. She edged past Nanny Greal and looked into the baby's face. The truth was—though she hated to admit it—Herbert suited him nicely. Which annoyed her even more. "I'll name him in my own good time and that's the end of that."

Melli pushed Nanny Greal out of the way, snatched the baby up, and crossed over to the other side of the inn.

"Melli. Don't be so hard on her." It was Tawl. Where had he come from? "She saved your baby's life. She hid him from Baralis, kept him safe, and looked after him as if he were her own. You owe her thanks, not resentment."

"Who turned you into a saint, Tawl?" Melli regretted the words as soon as they left her lips, but she'd said them and she wasn't about to take them back. To her surprise, Tawl actually smiled.

"They'll turn me into a saint the day you learn to think before you speak." Reaching up, he brushed a lock of hair from her face. "Seriously, if you can't be kind to Nanny Greal, at least don't be mean. It took her a lot to admit who the baby was and then give him up to me."

Nanny Greal! Melli tried, but couldn't quite stop the snort of indignation from puffing down her nostrils. "Well, she's certainly taken a shine to you, that much is clear. Ever since last night it's been Tawl this, Tawl that. If that woman has one soft spot in that hard bony head of hers, then you've surely found it."

Tawl was laughing at her. He wrapped his arms around her and the baby and hugged them both very hard. "I'm so glad you haven't changed," he said.

They had left the city at midmorning. Melli had managed only a few hours sleep, her body curled around the baby, her head resting against Tawl's chest. When she awoke she found that Tawl was no longer beside her; he was on the opposite side of the room talking with the knights. His voice was hushed, but one look at his face was enough for Melli to guess what Tawl was saying: he was telling the men what had happened last night. The knights' faces were grave, their eyes downcast, the tendons on their hands and necks sharply strained. Occasionally their lips would move, and although Melli could hear nothing, she knew they spoke Baralis' name.

After that events moved swiftly. Borlin came to her and put a new and much larger splint on her arm. He said there was no time to reset the bone before they left. A mighty scramble to get ready followed: horses were saddled, disguises were donned, breakfast eaten quickly, plans decided, supplies acquired, scouts sent out, and proposed escape routes checked for guards.

While all this was going on, Melli tried to deal with the baby. She felt like a fool; she knew nothing about caring for a newborn. Her own milk had dried up four days ago, and she didn't know what to feed him. The baby cried angrily at her attempts to calm him, dribbled viciously when offered a finger to suck on, and had a fist-throwing, feet-kicking fit when presented with a spoonful of sheep's milk. The newly styled Nanny Greal offered to help. Melli slapped her away. From a safe distance Nanny Greal suggested giving the baby a rag soaked with watered-down milk to suck on. Melli suggested that Nanny Greal should shut up. Five minutes later, when the baby had worked itself up into a tiny bundle of hungry and indignant rage, Melli was forced to concede.

Nanny Greal dealt firmly, yet gently, with the baby, calming, feeding, then rocking him off to sleep. Melli was so upset over Greal's success, she wanted to throw her out on the street then and there. It wasn't Nanny Greal's baby, it was _hers_.

Tawl stepped in and practically ordered her to calm down. Melli could see he was worried about the escape from the city, so she let the matter pass.

Minutes later they were on their way. Tawl made everyone split into small groups: some went through the east gate disguised as merchants, some went through the south gate as mercenaries or farmers, and Melli, Tawl, and the baby went under the wall. It was like fleeing from the palace all over again: freezing water, foul smells and utter darkness. Melli relished every step. She was free. Free from Baralis and Kylock and her small, confining chamber. It was a joy to walk hand in hand with Tawl, the baby snuggling against her back in a blanket-lined sling designed by Nabber.

For a while, Melli managed to forget everything that had gone before, but when Tawl asked her how she was coping in the dark, she began her reply: "Oh, this is nothing compared to the tunnels Jack and I . . . "

Melli couldn't finish the sentence. There was no more _Jack and I_. Jack was gone, killed by Baralis as they tried to escape. Closing her eyes very tightly, Melli willed herself not to cry. Tawl reached out and felt for her hand, and although she knew he was trying to comfort her, his thoughtfulness only made her feel worse. She and Tawl were safe, her baby was safe—it didn't seem fair that they had emerged from the palace unscathed while Jack's body was left behind.

Suddenly the baby began to cry, and despite Tawl's warnings that she would need both hands free to climb up to the surface, Melli took the baby from the sling and hugged him close to her chest. She needed to feel his warmth against her heart.

Andris was waiting for them on the other side of the wall. He had a spare horse with him, and he handed Tawl the reins before riding off. Melli rode on the horse whilst Tawl led it forward like the good husband he was pretending to be.

The journey to Fair Oaks took three hours. Occasionally, when they were walking on high ground, Melli would catch glimpses of Borlin. The stout archer was taking a parallel route to theirs and was ready to provide cover with his bow if trouble came. Nothing happened. The only people they passed were road-weary travelers, bone-thin farmers, and mercenaries looking for a fight. No one paid any attention to the fieldhand dressed in rags and his wild-looking wife.

Eventually they came to a small village that boasted one inn, a smithy, and a dressmaker. Fair Oaks. They were greeted by two knights whom Melli had never seen before. The men wanted to take them straight to the inn. Tawl refused at first, but after some discussion that Melli wasn't party to, he reluctantly agreed.

Never in her life would Melli forget the welcome she got at the inn. The innkeeper, his wife, his three pretty daughters, the cook, the stableboy, and an old man who could have been anyone's grandfather, all bowed as she walked in the door. Melli was confused. What had they been told?

"Drink! Food for the lady. Quick, quick." The innkeeper clapped pudgy hands together and the prettiest daughter went running off. Pulling a chair close to the fire, he dusted it down with his sleeve. "Please sit, my lady." He wasn't looking directly at her. No one was. They were all looking at what she held in her arms.

The baby started to cry. Everyone in the room leant forward. Tawl touched her sleeve. "Andris got here before us," he murmured. "He thought it best to tell them who the baby is."

Melli didn't know what to do. Everyone was waiting for her to move.

The youngest of the innkeeper's daughters stepped forward. "Can I have a look at the baby, my lady?"

Melli glanced at Tawl. He nodded almost imperceptibly, and Melli held out the baby for the young girl to see. Soon everyone was around her. Awestruck at first, they spoke only in whispers, keeping a polite distance between themselves and the child, then as they grew more confident the atmosphere changed. They stroked the baby's hair, giggled over his tiny fists, gave advice on how to feed him, and shared newborn stories of their own. They were all united in their desire to do something for the baby: the cook went off to warm some milk, the innkeeper's wife brought down her softest lambswool blanket, the stableboy went away to look for something suitable for the baby to lie in, the old man hummed a lullaby for sleeping, and the innkeeper's daughters, all three of them, ran upstairs to make sure the room the baby would rest in was as warm and dry as it could possibly be.

Melli felt tears coming to her eyes. She had gone on for so long without kindness, that now, to find it here amongst strangers seemed a gift of the most precious kind. She knew these people were taking a great risk welcoming the duke's son—Kylock would tolerate no one who aided the sole challenger to his title—and she paid back their bravery with trust: handing the baby over to the innkeeper's wife while she slept a few hours by the fire.

By the time she awoke all the knights, Nabber, and Nanny Greal had arrived. Judging from the number of lit candles, it was an hour or two after dusk. The baby was crying heartily for his dinner and all the women were fussing around, trying to calm him down. Once again, Nanny Greal was the only person who could comfort him: one squawk of her shrill voice and the baby was as quiet as a lamb.

Little Herbert was quiet now, resting against Melli's chest as Tawl caught them both in a hug. Melli felt safe and happy. Her baby was alive and well, and as long as Tawl was beside him, he'd never come to harm.

"Tawl!" cried someone from outside. "They're here! Maybor's men are here."

All thoughts dropped from Melli's mind at the sound of her father's name. She looked up at Tawl. "Is my father coming?" She had visions of Maybor meeting his grandson. He was sure to insist that the baby resembled him!

Tawl's face darkened. "Melli, I—"

Melli shook her head. "No," she said softly. *"No."* The look in Tawl's eyes scared her. Some deep protective instinct warned her she didn't want to hear anymore. She tried to pull away, but Tawl held her firm.

"Maybor died two weeks ago. He'd spent a month up in the mountains hiding away from Kylock, and he caught pneumonia." Tawl's voice was gentle. His fingers traced the line of her cheek. "By the time he came down it was too late."

Melli's legs buckled beneath her. The only thing that kept her from falling was Tawl. Her father dead—she just couldn't imagine it. He had always been so hearty, so full of life. . . .

Someone came forward and took the baby—Melli didn't know who. Tawl picked her up and carried her over to the fire. A cup of wine was pressed to her lips and reluctantly she drank. It tasted like blood. "How do you know what happened to him?" she said to Tawl.

"Jack and I saw him the night he died. He said he loved you very much." Tawl was kneeling beside her now. His eyes were filled with love and understanding. "I should have told you sooner, only everything happened so fast, and I wanted to wait for the right moment."

Two weeks. He'd been dead two weeks and she hadn't even known it. She felt like a traitor. Her mind was acting strangely, switching from thought to thought without the normal links in between. "Who are the men?" she asked. "The ones who are coming?"

"They're the Highwall troops he led off the battlefield into the mountains. He saved their lives."

"Why are they coming here?"

"They're going to help us take over Tyren's camp." Tawl took her hand. "Maybor brought them down from the mountain to give them a chance to fight."

Melli nodded; her mind had already moved on. "Did he suffer much?"

"If he did he never showed it. When I saw him he was clear-headed and alert, almost his old self."

"What did he look like?"

"The same as ever. His hair was well brushed, he was clean-shaven. Even wearing fragrance."

Melli smiled. She could see him now, lying in his bed, surrounded by pots of hair oil and scented creams, calling for his mirror whilst supervising his shave. In the back of her mind she knew that Tawl was leaving things out—no one dies of lung fever without pain—she also knew that if she asked him, he would tell her everything. But the same instinct that had warned her earlier to stop Tawl speaking warned her now to accept the image she had. Better to accept the half-truths than root out cold facts that could haunt her for life. She knew the thought of her father suffering would be too much for her to bear.

"I think you should go upstairs and lie down," said

Tawl. "I'll ask the innkeeper's wife to send up the baby and you and he can rest for a while."

Melli stood up. Strange, but she didn't feel like crying: not now, not yet. Crying marked the end of things, and there was still a long way to go. "No," she said gently. "I won't rest just yet. I want to meet my father's men and show them the baby."

And that was what she did. One by one, she met them, talked to them, kissed their weary cheeks, shared jokes about her father's stubbornness, and showed them all his grandson. She made sure they were well fed and rested, ordered hot water for them to wash with and strong brandy to help them sleep. She set the cook cooking, the innkeeper's daughters mending, Tawl and Borlin physicianing, and Nanny Greal doing all the unpleasant things like scraping the mud off their shoes.

Melli didn't stop until she was too tired to think. Close to midnight, Tawl took her hand and told her to sleep. She was about to protest—Grift had turned up with the men and she hadn't had a chance to speak to him yet—but something in his face stopped her. Glancing over at the far side of the room, she saw that Andris and Borlin were talking to a handful of the Highwall troops.

"I'll sleep if you tell me what's going on," she said.

"We're planning to raid Tyren's camp before dawn."

Melli was shocked. "So soon? The men have only just arrived."

"I know. I would have preferred to give them a full night's sleep, but we've got no choice. Now that Kylock and Tyren know we're here we have to move fast. We've already given them a day to prepare themselves." Tawl came and sat beside her. Melli noticed how tired he looked. "If we're going to put your son in his rightful place, we need to win the support of the knights. We need their manpower, their resources—without them we haven't got a chance. We can't enter the city with less than a hundred men; it would be suicide."

"You don't have to enter the city." Melli didn't want Tawl leaving her so soon. "We could just run away. Head south—"

"No." Tawl's voice was harsh. "I won't do that. Too many people have died, too many lives have been destroyed. I can't just run away."

"What if you get killed? You're in no state to fight—your sword arm's wounded. It's been dragging at your side all day."

Tawl seemed surprised that she'd noticed. He made a circular movement with his shoulder. "It will be all right."

"What about me and the baby, though?" As always, when Melli was worried she became angry. "Will we be all right if you don't come back? Or do you think you've fulfilled your obligation now that you've saved us once?"

Seeing Tawl flinch at her words, Melli went to apologize, but Tawl spoke first. "Borlin and a few chosen men are supposed to stay here with you, and if things don't go well at the camp, you'll be taken straight to Ness, and then moved south from there." Tawl leant forward. "But I'll change that if you're worried. I'll stay here at the inn. My first obligation will always be to you and the baby. You must believe that."

Melli suddenly felt out of her depth. There was something in Tawl's voice she couldn't understand, something almost desperate. She knew she had to let him go, but she didn't understand why. Taking a deep breath, she said, "The baby and I will be fine. Borlin's a good man. I'll feel safe with him watching over us while you're gone."

Tawl gave her a softly knowing smile. "You are the most remarkable woman I have ever known."

Melli returned the smile with a similar one of her own. "When you get back, I expect you to tell me the real reason why you had to go."

"When I get back I'll tell you everything." He kissed her

lightly on the cheek and led her up to bed, and when she woke in the morning he was gone.

Tawl counted the tents and the campfires. It was the last hour of darkness before dawn and the world was arranging itself into forms. Ten regular tents, one surgeon's tent, the command tent, and Tyren's tent could be seen amidst the glow of the fires.

"My guess is there's three hundred men in all," hissed Andris.

Tawl nodded. He and Andris were southeast of the camp, hiding in the cover of a small copse of trees. The city of Bren was a dark mass on the horizon and the mountains of the Divide were just so many shadows emerging from the night. Snow was falling: lazy, weightless flakes that were borne sideways by the wind. It was very cold.

Tawl glanced at the sky to the east. "How long do you think it will be before the men are in place?"

"Forty minutes," said Andris. "Mafrey and Corvis will signal when they're ready."

"Let's hope they're both ready at the same time, then. As soon as one of them lights up a torch, the knights will know something's wrong." Tawl was tense. He wished he'd had longer to plan the raid. He didn't know enough about the camp and the number and makeup of the knights. He felt he was leading Maybor's men in blindly.

"Follis and the two Highwall archers will be in position soon. They should be able to take out the watch the minute the signal is given."

"Will three archers be enough, though? How many knights are normally set to watch a camp this size?" Tawl had never campaigned with the knighthood, and he knew little about their camps.

"It's hard to say. Maybe twenty. Sometimes they use squires or first-year initiates, sometimes knights. It depends on what the dangers are." Andris' voice betrayed tension of his own. Since Crayne's death, he was in charge of the party, and his first mission as leader was not only reckless, it was treason. He was leading his men against Tyren.

An owl hoot startled them both. Tawl looked at Andris. "Come on, let's get back to the others. The signal's less than half an hour away now and I want a good head start."

They had less than ninety men in all. Mafrey and Corvis had thirty apiece and had ridden over to the west side of the camp: Corvis to the northwest, Mafrey to the southwest. Once in position they were to spread out and encircle the north, west, and south of the camp. Andris' men were due to head in from the east on their signal. Tawl was going to take a handful of men—Gervhay and four Highwall swordsmen—into the camp first, and attempt to take Tyren's tent.

Twenty men waited in the dark behind the grove. Tawl didn't know most of their names. They were lean from seven days of hard riding and tough from living on the mountains. By all rights they should have been tired—most had only had two or three hours rest—but one look into their dark, weather-beaten faces was enough to see that sleep was the last thing on their minds. They wanted revenge.

The journey to the southern plains of Bren took under three hours, and for the last of those hours the Highwall troops had ridden past the decomposing corpses of their countrymen. Kylock hadn't even bothered to bury the bodies. Five thousand men left for the weather and the carrion-pickers to take their toll. It sickened Tawl, but it had an entirely different effect on Maybor's men: it enraged them. Their friends, their brothers, their comrades, and their leaders had been denied the right to an honorable end.

Approaching them now, Tawl knew in his heart they would fight to the death. Their eyes were bright with fury.

"Gervhay," hissed Tawl, dismounting his horse. "Are you ready?"

Gervhay nodded enthusiastically. "Aye, Tawl. We're all set to go."

Tawl smiled at him. The young knight hadn't been branded with the second circle long: the skin was still raised around the mark. "I hope you've strung your bow tight for the cold."

Gervhay grinned. "Borlin warned me you'd state the obvious."

Both men laughed. Tawl bent down and raked a fistful of cold earth off the ground. It was too cold to stick well when he rubbed it into his face, so he spit a couple of times to soften it to mud. He was pleased to note that the four Highwall swordsmen had already done the same. Seeing what he was doing, Gervhay followed suit. The young knight covered his hands and his neck for good measure.

Tawl turned to Andris. "Take care, my friend. I trust I'll see you later just before you save my hide."

Andris clasped his arm. Two days ago he would have smiled at such a remark. Today he was simply grave. "You've got half an hour of darkness left. Use it well."

Looking at Andris' fair northern face, Tawl suddenly realized the full extent of what he was asking him and his men to do. They were about to break the founding tenet of the knighthood: loyalty to one's leader. Tawl's mind clouded with doubt: was he asking too much? Was it fair to involve other knights in his own personal war? He opened his mouth to speak, to offer Andris a chance to withdraw, but the knight forestalled him with a blessing.

"Borc be with you," he said.

Something about the manner in which he spoke made Tawl wonder if Andris had guessed what he was thinking. Glancing quickly up into his light gray eyes, Tawl saw that he was right. The knight's gaze was as firm as a warning. "Go," he said. "The time has long passed for doubts."

Tawl bowed his head. First Melli, now Andris—what had he done to deserve such selfless gifts? Briefly he remembered the demon in the lake: perhaps one day if he was lucky he might be worthy of them all.

Gervhay called from behind and Tawl raised a hand in parting to Andris, then turned and walked to the west.

Strange dreams hounded him like packs of muzzled dogs. They barked, they harried, they snapped at his ankles, but never once did they manage to bite.

Baralis knew warnings when he saw them—even now, with a body driven beyond the limits of exhaustion, his mind was as sharp as a tack. Dreams held messages and persistent dreams held the most potent messages of all. What was wrong? What had he overlooked? What had he left undone? Normally he would turn and face the hounds of chance, look them in the eye and demand to know their meaning. But such things demanded physical as well as mental strength, and he had nothing, absolutely nothing, to spare.

The drawing against Jack had brought him within touching distance of death. When he saw Jack emerge from behind the curtain he knew he had to destroy him. No matter that only moments earlier he had spent the better part of his strength killing the two knights standing guard; he had to reach within himself and find one drawing more.

And what a drawing it had been! Keen as an assassin's blade, dense as a defending wall. Split seconds were his accomplices, expectation was his friend. He spotted the enemy before the enemy spotted him. It hadn't been a contest of strength or skill, it had been a matter of *time*. He hadn't allowed Jack the chance to defend himself—his arrow had already left the bow.

Yet such a loosing had its price, and he was paying the cost of it now. Unable to move a muscle, he lay in his bed like a drooling invalid while Crope attended his needs.

Strength would return in a few days, and if anything should happen unexpectedly, there were always potions to bridge the gap. In the meantime, he took his normal recuperative medicines—mineral-rich infusions and sorcery-enhanced drugs—Crope drizzling them between his lips while he slept.

Baralis' senses were weak, but they were still on alert. He was half-expecting to feel something from Kylock: a drawing generated from frustration or rage. The king would be taking Melliandra's rescue badly. He had secret plans for Maybor's daughter—plans that Baralis could only guess at—and to have her stolen away from under his feet might have sent him deeper into madness. So far there had been nothing, though. No great lashing out, no palace-shaking tantrum, nothing to indicate a sudden flare of emotion.

Dimly, Baralis was aware of Crope moving around the room. He tried to force himself awake: he needed to discover if his servant knew anything about Kylock's mental state.

Up through the brittle layers of unconsciousness he went, cracking the fragile sheets like footsteps on thin ice. The hounds were still behind him, barking out their warnings, foaming at the mouth. One layer of sleep to go, one glassy, wafer-thin layer that bordered the waking world. He pushed against it with his mind and it shattered into slivers. First he saw his chamber and Crope, and then he spied the reflection in the glass. The reflection of his dream. The hounds full on.

A single image flashed like sunlight upon a lake. And that was exactly what it was: a lake, a dead body, a drawing that worked beyond its time. It was Skaythe.

Baralis blinked and the image fractured into so many streams of light.

"Master, master. Can you hear me?" Crope loomed over the bed, hastily stuffing his wooden box in his tunic.

Baralis couldn't be sure, but he thought he saw tears in Crope's eyes. He had neither the time nor energy to ponder their meaning: the dream was what counted now. Even Kylock could wait. "Crope," he whispered, his voice a lead weight upon his tongue. "Where is Jack's body?"

"Down belowstairs, master. In the dungeon. Locked away."

Baralis let out a sigh of relief. "Listen carefully. I want you to destroy it. Fire up the forge they use for heating extra water when the court is full. Fill it with as many logs as it will take, stoke it to a frenzy, and then throw the body upon it. You mustn't leave until you see the bones turn black. Do you understand?"

Crope nodded slowly. He opened his mouth to say something, but then nodded once more instead. "Yes, master," he murmured after a moment. "Until the bones turn black."

"Good. Now bring me my medicines and warm me some holk, and then go down to the cellar and get started." Baralis watched Crope hurry away before closing his eyes to rest.

The image of Skaythe's dead body returned to him with the dark. The hounds had sent the vision as a reminder to take no chances with Jack. Skaythe was weak, inexperienced, yet his last drawing had lingered on past his death, seeping from his body into the lake. If even he could manage that, then how much more could Jack do? Of course there was a chance that Jack's last drawing hadn't been full formed—after all, there was so little time—but it never hurt to take precautions.

Baralis knew better than to ignore his dreams.

Tawl spied the first of the watches: two men, neither of them looked like knights. "Gervhay, can you take them from here?"

Gervhay shook his head. "If I miss at this angle, there's a chance the arrows will go straight into the tent. I'll head north as far as those bushes on the rise and take a couple of shots from there. That way we'll stop any stray arrows from going wild."

Tawl nodded. "Keep your head low. We'll head forward and wait for you by the ditch." When Tawl looked around to confirm it, Gervhay was already gone, bellying over the ground, his bow slung over his back like the wing of a dragonfly.

A quick glance at the eastern sky revealed the gray blush of dawn. The snow clouds would slow down the light, but at most they had twenty minutes of darkness left.

"Follow me," hissed Tawl to the swordsman at his heels. His eye had spotted the yellow-and-black of Tyren's tent, and from this distance it looked like fair game. Scrambling over the freezing earth, he ignored the pain in his arm and the spreading numbness in his fingers and toes. Tyren was close now, close enough to make Tawl's blood run cold. The demons were gathering for the kill.

Ahead the ditch showed itself as a black line—judging from the smell it was where the camp dumped its waste. Just as Tawl crawled up to the staggered bank, he heard a soft whirring sound. Then another. The two watches went down. Gervhay had aimed his arrows well.

"Keffin, Baird. You two go ahead. I need to know how many guards we're going to run into before we get to Tyren's tent." Tawl was about to tell the two Highwall troopers not to take any risks, then thought better of it: risks were all they had. He settled for a warning to watch their backs, and then waved them on ahead. He wished he was going with them. Waiting, even for a few minutes, was unbearable to Tawl.

The remaining two Highwall swordsmen came and crouched beside him. Fair haired and stony faced, they drew out their swords and waited.

Gervhay sprung out of the darkness, surprising everyone. He grinned triumphantly. "Two down. Two hundred and ninety-eight to go."

"If all goes well, we won't have to kill that many," said Tawl. He tried to sound stern, but Gervhay's natural enthusiasm was something he didn't want to stifle. "You did well. Get ready to pick off a few more."

"Point and shoot. That's me." Somehow, the young knight had managed to get several twigs caught in his hair, giving him the look of a mad woodsman. "Now, if you gentlemen are well-rested, I say we go and find some trouble."

Tawl had to put a restraining arm on Gervhay: an archer had no business going first. "Take the rear, my friend," he said. "And keep to the shadows when you can." With that, Tawl leapt across the ditch, and running as fast as he could with his back bent low, he made for the nearest tent.

Open ground was the greatest danger at this point. A keen eye could easily pick out a fast-moving form in the quarter-light. The distance between the ditch and the tent seemed impossibly long, and Tawl dreaded the alarm being sounded with every stride. The two Highwall men ran without making a sound. They were faster than Tawl and overtook him as he stepped upon the cleared ground of the camp. By the time he reached the tent, they were already talking to Keffin and Baird.

Straightaway, Tawl noticed blood on Baird's long-knife. "What happened?"

"Just silenced a couple of guards, that's all." Despite the calmness of his voice, Baird was shaking. "They were outside the command tent, and they caught sight of Keffin. When they came close to investigate, I slit both their throats."

One after another without making a noise? Tawl was impressed. He would have liked to ask the Highwall swordsman how he managed such a feat, but there was no time. Any minute now the camp would start to wake. He nodded toward the interior. "How's it looking?"

Baird shrugged. "Two guards on Tyren's tent—same

as all the others. The problem is that the entrance to Tyren's tent looks directly onto three of the main tents— that's eight guards to take out from the start."

"Plus the two sets we'll have to pass along the way," added Keffin.

"I think we'll be going in the back door, then," said Tawl. From where he was he could see the back of Tyren's tent. It was overlooked by the command tent and the supply tent. Baird had already killed the guards on the command tent, so that meant less men to deal with. He looked at Baird. "How quickly can you slice me a way in?"

Baird smiled. "Quicker than I slit a throat."

"Good." Tawl glanced toward the eastern horizon. Ten minutes to first light. Five minutes before Mafrey and Corvis were due to make the signal. The timing had to be right: as soon as someone called the alarm they were dead unless the Highwall troops moved in. "Gervhay," called Tawl softly.

"Aye," came a voice from the shadows.

"I want you to stay back and cover us going in. Keep to the east side, pick off anyone who comes close to Tyren's tent, and whatever you do, lie low. I don't want anyone spotting you while you're out here on your own."

"It's as good as done."

Tawl watched Gervhay's bow hand make a salute, then he disappeared into the shadows. Tawl turned to the swordsmen. "Now. Baird, you know what you're doing. Keffin, you're with me. Murris, Sevri, I want you two to flank out around the tent. Keep an eye on the west side and the entrance, silence any wary guards, and watch out for the signal. If there's too many men to deal with, then you come in the tent with us. Right?"

"Right."

Tawl nodded at both men. "Let's go."

He chose an indirect path to Tyren's back door, hugging shadows and tent sides whenever he could. His mind was ticking seconds: he had to have Tyren in his keeping before Andris and the Highwall troops came in. Once the exchange started, the knights would rally around their leader. Tawl knew his only hope was to have a dagger at the leader's throat.

As he made his way to the center of the camp, a strange lightness invaded Tawl's chest. He felt excited, free, almost happy—he was here now, and there was no going back. By the time dawn passed into day he would have met his fate full on.

Something moving to the south caught his eye. It was a guard on the camp's far border dropping to the ground. Tawl grinned. Follis and the two Highwall marksmen were doing a little preraid thinning.

The yellow-and-black of Tyren's tent was only paces away now. Tawl beckoned Baird ahead. Just as the burly swordsman came forward with his long-knife, a cry sounded to their near left. It was cut off in midcall.

"Go," hissed Tawl to Baird. Tawl followed him to the back of Tyren's tent. Keffin was at his heels.

Another shout came from the left. There was movement in one of the main tents. An arrow shot past from the west.

Baird's hands were firm as he sliced through the tent. The fabric was oiled and half a finger thick, but his blade cut it as if it were silk. The downward stroke was accompanied by a soft tearing noise, and even as Tawl brought his sword forward, he heard a cry from inside the tent:

"Guards!"

Tawl pushed past Baird and forced his way through the slit. His sword touched tips with another, and before he could even see who he was fighting, he began defensive strokes. Immediately, he stepped to the side of the slit. He needed to give Baird and Keffin a chance to enter: he didn't want to attend the banquet alone.

As Baird pushed into the tent, a streak of dawn light

fell upon the face of the man Tawl was fighting: dark eyes, dark hair, olive skin.

Tyren smiled. "It's been a long time, Tawl."

Tawl took a quick breath. Tyren looked exactly the same as when he'd seen him last. The urge to bow, to supplicate himself before his leader, was strong but fleeting. It took Tawl by surprise. Tyren had betrayed him: he had to remember that.

Pressing his lips firmly together, Tawl resisted the urge to speak. He parried Tyren with a series of close body thrusts while he tried to orientate himself in the tent. Several chests, a slim table, a bench, and a pallet were positioned against the walls. The middle space was free and Tyren was using it to his full advantage, forcing Tawl to fight from the side.

Outside the sound of men running and shouting could be heard. Underneath the noise of the camp awaking was a low, distant rumble: Andris and the troops were on their way.

Tawl's eyes fell on the entrance flap—no men had come through yet. Murris or Sevri must have cut the two guards down. Tawl pushed Tyren back with a reckless, curving lunge. Pain shot up his arm, but he forced himself to keep his sword point up. Baird and Keffin took advantage of the newly freed space to move toward the flap.

Tyren tested Tawl's sword arm by hacking downward with his blade. Tawl had no choice but to bring his weapon up and block the full force of the blow. Steel rang out. Tawl's arm gave; a sharp spasm ripped through his shoulder, driving him to his knees. Tyren freed his sword for a thrust.

Baird came up behind Tyren and slammed the flat of his blade into the leader's back. Tyren went stumbling forward. His face registered pain, confusion, then anger. Quickly righting himself, he shouted at Tawl: "Call yourself a knight? Fight me one on one, or not at all."

Tawl got to his feet, his eyes not leaving Tyren for an instant. "I'm not falling for your talk of honor this time, Tyren. I'm a lot wiser now, and I see you for what little you are." With his left hand he made a minute gesture to Baird. The two Highwall swordsmen pressed their blade-tips against Tyren's flank. "I only fight one on one with people I respect."

Tawl turned his back on the leader of the knighthood. "Tie his hands, lads. We're going for a walk."

Thirty-five

Slowly, cell by cell, particle by particle, layer by layer, time turned.

Caught between metal and flesh, the magic worked its subtle purpose less than a step ahead of the grave. As the blood darkened and thickened, it was set running; as the last meal curdled, it was reclaimed. Moisture rose to line the drying membranes of the nose and throat, and the muscles of the intestines began to push.

The magic had none of the force of a drawing. It wasn't aimed like a weapon or brandished like a shield. It had escaped upon a dying breath: unspoken, unfocused, half-formed.

Diffused intent was all that was left. Shaped from a reflex action of survival, cut off before fully ripe, it seeped from the body and nestled close to the body, and sent curves bending through time.

The chain mail kept it pressed against the skin. Warming as it worked, edging back into moments past: it reconstructed and resuscitated in one. Time was thick around the body. Time was thin around the brink. The magic stayed the future with one hand and stretched the present with the other. First a hundred, then a thousand, then a million tiny changes. And then the heart was ready to beat.

The rhythm rang through the body even now. Strong

and deep, it provided the framework for momentum to build. Power gathered around the heart, bracing tissue, opening valves, clearing debris from the arteries—smoothing the way for the first mighty thrust.

Steeped in a solution of slow-reversing time, the heart began to vibrate. Old magic met new magic. The power of Larn met power born of man. The heart was where they converged and the first beat marked the moment they joined.

Terrible soul-wrenching suction, then one single lusty punch. The body jolted into life. Convulsing in its center, muscles contracted, blood rushed, senses reeled, nerve cells sparked, and sweat came oozing to the surface.

Red and black. Black and white. Light flared only to recede to a pinpoint. A single moment cleaved in two as time was ripped asunder, and then Jack opened his eyes.

Everything stopped as Tyren emerged from the tent. Men running came to a halt, weapons wielded came to rest, cries of pain and anger dried upon the lips. All eyes looked upon Tyren and all gazes dropped to his throat. The dagger caught dawn's first light and sent it glinting into the faces of all who were there.

Tawl pressed the blade-tip into Tyren's flesh. A tear's worth of blood ran red upon the skin. "Stay back!" he called to Tyren's knights. "Stay back, or Borc so help me I will kill him."

Tawl had one hand on the ties that bound Tyren's wrists, and he pushed against them now, driving Tyren forward, clearing the flap of the tent. With one quick glance he took in the scene. On either side of the entrance, bodies lay in piles. Those who didn't have arrows jutting from their chests or backs had great bloody gashes on their arms and their legs. Gervhay and the two swordsmen had fought well. Murris was lying motionless in a pool of his own blood, and Sevri was standing directly ahead of Tawl, his broadsword caked with flesh and hair, his body striped with cuts. Gervhay was nowhere to be seen.

Knights were everywhere. Caught unawares, some were wearing armor over their bedclothes, others wearing no armor at all. They all had swords, though. Some had shields.

Beyond the tents, at the boundaries of the camp, the raid was still in progress. The Highwall troops were matching metal with those knights who had managed to mount their horses. Tawl scanned the lines: Mafrey and Corvis had made it look as if the entire camp was surrounded.

"Let Tyren go or I will shoot you in the back."

Tawl didn't bother to turn around to see who was shouting. "Do it, then," he cried to the half circle of knights in front of him. "But I warn you, I'm wearing mail, and unless you aim your bow with the grace of Valdis himself, my injury will allow me time enough to slit Tyren's throat."

A moment of silence followed. The archer at the back did not risk a shot.

"What do you want?" demanded one of the knights stepping forward. Tawl didn't recognize him, but the paleness of the three circles on his sword arm marked him as an elder.

"He wants power for himself," said Tyren. "He wants to take my place."

It was close enough to the truth to make Tawl flinch. He felt blood rushing in his ears and heard the dry flapping of his demon's wings. How much of this was for his family? And how much was to fulfill his lifelong craving for glory? Hearing Tyren's smooth and convincing voice, he suddenly wasn't sure.

Dimly, Tawl was aware of Baird and Keffin shifting their positions to guard his back.

Tawl looked around the camp: the knights looked back at him, their eyes bright with fierce emotions. Did he want to take Tyren's place? He couldn't say no — part of him still wanted to see those old dreams come true. But there were new dreams competing with the old ones now, dreams that held power all of their own. Tawl's thoughts turned to Melli, and as his mind conjured up an image of her pale and lovely face, he heard Megan's voice sounding in his ears: *"It's love, not achievement, that will rid you of your demons."* Tawl felt a tightening around his heart. Would he leave everything behind to keep Melli and the baby safe? Yes. After today, yes.

He knew then that this was no longer about ambition. He didn't want Tyren's place. He didn't want Tyren's glory. He just wanted to believe there was goodness at the heart of it all. Pushing the dagger blade close to Tyren's throat, he said, "I want the knighthood to return to what it once was. I want to see men fighting for honor, not gold."

"Honor?" Tyren's voice was scathing. "How can a man who's shamed his circles by cold-blooded murder talk of honor? Do not presume to preach to me, Tawl, for your sermons are as flawed as your soul."

The knights greeted Tyren's words with a rally of calls and encouragement. Slowly they began to edge closer, claiming the ground around the tent.

"He murdered no one."

Everyone turned to look as a man rode into their midst. He was coming in from the east with the light behind him, so his features were hard to make out. Tawl recognized his voice at once: it was Andris. He pulled on the reins of his horse, then dismounted. "Tawl is a man of honor," he said, moving into the half circle, "I will swear that on my life."

A ripple of excitement passed through the gathered crowd.

"And how would you know?" It was the elder knight. He spoke harshly to quiet the whispers.

"I know because I've been with him for many weeks. I've seen him fight hard and fair and always bravely. And I now count him my friend."

Tawl locked gazes with Andris and then looked away.

The knight had taken a grave risk riding through the lines. If things went wrong, then everyone in the camp—Murris, Sevri, Baird, Keffin, Gervhay, Tawl himself, and now Andris—would end up dead. The knights could close the circle and hack them to pieces before the troops broke through.

Tyren broke the silence. "Andris, he has fooled you. He is not a true knight; he denounced his circles before the entire city of Bren. Come forward and take the knife from his hand—he will give it to you."

Andris didn't hesitate. "Tawl didn't sanction the killing of women and children in Helch. He didn't make bargains with Kylock for gold." Wheeling around, he turned to face the knights. When he spoke again, his voice was soft. "With my own eyes I have seen what Kylock's army is capable of. Riding north from Camlee, we came upon one of their campsites. The bodies of thirty women were mutilated and thrown into a ditch to rot."

"That is not our concern," said the elder.

"It is when there are knights in the party." Tawl's voice carried far in the cold air of dawn. An uneasy murmur rose up from the camp. The crowd had grown large now. Men were putting down their weapons and making for the tent.

"Andris," said Tyren sharply, "this man is a liar. Take the knife from him now, or be expelled from the knighthood for life."

No one moved. Andris looked down at the ground. The scar on his cheek looked almost white in the oblique morning light. Tawl released the pressure on the blade. He was ready to give it up to Andris: he didn't want to make the knight's decision any more difficult than it was.

Tawl knew all about hard choices.

All the fighting had stopped now, and the only sound was the soft and ragged hisses of three hundred breaths.

Andris moved forward. He raised his head and looked straight at Tyren. "Would a liar survive the Faldara Falls?"

A shocked murmur rose from the crowd.

"He's lying, too," cried Tyren to the camp. "Both of them are liars. No cheap villain can survive the falls."

"I saw him take them," said Mafrey, coming through the crowd.

"As I did," said Corvis, one step behind him.

"And I." The last voice belonged to Gervhay. The young marksman was standing on the far edge of the circle. Tawl felt pure joy at seeing him: he had thought Gervhay might be dead.

"Are we all liars, then, Tyren?" asked Andris.

The knights shifted nervously. Everyone looked to Tyren.

The muscles in Tyren's shoulder and back contracted minutely. "These men are a disgrace to the knighthood," he said, appealing to the crowd. "Look at how they came here—under the cover of the dawn, catching us unawares, unwilling to fight honorably and openly on the field. And look at who leads them"—Tyren's lip curled in a dismissive snarl—"a man who sneaked into my tent like a burglar. Who fought me to my face and then sent henchmen round my back. A man who talks glibly of honor when he has none of his own."

Tyren's low and powerful voice was building to a crescendo. "Ask this man, ask proud and glory-hungry Tawl of the Lowlands, what he did to his family. Ask him why he left three young children helpless without an older brother to care for them. Ask him what happened to them while he was strutting like a peacock at Valdis. Ask him who was responsible for their deaths. And then and *only* then, ask him about his honor—"

Tawl snapped. A cold, dense rage came upon him. Tyren's words stung like salt in an open wound. He had to stop them coming. Tears blurred his vision as he dropped the knife to Tyren's chest. He felt Tyren pull against him, but Tawl had hold of his hands and wouldn't let him go. Knights in the crowd were ghosts on the periphery—they didn't matter. All Tawl knew was pain, and all he wanted was for the feeling to end. He tilted the edge of his blade to an angle for cutting and pressed it into Tyren's flesh.

Just as he sliced the knife across his chest, Tyren jerked backward. Tawl, mad with fury, hardly aware of what he was doing, pushed against the man's bindings, sending Tyren staggering forward onto the blade. Tyren's own body weight carried the knife far deeper than Tawl intended. The blade had been wielded to cause a flesh wound—nothing more—but Tyren fell upon it, and the blade-tip slipped through his ribs and into his heart.

Stunned gasps escaped from the lips of every knight.

Tawl stepped back. He released his hold on Tyren's hands, and the leader of the knights stumbled forward, falling on his side. Blood gushed from the wound. A trickle ran down his neck. His chest heaved quickly as he struggled for air, and his entire body convulsed in sudden spasms.

Looking up at Tawl, Tyren's mouth formed a slow grin. "You are just as worthless as your father."

Shaking, disorientated, reeling in the wake of strong emotions, it took Tawl a moment to comprehend Tyren's words. *His father?* How could Tyren possibly know his father? It didn't make any sense. "What do you know of my father?" he said.

"I know he can be bought for fifty pieces of gold."

No, mouthed Tawl. *NO!*

He felt himself shift out of his body. The world began to whiten and turn. A sickness, like a fever, took his mind upward then backward to the past. He remembered the sun on his back the day he met Tyren. The questions on Tyren's lips: *"What about your father? Is he dead, too?"*

"No. We don't see him very often. He spends his days drinking in Lanholt."

Tawl saw the scene as clearly as if he were there, as vivid as a morning after rain. And this time he saw things he'd never noticed before: the quick, darting look in Tyren's eyes, his lips moving twice as he repeated the word *Lanholt* back to himself.

The image blasted into shards of whiteness, revealing yet another scene beneath. The cottage by the marsh four days later; the fire burning low, Anna, Sara, and the baby crowding around the figure of their father, squealing with excitement as gifts emerged from a sack.

"Gambling, carding, call it what you will. Luck kissed me, then made me her lover. I won a small fortune. And I'll be putting it to good use."

"How?"

"I've come home to stay. There's no need for you to do everything anymore, Tawl. I'll be head of the family from now on."

The action played itself out one beat slower than real time. Tawl was both observer and player in one. Details caught his eye like flashing jewels: his father refusing to meet his gaze, the time—midmorning, when his father never rose before noon—and gold. Gold in his father's hands. The gaming tables in Lanholt never allowed stakes any higher than silver.

Just as quickly as the scene emerged, it shifted sideways and a third snapped into place. The Bulrush at Greyving. An hour past midnight, Tyren woken by the innkeeper to greet an unexpected guest. Tawl watched him descend the stairs. His face showed no surprise.

"I'm free to come with you to Valdis," said Tawl. *"My obligation has been taken away."*

Tyren smiled and nodded, ordered food and drink, but he never once asked why.

Tawl felt as if his past had been wiped out and been replaced by something new and monstrous. Nothing was as it seemed. The shock was so great it brought him to his knees. Physically sick, a wave of nausea flared up from his gut, contaminating his body with its rancid acid-burn. He bit on his tongue to keep it down.

Anna and Sara and the baby. All dead, but no longer resting the same. Their deaths—his private torment, the thorns in his heart and the demons on his back—had been turned inside out. Everything had been tainted. Right from the start, right from the very moment he'd met Tyren on the south road, there had been one foul lie at the center of his life.

Tyren had made him a monster.

Hardly aware of what he was doing, drunk with sickness and tormented by pain, Tawl took the dying man in his arms and shook him. "You paid my father to look after my sisters. You knew I would never have gone with you to Valdis unless my sisters were taken care of, so you paid him to take my place."

Tyren was weak, his chest barely moving, his eyes slow to focus. A lazy smile graced lips red with blood. "Didn't do such a good job, did he?"

The air was filled with the sound of flapping wings. Each whip of leathered scales drove Tawl closer to madness. The demons were on his back. Bringing up his knife, he began to stab Tyren. Over and over again, the knife came down, thrust through ribs, collarbone, heart, and lungs. Tawl couldn't stop. It was the only way to save himself. The only way to shut out the terrible, searing pain.

Then, as Tyren's torso became a bloody pulp, Tawl felt something pass through him. A thin exhalation of breath flitted through his body like air through gauze. It didn't pass through Tyren. It gathered about him, whirling and solidifying, and changing his bloody features into a mask.

Tawl dropped the knife.

The demon was no longer on his back; it had merged with Tyren's corpse. Tyren was the demon, and had always been the demon, and that was what the green waters of Lake Ormon had tried to show him.

Tawl looked up. The eyes of three hundred men were upon him. No one spoke.

He felt so tired. Empty of every emotion except the grief of losing his sisters. It was as if they had died again—here, today, by Tyren's hand. As he raised himself to one knee and began to clean his blade on his tunic, a cry came up from the crowd:

"Tawl for leader!" It was Andris. He called a second time and Gervhay, Mafrey, and Corvis joined in.

Tawl shook his head. He couldn't speak. Not now.

"Tawl for leader!" More took up the cry the third time, and the voices doubled on the fourth.

Tawl couldn't bear it. All he wanted was to be left alone to grieve. Still shaking his head, he stood up. Weak from head to foot, his knees almost buckled beneath him. Baird came forward and loaned him a hand, and Tawl was glad to take it. Without a word passing between the two, Baird guided him toward Tyren's tent.

"Tawl for leader!" A full third of the knights had now joined in the chant.

Baird lifted the tent flap open, and Tawl stepped into the shaded warmth. Almost at once, his legs gave way beneath him. He fell onto Tyren's pallet, closing his eyes as he brought his head to rest.

"Tawl for leader."

He didn't want to hear it, didn't want to think about it. In his mind he saw only his sisters: Sara, golden hair bouncing as she followed him down to the waterhole; Anna, grinning her wicked grin as she tried to goad him into a fight; and the baby, lips quivering, cheeks flaming, as it worked itself into a tantrum over being left too long in the cot. Tawl smiled. It seemed just like yesterday.

Jack opened his eyes. He was enveloped by a white cocoon. It stretched out in every direction, brushing softly against his lashes and his nose. Jack thought he might have been in heaven if it hadn't been for the smell. Somehow, he'd never imagined the afterlife as smelling of musty linen. Could be wrong, though. Trying a quick upward movement with his hand, the whiteness grew taut across his face. The coarse nap of cheap linen brushed against his lips. Sticking out his tongue, he ran the tip along the surface. Lye and old mold. No, this was no afterlife, this was a poorly laundered sheet.

Grabbing the fabric in his fists, he yanked it away from his face. Cool air, dim light, and the strong smell of woodsmoke met his senses. Noises, too. A grating metal noise, like a shovel on stone, and the crackle and sputter of a well-stoked fire. Strange how he'd never heard them before.

The ceiling was oddly familiar: low and barreled with elaborately carved braces. He was sure he'd seen it recently.

A movement to the far left caught his eye. A dark figure moved across the glowing orange light source. Jack lifted his head to see it better. The movement took a lot more effort than he'd planned; surely his head wasn't normally this heavy? His senses had a minor blackout for a moment—a sort of dark, spiraling sensation like being spun around in a blindfold—and by the time his eyesight had returned to normal, the figure had moved to the side of the light.

Jack caught his breath. He could clearly see the man's profile: tall, bulky, shoulders slouched, chin drooping close to the chest—it was Crope!

Swinging his feet to the side, Jack attempted to rise from whatever surface he'd been laid on. He was ready for the blackout this time, clenching his teeth and pressing knuckles into wood. He lost the seconds from his feet hanging in midair to his feet touching stone.

Gathering his strength about him, he tilted his weight onto his feet. Just like his head, his body seemed heavier than he remembered. With his hand holding the table, he tried a step. Not bad really, all things considered. He took another one and then let go of the table.

Crope had his back to him and did not see him

approach. The distance between them was longer than Jack had first thought, and the walk gave him a chance to take in his surroundings. He now knew he was somewhere beneath the palace. The low ceilings, the distant drip of water, and the mushroomy smell of mold and excrement gave it all away. How long had passed since he was here last? One night? One day? Many days? There was no way of knowing. He could remember nothing after lifting the curtain and coming face-to-face with Baralis.

Still, he was alive, and that meant Tawl and Melli could be alive as well.

"*Mhmp.*"

Jack's thoughts bounded back to Crope. Close now, he could see the huge servant's shoulders shaking.

"*Mhmp.*"

The noise came again, and Jack suddenly realized it was the sound of Crope sobbing. Taking special care to pad his steps, Jack crept toward a post only paces behind the servant and the light source.

A stone furnace blazed with golden light; its metal door flung open to provide air to fuel the flames. A shovel lay at the side, and to the side of that lay a large heap of logs, wood chips, and wood dust. Crope was on the opposite side, shoulders moving up and down, head shaking from side to side. As Jack watched, he reached inside his tunic and pulled out a wooden box. With hands gentle enough to cup kittens, Crope sorted through the contents of the box. After a moment, he pulled something out. From his position behind the beam, Jack couldn't make out what it was. He saw Crope return the box to his tunic and then move toward the furnace door.

It was then that Jack saw the white square in Crope's hand. It was a letter—the bloodred daub of wax clearly marked it as such.

"*Mhmp.*" Crope held out the letter at arm's length and offered it up to the furnace.

"Crope." Jack was hardly aware he'd stepped forward and surprised to his very core that he'd spoken.

Crope turned around. The letter was still in his hand, but the flames of the furnace had already begun to blacken the edges. Crope took one look at Jack and screamed. His hand whipped from the furnace to his face, and the letter ended up clamped over his eyes. "Go away. Leave Crope alone. Crope's sorry."

"Crope it's me, *Jack.*" Jack took another step forward so he was properly in the light.

Screaming again, Crope moved his hands from his eyes to his ears. "Crope's sorry. Crope meant to give Jack the letter. Didn't know Jack was going to die."

Guessing that Crope thought he was a ghost, Jack leant forward and touched Crope's arm. "I'm alive, Crope. I'm not a ghost."

Crope pulled away. "Master said burn the body—only burns 'em when they're dead."

Baralis thought he was dead. Jack pushed the thought aside for a moment; he would think about that later. For now, he had to find out what was in the letter. Still holding out his arm, he said gently, "Here, touch me, Crope, I swear to you I'm not dead."

Crope eyed him suspiciously. "Ghost's playing tricks on Crope."

"No tricks. Look." Jack spit into his palm and held it out for Crope to examine. "Ghosts never spit—everyone knows that."

Edging forward, hands still clamped to his ears, Crope proceeded to examine the gob of spit. After a few moments of intense observation, he looked up at Jack's face. "Jack not dead, then?"

"No. Jack was alive, but very still."

"Cold, too. Very cold."

Jack shuddered. He never wanted to know what had happened after Baralis blasted him. *Never.* Gesturing toward the letter, he said, "Is that meant for me?"

Crope's hands came down from his ears. The letter shifted in his fingers as he presented it to Jack. "Jack's letter. Lucy said only to give it to him if Larn was ever destroyed."

Lucy? A shiver started at the base of Jack's spine and worked its way up to his skull. His heart pounded hard in his chest, Larn's rhythm rang on every beat. "My mother gave you this letter?"

Crope nodded. He thrust the letter out once more. "Lucy very sick, made Crope promise to keep the letter for Jack." Crope's lips widened into a tender smile. "Lucy gave Crope box. See." He pulled out the box. Seabirds and seashells were etched upon its lid. "Said the birds reminded her of home. Crope likes birds."

Jack could barely hear what Crope was saying. Like a war drum, his heart was sounding an assault. "You've had this letter for over ten years?"

Crope's face blushed with pride. "I kept it as safe as Grammy's teeth. Only lost it once—had to dig it out of the snow."

"And you were about to burn it because you thought I was dead?"

Crope hung his head. "Crope's sorry. Crope didn't know."

Jack brought his hand up and took the letter. "Don't be sorry, Crope. You've done what Lucy asked. She would have been pleased you kept it so long. And she would have thanked you—just like I'm doing now."

"Lucy was kind to Crope. She never called him names."

Jack nodded absently. As his fingers slid over the parchment, his mind slid back to the past. Ten years. Crope was the last person to see his mother alive. Jack remembered him emerging from her room, his hand tucked beneath his tunic. Was that when she gave him the letter? he wondered. The hour before she died?

With shaking hands, he broke the seal. The wax was

brittle, splintering into a dozen pieces that fell tinkling to the floor. Jack unfolded the paper and read the letter.

Dear Jack,

If you are reading this letter then Larn has been destroyed. If it is you that has brought about its fall, as I believe it will be, then I owe you the truth, as well as much, much more.

I was born on Larn. Daughter to a servant girl and a priest, I grew up to womanhood on the isle. From as early as I can remember, I tended the seers with my own hands, washing, feeding, rubbing salve into their wounds. I thought nothing of it for years; to me the seers were just babbling madmen who were somehow less than human. Then the priests grew to trust me enough to let me tend the new seers; young men, whose minds had not yet been corrupted by the stone, and whose bodies were still strong and virile. It was a shock to discover that these seers were just like me; they could talk, laugh, cry. Be afraid.

I grew to know these young men, and to love one in particular. He was a match for me in age, and we spent our days holding hands and talking of escape. We loved each other with the fierce, desperate passion of youth: nothing would come between us. Then one day, the red fever took me, and I was bedridden for fourteen days. When I eventually saw my love again, his mind had left him. His seering stone had robbed his sanity and the seering ropes had eaten his flesh. He didn't recognize me. I was frantic, screaming, pulling at the ropes, cursing Larn. When I finally got the rope to loosen, it pulled away a portion of his skin, exposing the raw flesh beneath. After that I became hysterical. The priests tried to pull me away and I cursed them, swearing a terrible oath to destroy the island. As I spoke, the cavern began to shake. Someone thrust a rag into my mouth, and then I was beaten until I was senseless.

When I awoke, I was in a dungeon, sentenced to die. I think the priests were afraid of me, afraid of my power and my curse. My mother helped me escape, and I was cast adrift on a skiff.

A few days later, I was picked up by a passing ship and taken to Rorn. One of the sailors, a good man with a good heart, brought me to his house and cared for me. When the time came for me to leave, he gave me his savings and bid me luck and helped me on my way. Even now, the thought of his kindness warms me when I am cold.

After I left Rorn I traveled as far away from the island as I could. I headed north and then west, changing my name and my appearance as I went. I finally arrived in the Four Kingdoms and became a chambermaid at Castle Harvell. Queen Arinalda favored me, and I was appointed as one of her personal servants.

That was when I met the king. Lesketh was a tortured man back in those days; he and his wife were like strangers, torn apart by their inability to conceive a child. I was lonely, with no friends and no one to trust, and when King Lesketh stopped to talk to me in the gardens one day, I was more than flattered, I was grateful. Like everyone else, I heard rumors that the king had affairs with other women, but Lesketh was so kind and considerate with me that I thought nothing of it. Over a period of many months we became close. Lesketh would talk to me about the queen and his problems at court, and I would simply listen, hardly daring to speak. Occasionally I would ask him about faraway lands—my mind always on Larn—and he would take delight in telling me about all the politics of the day, even bringing scrolls and maps to show me.

Gradually, there became more between us. We took to meeting in an old hunting lodge in the woods. And it was there, one wet and gusty evening in late autumn, where Lesketh first showed me Marod's Book of Words. Immeasurably old, with failed binding and fraying pages, it was, he said, one of the original four copies of the great scholar's work.

The moment I took the book in my hands, I felt something change inside me. My whole body began to tremble and a

*tight band of pressure wrapped around my forehead like a
vise. The book seemed almost to open itself, and the moment
the yellow page came into view, my eye fell upon the line that
would forever change my life:*

The stones will be sundered, the temple will fall.

*Straightaway, I knew what it meant, and even before
I'd finished the complete verse, I knew what I had to do. By
predicting the downfall of Larn, Marod had offered me a
chance to redeem my oath. All I had to do was to conceive a
child whose destiny was to fulfill the prophecies in the verse:*

*When men of honor lose sight of their cause
When three bloods are savored in one day
Two houses will meet in wedlock and wealth
And what forms at the join is decay
A man will come with neither father nor mother
But sister as lover
And stay the hand of the plague*

*The stones will be sundered, the temple will fall
The dark empire's expansion will end at his call
And only the fool knows the truth.*

*From that day on, I set about begetting a child with the
king. I knew he would never acknowledge the bastard son of
a chambermaid, so the child would be without a father to
claim him—just like the verse stated.*

Without mother would come later.

*The night you were conceived—for the one in the verse
was and is you, Jack—the king stole down to the castle
kitchens to see me. We made love in the dark shadows of the
chambermaid's corner, and when we had finished, I threw
back the shutters to get some air. That was when I saw the
sign in the sky: a star split in two and falling toward the
earth. I knew then that the prophecy had been set in motion.*

Just as the king slipped away, Crope came down into the kitchens. Baralis had sent him to get some food and drink, and he passed the king on the stairs. I took the servant aside and begged him not to tell his master of what he had seen. Reluctantly, he agreed, and from that day on Crope and I became friends.

I never saw the king again after that night. As soon as I knew I was pregnant, I gave up my position as a chambermaid and took on the lowliest job in the castle. As ashmaid, I never had to leave the kitchen, so there was no chance I would ever cross the king's path again. I didn't want him to know I was carrying his child.

As it turned out, it didn't matter. Two months later, the queen announced she was with child and the king fell in love with her all over again. He never made any attempt to contact me. I was sad for a while, but the prophecy had hold of me, and my life was no longer my own.

The queen and I gave birth on the same day. As soon as I learnt that she had also borne a son, my mind returned to the star in the sky. Two fragments, two conceptions, two births.

Years passed, and you grew from a baby to a boy, and I loved you more dearly than I could ever have imagined. Over time the prophecy became less important, and months went by when I never gave the verse more than a passing thought. Then one day I grew ill. It was as if Marod himself was tapping me on the shoulder, reminding me to finish what I had started. Right from the beginning, I didn't take the medicines the physicians gave me—for the prophecy to be fulfilled I had to be gone from your life. It was the hardest decision I ever had to make, but the prophecy had a life of its own and if I had resisted it then, it would have taken me later without warning.

As my strength was taken, I began to think I had made a terrible mistake: I had brought you into the world with a heavy burden on your back. I had used you, the prophecy had used you—you were nothing but a tool of fate. That was when I decided not to tell you about the verse before I

*died. I didn't want Marod's words ruling your life. I wanted
to give you the chance for your destiny to be your own.*

*So I wrote this letter. And gave it to Crope with instruc-
tions that he pass it on to you only if Larn was destroyed: an
explanation if you ever needed one, a lifetime of blissful igno-
rance if you did not.*

*I ask for your forgiveness, Jack, for I know the prophecy
demands more from you than Larn alone, and as I lie here
now, with my mind and body silently drifting away from me,
I would change it if I could.*

I will love you always,

Aneska

Jack leant back against the wooden brace and slowly
slid to the floor. Dropping the letter to his lap, he closed
his eyes. The darkness was soft and welcoming, like a
velvet-lined glove. There had been so much he hadn't
known.

The hunting lodge—he and Melli had been there. He
had picked up the copy of Marod's *Book of Words*, held it
in his hands, and read the note that dropped from its
pages. The letter his mother never received, the farewell
she thought had never been given. Jack shook his head.
So much he had simply failed to see.

So much he had misunderstood. His mother's illness—he had thought she refused the medicines because
she didn't want to go on living. Now he knew the truth.
And even as the old pain was taken away, it was replaced
by something new. She had died because she thought the
prophecy was hounding her into it. Afraid, in pain, and
with no one to confide in, she had spurned the help of the
physicians and surrendered to her fate.

A hard lump rose in Jack's throat. So much he had
misjudged.

From as early as he could remember he thought his
father had abandoned him. Unwanted and unwelcome,

he thought his birth had driven his father away. Yet now he had been told that his father never knew he existed—hadn't even known his mother was pregnant. Everything had been hidden from the start.

Jack brought up his knees and rested his head against them. How could he blame a man for not knowing he had a son? He had read the note from his father to his mother: Lesketh did not seem the sort of man who would have shunned a woman he cared for. *She* had shunned him.

A lifetime's worth of anger began to dissipate. Hate, which Jack had held so close for so long he was hardly aware of it, drained from him with every breath. He remembered Falk's words about his own father: *"He was just a man—not evil, not cunning, not deserving of punishment."* Jack had wanted to believe them at the time, now finally he could.

His father wasn't a callous monster who had deserted them. He was simply a man who had never known.

Jack stood up. As the anger left him, a rigid sense of purpose rose up to fill the void. He felt strong and clear-headed. He knew everything now: where he came from, who his parents were, what he had to do and why. It didn't matter that he was a bastard son of a king—that was nothing. The only thing that mattered was that he had finally learnt the truth.

Looking up, he went to thank Crope one more time, but the giant servant was nowhere to be seen. Jack wasn't really surprised: Crope's first loyalty would always be to Baralis.

Jack reached down into his boot and felt for his second knife. It was still there, strapped against the lining, pressing against his shin. Pulling it out, he unwrapped the linen-clad blade. Against all odds it had managed to keep its edge. Jack smiled. It was time to put Marod's prophecy to rest.

Thirty-six

*D*arkness was the only thing left to him now. The world of light had passed beyond his reach.

He sat in the center of a halo of shadow, his hands scrubbed raw and dripping blood. There was no cleaning them now. The taint was no longer on the skin, it was *in* it. In the skin, in the tissue. In the blood. Melliandra had fled, and with her had gone his one chance of redemption. Only the filthy nightmare world remained.

He had taken neither food nor drink since she had escaped. Even his little white parcels of *ivysh* lay disregarded by the side of his bed. He couldn't bring himself to take anything that might have been touched by a hand without a glove.

Strange, but he felt a certain sense of expectancy now that his head was clear. It was almost as if he were waiting for someone, or something, to come and try him like a god. *Let them come,* he thought negligently. He had nothing to fear from any man. Women were the blade sent to kill.

Shifting his position upon the fanned-out cloak of silk, Kylock brought a skinless fingertip to his lips. It smelled and tasted of his mother. Long dead, but still present in the slow corruption of his flesh. Everything led back to her. Right from the first moment his life had been flawed: cradled in a womb that stank like a brothel, then sent to a nursemaid for suckling because the whore's milk would not run. He didn't have a chance. Character flowed from mother to son, and he was what she had been, and all her sins were his.

People would have to pay—as people always did—for if he wasn't a king by birthright, then he would make himself one by blood.

The empire was young yet; it needed to be crafted by an iron will and stretched wide to span a continent. Already the darkness was closing in with its gifts. Kylock saw strategies before him like paintings in black and white: cities, towns, rivers, roadways, battlements, and men. Patterns emerged from the lines and curves—patterns of power and control. Just today word had come that Camlee had fallen. Now he saw that heading back toward Ness was a mistake: the city of Falport was ripe for the taking. Everyone was expecting his forces to turn north—surprise would be his greatest ally. The conquest of Falport would not only give him a fleet, it would position him to take the south.

Suddenly Kylock felt the skin of his face flare into a blush. A warm ripple passed over him and a sense of imminent danger wetted his tongue. He was neither displeased nor afraid.

Sitting in the dark, a soft smile playing at his lips, Kylock began to plan his next campaign: battalions to be readied, mercenaries to be recruited, alliances to be made and broken. He plotted a line of towns and villages to be destroyed in order to spread fear and prompt swift surrender, and made a mental note to have all women of childbearing age slaughtered on sight. No opposing army would be bred in his lifetime.

Gradually, as the hour passed, Kylock became resigned to his fate. Now that salvation was no longer possible, glorious damnation was all he had left.

Try as he might, Jack could not remember the route he had previously taken through the tunnels. He found the entrance quickly enough, and even thought to light a torch on the furnace flame, but once he was inside the confined, stagnant passageways, he lost all sense of direction. Every wall looked the same and every turning promised to be the one to take him upward.

Time was against him. Crope had almost certainly gone to tell his master that he still lived, and as soon as Baralis realized that Jack was no longer in the dungeon, he would head straight for Kylock's chamber. Jack's mind flashed back to the incident by the stairs: he didn't want Baralis lying in wait for him ever again.

Finally, after taking yet another turning that ended in a brick wall, Jack forced himself to stop and think. How could he find his way to Kylock's chamber? He had no choice but to use the tunnels; walking through the palace in daylight was as good as suicide, especially now with all the guards on alert. Taking a few long breaths to calm himself, Jack tried to replay his footsteps in his head. Nothing. His mind had been so full of Kylock at the time, so overwhelmed with the nearness of his presence . . .

That was it. He had to concentrate on Kylock—on the thread that lay between them. He had to reel himself in.

It wasn't easy to concentrate with time ticking away in his head. Everything was a distraction: the confined space, the thick black smoke of the torch, the flickering shadows that all looked like Baralis. Seconds gave way to minutes, and worry gave way to desperation. Casting the torch to the floor, Jack stamped out the light.

The darkness was a relief. No more shadows, or endless passageways, or wrong turns on show. With nothing for his eyes to see, Jack's other senses were forced into service. Sounds, smells, tastes, and textures began to take on the importance of visual cues. When he had first sensed Kylock's presence last time, it had been in the dark. It was the same this time, too. The first thing Jack felt was a warm flush across his left temple. The warmth spread over his cheek and down the left side of his neck.

Turning to face the warmth, Jack became aware of a rushing noise in his ears. The sound pulsed as he took a step forward, gradually increasing in intensity as he made his way along the corridor.

Before long, Jack forgot he was in the dark. He *saw* things with his skin. Blood bloomed to the surface, pointing the way like a needle in a compass. He never saw turnings approach, he just took them blindly, trusting in the shifting warmth of his face.

By the time he came to the second flight of stairs, he was as good as sleepwalking. Up and up he went, not caring about the dangers of misstepping, not interested in keeping track of his route. Not long now. Not long before the trail of blood warmth, blood pressure, and gut instinct led him straight to Kylock's door.

"What was his physical state?" Baralis pulled on his robe. Already the drug was working, strengthening the body, clearing the mind, its artificial brilliance shaping a world full of edges.

"He looked fair pale, master. But his wits were about him and I never saw him limp."

Crope was the picture of poorly concealed guilt. Baralis guessed that his servant had not told him the whole story of Jack's miraculous return to life. No matter, there would be time for questioning later. Right now he had more immediate matters to attend to. "Is he armed?"

"No master. I took his sword and his knife from his belt—just like you told me." Crope rolled his big thumbs round in circles. "He's still wearing mail, though. I was going to take it off him, only I forgot."

All thoughts deserted Baralis as the drug sank its barbs into his mind. His heartbeat raced and his vision blurred, and he was forced to reach for Crope's bulk to keep himself standing: Seconds later the turn had passed. A thimble's dose of the drug was all he had taken, but its potency was enough to make even such small amounts dangerous. In return for the physical risks, it bestowed temporary strength upon its taker. Enough for one tolerable drawing, no more. Normally Baralis would never take such a crude and potentially harmful potion, but the moment he learnt that Jack was not dead, he knew he had no other choice. The drawing of two nights back had left him physically and mentally weak, and right now he needed something, *anything*, that could give him a short burst of power. Subtle healings took time, and with Jack roaming the depths of the palace, time was the one thing he didn't have.

It was the one thing Jack had, though. The one amazing thing. Not once, but twice it had turned in his favor. First the loaves and now himself. The baker's boy had been dead—or as close enough as counted—yet now he lived; his body free of scars and wounds. A drawing must have been poised upon his tongue at the moment of his death and had leaked from his lips with his last breath and spittle.

Baralis cursed his own frailty. If he had been stronger, he would have been able to detect the subtle festering of time. He had been looking for the wrong thing: the mighty blast, the terrible sundering, the drawing that would shake a wall. Jack's magic had been a delicate embroidery, unraveling its power over two nights and a day. It had passed Baralis by like a shadow at dusk.

Pulling himself up to his full height, Baralis tested the work of the drug. He wasn't weak now; he could perceive the lines of force, feel the unnatural curvature of time. All his senses were heightened, and his thoughts were as sharp, clear, and deadly as a jagged spike of glass.

He turned to Crope. "Are you sure you came straight here from the cellar? You didn't dawdle around the courtyard to look at the birds?" He needed to know how long Jack had been left on his own.

"No, master. I gave Jack the letter, and —"

"The letter?"

Already looking guilty, Crope now looked condemned.

"The letter his mother asked me to give him if Larn was ever destroyed."

"What?"

"Lucy, the ashmaid. She asked me to keep a letter for Jack until—"

"What was in this letter?"

"Don't know, master. Never looked."

Baralis' eyes narrowed. It was pointless speculating on the contents of the letter, but perhaps some use could be made of its existence. "What did this letter look like?"

"Like every other letter, master."

"Was it sealed? Was it rolled, folded, or tied with string?"

"Folded, with a dark red seal."

Baralis went over to his desk. He picked a faded parchment at random, folded it and, tipping the edge of his sealing block to the flame, dripped bloodred wax onto the crease. Holding it up toward Crope, he asked, "Is this what it looked like?"

Crope nodded enthusiastically. "Yes, master. Yes."

"Good. Come with me."

Jack had reached the end of the tunnels. A glimmer of light sliced through the cracks in the stone, marking the presence of torches on the other side. Jack had no way of knowing if he had taken the same route laid out by Nabber, so he sent a quick prayer to Borc as he placed his hands on the wall: *No guards. Please.*

A gentle push set the stone in motion. Warmth, light, and freshness flooded in through the breach. Jack was dazzled. Lulled into a half-dream by the warm shift of his blood in the darkness, it was like being forced out of bed in the middle of the night.

Straightaway, he knew it wasn't the same entrance as before: there was no curtain to mask the movement of the stone. Jack stepped out into a corridor. His foot landed on something soft: a silken rug.

"Argh!"

Jack whipped around to see where the cry had come from, and he came face-to-face with a woman dressed in green satin. They stood and looked at each other for a moment, and then the woman took a screaming breath.

"Gua—"

Jack clamped his hand over her mouth. His senses felt as if they were on overload: for the past hour he had lived on the barest minimum of input, and now the real world seemed too brazen for him to bear. Trembling, unsure of what to do, worried that someone would come, Jack dragged the kicking woman into the passage. Even as he brought his knife to her throat, he knew he couldn't kill her. Grabbing at the fabric of her dress, he tore a strip good for gagging. The woman's gray eyes were large with terror. There was something about the slant of her cheekbones that reminded him of Tarissa.

"I'm not going to hurt you," he said softly. "I just want you to be quiet for a while." He had balled a wad of fabric in his fist, ready to stuff into her mouth, but now he reduced the mass by half—he didn't want to risk suffocating her.

As he worked, Jack was keenly aware of minutes passing. Once the gag was in place, he tied the woman's hands behind her back, using the stiff ribbons from her hair. "I'm sorry about this," he said, pulling the knot tight. "But I've got no time to do anything else." The woman simply glared back at him.

Jack stepped out into the well-lit corridors of the palace and dragged the stone-clad panel shut. Glancing to either side, he made a brief scan of the passageway. It was no more than thirty paces long, with two doors leading off to the right. The rug trailed to an end just beyond the second door, but in the opposite direction it ran straight along until another, more elaborate, rug intercepted it at right angles. Jack felt for the telltale pull in his blood. Weaker now, the incident with the woman and the bright light in the corridor had disturbed the fine balance of his senses.

What was left was just enough to confirm his best guess: Kylock's chamber lay the way of the elaborately woven rug.

Jack's heart beat fast as he raced along the passage. Kylock was very close now.

Reaching the corner, he slowed down his pace, bringing his body close against the wall. With breath wheezing in his throat and knife shaking in his hand, Jack stuck his head around the corner. Another corridor, a little longer than the last, with only one door to mark its length. A magnificent double door, torches to either side, guards to the side of the torches. An entrance fit for a king.

Jack's glance raked over the two guards. Both men had swords at their waists and halberds in their hands. It wasn't going to be an easy fight.

Or was it?

Closing his eyes, Jack tried to concentrate on the metal of their weapons. His thoughts skimmed through the air to the space around the door. He felt the quick buzz of loaded particles, perceived the unique vibration of the steel. It was like being in Stillfox's cottage all over again: feeling the substance, entering the substance, changing its nature from within. Jack's thoughts fell into vibration with the metal, and slowly he slipped inside. He tried to draw on his power to warm the metal, but there was no feeling of anger, no sudden rage to use as a spark. Without the push of strong emotions, he had nothing with which to kindle the flame.

In his mind, Jack searched for the old image of Rovas touching Tarissa. It came to him as quickly as always—the smuggler's hand reaching out to encircle Tarissa's waist—but this time it didn't ring true. He saw it for what it was: a false product of his own hate. Tarissa would never willingly submit to Rovas' caresses—he knew that now. Time and distance had allowed him to see things more clearly. Tarissa had never been out to snare him: her love had been true. He should have known that the day he left her, when she'd gone down on her knees and begged to come with him. . . .

Jack shook his head. He had been such a fool.

Shame at his own pride swelled like heat within his body. He couldn't be angry with Tarissa and he wouldn't use her image like a firelighter uses a spark.

There were other things to get angry about.

Baralis lying in wait to kill him.

Kylock's forces slaughtering thirty women, then leaving their bodies to rot in a ditch.

Melli locked up in a room for half a year, her baby torn away at birth.

The power began to flow through Jack. His stomach contracted and his skull grew tight around his brain. With saliva running like molten metal on his tongue, Jack switched his thoughts to the enemies' blades.

The air around the weapons shimmered, then the cool silver of the steel flared to hot red. There was no transition, no gradual change, the shift happened in less than a blink of an eye. The guards screamed, both dropping their halberds immediately. Burnt hands dropped down to belt buckles as swords burnt into thighs.

Jack stopped the power. The stench of hot metal, burnt flesh, and scorched fabric wafted up his nose on a wave of warm air. Dazed for a moment, he leant against the wall for support. One of the guards began to run down the corridor in Jack's direction. Jack forced his protesting body into action and leapt out into the man's path.

The guard was an easy target: defenseless, injured, and unprepared, he barely had time to register Jack's blade before it slipped through his ribs to his heart. Jack freed his knife and let the man drop to the floor. The second guard had witnessed the scene and now took flight in the opposite direction. Jack raced after him. Seconds later he pulled the guard down, tackling his legs from behind. A quick thrust into the back of his lungs finished him off.

Jack stood up. He was sweating and heaving like a madman. He felt mad, too: scared out of his wits and exuberant in one.

Looking down the length of the corridor, he decided not to waste time hiding the bodies. Anyone could come along at any moment, and he had to get to Kylock before someone raised the alarm.

As he walked the few steps to the towering double doors, Jack wiped the blood from his knife. He tried to stop his hand from trembling, but although his body obeyed him in most things, it wouldn't obey him in this. So it was a shaking right hand he raised to the latch, and arms weak at the elbows that pushed against the door.

"Follow me. We must get to the nobles' quarters at once." Baralis felt the waves of sorcery roll over him, raising the hairs on his flesh, drying the saliva on his teeth.

"But Jack was in the cellar."

"Well, he isn't there now." And he wasn't escaping, either. He was above them, drawing his special brand of sorcery close to the very heart. Jack had come for Kylock. Every nerve cell in Baralis' body confirmed it.

Marod's prophecy was unraveling before him.

Master and servant began to retrace their steps. Already halfway down to the kitchens, it would cost them precious minutes to make their way up through the palace. Baralis cursed his own stupidity—he should have gone straight to Kylock's chamber from the start. He just hadn't thought. He had assumed that Jack would try to escape, and had planned to lure him into staying by sending Crope ahead with a little something to catch his eye.

Reaching into his robe, Baralis pulled out the fake letter. Just as he was about to crumple it in his fist, he stopped himself. Perhaps a use might be found for his hasty decoy after all. Even if it only managed to distract

Jack's thoughts for a quarter-instant, it was well worth the keeping.

Jack found himself in a small hallway with a flight of steps leading up to a second set of doors. The place was quiet and cool with a torch burning low, and Jack took a moment to calm himself on the stairs.

Strange, but his sense of being led had gone; his blood was no longer pulling him forward and his skin rested slack upon the bone. It was as if their job was done.

On his own now, Jack climbed the stairs, took the second door, and entered Kylock's chambers. A dimly lit reception room met his eyes. Everything looked perfect, as if no one had ever stepped upon the silken carpets, or sat upon the cushioned chairs. Even the papers and charts on the desk looked as if they had never been touched. Everything was placed in neat stacks. There was something about the room, some tiny little discrepancy, that jarred at Jack's senses. Only as he crossed over to the door on the far side did he realize what it was.

All the furniture—the chests, the chairs, the benches, and tables—was arranged in lines to form a grid. The armrest of one chair was perfectly aligned with the armrest of another chair on the far side of the room. Table edges mirrored each other, chests were turned lengthwise and placed equal distances apart. Jack had the distinct feeling that if he had a measuring line upon him, he'd find all the lengths and angles exactly the same.

A cold chill ran over his cheeks, and he moved quickly on. A pair of doors waited on the far side of the room, and he picked one at random. The handle was cool as he turned it, so cool it raised goosebumps upon his hand and forearm.

Darkness enveloped him as he stepped inside the room. It clung, it seeped, it shrouded. The door clicked shut behind him.

"Who dares disturb me unannounced?"

For a brief moment, Jack thought the voice was Baralis': the rich and beautifully modulated timbre, the undertone of power. But there was a filigree of difference—a subtle thread of wildness that marked it all its own.

"Name yourself." There was no fear in the voice, simply authority used to being obeyed.

Jack tried to pinpoint the source. The darkness seemed to be created from more than lack of light, it had texture and thickness and movement. Jack imagined himself breathing it in: black smoke curling down to his lungs.

"Are you a demon come to try me? Step forward and take your chance."

Jack was unnerved by Kylock's calmness. He had expected many things, but never relaxed encouragement. His grip on his knife wavered—sweat oiling the shift. Realizing Kylock had him at a disadvantage, Jack tried hard to search for forms in the darkness. Spots of light danced before his eyes. When they cleared, he thought he saw a half-circle of pale light straight ahead.

"Come. I am not afraid."

Jack *was*. Power lay in this room. Raw terrible power. As he stepped forward, he began to shape a drawing. It was difficult to know what to focus on, or how much power to use, or where to aim the blow. He might miscalculate and miss Kylock altogether, leaving himself open to an attack.

Better by far to use a knife. Instinct warned him to keep something in reserve, though, to hold his power close in case Kylock lashed out.

The pale fan of light was clearer now. Jack *willed* Kylock to speak again so he could focus in on his position. Nothing. The only sound in the room was the pumping of Jack's heart. Then, from the center of the paleness, came the soft swish of silk on silk.

Jack leapt forward. He felt his knife edge nick soft flesh before he landed hard on his shoulder. Rolling to his feet, he sprang into a defensive position, sweeping his knife wide to form an arc. Noise came from his left, a ragged breath or a softly mocking laugh. Jack cursed the darkness.

Like an answer to a prayer, light slanted across the room. A thin line at first, it broadened into a band. Kylock was nowhere to be seen—standing in shadows that had darkened with the light. Jack felt a warm draft of air ripple over his back. Spinning around, he saw a black figure silhouetted in the doorway.

Metal slivered along Jack's tongue. All thoughts of caution were blasted from his mind by the pressure of power inside.

"Jack. Crope's got something for you. Crope forgot to give you the second letter." The figure held out a hand. Something white gleamed between the fingers.

Jack swallowed hard, pushing the power back. His head was flooded with pressure. Pain streaked along his forehead, meeting between his eyes. Blood poured down from his nostrils.

"Another note from Lucy, Jack." Crope waggled a folded piece of paper in front of him.

Jack could just about make out the wax seal. Everything about the letter looked the same as the one he held in the cellar earlier. Two letters from his mother? A noise buzzed through Jack's head. He ignored it. A rustle of fabric came from behind. He paid it no heed.

The buzzing sound grew louder as he stepped toward the door. It was nothing—probably an effect of biting back the drawing.

Crope's shadow was a black strip running through the light. Jack moved onto it, raising his hand in readiness to accept the letter. The shadow cast by Crope's arm caught his eye; it swayed in time to Crope's movements, but one small part seemed to trail behind. A lace cuff, perhaps? Jack looked up. The sleeves of Crope's undershirt were rolled above his elbows.

Jack felt a cold trickle of sweat run down his spine. There was a hand behind the hand.

Baralis.

Jack pivoted, leaping back from the doorway and the light. Letting his body fall to the floor, he scrambled desperately into the shadows near the wall. As he moved, he called up the drawing—soft now, it was slow to build. Teeth clenched, fists clenched, Jack forced the power to come back. Thought played no part in his actions. Reflexes were all that he had.

Movement came from the door. Crope's shadow moved out of sight and was instantly replaced by another.

"Come in and join the party, Baralis."

Kylock's words were the last thing Jack heard before he let the drawing out.

Baralis was ready for Jack's assault. Whilst Crope stood distracting him at the door, Baralis had taken stock of the situation and formed a drawing ready to be sent.

He stepped into the room.

Air crackled and condensed. Baralis saw the thickening, felt the sharp pressure pain in his eardrums. His own drawing rose up like a mirror image, not even a split second behind.

An instant was stretched to its limits. Directly ahead of him, Baralis saw Kylock step forward from the shadow. To the right, Jack was hunched against a wall. Baralis moved toward him. Even as he made himself a target, he fixed his own sights upon Jack. And he was quicker, better, and craftier than the baker's boy would ever be.

Baralis unleashed his power. With mouth open and tongue ringing, he watched in horror as Jack's drawing flared wide. A sickening sensation rose up from his gut. Jack wasn't targeting him—he *had* no target. He was blasting everything before him.

Kylock!

Baralis shifted his drawing in midcast, shaping a barrier to defend the king. Altering the nature of the sorcery
at such an instant was dangerous beyond measure, but he
had no choice. Without Kylock he had nothing. Baralis
fashioned the shield, speeding it toward Kylock, using
all his powers of mind and will to force it ahead of Jack's
blast. Something ripped inside his chest. Pain needled
close to his heart.

Baralis cursed Jack. He was a fool! Only an untrained
simpleton would send such a crude and directionless
drawing. He should have targeted it first. He should have
aimed it straight at him!

The first surge of Jack's drawing hit. Baralis was
thrashed by light and air. He was knocked back and his
head smashed into the doorframe. On and on the power
came. It was relentless—a solid block of force. There was
not enough power left within him to shield himself as
well as Kylock. What had happened two nights back had
left him too weak. Drugs could only do so much, and he
had nothing but the barest glimmer in reserve.

With the very last finger of power that was left to him,
Baralis secured the shield around Kylock, protecting his
own creation, gritting himself for the blow.

Jack was hardly aware of what was happening. In the
space of two seconds, a world of change had raced by.
The drawing flowed through him, fast and terrible and
filled with light. Kylock was in the center of the room,
standing upright against the blast. Baralis was pinned
against the doorframe. Jack could sense him trying to
shield himself. He perceived the lines of power, inter-
twining cords, like ligaments, that cut across the room.
Somehow Kylock was still protected by Baralis' power—
the mesh was still intact.

In that instant, Jack realized that he had been wrong
about one important thing. He would never be able to
destroy Kylock without destroying Baralis first. The man

would not give up his one chance for glory lightly. It was time to kill the master of the beast. All that was left—all that Jack had in body and soul—he directed toward Baralis.

His spine cracked like a whip as he forced the drawing to bend. Fighting against the broad blade of power, Jack whittled it down it to an arrow-point of light. And sent it straight for Baralis.

A sharp schism ripped through the air. Baralis' body was lifted up and thrown against the wall. Bones cracked, skull cracked, blood shot from ears and mouth. A terrible scream sounded. Jack saw the lines of power fade to light traces in the dark. The mesh that had been Kylock's protection was less than an arm's length from Baralis' chest when it withered into shade.

Air gusted around the room like a gale. Jack couldn't breathe. A convulsion tore through his belly—a void that sucked him in. Weakened beyond telling, he capped the power's flow. The light and air closed in on itself, thinning, fading, and then dying to nothing. A soft *hiss* sounded as it went.

Baralis slumped to the floor, his body landing in a heap of unnatural angles, jagged with broken bones.

Jack felt himself falling, only he was already on the floor. Down and down he went, his body collapsing around him, pulled under by the void. Pain washed over him, blurring his vision to darkness and weighing his eyelids down. The last thing he saw was Baralis raising a shaking hand toward Kylock. His mouth worked for a moment and then two tortured words came out:

"My son."

The hand dropped to the floor as Jack let in the dark.

Thirty-seven

*J*ack blinked into waking. There was no coming round period, no time to take stock before his eyes were open.

Kylock was standing above him, a letter in his hand. "Aah, awake at last I see. Tell me, were your dreams all you expected?" He looked calm, but there was a hint of madness in his voice and an artificial gleam in the corner of his eye.

Jack tried to rally his thoughts, tried to recall all that had happened to bring him here. *Baralis*. His gaze shot to the wall by the door: Baralis' body was nowhere to be seen. How much time had passed? How long had he lain here vulnerable to Kylock's scrutiny?

Kylock made a short clicking sound in his throat. "So you're Lesketh's bastard, eh?"

Jack raised his arm to his tunic. Pain shot from his shoulder to his stomach.

"Is this what you're looking for?" Kylock curled the letter up in his fist. "Such a touching little note from mother to son." His voice rose higher as he spoke. Abruptly he turned on his heel.

Pulling himself into a sitting position, Jack tested the power inside. There was nothing left: the drawing that had destroyed Baralis had used up all his strength. Cautiously, he felt for his knife.

Two noises distracted him at the same time. The first

was a dragging noise, the sound of something being scraped across the floor. It came from the other room, and Jack knew without a doubt it was Crope hauling Baralis' body away. The second noise came from Kylock himself: a low, hacking laugh, almost a cough.

Kylock's shoulders were shaking. His knuckles were white where he gripped the letter. His fingertips were raw flesh and blood. "And I—I am Baralis' bastard. Whilst the king took his pleasures where he found them, my mother whored with his chancellor." Kylock's laugh was bitter now. He swung around to face Jack, his eyes very bright. "Baralis. Who would have thought it? Who would have guessed?"

Jack felt his skin crawling. Slowly, gradually, power was building within Kylock.

"You have what is mine!" he cried. "Your father should have been my father. Your face should have been mine." Spittle flew from his lips. The two tendons on the side of his neck were raised like cords of rope. "My hands, my lips, my teeth—*all yours.*"

Jack flinched. He backed against the wall. His mouth felt as dry as parchment. Kylock was losing control. Desperate for the knife now, Jack spread out his search. Nothing. He risked a sideways glance—the knife gleamed to the right of his hand, just beyond his reach.

Moving in close, Kylock began shaking his head. "You think you're going to walk out of this room and take your proof to the world. Show me up for what I am. Well, I swear to you that's not going to happen. Not today. Not tomorrow. Not ever."

As Kylock spoke, Jack became aware of heat building on his cheeks. At first he thought it was a blood-flush, like the ones that had led him to Kylock, but it didn't stop at simple warming. It began to burn. Terror bubbled in Jack's throat. His every instinct warned him to run away, yet he was too terrified to move.

"King's son." Kylock was a finger-length from his face

now. "Mother a common servant who made her money whoring on the side."

Listening to Kylock's words, something snapped inside Jack. His mother wasn't a whore—he knew that now—and this monster before him had no right to say it. Springing up, Jack went straight for Kylock's throat. A wall of blistering heat knocked him back. His nose and forehead were scorched; he smelled the quick singeing of his hair. And his hands. Falling back against the wall, his hands blazed with pain. Red and throbbing, he brought them to his face. His eyes were aching and he could barely see the burns on his palms.

"Those should have been my hands," said Kylock.

Anger whipped through Jack. He was sick of listening to the ravings of a madman. "I don't care," he cried. "I don't want what you've got. I don't give a damn about being a king."

Even as he spoke, Jack felt the linings of his nose and throat drying out. Air scorched his lungs. The blazing wave of moments earlier had gone, only to be replaced by a steady buildup of heat. Everything was hot to the touch: the floor, the walls, his clothes. The chain mail next to his skin was a blistering, scorching sheath.

Kylock's eyes grew blank. The air surrounding him rippled. Something sparked in his fist: the letter. A lick of flame ran up his arm. He didn't even flinch.

Jack felt the buildup of terrible pressure. The heat was unbearable—the skin on his face was being seared like a piece of meat. He had to stop Kylock. Raising the palms of his hands to face him, he cried, "Look, these are a baker's hands, not a king's."

The terrible bright blankness left Kylock's eyes for an instant. The heat wavered.

Jack edged to the side, his sights set on the knife.

Kylock began shaking his head. "No, king's son," he said, speaking very softly. "You'll never have what is mine."

Jack lunged for the knife. Heat blasted against him. His skin was on fire, the air was sucked from his lungs. Still he went on. His fingers touched the hilt. Railing against instinct, he clasped the red-hot metal in the palm of his hands. Pain ripped through his mind. A second, maybe two, was lost to him as he spiraled down toward a fiery hell. The smell of his own burnt flesh brought him round.

Flames. He was surrounded by flames. The silk rug on the floor was ablaze. Wall hangings and furnishings caught light as he watched. Panicking, terrified, breathing in smoke, Jack fought to keep his mind intact. Strangely it was the pain throbbing in his hand that kept him focused. It throbbed in time with his heart. It was as if Larn was behind each agonizing pulse—slapping him on the cheek to keep him conscious.

Jack felt himself growing stronger. He knew he had never been abandoned by his father. He knew who his mother was and where she had come from, and what she had planned a decade to do. After a lifetime of lies and evasions, the truth was his at last. And there had to be power in that.

Forcing himself to his feet, he ran through the flames toward Kylock. The blaze blinded, the smoke choked, the scorching heat shredded his flesh. A warm breath of air buffeted his body, and then he came face-to-face with Kylock. Surprise flitted across Kylock's face. A dark glimmer in his eyes might have been fear, but by the time Jack had blinked away the smoke-tears it was gone.

Time stretched to a fine film like oil over water. Flames formed a hissing, crackling ring around the two men. Jack could feel the fire's heat on his back. Kylock was surrounded by a halo of golden light; it spilled over his shoulders and down along his torso. It flickered like candlelight upon his face. Never had he looked more like Baralis.

Watching him, Jack felt a hard block of fear rise in his

throat. There was no doubting Kylock was Baralis' son.

Baralis. Even now that he had killed the man, Jack could only guess at the full range of Baralis' powers. Focusing his gaze on Kylock's face, Jack wondered if the son was capable of more. Kylock's eyes were sharp with madness—Baralis' brilliance was there, but it had been distorted into something new and monstrous. As Jack watched, Kylock's lips curved into a smile. Yes, he could do much worse.

Jack shuddered.

The pain pulsed hot in his hand. Larn again, pushing, reminding, keeping him on track. The reflex reaction of the pain caused him to raise his hand. The knife came up with it.

Kylock's gaze flicked to the blade. He raised his arm to defend himself. Jack moved ahead of him. Driven to madness by the pain of his burns, he had developed a madman's reflexes. The moment Kylock's arm came up to his heart, Jack raised the dagger to his throat. Blind panic registered on Kylock's face. For the briefest instant he looked as shocked as a child who had been slapped for no reason.

And then the knife went in. Kylock's mouth fell open. Jack flinched, expecting sorcery. Quickly, he worked to turn the blade within the muscle of Kylock's neck, seeking to sever the windpipe. Kylock fought him all the way.

Jack smelled the metal tang of sorcery. He saw Kylock's lips move. Within the wet redness of his mouth, Kylock's tongue began to vibrate.

The pain in Jack's arm and hand was unbearable. His eyes were stinging with sweat and smoke. Kylock's body tensed. Panicking, Jack fumbled with the knife for what seemed like an eternity. Blood gushed over Jack's fist and down Kylock's chest. Jack's knife hand wouldn't stop shaking. Finally the blade scraped against the elastic wall of Kylock's windpipe.

In that instant Kylock's mouth opened wide. The air thickened around his lips. The odor of hot metal sharpened into a stench.

With one razor-quick movement, Jack sliced Kylock's windpipe in two.

A soft hiss escaped from Kylock's lips. He blinked once, his eyes revealing a raw, animal terror, and then the light disappeared from his face.

Jack couldn't stop shaking. His grip on the knife was so tight, his knuckles were as white as bone. He took a deep gulp of air, and as he did so, he breathed in what remained of Kylock's last breath.

The breath was the final link between them. Jack felt it settling within his lungs, sending messages to his blood. It was rich with the promise of sorcery, heavy with the remains of the man. Breathing it in, Jack realized the full wrath of Kylock's last drawing, shivered at the knowledge of all it could have destroyed. No one in this palace would have escaped alive. The power was as thick and black as tar. Yet there were other things besides destruction borne upon the sorcery-tainted air. Jack felt the force of Kylock's will, the breadth of his genius, and the dark depths of his madness. He saw the full tragedy of a brilliant mind ruined by drugs, manipulation, and lies. Baralis' creature entirely, Kylock had been lured into a delusional state where his emerging insanity was encouraged and his sadism overlooked.

Jack knew all this in an instant, and much, much more. There was little triumph here, only the end of a life that had been doomed from the start.

Tired beyond measure, Jack exhaled. He didn't want Kylock's breath in him a moment longer. The truths it had shown him were too disturbing. They left a bad taste in his mouth.

Baralis had turned his own son into a monster.

Jack yanked out the blade and blood gushed from the wound. Kylock's eyes were closed. His muscles stiffened, then relaxed. The blackened letter dropped into the flames by his feet. Jack made no attempt to retrieve it.

Kylock fell. The blaze closed in to take him.

Jack turned. There was nowhere to go. Shoulder-height flames circled the room. There were no walls, there was no door: everything was red and white. Thick smoke rolled from under flames, hot and acrid; Jack didn't want to take it in, but he had no choice. He had to breathe.

Pain had taken his sanity, now the smoke took his consciousness. In and out he drifted, the flames flickering higher and nearer each time he opened his eyes. He felt himself swaying, ready to fall. The heat was too intense; he couldn't fight it. All he wanted to do was collapse by Kylock's side.

Drifting . . . further and further away. Peace lay ahead. Peace, relief, and truth.

"Jack!"

A dark shadow broke through the flames. For one brief moment, Jack's heart thrilled: it was Tawl, come to carry him from the temple. But no, this wasn't Larn. And as the figure came closer, he realized it couldn't be Tawl. Yellow and black, the colors of Valdis—Tawl would never dress as a knight.

"Jack!"

The figure hovered outside the ring of flames. Other figures joined him, all wearing yellow and black. There was shouting and moving and beating of cloaks.

Jack felt himself falling. The flames leapt up to meet him; hot little fingers eager to burn.

He never hit the floor. Hands broke his fall, gentle hands that cupped him like a baby and carried him through the blaze. With eyes that could barely see, through tears that wouldn't stop coming, Jack looked up into the face of the person who held him. That was when he knew it *was* Tawl. Tawl wearing the knight's colors, surrounded by other knights, shouting out commands, his voice filled with urgency, his blue eyes more fierce than Jack had ever seen them. Tawl. Together they went through the flames, and together they emerged into a world bright with hope, light, and laughter far on the other side.

"You—" Jack fought against the blistered dryness that was his throat, "you weren't supposed to come back for me."

Tawl's smile was gentle. "I warned you about my heart, Jack. I said it might lead me astray."

Fire followed them from the palace, barreling down corridors, licking at their heels. Stairwells and passageways were filled with smoke and motes of blackened dust. People were everywhere—screaming and panicking and running for their lives. No one paid heed to their passing. No one cared about the dozen fully dressed knights who raced ahead of the blaze. If they looked at all, it was at the one tall, golden-haired knight who carried a lifeless body in his arms. Something about his face gave hope to those who saw him. Something in his eyes spoke directly to the soul.

Melli stood in the knights' camp and watched the palace burn. Bright, fierce, and liberating, it lit up the northern sky. Strange, but she wasn't worried anymore: there was something in the air besides the smoke: a sense of anticipation, a feeling that everything would turn out all right.

"They're coming back, miss," said Borlin. "I can spot them now, just north of the plain."

Melli didn't ask if Tawl was amongst them, she didn't have to. She just knew. "Have some brandy and blankets ready," she said to Grift, who was hovering near to the fire.

"Aye, miss."

Walking to the front of the camp, Melli heard the first strains of a song. A rich and mellow voice shaped words that pulled at the heart. Melli changed her course, drawn to the beauty of the voice. As she walked nearer, other voices joined in the song, and when she rounded the command tent, she saw a sight that made her smile with joy.

Twenty or so knights were gathered around a makeshift crib, singing little Herbert to sleep.

Andris, who had ridden out to Fair Oaks to fetch her earlier that day, caught sight of Melli and beckoned her over. She was drawn into the circle next to her baby, and the knights sang for her as well. Melli felt her heart would break. Anyone who heard them sing could not doubt that the knighthood was good. Looking at their fine faces, hearing the tenderness in their voices, Melli suddenly knew why Tawl had risked everything to save them. Some things were worth more than one life alone.

And, as the song came to an end and Tawl rode into the camp, Melli made up her mind that she would not stand in his way. She would release Tawl from his oath and give him the freedom to become leader of the knighthood. After all he had done for her she owed him that.

"Get the surgeon. Quick!" shouted Tawl from his horse. Melli saw someone riding at his back. She caught her breath. *No.* It couldn't be . . .

But it was. It was Jack, nothing on his back except grimy, warped chain mail, no part of his skin that wasn't black with smoke or burns. Melli rushed forward, her eyes filling with quick tears, her throat closing in around her breath. The world suddenly seemed a place where miracles could happen. And the golden-haired knight who rode toward her seemed worthy, at long last, of all God's gifts. She loved him completely.

That night, as the fire blazed a league to the north, the surgeon worked on Jack. Melli held his hand through the long hours of torment, forcing water through his blistered lips, rubbing salve into his wounds. His forehead and hands were burnt the worst, but there were many lesser burns running the entire length of his body. One or two knights came over offering help and advice, and Borlin brought a drug to make him sleep. Only when Jack's breathing was easy and regular did Melli fall asleep herself.

Tawl woke her at dawn. "Come, Melli. We've got to go to the city."

"But—" Melli looked down at her lap. Jack's bandaged hand rested against the fabric of her dress.

"Jack needs to sleep. You've done what you can. Nabber can look after him while we're gone." Tawl's voice was gentle but firm. "You and the baby must come with me."

She didn't argue. She had many different responsibilities now.

Melli took great care with her appearance before she rode into the city. She brushed her hair until it shone, and disguised her burns with powder and paste. The innkeeper's eldest daughter had parted with her best winter dress, and Melli put it on in Tyren's tent. She struggled to pull it over her broken arm, far too proud to ask for help. When she finally emerged into the camp, Tawl was waiting with a beautiful bay gelding. He had just helped her onto the horse when, to her great displeasure, Nanny Greal rode over to join them.

"What's she doing coming with us?" hissed Melli under her breath.

"She's the only person in Bren who knows Baralis was the one who ordered the duke's murder."

Melli could think of no suitable objection to that, so she settled for an indignant snort instead. "She's not riding with the baby. I'm taking him."

Tawl actually laughed. Melli was struck by how young and happy he looked: almost like a child. "Well, if that's what you want, little Herbert will have to be slung over your back."

"Fine." Melli tried to sound firm, but Tawl's smile

was infectious and she found herself giving in. "All right, all right, Nanny Greal can take him."

Nanny Greal beamed at Tawl.

Tawl beamed at Nanny Greal.

Melli glared at both of them. And then smiled when their backs were turned. She felt madly, recklessly, happy.

The ride into the city took less than an hour. Melli rode at the head of a cohort of two hundred and fifty knights and seventy Highwall troops. Word was out that Baralis and Kylock were dead, and with no one to give orders, the city was in chaos. A company of blackhelms challenged them at the gate, but Valdis' marksmen picked off a few of their numbers and their enthusiasm quickly waned.

Melli felt nervous entering the city. She rode through street after street where people stood and stared at her, many openly hostile, some cursing as she passed. Gone was the mad euphoria of earlier. Instead she was sobered by the sheer brevity of events: the future of a great and ancient city lay in the balance—its fate dependent upon her and her son.

Melli's nervousness showed itself as pride. Her chin tilted upward and her eyes flashed at those who cursed her. She had been married to their duke and had given birth to Bren's true heir—she had every right to be here.

As the cohort turned into a large public square, Melli got her first sight of the smoking skeleton that had once been the duke's palace. It had been reduced to a stone shell. The walls were intact, but the middle was now a gaping hollow: all the wood—all the roof beams and floorboards and furnishings and doorframes—had perished. All gone, and she couldn't say she was sorry to see it.

Mesmerized by the sight for some time, Melli looked around to see a large crowd gathering in the square. She glanced at Tawl.

"It's all right," he said. "The more the better."

Melli looked at the hundreds of people who were blocking the streets and pathways, swarming around the fountains, and rapidly filling every available cobbled space. She was afraid now, but determined not to show it.

The knights—resplendent in full dress armor, lances at their sides, their horses proud and gleaming—formed a defensive semicircle around Melli, Tawl, and Nanny Greal. A flash of yellow-and-black high up on a roof caught Melli's eye: Valdis' marksmen were leaving nothing to chance.

When the square was full of people, Tawl urged his horse up the few steps to the raised dais at the head of the square. The crowd, recognizing the man who had once been the duke's champion, began to hiss.

Tawl raised his hands. "Silence," he commanded. "Hear me first before you condemn me." His voice carried to all four corners of the square and the noise of the crowd died down. "Baralis and Kylock are dead. They were both killed last night in the fire. Your city and your armies are no longer commanded by a foreign king—"

"Why should we listen to you?" snapped a man near the front of the crowd. "You murdered our duke."

"Aye," murmured a hundred others.

Tawl's face darkened. He pressed his lips together as if he were forcibly containing a reply. With a quick gesture he beckoned Nanny Greal forth. Melli took the baby from her before she guided her horse up the steps.

Nanny Greal brought her horse to rest next to Tawl's, and arranging her bony body high in the saddle, she told her story to the crowd. First she told how she had overheard Baralis plotting to kill the duke, about the payment that changed hands, and the true name of the assassin.

Then, with the crowd still reeling in disbelief, she told them how Kylock had murdered dozens of noblemen and had their mutilated bodies thrown into the lake. When someone called her a liar, she took out a little pigskin book and recited their names one by one. When she came to the name, "Lord Bathroy," a voice cried out from the crowd:

"The lady is right." The voice belonged to an old man who made his way to the front. Painfully thin, covered only by rags, the man was missing his left hand. Slowly he climbed the steps of the dais. "Bathroy is dead."

Tawl glanced at Melli.

Someone in the crowd jeered, "How would you know?"

Turning to face the mob, the old man held up the scarred stump that had once been his left wrist. "I know because I was one of Kylock's victims." His gaze darted around the crowd, challenging anyone to contradict him. No one could meet his eye. "I shared a cell with Bathroy. I was there when he was taken away, and I stayed awake as he screamed through the night." The man's voice was thin and piercing. "And let me tell you, he wasn't the only one. Night after night I heard men scream, and night after night I gave thanks to God that Kylock hadn't come for me."

The crowd was silent now. They shifted uneasily where they stood.

"Only one night he did come," said the man. "One night our king, our duke, our warlord came and asked for me."

Hearing the old man speak, Melli felt the hairs on her arms prickle. Her throat and lips were dry.

"Bound and gagged, I was led into a room lit up like a surgeon's tent. In the middle of the floor was a butcher's block. After the guards left, Kylock laid my arm against the wood and hacked off my hand with a cleaver."

A shocked murmur rippled through the crowd.

Tawl grasped Melli's hand tightly. She felt as if she would faint.

The man brought his arm down to his side. "Kylock wasn't going to stop there, but word came that he was needed urgently upstairs, so I was led back to my cell. He never called for me again after that night—whether he forgot, or whether he just wanted to prolong my suffering, I will never know." The man shook his head slowly, and when he next spoke, his voice had lost all its former power. He sounded tired and very old. "So, whatever you do today, remember this one thing: Kylock may have led us to victory, but he would have led us to damnation as well."

A single tear streaked down Melli's face. Quickly, she brushed the wetness away. Of all who were gathered here today, she alone knew just how right the old man was.

The eyes of the crowd were cast down to the ground. No one spoke.

Melli wanted to go to the man, to comfort him. She wasn't the only one: a young girl with dark shiny hair and pink cheeks came forward and took the man's arm. Without looking up at the dais, he let himself be led away. The crowd was silent as the old man and the girl made their way through their midst. There was something immeasurably sad about the sight of them, arms linked, shoulders touching, the old man leaning against the girl for support.

Watching them, Melli felt her throat tighten. How many other people in the city had been touched by Kylock's madness? How many years would need to pass before they were free of the memories and the pain?

After a few minutes of silence, Mistress Greal chose to speak. Clearing her throat loudly to ensure she had everyone's full attention, she began telling the crowd the story of how Melli had been imprisoned in the castle for five months—pregnant with the duke's child and victim of Kylock's cruelty. The crowd listened, subdued. Nanny Greal told of the night Melli gave birth and the orders Baralis had given her: *"As soon as the baby is born, take it away and smother it. Destroy the body when you're done."*

A dark murmur united the crowd.

Melli shuddered. She heard the words as if they came straight from Baralis' mouth. For the first time, she realized just how much danger Nanny Greal had placed herself in by defying Baralis' orders. Later, when all this was over she would thank her—properly and from the heart.

For now, though, her first task was to show her son to the city of Bren. Kicking her horse forward, she joined Tawl and Nanny Greal on the steps. Tawl took her reins and Melli held up the baby for all the crowd to see.

"Look," she cried. "Look at the face of your future duke. Look at the son of the Hawk."

Many in the crowd cheered, others hissed, a few cursed.

"Foreign whore! That baby could be anyone's brat."

Tawl stiffened. He took a mouthful of air to shout, but Melli put a hand on his arm. "No," she whispered. "Let me handle this."

Turning back to the crowd, she took the left sock from the baby. When Nanny Greal leant forward to give her a hand, Melli didn't slap her away.

"Here!" she said, presenting the barefoot and now very indignant baby to the crowd. "See the mark of the Hawk for yourself."

Most of the people cheered now. It wasn't enough for Melli. Looking directly at the man who had just insulted her, she beckoned him forward. "Come, sir, take a look at the baby close up. Run your finger over the mark—satisfy yourself that it won't rub off." Laughter rose from the crowd. "Come on," she said when the man hesitated. "With a tongue as fast as yours, I would have expected quicker feet."

The man who came forward became the most famous man in Bren. Quick-tongued Tarvold, as he was subsequently known to all and sundry, went down in history as being the man first to doubt, and then to proclaim, Melliandra's baby as the true heir to Bren. His words,

"Aye, my friends, the lady's right about the mark—it won't come off," went on record as setting off the longest and loudest cheer in the city's thousand-year history.

Tradition later held that the one thing that stopped the cheering was when the Lady Melliandra turned her open palm toward the crowd and swore she would bring peace. Everyone was quiet after that. There was nothing more to say.

Epilogue

"Aah, so what you're saying is that I'm definitely not the chosen one?" Tavalisk held out his little silver sieve and scooped a fistful of tadpoles from the tank. It was hatching season at last and the archbishop was looking forward to one of his favorite delicacies: frogspawn.

"Well, as Your Eminence can see, there is a great difference between the two verses." Gamil waved toward the two copies of Marod's prophecy on the desk. "The version that fell into your hands was a much later edition than the first, Your Eminence. Scribes had changed words, sentences, meanings."

"Hmm." Tavalisk inspected the sieve full of wriggling tadpoles, looking for the ones that were already sprouting limbs. "Well, I have no sister, so it surely can't be me. And even if I did have one, as a man of the Church I could never condone taking her as a lover."

"Exactly, Your Eminence." Gamil took the liberty of edging the copies to the side. A few stray tadpoles had landed on the parchment.

"Well, I can't say I'm surprised, Gamil. Can't say I'm disappointed, either. After all, everything has turned out fine: the lovely Lady Melliandra is acting as regent in Bren, the Four Kingdoms have dragged up an old cousin of the late King Lesketh to take the throne there, the north is free of Kylock's forces, and the south is no longer

under threat. I couldn't have planned it better myself.
Though I still think I'm due part of the credit."

"How so, Your Eminence?"

"Well, according to all the rumors it was that golden-
haired knight's doing, and you alone know, Gamil, how I
encouraged him all the way."

"I pray Your Eminence never sees fit to encourage me."

"Nonsense, Gamil. I did my duty by the knight: kept
him safe in my dungeons for a year, monitored his every
move, even saved his ladyfriend from a life on the
streets." Tavalisk filled his silver spoon with tadpoles,
squeezed fresh lemon juice, seasoned with salt and
pepper, then swallowed them whole. Slimy little devils.
Quite tasteless, really. "In fact, in many ways I *was*
chosen. Who's to say the newly altered version of a
prophecy doesn't have as much validity as the old one?
Words don't change without reasons, Gamil. Fate meant
to draw me in."

"And then let you off the hook at the last moment?"

"Gamil, you forget how tirelessly I have worked over
the past two years to keep Baralis and Kylock from taking
power." Tavalisk managed an affronted snort. "Anyway,
the Lady Melliandra has been regent for over two months
now, and it's high time I sent her an official greeting.
Scribe me an appropriate missive. Make the usual offer-
ings of friendship and so forth, and then bring it to me to
sign."

"Certainly, Your Eminence. Though the lady might
not be willing to respond to your overtures."

"Really, Gamil, like a shortsighted archer your arrows
always land wide of the mark. We're dealing with heads
of state now; they know better than to keep up petty
squabbles. Rorn is powerful, Bren is powerful—the two
cities need to work together, not apart. People and politics
will always change, but the dance of power goes on."

"Your Eminence is undoubtedly the most light-footed
on the floor."

"Thank you, Gamil. Wily movers like me always live to dance another day." Tavalisk handed the bowl of tadpoles to his aide. "You may go now, Gamil. Take the tadpoles with you—they're beginning to look far too slippery for comfort."

Just as his aide was about to step from the room, a thought occurred to Tavalisk. "Oh, by the way, Gamil, did they ever recover Baralis' body from the palace ruins?"

"I don't think anyone knows for sure, Your Eminence. After all, one set of blackened bones looks much like another."

Tavalisk shuddered. "Be gone, Gamil," he said. "You're letting in a draft through the door."

The sun shone through the open shutter and into the kitchen of the old duke's hunting lodge. With the light came a soft mountain breeze and with the breeze came the scent of spring flowers. Jack knew, as only a baker can, that somehow the scent, the breeze, and the light would find their way into the dough.

For the first time in many months Jack was baking bread. He had awoken with the strong desire to feel flour between his fingers, to cup yeast in his palms, and knead dough beneath his knuckles. He worked quickly, his hands remembering moves that his mind had long forgotten. The burns troubled him little now. There was some tautness where scars pulled at his skin and some lost sensitivity in his fingertips, but the blisters had all gone, and new pink skin covered once-raw flesh. He was lucky in many ways, and the quick healing of his wounds was just one of them.

Setting the dough in a bowl, he covered it with a damp cloth. It was the second rising, so it would be ready for the oven in less than an hour.

That done, Jack moved around the table, rubbing the flour from his fingers. The far corner of the working surface was set out for writing, not for baking, and Jack sat down on the bench before the square of parchment, the linen blotter, the ink, and the quill. The quill felt strange in his hand, small and awkward; it had been a long time since he'd last handled a pen. Turning it in his fingers, Jack couldn't help recalling the very first time he picked up a pen to write with: all those years ago in Baralis' study, the day King Lesketh was shot.

Jack surprised himself by smiling at the memory. He hadn't known it then, but that bright and icy afternoon had marked the beginning of everything. All the fear, madness, and triumph could be traced back to that day.

And all the heartache, too.

Jack dipped the quill into the ink and tested the edge in the side margin of the parchment. *Tarissa*. The nib was fine and sharp. Jack blanked out the jotted-down name, and then rewrote it in finehand at the top.

Dear Tarissa,

Pausing to brush the hair from his face, Jack took a long, deep breath. This was going to be harder than he thought. At some point in the middle of the night, he had managed to convince himself that if he woke up early enough, and tired himself out by working hard enough, that somehow when the time came to write the letter, the words would flow quickly from his pen.

He'd been wrong, of course. He was wrong about so many things that sometimes he wondered how he'd managed to muddle through. Mistakes, misconceptions, and misjudgments had hounded him all the way.

For the past seven weeks, Jack had stayed in the old duke's hunting lodge. Alone except for an elderly caretaker who aired the rooms and lit the fires, Jack had found plenty of time to think. Marod's prophecy, his mother's letter, and Tarissa's reluctance to disclose her origins all needed making sense of. He didn't want to make any more mistakes.

Now, as the time came for him to leave this place, Jack thought he had an answer to the puzzle that had occupied his mind for so long: he and Tarissa shared the same father.

But sister as lover. The line had stayed with him since that long night in the palace. Disregarded at first, it had needled away at his thoughts until it could no longer be ignored. Tarissa was his half-sister; an illegitimate child of the king—just like himself. It explained so much: Magra's noble birth, her bitterness, their exile from the kingdoms. Even his mother's letter had hinted at the truth: *"Like everyone else, I heard rumors that the king had affairs with other women . . ."*

Suddenly tired, Jack closed his eyes. Straightaway a vision came, unbidden, into the blackness. It was the glade where Tarissa had said she loved him. Jack could see the willow branches trailing in the pool, smell the daffodils casting their scent to the breeze. He saw himself looking down into the spring clear water and mistaking Tarissa's reflection for his own.

Jack blinked the image away. A soft pain, mostly sadness, pulled at the muscles of his chest. They had looked so alike, yet neither of them had known it.

Jack took up the quill once more, wondering what to write first. How could he possibly say what he had to? Was there any way he could word the letter without causing Tarissa more pain? In his head, Jack tried out several beginnings, but none of them seemed right. After not hearing from him for so long, after his self-righteous exit from her life, when she pleaded with him to stay, what would she want him to say?

Jack stretched back in his chair, thinking. Specks of dust and flour floated in the strip of morning sunlight that split the kitchen in two. After watching them rise and fall for a short while, each mote entirely separate yet following the same path as the rest, Jack leant forward and began to write.

I'm writing this letter for many reasons, but most of all to say I am sorry. I should never have walked away from you that day I fought with Rovas. I know now that you spoke the truth when you said you loved me. . . .

The words flowed out of Jack. The ink was a shiny black ribbon unraveling from his pen. He knew what to say and how to say it. There was no need for fancy words or high-blown sentiment, he just needed to tell the truth. It was what he would want if he were in Tarissa's shoes. It was what he had searched for all along.

Jack sat and wrote for an hour, speaking of forgiveness and love and friendship. He told Tarissa all he had guessed about her parentage and disclosed all he knew about his own. No matter how conclusive the proof sounded, a small part of Jack couldn't help but wish he was wrong, so right at the end of the letter he added an extra sentence, stating that Tarissa could always contact him through Stillfox in Annis if he had made a terrible mistake. He signed his name quickly, determined not to dwell upon that one single hope. They had to move on with their lives now. Both of them.

While he was writing the dough had formed a fat globe beneath the cloth. Jack blotted and folded the letter, then slipped it into his tunic before cutting the dough into loaves. Now that the letter was finished, he felt clear-headed. He would leave the lodge today, leave his friends and his life here, and try to find himself anew. Writing the letter had been the right thing to do: it was an explanation, an apology, and a farewell.

Jack shaped the loaves, placed them on the floured paddle, and then transferred them to the oven. Just as he fixed the oven door in place, he heard the sound of horses trotting up the path. A few seconds later Nabber burst into the kitchen.

"Hey, Jack. How are you, my old friend?"

"Nabber!" Jack was genuinely surprised. It had been many weeks since he had last seen the young pocket. "I hadn't expected to see you all the way out here. Are Tawl and Melli with you?"

"Tawl is." Nabber strolled over to the table where Jack was preparing the bread and began prodding at various things he found there. "We're on our way south—heading back to Rorn. Thought we'd just stop by and say farewell."

It was a day for parting, then. Jack glanced toward the doorframe where his pack lay ready for the taking. "So what business do you have in Rorn?"

Nabber ran his finger through the layer of flour on the table top. "Well, I can't speak for Tawl, but personally I'm hoping to move up in the world. Last time I was in Rorn I got a very interesting offer. Very interesting, indeed. The Old Man said he might have a place for me in his organization. You know, helping with his personal finances and so on." Nabber waited a moment to give Jack time to look suitably impressed. "'Course I'd appreciate it if you kept it to yourself."

"Of course."

"Jack!" Tawl stepped through the door. Crossing the room in two mighty strides, he caught Jack in a huge bear hug. "It's good to see you, friend."

Jack looked into the knight's face. All the hardness and strain that had once been there had now disappeared completely. It was as if he had been made anew. "It's good to see you, too," he said, meaning it more than he could ever hope to convey.

The two men stood and looked at each other for a moment. Jack got the feeling Tawl was appraising him, looking for damage . . . or signs of repair. After a moment he nodded, seeming satisfied with what he saw. "Has Nabber told you where we're headed?"

"Where but not why."

Tawl grinned like a naughty choirboy. "I think it's

high time someone finally put the archbishop of Rorn in his place."

Jack smiled, catching his mood. "And what place is that?"

"I'm not fussy—the gutters or the streets, either will do." Grabbing a wedge of cheese from the table, Tawl began to chew on it. Jack noticed that he had an extra circle on his forearm: three of them now, the third one red around the edges, newly branded. The white scar that had once cut through the circles had disappeared completely. "Seriously, I'm leading a party of knights down to Rorn. Nabber here knows a thing or two about the archbishop, that will—how should I put it?—help hasten His Eminence's departure."

Nabber was on his way out of the back door. "You'd better not tell anyone it was me who snitched on him, Tawl. Lose my reputation, I would." With that, Nabber strolled out in the courtyard and into the fields beyond.

Jack watched him go. "What will happen to Melli while you're away?" he said, turning to Tawl after a few minutes.

Tawl raked his fingers through his hair. "You know how strong-willed she is, Jack. She practically forced me into taking the leadership—even rescinded my oath." Tawl shook his head, smiling softly. "She's right though; getting rid of Tyren is only half the job. There's a lot of work to be done at Valdis, things that I think I can help with, changes I'd like to make. At one time men used to be proud to call themselves knights: I'd like to see that day again."

"I think you can make it happen."

"I hope so." Tawl's voice was soft. "I really hope I can."

"So, you and Melli . . . " Jack's words trailed off as he realized he couldn't think of a polite way of putting things.

"Won't get married." The grin had returned to Tawl's

face. "Well, I wouldn't say no for definite, Jack. After all, I did say I wanted to make changes." His blue eyes twinkled brighter than Jack had ever seen them.

"You mean—"

"Yes. I always thought it was a senseless rule that knights couldn't marry. Give me a couple of years and I'm sure I'll bring others around to my way of thinking."

"I'm sure you will." Both men laughed. Tawl's excitement was infectious.

"So you're leaving, too?" Tawl nodded toward Jack's pack.

"Yes. I'm heading to Annis. There's a man I know there—Stillfox, his name is. He started to teach me things, only I ran off before he could finish. Now I think it's time I went back and learnt something."

"Will you come back here when you're done?"

Jack shook his head. "I don't know. I think I might do some traveling first. See some places, head west to Silbur, then south to Isro."

Tawl turned his face to the window. When he spoke, his voice was low and rough. "We'll be a long time parted."

Jack felt a sharp ache in his heart. He and Tawl were connected in so many ways: through prophecies, dreams, and shared adventures. And blood. Jack remembered the first time they met in Cravin's wine cellar. They were joined by blood, too.

It was hard to believe the time had come for them to part. He owed Tawl so much. The knight had saved his life, not once but twice, and ultimately led him to the truth. He was always there when he was needed.

Jack took a quick breath and asked Tawl what had been on his mind for many weeks now: "What made you come for me that night in the palace?"

Tawl continued to stare out of the window. His answer came quickly, as if his thoughts had been following the same path. "I'm not really sure, Jack. After I killed Tyren

I lay in the tent for hours sleeping, daydreaming, thinking of my family. Somehow my thoughts drifted to you, and there was something—" Tawl shrugged. "I didn't feel any grief, just a sort of niggling emptiness. The next thing I knew, I was in the middle of the camp arranging a raid into the palace. It all happened so fast; my clothes were covered in Tyren's blood, so someone gave me the knights' colors to wear, many of Maybor's men were injured, so a couple of knights volunteered to come along. An hour later we were in the heart of the palace.

"I wasn't sure you were alive though, not until we saw a girl in a green dress wandering around the passageways. We took the gag off her and she said a tall, brown-haired man had tied her up. After that there was no stopping us." Tawl made a deprecating gesture with his hand.

"You got there just in time." Jack's memories of the night were patchy, but the sight of Tawl coming toward him as he fell was something he'd remember for the rest of his life. So much fire and brightness and pain, and in the middle of everything came Tawl.

Tawl's blue eyes met his. "I was blessed that night, Jack. We all were."

The truth of the knight's words stopped all talk for a while, and Jack returned to his baking while Tawl stared out of the window to the green and flowering meadow beyond. When finally he spoke again, the subject, although different, was in essence the same. "Grift found Bodger wandering the streets a couple of weeks back. He'd been locked in a dungeon for Borc knows how long, and when the fire in the palace started, the jailer had no choice but to let the prisoners out. In the confusion Bodger managed to run away."

So many of them had been blessed that night. So many separate miracles had taken place within the whole. Jack closed his eyes a moment, overwhelmed with the closeness of it all. Although he was feeling more awed than happy, he smiled and said, "So Bodger and Grift are back together again, then?"

"Much to the horror of the entire female population of Bren," said Tawl, laughing gently. As he spoke, Tawl beckoned to Nabber through the open window. Turning back to Jack, he said, "We've got to be going now. We've a long day's ride ahead of us." Again came the searching look of minutes earlier, only this time there was sadness at the heart of the scrutiny. "If you are in trouble, send a message and I will come. If you are weary of being alone, seek me out, and we will journey together once more."

Jack couldn't reply. He couldn't trust himself to speak.

A minute later, Nabber appeared at the window. His sharp young eyes immediately took in the nature of the silence that lay between them, and he set about lightening it as only he could. "Once this journey's over," he said, "I swear on Swift's mother's grave that there's no way I'm getting on a horse ever again. Why anyone would choose to ride when they could be sailing on the high seas, I'll never know."

Jack and Tawl looked at each other an instant longer, and then laughed with simple joy.

"Well," said Tawl, laying his hand on Jack's shoulder, "it's time we were off. Take care, my friend. My thoughts will always be with you."

"And mine with you." Jack wanted to say more, wanted to thank Tawl for everything he had done and all he had just offered, but something in the knight's face stopped him. There would never be any need for thanks between them.

Jack walked around to the front of the lodge to watch them go. Tawl looked exactly as Jack had always imagined knights to look: fair, powerful, self-assured. Raising his newly marked forearm in parting, Tawl turned his horse and rode away.

Jack swallowed hard, torn between sadness and joy. He watched the two riders disappear into the deep green shadows of the distant pines. His eyes strained to catch every possible detail he could, saving them as precious memories in his heart. When finally there was nothing more to see, Jack began the short walk back to the lodge.

The smell of baking bread filled the kitchen. Jack took the loaves from the oven and set them to cool on the table. He sat and watched the steam rise from the crusts for a few moments and then, suddenly overcome with a deep need to be gone, he made his way to the door. He'd leave this batch for the caretaker.

Hoisting his pack over his shoulder, he made his way out into the noonday sun. He didn't feel much like riding, so he led his horse along the path and into the grassland beyond. The breeze from the mountains was soft and fragrant and fresh. Insects buzzed, small birds called from bushes, and a solitary hawk circled high overhead. The sun was warm on Jack's neck and the side of his face, the grass crackled beneath his feet. The letter to Tarissa pushed gently against his heart as he followed Tawl's path to the pines. By the time he reached the tree line, the shade had shifted from west to east, and although his horse was inclined to follow the eastern trail left by Nabber and Tawl's horses, Jack guided the gelding due south. He felt like traveling alone for a while.

The End

THE BARBED COIL

J.V. Jones

The Barbed Coil is a fast moving tale of passion, intrigue and adventure that triumphantly confirms J.V. Jones as fantasy's brightest new star.

When Izgard of Garizon put on the Coil and crowned himself King, he set in train a course of tumultuous events that would reverberate around the continent. For the Coil must have blood.

And the first blood to flow is that of Berick of Thorn, the legendary conqueror of Garizon. His son, Camron, wants revenge and knows that Izgard can only be stopped by force of arms. He seeks out the man who knows most about Izgard's murderous hordes – Lord Ravis, a ruthless mercenary with a dark and secret past.

And Tessa McCamfrey is about to become caught up in this dangerous and exotic world – with the piratical Ravis, a beautifully patterned gold ring and a role to play in the momentous events that unfold.

A CAVERN OF BLACK ICE

Book One of Sword of Shadows

J. V. Jones

A MAJOR NEW FANTASY EPIC BEGINS

When Raif Sevrance and his brother return home to their
clan as the only survivors of a vicious attack in which
both their father and the clan chief were killed, it is not
only grief that clouds Raif's thoughts. For the new clan
chief's reign is a brutal one – made worse by his brother's
acceptance of it. When his uncle, Angus Lok, invites Raif
to accompany him to Spire Vanis, it seems that he has no
choice but to leave his home.

On their arrival at Spire Vanis, however, Raif is
immediately plunged into events more perilous than
those he has left behind. For Angus Lok, to Raif's
amazement, has helped Asarhia March to escape from
the Overlord of Spire Vanis. And it is up to Raif to
protect the young woman – and the world – from
the forces growing within her.

TRANSFORMATION

Carol Berg

Seyonne is a man waiting to die.

He has been a slave for sixteen years
and has lost everything of meaning to him: his dignity,
the people and homeland he loves, even the power he
once wielded as a Warden of souls.

Now he must bend his knee to a Derzhi Prince,
heir to the Empire that wiped out his people
and destroyed his life.

As the Empire begins negotiations for an alliance
with the savage Khelid nation, a deadly menace stalks
the corridors of the Prince's palace. Only Seyonne
seems aware of this danger. But can he ignore his years
of subservience, put aside his hatred of the selfish
Prince Aleksander and raise his voice in warning?

If he does, he will risk his life,
but it may save his soul.

As Seyonne's tale unfolds, it is the actions of one
man that will determine the fate of an empire.

THE HEART OF MYRIAL

Book One of the Shadowleague

Maggie Furey

The magical barriers that have held the world together
for aeons are beginning to fail. But this is far more than
just a natural disaster. For the boundaries have also
served to keep hostile nations apart.

Catastrophe is imminent, and the only hope of salvation
lies in the hands of the Shadowleague and its emissaries,
in particular the Loremaster Veldan and her firedrake
partner Kazairl. The next few days will change their
future and threaten to tear the Shadowleague apart.

Orbit titles available by post:

☐ The Barbed Coil	J.V. Jones	£7.99
☐ The Baker's Boy	J.V. Jones	£7.99
☐ A Man Betrayed	J.V. Jones	£7.99
☐ A Cavern of Black Ice	J.V. Jones	£7.99
☐ A Fortress of Grey Ice	J.V. Jones	£17.99
☐ Transformation	Carol Berg	£6.99
☐ The Heart of Myrial	Maggie Furey	£6.99

The prices shown above are correct at time of going to press. However, the publishers reserve the right to increase prices on covers from those previously advertised, without further notice.

orbit

ORBIT BOOKS
Cash Sales Department, P.O. Box 11, Falmouth, Cornwall, TR10 9EN
Tel: +44 (0) 1326 569777, Fax: +44 (0) 1326 569555
Email: books@barni.avel.co.uk

POST AND PACKING:
Payments can be made as follows: cheque, postal order (payable to Orbit Books) or by credit cards. Do not send cash or currency.

U.K. Orders under £10	£1.50
U.K. Orders over £10	**FREE OF CHARGE**
E.C. & Overseas	25% of order value

Name (Block letters) . . . .

Address . . . .

. . . .

Post/zip code: . . . .

☐ Please keep me in touch with future Orbit publications

☐ I enclose my remittance £ . . . .

☐ I wish to pay by Visa/Access/Mastercard/Eurocard

Card Expiry Date
